William Francis Collier

A History of English Literature

William Francis Collier

A History of English Literature

ISBN/EAN: 9783742813992

Manufactured in Europe, USA, Canada, Australia, Japa

Cover: Foto ©Andreas Hilbeck / pixelio.de

Manufactured and distributed by brebook publishing software
(www.brebook.com)

William Francis Collier

A History of English Literature

A

HISTORY

OF

ENGLISH LITER[ATURE]

IN A SERIES OF

BIOGRAPHICAL SKE[TCHES]

BY

WILLIAM FRANCIS CO[LLIER]

TRINITY COLL[EGE], [DUBLIN];

AUTHOR OF "[SCHOOL HISTORY OF THE BRITISH EMPIRE]"

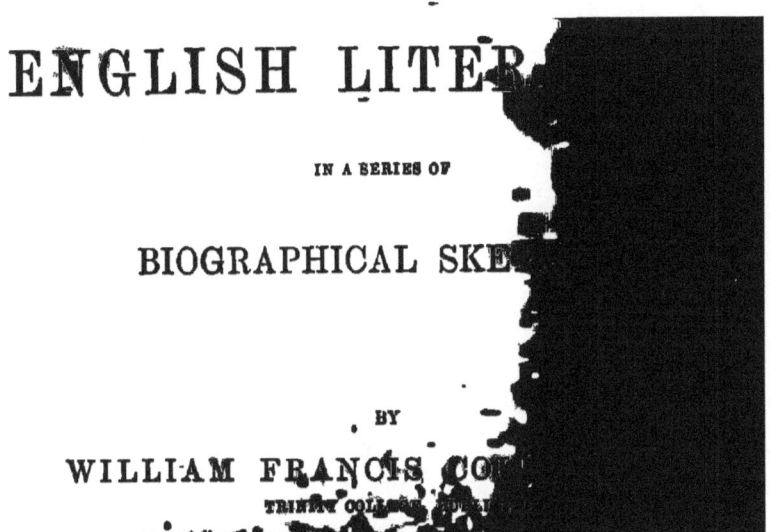

T. NELSON A[ND SONS]

PREFACE.

THIS History of English . Literature is essentially biographical, for true criticism cannot separate the author
from his book.   Leaving entirely out of sight what is no
light matter in a work written for the young,—the
living interest thus given to a subject for which some
have little love,—so much do the colour and the flavour
of that wonderful Mind-fruit, called a Book, depend upon
the atmosphere in which it has ripened, and the soil
whence its sweet or sour juices have been drawn, that
these important influences cannot be overlooked in tracing,
however slightly, the growth of a Literature.   It has,
accordingly, been my principal object to shew how the
books, which we prize among the brightest of our national
glories, have grown out of human lives—rooted oftener,
perhaps, in sorrow than in joy; and how the scenery and
the society, amid which an author played out his fleeting
part, have left indelible hues upon the pages that he
wrote.

Instead of trying to compress the History of our

Books into the framework formed by the accession of our Sovereigns, I have adopted a purely literary division. Selecting such great landmarks as the Birth of Chaucer, and the Introduction of Printing, I find that Ten Eras, each possessing a very distinct character, will embrace every name of note, from the oldest Celtic bards to Tennyson and Carlyle. The Pre-English Era takes a rapid view of British books and book-makers before the birth of Chaucer, about whose day the true English Literature began to exist. In the nine remaining Eras an entire chapter is devoted to each greatest name, writers of less mark being grouped together in a closing section. Short illustrative specimens, intended mainly to form the basis of lessons on variety of style, are appended to all the leading lives. Since names that cannot be passed over grow very thick towards the end, the closing chapters of the last two Eras have been arranged upon a plan which prevents confusion, and, by the use of Supplementary Lists, admits the mention of many authors who must otherwise have been left out.

The method of the entire book aims at enabling a student to perceive at a glance the relative importance of certain authors, so that his reading may be either confined to the lives of our great Classics, or extended through the full range of our Literature, without much risk of confusion or mistake as to proportionate greatness.

And here, in passing, I may say that only those who have tried it can estimate the difficulty of striking a balance in the case of certain names, when space and plan will admit of no choice but between a chapter and a paragraph. With great regret, and not without some misgivings, was I forced to assign to a secondary place Defoe, Adam Smith (in spite of Buckle's praise), Lamb, Wilson, De Quincey, Chalmers, Kingsley, Hugh Miller, and many others. The same difficulty met me in the formation of the Supplementary Lists, which, however, will serve to give what, I hope, is a tolerably accurate idea of those third-class writers, or rather first-class writers of the third degree, who adorn the present century.

In the opening chapter of the various Eras I have ventured to add to the simple history of our Literature what I believe to be a novelty in a book of this kind. Recognising the value of such pictures to the student of national history, I have attempted to reproduce, with some vividness, scenes of vanished author-life, and to trace the chief steps by which a green leaf has become a printed volume. For, to know something of the dress our books have worn at various times, and the stuff of which the older ones were made; to see the minstrel singing in the Castle hall, and the monk at work in the still Scriptorium; to peep at Caxton in the Almonry, and watch the curtain rise on Shakspere at the Globe; to trace the lights and shadows flung upon English books from

Cavalier satins and the more sober-coloured garments of their opponents; to see courtly poison withering Dryden's wreath of bay, and men like Johnson starving their way to fame: these are surely things of no slight interest and value to the earnest student of English Literature. And to such this book is offered.

W. F. C.

October 5, 1861.

CONTENTS.

FIFTH ERA.

SIXTH ERA.

SEVENTH ERA.

EIGHTH ERA.

NINTH ERA.

HISTORY

OF

ENGLISH LITERATURE.

———◆———

THE PRE-ENGLISH ERA.

———

CHAPTER I.

FIRST STEPS IN BOOK-MAKING.

WHEN in the depth of some Asiatic forest, shadowy with the green fans and sword-blades of the palm tribe, and the giant fronds of the purple-streaked banana, a sinewy savage stood, one day long ago, etching with a thorn on some thick-fleshed leaf, torn from the luxuriant shrubwood around him, rude images of the beasts he hunted or the arrows he shot,—the first step was taken towards the making of a book.

Countless have been the onward steps since then; but the old fact that the *tree* is the parent of the *book* still survives in many well-known words, which ever point us back to the green and perfumed woodland where sprang the earliest ancestor of those wondrous and innumerable compounds of author's brain, printer's ink, and linen rag, now answering to the term book. For example, take the Latin *liber*, and the English *book* and *leaf.* Who does not know that *liber* means originally the inner bark of a tree? *Book* is merely a disguised form of the word *beech*, into which it easily changes when we tone down *k* to *ch* soft; and what could our Saxon forefathers have found, in the thick forests of their native Germany, better fitted for their rude inscribings than the smooth and silvery bark of that lovely tree? The word *leaf* tells its own tale. The trim squares of paper, sewed or glued together, which we call by that common name, find their earliest types in those green tablets we have spoken of, pulled fresh and sappy from the forest bough, and marked with the point of a little thorn; which, perhaps, by also pinning the pretty sheets together, may have done the double work of pen and binding-needle.

But fading leaves were too perishable to do more than suggest the notion of a book. Some more durable material was needed to keep alive the memory of those events—battles, huntings, changes of encampment, death of chiefs—which chequered the simple life of the early world. Groves were planted, altars raised, cairns heaped up,—each to tell some tale of joy or grief; but a day soon came when the descendants of the men who had raised these memorials wondered what the decaying trees, and the grey, moss-covered heaps of stones could mean—for the story had perished when the fathers of the tribe were gathered to their rest.

In some nations the earliest records were knotted cords. Strings of different colours, with knots of various sizes and variously arranged, contained the national history of the Peruvians. The Chinese and some negro tribes made use of similar cords.

But it was not in man, endowed by his Creator with the glorious faculties of reason and of speech, to remain contented with these imperfect means of keeping alive the memory of great events. The old book of green leaves was soon exchanged for a book of tough bark, and this for tablets of thin wood. Records, which men were very anxious to preserve, came to be engraven on slabs of rock or cut into plates of metal. The skins of various animals, tanned into a smooth leather, afforded to the ancients a durable substance for their documents and books.   Out of this class of writing materials came the parchment and the vellum, which have not yet been superseded in the lawyer's office, for no paper has been made to equal them in lasting power.   Parchment takes its name from the old city of Pergamos in Asia Minor, whose king, when the literary jealousy of the Egyptians stopped the supply of papyrus, caused his subjects to write on sheep-skins, hence called *Pergamena* or parchment.   Vellum, a finer material, is prepared calf-skin.   Besides these, a common form of the book in Greek and Roman days consisted in tablets of wood, ivory, or metal, coated thinly with wax, on which the writer scratched the symbols of his thoughts with a bronze or iron bodkin, (γραφίον or *stilus*.)   A cut reed, dipped in gum-water which was coloured with powdered charcoal or the soot of resin, represented long ago the pen and ink of modern days.   With such appliances, Egyptian, Greek, and Roman scholars penned their early works on rolls of parchment or of papyrus, the famous rush-skin, which has given us a name for that common but very beautiful material on which *we* write our letters and print our books.

In swampy places by the Nile, where the retreating flood had left pools, a yard or so deep, to stagnate under the copper sky, there grew in old times vast forests of tall reeds, whose triangular stems, some six or eight feet high, bore tufted plumes of hair-like fibres.   Wading in these shallows, where the ibis stalked, and the mailed crocodile crashed through the canes to plunge like a log in the deep current beyond, day after day bands of dark and linen-robed Egyptians came to hew down the leafless woods with knife or axe, and bear their heavy sheaves to the dry and sandy bank.   It was the famous *papyrus* they cut, whose skin vied with parchment, as the writing material of the ancients.   The several wrappings of the papyrus stalk being stripped off, the lengths were cemented either with the muddy water of the Nile, or more probably with the sugary juices of the plant itself.   As skin after skin peeled away, the more delicate tissues, of which the finest paper was made, were found wrapping the heart of the stem.   Pressing and drying completed the simple process of making this much-used paper.   It was then ready to receive the semi-liquid, gummy soot, with which the Xenophons and the Virgils of old Greece and Rome traced their flowing histories or sparkling poems.

Such were the chief materials of which ancient books were made,—the hard and stiff substances being formed into angular tablets, which opened either like the leaves of a European book or like the folding compartments of a screen,—the soft and pliable, such as leather or linen, being rolled on ornamented, smoothly-rounded sticks, as we roll up our maps and wall-diagrams.   Instead of showing, like our modern libraries, trim rows of books standing shoulder to shoulder with the evenness of well-drilled soldiers on parade—the juniors gleaming with magenta and gold, the seniors hoary in ancient vellum or sombre with dingy calf—the book-room of a Plato or a Seneca would have displayed a few circular cases, resembling our common bandbox, and filled with papyrus or parchment rolls, which, standing on end, displayed the bright yellow, polished vermilion, or deep jet of their smoothly-cut edges.

Let us now see what the men, who wrought out the wonders of ancient history, cut or painted on their granite slabs, their cloths of cotton or linen, their sheep-skins, or their slips of bark.

.Drawing and painting were, undoubtedly, the earliest methods of conveying ideas in books.   And still, pictures and sketches aid many of our books and serials to convey a clearer meaning; else why do we love to read the *Illustrated News*, or turn the first thing in the *Cornhill* to the drawings of Millais and of Doyle? The various gradations by which the first rude sketch changed into that wonderful invention—a word formed of alphabetic symbols —cannot here be traced.   Take two specimens of the phases which the growing art assumed.

A piece of cotton cloth is before us, brilliant with crimson and yellow and pale blue, and oblong like our modern page.   It is a picture-writing of old Mexico, relating the reign and conquests of King Acamapich.   Down the left border runs a broad stripe of blue, divided into thirteen parts by lines resembling the rounds of a

ladder. This represents a reign of thirteen years. In each com-
partment a symbol expresses the story of the year. A flower,
denoting calamity, is found in two of them. But the chief story
is told by the coloured forms of the centre, where we have the
sovereign painted twice, as a stern-looking head, capped with a
serpent crest, with a dwarfish, white-robed body, and, separate
from the shoulder, a hand grasping a couple of arrows. Before
this grim warrior at the top of the scroll lie a shield and a bundle
of spears. Face and feet are painted a dull yellow. Before his
second effigy we have four smaller heads, with closed eyes and an
ominous, bloody mark upon lip and chin, denoting the capture and
beheading of four hostile chiefs. The four sacked and plundered
cities are depicted by roofs falling from ruined walls; and beside
each stands a symbol representing some botanical or geographical
feature by which its site is characterized. Pictures of different
species of tree distinguish two of the cities; the third stands
evidently by a lake, for a pan of water is drawn close to it, united
by a line to mark close connection.

By some such suggestive painting upon cotton cloth or aloe
leaves did the frightened Mexicans, who dwelt on the coast of the
great Gulf, convey to the inland towns the terrible news that Cortez
and his Spaniards had appeared. They painted the great ships,
the pale, bearded men, the cannon breathing flames and smoke
and hurling distant trees in splinters to the earth; and no
sadder picture was ever unrolled in the splendid palace of Monte-
zuma than the cotton cloth emblazoned with terrible meanings,
which had been borne, with galloping of swiftest mules, up, up
the rocky terraces of the plateau from the blue edge of the tepid
sea.

The link, which connects such picture-writing with that use of
alphabetic symbols so familiar to us that we do not realize its
wonder, lies in the hieroglyphic writing of the Egyptians. Figures
of natural objects abound in that system too, but they have now got
a deeper meaning—the power of expressing abstractions, or qualities
considered alone. Thus the queen bee represents royalty; the bull,
strength; an ostrich feather, from the evenness of its filaments, truth

or justice. The figures are often, especially in later writings, reduced to their principal parts, or even to lines, the latter being the first step toward the formation of an alphabet. For instance, a combat is represented by two arms, one bearing a shield, the other a pike; Upper and Lower Egypt are denoted by single stems topped with a blossom or a plume, representing respectively the lotus and the papyrus. The colouring of the hieroglyphics is not in imitation of nature, as is the case with the earlier picture-writing, but follows a conventional system seldom departed from. The upper part of a canopy in blue stood for the heavens; a thick waving line of the same, or a greenish hue, represented the sea. The sun is red with a yellow rim. Men's flesh is red; women's, yellow. Parts of the body are painted deep red; wooden instruments are pale orange or buff; bronze utensils, green. The effect of a hieroglyphic writing as it strikes the eye is very brilliant, the primary colours—red, yellow, and blue—being the prevailing hues.

A hieroglyphic painting taken from the wall of an excavated temple in Nubia is before us. It represents the introduction of ambassadors to the great Sesostris, whose figure, seated on a throne, fills all the left side of the record. He bears as sceptre a red wand with yellow top; his white robe is embroidered with blue and gold; a square blue cap, rimmed with gold and adorned with a symbolic bird, covers his head; his arms, his face, and lower legs are bare, and painted of a deep red. Two coloured ovals above his head express by figures and signs the names of the king. Four or five upright columns of hieroglyphic symbols tell the story of the ambassadors; and, crossing two of these from the right, there comes a red arm to announce the introduction to the royal presence. To attempt a description of the symbols here would be absurd. No fewer than twenty-three figures of birds with spread or folded wings are there. The sign for water is frequently repeated. Figures of men kneel and sit and stand. There are fish, and arms and legs and eyes, crowns and flowers, a crocodile and a horse,—all in red, or blue, or yellow, or green. No other colour appears in the painting, except the grey used to shade the great figure of the king.

Then by slow, yet very sure degrees, the hieroglyphic system altered until certain signs became *phonetic ;* that is, expressive of sounds, not things. The Phœnicians, who had much to do with early Egypt, in adopting the art of writing probably abandoned the pictorial part of the hieroglyphic system, and retaining only the phonetics, formed out of these the first pure alphabet ; and so from Phœnicia through Greece and Rome we, in all likelihood, got the ground-work of those twenty-six letters of which our thirty-eight thousand words are made.

Much of this opening chapter deals with countries far from Britain, and an age anterior, in the Old World at least, to the birth of British literature. But it is not a rash conjecture, that, among the ancestors of those blue-limbed Celts who dashed so bravely into the surf near Sandwich on that old September day, to meet the brass-mailed legions of Cæsar, there were some untutored attempts at picture-writing on such materials as the country could supply. For savage man must, in every age and clime, travel on to civilization by much the same pathway. And, in any case, it is well, when beginning to record the great victories of the British pen, to trace a few of those faltering steps which were taken, as the world grew from morning into prime, towards the production of that grand triumph of human thought and skill we call a modern book.

CHAPTER II.

CELTIC WRITERS.

Origin of the Ballad.	The "Annals."	"Triads."
Irish manuscripts.	Poems of Ossian.	Latin writers.
"The Psalter of Cashel."	Welsh bards.	Gildas.

AMONG every people the earliest form of literature is the Ballad. The History and the Poetry of a nation are, in their infant forms, identical.   When the old Greeks taught, in their mythology, that Memory was the mother of the Muses, they embodied in a striking personification the fact that the rude language, in which men emerging from savagery used to chant the story of their deeds to their children, was couched in rough metre, in order that the ring of the lines might help the memory to retain the tale.

Oldest of all British literature, or, indeed, of all literature in modern Europe, of which any specimens remain, are some scraps of Irish verse, found in the Annalists and ascribed to the fifth century.   *The Psalter of Cashel*, the oldest existing manuscript of the Irish literature, is a collection of metrical legends, sung by the bards, which was compiled towards the end of the ninth century, by a man who seems to have held the offices of Bishop of Cashel and King of Munster.   More important, however, as giving in careful prose a calm account of early Irish history, are the *Annals of Tigernach and of the Four Masters of Ulster.*

The very scanty remains of the Scottish Gaelic are of much later date than the earliest Irish ballads.   The poems of Ossian— *Fingal* and *Temora*—which were published in 1762 and 1763 by James Macpherson, as translations from Gaelic manuscripts as old as the fourth century, are now generally looked on as literary forgeries, executed by their clever but not very scrupulous editor. The ancient manuscripts, from which he professed to have trans- lated these graphic pictures of old Celtic life, have never been produced.   A narrative in verse, called the *Albanic Duan*, is thought to have been composed in the eleventh century.

In Wales, which was the stronghold of Druidism, the profession of the bard was held in high honour. The poems of Taliesin, Merlin, and other bards of the sixth century, still remain. The Welsh *Triads*, some of which are ascribed to writers of the thirteenth century, are sets of historical events and moral proverbs, arranged in groups of three. Both in these and in the ballads of the bards, one of the leading heroes is the great Prince Arthur, whose prowess against the Saxons was so noted in those dim days.

Besides those who wrote and sang in their native Celtic tongue, there were also among the ancient British people a few Latin authors. Three may be named. First on the long and brilliant roll of British historians stands Gildas, born at Alcluyd (Dumbarton) about the beginning of the sixth century. He is known to us as the author of a *History of the Britons*, and an *Epistle* to his countrymen, both in Latin, and both containing fiery assaults upon the Saxon invaders. Nennius, thought to have been a monk of Bangor, is said also to have written a *History of the Britons*. *The Latin poems* of St. Columbanus, an Irish missionary to the Gauls, are spoken of by Moore as "shining out in this twilight period of Latin literature with no ordinary distinction."

CHAPTER III.

ANGLO-SAXON WRITERS.

The Saxon gleeman.	King Alfred.	Alcuin.
Saxon verse.	Alfric the Grammarian.	Erigena.
The Epic Beowulf.	The "Saxon Chronicle."	Dunstan.
Caedmon.	Aldhelm.	Decay.
His "Paraphrase."	Beda.	

THE *Gleeman* or Minstrel of the Anglo-Saxons was a most important person. When the evening shadows fell, and the "mead-bench" was filled, his scene of triumph came. His touch on the "wood of joy" had power alike to rouse the fiery passions of the warriors or soothe their ruffled moods. He related the deeds of dead heroes, or sung the praise of their living descendants; stung the coward with his sweet-voiced scorn, or exulted in his proudest tones over the beaten foe. From earliest days his training was directed to the storing of his memory with the poetic legends of his country; and when, grown more skilful, he learned to string into rude verses the story of his own day, it went, without his name to mark it, into the common stock of his craft. Hence the Anglo-Saxon poetry is anonymous.

The structure of the verse in which these gleemen sang is thus described by Wright:—"The poetry of the Anglo-Saxons was neither modulated according to foot-measure, like that of the Greeks and Romans, nor written with rhymes, like that of many modern languages. Its chief and universal characteristic was a very regular *alliteration,* so arranged that in every couplet there should be two principal words in the first line beginning with the same letter, which letter must also be the initial of the first word, on which the stress of the voice falls in the second line. The only approach to a metrical system yet discovered is, that two risings and two fallings of the voice seem necessary to each perfect line. Two distinct measures are met with, a shorter and a longer, both commonly mixed together in the same poem; the former being used for the ordinary narrative, and the latter adopted when the poet sought after greater dignity. In the manuscripts the Saxon poetry is always written continuously, like prose; but the division of the lines is generally marked by a point."

The chief Anglo-Saxon poems that have come down to us are the *Romance of Beowulf,* and *Caedmon's Paraphrase.*

Beowulf is a nameless poem of more than 6000 lines, thought to be much older than the manuscript of it which we possess. Its hero, BEOWULF, is a Danish soldier, who, passing through many dangers by land and sea, slays a monster, Grendel, but is himself slain in an attack upon a huge dragon. It is a striking picture of dim old Gothic days, much heightened in its effect by the minuteness of the descriptive lines. As we read, the gleaming of mail flashes in our eyes, and we hear the clanging march of the warriors, as the "bright ring-iron sings in its trappings." Metaphors are common in the language of Beowulf, and some are of noble simplicity, such as, "They lay aloft, put to sleep with swords;" but in all this long poem there are only five similes. This scarcity of similes is a characteristic of all Anglo-Saxon verse.

CAEDMON, the author of the *Paraphrase,* was originally a cowherd near Whitby in Northumbria. Bede tells the story of his inspiration. It was the custom in those days for each to sing in turn, as the harp was pushed round the hall at supper. This Caedmon could never do; and when he saw his turn coming, he used to slip out of the room, blushing for his want of skill and eager to hide his shame. One night, having left the hall, he lay down to sleep in the stable; and as he slept, he dreamed that a stranger came to him, and said, "Caedmon, sing me something." "I know nothing to sing," said the poor herd, "and so I had to slink away out of the hall." "Nay," said the stranger, "but thou hast something to sing." "What must I sing?" "Sing the Creation," replied the stranger; upon which words of sweet music began to flow from the lips that had been sealed so long. Caedmon awoke, knew the words he had been reciting, and felt a new-born power in his breast. The mantle of song had fallen on him; and when next day, before the Abbess Hilda and some of the scholars of the place, he told what had occurred, they gave

him a passage of the Bible to test his new-found skill. Within
a few hours he composed, on the given subject, a poem of surpassing sweetness and power. Thenceforward this monk of Whitby
spent his life in the composition of religious poetry.

The " Paraphrase " of Caedmon contained, besides other portions
of the Bible, the story of the Creation and the Fall, the history of
Daniel, with many passages in the life and death of our Saviour.
From the similarity of subject, a likeness has been traced between
him and Milton, upon which a charge of plagiarism against our
great epic poet has been most foolishly grounded.

It is believed that Caedmon died about 680. Some think that
there were two poets of the name, the elder of whom composed
those lines on the Creation, which are acknowledged to be among
the oldest existing specimens of Anglo-Saxon, while the younger
was the author of the " Paraphrase."

The principal fragmentary Anglo-Saxon poems, which still
survive, are the *Battle of Finsborough;* the *Traveller's Song*, which
contains a good many geographical names; and the fragment of
Judith. In the Saxon Chronicle of 938 we find a poem called
Athelstan's Song of Victory.

The following extract from Caedmon's " Paraphrase "—part of the
Song of Azariah—may be taken as a specimen of Anglo-Saxon
verse :—

	Thorpe's Translation.
Tha of roderum wæs.	Then from the firmament was
Engel ælbeorht.	An all-bright angel
Ufan onsended.	Sent from above,
Wlite scyne wer.	A man of beauteous form,
On his wuldor-haman.	In his garb of glory :
Se him cwom to frofre.	Who to them came for comfort,
& to feorh-nere.	And for their lives' salvation,
Mid lufan & mid lisse.	With love and with grace ;
Se thone lig tosceaf.	Who the flame scattered
Halig and heofon-beorht.	(Holy and heaven-bright)
Hatan fyres.	Of the hot fire,
Tosweop hine & toswende.	Swept it and dashed away,
Thurh tha swithan miht.	Through his great might,
Ligges leoma.	The beams of flame ;
That hyra lice ne wæs.	So that their bodies were not
Owiht geegled.	Injured aught.

ALFRED.—King Alfred is the leading writer of Anglo-Saxon prose, whose works remain. The Welshman Asser has preserved for us an account of this royal scholar's life and works.

What Alfred did for England in those dark days, when Danish pirates ravaged the land so sorely, every reader of our history knows. Here it is not as the warrior, victorious at Ethandune and on the banks of the Lea, that we must view this greatest of the Anglo-Saxons; but as the peaceful man of letters, sitting among his books and plying his patient pen, as his time-candle burns down, ring after ring, through the hours allotted to literary toil. Both sword and pen were familiar tools in that cunning right hand.

Alfred the Great was born in 848, at Wantage in Berkshire. Two visits to Rome in his early days gave him a wider range of observation and thought than Anglo-Saxon children commonly enjoyed. When he had reached his twelfth year, he won as a prize a beautiful book of Saxon poetry, which his mother had promised to that one of her sons who should first commit its contents to memory. Already Alfred had been noted in the family circle for the ease with which he remembered the songs sung by the wandering gleemen.

When in 871 he ascended the throne of Wessex, his great mind found its destined work. Through many perils and disheartening changes he broke the power of the insolent Danes, taming the pirates into tillers of the Danelagh. And then, his warlike task for the present done, turned to the elevation of his people's mind.

There being few scholars in the troubled land, he invited learned men from France to preside over the leading schools. Much of his scanty leisure was spent in literary work, chiefly translations into Anglo-Saxon. His chief works were his versions of *Bede's History of the Anglo-Saxon Church*, and *Boethius on the Consolation of Philosophy.* Translations of *Orosius*, of *Pope Gregory's Pastorale*, and an unfinished rendering of the *Psalms*, are also named among his contributions to literature.

ALFRIC.—There was an author in the latter days of the Anglo-Saxon period, known as Alfric the Grammarian, about whom much confusion exists among writers on the Anglo-Saxon literature. Whoever this man was,—whether, as is generally thought, that monk of Abingdon who was made Archbishop of Canterbury in 995, or another man of York, or yet another of Malmesbury,—he contributed largely to the literature of his day. Most of his writings are still extant. His name, the Grammarian, was taken from a *Latin Grammar*, which he translated from Donatus and Priscian. His *Latin Glossary* and *Book of Latin Conversation* are works of merit. But his *Eighty Homilies*, written in the simplest Anglo-Saxon, for the use of the common people, are undoubtedly his greatest work. Among these is his famous *Paschal Sermon*, which embodies the Anglo-Saxon belief on the subject of the Lord's Supper. Alfric of Canterbury died in November 1006.

The famous *Saxon Chronicle* was the work of centuries. An Archbishop of Canterbury, named Plegmund, drawing largely from Bede, is said to have compiled the work up to 891. It was then carried on in various monasteries until 1154, when the registers ceased to be kept. As a work of history, embracing the events of many hundred years, and written for the most part by men who lived in the midst of the scenes they described, it is perhaps the most valuable inheritance we have received from the native literature of our Saxon forefathers.

A romance founded on the story of Apollonius of Tyre,—King Alfred's Will,—some Laws and Charters,—some Homilies,—and a few works on Grammar, Medicine, and Botany,—are nearly all the specimens of Anglo-Saxon prose that remain.

LATIN WORKS.

The learned tongue of Europe was then, as it long continued to be, Latin, the writing of which was revived in England by Augustine and his monks. In the stern soldiering days of the Roman period, much Latin had been spoken and read, but little had been written within British bounds. But the Anglo-Saxon monks,—

nay, the Anglo-Saxon ladies, — wrote countless pages of Latin prose and verse. The great subject of those Latin works was theology, as was natural from the circumstance that they were chiefly the productions of the cloister.

ALDHELM.—Most ancient of the Anglo-Saxon writers in Latin was Aldhelm, Abbot of Malmesbury and Bishop of Sherborn. He was born in Wessex about 656, of the best blood in the land. His chief teacher was an Irish monk named Meildulf, who lived a hermit life under the shade of the great oak trees in north-eastern Wiltshire. When the followers of Meildulf were formed into a monastery bearing its founder's name (Meildulfesbyrig or Malmesbury), Aldhelm was chosen to be their abbot. There he lived a peaceful life, relieving his graver cares with the sweet solace of literature and music. He died at Dilton in May 709. His chief works are three; a prose treatise in praise of *Virginity*,— a work in verse on the same subject,—and a book of *Riddles*. His Latin is impure, filled with Greek words, and stuffed with those alliterations and metaphors which are characteristic of Anglo-Saxon poetry.

BEDE.—Second in time, but first in place, comes the name of the Venerable Bede, or Beda. This illustrious man was born about 672 or 673, at Jarrow in Durham, near the mouth of the Tyne. To the newly founded monastery of Wearmouth, not far distant, the studious boy went at the age of seven, to profit by the teaching of Benedict Biscop. Thenceforward—until his death fifty-six years later—the cloisters of Wearmouth were his home; and within their quiet seclusion he wrote the great work, on which his title to the name Venerable is justly founded. In his fifty-ninth year he brought to a close his famous *History of the Anglo-Saxon Church*, written—like nearly all his works—in Latin. Its style is simple and easy, unsullied by the far-fetched figures which are such favourites with Aldhelm. From it we learn nearly all we know of the early history of the Anglo-Saxons and their Church. At the end of this book Bede gives a list of thirty-eight works, which he had already written or compiled. These are chiefly theological; but there are, besides, among them, histories, poems, works on physical science, and works on grammar.

Cuthbert, one of Bede's disciples, gives us a sketch of his dying bed. From the beginning of April until the end of May 735, he continued to sink under an attack of asthma, which had long been sapping his strength. To the very last he worked hard, dictating with his failing breath a translation into Anglo-Saxon of John's Gospel. It was morning on the 27th of May. "Master," said one of the young monks who wrote for him, "there is but one chapter, but thou canst ill bear questioning." "Write quickly on," said Bede. At noon he took a solemn farewell of his friends, distributing among them his treasured spices and other gifts. By sunset there remained but one sentence of the work to do, and scarcely had the concluding words of the Gospel flowed from the pen of the writer, when the venerable monk sighed out, "It is done." The thread was just about to snap. Seated on that part of the floor where he had been wont to kneel in prayer, he pronounced the "Gloria Patri," and died as the last words of the sacred utterance were breathed from his lips.

735
A.D.

ALCUIN.—The year 735, which sealed the eyes of Bede in death, is thought to have given life to the great scholar Alcuin. It is doubtful whether Alcuin was born at York or in Scotland. He won a prominent place in the great school presided over at York by Archbishop Egbert, and when he was called to fill the chair—from which his master, Egbert, had taught so well—he drew even greater crowds of students to this capital of the north. Besides his work as a teacher, he acted as keeper of the fine library collected in the Cathedral of York. While returning from a visit to Rome, he became acquainted at Parma with the Emperor Charlemagne, who invited him to France. Going thither in 782, he speedily became one of the most cherished friends of his imperial patron, who was never happier than when he was chatting and laughing unreservedly with men of thought. After a short visit to England (790–792) in the character of Imperial Envoy, Alcuin seems to have settled permanently in France. There his position was a proud one, for he was recognised as chief among the distinguished group of wits and lettered men who encircled the throne of Charlemagne. The name by which he was known in this brilliant circle was Flaccus Albinus, a title under which he could converse more freely with his friend David (Charlemagne), than if the monk and the emperor always retained their distinctive names and titles. In his old age Alcuin desired earnestly to retire from the glare and bustle of court life to that quiet monastery round which his earliest associations were twined. He had all ready for the journey, when news came of terrible massacres and burnings in the north of England, such as had not before been suffered, although the Raven's beak had left many a deep and bloody gash upon the fair English shore. Frightened at such tales, he asked from the emperor a post, in which he might calmly pass the evening of his days. The Abbey of Tours, falling vacant just then, became his place of retirement, where he spent his learned leisure in training a new generation of scholars, and in writing most of those books by which his name has come down to us. At Tours he died in 804.

The Letters of Alcuin give a life-like picture of the great events of his day. The wars of Charlemagne against the Saracens and the Saxons are there described; and there, too, we find a graphic account of the inner life of the imperial court. A *Life of Charlemagne* has been ascribed to the pen of Alcuin; but, if there was ever such a work, it has long been lost. Of his poems, the best is an *Elegy on the Destruction of Lindisfarne by the Danes.* He wrote, besides, a long metrical narrative of the bishops and saints of the Church at York; which, on the whole, is not very elegant Latin, and poor enough poetry. Theology, of course, was his principal study; and on this theme he wrote much, pouring from his pen a host of Scriptural commentaries and treatises on knotty points of doctrine. As a teacher he ranks much higher than he ranks as an author. His chief glory—and the thing of which his countrymen were especially proud—was the fact that he, a Briton, had been chosen to give instruction to the great Emperor of the West.

ERIGENA.—John Scotus or Erigena, although not a Saxon, but, as his name shows, an Irishman, claims our special notice here. Little is known of this great man. He probably settled in France about 845, and lived there, under the patronage of Charles the Bald, for thirty years. He should be well remembered for two things: he was a learned layman, and a well-read Greek scholar, both characters being very rare in those benighted days. His chief works are a treatise on *Predestination*, in which he argues that God has fore-ordained only rewards for the good, and that man has brought evil on himself by the exercise of his own perverted will; a treatise on the *Eucharist*, denying the doctrine of transubstantiation; and—more remarkable than either—a book *On the Division of Nature*, which embraces a wide range of scientific knowledge, and is copiously enriched with extracts from Greek and Latin writers.

The bold, fearless nature of the man, and the familiar tone of the Frankish court-life, are well illustrated by an anecdote told of Erigena. One day the king and he sat on opposite sides of the table, with the courtiers ranged around. The scholar—through forgetfulness or ignorance—transgressed some of the rules of etiquette, so as to offend the fastidious taste of those who sat by, upon which, the king asked him what was the difference between a Scot* and a sot. "Just the breadth of the table," said Erigena; and it is more than likely that the royal witling ventured on no more puns, for that day at least, at the scholar's expense. Erigena is said to have died in France some time previous to the year 877.

DUNSTAN.—One of the foremost Saxons of his day, though more noted for his learning than for his writings, was Dunstan, Abbot of Glastonbury, and afterwards Archbishop of Canterbury. Born in 925, near Glastonbury in Somersetshire, and educated there in the Irish school, he became a monk at an early age. His advances in learning were surprisingly rapid, in spite of the convulsive fits to which he was subject, and under the influence of which he thought that he was hunted by devils. Arithmetic, geometry, astronomy, and music were his favourite studies. While living at Winchester, he was persuaded by his uncle the Bishop to crush down his early love for a girl of great beauty, and to devote himself with might and main to the austerities of a monkish life. Be-

---

* A *Scot* then meant a native of Ireland.

side the church wall he built a cell, into which he shut himself
with his tools of carpentry and smith-work, his paints and brushes
for the illumination of manuscripts. Seldom venturing from this
retreat, he soon won a reputation for wonderful sanctity and
alliance with supernatural beings. King Edmund made him
Abbot of Glastonbury; and with Edred also—the next king—he
was in high favour. Banished by Edwy to Ghent, he was by
Edgar recalled to become Archbishop of Canterbury. Thenceforward
ward he was first man in the English realm, able not merely to rebuke the king, but even to bestow the crown at his pleasure. He
died in 988.

His works are nearly all theological, the best known being
the *Benedictine Rule*, modified for English monks, and having
its Latin interlined with a Saxon translation. He wrote also a
Commentary or Set of Lectures on the Rule; which were probably read by him in the various schools with which he was connected.

The latter days of the Anglo-Saxon literature were feeble
compared with the vigour of its youth. Even in the day of
Alfred, when it may be said to have reached its prime, decay was
at work, and the ravages of the Danes completed the blight of its
promise. Those were days when many kings made their mark at
the foot of charters, for want of skill to write their names. Alfred
could find no tutors able to teach the higher branches of education;
and he was forced to state publicly, in his preface to " Gregory's
Pastorale," that he knew no men south of the Thames, and few south
of the Humber, who could follow the sense of the public prayers,
or construe a Latin sentence into English. Yet that an Anglo-
Saxon literature—however scanty—*did* flourish, is no slight wonder, for during those ages clouds of thickest darkness hung over
all Europe with a seemingly impenetrable gloom.

CHAPTER IV.

ANGLO-NORMAN WRITERS.

Effects of the Conquest.	The Chronicles.	Nature of the Romance.
John of Salisbury.	Ingulphus.	Stories of Arthur.
The Norman Romance.	Ordericus Vitalis.	Master Wace.
Romance tongues of France.	William of Malmesbury.	Langton and Richard I.
Prevalence of Latin.	Geoffrey of Monmouth.	Layamon's "Brut."
Latin poetry.	The "Gesta."	The "Ormulum."

THE Norman Conquest wrought great changes on both the learning and the literature of England.   Saxon scholarship had been
growing rustier every day since the great Alfred died; and those
Saxon prelates who held sees at the time of the Conquest were far
behind the age as men of letters.   William therefore displaced many
of them, to make room for polished scholars from the Continent—
such as Lanfranc and Anselm, who held the see of Canterbury in
succession.   The Conqueror, moreover, founded many fine abbeys
and convents, within whose quiet cells learned men could think and
write in safe and honoured leisure.   Schools sprang up on every side.
The great seminaries at Oxford and Cambridge—already distinguished as schools—were elevated to the rank of universities, destined to be formidable rivals of the older institutions at Paris and
Bologna.   Latin being the professional language of churchmen,
by whom in those days nearly all learning was monopolized, we
find a vast number of Latin works written during the centuries
which immediately followed the Norman Conquest.

At this time what is called the Scholastic Philosophy, founded
on Aristotle's method of argument, grew to a most extravagant
degree of favour.   Hence imaginative writing of all kinds suffered
a great blight.   It was only in the ballads of the people that fancy
found utterance at all.

John of Salisbury, who, going to Paris in 1136, spent several
years in attending the lectures of the best masters there, wrote
a book called *Metalogicus*, exposing the absurd and childish

wrangling which then bore the dignified name of Logic. Such questions as the following were seriously discussed in learned assemblies : "If a man buy a cloak, does he also buy the hood?" and, "If a hog be carried to market with a rope tied round its neck and held at the other end by a man, is the animal carried to market by the man or by the rope?" John of Salisbury's chief work was called *Polycraticon*, a pleasant and learned treatise upon the "Frivolities of Courtiers, and the Footsteps of Philosophers." This accomplished monk died in 1182, being then Bishop of Chartres.

The great feature in the literary history of this time was the introduction into England of the Norman Romance. With Chivalry, from which it was inseparable, and from whose stirring life it took all its colours, the Romance rose and fell.

From the corrupted Latin a group of dialects arose, called the Roman or Romance tongues; which, owing to slight intermixture with the barbarous languages, assumed somewhat different forms in Italy, France, and Spain. In France two dialects of the Romance language were spoken, distinguished in name by the peculiar words used for our "yes"—*oc*, (*hoc*), and *oyl*, *oy*, or *oui* (probably *illud*). The language of *oc* was spoken in the south, and the language of *oyl* in the north of France. The Langue d'Oc, otherwise known as the Provençal which was sung by the famous Troubadours, blazed out a brief day of glory, was then trampled down with all its lovely garlands of song by Montfort and his crusaders, and now exists merely as the rude *patois* of the province that bears its name. The Langue d'Oyl, growing into the modern French, has influenced our literature in more ways than one. The lays, sung by the *trouvères* of northern France in praise of knights and knighthood, were the delight of the Norman soldiers who fought at Hastings; and when these soldiers had settled as conquerors on the English soil, what was more natural than that they should still love the old Norman lays, and that a new generation of poets should learn in the Normanized island to sing in Norman too?

It is no wonder that the list of Saxon writers, during the time when the nation lay stunned by the Conqueror's sword, should be short. The Saxons were then slaves; and slaves never have any literature worth speaking of. Some romances and chronicles, echoes of the lays sung by their Norman masters, were all that remained to show that the Saxon tongue was living. Yet living it was, with a wealth of life pent up in its hidden root, which was destined at no very distant day to clothe the shorn stem with the brightest honours of leafage and bloom.

LATIN WRITERS.

Let us first glance at the Latin writers of the Norman times. As has been already said, Latin was the language of churchmen, the most honoured class in the nation; and therefore the amount of Latin writing, both in prose and verse, was very great. Sermons were often preached in Latin.

JOSEPH OF EXETER.—Josephus Iscanus, or Joseph of Exeter, was the leading Latin poet of this day. His chief works were two epic poems—one on the *Trojan War*, remarkable for its pure and harmonious Latin; the other, now almost altogether lost, called *Antiocheis*, a story of the third Crusade. Walter Mapes, or Map, Archdeacon of Oxford, also wrote Latin verses, but of quite a different stamp. A drinking-song in rhyming Latin is a well-known part of his satirical work, called the *Confession of Golias*, which was directed chiefly against the Church and the clergy.

The chief use of Latin at this time was in the compilation of the Chronicles or historical records. We owe much to the patient monks, whose pens traced weary page after page of these old books. There is, indeed, nothing like fine writing in any of these chronicles; and in many of them fiction mixes inextricably with true history like tares in the wheat-field. Yet much good sound truth has been extracted from the old chronicles; and from such legends as Arthur, Lear, and Cymbeline some of the finest blossoms of our literature have sprung.

INGULPHUS.—A history of the Abbey of Croyland, or Crowland, in Lincolnshire, extending from 664 to 1091, is said to have been written by Ingulphus, who was abbot there for thirty-four years (1075–1109). But it is doubtful whether or not this was really the work of Ingulphus; and certainly it must not be taken as a trust-worthy record of passing events, for it is full of false and impro-bable statements.

ORDERICUS VITALIS.—This monk, who was born in 1075, at the village of Atcham on the Severn, and spent all his life, after his eleventh year, abroad, was the writer of an ecclesiastical history, extending from the Creation to the year 1141. His account of the Norman Conquest is minute; and that part of his history nar-rating the events of the first four years of the Conqueror's reign (1066–1070), is much prized.

WILLIAM OF MALMESBURY.—The name of William of Malmes-bury, born probably about the date of the Conquest, is remarkable among the many chroniclers of this period. His *History of the Eng-lish Kings*, in five books, extends from the landing of the Saxons to 1120; and then three other books, called *Historia Novella*, are added, carrying the story down to 1142. As an historian, he ex-cels in what is, comparatively speaking, careful writing, and a more exact balancing of facts than was common with the cowled chroniclers of the day. But his pages, too, abound in stories of miracles and prodigies, reflecting the " all-digestive" superstition of the time, from which the wisest heads were not free.

GEOFFREY OF MONMOUTH.—This learned Welsh monk, who died in 1154, is noted for having preserved the fine antique legends of the Celtic race in his *History of the Britons*, which he professed to have translated from an old Welsh chronicle. Here we find the story of Arthur and his Knights of the Round Table, upon which many noble works of our literature have been composed. The charm of such a book must necessarily be fatal to its value as a history; for the writer, letting his fancy play upon the adornment of these dim legends, mixes fact with fiction in a confusion that cannot be disentangled.

Gerald Barry (Giraldus Cambrensis), Henry of Huntingdon, Roger of Hoveden, and Benedict, Abbot of Peterborough, may also be named among the crowd of chroniclers who have written on the early history of England.

A favourite kind of light reading, often conned by the refectory fire in the long winter nights, was an *olla podrida* of interesting stories, gathered from every possible source and done into Latin by unknown hands. These books, called *Gesta*, were made up of monkish legends, chivalric romances, ghost-stories, parables, satirical flings at the foibles of women, and such stories from the classics as the Skeleton of Pallas and the Leap of Curtius. The chief reason why they are worthy of our notice here is, that Shakspere, Scott, and other great wizards of the fancy, drawing some of these dim old stories from their dusty sleep, have touched them with the wand of genius and turned the lumps of dull lead into jewels of the finest gold.

NORMAN-FRENCH WRITERS.

When the chase was over, and the Norman lords caroused in their English halls around the oak board, flinging scraps of the feast to their weary hounds, that couched on the rush-strewn floor, the lays of the French *trouvères* were sung by wandering minstrels, who were always warmly welcomed and often richly paid. Many poets of English birth soon took up this foreign strain, and wrote lays in Norman-French. The deeds of Alexander, Charlemagne, Havelok the Dane, Guy of Warwick, Cœur de Lion, and other such heroes, were celebrated in these romances. In the earlier stories there is more probability; but by degrees, what critics call the "machinery" of the poem, that is, the introduction of supernatural beings as actors in the drama, becomes wild and fanciful, borrowing largely from the weird superstitions of the North and the East. As we read, knights and ladies, grim giants dwelling in enchanted castles, misshapen dwarfs, fairies kindly and malevolent, dragons and earthdrakes, magicians with their potent wands, pass before us in a highly-coloured, much-distorted panorama.

The romances relating to King Arthur possess a special interest for us, since our Laureate and a brother bard have founded poems on these old tales. The strange and profane legend of the Saint Greal is mixed up throughout with the story of Arthur and his Knights. The Greal was said to be the dish from which our Saviour ate the

Last Supper. It was then taken, according to the legend, by Joseph of Arimathea, who used it to catch the blood flowing from the wounds of the Saviour. Too sacred for human gaze, it became invisible, and only revealed itself in visions to the pure knight Sir Galahad, who, having seen it, prayed for death. The names of Merlin the enchanter, the false knight Lancelot, and others, familiar to the thousands who have read the " Idylls of the King," constantly occur in the romances of Arthur. As has been already stated, the chronicler Geoffrey of Monmouth, who drew his materials from ancient Welsh and Breton songs, is the chief authority that we find for the story of Arthur.

WACE.—The best known of the Norman-French poets is Master Wace, as he calls himself, who was born probably at Jersey about 1112. He was educated at Caen, and there he spent nearly all his life. His chief poems are two—*Brut* d'Angleterre*, and *Roman de Rou.* The former, a translation into eight-syllabled romance verse of Geoffrey of Monmouth's History of Britain, contains nearly eighteen hundred lines; the latter, the Romance of Rollo, written partly in the same verse, narrates the history of the Dukes of Normandy from Rollo to the sixteenth year of Henry II. The central picture of this poem is the minute account of the battle of Hastings. Wace, who became Canon of Bayeux on the recommendation of Henry II., is thought to have died in England about 1184.

There are two among the Anglo-Norman romancers who are worthy to be named besides, not so much for the excellence of their verse as for their prominence in English history—Cardinal Stephen Langton, and Richard Cœur de Lion. In the British Museum there is a manuscript sermon of Langton's, in the middle of which he breaks into a pretty French song about " la bele Aliz," the fair Alice, and then turns the story of this lady and the flowers she has been plucking in a garden, so as to bear upon the praises of the Virgin Mary.

Richard I. is said to have composed several military poems

---

* The word *Brut* is said to be derived either from the name of Brutus, great-grandson of Æneas, whom tradition makes the first king of Britain, or from the old word *brud* (a rumour or history), from which has come our *bruit.*

called *Serventois*, in addition to a complaint addressed from his dungeon to the barons of France and England, bewailing his long captivity. Of this latter poem Horace Walpole printed, in his "Royal and Noble Authors," a Provençal form, which he took from a manuscript in the library of San Lorenzo at Florence.

As was natural from the miserable state of the Saxon nation immediately after the Conquest—her braver spirits forced, like Hereward and Robin Hood, to take to the greenwood and the marshes, while her weaker souls were cowed into tame submission and slavery—the works written in English of the second stage were very few. The Saxon Chronicle, already noticed, runs on to the year 1154, when the registers come to an abrupt stop.

Two works are named as the chief remains of the Semi-Saxon literature. One, a *Translation of Wace's "Brut,"* by Layamon, a priest of Ernlcye (Areleye-Regis), near the Severn in Worcestershire, is placed by Hallam between the years 1155 and 1200. It rises in many passages beyond a mere translation of Wace's text, and runs to more than fourteen thousand long verses. Its language is said to be a western dialect of the Semi-Saxon. The *Ormulum*, so called from its writer, Ormin or Orm, is a metrical paraphrase of Scripture, which has been assigned to the second stage of the language. Dr. Craik, however, suggests that it probably belongs to the end of the thirteenth century. The language of the "Ormulum" is, beyond question, in a more advanced stage than that of Layamon's "Brut."

FIRST ERA OF ENGLISH LITERATURE.

**FROM THE BIRTH OF CHAUCER ABOUT 1328 A.D. TO THE INTRO-
DUCTION OF PRINTING BY CAXTON IN 1474 A.D.**

CHAPTER I.

THE MINSTREL AND THE MONK.

Minstrel v. Monk.	Modern minstrels.	The monk.
Honour to the minstrel.	English metrical romance.	The Scriptorium.
Other names.	Robert of Gloucester.	The workmen.
Picture of a castle hall.	Robert Mannyng.	Picture of a copyist.
Classes of minstrels.	Thomas the Rhymer.	Purple and gold.
Their dress.	Craik's summary.	Illuminations.
Decay of the craft.		

THE literature of England, as indeed of all Europe, lay during the earlier and central periods of the Middle Ages in the hands of the Minstrels and the Monks. The minstrel, roaming through the land, sang ballads of love and war; the monk sat in his dim-lit cell penning tomes of unreadable theology, very useless logic, or dry but valuable history, and varying these sterner labours with the graceful task of copying and illuminating the manuscripts, which then held the place of our printed volumes. There was no love lost between the brotherhoods of the Harp and the Missal; for the minstrel wielded a weapon in his song which often hit monkery sly and terrible blows, and could, moreover, open wide the purses of rich nobles, whose coins were doled out with niggard hand to the Church. So it happened that the cloister doors were too often shut in the faces of the wearied gleemen; and grumbling Brother Ambrose, having shot the bolt, betook himself in wrath to his cell to write a Latin treatise, as ponderous as himself, against the abominations of minstrelsy and minstrels.

In very early days the Bards and Scalds of northern Europe sang
their own verses to the music of the harp, much as Homer used to
sing by the shore of the sounding Ægean. The minstrels of later
days recited sometimes their own compositions, but oftener the
poems of others.   And by no means ignoble was the occupation
of these musical wanderers.   When Alfred donned the minstrel's
dress, he took a downward step, to be sure, but by no means so
great a downward step as the Emperor Napoleon would take, if he
laid aside the imperial purple for the robes of a first tenor in the
Italian Opera.   And when Alfred walked among the tents of
Guthrum's camp, a servant bore his harp behind him—a thing
which would have at once revealed the secret of the singer, if it
had not been a very usual occurrence.   Gleeman and Jogeler (our
juggler; the French, *jongleur;* the Latin, *joculator*) were other
names for the minstrel craft in old English days.

Nor was there any more honoured or more welcome guest than
this wanderer, whose time of triumph came when the rough sub-
stantial supper had vanished before the hungry hunters and their
dogs, and the cups of mead or wine began to circle round the hall.
Mimicry and action accompanied the music and the song.   And
as the wine fumes mounted to the brain, and the wild torrent of
melody drove their pulses into madder flow, the battle-day seemed
to have come again.   War-cries rang through the smoky hall; and
in the ruddy light, which streamed from crackling logs or flaring
pine-knots, flushed brows grew a darker red; and hands, veined as
if with whip-cord, clutched fiercely at knife or bill-hook, and
wheeled the weapon in flashing circles through the air. Love, too,
was the minstrel's theme; and here the power of his song struck
even deeper to those simple hearts than when he sang of war,
although the eye gleamed with another light, and the stern war-
shout faded into gentler tones.

The minstrels in feudal times were probably divided into various classes, which were distinguished as Squire minstrels, Yeoman
minstrels, &c.   Those attached to noble houses wore the arms of
their patron, hung round the neck by a silver chain. The distinctive badge of the profession was the *wrest* or tuning-key.   Many

minstrels carried a tabor; but some played on a *viele*, supposed to have been like a guitar, in the top of which one hand turned a handle, while the other touched the keys of the instrument. The minstrel's dress, of which an idea may be gathered from the following passage, bore some resemblance to that of the monks.

An old letter, written by a man who was present at the grand entertainment given at Kenilworth in 1575 to Queen Elizabeth, describes the dress of a minstrel, who took a prominent part in the pageant. He was dressed in a long gown of Kendal green, with sleeves hanging down to the middle of the leg; a red belt girt his waist; his tonsure, like a monk's, was shaven round; his head was bare; a red ribbon hung round his neck; his shoes were cleanly blacked with soot; all his ruffs (this fashion belonged to Elizabeth's own day) stuck stiffly out with the setting-sticks, which then did the work of starch; and round his neck were suspended the arms of Islington. Although this depicts the minstrel at a later stage than that of which we write, when the profession had fallen low in public esteem, it may yet serve to give us an idea of the kind of men who wandered from hall to hall, embalming in song those picturesque old histories of early English days, whose very roughness of flow is a new charm, and whose large admixture of highly-coloured fable, if detracting from their historic worth, yet endeared them all the more to the hearts of the simple people, whose delight it was to sing and hear them by the winter fire or beneath the summer trees.

The application of the word *Minstrel* changed a good deal during the decay of chivalry. At first used to denote those wandering historians of whom we have spoken, "abstracts and brief chronicles of the time," who sang of love or war in lordly halls, playing a musical accompaniment and gesturing with imitative motions, it came to apply afterwards chiefly to the musician. The song was dropped, and so were the gestures. The Poet took up the song; the Juggler and Tumbler took up the bodily movements; while the Minstrel remained a player of music only. Had Alfred Tennyson lived six hundred years ago, in order to win the laurel-crown which he worthily wears as first minstrel in the land, he would have needed, in addition to his fine poetic genius, something of the pliant muscle that bears Blondin along the perilous rope, and the rapid finger with which Ernst draws the music of the spheres from tightened cat-gut.

An Act of 1597, by which Elizabeth included wandering minstrels among rogues, vagabonds, and beggars, gave a mortal wound to the minstrel craft. Cromwell, too, denounced terrible penalties against fiddlers or minstrels. So low had the brotherhood of old Homer fallen!

In more enlightened days the poet and the musician have found once more something like their fitting station in society; but the tumbler, representing the mere physical element of the old minstrel craft, still remains among the dregs of the middle classes—but a step or two above the point where Elizabeth and Cromwell left the poor degraded minstrels.

MINSTRELSY.—The poetry of the Saxons was distinguished from their prose by a peculiar kind of *alliteration*. Metre or rhyme they had none. These attributes of English verse were imported from the Continent by the Normans, who copied both from the decayed Latin. Even before the age of Constantine a species of rhythmical poetry, in which the metrical quantity of syllables was almost wholly disregarded, and the accent alone attended to in pronunciation, became common, especially in the mouths of the lower classes of those that spoke Latin. In this rhythmical verse the number of syllables was irregular. That rhyme was used in Latin poetry from the end of the fourth century is a distinctly proved fact.

No work, in which rhyme or metre was used, can be traced in our literature until after the Norman Conquest. A few lines in the Saxon Chronicle on the death of the Conqueror, and a short canticle, said by Matthew Paris to have been dictated by the Virgin Mary to a hermit of Durham, are perhaps the earliest specimens of rhyme in English verse. Through Layamon's poem, written in the time of Henry II., numbers of short verses are scattered which rhyme together pretty exactly. There are, besides, some eight-syllable lines in imitation of Wace's metre. But, on the whole, the *Brut* is, like old Saxon verse, without either metre or rhyme. Then comes a gap of a century, during which no maker of English rhymes appeared, at least so far as we know. Metrical romances in Latin and French were plentiful enough, and on them all the literary talent of the time was spent; for the one tongue was the speech of courtiers, and the other that of church-men. The English, thoroughly out of fashion, was left in its fall to the serfs and boors of the land.

But a day came, about the opening of the thirteenth century, when the enslaved speech began to raise its diminished head and assert its native power, and then metrical romances were written in an English form. These first faltering steps of an infant lite-rature were nearly all translations from the French romances, some of which have been already noticed.

Tyrwhitt says: "I am inclined to believe that we have no English romance prior to the age of Chaucer, which is not a translation or imitation of some earlier French romance."

The story-books, called *Gesta*, whose anecdotes were the delight of the cloister, and often lent a charm to the teachings of the pulpit, were the grand store-houses, from which the romancers drew the material of their tales.

A monk, named Robert of Gloucester, whose known life is summed up in the single fact that he lived in the abbey of that city, wrote, after 1278, a *Rhyming Chronicle* in English, narrating British history to the end of Henry III.'s reign. The earlier part of this work, which seems to be written in west country English, and is printed in lines of fourteen syllables, is a free translation from Geoffrey of Monmouth. Warton condemns it as "totally destitute of art or imagination."

Robert Mannyng of Brunne in Lincolnshire, writing half a century later, also produced a *Rhyming Chronicle*, translated from the French of Wace and Langtoft. The latter of these was a canon regular of St. Austin, at Bridlington in Yorkshire. An-other name well known in the list of minstrels is that of Thomas the Rhymer, who flourished during the thirteenth century in the south of Scotland. His full name is thought to have been Thomas

Learmount of Ercildoun (now Earlston near Melrose). He and an unknown poet, Kendal, are mentioned by Robert of Brunne as the authors of "Sir Tristrem," a romance which was little known until it was published by Sir Walter Scott at the outset of his literary career.

Dr. Craik thus sums up the leading facts in the history of English metrical romance :—

1. At least the first examples of it were translations from the French.

2. If any such were produced so early as before the close of the twelfth century (of which we have no evidence), they were probably designed for the entertainment of the mere commonalty, to whom alone the French language was unknown.

3. In the thirteenth century were composed the earliest of those we now possess in their original form.

4. In the fourteenth century the English took the place of the French metrical romance in all classes. This was its brightest era.

5. In the fifteenth it was supplanted by another species of poetry, among the more educated classes, and had also to contend with another rival in the prose romance; but, nevertheless, it still continued to be produced, although in less quantity and of an inferior fabric.

6. It did not altogether cease to be read and written until after the commencement of the sixteenth century.

7. From that time the taste for this earliest form of our poetical literature lay asleep, until, after the lapse of three hundred years, it was re-awakened in this century by Scott.

THE MONK.—Let us now turn from the noisy brilliant scenes, in which the old minstrel was most at home, to the quiet gloom of monastic life, and see what literary work went on within those thick oaken doors, studded with heavy nails, whose hinges creaked out but a churlish welcome to the belated harpist, or often refused to creak at all.

We pass through the arched gateway—rounded if the building be of the earlier Norman style, pointed if of the later Gothic—and across the broad quadrangle, through a smaller door into the arched and pillared cloister, where draughts are not unfrequent invaders through the unglazed loop-holes, and the green damp has traced its grotesque velvet-work upon the cold stone walls. A few sombre figures glide silently through the shadowy stillness; but we linger not here. Up a narrow stair of winding stone into a higher room, arched and pillared too, but lighter, and dotted with long-robed monks, all intent upon real and useful work— doing that service to our literature for which the mediæval monastery deserves our warmest gratitude. We have reached the *Scriptorium;* and its chilly bareness certainly presents a striking contrast to the snug, carpeted, and thick-curtained libraries, in which modern clergymen pen their weekly sermons, or their occasional essays and reviews. Round the naked stone walls wooden chests are ranged, heaped with the precious manuscripts, to multiply and adorn which is the task of those cowled and dark-skirted men who toil in that work-room of the Abbey. And over the rude desks and tables of the time heads of many hues are bending—choir-boys with locks of curly flax; grave-browed men, whose ring of raven hair, surrounding the shaven crown, proclaims the noon of life ; and the thinly silvered scalp of weak old age—all intent upon their work. Now and then a novice, to whom a common work, or some much-used Service-book for the choir, has been intrusted, crosses to the side of that keen-eyed, wrinkled monk, who has power in his very glance, and humbly begs advice as to the form of a letter or the colouring of a design. And ever and anon the grave tone of this same instructor checks with a few calm words the buzz that sometimes rises from the boyish monks whom he guides. There are things in that Scriptorium which we miss in our writing-desks and on our study-tables. Besides the quills and coloured inks, there are reed-pens, pots of brilliant paint, phials of gold and silver size, hair pencils of various shapes and kinds : for the work of the copyist-monks is rather that of the artist than of the mere penman ; and although the figures, which adorn the brilliant illuminations of those Missals and Psalters that preserve in the nineteenth century the arts of dead ages, have much of the stiffness of all mediæval drawing, yet, for beauty of design and richness of colouring, many productions of the quiet Scriptorium remain unsurpassed by modern pencils.

Let us draw near to this cowled transcriber—evidently a monk of note from his solitary state—who sits apart on his straight-backed wooden chair, and note the progress of his work. He is copying the Gospels upon vellum, and has just put the finishing touches to a painting, glowing with scarlet and gold and blue lace-work, fantastically formed of intermingled flowers and birds, which has occupied the hot noontide hours of a full week. The brilliant tracery forms the initial letter of a chapter. This done, he takes the pen, and rapidly, with practised hand, traces in black ink the thick perpendicular strokes of that old English text-hand, which has given their name to our black-letter manuscripts. While the right hand guides the pen, the left holds a knife, whose point, pressed upon the quickly blackening vellum, is ever ready to shape a clumsy line or erase a wrong word. There are no capitals except the brilliant and fanciful initials; nor any points except a slight dash, occasionally used to divide the sentences. When the book is finished, which may be the work of years if the decorations are minute and profuse, the title will probably be painted in red ink (hence the word *Rubric*); and the name of the copyist, with date and place of completion, will also shine in brilliant scarlet or other coloured ink at the foot of the last page. The headings of the various chapters are also written for the most part in red ink.

. Perhaps the richest specimens of the ancient manuscript are those copies of the Gospels on purple vellum, written in silver letters with the sacred names in gold, which were favourite productions of the eighth, ninth, and tenth centuries. These, however, were not originally of English growth, but were the offspring of Greek luxury.

It was upon the initial letters and the marginal ornaments, with which the pages of these mediæval manuscripts were adorned, that the taste and labour of the illuminators were chiefly bestowed. Angelic and human figures, birds, beasts, and fishes, flowers, shells, and leaves, were all pressed into the service of the patient monks. Rare and exquisite patterns grew under their unwearying pencils in the still Scriptorium, until each page of the Missal or Service-book presented an embroidery of gorgeous colouring, resembling nothing so much as the many-hued splendours of a great cathedral window, through which the rays of the setting sun stream in a flood of rainbow glory.

It would be vain to attempt a description of these beautiful works. Many pages of this book might be filled with a mere enumeration of the various figures and colours combined in one of the splendid designs. How hard and how long the monks must have worked at their copying-desks can only be judged by those who have turned over the leaves of an illuminated Missal, executed in the Scriptorium of some old abbey.

CHAPTER II.

SIR JOHN DE MANDEVILLE.

Born about 1300 A.D..........Died 1372 A.D.

First English prose.	IIIs book written.
Mandeville's birth.	IIIs wild stories.
His travels.	Value of his book.
IIIs return.	Illustrative extract.

THE earliest writer of English prose, whose work survives, was Sir John de Mandeville.

He was born at St. Albans in Hertfordshire about the year 1300. Educated for the medical profession, he had scarcely finished his studies when, impelled by the irresistible desire of change, or, perhaps, by some deeper motive of which we know nothing, he set out at the age of twenty-two to travel in distant lands. He joined a Mahometan army in Palestine. He saw some service under the Sultan of Egypt. He penetrated even as far as Cathay (China), where, we are told, he lived for three years at Pekin. Turkey, Persia, Armenia, India, Ethiopia, Libya, and many other places, were also visited by him. His knowledge of medicine often stood his friend, no doubt, among the rude tribes with whom he met. For thirty-four years Mandeville roved over the wildest regions of the Old World, looked upon as lost and dead by all his friends at home. And when he came back a worn greybeard, he found, instead of the many fresh cheeks and bright eyes of the friends from whom he had parted so long ago, only the grave welcome of a few thin and withered men.

1356 A.D. In or about the year 1356, immediately after his return, he wrote in Latin a *Narrative of his Travels*. This work was afterwards translated by himself into French, and thence into English.

Mandeville's great fault as a writer was, that he loaded his pages with the wildest and most absurd stories, picked up by the way, and admitted upon the shallowest testimony—often, indeed, upon none at all. The most extravagant offshoots of the chivalrous Romance find a parallel in many passages of the oldest work of English prose, in which monsters, giants, and demons are found to swarm. Such stories as of men with tails, and of a bird native to Madagascar that could carry an elephant in its talons, are given with the greatest seriousness. Much, however, as we may laugh at the extravagant tone of the work, it possesses for us a deep interest, both as a remarkable monument of our noble old speech in its infancy, and as a specimen of the style of thought common in an unripe age.

Mandeville, roving again from England, died and was buried at Liège in 1372.

The following extract is from the seventh chapter of his Travels, entitled, "Of the Pilgrimages in Jerusalem, and of the Holy Places thereaboute :"—

And zee schull undirstonde that whan men comen to Jerusalem her first pilgrymage is to the chirche of the Holy Sepulcr wher oure Lord was buryed, that is withoute the cytee on the north syde. But it is now enclosed in with the ton wall. And there is a full fair chirche all rownd, and open above, and covered with leed. And on the west syde is a fair tour and an high for belles strongly made. And in the myddes of the chirche is a tabernacle as it wer a lytyll hows, made with a low lityll dore; and that tabernacle is made in maner of a half a compas right curiousely and richely made of gold and azure and othere riche coloures, full nobelyche made. And in the ryght side of that tabernacle is the sepulcre of oure Lord. And the tabernacle is viij fote long and v fote wide, and xj fote in heghte. And it is not longe sithe the sepulcre was all open, that men myghte kisse it and touche it. But for pilgrymes that comen thider peyned hem to breke the ston in peces, or in poudr; therefore the Soudan [*Sultan*] hath do make a wall aboute the sepulcr that no man may towche it. But in the left syde of the wall of the tabernacle is well the heighte of a man, is a gret ston, to the quantytee of a mannes hed, that was of the holy sepulcr, and that ston kissen the pilgrymes that comen thider. In that tabernacle ben no wyndowes, but it is all made light with lampes that hangen befor the sepulcr. And there is a lampe that hongeth befor the sepulcr that brenneth light, and on the Gode ffryday it goth out be him self, at that hour that our Lord roos fro deth to lyve. Also within the chirche at the right syde besyde the queer of the churche is the Mount of Calvarye, wher our Lord was don on the cros. And it is a roche of white coloure and a lytill medled with red. And the cros was set in a morteys in the same roche, and on that roche dropped the woundes of our Lord, whan he was pyned on the cros, and that is cleped [*called*] Golgatha. And men gon up to that Golgatha be degrees [*steps*]. And in the place of that morteys was Adames hed found after Noes flode, in tokene that the synnes of Adam scholde ben bought in that same place. And upon that roche made Abraham sacrifise to our Lord.

CHAPTER III.

JOHN DE WYCLIFFE.

Born about 1324 A.D..........Died 1384 A.D.

Wycliffe's birth.	Wycliffe at St. Paul's.	His death.
Enters Oxford.	Synod of Lambeth.	His bones burned.
His rapid rise.	His sickness.	The English Bible.
The Mendicant Friars.	The Poor Priests.	Character of his prose.
Begins to lecture.	Life at Lutterworth.	Illustrative extract.
Envoy at Bruges.		

ON a rocky point, overhanging the Tees in Yorkshire, a manor-house stood, in which once lived the Wycliffes of Wycliffe.* There, probably in 1324, a boy was born, who has gilded the family name with undying lustre. Among the rich woodlands of that fertile valley he grew up, taught, we know not certainly where or by whom, until he reached his sixteenth year. Then a new world opened upon the country squire's son.

Travelling to Oxford on horseback, and spending, no doubt, many weeks upon the rough and perilous journey, young **1340** Wycliffe was entered as a Commoner upon the books of A.D. Queen's College, a newly founded school. From Queen's he soon removed to Merton. The students of Oxford in that day were, as we learn from Chaucer's pictured page, as strongly marked out into reading men and fast men as they are in our own century. Among the motley company that rode out of the Tabard gateway down the Canterbury road, there was "a clerk of Oxenforde," lean and logical, who would rather have had twenty red or black-bound books at his bed's head than wear the richest robes or revel in the sweetest joys of music; and in violent contrast to this good threadbare bookworm, the Miller in his tale gives a full-length portrait of the dissolute "parish clerk Absolon," who, clad in

* The name *Wycliffe* means the "cliff by the water." The family took their surname from their manor.

hosen red and light-blue kirtle, with a snowy surplice flowing around his dainty limbs, and the windows of St. Paul's carved upon his shoes, minced through the service of the parish church. Many such did John Wycliffe meet in the streets and schools of Oxford; but his place must have been, not among the fast men in the brew-houses, ringing with the sounds of fiddle and dance, but among the red-bound books in his quiet rooms, else how could he have won a Fellowship in Merton, which was then considered the most learned college in Oxford?

His rise was rapid. In 1361 he was presented to the college living of Fylingham; and towards the close of the same year he was elected Master of Balliol College. Four years later, the Primate appointed him to the Wardenship of Canterbury Hall, in the room of the deposed Wodehall.

Mendicant friars at that time swarmed all over England, who, by the sale of relics and pardons "all hot from Rome," fleeced the poor country folk of their hard-earned groats. Such a one was the Pardoner of the "Canterbury Tales," who sold clouts and pigs' bones as holy relics, for money, wool, cheese, and wheat, swindling even the poorest widow out of her mite; and all the while, amid the farrago of old stories, with which he pleased his gaping audience, taking up the hypocritical cry, "Radix malorum est cupiditas." Such canting and cheating kindled rage in the honest heart of Wycliffe, who directed his sturdy eloquence against them. In his treatise called *Objections to Friars*, he maintained that the Gospel in its freedom, without error of man, is the sole rule of religion. And thus he struck the key-note in the noble music of his life.

In 1372 Wycliffe took the degree of D.D. at Oxford, and thus became qualified to lecture as a Professor of Divinity. Armed with this new power, the plain-speaking, true-hearted Englishman gathered a band of pupils in a wooden hall, roughly plastered and roofed with thatch, like all Oxford at that date, and there lifted up his voice boldly against the corrupted doctrines and the swollen avarice of the Church.

His fame led the rulers of England to send him, in 1374, as

envoy to Bruges, to protest against certain encroachments of the
papal power. A momentous journey it was to Wycliffe, for at
Bruges he seems to have become acquainted with John of Ghent,
Duke of Lancaster, who shielded the daring reformer in many a
perilous hour.

Already there was thunder in the air, gathering and blackening
round Wycliffe's path. A charge of heresy was laid
1377 against him, and he was summoned before the Houses of
A.D. Convocation. On the 19th of February, 1377, a venerable man, his face "sicklied o'er with the pale cast of
thought," stood within old St. Paul's, a grey beard sweeping
his breast, a dark belted robe flowing to his feet, and a tall
white staff held firmly in his thin hand. But he did not stand
alone. The eldest living son of the King, and the Earl Marshal of
England stood by his side; for Lancaster and Percy loved and
honoured the brave Oxford Doctor. The storm passed harmless
by. A dispute which rose between Lancaster and Bishop Courtney as to whether the accused should sit or stand, Courtney in-
sisting on the latter, excited so fierce a tumult that the meeting
was dissolved. During all the evening shouting mobs ran riot
through the streets of London.

Then King Edward died, and his grandson Richard reigned.
So marked a man had Wycliffe become in this Reformation
struggle, that the first Parliament of Richard II. submitted to him
a question, "Was it lawful to keep back the treasure of the kingdom for its own defence, instead of sending it away to the Pope?"
Who can need to be told the reply?

This could not go on without drawing forth thunder from the
banks of Tiber. Five bulls, couched in the fiercest words, were
launched against that "master in error," John Wycliffe, who was
forthwith to be committed to jail. Summoned before a synod at
Lambeth in April 1378, he replied to all charges manfully, and to
honest minds most convincingly. And yet, in spite of this
increased boldness, he was not seized and martyred; because
nearly all English laymen were on his side—some from political
motives, others on religious grounds. The pope and his creatures,

though their hearts burned to smite him down, dared not do so, for they feared the people.

It was then that a wasting sickness seized him at Oxford. His health, worn out with study, gave way under the mental wear of these troubled years. He lay, as it seemed, on the point of death, when eight men—four doctors to represent the mendicant friars, and four aldermen of the town—entered his chamber. They came to talk the old man into an undoing of his life's work—into a penitent recantation of what they called his errors. He listened until they had done, then " holding them with his glittering eye," he signed to his servant to raise him in the bed, and in strong, defiant tone he cried, " I shall not die, but live; and again declare the evil deeds of the friars !" What could they do but grow pale and go ? As he lay panting on the pillow, new life shot through his tingling nerves ; and in no long time he rose again from that bed to do glorious battle in the cause of truth.

His attack upon transubstantiation drew upon him the wrath of his University. One day in 1381 the Chancellor entered his class-room, and in the hearing of his scholars condemned his teaching as heretical. This finally led to the shutting of his class. But it was not in the power of Chancellors or Primates to stop the spread of light in the land. Though proceedings were taken against the disciples of Wycliffe—and all the more bitterly when that fiery adherent of the pope, Courtney, became Archbishop of Canterbury—yet their number constantly increased. Not one voice, but many were now heard in the land. " Poor priests," as they were called, trudged barefoot even into the remotest hamlets, preaching, in defiance of the clergy, wherever they could gather a crowd to hear them, in church, church-yard, market-place, or fair. So the good seed was sown broad-cast over England ; and, though often trampled fiercely down by the infuriated priesthood of a later day, especially in London and the great towns, in many a green far-off country nook it sprang and ripened and safely bore its golden fruit.

Nearly five years before he was silenced at Oxford, Wycliffe had become Rector of Lutterworth, a Leicestershire parish, watered

by the little river Swift.   Until 1381 his time was about equally
divided between his cottagers in Leicestershire and his students
at Oxford.   But after that date he devoted himself with earnest
heart to the work of a country parson; and never does the great
Dr. Wycliffe, first scholar of his day and keenest logician of the
Oxford halls, seem so truly great as when we trace his footsteps
among the hovels of Lutterworth.   A sorry place it would have
seemed to a townsman of smart modern Lutterworth, glowing
with red brick and gaslight.   Two or three rows of thatched
cabins, built chiefly of lath and plaster, straggled along the sloping
banks of the Swift.   From the uneven street one stepped in upon
a foul earthen floor.   The rafters above hung thick with black
soot, for there were no chimneys, and the smoke found its way
out of door or window as it best could.   There, in the meanest
hut, might the good rector be often seen, cheering with kind
words the sick peasant, who had then no better bed than a heap
of straw, and no softer pillow than a log of wood.   The morning
he spent among his books, revising a Latin treatise, or adding
some sentences to the English Bible that was fast growing beneath
his patient pen.   In the afternoon he girt his long dark robe about
him, took his white staff, and went out among his flock.   And on
Sundays, clad in a gorgeous vestment, adorned with golden
cherubs, of which some tarnished fragments are still shown, he
preached the truth in homely, nervous English words, from that
pulpit of carved oak which stands in Lutterworth Church—a
sacred memorial of one who has worthily been called " The morning
star of our English Reformation."

So passed the last years of this great life.   In his sixtieth
year, while he was engaged in sacred service within the chancel
of Lutterworth Church, paralysis, which had already
Dec. 31,   shaken his frame severely, struck him down to die.   A
1384   day or two later, in the last hours of the dying year, his
A.D.   great intrepid spirit passed away from the clouds and
toils of earth.

More than forty years had swept by, when the pent-up vengeance
of his enemies, from which the living man had been mercifully

shielded, burst in impotent fury upon his mouldered corpse. The coffin was torn up, and carried to the little bridge over the Swift, where his bones were burned to ashes and scattered on the waters of the brook. "Thus," says worthy Thomas Fuller, "the brook conveyed his ashes to Avon, Avon into Severn, Severn into the narrow seas, they into the main ocean; and thus the ashes of Wycliffe are the emblem of his doctrine, which now is dispersed all the world over."

As a writer, Wycliffe's great merit lies in his having given to England the first *English* version of the *whole* Bible. There were already existing a few English fragments, such as many of the Psalms, certain portions of Mark and Luke, and some of the Epistles. But to the mass of the people the Bible was a sealed book, locked up in a dead and foreign tongue. Wycliffe soon saw the incalculable value of an English Bible in the work of the English Reformation, and set himself to the noble task of giving a boon so precious to his native land. No doubt he sought the aid of other pens, but to what extent we cannot now determine. The greater part of the work—perhaps the whole—was done during those quiet years at Lutterworth, between 1381 and his death. It is nearly certain that he saw the work finished before he died. A complete edition of Wycliffe's Bible, in five volumes, was issued in 1850 from the Oxford Press.

His Latin works are very numerous. One of the principal was called *Trialogus*, which embodies his opinions in a series of conversations carried on by Truth, Wisdom, and Falsehood. It contains, no doubt, the essence of his class lectures.

From his country parsonage by the Swift he poured forth an incredible number of English tracts and treatises, addressed to the people, and thoroughly leavened with his earnest love of truth. The characteristic feature of his English is a manly ruggedness. Content to know that his meaning is strongly and clearly put, he often disdains all elegance of style, and sometimes lapses into lame and slovenly language. We may compare him, as an opponent of error, not to a gallant master of fence, glistening in well-cut taffeta, who with keen glittering rapier lunges home to the heart, while he never loses the elegance of posture and movement, the poise of body and of blade, which his graceful art has taught him; but rather to the sturdy leather-clad rustic, who wields his oaken quarter-staff with such sweeping vigour, that in a twinkling he beats down his opponent's guard, and with a rattling shower of heavy blows lays the luckless fellow bleeding and sense-less on the earth.

SPECIMEN OF WYCLIFFE'S PROSE.

PART OF LUKE XXIV.

    But in o day of the woke ful eerli thei camen to the graue, and broughten swete smelling spices that thei hadden arayed. And thei founden the stoon turnyd awey fro the graue. And thei geden in and foundun not the bodi of the Lord Jhesus. And it was don, the while thei weren astonyed in thought of this thing, lo twey men stodun bisidis hem in schynyng cloth. And whanne thei dredden and bowiden her semblaunt into erthe, thei seiden to hem, what seeken ye him that lyueth with deede men? He is not here; but he is risun: haue ye minde how he spak to you whanne he was yit in Golilee, and seide, for it behoueth mannes sone to be bitakun into the hondis of synful men: and to be crucifyed: and the thridde day to rise agen? And thei bithoughten on hise wordis, and thei geden agen fro the graue: and teelden alle these thingis to the ellevene and to alle othere. And there was Marye Maudeleyn and Jone and Marye of James, and othere wymmen that weren with hem, that seiden to Apostlis these thingis.

CHAPTER IV.

GEOFFREY CHAUCER.

Born about 1328 A.D..........Died 1400 A.D.

CHAUCER is a star of the first magnitude. First great writer of English verse, he proudly wears the honoured title,—"Father of English Poetry;" nor can the most brilliant of his successors feel ashamed of such a lineage.

The accounts of his early life are very uncertain. He calls himself a Londoner; and an inscription on his tomb, which signified that in 1400 he died at the age of seventy-two, seems to fix his birth in the year 1328. The words "Philogenet, of Cambridge, Clerk," which occur in one of his earliest works in reference to himself, have caused it to be inferred that he was educated at Cambridge. But Warton and others claim him as an Oxford man too; and, if he studied there, it is more than probable that he sat at the feet of Wycliffe, and imbibed the doctrines of the great reformer. An entry in some old register of the Inns of Court is said to state, that " Geffrey Chaucer was fined two shillings for beating a Franciscane friar in Fleet Street;" which ebullition of young blood is the only recorded event of his supposed law-studies in the Inner Temple.

The favour of John of Ghent, won we know not how, introduced him to Court and the favour of King Edward III. The handsome and accomplished poet, with his red lips and graceful shape, was the very man to win his way in a courtly circle. He went with the army to France, where in 1359 he was made

prisoner at the siege of Retters.   On his release and return home,
whenever that happened, we find his prospects grow brighter and
brighter.   One grant following another, showed how dear the
man of letters, who could also wield a sword, was to the brave old
king.   When in his thirty-ninth year (1367), the poet received a
pension of 20 marks ; which, as each silver mark weighed eight
ounces and was worth £10 of our money, was equivalent to £200
a year.   Five years later, he was sent with two others to Genoa,
on an important commercial mission; during which trip

1372   he is thought to have travelled in northern Italy, to

A.D.   have visited Petrarch at Padua, and to have heard from
the very lips of that " old man eloquent," the story of
" Patient Grisilde," which he afterwards embodied in the Clerkes Tale.

Then came other royal grants,—a pitcher of wine daily for life
—the office of Comptroller of Customs of wool, wine, &c., in the
Port of London—the wardship of a rich heir, for three years'
guardianship of whom he got £104.   During this sunshine of
kingly favour he married a maid of honour, whose sister afterwards
became the wife of his patron, John of Ghent.   By this union a
pension of 100 shillings, lately conferred on his wife, was added
to his income.   Two more diplomatic missions, to Flanders and to
France, proved the confidence reposed in him by his royal master.
Thus rich, honoured, useful, and, we may conjecture, happy, Geoffrey Chaucer saw in 1377 the grey head of the third Edward go
down with sorrow to the grave.

At first, under the new reign, all was bright, and continued so
for some seven years.   In the first year of Richard II. his daily
gallon of wine was exchanged for a pension of 20 marks, and
other gifts were bestowed on the prosperous comptroller.   But
soon his sun was darkly clouded.   It was not likely that he could
avoid taking an active part in the difficulties that arose between
Richard and Lancaster ; and, as his feelings were strongly enlisted
on the side of the duke, he fell into disfavour with the king.
Embroiled especially in a London riot, raised by John of Northampton, who was a friend of Lancaster, the poet was forced to
flee to the Continent.   There, in Hainault, in France, and in Zee-

land, he lived with his wife and children for eighteen months, becoming at last almost penniless through generosity to his fellow-exiles, and the failure of supplies from home, where his agents had treacherously appropriated his rents. Returning, he was flung into the Tower, and lay there until he was forced to sell his two pensions to save his family from starvation; nor was he freed until, indignant at the base ingratitude of those in whose cause he was suffering, and pressed both by the threats and the entreaties of the Court, he confessed his guilt and denounced his accomplices. Then, Lancaster being once more in the ascendant, royal favour smiled on the poet. He was made Clerk of Works at Westminster and other places, receiving, in lieu of the pensions he had been forced to sell, a pension of £20 and an annual pipe of wine.

Wearied with public life, he retired about 1391 to his house at Woodstock, where he sat down in sober age and country quiet to write his great work—*The Canterbury Tales.* His remaining days were spent at Woodstock and Donnington Castle, both gifts from the princely Lancaster ; and within these sheltering walls he rested and wrote. The accession of Henry IV. brought good fortune to the poet, whose pension was doubled; but he did not live long to enjoy this greater wealth. Within a house which is said to have stood in a garden near the site of Henry the Seventh's Chapel at Westminster, he died on the 25th of October, 1400. His body was buried close by in the Abbey, where the dust of England's noblest dead is laid.

Chaucer's chequered life was such as to wear off all the little roughnesses and conceits of his earlier character, and bring the fine grain of the manly nature below into full view. He saw both the lights and the shadows of human existence,—at one time the admired of a brilliant Court, at another a prisoner and an exile. But through every change he seems to have borne a heart unsoured by care ; and even in old age, when his locks hung in silver threads beneath his buttoned bonnet, a joyous spirit shone in his wrinkled face. A small, fair, round-trimmed beard fringed those lips, whose red fulness was remarked as a special beauty in the handsome face of the young poet. His common dress consisted of red hose, horned shoes, and a loose frock of camlet, reaching to the knee, with wide sleeves fastened at the wrist.

Chaucer's fame as a writer rests chiefly upon his *Canterbury Tales*. The idea of the poems is, perhaps, borrowed from the "Decameron" of Boccaccio, in which a hundred tales are supposed to be told after dinner by the persons spending ten days in a country house near Florence during a time of plague. Chaucer's plan is this : A company of some twenty-nine or thirty pilgrims collect at the Tabard Inn in Southwark, bound for the shrine of St. Thomas à-Becket at Canterbury. The motley gathering contains specimens of nearly every character then common in the streets and homes of England. After the Prologue has described the company and their start, a brave Knight, bronzed by the Syrian sun, tells the first tale. Then follows the Miller, "dronken of ale;" and so the tale goes round, often merrily, but sometimes of a sadder tone, beguiling the miles of the weary road. As Chaucer sketches the plan of the work in his Prologue, each pilgrim ought to tell two stories when going to Canterbury, and two more on the homeward way; and the whole proceedings were to be wound up with a supper at the Tabard, where the teller of the best tales was to be entertained by the rest of the band. The poet did not live to complete his design. Twenty-four tales only are given; the arrival at Canterbury, the scenes at the shrine, the tales of the return, the wind-up supper, are all untold. Two of the stories —the *Tale of Melibeus* and the *Persones Tale*—are in prose, and afford a very favourable specimen of Chaucer's power in that kind of writing. Nothing could surpass the "Canterbury Tales," as a series of pictures of the middle-class English life during the fourteenth century. Every character is a perfect study, drawn from the life with a free yet careful hand,—in effect broad, and brilliant in colour, but painted with a minuteness of touch and a careful finish that remind us strongly of the elaborate pencilling of our Pre-Raphaelite artists, whose every ivy-leaf and straw is a perfect picture.

This great work was written during the quiet sunset of

the poet's life, when, after his sixtieth year, he rested from the toils and troubles of a public career. It is composed in pentameter couplets,—a form of verse thoroughly suited to the spirit of our English tongue, and used by almost all the great masters of our literature. The abundance of French words in the language of Chaucer is easily accounted for by the fact that French was not in the poet's day quite superseded as the speech of the upper classes in England. Many of Chaucer's words require a French accentuation; such as *aventúre, licóur, coráge.* There has been much discussion about the true way of reading Chaucer; some maintaining that the rhythm is to be preserved by certain pauses, while others, following Tyrwhitt, sound as a separate syllable the *e*, which is now silent at the end of so many words Most prefer the latter method, which has the advantage of giving to the language an antique air, suitable to the cast of the plot and the period of the poem. The *ed* at the end of certain verbs, and the *es* terminating nouns in the plural number or the possessive case, are always to be made separate syllables.

Most of Chaucer's minor and earlier works are either in part or altogether translated from French, Italian, and Latin. The *Court of Love*, and a heavy tragic poem in five books, called *Troilus and Creseide*, are thought to have been the work of his college days. The *Romaunt of the Rose* is an allegory, in which the troubled course of true love is painted in rich descriptive verse. The *House of Fame* depicts a dream, in which the poet is borne by a huge eagle to a temple of beryl, built on a rock of ice, where he sees the Goddess of Fame dispensing her favours from a carbuncle throne. The *Legende of Goode Women* narrates some passages in the lives of Cleopatra, Dido, Ariadne, and other dames of old classic renown. But most beautiful of all these is the allegory called *The Flour and the Lefe*, of which the plot is thus given: " A gentlewoman out of an arbour, in a grove, seeth a great companie of knights and ladies in a daunce upon the greene grasse; the which being ended, they all kneele down, and do honour to the daisie, some to the flower, and some to the leafe. The meaning hereof is this:—They which honour the flower, a thing fading with every blast, are such as looke after beautie and worldly pleasure. But they that honour the leafe, which abideth with the root, notwithstanding the frosts and winter storms, are they which follow vertue and during qualities without regard of worldly respects." While a prisoner in the Tower, Chaucer wrote, in imitation of Boethius, his longest prose work, called *The Testament of Love.*

In closing our sketch of Geoffrey Chaucer, the recorded opinions of a great poet and a great critic are well worthy of remembrance. While Spenser says,—

> That renowned Poet
> Dan Chaucer, well of English undefyled,
> On Fame's eternall beadroll worthy to be fyled,

no less a literary judge than Hallam classes him with Dante and Petrarch in the great poetic triumvirate of the Middle Ages.

The following are specimens of Chaucer's verse:—

"THE KNIGHT AND THE SQUIER."

FROM THE PROLOGUE OF THE "CANTERBURY TALES."

A KNIGHT ther was, and that a worthy man,	
That fro the time that he firste began	
To riden out, he loved chevalrie,	
Trouthe and honoúr, fredom and curtesie.	
Ful worthy was he in his lordes *werre,*	[*war*
And therto hadde he ridden, no man *ferre,*	[*further*
As wel in Cristendom as in Hethenesse,	
And ever honoured for his worthinesse.	
This *ilke* worthy knight hadde ben also	[*same*
Somtime with the lord of Palatie,	
Agen another hethen in Turkie:	
And evermore he hadde a sovereine *pris.*	[*praise*
And though that he was worthy he was wise,	
And of his port as meke as is a mayde.	
He never yet no vilanie ne sayde	
In alle his lif, unto no *manere wight.*	[*kind of person*
He was a veray parfit gentil knight.	
But for to tellen you of his araie,	
His hors was good, but he ne was not gaie.	

Of fustian he wered a *gipon*,   [*a short cassock*
Alle *besmotred* with his habergeon.   [*smutted*
For he was late ycome from his *viage*,   [*voyage*
And wente for to don his pilgrimage.
   With him ther was his sone a yongé SQUIER,
A lover, and a lusty bacheler,
With lockes *crull* as they were laide in presse.   [*curled*
Of twenty yere of age he was I gesse.
Of his stature he was of even lengthe,
And wonderly *deliver*, and grete of strengthe.   [*nimble*
And he hadde be somtime in *chevachie*,   [*an expedition*
In Flaundres, in Artois, and in Picardie,
And borne him wel, as of so litel space,
In hope to stonden in his ladies grace.
   Embrouded was he, as it were a mede   [*embroidered*
Alle ful of fresshe floures, white and rede.
Singing he was, or *floyting* alle the day,   [*playing on the flute*
He was as fresshe as is the moneth of May.
Short was his goune, with sleves long and wide.
Wel coude he sitte on hors, and fayre ride.
He coude songes make, and wel *endite*,   [*relate*
Juste and eke dance, and wel pourtraie and write.
So hote he loved, that by *nightertale*   [*the night-time*
He slep no more than doth the nightingale.
Curteis he was, lowly, and servisable,
And *carf* before his fader at the table.   *carved.*

STANZAS FROM "THE FLOUR AND THE LEFE"

And at the last I cast mine eye aside,
And was ware of a lusty company
That came roming out of the field wide,
Hond in hond a knight and a lady;
The ladies all in *surcotes*, that richely   [*kirtles*
Purfiled were with many a rich stone,   [*worked on the edge*
And every knight of green ware mantles on.

Embrouded well so as the surcotes were,
And everich had a chapelet on her hed,
Which did right well upon the shining *here*,   [*hair*
Made of goodly floures white and red,
The knightes eke, that they in honde led,
In *sute* of *hem* ware chapelets everichone,   [*imitation—them*
And before hem went minstrels many one,

"THE FLOUR AND THE LEFE."

As harpes, pipes, lutes, and *sautry*
Alle in greene; and on their heades bare
Of divers floures made full craftely,
All in a sute goodly chapelets they ware;
And so dauncing into the mede they *fare*,
In mid the which they found a tuft that was
All oversprad with floures in compas.

Whereto they enclined everichone
With great reverence, and that full humbly;
And, at the last, there began, anone,
A lady for to sing right womanly,
A *bargaret* in praising the daisie;
For as me thought among her notes swete,
She said "*Si douce est la Margarete.*"

CHAPTER V.

JOHN GOWER.

Born about 1325 A.D.∴........Died 1408 A.D.

Gower's poetic rank.	His death.	Confessio Amantis.
His family and calling.	Three chief works.	Opinion of Ellis.
His patron.	His French sonnets.	Illustrative extract.

THOUGH ranking far below the great Father of English Poetry, "the moral Gower," as his friend Chaucer calls him in the "Troilus and Creseide," yet holds an honoured place among our earlier bards. We know very little of his personal history.

He was, perhaps, born in 1325. One of the most illustrious houses in the realm now bears his name ; and even in the far-off days of the poet's birth the family was of noble blood. Supposed to have been a scion of the gentle Gowers, resident in the twelfth century at Stittenham in Yorkshire, he seems to have studied at Merton College, Oxford, and to have adopted the law as his profession. Indeed there is a story to the effect that he was a judge of the Common Pleas. But evidence is not forthcoming to prove that Sir John Gower the judge and John Gower the poet were one and the same man.

Like Chaucer, with whom he was long very intimate, although it is said that their friendship cooled at last, Gower espoused the cause of one of King Richard's uncles. *His* patron was the Duke of Gloucester, whose mysterious murder at Calais is one of the darkest spots in a miserable reign. Fired, no doubt, with the strong suspicion, perhaps with the certain knowledge, that his friend and patron was slain by a royal order, Gower seems to have been right glad when the luxurious king was hurled from his throne to die in Pontefract.

During the last nine years of his life, Gower was blind (1399–1408.) He died rich, leaving to his widow the then large sum of £100, along with the rents of two manors, one in Nottinghamshire and one in Suffolk. His tomb in the Church of St. Saviour, Southwark, which was called in the fourteenth century St. Mary Overies, represents the poet pillowed upon three volumes, in memento of his three great works. His grave face, framed with a mass of long auburn hair, well befits his name of " Moral Gower."

Gower's three great works were .called, *Speculum Meditantis*, *Vox Clamantis*, and *Confessio Amantis.* Of these, the first, said to have been in French, has been lost ; the second, in Latin, is still preserved in manuscript, but has never been printed; the third is that work of the poet which has entitled him to an enduring place in our literature, for it is nearly all in English. There is, in the library of the Duke of Sutherland at Trentham in Staffordshire, a volume, in which there are many French love sonnets, written by Gower when young, so full of sweetness and feeling as to have drawn the warmest praises from Warton.

The plot of the *Confessio Amantis* is rather odd. A lover holds a dialogue with his confessor, *Genius*, who is a priest of Venus. The priest, before he will grant absolution, probes the heart of his penitent to the core, trying all its weak spots. He plies him with moral tales in illustration of his teaching, giving him, *en passant*, lessons in chemistry and the philosophy of Aristotle. After all the tedious shrift, when our hero seems to be so arrayed in a panoply of purity and learning as to render his victory a certain thing, we suddenly find that he is now too old to care for the triumph suffered for and wished for so long. Ellis, in his " Specimens of the Early English Poets," characterizes the narrative of Gower as being often quite *petrifying.* And although this poet's place, as second to Chaucer during the infancy of our literature, cannot be disputed, still it must be confessed that old John is often prosy, and sometimes dull.

FROM GOWER'S "CONFESSIO AMANTIS."

A ROMAN STORY.

In a Croniq I fynde thus,
How that Caius Fabricius
Wich whilome was consul of Rome,
By whome the lawes *yede* and come,   [*went*

Whan the Sampnitees to him brouht
A somme of golde, and hym by souht
To done hem fauoure in the lawe,
Towarde the golde he gan hym drawe:
Whereof in alle mennes loke,
A part in to his honde he tooke,
Wich to his mouthe in alle haste
He put hit for to smelle and taste,
And to his ihe and to his ere,
Bot he ne fonde no comfort there:
And thanne he be gan it to despise,
And tolde vnto hem in this wise:
" I not what is with golde to thryve
Whan none of alle my wittes fyve
Fynt savour ne delite ther inne
So is it bot a nyce sinne
Of golde to ben to coveitous,
Bot he is riche an glorious
Wich hath in his subieccion
The men wich in possession
Ben riche of golde, and by this *skille*,   [*reason*
For he may alday whan he wille,
Or be him leef or be him loth,
Justice don vppon hem bothe."
Lo thus he seide and with that worde
He threwe to fore hem on the borde
The golde oute of his honde anon,
And seide hem that he wolde none,
So that he kepte his liberte
To do justice and equite.

CHAPTER VI

KING JAMES I. OF SCOTLAND.

Born 1394 A.D..........Died 1437 A.D,

Bound for France.	The King's Quhair.
A captive at Windsor.	His minor poems.
Falls in love.	Illustrative extract.

THE romantic story of this royal poet is well known.   His poor father, Robert III., whose heart had been well-nigh broken by the murder of his darling son Rothesay, put his only remaining son, James, on board a ship bound for France, that the boy might be safe from the wiles of Albany.   The ship being seized off the Norfolk coast, the prince was led a captive to the English Court —an event which brought his father's grey head in sorrow to the grave.   This happened in 1405, when young James was only eleven years of age.   From that time, until his release in 1424, he remained in England, living chiefly at Windsor and receiving an education befitting his royal birth.   He seems to have excelled in every study and every sport ; but the music of the harp and the making of verses were his chief delights.   Chaucer's poetry and Gower's were studied eagerly by the captive king, and " from admiration to imitation there is but a step."   But a power greater than delight in Chaucer's verse was at work in the poet's breast. He fell in love ; and, while all life was bright with the rosy hue of a new-blown passion, he sang his sweetest song.

Early one morning, looking from a window in the Round Tower of Windsor out upon a garden thick with May leaves, and musical with the liquid song of nightingales, he saw walking below a lady, young, lovely, richly dressed and jewelled.   This was Joan Beaufort, daughter of the Duke of Somerset.   His love for her, speedily kindled, inspired his greatest work, *The King's Quhair* (quire or book).   The poem, written in one hundred and ninety-seven stanzas of seven lines each, contains many particulars of the poet's life, the most admired passage being that in which he describes his first glimpse of his future wife walking in the leafy garden. The polish of many stanzas is exquisite.

Although King James ranks so high as a pathetic and amatory poet, he seems equally at home in a broad comic vein of description. Two poems of this class,—*Christis Kirk on the Grene* and *Peblis to the Play*,—are ascribed to him rather than to James V. The former is in the Aberdeenshire dialect, the latter in that of Tweeddale, and both humorously describe certain old Scottish country merry-makings.

Ruling not wisely (for himself at least), but too well, this cleverest of the royal Stuarts was stabbed to death in the Monastery of the Dominicans at Perth early in the year 1437. The murderers, chief among them Sir Robert Graham, burst late at night into his private room, found him, where he had hidden, in a vault below the flooring, and after a fearful struggle cut him almost to pieces with their swords and knives.

VERSES SELECTED FROM "THE KING'S QUHAIR."

Cast I down mine eyes again,
Where as I saw, walking under the Tower,
Full secretly, new comen here to plain,
The fairest or the freshest young flower
That ever I saw, methought, before that hour,
For which sudden *abate, anon astart,*   [*went and came*
The blood of all my body to my heart.

  * * * * *

Of her array the form if I shall write,
Towards her golden hair and rich attire,
In fretwise *couchit* with pearlis white,   [*inlaid*
And great *balas leaming* as the fire,   {*gems of a certain*
With mony ane emeraut and fair sapphire ; { *kind—shining*
And on her head a chaplet fresh of hue,
Of plumis parted red, and white, and blue.

Full of quaking spangis bright as gold,
Forged of shape like to the amorets,
So new, so fresh, so pleasant to behold,
The plumis eke like to the flower *jonets,*   [*lily*
And other of shape, like to the flower jonets ;

And above all this, there was, well I wot,
Beauty enough to make a world to dote.

    *   *   *   *

And for to walk that fresh May's morrow,
Ane hook she had upon her tissue white,
That goodlier had not been seen *to-forow*,   [*before*
As I suppose; and girt she was *alite*,   [*slightly*
Thus halflings loose for haste, to such delight
It was to see her youth in goodlihede,
That for rudeness to speak thereof I dread.

    *   *   *   *   *

And when she walked had a little thraw
Under the sweete greene boughis bent,
Her fair fresh face, as white as any snaw,
She turned has, and furth her wayis went;
But tho began mine aches and torment,
To see her part, and follow I na might;
Methought the day was turned into night.

CHAPTER VII.

OTHER WRITERS OF THE FIRST ERA.

(1328–1474.)

Minot.	Its versification.	Lydgate.
Longlande.	Barbour.	Blind Harry.
Plot of Piers Plough-	Wyntoun.	Trevisa.
man.	Occleve.	Fortescue.

POETS.

LAURENCE MINOT.—This writer, who flourished under Edward III., is called by Dr. Craik the earliest writer of English verse, who deserves the name of a poet. We have his ten poems, describing the martial achievements of Edward, such as the battles of *Halidon Hill*, and *Nevil's Cross*, *The Sieges of Tournay and Calais*, and *The Taking of Guisnes;* written, no doubt, between the years 1333 and 1353, and thrown off under the fresh impression of the great events they record. They have all the fine warlike ring of the older. minstrelsy, combined with a polish to which the ballad-singers of former days were strangers.

ROBERT or WILLIAM LONGLANDE.—The author of the *Vision of Piers* (*Peter*) *Ploughman* was born in Shropshire about 1300. A secular priest and a Fellow of Oriel College, Oxford, he had many opportunities of knowing thoroughly those abuses which he lashes with an unsparing hand. The time was indeed a terrible one,—the nobles and the clergy were alike corrupt to the very core.

The poet supposes himself to have fallen asleep after a long ramble over the Malvern Hills on a May morning. As he sleeps, he dreams a series of twenty dreams. The general subject of the poem has been described as similar to that of "The Pilgrim's Progress." The gaudy, changeful scenes of "Vanity Fair," are much the same, in spirit at least, on the canvas of Longlande as in the later pictures of Bunyan and of Thackeray. Losing no opportunity of tearing the cloak from the ignorant and vicious churchmen of his day, this old poet may be said to have struck the first great blow in the battle of the English Reformation.

" Piers Ploughman " is unrhymed, having, as its distinctive feature, a kind of *alliteration;* probably borrowed, as Dr. Percy shows in his " Reliques," from the Icelandic. The following lines will show the nature of this alliteration :—

> *Ac* on a May Morwening   [*and*
> On Malvern hills
> Me beFel a *Ferly,*   [*wonder*
> Of Fairy me thought.
> I was Weary *for-Wandered,*   { *worn out with*
> And Went me to rest   *wandering*
> Under a *Brood* Bank,   [*broad*
> By a *Burn's* side;   [*stream's*
> And as I Lay and Leaned,
> And Looked on the waters,
> I Slombered into a Sleeping,
> It S*wayed* so *mury.*   [*sounded—pleasant*

JOHN BARBOUR.—Two dates, 1316 and 1330, are assigned for the birth of Barbour, and Aberdeen is named as his native place. He was made Archdeacon of Aberdeen in 1356. Next year we find him acting as one of the commissioners that met at Edinburgh to deliberate upon the ransom of the king, and also receiving a passport from Edward III. that he might visit Oxford for purposes of study. Three other passports were also granted to him by the English king at various times.

Barbour's great poem is *The Bruce*, an epic, written pro- bably about 1376, in that eight-syllabled verse which Scott has made so famous. The work embraces the events of about forty years, from the death of the Maid of Norway in 1290 to the death of Lord James Douglas in 1330; and though styled by the poet himself a Romaunt, its main narrative has been accepted as true history by all the leading writers upon Scottish affairs. Another poem, called *The Stewart*, is said to have been written by Barbour ; but it has been lost. Two pensions, one of £10 Scots, the other of 20 shillings, were granted to the poet, both probably by Robert II.   The language in which Barbour wrote does not differ much from the English of Chaucer, the chief dis· tinction consisting in the broader vowel-sounds of the Scottish poem.   Barbour is thought to have died in 1395.

ANDREW WYNTOUN.—This priest, supposed to have been born about 1350, was Prior of St. Serf's at Lochleven, a house under the rule of the great Priory of St. Andrews.   In ruder strains than Barbour, he wrote about 1420 an *Orygynale Cronykil of Scotland*, extending from the creation to 1408.   This work, part of which was the composition of another poet, is, when we make allowance for the fabulous legends interwoven with it, a clear, trustworthy historical record.   It is divided into nine books, and written in eight-syllabled rhymes.

THOMAS OCCLEVE.—This writer of verses, for poet we can scarcely call him, is thought to have lived and written about the beginning of the fifteenth century.   We learn from his works that he was a lawyer; that he held a government situation under the Privy Seal; and that he led a wild, extravagant life.   His chief poem is founded on a Latin work, *De Regimine Principum*, written by Egidius, an Italian monk of the thirteenth century. On the whole, Occleve's verse must be judged rather by its quan- tity than its quality.   His admission into the ranks of our Eng- lish writers of note is owing to the circumstance of his writing in a barren age, when every versifier was a man of mark.

JOHN LYDGATE.—Lydgate, the monk of Bury, flourished in the reigns of Henry V. and Henry VI.   Educated at Oxford, he added to his college training a wider view of life by travelling in France and Italy.   On his return home he opened a school for the instruction of the young in verse-making and polite composi- tion.   His ready pen, kept unceasingly busy, supplied verses of every style and sentiment, producing ballads and hymns with equal ease.   He wrote for masks and mummings, coronations and saints' days, for king, citizen, and monk; and no doubt found the fruit of his work multiplying in the solid shape of gold and silver coin.   The chief works of Lydgate, whose *forte* lay in flowing and diffuse description, were the *History of Thebes*, the *Fall of*

Princes, and the *History of the Siege of Troy*—the last named being borrowed from Colonna's prose.

BLIND HARRY.—A poor man, so named, wandered about Scotland during the third quarter of the fifteenth century, reciting poems for bread. This was the author of *The Wallace*, a companion work to Barbour's "Bruce," but rougher in the grain and less trustworthy, owing to its being chiefly woven from the popular legends afloat concerning the tall hero of Elderslie. "The Wallace" contains about twelve thousand lines.

PROSE WRITERS.

JOHN DE TREVISA.—A Latin work, the *Polychronicon* of Higden, a monk of Chester, was translated into English prose about 1387 by Trevisa, who was vicar of Berkeley in Gloucestershire. Many other translations were executed by the same pen.

SIR JOHN FORTESCUE.—Born, it is supposed, in Devonshire, this eminent lawyer became in 1442 the Chief-Justice of the King's Bench. Remaining faithful to the Red Rose through every change, he followed Queen Margaret into France, where he lived in exile for some time. Out of evil came good. We owe to this banishment one of the finest of our early English law-books, *De Laudibus Legum Angliae*, written in the form of a conversation between himself and his young pupil Prince Edward. Much more interesting, however, to us is an English work from his pen entitled, *Of the Difference between an Absolute and a Limited Monarchy*, in which he compares the French and the English in regard to liberty, much to the disadvantage of the former people.

SECOND ERA OF ENGLISH LITERATURE.

FROM THE INTRODUCTION OF PRINTING IN 1474 A.D. TO THE ACCESSION OF ELIZABETH IN 1558 A.D.

CHAPTER I.

THE OLD PRINTERS OF WESTMINSTER.

Caxton's house.	Serves the Duchess.	The Game of Chesse.
His face.	First literary work.	Publishing.
Birth and boyhood.	At Cologne.	Caxton's death.
On the Continent.	History of Troy.	Wynkyn de Worde.
Invention of printing.	The Almonry.	Richard Pynson.
Trade in books.	Old printers at work.	A contrast.
Envoy at Bruges.	Book-binding.	

IN one of the most squalid recesses of Westminster there stood, until 1845, a crazy building of wood and plaster, three stories high. Its pointed roof and wooden balcony were seldom free from poor fluttering rags of clothing, hung out to dry by the wretched tenants. The very sunlight grew sickly when it fell into the poverty-stricken street, where slipshod women, unshaven lounging men, and pale stunted children slunk hopelessly about. Foulness, gloom, and wretchedness were the prominent features of the place around the frail timbers of the house in which the first English printer is said to have lived and wrought. It was almost a mercy when a new street was driven through the poor old house and its tottering neighbours. Not far from this, in the Almonry or Eleemosynary of the Abbey, where the monks of Westminster used to distribute alms to the poor, that London merchant, whose name has grown to be a household word, set up, most probably in 1474, the first printing-press whose types were inked on English ground.

As we write the name of CAXTON, a grave and beardless face, with an expression somewhat akin to sadness, rises from the past, looking calmly out from the descending lappets of the hood, which was the fashionable head-dress of his day. All honour to the memory of the Father of the English Press!,

Born about 1412 in some lonely farm-house, a few of which were thinly scattered over the Weald or wooded part of Kent, William Caxton grew to boyhood among the simple peasants of that wild district. Probably about 1428 he assumed the flat round cap, narrow falling bands, and long coat of coarse cloth, which then formed the dress of the city apprentice; and was soon, no doubt, promoted to the honour of carrying lantern and cudgel at night before the worshipful Master Robert Large, the rich mercer to whom he was bound. A mercer then did not confine his trade to silk : he dealt also in wool and woollen cloth ; and, no doubt, in the parcels from the Continent there often came, for sale among the rich English, a few copies of rare and costly manuscripts. From such the apprentice probably obtained his first knowledge of books in their old written shape.

Upon the death of his master, Caxton went abroad, and continued to reside chiefly in Holland and Flanders for fully thirty years. What his exact position was cannot be determined ; but it is supposed that he acted as travelling agent or factor for the Company of London Mercers. While he was thus employed, the great invention of printing began to attract the notice of the world. Laurence Coster, in the woods of Haarlem, had shaped his letters of beech-bark, and had looked with delight upon the impression left by the sap upon the parchment in which he had wrapped them. Gutenberg of Mentz, catching a sight of old Coster's types, had shut himself up in the ruined monastery by Strasbourg, to make the inks, the balls, the cases, and the press. Faust and Schoeffer had joined with Gutenberg, and had betrayed him when they knew his secret. Faust, by offering for sale as many Bibles as were asked for, at one-eighth of the usual price, had excited the wonder of the Paris world, and had evoked a cry that he was in league with the Enemy of man. And those strange pages, written in the blood of the salesman, as the shuddering gazers whispered to one another, pointing with trembling finger to the letters of brilliant red, had spread their fascinations, too, across the English Channel. A sharp business man like Caxton would not waste much time in sending these novelties to the English market. So printed books began to find their way to England among the silks and perfumes, which crossed the sea from Flanders.

A shrewd and clever man this mercer must have been in matters relating to his trade, for we find him in 1464 nominated one of the envoys to the Court of Burgundy, to negotiate a treaty of commerce between the King of England and Duke Philip. It must not be forgotten that the duchy of Burgundy then included nearly all of modern Belgium. And when, four years later, Philip's son, lately made Duke Charles by his father's death, married Margaret Plantagenet, the sister of the English king, William Caxton, who was already a resident in **1468** Bruges, where the rich and luxurious Court of Burgundy A.D. had its seat, entered the service of this English princess, who had changed her country and her name. He had probably already laid down the ell-wand, and had ceased to be seen among the mercers' stalls; but in what capacity he served the duchess we cannot say. His own words tell us that he received from her a yearly fee, for which he rendered honest service. It was when his active mercer's life was over that he took up the pen, and began to work with types and ink-balls.

Our printer's entrance on literary work happened thus : Some months before the gorgeous ceremonies with which Duke Charles brought his English bride to her home in Bruges, Caxton, feeling himself to have no great occupation, sat down in some quiet turret chamber to translate a French book into English. This work was *Recueil des Histoires de Troye*, written by Duke Philip's chaplain, Raoul le Fevre. When five or six quires were written, he grew dissatisfied with his English and doubtful of his French; and so the unfinished translation lay aside for two years, tossed among his old invoices and scattered papers. One day " my Lady

Margaret," talking to her trusty servant about many things, chanced to hear of this literary pastime, and asked to see the sheets of manuscript. When she had read them, pointing out some faults in the English, she encouraged Caxton to proceed with the translation, which he did with renewed hope and vigour.

From Bruges he removed to Cologne, where it probably was that he first appeared as a printer, having learned the art, as he tells us, at considerable expense. His instructor, from whom he, no doubt, bought his first set of types, may have been one of Faust's workmen, who had been driven from Mentz in 1462, when the sack of the city by Adolphus of Nassau scattered the printers over the land. At Cologne in 1471 Caxton finished the "History of Troy;" and it was printed most probably in the same year—the first English book that came from any press. For this, the first great work of his own pen, and the first *English* production of his press, he was bountifully rewarded by the "dreadful duchess," who had encouraged him to resume his task.

When or how the happy idea occurred to Caxton of carrying press and types to England we do not know; but, soon after his sojourn in Cologne, we find him in the Almonry of Westminster, surrounded by the materials of his adopted craft, and directing the operations of his workmen. He united in himself nearly all the occupations connected with the production and sale of books; for in the infancy of printing there was no division of labour. Author, inkmaker, compositor, pressman, corrector, binder, publisher, bookseller,—Caxton was all these.

1474
A.D.

Let us pass into his workshop, and see the early printers at their toil. Two huge frames of wood support the thick screws which work the pressing slabs. There sits the grave compositor before the cases full of type, the copy set up before him, and the grooved stick in his hand, which gradually fills with type to form a line. There is about his work nothing of that quick, unerring nip which marks the fingers of a modern compositor, as they fly among the type, and seize the very letter wanted in a trice. With quiet and steady pace, and many a thoughtful pause, his fingers travel through their task. The master printer in his furred gown moves through the room, directs the wedging of a page or sheet, and then resumes his high stool, to complete the reading of a proof pulled freshly from the press. The worker of the press has found the balls or dabbers, with which the form of types is inked, unfit for use. He must make fresh ones; so down he sits with raw sheep-skin and carded wool, to stuff the ball and tie it round the handle of the dab. Till this is done, the press-work is at a stand. But there is no hurry in the Almonry; and all the better this, for the imperfection of the machinery makes great care necessary on the part of the workmen. Then, suppose the proofs corrected, and the sheets, or pages rather, printed off, the binder's work begins. Strong and solid work was this old binding. When the leaves were sewed together in a frame—a rude original of that still used—they were hammered well to make them flat, and the back was thickly overlaid with paste and glue. Then came the enclosing of the paper in boards—veritable boards—thick pieces of wood like the panel of a door, covered outside with embossed and gilded leather, and thickly studded with brass nails, whose ornamental heads shone in manifold rows. Thick brass corners and solid clasps completed the fortification of the book, which was made to last for centuries. Half a dozen such volumes used then to form an extensive and valuable library.

The book which is considered to have been the earliest work from the Westminster press, is that entitled *The Game and Playe of the Chesse, translated out of the French, fynysshid the last day of Marche*, 1474. A second edition of this work was the first English book illustrated with wood-cuts. A fable about the origin of chess; an account of the offices, or powers, of the various pieces; and a prayer for the prosperity of Edward and England, make up the four treatises into which the "Game of Chesse" is divided.   **1474** A.D.

Sixty-five works, translated and original, are assigned to the pen and the press of Caxton, who seems to have supplied nearly all the copy that was set up in the side-chapel, or disused Scriptorium, where his printing was done. His old business tact stood well to him in his publishing and bookselling transactions. We have still a hand-bill in his largest type, calling on all who wanted cheap books to come and buy at the Almonry. We find him, when undertaking the publication of the *Golden Legend* — a large, double-columned work of nearly five hundred pages, profusely illustrated with wood-cuts—securing the promise of Lord Arundel to take a reasonable number of copies, and, moreover, to reward the printer with a yearly gift of venison—a buck in summer, and a doe in winter.

So, for some seventeen years, Caxton laboured on at his English printing. The man who, at fifty-nine, had gone to Cologne to learn a new trade when his life's work seemed nearly done, still inked the types and worked the lever of the press, when the weight of nearly fourscore years hung upon his frame.

But there came a day when the door of the printing-office was shut, and the clank of the press was unheard within. **1491** William Caxton was dead. The rude school-boy of the A.D. Kentish Weald—the blithe apprentice of Cheapside—the keen mercer, well known in every Flemish stall—the trusted retainer of the house of Burgundy—the grey-haired learner at Cologne—the old printer of Westminster—had played out his many parts, and had entered into his rest. Another sorrowful time came for his faithful little band of printers, when, with the glare of torches and the deep tolling of a bell, they laid their hoary chief in the grave at St. Margaret's Church, not far from the scene of his daily toils and triumphs.

WYNKYN DE WORDE, a foreigner who had long assisted Caxton at his press, kept up the good work, and probably at first in the old place. There is something touching in the devotion to his dead master which he displays, in uniting the monogram of Caxton with the blazing suns and clustering grapes that adorn his own trade-device. Four hundred and eight works are assigned to Wynkyn's press.

Another of Caxton's assistants—one RICHARD PYNSON, a native of Normandy—set up after a time in business for himself, and throve so well, that he received the somewhat valuable appointment of King's Printer, being first on the long list of those who have borne the title. Two hundred and twelve works are said to have been printed by Pynson.

These were the men who printed our earliest English books. Their types have been multiplied by millions, and their presses by hundreds. A little silver coin can now buy the book for which Caxton charged a piece of gold. The British cottage is indeed a poor one which cannot show some volumes as well printed and as finely bound as his finest works. Rejoicing, as we do, in the countless blessings which the Press has given to Britain, let us not forget that arched room in old Westminster, where our earliest printer bent his silvered head over the first proof-sheets of the " Game of Chesse."

CHAPTER II.

SIR THOMAS MORE.

Born 1480 A.D.........Beheaded 1535 A.D.

Boyhood of More.	Reverses.	History of Edward V.
His Oxford life.	Last glimpse of home.	The Utopia.
Career as a lawyer.	Imprisonment.	Parliamentary fame.
His home at Chelsea.	His trial.	Illustrative extract.
Chancellor.	His execution.	

THOMAS MORE, who takes rank as the leading writer during this second era of our literature, was born in Milk Street, London, in 1480. Having learned some Latin in Threadneedle Street from Nicholas Hart, he became in his fifteenth year a page in the household of Cardinal Morton, the Archbishop of Canterbury. Here his sharp and ready wit attracted so much notice that the archbishop prophesied great things for him; and a dean of St Paul's, one of the most noted scholars of the day, used to say that there was but one wit in England, and that was young Thomas More.

Devoted to the law by his good father, who was a justice in the King's Bench, More went to Oxford at seventeen; and here, in spite of the frowns of old Sir John, who dreaded lest the seductions of Homer and Plato might cast the grave sages of the law too much into the shade, he studied Greek under Grocyn. And not only did he study it *con amore*, but he wrote to the University a powerful letter in defence of this new branch of learning, inveighing strongly against the Trojans, as the opponents of Greek had begun to call themselves. The leading Anti-Grecians were the senior clergy, who were too old or too lazy to sit down to the Greek alphabet and grammar; and who, besides, feared that if Greek and Hebrew were studied, the authority of the Latin Vulgate might be shaken. At Oxford, More won the friendship of the eminent Erasmus; and though the Dutchman was thirty and the English boy only seventeen, the attachment was mutual, and so strong, that it was only severed by death. Here, too, he wrote many English poems of considerable merit. These snow-drops of our literature, flowerets of a day hovering between winter and spring, might pass unnoticed among the gay blooms of a sum-mer garden, but rising in pale beauty from the frozen ground, they are loved and welcomed as the harbingers of brighter days.

A few notes of his rapid rise must suffice here. Appointed reader, that is, lecturer, at Furnival's Inn,* he soon became a popular lawyer; and we find him expounding not only the English law, but the works of St. Augustine. This mixture of theology and law was common in those days, when churchmen alone were chancellors. Running down occasionally into Essex from his chambers near the Charter House, for a breath of country air, he fell in love with a lady named Jane Colt, whom he soon married. Under Henry VII. he became Under-Sheriff of London; and when miser Henry's spendthrift son wore the crown, he still rose in favour and in fortune. Employed on many continental missions, he became a Privy Councillor, Treasurer of the Exchequer, and in 1523 Speaker of the Commons. While filling the Speaker's chair he incurred the anger of Wolsey, who strove to injure him with the king. But the magnificent cardinal's own feet were then on quaking, slippery ground, and when in 1529 he fell with a great ruin, More stepped on to the chancellor's bench.

We have pleasant domestic pictures of the home at Chelsea, embosomed among flowers and apple-trees, where the great lawyer lived in tranquil happiness with his wife and children. Thither often on a summer afternoon, after his day at court was done, he used to carry his friend Erasmus in his eight-oared barge. Gravely sweet was the talk at the six o'clock supper, and during the twilight stroll by the river. The king, too, often came out to dine with the Mores, sometimes uninvited, when the good but fussy lady of the house (not Jane Colt, but a second wife, Alice, seven years older than her husband) was in a desperate state until she had got her best scarlet gown put trimly on, to do honour to his

---

* The law-schools, such as Furnival's Inn and Lincoln's Inn, were so called because they were once used as the inns or town-houses of noblemen. Compare the French use of "hotel."

highness. So familiar were the king and his chancellor, that, as they walked in the garden, the royal arm often lay round More's neck. Yet, a few years later, that neck bled on the block by a royal order.

For more than two years More held the office of chancellor, discharging its high duties with singular purity. While it has been said of his predecessor, Wolsey, that no suitor need apply to him whose fingers were not tipped with gold, we read of More refusing heavy bribes, and sitting in an open hall to hear in person the petitions of the poor. The rock on which Wolsey had gone down lay ahead of More, who saw it with an anxious but undaunted heart. His mind was quite made up to steer an honest, straight-forward course. The king, who was bent upon marrying Anne Boleyn, pressed the chancellor urgently for an opinion on the case, expecting, no doubt, that a man who owed his commanding position to royal favour would not dare to thwart the royal will. But Henry was mistaken in his man. Rather than give an opinion which must have been against the king, More laid down the seals of his high office. A reverse of fortune so great seemed to cast no shadow upon his joyous spirit. Quietly reducing his style of living, he brightened his humble home with the same gentle, gleaming wit, which had given lustre to his splendid days. Poor Mistress Alice, who had loved the grandeur of being a chancellor's lady, did not take so kindly to the change. But worse was yet to come. To thwart Henry the Eighth was a capital offence. More must yield or die. An attempt, soon abandoned however, was made to involve him in the doom of the girl called "The Holy Maid of Kent." Summoned to Lambeth in April 1534, he left for the last time his well-loved Chelsea home. Turning, as he hurried to his boat, he caught the last glimpse of its dear flower-beds through the wicket, beyond which he would not suffer his family to pass. His refusal to take an oath, which acknowledged the king's marriage with Anne Boleyn to be lawful, so enraged Henry that he was cast into the Tower, where he lay for a year. His letters to his daughter Margaret, written from that prison with a coal, are touching memorials of a great and loving heart.

1532

A.D.

At last he was placed at the bar at Westminster, on a charge, of which the leading points were his opposition to the royal marriage, and his refusal to acknowledge Henry as the head of the Church. He was found guilty and hurried back to prison. As he landed at the Tower wharf, his daughter, Margaret Roper, rushing forward in spite of the bristling halberds that shut him in, flung her arms round him, and, mingling her bright hair with his grizzled beard, kissed him over and over again amid the sobs and tears of all around.

Without endorsing the opinions of this man, we may freely and honestly admire his excelling genius, his noble courage, and his gentle heart. The wit that sparkled from Cardinal Morton's rosy page, that in bachelor days lit the gloomy chambers in Lincoln's Inn, and added new lustre to the hospitalities of Chelsea, shone bright as ever on the scaffold, undimmed even by the cruel glinting of the headsman's axe. As he climbed the crazy timbers where he was to die, he said gaily to the lieutenant, "I pray you see me safe up ; and for my coming down let me shift for myself." His head was fixed on the spikes of London Bridge; but his brave daughter Margaret caused it to be taken down, and when she died, many years after, it was buried in her grave. And so mouldered together into common dust as great a brain and as true a heart as ever England held.

More's fame as a writer rests on two works, written during that happy period of his life, when, as Under-Sheriff of London and a busy lawyer, he enjoyed the sunshine of royal favour and the solid advantage of an income amounting to £4000 or £5000 a year. His *Life and Reign of Edward V.*, written about 1513, is not only the first English work deserving the name of history, but is further remarkable as being our earliest specimen of classical English prose. The character of Richard III. is here painted in the darkest colours. But More's *Utopia* has had a wider fame. In flowing Latin he describes the happy state of an island, which is discovered by one Raphael Hythloday (learner of trifles), a supposed companion of Amerigo Vespucci. The place is called Utopia, which simply means "Nowhere," from οὐ τόπος. A republic, of

which the foundation idea is borrowed from Plato, although the
details are More's, has its seat in this favoured land. The Utopian
ships lie safe within the horns of the crescent-shaped island; for
no enemy can steer through the rocks that guard the harbour's
mouth.   Every house in the fifty-four walled cities has a large
garden; and these houses are exchanged by lot every ten years.
All the islanders learn agriculture; but all have, besides, a certain
trade, at which six hours' work, and no more, must be done every
day. There are in Utopia no taverns, no fashions ever changing, few
laws, and no lawyers.   There, war is considered a brutal thing;
hunting, a degrading thing, fit only for butchers; and finery, a
foolish thing,—for who that could see sun or star would care
for jewels.   This work was composed shortly after More's return
from the Continent, whither he was sent on a mission to Bruges
in the summer of 1514.   His other works are chiefly theological
treatises, written against the Lutheran doctrines, and Latin
epigrams, modelled after those of his sarcastic friend, Erasmus.
He stands first, too, in the glorious roll of our parliamentary
orators.   But, unfortunately, of his speeches we know next to
nothing; for an orator's fame is perishable, too often fading into
oblivion almost as soon as death has quenched his eye of flame
and stilled the magical music of his voice.

A LETTER FROM SIR THOMAS MORE TO HIS WIFE.
(1528.)

Maistres Alyce, in my most harty wise I recommend me to you; and whereas
I am enfourmed by my son Heron of the losse of our barnes and of our neighbours also, with all the corn that was therein, albeit (saving God's pleasure) it is
gret pitie of so much good corne lost, yet sith it hath liked hym to sende us
such a chaunce, we must and are bounden, not only to be content, but also to be
glad of his visitacion. He sente us all that we have loste: and sith he hath by
such a chaunce taken it away againe, his pleasure be fulfilled. Let us never
grudge ther at, but take it in good worth, and hartely thank him, as well for ad-
versitie as for prosperitie. And peradventure we have more cause to thank him
for our losse, then for our winning; for his wisdome better seeth what is good for
vs then we do our selves.   Therfore I pray you be of good chere, and take all
the howsold with you to church, and there thanke God, both for that he hath
given us, and for that he hath taken from us, and for that he hath left us, which
if it please hym he can encrease when he will. And if it please hym to leave us
yet lesse, at his pleasure be it.

I pray you to make some good ensearche what my poore neighbours have loste, and bid them take no thought therfore : for and I shold not leave myself a spone, there shal no pore neighbour of mine bere no losse by any chaunce happened in my house.   I pray you be with my children and your household merry in God. And devise some what with your frendes, what waye wer best to take, for provision to be made for corne for our household, and for sede thys yere comming, if ye thinke it good that we kepe the ground stil in our handes.   And whether ye think it good that we so shall do or not, yet I think it were not best sodenlye thus to leave it all up, and to put away our folk of our farme till we have somwhat advised us thereon.   How beit if we have more nowe then ye shall nede, and which can get them other maisters, ye may then discharge us of them.   But I would not that any man were sodenly sent away he wote nere wether.

At my comming hither I perceived none other but that I shold tary still with the Kinges Grace.   But now I shal (I think) because of this chance, get leave this next weke to come home and se you: and then shall we further devyse together uppon all thinges, what order shal be best to take.   And thus as hartely fare you well with all our children as ye can wishe.   At Woodestok the thirde daye of Septembre by the hand of

your louing husbande,

THOMAS MORE Knight.

CHAPTER III.

WILLIAM TYNDALE.

Born about 1477 A.D..........Strangled 1536 A.D.

Birth and boyhood.	Settled at Antwerp.	The stake.
Tutor to Sir John Welsh.	The New Testament.	Literary character.
In London.	Sir Thomas More.	Illustrative extract.
Humphrey Monmouth.	Other works.	

WILLIAM TYNDALE is celebrated among our writers as a translator of the New Testament into English. What Wycliffe had done for his countrymen in the fourteenth century, Tyndale undertook during the troubled reign of the eighth Henry.

Of Tyndale's birth and boyhood we know positively nothing beyond the statement of Fox, that he was born on the borders of Wales, and brought up from childhood at Oxford. Graduating at that university, he went to spend some time at Cambridge. His powers as a linguist and his great love for the Scriptures are specially noted by his early biographer. The next scene of his life was the house of Sir John Welsh, a knight of Gloucestershire, who employed him as tutor to his children. This honourable but troublesome office was most creditably filled by the Oxford man, who met at the hospitable board of the good knight most of the leading country clergymen. The talk naturally turned very often upon the religious opinions of such men as Luther and Erasmus; and in these conversations Tyndale took a most conspicuous part, freely declaring his sympathy with the Reformers, and his desire—nay, his purpose—that every English ploughboy should soon know the Scriptures well. Resigning his tutorship to seek a safer place, he preached for some time at Bristol and through the surrounding country, and then went to London, his big brain bursting with a glorious thought. He would translate the New Testament from the original Greek, and thus feed the hungering English people with the bread of life.

Wycliffe's Bible had become, in the changes which more than one hundred stirring years had brought upon the English language, a book unreadable but by a learned few. Disappointed in his attempt to secure the protection of Tonstal, the learned Bishop of London, Tyndale found a refuge in the house of Alderman Humphrey Monmouth, a rich London merchant, whose heart was in the good work. This honest man, keeping the poor scholar in his house for six months, would gladly have seen his friend fare better than on sodden meat and small single beer. But Tyndale would, if given his own way, take nothing else. The kindness of Monmouth did not stop here, for he made Tyndale an allowance of £10 a year, which enabled him to set in earnest about his grand design. Travelling into Germany, Tyndale saw and talked with Luther, and settled finally at Antwerp. There he finished his *Translation of the New Testament*. The first edition, printed probably at Wittenberg, was published in 1525 or 1526. An improved and altered version appeared in 1534. The run upon the book, both on the Continent and in England, was very great. Copies poured by hundreds from the foreign presses into England. In vain the terrors of the Church were threatened and inflicted upon the sellers and owners of Tyndale's Testament. The translator's brother and two others were sentenced, for distributing copies, to pay a fine of £18,840, 0s. 10d.; and, moreover, had to ride, facing the horse's tail, with many copies of the condemned volume tacked to their clothes, as far as Cheapside, where a fire blazed to burn the books. Conscious how utterly feeble such exhibitions were as a means of checking the new doctrines, Tonstal applied to Sir Thomas More for help; and More, a devoted member of the Romish Church, dipping his pen in gall,—with which, however, the honey of his better nature often mingled,—wrote many fierce and bitter things of Tyndale and Tyndale's works.

The Five Books of Moses, translated from the Hebrew partly by Tyndale, were printed at Hamburg in 1530; and in the following year the same industrious pen produced an *English version of the Book of Jonah*. Such work, added to the composition of many English tracts for sale in England, written in defence of his re-

ligious opinions, filled the days, and many of the nights too, of this
good man. Nor was the wear and tear of body and brain by night
and day all that Tyndale gave to the service of his Master. Without straining the figure far, we can truly say that his Bible was
written with his blood. One Henry Philips, English student at
Louvain, by the basest treachery betrayed him in 1534 into the
hands of the Emperor's officers at Brussels; near which city, in
the Castle of Vilvoord, he was kept a close prisoner for
A .D. eighteen months. Then, tried and condemned for heresy,
1536 he was strangled at the stake, and his dead body was
burned to ashes. His dying words were, " O Lord, open
the King of England's eyes!"

Tyndale's English is considered, by the best authorities, to be
remarkably pure and forcible. His New Testament ranks
among our best classics. Tyndale also possessed such a knowledge of the Greek and Hebrew tongues as was rare in his day;
and this, securing the fidelity of the translation, stamps his books
with no common value.

FROM TYNDALE'S NEW TESTAMENT.

Jesus answered and sayde: A certayne man descended from Jerusalem into
Jericho. And fell into the hondes off theves whych robbed hym off his rayment
and wonded hym and departed levynge him halfe deed. And yt chaunsed that
there cam a certayne preste that same waye and saw hym and passed by. And
lyke wyse a levite when he was come neye to the place went and loked on hym
and passed by. Then a certayne Samaritane as he iorayed cam neye vnto him
and behelde hym and had compassion on hym and cam to hym and bounde vppe
hys wondes and poured in wyne and oyle and layed hym on his beaste and
brought hym to a common hostry, and drest him. And on the morowe when he
departed he toke out two pence and gave them to the host and said unto him,
Take care of him and whatsoever thou spendest above this when I come agayne
I will recompence the. Which nowe of these thre thynkest thou was neighbour
unto him that fell into the theves hondes? And he answered: He that shewed
mercy on hym. Then sayd Jesus vnto hym, Goo and do thou lyke wyse.

CHAPTER IV.

THOMAS CRANMER, ARCHBISHOP OF CANTERBURY.

Born 1489 A.D..........Burned 1556 A.D.

Fellow of Cambridge.	Book of Common Prayer.
Archbishop of Canterbury.	The Twelve Homilies.
His glory and his death.	Cranmer's Bible.

AFTER some years of study, sporting, and teaching at Cambridge, Thomas Cranmer, a Fellow of Jesus College, born in 1489, at Aslacton in Nottinghamshire, went on a visit to Waltham Abbey in Essex, where lived a Mr. Cressy, the father of some of his college pupils. It happened that King Henry VIII., returning from a royal progress, stayed a night at Waltham; and, according to the custom of the day, his suite were lodged in the various houses of the place. Cranmer met Fox, the royal almoner, and Gardiner, the royal secretary, at supper in his friend Cressy's ; and when the table-talk turned upon the king's divorce, which was then the great topic of the time, he suggested that the question should be referred to the Universities of Europe. "The man has got the right sow by the ear," said Henry, next day, when he heard of the remark. And from that day Cranmer was a made man.

It is not our purpose here to trace the great career of Cranmer as a politician and a churchman. His literary character and works alone claim our notice. The part which he played in the shifting scenes of the English Reformation may be read in the annals of our Tudor Sovereigns. In March 1533 he was consecrated Archbishop of Canterbury, qualifying his oath of obedience to the pope with the statement, "that he did not intend by this oath to restrain himself from anything that he was bound to either by his duty to God or the king or the country."

After escaping, in the reign of Henry VIII., the double danger arising from the king's capricious ferocity and the insidious hatred of the anti-reform party, Cranmer became, during the reign of Henry's gentle son Edward, a leader of the English Reformation and a founder of the English Church. A few years later, under

1556
A.D.

poor, ill-tempered, misguided Mary, having been induced in the gloom of a prison cell to sign a denial of his Protestant belief,—a deed which he afterwards utterly repealed —he underwent at Oxford that baptism of fire which has purified his memory from every stain. Cranmer's great fault was a want of decision and firmness.

There is a book, which ranks with our Bible and the Pilgrim's Progress, as containing some of the finest specimens of unadulterated English to be found in the whole range of our literature. It is *The Book of Common Prayer*, used by the Episcopal Churches of Great Britain and Ireland. To Cranmer the merit of compiling this beautiful service-book is chiefly due. The old Latin Missal, used in various forms all over England, was taken to pieces; many parts of it were discarded, especially the legends and the prayers to saints, and what remained was re-cast in an English mould. The Litany, differing only in a single petition from that now read, was added as a new feature of the service. By an Act of Parliament, passed in 1548, all ministers were ordered to use the Book of Common Prayer in the celebration of Divine service. And ever since, that sweet and solemn music of King Edward's Liturgy has been heard in our lands, rising through the sacred silence of many churches when the Sabbath bells have ceased to chime.

A book of *Twelve Homilies*, or sermons, was also prepared under the superintendence of Cranmer, for the use of those clergymen who were not able to write sermons for themselves. The need of such a work shows us how far behind the lower clergy then were, even in the knowledge and use of their own tongue. Four of these Homilies are ascribed to the pen of Cranmer.

His third great literary work was his superintendence of a revised translation of the Bible, which is commonly called either *Cranmer's Bible* from his share in its publication, or the *Great Bible* from its comparative size. This edition, which came out in 1540, appears to have been founded on Tyndale's version. The Hebrew and Greek originals were carefully consulted, and the English was compared with them, many of the proof-sheets—perhaps all of them—passing under Cranmer's pen.

Cranmer's extant original works are very many, and possess considerable merit ; but his literary reputation will always rest mainly on the fact that he was what we may call editor-in-chief of those three great works of the English Reformation already noticed,—the Book of Common Prayer, the Twelve Homilies, and the Great Bible.

CHAPTER V.

HENRY HOWARD, EARL OF SURREY.

Born about 1516 A.D..........Beheaded 1547 A.D.

Surrey's fame.	English metre.
Early life.	Geraldine.
Troubles.	Æneid in blank verse.
Trial and death.	Illustrative extracts

For two reasons the brilliant but unhappy Surrey holds a fore-most place in the annals of our English literature. He was, so far as we know, the earliest writer of English blank verse, and he gave to English poetry a refinement and polish for which we search in vain among his predecessors.

His father was the third Duke of Norfolk; and his mother, Elizabeth, was a daughter of the great house of Buckingham. But Surrey had more from Heaven than noble birth could give, for the sacred fire of poetry burned in his breast. Of his boyhood we know nothing certain. Nursed in the lap of luxury, and the darling of a splendid Court, he yet won a soldier's laurels both in Scotland and in France. But his fame was not to be carved out only with a sword. Travelling into Italy, he "tasted the sweet and stately measures and stile of the Italian poesie," and returned home to re-cast in the elegant mould of his accomplished mind the metres of his native land.

At home, however, he became involved in many troubles. Some of these resulted from the escapades of his own youthful folly. He was once imprisoned for rioting in the streets at night and breaking windows with a cross-bow. But other and graver evils came. In the latter days of the reign, when "Bluff King Hal" had become "Bloated King Hal," and all the courtly circle saw that the huge heap of wickedness was sinking into the grave, there arose a keen contest between the noble houses of Howard and Seymour. The element of religious strife added to the bitterness of the feeling which grew up between these two rival families; for the Howards were Roman Catholics, and the Earl of Hertford, the head of the Seymours, was a secret friend of the Reformation. The grand aim of Hertford was to secure the protectorship of his young nephew Prince Edward when the old king was dead. Surrey and his father Norfolk, standing in the way, must perish. The thing was easy to do; the name of Howard was poison to the king, who had already soiled their proud escutcheon with an ugly smear of blood, drawn, four years earlier, from the fair neck of his fifth wife. Arrested for treason, the father and the son, each ignorant of the other's capture, were hurried by different ways to the Tower. Surrey was tried at Guildhall on a flimsy charge of treason, supported chiefly by the fact that he had quartered the arms of Edward the Confessor on his shield with those of his own family. This was tortured into a proof that he aimed at the throne. He had long worn these arms, he said, even in the king's own sight; and the heralds had allowed him to do so in virtue of his royal descent. In spite of these simple truths, and the noble eloquence of his defence, the poet was doomed to die; and on the 19th of January 1547 his bright hair, all dabbled in blood, swept the dust of the scaffold. Eight days later, the blood-stained Henry died, just in time to save from the block the head of Norfolk, whose execution had been arranged for the following morning.

Surrey's literary merits have been already noticed. Dr. Nott, who edited Surrey's works, claims for the poet the honour of having revolutionized English poetry, by substituting lines of fixed length, where the accents fall evenly, for the rhythmical lines of earlier poets, in which the number of syllables is irregular, and the equality of the lines requires to be kept up by certain pauses or cadences of the voice. But recent writers have shown that this theory cannot be maintained. In the words of Dr. Craik, " The true merit of Surrey is, that he restored to our poetry a correctness, polish, and general spirit of refinement, such as it had not known

Dec. 12,
1546
A.D.

since Chaucer's time; and of which, therefore, in the language as now spoken, there was no previous example whatever." Like Chaucer, he caught his inspiration from the great bards of Italy, and sat especially at the feet of Petrarch. In his purification of English verse, he did good service by casting out those clumsy Latin words, with which the lines of even Dunbar are heavily clogged.

The poems of Petrarch ring the changes in exquisite music on his love for Laura. So the love-verses of Surrey are filled with the praises of the fair Geraldine, whom Horace Walpole has tried to identify with Lady Elizabeth Fitzgerald, a daughter of the Earl of Kildare. If this be so, Geraldine was only a girl of thirteen when the poet, already married to Frances Vere for six years, sang of her beauty and her virtue. It is no unlikely thing that Surrey, an instinctive lover of the beautiful, was smitten with a deep admiration of the fresh, young, girlish face of one—

> "Standing with reluctant feet,
> Where the brook and river meet,
> Womanhood and childhood fleet."

Such a feeling could exist—it often has existed—in the poet's breast, free from all mingling of sin, and casting no shadow of reproach upon a husband's loyalty.

Surrey's chief work was *the translation into English blank-verse of the Second and Fourth books of Virgil's " Æneid."* Some think that he borrowed this verse from Italy; Dr. Nott supposes that he got the hint from Gavin Douglas, the Scottish translator of Virgil. Wherever the gem was found, Surrey has given it to English literature; a rough gem, indeed, at first, and shining with a dim, uncertain gleam, but soon, beneath Shakspere's magic hand, leaping forth to the sight of men, a diamond of the first water, flashing with a thousand coloured lights.

Surrey is said to have written also the first English Sonnets.*

---

* The Sonnet is borrowed from the Italian. It is a poem of fourteen lines, two of its four stanzas having four lines each, and the others three lines. The rhymes are arranged according to a particular rule.

FROM SURREY'S TRANSLATION OF VIRGIL.

(FOURTH BOOK.)

But now the wounded quene with heavie care
Throwgh out the vaines doth nourishe ay the plage,
Surprised with blind flame, and to her minde
Gan to resort the prowes of the man
And honor of his race, wbiles on her brest
Imprinted stake his wordes and forme of face,
Ne to her lymmes care graunteth quiet rest.
The next morowe with Phoebus lampe the ertbe
Alightned clere, and eke the dawninge daye
The shadowe danke gan from the pole remove.

SONNET ON SPRING.

(MODERN SPELLING.)

The *soote* season, that bud and bloom forth brings,   [*sweet*
With green hath clad the hill and *eke* the vale.   [*also*
The nightingale with feathers new she sings ;
The turtle to her *make* hath told her tale.   [*mate*
Summer is come, for every spray now springs ;
The hart hath hung his old head on the pale,
The buck in brake his winter coat he flings ;
The fishes *flete* with new repaired scale ;   [*float*
The adder all her slough away she flings ;
The swift swallow pursueth the flies *smale ;*   [*small*
The busy bee her honey now she *mings ;*   [*mixes*
Winter is worn that was the flowers *bale.*   [*evil*
And thus I see among these pleasant things
Each care decays, and yet my sorrow springs.

CHAPTER VI.

OTHER WRITERS OF THE SECOND ERA.

(1474–1558.)

Poets.	Sir David Lyndsay.	John Bellenden.
Robert Henryson.	Nicholas Udall.	John Leland.
William Dunbar.		Hugh Latimer.
Gavin Douglas.	Prose Writers.	Miles Coverdale.
Alexander Barclay.	Robert Fabian.	John Bale.
Stephen Hawes.	Edward Hall.	John Knox.
John Skelton.	Lord Berners.	George Cavendish.
John Heywood.	John Fisher.	Sir John Cheke.
Sir Thomas Wyatt.	Sir Thomas Elyot.	John Fox.

POETS.

ROBERT HENRYSON was chief schoolmaster at Dunfermline about the end of the fifteenth century. His longest poem is the *Testament of Fair Creseide*, in which Chaucer's tale of "Troilus and Creseide" is continued. The fine ballad of *Robin and Makyne*, which may be found in Percy's "Reliques," is ascribed to this accomplished man. *The Moral Fables of Æsop*, and *The Garment of Gude Ladyes*, are his chief remaining works. He is said to have died some time before 1508.

WILLIAM DUNBAR, placed by Sir Walter Scott at the head of Scottish poets, and perhaps, therefore, deserving more prominence than he receives here, is thought to have been a native of East Lothian, and to have been closely allied to the noble house of March. This Chaucer of the North graduated at St. Andrews as M.A. in 1479. Then, assuming the grey robe of the Franciscans, he travelled for some years in Britain and France, preaching and begging, according to the custom of the friars; and he afterwards visited the English and some of the Continental courts, as an *attaché* to certain Scottish embassies. The many-coloured life he thus spent is clearly reflected in his works, which show remarkable knowledge of human nature and society. Pensions, rising at last to £80, rewarded the public services of the poet. Spending his last days in the irksome bondage of a court life, and pining for a chance of escape from his gilded cage, he died about 1520, having reached the age of sixty years.

Dunbar's leading poems are three—*The Thistle and the Rose; The Golden Terge;* and, finest of all, *The Dance of the Seven Deadly Sins.*

The first-named commemorates the marriage of King James IV. with the English princess Margaret in 1503,—an historical event which paved the way for the close union of two sister lands.

In the poem of "The Golden Terge," the sleeping bard is attacked by Venus and her train. Reason, holding over him a golden shield, repels all assailants, until blinded by a powder which Presence flings in his eyes. The poor poet then becomes the captive of Lady Beauty, and is much tormented until the scene vanishes with a clap of thunder, and he awakes amid the song of birds and the perfume of bright May flowers.

"The Dance" describes a vision, beheld during a trance into which the poet fell on a winter night. In presence of Mahoun (that is, Mahomet, or the Devil, for these were often interchangeable terms about the days of the Crusades) Pride leads on the other deadly sins in a fearful dance. Each sin is represented by a distinct personification, painted in horror's darkest hues, and lighted in the dance by the lurid flames through which he leaps.

GAVIN DOUGLAS was a younger son of the fifth Earl of Angus, well known in Scottish story as Archibald Bell-the-Cat. He was born about 1474. Having finished his education at Paris, he rose by many minor steps to be Abbot of Aberbrothock, and was afterwards consecrated Bishop of Dunkeld. But for the Pope's refusal to sanction his appointment, he would have become Archbishop of St. Andrews.

The work for which Douglas is most celebrated, is his *poetical translation of Virgil's " Æneid" into the Scottish dialect;* remarkable as being the first rendering of a Latin classic into our native tongue. Two long allegories—*King Hart*, and *The Palace of*

Honour—were also written by this poet-priest. The distinctive feature of his language is the abundant use of words from the Latin,—an innovation by which the foreign-bred scholar strove to lift the diction of his poems above the homely level of Dunbar and other earlier bards. Original prologues stand before each book, bright with pictures of nature; to which, no doubt, the lovely wooded hills, among which the Tay winds at Dunkeld, contributed not a little of their exquisite colouring.

Flodden was a fatal day for the house of Douglas. The Master of Angus and his brother William wet the Cheviot heather with their life-blood. The old earl, whose wise caution had been rudely repelled by the wilful king before the dark day of battle, retired to Galloway to die. And the gentler scholar, Gavin, had soon to flee to the English Court, and in 1521 or 1522 died in London of the plague.

ALEXANDER BARCLAY, who died in 1522, flourished in the reigns of Henry VII. and his son. He is remembered as the writer of a poem, *The Ship of Fools*, of which the name shows it to be a satirical allegory. It was founded on the German of Brandt.

STEPHEN HAWES, writer of the *Pastime of Pleasure*, and groom of the chamber to Henry VII., was a Suffolkman. His skill in versifying, combined with his knowledge of French and Italian, made him a great favourite at court.

JOHN SKELTON, a coarse, bold satirist, was in his prime in the latter days of Henry VII., and the earlier days of Henry VIII. In a short-lined poem, called *Colin Clout*, he belabours the clergy unmercifully with cudgel-words, making no choice of weapons, but striking with the first that came to hand. He is one of that useful band of satirists, among whom we reckon also Longlande and Heywood, whose trenchant lines cut deep into the foul growths of monkish ignorance and lust. So vigorous was the assault of Skelton, that even the magnificent Wolsey found it necessary to turn on the strong-voiced poet, who was forced to shelter himself in the sanctuary of Westminster. There he died in 1529.

JOHN HEYWOOD, styled the Epigrammatist, who flourished during the reign of Henry VIII., was remarkable for his *Interludes*, or short satirical plays, in which, as in "Colin Clout," the clergy suffer tremendously.

SIR THOMAS WYATT was born in 1503 in Kent, and was educated at Cambridge. His elegant scholarship and quick wit, added to a fine person and remarkable skill with lance and rapier, speedily won for him a brilliant reputation. But his life was not all sunshine: he was named as one of the lovers of Anne Boleyn, whose praise he had sung in his verses; and for this and other reasons he was cast into prison. He was afterwards restored to royal favour, and being employed on some mission by the king, he overheated himself in riding on a summer day, took fever, and died at Sherbourne in Dorsetshire in 1541. He aided his friend Surrey in raising the tone of English poetry.

SIR DAVID LYNDSAY of the Mount, born about 1490, was page of honour to young James V., by whom he was knighted. He was employed as envoy to Holland and Denmark, and was for two years member of Parliament for his native shire of Fife. He died in that county in 1557 at his seat, the Mount. His chief work is the *Play of the Three Estates*, a dramatic satire on the king, lords, and commons, which was acted in 1535 at Cupar-Fife and Edinburgh. His *Squire Meldrum*, last of the metrical romances, is lively but licentious. *The Monarchie*, opening with the Creation and closing with the Day of Judgment, is valuable for its spirited account of Scotland. A smaller piece, full of pungent satire upon the court, is called the *Complaynt of the King's Papingo* (peacock or parrot).

NICHOLAS UDALL, author of the earliest existing English comedy, was born in Hampshire about 1506, and was educated at Oxford. Udall was master of Eton, where his cruel floggings won for him a more dubious kind of renown than his learning or his wit. His comedy of *Ralph Royster Doyster*, in five acts, is thought to have been written some time before 1551, for the Christmas performance at Eton. Udall died in 1557.

PROSE WRITERS.

ROBERT FABIAN and EDWARD HALL are the earliest writers of history in English prose. The former, a London alderman, who died in 1512, wrote a chronicle of English history, called the *Concordance of Stories;* in which fact and fiction are industriously heaped together with honest, well-meaning dullness. The latter, a lawyer, who died in 1547, gives us a more valuable book in his *History of the Houses of York and Lancaster.*

LORD BERNERS, Chancellor of the Exchequer and Governor of Calais under Henry VIII., *translated* into vigorous English prose *Jean Froissart's brilliant pictures of Chivalry.*

JOHN FISHER.—Let us not forget the English sermons· of the Bishop of Rochester who bore this name. Leaving out of sight higher results, the good done to our language by its weekly growing hosts of sermons, has been incalculable. Fisher, born in 1459, lived a long life in steady adherence to the Church of Rome. In the bloody year 1535 he was tried and convicted on a charge of denying that Henry VIII. could be the head of the Church. As the poor old bishop lay in the Tower, the pope sent him a cardinal's hat. "Ha!" said the royal wild beast, "Paul may send him a hat, but I will leave him never a head to wear it!" The savage threat was executed on the 22d of June, fourteen days before his friend More met the same fate on the same charge.

SIR THOMAS ELYOT, the friend of Leland and of More, was eminent as a medical man during the reign of Henry VIII. He wrote a work called *The Castle of Health*, which contains much good advice about food and such matters. Of more importance, however, was his educational work, *The Governor*, published in 1531, in which he recommends that children should be taught to speak Latin from their infancy, and that music, drawing, and carving (that is sculpture), should have place in a scheme of enlightened education.

JOHN BELLENDEN, Archdeacon of Moray and a Lord of Session under Queen Mary, produced in 1536, by order of James V., *a translation of Hector Boece's History of Scotland.* This is considered the earliest existing specimen of Scottish prose literature. An anonymous work, called *The Complaynt of Scotland*, published at St. Andrews in 1548, was the first *original* work in Scottish prose. Bellenden also *translated the first Five Books of Livy*, writing, besides, *Poems*, *Epistles to James V.*, and a *Sketch of Scottish Topography*.

JOHN LELAND, the father of our archæological literature, was born in London. Passing from St. Paul's school, he studied at Cambridge, Oxford, and Paris, and then became a chaplain to Henry VIII. His powers as a linguist were remarkable. His great work is the *Itinerary*, in which he gives the results of his many antiquarian tours. Insane during his last two years, he died in his native city in 1552.

HUGH LATIMER, famous as a leader of the English Reformation, was born in Leicestershire about 1472, received his education at Cambridge, and became Bishop of Worcester in 1535. When the Act of the Six Articles was passed, he resigned in disgust, and spent the last six years of the reign of Henry VIII. in prison. Liberated by Edward VI., he devoted himself earnestly to the work of preaching. His style—many of his *Sermons* and *Letters* remain—is remarkable for its homeliness and its wealth of droll anecdotes and illustrations. He was too great a champion of the truth to escape the flames that Mary lit. Ridley and he burned together at Oxford in 1555. His were the glorious, ever-memorable words, spoken ere the lips of the aged prophet were shrivelled into ashes,—"We shall this day light such a candle, by God's grace, in England, as I trust shall never be put out."

MILES COVERDALE, Bishop of Exeter, was born in Yorkshire in 1487. His changeful life extended far into the succeeding century (1568). His name is imperishably associated with the story of the English Bible; for in 1535 he published, with a dedication to the king, the first printed translation of the *whole Bible*. He was also much engaged in the preparation of the Great, or Cranmer's Bible (1540); and when exiled in the time of Mary, he took part in the Geneva translation, printed there in 1557 and 1560. He is supposed to have died in London in 1568.

JOHN BALE, Bishop of Ossory in Ireland, was born in Suffolk in 1495. He is chiefly remarkable for a Latin work, *Lives of Eminent Writers of Great Britain,* the list beginning with Japheth! Many interludes and scriptural dramas were also written by him, besides a *Chronicle of Lord Cobham's Trial and Death.* He died at Canterbury in 1563.

JOHN KNOX, the great reformer of Scotland, cannot be forgotten here, although his literary works were few. *A History of the Scottish Reformation* was the chief of these. Born at or near Haddington in 1505, he received his education at St. Andrews, became the leader of the Scottish Reformation, and died at Edinburgh in 1572.

GEORGE CAVENDISH is remarkable as the writer of a very truthful and unaffected *Life of Cardinal Wolsey,* whose gentleman-usher he was, and whom he served to the last with devoted fidelity. This work, from which Shakspere has largely drawn in his play of Henry VIII., was not printed until 1641. Cavendish, who was also a member of the royal household, died in 1557.

SIR JOHN CHEKE, who was born in 1514, is more worthy of remembrance for his success in fostering the study of Greek at Cambridge, when the hated novelty was in danger of being trampled to death by an opposing party, than for his contributions to English literature. A pamphlet called *The Hurt of Sedition* is his only original English work. He left also some manuscript translations from the Greek. He died in 1557.

JOHN FOX, born at Boston in 1517, is distinguished as the author of the *Acts and Monuments of the Church,* which is familiarly known as *Fox's Book of Martyrs.* His education was received at Oxford, whence he was expelled for heresy in 1545. At one time he was all but starving in London; at another he had to flee for his life to the Continent from the persecutions of Mary's reign. His great work occupied him for eleven years, and was published in 1563. Under Elizabeth he became a prebend of Salisbury, after declining many other offers of promotion in the Church. He died in 1587.

THIRD ERA OF ENGLISH LITERATURE.

FROM THE ACCESSION OF ELIZABETH IN 1558 A.D. TO THE SHUTTING OF THE THEATRES IN 1648 A.D.

CHAPTER I.

THE PLAYS AND PLAYERS OF OLD ENGLAND.

Miracle plays.	The old stage.
Moralities.	Early scenery.
Interludes.	Wall and Moonshine.
The Four Ps.	At the play.
Comedy and Tragedy.	Standing of the players.

THE *Miracle Play* or *Mystery*, acted in churches and convents, either by the clergy themselves or under their immediate direction, was the earliest form of the English drama. The only knowledge of Bible history possessed by the rude and ignorant masses of the people, during the later centuries of the Middle Ages, was got from these plays. The subjects chosen were the most striking stories in the Book—such as the Creation, the Fall, the Deluge, Abraham's Trial, the Crucifixion; and these were dramatized with little regard to the sacred and awful nature of the themes. Profane and terrible, indeed, were these mistaken teachings. Three platforms rose, one above another, forming a triple stage. The topmost, representing the heaven of heavens, was occupied by a group of actors, who personated the Almighty and his angels. Below stood those who played the parts of the redeemed. Upon the lowest, which imitated the world, the deeds of men were represented; and not far from the side of this lowest stage there smoked a fiery gulf, which stood for hell. All this is bad enough, but worse remains behind. The comic element must not be forgotten; for the poor yokels, who gather to be taught and amused, would yawn and sleep, if there were no broad jokes and boisterous fun to relieve the solemnities of the performance. And of all beings, whom should these priests of the Church choose to be their first comedian, but the Prince of Darkness! He it was who, equipped according to the vulgar notion with hoofs and horns and tail, created the fun by which the congregation was kept awake and in good temper. This trifling with awful subjects shows us how low the religion both of priests and people was in tone and feeling. It took a week to act some of these Mysteries; and there are instances in which the whole circle of religious doctrine and history was traversed in this barbarous fashion. All the countries of western and south-western Europe, as well as Britain, have some remains of the old Mystery literature.

Gradually these Miracle Plays changed into the *Moralities*, which formed the second stage in the development of the English drama. Here, instead of Scripture characters, we find abstract qualities personified and strutting in varied garments on the stage. Noah and Abraham have given place to Justice, Mercy, Gluttony, and Vice. The amount of morality, learned by the audiences who gathered round such actors, cannot have been great; but we must respect to some extent the intention of the authors who produced these plays, and meant them to do good. Students in the universities, boys at the public schools, town councillors, or brethren of the various trade guilds, acted these Moralities on certain great days and state occasions. An open scaffold knocked up in the market-place, or a platform of planks drawn upon wheels, served as a stage, on which such pieces as *Hit the Nail on the Head*, or, *The Hog hath Lost his Pearl*, were acted by these dramatic amateurs. The Devil of the Miracle Plays was still retained, to aid the Vice in doing the comic business of the Moralities. The fun, most relished by such audiences as Old England could then produce, consisted in calling bad names and hitting hard blows. Such contests of tongue and fist went on continually between the Devil and the Vice; but in many cases the former carried off his victim in triumph at the close of the performance.

Thus the two branches of our drama sprang from one and the same root. A Morality, broken in two, supplies the elements of both. Its serious portions form the groundwork of English tragedy; its lighter scenes, of English comedy. But, between the Moralities and the appearance of our earliest Comedy, came the *Interludes*, which strongly resembled our modern Farce. Of these John Heywood was the most noted writer. He lived in the reign of Henry VIII., whose idle hours he often amused with his music and his wit. The controversial spirit of the Reformation age deeply penetrated the nascent drama. Moralities and Interludes abound, which are just so many rockets, charged with jest and sneer and railing, that the opposing sides launched fiercely at each other in the heat of the religious war.

An idea of the Interludes may be formed from a single specimen. *The four Ps* describes in doggerel verse a contest carried on by a Pedlar, a Palmer, a Pardoner, and a 'Poticary, in which each character tries to tell the greatest lie. On they go, heaping up the most outrageous falsehoods they can frame, until the chance hit of the Pardoner, who says that he never saw a woman out of temper, strikes the others dumb. This tremendous bouncer nobody can beat, so the Pardoner wins the prize.

The Greek and Latin drama, with the refined productions of Italy and Spain, had much to do with the moulding of our English plays into a perfect shape.

Ralph Royster Doyster, a dramatic picture of London life, written before 1551, by Nicholas Udall, is—so far as we know—the first English comedy. And the old British story of *Ferrex and Porrex*, dramatized by Sackville and Norton, which was acted in 1561 by the students of the Inner Temple, is considered the earliest tragedy in the language. The introduction of human characters, instead of the walking allegories that trod the Moral stage, is the grand distinctive feature which marks the rise of the true English drama. There is something in the very words—*abstraction* and *allegory*—to make men yawn; and few were deeply moved at the sufferings or triumphs of Justice and Peace. But when real life was put upon the stage,—when crimes were per-

petrated, marriages managed, sufferings endured, difficulties overcome by actors who bore the names and did the deeds of human
flesh and blood,—a new interest was given to our plays, and the
audience wept and laughed not *at* the performance, but *with* the
performers.

By a sudden and enormous stride, the English drama reached
the magnificent creations of Shakspere in a few years after the
production of its earliest perfect specimens.   Not half a century
after the court of Henry VIII. had been amused with the grotesque
drolleries of John Heywood, Elizabeth and her maids of honour
assembled to laugh at the fortunes and misfortunes of old Jack
Falstaff, and to tremble in the shadow of the finest tragedies
the English stage has ever seen.

We must not suppose, however, that the Theatres kept pace with
the wonderful improvement of the Drama.   To form a true idea of
the stage on which the Elizabethan plays were acted, we
must carry our recollection back to those yellow-painted wooden
caravans, that travel round the country fairs, and supply the delighted rustics, in exchange for their pennies, with a tragedy full
of ghosts and murder, and thrilling with single combats between
valiant warriors in tin armour, who fight with broadswords made
of old iron hoops.   The travelling stage was often set up in
the court-yard of an inn.   A wooden erection—little better than
what we call a shed—there sheltered the company and their
audience.   When in 1576 the first licensed theatre was opened
at Blackfriars in London, it was merely a round wooden wall
or building, enclosing a space open to the sky.   The stage,
indeed, was covered with a roof of thatch; but upon the greater
part of the *house*—as in modern days we call the spectators—the
sun shone and the rain fell without let or hindrance.

The rude attempts at scenery in such theatres as the Rose and
the Globe, which were among the leading London houses, make us
smile, who have witnessed the gorgeous scenic triumphs of Kean
and his brother managers.   Some faded tapestry, or poorly daubed
canvas hung round the timbers of the stage, at the back of which
ran a gallery—eight or ten feet high—to hold those actors who

might be supposed to speak from castle walls, windows, high rocks, or other lofty places. A change of scene was denoted by hanging out in view of the spectators a placard with the name of the place—Padua, Athens, or Paris—painted on it. A further stretch of imagination was required from the assembly, when the removal of a dingy throne, and the setting down of a rough table with drinking vessels, were supposed to turn a palace into a tavern ; or the exchange of a pasteboard rock for a thorn branch was expected to delude all into the belief that they saw no longer a pebbly shore, but a leafy forest. An exquisitely comical illustration of this scenic poverty may be found in "Midsummer Night's Dream," where the Athenian tradesmen rehearse a play, and act it before Duke Theseus. Funny as it seems, the picture was drawn from the realities of the author's day. The play of "Pyramus and Thisbe" requires the introduction of a wall upon the stage, that the lovers may whisper their vows through a chink in its masonry. So Snout the tinker is daubed with plaster, and coming on the stage, announces to the audience that he is to be considered the Wall ; and for a chink, he forms a circle with thumb and fingers, through which the appointment to meet at Ninny's tomb is made by the ardent lovers. Then in comes one with a lantern, a thorn bush, and a dog, who calls himself the Man in the moon, and proceeds to light the midnight scene. An unbelieving critic, who sits among the onlookers, suggests that the man, the bush, and the dog should get into the lantern, since the appearance of the Man in the moon, carrying the moon in which he lived, was likely to cause some confusion of ideas. The notion of Wall and Moonshine announcing their respective characters to the audience, is, no doubt, a bit of Shakspere's native humour; but every day that our great dramatist acted in the Globe he saw as sorry makeshifts for scenery as the lime-daubed tinker who acted Wall, and the dim tallow candle, in sore need of snuffing, that sputtered in the lantern of Moonshine.

At one o'clock—on Sundays especially, but also on other days —the play-house flag was hoisted on the roof, announcing that the performance was going to begin; and there it fluttered till the

play was over.   Placards had already told the public what was to
be the performance of the day.   The audience consisted of two
classes; the *groundlings*, or lower orders, who paid a trifle for admission to the pit; and the *gallants*, who paid sixpence apiece
for stools upon the rush-strewn stage, where they sat in two rows
smoking, and showing off their ruffs and doublets, while the actors
played between them.   The circle of the pit resounded with oaths
and quarrelling, mingled with the clatter of ale-pots and the noise
of card-playing.   Nor did the occupants of the full-dress stools
show better breeding than the unwashed groundlings.   Noise,
tobacco smoke, and the heavy fumes of ale, formed the main parts
of the atmosphere, in which our noblest plays were ushered into
fame.   When the trumpets had sounded, a figure in a long black
velvet cloak came forward to recite the prologue.   Then the play
began; and, if its early scenes did not suit the taste of the
audience, a storm of noises arose; hisses, yells, cat-calls, cock-
crowing, whistling drowned the actors' voices, and stopped the
progress of the play.   In short, Elizabeth's loyal subjects used
or abused their lungs just as vigorously as those of Queen Victoria
can do in Parliament, and out of it as well.   The actors—attired
in the costume of their own day—played in masks and wigs; and
the female parts—the Violas, the Portias, the Rosalinds—were
filled by boys, or smooth-faced young men, in women's dress.   All
was over by three or four o'clock, and then the audience went home
to an early supper.

The players—of whom Shakspere was one—held no very exalted place in the society of the day.   The very familiar way in
which their Christian names have come down to us—as *Will* and
Ben—shows that they were lightly esteemed by the courtiers
and nobles; looked upon, if not exactly as menial servants in
livery, yet as something not far above the jester who shook his
cap and bells at the supper tables of the great.   They were formed
into companies generally under the patronage of some nobleman,
at whose parties they acted in presence of the guests.   Neither
their acting nor their play-writing—they nearly all held the
dramatist's pen—did so much for the more prosperous players as

their shares in the Globe, or some other of the London theatres. The sum which managers paid before 1600 for a new play, never exceeded £8 or £10; when, a little later, the number of theatres increased, the price rose to £20 or £25, and the receipts of the second day became the author's perquisite. A few stray shillings might be also made by writing prologues to new pieces. It was the pennies of the groundlings, and the sixpences of the gallants, not the sale of his splendid dramas, that enabled Shakspere to buy his house at Stratford, and retire a rich man to die in his native town. Many a university man, however, like Jonson and Chapman, earned his manchets and his sack, his steaks and ale, by acting and writing for the stage. The two occupations were nearly always united; and the wiser brethren of the buskin and the sock added, as Shakspere did, a third and more fruitful source of income, by investing their early gains in theatre shares. Shakspere acted at the Globe, wrote for the Globe, and pocketed so much of the money taken at the doors of the Globe. A sensible and prudent man was this glorious dramatist, utterly unsympathizing with the ridiculous notion, hardly yet extinct, that a real poet must of necessity be a reckless, improvident fool.

CHAPTER II.

ROGER ASCHAM.

Born 1515 A.D.........Died 1568 A.D.

Ascham's fame.	In Germany.	Titles of his books.
Birth and education.	Mary's reign.	Plan of the Toxophilus.
Toxophilus.	The pupil-queen.	The School-master.
Elizabeth's tutor.	Ascham's death.	Illustrative extract.

ROGER ASCHAM, an eminent teacher as well as a great writer, has thus won double fame as a man of letters. He acted as classical tutor to Queen Elizabeth, whose fondness for him was very great; and he left behind him two works, which rank high among our English classics.

At Kirby Wiske, near Northallerton in Yorkshire, he was born in 1515, the son of an honest yeoman who acted as steward to the Scroopes. A certain Sir Anthony Wingfield, noticing the studious boy, took him among his own sons, gave him a good education, and in 1530 sent him to St. John's at Cambridge. To the study of Greek—which was just then taking root in our universities—the young student applied himself with such ardour, that he was soon qualified to read Greek lectures to his younger associates. In 1534 he took B.A., and M.A. in 1536. And then he entered on the life of a teacher, for which he was remarkably well qualified. When Cheke resigned in 1544, he was chosen to fill the honourable office of University Orator.

One year later, his first great book, *Toxophilus*, was published. This work won for him the kind wishes and cordial support of troops of friends, besides the notice of King Henry, who granted the writer a pension of £10 a year.

1545 A.D.

Ascham was shortly afterwards chosen to act as private tutor to the Princess Elizabeth. It was a fortunate choice for both the royal girl and the Cambridge man. Fortunate for her, because her fine intellect was intrusted to the culture of one who knew his profession and loved it well; fortunate for him, because during two happy years (1548–50) he enjoyed the delight of teaching one who loved to learn, and in after days he found, in his submissive and hard-working pupil, a royal mistress, who loved and honoured her Greek master to the last.

The last three years of King Edward's reign (1550–53) Ascham spent in Germany, acting as secretary to Sir Richard Morysine, who was English ambassador at the Imperial Court. His experiences of German life are embodied in a work on that country and court. During these three years of absence his friends at home were endeavouring to do him good. His pension, which had ceased at the death of Henry VIII., was restored, and he received in addition the important office of Latin Secretary to the king.

Upon the accession of Queen Mary a cloud seemed to hang over the fortunes of the scholar, who was a keen Protestant. But the shadows passed. Bishop Gardiner was induced to look kindly on him, and on the strength of his book "Toxophilus," his pension was doubled, and his appointment as Latin Secretary was renewed. Nor was his college standing altered, for he still held his fellowship, and still wore the honours of Public Orator.

Under the sceptre of Elizabeth his life was a smooth and quiet stream. But it was fast gliding to its rest. Her majesty read Greek and Latin with her honoured tutor for some hours almost every morning, and in the evening they often played at tables or shovel-board together. At last the studies, that he loved so well, proved too much for the scholar's weakened frame. A feverishness, which prevented him from afternoon study and broke his night's rest, had long hung about him. Anxious to finish by New Year's day 1569 a poem, which he was writing in honour of his royal pupil, he began to work at night. Ague seized him, and in a week laid him on his death-bed (December 30, 1568). So old Roger Ascham died, as many of his life's best hours had been spent, in the service of his pupil-queen. When she heard that the kind heart was still in death, whose warmest pulses had throbbed for her, she cried out, "I would rather have thrown ten thousand pounds into the sea than have lost my Ascham."

The titles of Ascham's three chief books are here given in full, as a specimen of the way in which the writers of this time named their works. We have, 1. "Toxophilus, the Schole or Partitions of Shootinge, contayned in II. Bookes. Written by Roger Ascham, 1544, and now newly perused. Pleasaunt for all Gentlemen and Yeomen of Englande, for theyr pastime to reade, and profitable for theyr use to followe both in Warre and Peace." 2. "A Report and Discourse, written by Roger Ascham, of the Affaires and State of Germany, and of the Emperor Charles his Court, during certain years while the sayd Roger was there." 3. "The Schole-Master ; or Plain and Perfite Way of teaching Children to Understand, Write, and Speake the Latin Tongue, but specially purposed for the private bringing up of Youth in Jentlemen and Noblemen's Houses."

The *Toxophilus* is, in many things, a sensible and pleasant book on archery, cast into the form of a dialogue, between a lover of study (Philologus), and a lover of archery (Toxophilus). But, while it very properly insists on the use of out-door recreation to the studious man, it gives an undue prominence to the pastime whose name it bears, and needlessly undervalues some fine old English athletic sports. The language of the book—in the preface he half apologizes for not writing it in Latin—is good honest English prose, pretending to no great elegance, but full of idiomatic strength.

Ascham's greatest work is *The Schoolmaster*, which was not published until after the author's death. It is noted as being the first important work on Education in our literature. The idea of the book sprang from a discussion at Cecil's dinner-table at Windsor. Some of the Eton boys having run away from school to escape a flogging, the conversation turned upon this bit of local news ; and Ascham spoke out his mind. On the encouragement of Sackville, who sat by, he committed his thoughts to paper, and so the book began. The first section of the work condemns severity in the treatment of the young, while the second develops a new way of

teaching Latin, without putting the pupils through the prepara-
tory drudgery of mastering the details of the grammar.

Ascham's work on *Germany* gives, besides much political information, some curious pictures of the Emperor and his court,
which are valuable as being sketched by an eye-witness.

EXTRACT FROM "THE SCHOOLMASTER" OF ASCHAM.

Before I went into Germany, I came to Broadgate in Leicestershire, to take
my leave of that noble Lady Jane Grey, to whom I was exceeding much beholden.
Her parents, the duke and duchess, with all the household, gentlemen and
gentlewomen, were hunting in the park. I found her in her chamber reading
Phœdon Platonis in Greek, and that with as much delight as some gentlemen would read a merry tale in Bocace. After salutation and duty done,
with some other talk, I asked her why she would lose such pastime in the park?
Smiling, she answered me: "I wiss, all their sport in the park is but a shadow
to that pleasure that I find in Plato. Alas! good folk, they never felt what
true pleasure meant." "And how came you, madam," quoth I, "to this deep
knowledge of pleasure? And what did chiefly allure you unto it, seeing not
many women, but very few men, have attained thereunto?" "I will tell you,"
quoth she, "and tell you a truth which, perchance, ye will marvel at. One of the
greatest benefits that ever God gave me, is, that he sent me so sharp and severe
parents, and so gentle a schoolmaster. For when I am in presence either of
father or mother, whether I speak, keep silence, sit, stand, or go, eat, drink, be
merry or sad, be sewing, playing, dancing, or doing anything else, I must do it,
as it were in such weight, measure, and number, even so perfectly as God made
the world, or else I am so sharply taunted, so cruelly threatened, yea, presently,
sometimes with pinches, nips, and bobs, and other ways which I will not name
for the honour I bear them, so without measure misordered, that I think myself
in hell, till time come that I must go to Mr. Elmer; who teacheth me so
gently, so pleasantly, with such fair allurements to learning, that I think all
the time nothing, whiles I am with him."

CHAPTER III.

GEORGE BUCHANAN.

Born 1506 A.D..........Died 1582 A.D.

The Scottish Virgil.	Coimbra.	Last days and death.
His education.	Translates the Psalms.	History of Scotland.
Offends the monks.	Tutor to Mary and James	The Psalms.
Bordeaux.	the Sixth.	Arthur Johnston.

GEORGE BUCHANAN has been styled the Scottish Virgil from the elegance of his Latin verse, in which among moderns he stands unrivalled, at least by any writer of British birth. Nor is his Latin prose much inferior in vigour and in flow.

Born in Dumbartonshire in 1506, he passed, after a poor and struggling boyhood, to the University of Paris, where he was supported by the kindness of his uncle, James Heriot. But in less than two years the death of this good friend flung him upon the world, sick and poor. Returning to Scotland, he joined a Scottish army that was marching into England; but the hardships of a soldier's life once more laid him on a sick-bed. When restored to health, he went to college at St. Andrews, graduated there, and went again to France, where he completed his academic course at Paris. About the age of twenty-three he was chosen professor in the College of St. Barbe, and then began his teaching life.

Having acted for five years as tutor to the young Earl of Cassilis, who lodged near St. Barbe, Buchanan returned with his pupil to his native land. His growing reputation as a teacher won for him the notice of James V. who intrusted one of his own natural sons to his care. This office he continued to fill until his poetic satires upon the vices of the friars, especially the poem called *Franciscanus*, drew upon him the fiery wrath of the clergy. Charged with holding the Lutheran heresy—he really had caught the flame in Paris—he was arrested; and but for his lucky escape through a window, while his keepers were asleep, the name of Buchanan might now be read **1539** with those of Hamilton and Wishart upon the sand- A.D. stone obelisk at St. Andrews.

Before the year closed, we find him teaching Latin in the College of Guienne at Bordeaux. While there he made the acquaintance of the Scaligers, father and son, who lived at Agen. Here, too, he wrote four tragedies. After some changes of fortune in France, Buchanan went to fill a chair in the newly established College of Coimbra in Portugal, on the invitation of his friend Govea, who had been appointed Principal. Here he was assailed, after a short interval of peace, by the revengeful monks, who had never forgiven the poems, in which he had heaped ridicule on their order. The fearful machinery of the Inquisition was now in full work, and Buchanan was in considerable danger of his life. But after the delay of a year and a half, he was sentenced to confinement in a monastery, where he was to be schooled by the monks into better behaviour and sounder views. It is said, but without a shadow of evidence, that these monks gave George, as a punishment, the task of translating the Psalms into Latin verse. He certainly began in that quiet Portuguese cloister the version of the Psalms which has made his name so great; and what more natural than that he should thus beguile the lagging hours of a captive's life? We can fancy the keen pleasure with which his eye would brighten, when the dull homilies of the monks were done for the day, and he found himself among his well-thumbed books in some sequestered nook, where, with the vine leaves tapping at the open grating, and a glimpse of the deep azure sky seen beyond their tender green, he loved to sit writing his great work. Upon his release, finding his chances of promotion in Portugal very doubtful, he sailed to England, whence after some time he passed to France. We find him soon in Italy, teaching the son of Marshal de Brissac, a great French soldier, by whom he was treated with respectful kindness. The termination of this engagement, which lasted for five years, marks the close of Buchanan's Continental life.

The return of Buchanan to his native land, which was then

convulsed with the throes of the Reformation, took place shortly
before the year 1562. His fame as a teacher had crossed the
Straits of Dover before him; and he was honoured, in spite of his
Protestant principles, with the office of classical tutor to Queen
Mary, who read a passage of Livy with him every day after
dinner. In 1564 he received from his royal mistress and pupil, in
recognition of his literary merit, the temporalities of Crossraguel
Abbey, which were worth £500 a year in Scottish money. The
Earl of Murray, who was then the leading man in Scotland, took
special notice of this great scholar, and made him, about 1566,
Principal of St. Leonard's College at St. Andrews. The terrible
murder of Darnley, and the infamous marriage of Mary with
Bothwell, soon split Scotland into rival factions. Buchanan, sid-
ing with the Regent Murray, undertook the tuition of
1570 the young king, James VI.; into whom, according to the
A.D.   fashion of those days—and later days, too, not far from
our own—he whipped so much Greek and Latin, that the
thick-speaking, shambling, unwashed pedant acquired the name of
the "British Solomon." There is more than a spice of irony in
the appellation; though, doubtless, many a servile courtier, with
a fat living or an easy place in his eye, used it in another sense.
Bitter and stern words flowed from Buchanan's pen against the
royal girl, once his pupil, who had so fearfully sullied the crown
she wore, and so recklessly outraged her people's love. The Latin
work, *Detectio Mariæ Reginæ*, is a fierce exposure of her guilt and
shame. Eight years later, in 1579, followed a masterly political
work, *De Jure Regni*, maintaining the right of the people to
control their rulers.

The last days of this great Scotsman were passed quietly,
although his pupil James did not look so kindly on him after the
publication of his republican book in 1579. He wrote a yearly
letter, transmitted by the wine-ships that traded from Leith to
Bordeaux, to his old friend and colleague, Vinetus. He penned a
modest account of his own life; and he completed his second
great work, *The History of Scotland* on which he had been engaged
for twenty years.

In his seventy-seventh year he breathed his last, so poor that his body was buried at the expense of the city of Edinburgh. His " History of Scotland " was then passing through the press. It is written in Latin, which many writers prefer to that of Livy, and consider equal to that of Sallust. The record of events is brought down to the year 1572, and occupies twenty books, into which the whole work is divided. Buchanan adopts that practice of the ancient historians, by which they put fictitious speeches into the mouths of their leading characters. This, however well adapted for displaying the historian's skill in composition, takes from the truthfulness, which should be the pervading and governing quality of all history.

In his magnificent Latin version of the Psalms he has used twenty-nine different metres. The translation is freely executed, so that it frequently becomes a paraphrase rather than an exact rendering. The 104th and 137th Psalms are considered the gems of this master-piece of elegant scholarship and poetic fire.

Among the miscellaneous works of Buchanan, it may suffice to name two,—the *Epithalamium*, which he wrote in honour of Queen Mary's first marriage; and a poem composed on the occasion of James the Sixth's birth. Both are in Latin, and both contain passages of excelling sweetness. A tract, called *The Chamæleon*, satirizing Secretary Maitland, affords a scanty specimen, but quite enough too, of the rugged Scotch, in which this Scottish Virgil transacted his daily business.

A physician to Charles I., born in 1587 at Aberdeen, by name Arthur Johnston, much of whose life was also spent abroad, wrote a complete Latin version of the Psalms in elegiacs, which Hallam values almost as highly as the version of Buchanan.

CHAPTER IV.

SIR PHILIP SIDNEY.

Born 1554 A.D..........Died 1586 A.D.

The boy Philip.	Tiles for Flushing.
On the Continent.	Skirmish near Zutphen.
Appearance and character.	His death.
The Arcadia.	Other works.
The Defense of Poesie.	Illustrative extract.

WHILE Elizabeth in the first year of her glorious reign was receiving the congratulations of a rejoicing land, a boy, not yet five years old, was plucking daisies and chasing butterflies on the green lawns of Penshurst in Kentshire. It was Philip Sidney, son of Sir Henry Sidney and Mary Dudley, who was sister to the magnificent Leicester, soon to be prime favourite of the Queen.

Philip, born in 1554, went to school at Shrewsbury, and passed thence to Oxford and Cambridge, where he won a scholar's name. Having spent three years in Continental travel, during which he saw Paris drenched in the blood of Huguenots, and himself narrowly escaped death on the fearful day of St. Bartholomew, he returned in his twenty-first year to England, a polished and accomplished man.

His *début* at court was an instant and decided success. No doubt his uncle, Leicester, then in the full blaze of royal favour, had much to do with this; but Sidney had personal qualities which won for him the smiles of all. His finely-cut Anglo-Norman face, his faint moustache, his soft blue eyes, and flowing amber hair, were enough to make him the darling of the women; while his skill in horsemanship, fencing, and manly games, gained the respect and admiration of the men.   Higher than these outward and accidental graces must we rank the intellect and scholarship which stamped him as one of England's greatest sons; and higher still, that gentle heart, whose pulses, always human, never throbbed more kindly than when, on the field of his death, he turned the cooling draught from his own blackened lips to slake the dying thirst of a bleeding soldier, past whom he was carried.

Yet this brilliance was not without its clouds. At tennis one day he quarrelled with the Earl of Oxford, who ordered him to leave the playing-ground. This Sidney refused to do;-upon which Oxford, losing temper, called him a puppy. Voices rose high, and a duel was impending, when Elizabeth interfered and took Sidney to task for not paying due respect to his superiors. Philip's haughty spirit could not bear the rebuke, and he withdrew from court. Far from the glittering whirl, sheltered amid the oaks of Wilton, the seat of his brother-in-law, Pembroke, he wrote a romantic fiction, which he called *The Countess of Pembroke's Arcadia.* Written merely to amuse his leisure hours, it was never finished, and was not given to the world till its gifted young writer had been four years dead. The censures, which Horace Walpole and others have passed upon this work, are quite unmerited. No book has been more knocked about by certain critics; but its popularity in the days of Shakspere and the later times of the Cavaliers, with whom it was all the fashion, affords sufficient proof that it is a work of remarkable merit. We, who read Scott and Dickens and Thackeray, cannot, certainly, relish the "Arcadia" as Elizabeth's maids of honour relished it; but all who look into its pages must be struck with its rich fancy and its glowing pictures. It is not a pastoral, as the misnomer "Arcadia," borrowed from Sannazzaro, seems to imply. There are indeed in this book shepherds, who dance and sing occasionally; but the life of a knight and courtier—such as Sidney's own—has clearly supplied the thoughts and scenery of the work.

But the book on which Sidney's reputation as an English classic writer rests, is rather his *Defense of Poesie,* a short treatise, written in 1581, to combat certain opinions of the Elizabethan Puritans, who would fain, in their well-meant but mistaken zeal, have swept away the brightest blossoms of our literature, along with pictures, statues, holidays, wedding-rings, and other pleasant things.

A favourite of Elizabeth, who called him the "jewel of her

dominions," he was looked coldly on by the Cecils, whose policy
it was to keep down men of rising talent. He had to struggle
long against this aversion before he gained the governorship of
Flushing. When this dear wish of his heart was at first refused,
he was so angry that he resolved to join Sir Francis Drake's expedition, just then equipping for the West Indian seas. Nothing
but a determined message from the Queen, whose messages were
not lightly to be disregarded, could turn him from this step. It
is said that about the same time he became a candidate for the
crown of Poland, but here again Elizabeth interfered.

The bright life had a sad and speedy close. Holland, then
bleeding at every pore in defence of her freedom and her faith, had
sought the help of England, ceding in return certain towns, of
which Flushing was one. Of this seaport Sidney became governor
in 1585. In the following year his uncle, Leicester, laid siege to
Zutphen (Southfen), a city on the Yssel, one of the mouths of the
Rhine. A store of food, under the escort of some thousand troops,
being despatched by Parma, the Spanish general, for the relief of
the place, Leicester resolved to intercept the supply; and rashly
judging one English spear to be worth a dozen Spanish, he sent
only a few hundred men on this perilous service. It was one of
those glorious blunders, of which our military history is full.
Sidney was a volunteer, and as they rode on a chilly October
morning to the fatal field, about a mile from Zutphen, the gallant
fellow, meeting an old general too lightly equipped for battle,
gave him all his armour except the breastplate. Thus his kindness killed him; for in the last charge a musket-ball smashed
his left thigh-bone to pieces, three inches above the knee. As he
passed along to the rear, the incident occurred which
1586 has been already noticed. Carried to Arnheim, he lay a
A.D.   few days, when mortification set in, and he died. His
last hours were spent in serious conversation upon the immortality of the soul, in sending kind wishes and keepsakes to his
friends, and in the enjoyment of music.

Besides the "Arcadia" and the "Defense of Poesie," Sidney
wrote many beautiful sonnets, and in 1584 replied, with perhaps

more vigour than prudence, to a work called "Leicester's Commonwealth," impugning the character of his uncle.

A STAG HUNT.

(FROM THE "ARCADIA.")

They came to the side of the wood, where the hounds were in couples, staying their coming, but with a whining accent craving liberty; many of them in colour and marks so resembling, that it shewed they were of one kind.   The huntsmen handsomely attired in their green liveries, as though they were children of summer, with staves in their hands to beat the guiltless earth, when the hounds were at a fault; and with horns about their necks, to sound an alarm upon a silly fugitive : the hounds were straight uncoupled, and ere long the stag thought it better to trust to the nimbleness of his feet than to the slender fortification of his lodging; but even his feet betrayed him; for, howsoever they went, they themselves uttered themselves to the scent of their enemies, who, one taking it of another, and sometimes believing the wind's advertisements, sometimes the view of—their faithful counsellors—the huntsmen, with open mouths, then denounced war, when the war was already begun.   Their cry being composed of so well-sorted mouths that any man would perceive therein some kind of proportion, but the skilful woodmen did find a music.   Then delight and variety of opinion drew the horsemen sundry ways, yet cheering their hounds with voice and horn, kept still as it were together.   The wood seemed to conspire with them against his own citizens, dispersing their noise through all his quarters; and even the nymph Echo left to bewail the loss of Narcissus, and became a hunter.   But the stag was in the end so hotly pursued, that, leaving his flight, he was driven to make courage of despair; and so turning his head, made the hounds, with change of speech, to testify that he was at a bay : as if from hot pursuit of their enemy, they were suddenly come to a parley.

CHAPTER V.

EDMUND SPENSER.

Born 1553 A.D..........Died 1599 A.D.

Birth and education.	Raleigh's visit.	Chief works.
In the north.	The Faerie Queene.	Plan of the Faerie Queene.
The Shepheard's Calender.	Return to Ireland.	Its style and stanza.
The loss of a friend.	Public offices.	Pastorals.
Goes to Ireland.	Marriage.	Prose work.
Kilcolman Castle.	Misery and death.	Illustrative extract.

WHEN Chaucer died, the lamp of English poetry grew dim, shining for many years only with faint, uncertain gleams. A haze of civil blood rose from the trodden battle-fields of the Roses and the dust of old, decaying systems, the clamour of whose fall resounded through the shaking land, obscured the light "and blotted out the stars of heaven." But only for a while. Truth came with the Bible in her hand. The red mist rolled away. The dust was sprinkled with drops from the everlasting well. Men breathed a purer air and drank a fresher life into their spirit, and a time came of which it may well be said, "There were giants on the earth in those days."

Edmund Spenser was, in point of time, the second of the four grand old masters of our poetical literature. He was born in 1553, in East Smithfield, by the Tower of London. It is said that he was of a noble race, but we know little or nothing of his parents. Nor can we tell where he went to school. At the age of sixteen (1569) he entered Pembroke Hall, Cambridge, as a sizar, and there in 1576 he took his degree of M.A. So meagre is our knowledge of his early life.

A friendship, formed at Cambridge with Gabriel Harvey of Trinity Hall, had considerable influence upon the poet's fortunes. When Spenser left college, having disagreed, it is thought, with the master of his hall, he went to live in the north of England, perhaps to act as tutor to some young friend. He had, no doubt, long been wooing the Muses by the classic banks of Cam, but now the time had come when his genius was to shine out in fuller lustre. His fame, as often happens, had its root in a deep sorrow. A lady, whom he calls Rosalind, made a plaything of his heart, and, when tired of her sport, cast it from her. She little knew the worth of the jewel she had flung away. "The sad mechanic exercise" of verse was balm to the wounded poet, who poured forth his tender soul in *The Shepheard's Calender*, begun in the north but completed under the oak-trees of Penshurst, where dwelt "Maister Philip Sidney."

Spenser owed this brilliant friend to the kindness of Harvey, who had induced him to come to London. Thus he was naturally brought under the notice of Leicester, Sidney's uncle, by whose interest he became secretary to Lord Grey of **1580** Wilton, the newly-appointed Lord-Lieutenant of Ireland. A.D. The next two years were therefore spent in that country. Grey owed much to the gifted pen of his grateful secretary, who zealously defended his policy and reputation. The poet's services were rewarded in 1586 by a grant from Elizabeth of more than 3000 acres in the county of Cork. These acres—the estate of Kilcolman—formed a part of the forfeited lands of the rebel Desmonds, of which Raleigh had already received a large share. This seeming generosity—which, however, cost Elizabeth nothing—is ascribed to the good offices of Grey and Leicester; but there are not wanting hints that the cool and cautious Burleigh, anxious to thin the ranks of his magnificent rival, managed thus to consign to an honourable exile an adherent of Leicester, whose genius made him a formidable foe. The life of Spenser, all but the last sad scene, is henceforth chiefly associated with the Irish soil.

Smitten in the autumn of 1586 with a great grief—the bloody death of Sidney near Zutphen—Spenser hurried across to his estate, of which he was called the *Undertaker*, and **1586** which he was compelled to cultivate, in terms of the A.D. grant. It was a lovely scene, and we cannot quarrel with the causes, friendly or the reverse, which led the author of *The Faerie Queene* to take up his dwelling among "the green alders by the

Mulla's shore." The castle of Kilcolman, from which the Desmonds had been lately driven, stood by a beautiful lake in the
midst of an extensive plain, girdled with mountain ranges. Soft
woodland and savage hill, shadowy river-glade and rolling plough-
land were all there to gladden the poet's heart with their changeful
beauty, and tinge his verse with their glowing colours. Dearly
he loved the wooded banks of the gentle Mulla, which ran by his
home, and by whose wave, doubtless, many sweet lines of his great
poem were composed. Hither there came to visit him the brilliant
Raleigh, then a captain in the Queen's Guard, who seems to have
quarrelled with Essex, and to have been " chased from court" by
that hot-headed favourite. The result of this remarkable meeting
was Spenser's resolve to publish the first three books of " The
Faerie Queene," with which Raleigh was greatly delighted.

The two friends—for Raleigh now filled in the poet's heart the
place which poor Sidney had once held—crossed the sea together
with the precious cantos. The voyage is poetically described in
the Pastoral of *Colin Clouts come home againe*, published in 1591,
where Raleigh figures as the "Shepherd of the Ocean." Introduced by his friend to the Queen, and honoured with her
1590 approval of what he modestly calls his "simple song," the
A.D. poet lost no time in giving to the world that part of " The
Faerie Queene " which was ready for the press. The success of the poem was so decided, that in the following year the
publisher issued a collection of smaller pieces from the same pen.
A pension of £50 from Elizabeth—no small sum three centuries
ago—rewarded the genius and the flattery of Spenser, who then
went back to Ireland to till his beautiful barren acres, and
"pipe his oaten quill." He had, besides his farming and his
poetry, a public work to do, and that of no easy or pleasant
kind. As Clerk of the Council for Munster, and afterwards as
Sheriff of Cork, he came much into collision with the Irish people,
whom it was his policy to keep down with an iron hand.

The chief events of his later life were his marriage, and the
publication of the second three books of " The Faerie Queene." In
the fair city of Cork, not far from his castle, he was united, pro-

bably in 1594, to a lady named Elizabeth, in whose honour he sang the sweetest marriage song our language boasts. In 1596 he crossed to England and published the fourth, fifth, and sixth books of his great work.

So, laurelled and rejoicing, he returned to his Irish castle. To all appearance a long vista of happy years, bright with the love of a tender wife and blooming children, lay stretching out before the poet. But in that day life in Ireland resembled the perilous life of those who dress their vines and gather bursting clusters on the sides of Etna or Vesuvius. Scarcely was he settled in his home, when a torrent of rebellion swept the land. Hordes of long-coated peasants gathered round Kilcolman. Spenser and his wife had scarcely time to flee. In their haste and confusion their new-born child was left behind, and, when the rebels had sacked the castle, the infant perished in the flames. It was only three months later that Spenser breathed his last at an inn in King Street, Westminster. A common tale in human life. Bright hopes—a crushing blow—a broken heart —and death!

Oct.

1598

A.D.

> " Alas for *man*, if this were all,
> And nought beyond the earth."

In Westminster Abbey, near the dust of Chaucer, the body of this great brother minstrel was laid.

The grandest work of Spenser is his *Faerie Queene*. Among his numerous other writings the *Shepheard's Calender,—Colin Clouts come home againe,—Epithalamion,*—and his *View of the State of Ireland* are worthy of special notice.

In a letter to Sir Walter Raleigh, prefixed to the first three books of " The Faerie Queene," which were published in 1590, the poet himself tells us his object and his plan. His object was, following the example of Homer, Virgil, Ariosto, and Tasso, to write a book, coloured with an historical fiction, which should " fashion a gentleman or noble person in vertuous and gentle discipline." The original plan provided for twelve books, "fashioning XII. morall vertues." Of these twelve books we have only six. The old story of the six remaining books being finished in Ireland,

and lost by a careless servant, or during the poet's voyage to England, is very improbable. Spenser had only time between 1596 and his death to write two cantos and a fragment of a third. Hallam justly says, "The short interval before the death of this great poet was filled up by calamities sufficient to wither the fertility of any mind."   Prince Arthur, who is chosen as the hero of the poem, falls in love with the Faerie Queene, and, armed by Merlin, sets out to seek her in Faery Land. She is supposed to hold her annual feast for twelve days, during which twelve adventures are achieved by twelve knights, who represent, allegorically, certain virtues.

The Red-Crosse Knight, or Holiness, achieves the adventure of the first and finest book.   In spite of the plots of the wizard Archimago (Hypocrisy) and the wiles of the witch Duessa (Falsehood), he slays the dragon that ravaged the kingdom of Una's father, and thus wins the hand of that fair princess, (Truth.)   Sir Guyon, or Temperance, is the hero of the second adventure ; Britomartis, or Chastity—a Lady-Knight—of the third ; Cambel and Triamond, typifying Friendship, of the fourth ; Artegall, or Justice, of the fifth ; Sir Calidore, or Courtesy, of the sixth. The six books form a descending scale of merit. The first two have the fresh bloom of genius upon them; the third contains some exquisite pictures of womanhood, coloured with the light of poetic fancy; but in the last three the divine fire is seen only in fitful and uncertain flashes.   It was not that the poet had written himself out, but he had been tempted to aim at achieving too much. Not content with giving us the most exquisite pictures of chivalrous life that have ever been limned in English words, and at the same time enforcing with some success lessons of true morality and virtue, he attempted to interweave with his bright allegories the history of his own day.   Thus Gloriana the Faerie Queene, and Belphœbe the huntress, represent Elizabeth ; Artegall is Lord Grey ; Envy is intended for poor Mary Stuart.   Spenser's flattery of Queen Bess, whose red wig becomes in his melodious verse "yellow locks, crisped like golden wire," is outrageous.   It was a fashion of the day, to be sure ; and, after all, poets are only human.

It is almost needless to say that the politics dull and warp the beauty of the poetry,—a fact nowhere more manifest than in the fifth book, whose real hero is Lord Grey of Wilton.

The language of Spenser was purposely cast in an antique mould, of which one example is the frequent use of *y* before the past participle. The expletives *do* and *did* occur in his pages to a ridiculous extent. The stanza in which this great poem is written, and which bears the poet's name, is the Italian *ottava rima*, with a ninth line—an Alexandrine—added to close the cadence. It may well be compared to the swelling wave of a summer sea, which sweeps on—a green transparent wall—until it breaks upon the pebbly shore in long and measured flow. Thomson, Campbell, and Byron have proved the power of the grand Spenserian stanza.

In his Pastorals—the "Shepheard's Calender" and "Colin Clout" —Spenser cast aside much of the stereotyped classic form. Instead of Tityrus and Corydon breathing their joys and sorrows in highly polished strains, we find Hobbinoll and Diggon, Cuddie and Piers, chatting away in good old-fashioned English about the Church and its pastors, poets and their woes, and similar themes. The Calender contains twelve eclogues—one for every month in the year.

That Spenser could write capital prose, as well as exquisite verse, is clearly proved by his " View of the State of Ireland," a dialogue in which that land and the habits of its natives are finely described. The views of Spenser as to the government of the Irish people seem to have harmonized with those of relentless Strafford, whose plan was aptly named "Thorough," from its sweeping cruelty. This prose work of Spenser, though presented to Elizabeth in 1596, was not printed until 1633.

THE OPENING STANZAS OF THE FIRST CANTO OF "THE
FAERIE QUEENE."

A gentle Knight was *pricking* on the plaine,   [*riding*
Ycladd in mightie armes and silver shielde,
Wherein old dints of deepe woundes did remaine,
The cruel markes of many a bloody fielde ;

Yet armes till that time did he never wield :
His angry steede did chide his foming bitt,
As much disdayning to the curbe to yield :
Full iolly knight he seemed, and faire did sitt,
As one for knightly iiusts and fierce encounters fitt.

And on his brest a bloodie crosse he bore,
The deare remembrance of his dying Lord,
For whose sweete sake that glorious badge he wore,
And dead, as living ever, him ador'd :
Upon his shield the like was also scor'd,
For soveraine hope, which in his helpe he had.
Right, faithfull, true he was in deede and word ;
But of his cheere did seeme too solemne sad ;
Yet nothing did he dread, but ever was *ydrad.*   [*fcarcd*]

Upon a great adventure he was bond,
That greatest Gloriana to him gave,
(That greatest glorious queene of Faery lond,)
To winne him worshippe, and her grace to have,
Which of all earthly thinges he most did crave :
And ever, as he rode, his hart did earne
To prove his puissance in battell brave
Upon his foe, and his new force to learne ;
Upon his foe, a Dragon horrible and stearne.

A lovely Ladie rode him faire beside,
Upon a lowly asse more white than snow ;
Yet she much whiter ; but the same did hide
Under a vele, that wimpled was full low ;
And over all a blacke stole shee did throw :
As one that inly mournd, so was she sad,
And heavie sate upon her palfrey slow ;
Seemed in heart some hidden care she had ;
And by her in a line a milke-white lambe she lad.

So pure and innocent, as that same lambe,
She was in life and every vertuous lore ;
And by descent from royall lynage came
Of ancient kinges and queenes, that had of yore
Their scepters stretcht from east to westerne shore,
And all the world in their subjection held ;
Till that infernal Feend with foule uprore
Forwasted all their land, and them expeld ;
Whom to avenge, she had this Knight from far compeld.

Behind her farre away a Dwarfe did lag,
That lasie seemd, in being ever last,
Or wearied with bearing of her bag
Of needments at his backe. Thus as they past,
The day with cloudes was suddeine overcast,
And angry Iove an hideous storme of raine
Did poure into his lemans lap so fast,
That everie wight to shrowd it did constrain;
And this faire couple eke to shroud themselves were fain.

Enforst to seeke some covert nigh at hand,
A shadie grove not farr away they spide,
That promist ayde the tempest to withstand;
Whose loftie trees, yclad with sommer's pride,
Did spred so broad, that heavens light did hide,
Not perceable with power of any starr :
And all within were pathes and alleies wide,
With footing worne, and leading inward farr :
Faire harbour that them seems ; so in they entred ar.

And foorth they passe, with pleasure forward led,
Ioying to heare the birdes sweete harmony,
Which, the rein shrouded from the tempest dred,
Seemd in their song to scorne the cruell sky.
Much can they praise the trees so straight and hy,
The sayling pine ; the cedar proud and tall ;
The vine-propp elme ; the poplar never dry ;
The builder oake, sole king of forrests all ;
The aspine good for staves ; the cypresse funerall;

The laurell, meed of mightie conquerours
And poets sage ; the firre that weepeth still ;
The willow, worne of forlorne paramours ;
The eugh, obedient to the benders will ;
The birch for shaftes ; the sallow for the mill ;
The mirrhe sweete-bleeding in the bitter wound ;
The warlike beech ; the ash for nothing ill ;
The fruitfull olive ; and the platane round ;
The carver holme ; the maple seeldom inward sound.

Led with delight, they thus beguile the way,
Untill the blustring storme is overblowne ;
When, weening to returne whence they did stray,
They cannot finde that path, which first was showne,
But wander too and fro in waies unknowne,
Furthest from end then, when they neerest weene,

That makes them doubt their wits be not their owne:
So many pathes, so many turnings seene,
That, which of them to take, in diverse doubt they been.

At last resolving forward still to fare,
Till that some end they finde, or in or out,
That path they take, that beaten seemd most bare,
And like to lead the labyrinth about;
Which when by tract they hunted had throughout,
At length it brought them to a hollow cave,
Amid the thickest woods.   The Champion stout
Eftsoones dismounted from his courser brave,
And to the Dwarfe a while his needlesse spere he gave.

CHAPTER VI.

RICHARD HOOKER.

Born about 1553 A.D.........Died 1600 A.D.

Contemporaries.	Boscomb.
Early days.	Bishop's-Bourne.
Marriage.	Death.
First living.	His great work.
Master of the Temple.	Illustrative extract.

WHEN Richard Hooker gave to the world his splendid work on the *Laws of Ecclesiastical Polity*, English prose literature acquired a dignity it had not known before. The last decade of Elizabeth was indeed a glorious time in the annals of British authorship. The genius of Shakspere was then bursting into the full bloom, whose bright colours can never fade; Spenser was penning the *Faerie Queene* on the sweet banks of Mulla; Bacon, a rising young barrister, was sketching out the ground-plan of the great *Novum Organum;* and in the quietude of a country parsonage, a meek and hen-pecked clergyman was composing, with loving carefulness, a work which, for force of reasoning and gracefulness of style, is justly regarded as one of the master-pieces of our literature. Richard Hooker was writing his great treatise.

Born at Heavytree near Exeter, in 1553 or 1554, Hooker was indebted to the kindness of Bishop Jewell for a university education. The modest young student, who was enrolled on the books of Corpus Christi at Oxford, did not disappoint the hopes of his patron : his college career was marked with steady application and closed with honour. His eminence as a student of Oriental tongues led to his appointment in 1579 as lecturer on Hebrew. Two years later he entered the Church.

And then a great misfortune befell Master Richard Hooker. Appointed to preach at St. Paul's Cross, he left his college, a perfect simpleton in the world's ways, and journeyed up to London. There he had lodgings in the house of one John Church·man, whose wife so won by her officious attentions upon the drenched and jaded traveller, that he thought he could not do better than follow her advice and marry her daughter Joan, whom she strongly recommended as a suitable wife and skilful nurse for a man so delicate as he appeared to be. Accordingly in the following year Richard and Joan were married; and not till it was too late did the poor fellow find that he had bound himself for life to a downright shrew.

The first year or so of his married life was spent in Bucks, where he was rector of Drayton-Beauchamp. But the affection of an old pupil, Sandys, son of the Archbishop of York, obtained for him in 1585 the post of Master of the Temple. It was his duty here to preach in the forenoon, while the afternoon lecture was delivered by Travers, a zealous Calvinist. The views of the two preachers were so diametrically opposed to each other, that it was said " the forenoon sermons spoke Canterbury, and the afternoon Geneva." Travers was forbidden to preach by Archbishop Whitgift; and a paper war began between the rivals, which so vexed the gentle Hooker, that he begged to be restored to a quiet parsonage, where he might labour in peace upon the great work he had begun.

In 1591 his wish was granted. He received the living of Boscomb in Wiltshire; and, gathering his darling books and papers round him, he sat down to his desk, no doubt, with a deep sense of relief. There he wrote the first four books of the *Ecclesiastical Polity*, which were published in 1594. In recognition, probably, of this great service to the Church of England, the Queen made him in the following year rector of Bishop's-Bourne in Kent. The important duties of his sacred office and the completion of his eight books filled up the few remaining years of his life. Never very strong, and weakened, perhaps, by ardent study, he caught a heavy cold, which, settling on his lungs, proved fatal on the 2d of November 1600. The fifth book of the " Ecclesiastical Polity" was printed in 1597; the remaining three did not appear until 1647.

1594
A.D.

" The first book of the ' Ecclesiastical Polity,' " says Hallam, " is at this day one of the master-pieces of English eloquence." The moderate tone of the work, which was written against the Puritans, is worthy of all praise. The author is somewhat censured for the great length of his sentences; but the best critics agree in admiring the beauty and dignity of his style, which, woven of honest English words chosen by no vulgar hand, is yet embroidered with some of the fairest and loftiest figures of poetry. This charm—the ornament of figures—English prose had probably never possessed till Hooker wrote.

ON CHURCH MUSIC.

(FROM THE " ECCLESIASTICAL POLITY.")

Touching musical harmony, whether by instrument or by voice, it being but of high and low in sounds a due proportionable disposition, such notwithstanding is the force thereof, and so pleasing effects it hath in that very part of man which is most divine, that some have been thereby induced to think that the soul itself by nature is, or hath in it, harmony; a thing which delighteth all ages, and beseemeth all states; a thing as seasonable in grief as in joy; as decent being added unto actions of greatest weight and solemnity, as being used when men most sequester themselves from action. The reason hereof is an admirable facility which music hath to express and represent to the mind, more inwardly than any other sensible mean, the very standing, rising and falling, the very steps and inflections every way, the turns and varieties of all passions whereunto the mind is subject; yea, so to imitate them, that, whether it resemble unto us the same state wherein our minds already are, or a clean contrary, we are not more contentedly by the one confirmed, than changed and led away by the other. In harmony, the very image and character even of virtue and vice is perceived, the mind delighted with their resemblances, and brought by having them often iterated into a love of the things themselves. For which cause there is nothing more contagious and pestilent than some kinds of harmony; than some, nothing more strong and potent unto good.

CHAPTER VII.

THOMAS SACKVILLE, LORD BUCKHURST.

Born 1536 A.D.........Died 1608 A.D.

Birth.	Gorboduc.
Education.	Its plan and story.
The law-student.	Mirrour of Magistrates.
Political career.	The Induction.
Lord High Treasurer.	Illustrative extract.

SACKVILLE was the herald of that splendour in which Elizabeth's glorious reign was destined to close. He was born in 1536, at Buckhurst in Sussex, the seat of his ancestors. His father, Richard Sackville, had held high office in the Exchequer. Some home teaching, a few terms at Oxford, and a continuation of his course at Cambridge, where he graduated as M.A., prepared the way for his entrance upon the profession of the law and a statesman's life. While at college, his skill in verse-making gained him some little fame; and when entered at the Inner Temple, and regularly set down to the study of dry and dusty law books, he did not forget those flowery paths in which he had spent so many glad hours, but often stole from his graver studies to weave his darling stanzas.

With his political career we have here little to do, and a few notes of it must therefore suffice. Created Lord Buckhurst in 1566 by Elizabeth, he laid aside his literary pursuits and gave himself up to the toils of statesmanship. Twice he crossed the seas as ambassador. He was selected, on account of his gentle manner and address, to tell her doom to the wretched woman who once was Queen of Scotland. And, in a later year, he sat as Lord Steward, presiding over those brother peers who were appointed to try the unhappy Essex. The dislike of Leicester clouded his fortunes, and cast him into prison; but when in 1588 death freed him from this foe, he regained the royal favour. He reached the pinnacle of his greatness in 1598, upon the death of Lord Burleigh, when he became Lord High Treasurer of England.

This great office he continued to hold until he died in 1608, at a good old age. Elizabeth and James, unlike in almost everything else, agreed in appreciating the services of this great and gifted man.

While still a student in the Temple, he had joined Thomas Norton in writing a play then called *Gorboduc*, which was acted before Elizabeth at Whitehall by a company of his fellow-students of the Inner Temple, as a part of the Christmas revels of 1561. This was the first English tragedy, so far as is known. It resembles the later tragedies in having five acts, of which probably Norton wrote three, and Sackville the last two; but it differs from them in the use of that very prosy and unnatural excrescence of the ancient plays, called the Chorus. Every act of *Gorboduc*, or *Ferrex and Porrex* as the authors called it in the revised edition of 1571, is closed with an ode in long-lined stanzas, filled, as was the old Greek chorus, with moral reflections on the various scenes. The plot of this play was founded on a bloody story of ancient British history.

But a greater work than *Gorboduc* adorns the memory of Sackville. During the last years of Mary, which might well be called gloomy, were it not for the fiery glare that tinges them red as if with martyrs' blood, he sketched out the design of a great poem, which was to be entitled *The Mirrour of Magistrates*, and was to embrace poetic histories of all the great Englishmen who had suffered remarkable disasters. The bulk of this work, which first appeared in 1559, was done by minor writers of the **1559** time; but the *Induction* and the *Story of the Duke of* A.D. *Buckingham*, contributed to the second edition in 1563, are from the powerful pen of Sackville. The "Induction" is a grand pictured allegory, which describes "within the porch and jaws of hell" Remorse, Dread, Revenge, and other terrible things, that are ever gnawing away at the root of our human life. It contains only a few hundred lines, and yet these are enough to place Sackville high on the list of British poets. As already hinted, these poems were the fruit of Sackville's early summer; the ripe luxuriance of his life was devoted to cares of the state, whose ample honours crowned his head when frosted with the touch of winter.

OLD AGE.

(FROM "THE INDUCTION.")

And, next in order, sad Old Age we found,
His beard all hoar, his eyes hollow and blind,
With drooping cheer still poring on the ground,
As on the place where nature him assigned
To rest, when that the Sisters had untwined
His vital thread, and ended with their knife
The fleeting course of fast-declining life.

There heard we him, with broke and hollow plaint,
Rue with himself his end approaching fast,
And all for nought his wretched mind torment
With sweet remembrance of his pleasures past,
And fresh delights of lusty youth *forewaste;*   [*utterly wasted*
Recounting which, how would he sob and shriek,
And to be young again of Jove beseek!

But, *an* the cruel fates so fixed be   [*if*
That time forepast cannot return again,
This one request of Jove yet prayed he—
That, in such withered plight and wretched pain
As Eld, accompanied with her loathsome train,
Had brought on him, all were it woe and grief,
He might awhile yet linger forth his life,

And not so soon descend into the pit,
Where Death, when he the mortal corpse hath slain,
With reckless hand in grave doth cover it,
Thereafter never to enjoy again
The gladsome light, but, in the ground *ylain,*   [*laid*
In depth of darkness waste and wear to nought,
As he had ne'er into the world been brought.

But who had seen him sobbing how he stood
Unto himself, and how he would bemoan
His youth forepast,—as though it wrought him good
To talk of youth, all were his youth foregone—
He would have mused, and marvelled much, whereon
This wretched Age should life desire so fain,
And knows full well life doth but length his pain.

Crook-backed he was, tooth-shaken, and blear-eyed,
Went on three feet, and sometime crept on four;
With old lame bones, that rattled by his side;
His scalp all *pilcd,* and he with eld forelore;   [*peeled*
His withered fist still knocking at Death's door;
Fumbling and drivelling as he draws his breath;
For brief, the shape and messenger of Death.

CHAPTER VIII.

OUR ENGLISH BIBLE.

Earliest translations.	Hampton Court.
The life of Truth.	Translation of 1611.
Bible-burning.	Proposed change.
Crypt of St. Paul's.	Hallam's criticism.
Geneva and Bishop's Bible.	English of the Bible.

WE have already seen how the first English Bible grew, sentence by sentence, in the quiet study of Lutterworth Rectory, where John Wycliffe sat among his books; how William Tyndale dared death and found it in a foreign land, that he might spread God's word freely among his awakening nation; how Miles Coverdale published in 1535 a version of the *whole* Bible, translated from the Hebrew and the Greek; and how in 1540 Cranmer, Archbishop of Canterbury, superintended the issue of a new translation, which was called Cranmer's, or the Great Bible.

The reign of the eighth Henry was a strange era in the history of the Book, evidencing perhaps above all other modern days the everlasting life of Truth. If the Bible were not immortal, it would surely have perished then.

One Sunday in February 1526, the great Wolsey sat in old St. Paul's under a canopy of cloth of gold. His robe was purple; scarlet gloves blazed on his hands; and golden shoes glittered on his feet. A magnificent array of satin and damask-gowned priests encircled his throne; and the grey head of old Bishop Fisher—soon to roll bloody on a scaffold—appeared in the pulpit of the place. Below that pulpit stood rows of baskets, piled high with books, the plunder of London and the university towns. These were Tyndale's Testaments, ferreted out by the emissaries of the cardinal, who had swept every cranny in **1526** search of the hated thing. None there fresh from the **A.D.** printer's hand—all well-thumbed volumes, scored with

many a loving mark, and parted from with many bitter tears!
Outside the gate before the great cross there burned a fire,
hungering and leaping for its prey like a red wild beast.   On that
day no blood slaked its ceaseless thirst, no crackling flesh fed its
ravenous maw—this was to be but a prelude to the grand performance of later days.   Bibles only were to burn; not Bible
readers.   When the sermon was over, men, who loved to read
these books, were forced, with a refinement of cruelty, to throw the
precious volumes into the flames, while the cardinal and his prelates
stood looking at the pleasant show, until the last sparks died out
in the great heaps of tinder; and then the gorgeous crowd went
home to supper, rejoicing in their work of destruction.   Poor misguided men! to think that the burning of a few shreds of paper
and scraps of leather could destroy the words of eternal Truth!

Scenes like this occurred more than once at St. Paul's Cross;
yet the Bible lived—was revised and translated with more untiring
industry than ever.

Fifteen years after the burning thus described, and five years
after the body of Tyndale had perished like his books in the
flames, a royal order was issued, commanding a copy of the Bible
to be placed in every church, where the people might read or hear
it freely.   Gladly was the boon welcomed; young and old flocked
in crowds to drink of the now unsealed fountain of life.

1541 Then was often beheld, within the grey crypt of St. Paul's,
A.D.   a scene which a distinguished living artist* has made
the subject of a noble picture.   The Great Bible, chained
to one of the solid pillars which upheld the arches of the massive
roof, lay open upon a desk.   Before it stood a reader, chosen
for his clear voice and fluent elocution; and, as leaf after leaf was
turned, the breathless hush of the listening crowd grew deeper.
Grey-headed old men and beautiful women, mothers with their
children beside them and maidens in the young dawn of womanhood, merchants from their stalls and courtiers from the palace,
beggary and disease crawling from the fetid alleys, stood still to
hear; while, in the dim back-ground, men who, if they had dared,

* George Harvey, Esq., of the Royal Scottish Academy.

would have torn the sacred Book to tatters and trampled it in the dust, looked sourly on.

This dear privilege of hearing the Bible at church, or reading it at home, so much prized by the English people then, was snatched from them again by their cruel and fickle king. But in 1547 the tyrant died, and during the reign of the gentle boy Edward Bible-reading was restored. Under Elizabeth the Bible was finally established as the great standard of our national faith. Two editions, appearing before that translation which *we* use, may be noted,— the Geneva Bible, so dear to the Puritans, finished in 1560 by Miles Coverdale and other exiles who were driven from England by the flames of persecution; and the Bishop's Bible of 1568, a translation superintended by Matthew Parker, Archbishop of Canterbury, who was aided by the first scholars of that learned age.

Then came the translation which we still use, and to which most of us cling with unchanging love, in spite of the occasional little flaws which the light of modern learning has discovered. How tame and cold the words of that Book, entwined as they are with the memory of earliest childhood, would fall upon our ear if rendered into the English in which we speak our common words and read our common books!

Within an oak-panelled and tapestried room of that splendid palace which Wolsey built at Hampton by the Thames, King James the First, most pedantic of our English monarchs, sat enthroned among an assembly of divines, who were met in conference upon the religious affairs of the kingdom. It was then little more than nine months after his accession to the English throne, and he took his seat, resolved to teach the Puritan doctors   Jan. 14 that in him they had to deal with a prince of logicians   **1604** and a master in theology. There were present, to back   A.D. the wisdom of the British Solomon and applaud his eloquence, some twenty bishops and high clergy of the Church of England, the lords of the Privy Council, and many courtiers; while, to speak in the cause of needed change there were only four—two doctors from Oxford, and two from Cambridge. It

would be out of place here to describe how, during the three days
of conference, amid the titters of the courtiers and the gratified
smiles of the clergy, the conceited king called the Puritan doctors
"dunces fit to be whipped," and indulged in other similar flights
of his peculiar, knock-down style of oratory. The scene, ridiculous
in most respects, is memorable to us, because it led to the publication
of our English Bible. During one of the pauses of the fusilade,
when the royal orator was out of breath, Dr. Reynolds proposed a
new version of the Scriptures; and James saw fit, by-and-by, to
yield his gracious consent.

Fifty-four scholars were appointed to the great work, but only
forty-seven of these actually engaged in the translation. Taking
the Bishop's Bible as the basis of the new version, they set to
their task in divisions, Oxford, Cambridge, and Westminster being
the centres of their labour; and, often meeting to compare notes
and correct one another's manuscripts, they completed their translation in about three years. Our Bible was therefore pub-
1611   lished, with a dedication to King James, in the year 1611.
A.D.   Of late years there has been some talk of a new translation. No doubt, a revisal, by which manifest mis-
prints or inaccuracies in translation might be remedied, would be
a good thing; but a completely new translation would so utterly
destroy those solemn associations which, rooted in every heart, are
twined, closer than the ivy around its elm-tree, round the antique
English of our Bibles, that to attempt it would be dangerous and
wrong. During the ascendency of the Puritans in Cromwell's day,
the same scheme was mooted, for the Puritans long preferred the
Geneva Bible to that of King James; but on the proposal being
laid before the leading scholars of that time, they pronounced the
translation of 1611 "best of any in the world;" and so the matter
dropped.

Hallam reminds us that, even in the days of King James, the
language of this translation was older than the prevailing speech.
"It may," this great critic says, "in the eyes of many, be a better
English, but it is not the English of Daniel, or Raleigh, or Bacon,
as any one may easily perceive. It abounds, in fact, especially in

the Old Testament, with obsolete phraseology, and with single words long since abandoned, or retained only in provincial use."

This may all be true; yet, in the face of Hallam's implied disparagement, we hold, with scores of better judges, that the English of the Bible is unequalled in the full range of our litera- ture. Whether we take the subtile argument of Paul's Epistles, the sublime poetry of Job and the Psalms, the beautiful imagery of the Parables, the simple narrative of the Gospels, the magnifi- cent eloquence of Isaiah, or the clear plain histories of Moses and Samuel, but one impression deepens as we read, and remains as we close the volume,—that, without regard to its infinite greatness as the written word of God, taken simply as a literary work, there is no English book like our English Bible.

CHAPTER IX.

WILLIAM SHAKSPERE.

Born 1564 A.D.........Died 1616 A.D.

Shakspere's tomb.	Rich and famous.	Study of Shakspere.
Birth-place.	Character as an actor.	His grand quality.
His father and mother.	Returns to Stratford.	Shakspere v. History.
Youthful life.	Speedy death.	Faults of his style.
Stories of his 'teens.	The First Folio.	Minor poems.
Goes to London.	Chief plays.	Illustrative extracts.

CLOSE by the river Avon in Warwickshire, a tall grey spire, springing from amid embowering elms and lime-trees, marks the position of the parish church of Stratford, in the chancel of which sleeps the body of our greatest poet. The proud roof of Westminster has been deemed by England the fitting vault for her illustrious dead; but Shakspere's dust rests in a humbler tomb. By his own loved river, whose gentle music fell sweet upon his childish ear, he dropped into his last long sleep; and still its melancholy murmur, as it sweeps between its willowy banks, seems to sing the poet's dirge. Four lines, carved upon the flat stone which lies over his grave, are ascribed to his own pen. Whoever wrote them, they have served their purpose well, for a religious horror of disturbing the honoured dust has ever since hung about the place :—

> Good friend, for Jesus' sake, forbeare,
> To digg the dust enclosed heare.
> Blest be ye man yt spares these stones,
> And curst be he yt moves my bones.

A niche in the wall above holds a bust of the poet, whose high arching brow, and sweet oval face, fringed with a peaked beard and small moustache, are so familiar to us all. How well we know his face and his spirit; and yet, how little of the man's real life has descended to our day !

Not very far from Shakspere's tomb part of the house in which he was born still stands. Sun and rain and air have gradually reduced the plastered timber of its old neighbours into powder; but its wood and lime still hold together, and the room is still shown in which baby Shakspere's voice uttered its first feeble wail. The dingy walls of the little chamber are scribbled all over with the names of visitors, known and unknown to fame. It is pleasant to think that this shrine, sacred to the memory of the greatest English writer, has been lately purchased by the English nation; so that lovers of Shakspere have now the satisfaction of feeling that the relics, which tell so picturesque a story of the poet's earliest days, are in safe and careful keeping.

Here, then, was born in April 1564 William, son of John Shakspere and Mary Arden, his wife. The gossiping Aubrey, no great authority, certainly, who came into the **1564** world about ten years after Shakspere's death, says that A.D. the poet's father was a butcher; others make out the honest man to have been a wool-comber or a glover, while an ingenious writer strives to reconcile all accounts by supposing that since good John held some land in the neighbourhood of Stratford, whenever he killed a sheep, he sold the mutton, the wool, and the skin, adding to his other occupations the occasional dressing of leather and fashioning of gloves. Perhaps John Shakspere's chief occupation was dealing in wool. At any rate, whatever may have been his calling, he ranked high enough among the burgesses of Stratford to sit on the bench as High Bailiff or Mayor of the town. Mary Arden, who should perhaps interest us more, if the commonly received rule be true, that men more strongly resemble their mothers in nature and genius, seems to have belonged to an old county family, and to have possessed what was then a considerable fortune.

The beautiful woodland scenery amid which the boy grew to early manhood made a deep impression on his soul. The beds of violets and banks of wild thyme, whose fragrance seems to mingle with the music of the lines that paint their beauty, blossomed richly by the Avon. The leafy glades, from which were pictured those through whose cool green light the melancholy Jacques wandered, and under whose arching boughs Bully Bottom and his

friends rehearsed their "very tragical mirth," were not in the
dales of Middlesex or Surrey, but in the Warwickshire Valley of
the Red Horse.   But of all men or boys, Shakspere was no mere
dreamer, fit only—

> "To pore upon the brook that babbles by."

We have no doubt that, when the daily tasks were done in the
Free Grammar School of Stratford, where Will probably got all the
regular instruction he ever had, the said Will might often have
been spied on Avon banks, rod in hand, thinking more of trout
and dace than of violets or wild thyme.   And, as we shall shortly
see, there is a strong suspicion, not far removed from certainty,
that more than once he saw the moon rise over the dark oak
woods of Charlecote Park, while he lurked in the shadow, waiting
for the deer, with more of the poacher than the poet in his guise.

And, while he was receiving from Hunt and Jenkins, then the
masters of the school, that education which his friend Jonson
characterizes as consisting of "little Latin and less Greek," an
occasional visit to scenes of a different kind, not far away, may
have mingled the colouring of town life and courtly pageants
with those pictures of woodland sweetness which his mind caught
from the home landscape.   Warwick and Coventry—Godiva's
town—were near ; and in the grand castle of Kenilworth in the
year 1575, when the princely Leicester feasted the Queen for
nineteen days, why may we not suppose that Alderman or Ex-
Bailiff Shakspere, his wife Dame Mary, and his little son Will,
then aged eleven, were among the crowd of people who had travelled from all the country round to see the Queen, the masquers,
and the fire-works ?   Strolling players, too, sometimes knocked up
their crazy stage, hung with faded curtains, in the market-place of
Stratford, and there flourished their wooden swords, and raved
through their parts to the immense delight of the gaping rustics.
Such visits, dear to all the boys of a country town, were, no doubt,
longed for and intensely enjoyed by young Shakspere.

How he spent his life after he had left school, and before he
went to London, we know as dimly as we know the calling of his

father. Aubrey says he helped his father the butcher, and that he acted also as a teacher. It is thought, from the constant recurrence of law terms in his writings, that he spent some of these years in an attorney's office. All stories may be true, for everything we know of the poet during this period goes to show that he was by no means a steady or settled character. He may have killed an odd calf or sheep, have taught an occasional class for his former master, and have driven the quill over many yards of yellow parchment. The very existence of *three* different stories about his early occupation implies that his life at Stratford was changeful and undecided. Nor was he free from youthful faults. To tell the truth, he appears to have engaged in many wild pranks, of which two stories have floated down to our day. One relates to an ale-drinking bout at the neighbouring village of Bidford, by which he was so overcome that, with his companions, he was obliged to spend the night by the road-side under the sheltering boughs of a large crab-tree. The other story is that of the poaching affair already alluded to. It seems that the wild youths of Stratford could not resist the temptation of hunting deer and rabbits in the park of Sir Thomas Lucy, who lived at Charlecote, about three miles off. Shakspere got into the poaching set, was detected one night, and locked up in the keeper's lodge till morning. His examination before the offended justice, and whatever punishment followed it, awoke the anger of the boyish poet, who in revenge wrote some doggerel, punning rhymes upon Sir Thomas, and stuck them on the park gate. This was throwing oil upon flame ; and the knight's rage grew so violent that Shakspere had to flee from Stratford. We have thought it right to notice these traditions, though modern authorities discard them with scorn. With much fictitious colouring they have, perhaps, a ground-work of truth sufficient to afford a strong presumption that Shakspere's opening manhood was wild and riotous. His early marriage, too, contracted **1582** when he was but a raw boy of eighteen, with Anne A.D. Hathaway of Shottery, a yeoman's daughter, some eight years older than himself, affords additional evidence of youthful indiscretion.

So, driven either by the fear of Sir Thomas Lucy's vengeance, or, more probably, by the need of providing daily bread for his wife and children, Shakspere went up to London in 1586 or 1587; and then began that wonderful theatrical life of six and twenty years, whose great creations form the chief glory of our dramatic literature. The brightest day at noon is that whose dawn is wrapped in heavy mists; and so upon the opening of this brilliant time—the midsummer of English poetry—thick clouds of darkness rest.

How Shakspere lived when first he arrived in London, we do not certainly know. Three Warwickshire men, one a native of his own town, then held a prominent place among the metropolitan players, and this, no doubt, coupled with his poetical tastes, led him to the theatre. Here, too, there are vague traditions of his life. According to one, he was call-boy or deputy-prompter; according to another, he held horses at the theatre door. However he may have earned his first shillings in London, it is certain that he soon became prosperous, and even wealthy. In the year 1589 **1589** he held a share in the Blackfriars Theatre, having A.D. previously, by his acting, by the adaptation of old plays, and the production of new ones, proved himself worthy to be much more than a mere sleeping partner in the concern. As his fame brightened, his purse filled. He became also a part-owner of the Globe Theatre; and at one time drew from all sources a yearly income fully equivalent to £1500 of our money.

"Respectable" is, perhaps, the best word by which Shakspere's *acting* may be characterized: the Ghost in "Hamlet," and Adam in "As You Like It," are named among his favourite parts. But his magic pen has taught us almost to forget that he ever was an actor; nor can we, without a violent stretch of fancy, realize our greatest poet stalking slowly with whitened cheeks across the boards, or tottering in old-fashioned livery through a rudely painted forest of Arden. Thus acting, writing, and managing, he lived among the fine London folks, honoured with the special notice of his Queen, and associating every day with the noblest and wittiest Englishmen of that brilliant time, yet never snapping the link which bound him to the sweet banks of Avon. Every year he ran down to Stratford, where his family continued to reside; and there he bought a house and land for the rest and solace of his waning life.

The year 1612 is given as the date of the poet's final retirement from London life. He was then only forty-eight, and might reasonably hope for a full score of years, in which to grow his flowers, his mulberries, and his apple-trees, to treat his friends to sack and claret under the hospitable roof of New Place, and to continue that series of Roman plays which had so noble a beginning in "Julius Cæsar" and "Coriolanus." But four years more brought this great life to an untimely close. He **1616** died on the 23d of April 1616, of what disease we have A.D. no certain knowledge. In a "Diary" by John Ward, a vicar of Stratford-on-Avon, written between 1648 and 1679, it is stated that the poet drank too much at a merry meeting with Drayton and Jonson, and took a fever in consequence, of which he died; but this story is considered an exaggeration. His wife survived him seven years; his only son had gone to the grave before him; and long before the close of the century that saw this great poet die, all the descendants of William Shakspere had perished from the face of the earth. From the dim, uncertain story of his life, and the speedy blighting of his family-tree, withered in its third generation, let us turn to the magnificent works, which have won for this London actor the fame of being, certainly England's—perhaps the world's—greatest poet.

Seven years after the poet's death, a volume, known to students of Shakspere as the "First Folio," was published by his two professional friends, John Heminge and Henrie Condell. **1623** This book contained thirty-six plays; seven more were A.D. added in the Third Folio; but of these seven, only the play of Pericles is received as genuine. The plays of Shakspere, therefore, so far as the battling of critics has agreed upon their number, are *thirty-seven*. And these have been corrected and re-corrected, altered and revised, mended and re-mended, until we must have a very true and pure text of the poet in this century of ours,—unless, indeed, something may have happened to certain passages, like that which the fable tells us happened to Jason's ship, the *Argo*, in which he sought the Golden Fleece. So carefully did a grateful and reverent nation patch up the decaying timbers of the old craft, as she lay high and dry on the Greek shore, that in process of time it became a serious question among learned men whether much of the old ship was left together after all. The books written about Shakspere and his works would of themselves fill a respectable library.

The thirty-seven plays are classed as Tragedies, Comedies, and Histories. The great Tragedies are five—*Macbeth*, *King Lear*, *Romeo and Juliet*, *Hamlet*, and *Othello*. *The Midsummer Night's Dream*, *As You Like It*, and the *Merchant of Venice*, are perhaps the finest Comedies; while *Richard III.*, *Coriolanus*, and *Julius Cæsar*, stand prominently out among the noble series of Histories. The student who knows these eleven plays, knows Shakspere in his finest vein. Yet fat and vinous old Jack Falstaff, whose portraiture is the happiest hit in all the varied range of English comedy, must be sought for in other scenes. Indeed, to know Shakspere as he ought to be known, we must read him right through from first to last; and in days when our most brilliant essayists draw gems of illustration from this exhaustless mine, when every newspaper and magazine studs its leaders with witty allusions to Shallow or Dogberry, Malvolio or Mercutio, and every orator borrows the lightning of some Shaksperian line to gild his meaner language with its flash,—not to have studied the prince of poets thoroughly, proves not merely the absence of a fine literary taste, but the total lack of that common sense which leads men to aim at knowing well and clearly every subject that may help them in their daily life.

The grand, surpassing quality of Shakspere's genius, was its *creative* power. Coleridge, who saw, perhaps, deeper into the unfathomed depths of the poet's spirit than any man has done, calls him the *thousand-souled* Shakspere, and speaks of his *oceanic* mind. And well the dramatist deserves such magnificent epithets, for no writer has ever created a host of characters, so numerous, so varied, and yet so completely distinct from one another. The door of his fancy opened, as if of its own accord, and out trooped such a procession as the world had never seen. The bloodiest crimes and the broadest fun were represented there; the fresh silvery laughter of girls and the maniac shriekings of a wretched old man, the stern music of war and the roar of tavern rioters, mingled with a thousand other various sounds, yet no discordant note was heard in the manifold chorus. So true and subtile an interpreter of the human soul, in its myriad moods, has never written novel, play, or poem; yet he drew but little from -the life around him. The revels with Raleigh and Jonson at the Mermaid and the Falcon, may have suggested some hints for the pictures of life in the Boar's Head Tavern, Eastcheap. The court of Elizabeth, and the greenwood that embowered Stratford, doubtless supplied material for many brilliant and lovely scenes. But those characters which were not drawn from the page of history, are chiefly the creations of his own inexhaustible imagination; and often, when he does adopt a historic portraiture, the colouring is nearly all his own. Many of us read Shakspere before we read history, and take our ideas of his-torical heroes rather from his masterly idealizations than from the soberer painting of the historian's pencil. So deeply rooted, for example, are our early-caught notions of Macbeth's villany, and Richard Crookback's appalling guilt, that it is with somewhat of a startle and recoil we come in our later reading upon other and milder views of these Shaksperian criminals. And, read as we may, we can never get wholly rid of the magic spell with which the poet's genius has enchained us.

The language of Shakspere has been justly censured for its ob-scurity. "It is full of new words in new senses." There are lines and passages, upon whose impenetrable granite the brains of critics and commentators have been well-nigh dashed out; and yet their meaning is still uncertain. Another fault is the frequent use of puns and verbal quibbles, where, quite out of place and keeping, they jar harshly upon the feelings of the reader. Yet these are spots upon the sun, forgotten while we rejoice in his cheerful beams and drink his light into our souls—discoverable only by the cold eyes of those critics who read for business, not delight.

Besides his plays, Shakspere gave to the world various poems : *Venus and Adonis, Lucrece, The Passionate Pilgrim, A Lover's Complaint,* and one hundred and fifty-four *Sonnets.* The " Venus and Adonis," which formed the first fruits of his ripening powers, was published in 1593, with a dedication to Lord Southampton.

Dr. Johnson says, in his Preface to Shakspere's Works, " He that tries to recommend him by select quotations, will succeed like the pedant in Hierocles, who, when he offered his house to sale, carried a brick in his pocket as a specimen." The comparison is witty and just ; yet, in pursuance of our plan, we must select specimens of Shakspere's style. The first extract illustrates the poet's tragic power ; the second shows him in a light and playful mood :—

MACBETH.—ACT II., SCENE 1.

Macbeth.—Is this a dagger, which I see before me,
The handle toward my hand ? Come, let me clutch thee :—
I have thee not, and yet I see thee still.
Art thou not, fatal vision, sensible
To feeling, as to sight ? or art thou but
A dagger of the mind ; a false creation,
Proceeding from the heat-oppressed brain ?
I see thee yet, in form as palpable
As this which now I draw.
Thou marshal'st me the way that I was going ;
And such an instrument I was to use.
Mine eyes are made the fools o' the other senses,
Or else worth all the rest : I see thee still ;
And on thy blade and dudgeon, gouts of blood,
Which was not so before.—There's no such thing :
It is the bloody business, which informs
Thus to mine eyes.—Now o'er the one half world
Nature seems dead ; and wicked dreams abuse
The curtain'd sleep ; now witchcraft celebrates
Pale Hecate's offerings ; and withered murder,
Alarum'd by his sentinel, the wolf,
Whose howl's his watch, thus with his stealthy pace,
With Tarquin's ravishing strides, toward his design
Moves like a ghost.—Thou sure and firm-set earth,
Hear not my steps, which way they walk, for fear
Thy very stones prate of my whereabout,
And take the present horror from the time,
Which now suits with it.—Whiles I threat, he lives :

Words to the heat of deeds too cold breath gives.
I go, and it is done ; the bell invites me.   [*A bell rings*
Hear it not, Duncan ; for it is a knell
That summons thee to heaven, or to hell.

ROMEO AND JULIET.—ACT I., SCENE 4.

Mercutio.—Oh, then, I see, Queen Mab hath been with you.
She is the fairies' midwife ; and she comes
In shape no bigger than an agate-stone
On the fore-finger of an alderman,
Drawn with a team of little atomies
Athwart men's noses as they lie asleep :
Her waggon-spokes made of long spinners' legs ;
The cover, of the wings of grasshoppers ;
The traces, of the smallest spider's web ;
The collars, of the moonshine's wat'ry beams :
Her whip, of cricket's bone ; the lash, of film :
Her waggoner, a small grey-coated gnat,
Not half so big as a round little worm
Prick'd from the lazy finger of a maid :
Her chariot is an empty hazel-nut,
Made by the joiner squirrel, or old grub,
Time out of mind the fairies' coach-makers.
And in this state she gallops night by night
Through lovers' brains, and then they dream of love :
On courtiers' knees, that dream on court'sies straight :
O'er lawyers' fingers, who straight dream on fees :
O'er ladies' lips, who straight on kisses dream,
Which oft the angry Mab with blisters plagues,
Because their breaths with sweetmeats tainted are.
Sometime she gallops o'er a courtier's nose,
And then dreams he of smelling out a suit :
And sometimes comes she with a tithe-pig's tail,
Tickling a parson's nose, as 'a lies asleep,
Then dreams he of another benefice :
Sometimes she driveth o'er a soldier's neck,
And then dreams he of cutting foreign throats,
Of breaches, ambuscadoes, Spanish blades,
Of healths five fathom deep ; and then anon
Drums in his ear ; at which he starts, and wakes ;
And, being thus frighted, swears a prayer or two,
And sleeps again.

CHAPTER X.

SIR WALTER RALEIGH.

Born 1552 A.D..........Beheaded 1618 A.D.

Early adventures.	His trial.	Burning of St. Thomas.
Court life.	In prison.	His execution.
Virginia colonized.	History of the World.	Minor works.
Fall of Raleigh.	His release.	Illustrative extract.

No English writer has lived a more romantic life than Raleigh.
Born in 1552, at Hayes Farm in Devonshire, and educated at
Oriel College, Oxford, he entered at the age of seventeen upon his
brilliant and adventurous career as a volunteer in the cause of the
French Protestants. For more than five years he fought in Continental wars; but in 1576 a new field of action was opened to
his daring spirit. It was the time when Britain began to take
her first steps towards winning that ocean-crown which she now
so proudly wears. And among the dauntless sailors, who braved
the blistering calms of the tropics and the icy breath of the
frigid seas in search of new dominions, Raleigh was one of the
foremost. With his half-brother, Sir Humphrey Gilbert, who
perished at sea in a later voyage, he sailed to North America; but
after two years of toil he returned home, richer in nothing but
hard-won experience. We then find young Captain Raleigh engaged in Ireland on active service against the rebel Desmonds,
winning high honours by his bravery and military talent, and rewarded by being chosen to bear despatches from the Lord Lieutenant to the Queen.

His court life now began. Hitherto, we picture him keeping
watch upon the icy deck in the starry light of a frosty night at
sea, or, in dusty and blood-stained doublet, sleeping off the ex-
haustion of a hard battle-day. A scene of courtly splendour now
opens to our view; and, prominent among the plumed and jewelled
circle gathered round the throne, stands Sir Walter Raleigh, high

in the favour of his Queen, the associate or rival of the proudest noble there. The legend of his first introduction to Elizabeth is too romantic to be omitted, although we must not forget that it rests only on tradition. When the Queen in walking one day came to a muddy place,—these were very common on English roads and pathways then,—she stopped and hesitated. Raleigh, seeing her pause, with ready tact flung down his rich plush cloak for her to step on. The graceful act, which was just the kind of flattering attention that Elizabeth liked best, showed that Raleigh was cut out for a courtier. A capital investment it was that the young soldier made. He lost his cloak, but he gained the favour of a Queen, who well knew how to honour and reward those she loved. Within a few years he became a knight, Captain of the Guard, and Seneschal of Cornwall, besides receiving a grant of 12,000 acres of Irish land, and the sole right of licensing wine-sellers in England.

His attempts to colonize North America, for which a patent had been granted to him, went far to exhaust his fortune. Twice he sent out expeditions, supplied with all necessary stores; but the red men, who swarmed in the woods along the shore, would not suffer the colonies to take root. The first settlers escaped with their lives on board Drake's ships; the second band perished under the deadly tomahawk. Tobacco and the potato were brought to Europe, as the only fruits of these unhappy enterprises. The name Virginia, given to the colony in honour of the unmarried Elizabeth, and the name Raleigh, applied to the capital of North Carolina, still remind our transatlantic kindred of the ancient ties that bind them to the mother-land.

A leader of English ships in the great conflict with the Armada— the courted and prosperous owner of the broad acres of Sherborne in Dorsetshire—the disgraced husband of Elizabeth Throgmorton— the gallant explorer of the Orinoco and its neighbouring shores— the hero of the siege of Cadiz and the capture of Fayal;—such were the various characters filled by this English Proteus during the last years of Elizabeth's reign.

Scarcely was James I. seated on the throne when a change came.

Raleigh's former associate, Cecil, poisoned the King's mind so much against him, that he was stripped of nearly all his honours and rewards. A worse blow was then aimed at him. Charged with having joined in a plot to seize the King and set Lady Arabella Stuart on the throne, he was brought to trial at Winchester Castle. From eight in the morning till nearly midnight he fronted his enemies with unshaken courage. The bluster of Attorney-General Coke roared around him without effect. "I want words," stormed the great prosecutor, "to express thy viperous treasons!" "True," said Raleigh, "for you have spoken the same thing half a dozen times over already." But rare wit and eloquence did not save Raleigh from the Tower, where he was left to lie for nearly thirteen weary years. Much of his time within these dark walls was devoted to chemical experiments, in course of which he sought eagerly for the philosopher's stone, and believed at one time that he had discovered an elixir, which would cure all diseases. But what made his imprisonment a memorable era in the annals of English literature, was the composition in his cell of his great *History of the World.* This work, in the preparation of which he was aided by other able hands, is chiefly valuable for its spirited histories of Greece and Rome. A fine antique eloquence flows from his pen, enriched with a deep learning, which excites wonder when displayed by Raleigh. The soldier, the sailor, or the courtier is hardly the man from whom we expect profound philosophy or deep research; yet Raleigh showed by this achievement a power of wielding the pen, at least not inferior to his skill with sword or compass. That part of the History which he was able to complete, opening with the Creation, closes with the second Macedonian war, about one hundred and sixty-eight years before Christ. A deep tinge of melancholy, caught from the sombre walls that were ever frowning on his task, pervades the pages of the great book.

1603 A.D.

A penniless king, dazzled by the story of an unwrought gold mine, discovered years ago during a cruise up the Orinoco, at length set the prisoner free, and sent him with fourteen ships to make sure of this far-off treasure. The capture of St. Thomas, a Spanish settlement on the banks of the great river, produced only two bars of gold; and with "brains broken," as he told his wife in a letter, Raleigh was forced to sail away, a baffled man, leaving in a foreign grave the body of his eldest son, Walter, who had been killed in the assault. The rage of the Spaniards, who considered all these rich regions their own by right of prior discovery, kindled into flame when the news of this daring move reached Europe. With a cry of "Pirates! pirates!" the Spanish ambassador at London rushed into the presence-chamber of King James to demand vengeance on the slayer of his kinsman, who had been governor of St. Thomas, and reparation for the insult offered to his country's flag. James had good reasons just then for desiring to please the Spanish court, since one of his dearest wishes was to marry his son Charles to the Infanta. So Raleigh was arrested upon his landing at Plymouth, and, after more than a week's delay, was carried to London. A few months later, Oct. 29, he was executed at Westminster upon the old charge of **1618** treason, for which he had already suffered so many years A.D. of imprisonment. Almost his last words, as he lifted the axe and ran his fingers along its keen edge, show with what feelings he fronted death. Smiling, he said, "This is a sharp medicine, but it will cure all diseases." Two blows severed the neck of the old man, who had seen so many phases of human life, and had played with brilliant success so many varied parts.

Besides his great work, a *Narrative of his Cruise to Guiana*, which proceeded from his pen in 1596, is worthy of being named. He wrote many other prose works, and cultivated poetry with such success that Edmund Spenser calls him the "Summer's Nightingale."

THE CONCLUSION OF RALEIGH'S HISTORY.

If we seek a reason of the succession and continuance of this boundless ambition in mortal men, we may add to that which hath been already said, that the kings and princes of the world have always laid before them the actions, but not the ends of those great ones which preceded them. They are always transported with the glory of the one, but they never mind the misery of the other, till they find the experience in themselves. They neglect the advice of God, while they enjoy life or hope it; but they follow the counsel of Death upon his first approach.

It is he that puts into man all the wisdom of the world, without speaking a word, which God, with all the words of His law, promises, or threats, doth not infuse. Death, which hateth and destroyeth man, is believed; God, which hath made him and loves him, is always deferred. . . . . It is Death alone that can suddonly make man to know himself.   He tells the proud and insolent, that they are but abjects, and humbles them at the instant, makes them cry, complain, and repent, yea, even to hate their forepast happiness.   He takes the account of the rich, and proves him a beggar, a naked beggar, which hath interest in nothing but the gravel that fills his mouth.   He holds a glass before the eyes of the most beautiful, and makes them see therein their deformity and rottenness, and they acknowledge it.

Oh, eloquent, just, and mighty Death! whom none could advise, thou hast persuaded; what none hath dared, thou hast done ; and whom all the world hath flattered, thou only hast cast out of the world, and despised ; thou hast drawn together all the far-stretched greatness, all the pride, cruelty, and ambition of man, and covered it over with these two narrow words—HIC JACET.

CHAPTER XI.

FRANCIS BACON, VISCOUNT ST. ALBANS,

Born 1561 A.D.........Died 1626 A.D.

Bacon's fame.	Conduct toward Essex.	Degradation.
Birth and education.	His ten Essays.	Latest works.
In France.	Marriage.	Death.
Studies law.	Lord Chancellor.	Plan of the Instauratio.
Enters the House.	Novum Organum.	Style of his Essays.
Early struggles.	Impeachment.	Illustrative extract.

" My name and memory I leave to foreign nations, and to mine own country after some time is passed over," wrote Bacon in his will. There is no greater name among the many writers of English prose,—no prouder memory among the host of grave-eyed philosophers, who have spent their best years and ripest powers in exploring the secrets and tracing the laws of the universe ; but many blots lie dark upon the reputation of the man. Of late, however, much has been done, especially by Mr. Hepworth Dixon of the *Athenæum*, to efface these stains from the fame of one of our leading English philosophers and writers.

At York House in the Strand, London, Francis, youngest son of Sir Nicholas Bacon, Lord Keeper of the Great Seal of England, was born on the 22d of January, 1561. As the boy grew, he was noted for a quick wit and precocious gravity, **1561** which led the Queen, a frequent visitor at his father's A.D. house, to call him her little Lord Keeper. At thirteen he went to Cambridge, where he studied for three years, and where the deepest impression he received was a dislike to the philosophy of Aristotle.

Then, in accordance with the custom of the time, he joined the suite of Sir Amias Paulett, who was going on an embassy to France. A worse school for a young man of rank could scarcely be found than was the brilliantly voluptuous court of France in that unhappy day. Yet Bacon seems to have been proof against its worst seduc-

tions, imbibing, however, during his residence abroad, that taste
for magnificence and display which kept him through all his life
a needy man, and proved a source of much misery and sin. Something of a woman's nature appears to have mingled with the qualities
of his early manhood; his love of beauty displayed itself in a
passion for rich dress and furniture, birds, flowers, perfumes, and
fine scenery. It might, certainly, have taken a less innocent and
more destructive shape. During his stay in France he spent much
time at Poictiers, employed chiefly in collecting materials for his
maiden work, entitled *Of the State of Europe.*

Recalled to England in 1579 by his father's sudden death, he
settled down to study law, with little money but a great
1582   mind, in Gray's Inn.   In 1582 he was called to the bar;
A.D.   and in 1585 he obtained a seat in the Commons for Mel-
combe.   When the dapper, richly-dressed youth of
twenty-four, whose round rosy face was new to the House, first rose
to speak, indifference speedily changed to curiosity, and curiosity
to deep attention. It was felt by all that the young lawyer, already
well known in the courts, was a man of no common powers.
Even then the main idea of his life, so nobly carried out in his
great system of philosophy, began to develop itself in every speech.
" Reform " was his motto ; and for this he fought hard in the earlier
years of his public life.

At the opening of his career he made a great mistake, fatal to
his happiness and fatal to his fame.   He lived beyond his means,
and thus became hampered with debt, from which he never quite
got free.   In conjunction with his brother he set up a coach ; for
which some excuse may be found in the fact, that even at this early
age he suffered severely from gout and ague.   He was forced to
borrow from the Jews ; and it might often have gone hard with
the young men in their city lodging, had not their kind mother,
Lady Anne, sent frequent supplies of ale and poultry in from
Gorhambury.

Looked coldly on by his relatives the Cecils, he became a parti-
san of Essex, who tried hard to get him made Solicitor-General.
But Burleigh and his clan were too strong for the Earl, and Bacon

was defeated. To console him for this reverse, Essex gave him the beautiful estate of Twickenham Park. The value of the gift was great—some £1800; and there, under the spreading cedars, the hard-worked lawyer, dried up for many a week in the hot and dusty courts, used gladly to enjoy his leisure by the gentle Thames.

But Bacon soon saw that Essex was a dangerous friend, and, after earnest remonstrances from the lawyer, which the Earl appears to have despised, the connection between them was dissolved. Through the remaining years of Elizabeth's reign, Bacon, who had already become member for Middlesex and a Queen's Counsel, continued to rise in the House. All that he could do to save Essex, he did; at the risk of offending the touchy old Queen he pleaded the cause of his former friend and patron. But every effort was rendered useless by the mad folly of the Earl, who had been spoiled by the doting Elizabeth. Forgiven again and again, this madman persisted in trying to kindle a rebellion; and after his failure in London he died on the scaffold. Bacon has been charged with base ingratitude and treachery in this case of Essex. But he could not save a man who rushed so blindly on to death. What he could do, he seems to have done. His public office of Queen's Counsel enabled him to deal more gently with the foolish Earl than a stranger might have dealt. And when at the Queen's command he drew up a paper declaring the treasons of Essex, its lenient tone made the angry Elizabeth cry out, "I see old love is not easily forgotten."

Through these changeful years Bacon had been writing some of the celebrated *Essays*, which form his chief English work, and entitle him to the fame of holding a first rank among the grand old masters of English prose. When first published in 1597, the "Essays" were only ten in number; but others were added in 1612, and after his fall he spent much time in expanding and retouching them. **1597** A.D.

These years were also marked by a disappointment in love. A rich young widow, named Lady Hatton, was the object of his hopes; but his great rival at the bar proved also a formidable rival in the court of love. Attorney-General Coke stepped in and bore away the golden prize.

However the wound soon healed; for in 1606 an elderly bride-groom of forty-five, richly clad in purple Genoa velvet, stood at the altar beside a fair young bride in cloth of silver. The lady was the daughter of a Cheapside merchant, Alice Barnham, who on that day changed her name to Lady Bacon. Sir Francis had been lately knighted by King James.

From the Solicitor-Generalship, won in 1607, he stepped on in 1613 to the rank of Attorney-General; in 1617 he received the Great Seal; and in the following year he reached the sum-

1618 mit of his profession, being made Lord High Chancellor

A.D.   of England with the title of Baron Verulam. Thus, at last, had Bacon beaten Coke, his rival in love, in law, and in ambition.

For three years he held the seals as Chancellor, and great was the splendour of his life. Baron Verulam soon became Viscount St. Albans. But the glitter of costly lace and the sheen of gilded coaches, of which these years were full, grow dim and tarnished before a splendour that cannot fade. The Lord Chancellor, with his titles of honour, is almost forgotten when the author of the *Novum Organum* rises in our view. This celebrated work,

1620 of which more will soon be said, appeared in 1620; and

A.D.   the pains which Bacon took to make it worthy of his fame may be judged from the fact, that he copied and corrected it twelve times before he gave it to the world.

The greatest of Bacon's works was yet fresh from the press when dark clouds began to gather round its author. Coke, his bitter foe, and others whom the poison of envy had also tainted, raised a clamour against the Chancellor for taking bribes. Un-doubtedly Bacon was guilty of the crime, for his extravagance and love of show drained his purse continually, and a needy man is often mean. But it may be said, in extenuation of his fault, that it was the common practice in that day for judges to

1621 receive fees and gifts; indeed, the greater part of their

A.D.   income was derived from such sources. A case, containing at least twenty-two distinct charges of bribery and cor-ruption, being prepared by the House of Commons, the Lords proceeded to sit in judgment upon the highest lawyer in the land. Humbled by the disgrace of his impeachment, and broken down by a fierce attack of his old enemy the gout, the great philosopher, but weak and erring man, sent to the Lords a full confession of his faults. " It is," said he to some of his brother peers who came to ask if this was his own voluntary act, " it is my act—my hand—my heart. O my lords, spare a broken reed!" So fell the Viscount St. Albans from his lofty place, sentenced to pay a fine of £40,000, and to lie in the Tower during the pleasure of the King. James was magnanimous enough to remit the fine, and to set the fallen lawyer free in two days.

The evening of this chequered life was spent chiefly in country retirement at Gorhambury. Books, experiments, and a quiet game at bowls were the chief recreations of the degraded statesman. His busy hours were spent in the revisal and enlargement of his *Essays*, the composition of his *History of King Henry VII.*, a philosophical fiction called *The New Atlantis*, and that part of his great work which relates to Natural History. Heavy debts still hung upon him. He applied for the Provostship of Eton, but failed. The story of his death is curious. Driving in his carriage one snowy day, the thought struck him that flesh **1626** might be preserved as well by snow as by salt. At once **A.D.** he stopped, went into a cottage by the road, bought a fowl, and with his own hands stuffed it full of snow. Feeling chilly and too unwell to go home, he went to the house of the Earl of Arundel, which was near. There he was put into a damp bed; fever ensued; and in a few days he was no more.

The scale upon which the ground-plan of Bacon's great work is drawn is very magnificent; but no single human mind, working within the compass of a human life, could hope to accomplish the grand design. Yet even to have grasped the idea of such a giant plan is enough to prove a mighty genius. While fagging at his law books and briefs in old Gray's Inn, the thought had dawned upon his mind; and through thirty years of up-hill labour at the bar and fierce political struggles in the House he was steadily collecting materials to fill in the outlines of his colossal sketch. An

English treatise on the *Advancement of Learning*, published in
1605, was the herald of the greater work, which appeared in his
brightest days to gild them with a lustre brighter still—a lustre,
too, which even his sad disgrace and doubtful character could not
wholly dim. The plan of the work, which was written in Latin
and was styled *Instauratio Magna*, may be understood from the
following view :—

I. *De Augmentis Scientiarum.*—This treatise, in which the English work on the Advancement of Learning is embodied,
gives a general summary of human knowledge, taking special notice of gaps and imperfections in science.

II. *Novum Organum.*—This work explains the new logic, or
inductive method of reasoning, upon which his philosophy is founded. Out of nine sections, into which he
divides the subject, the first only is handled with any fulness, the other eight being merely named.

III. *Sylva Sylvarum.*—This part was designed to give a complete
view of what we call Natural Philosophy and Natural History. The subjects he has touched on under this head are
four—the History of Winds, of Life and Death, of Density
and Rarity, of Sound and Hearing.

IV. *Scala Intellectûs.*—Of this we have only a few of the opening
pages.

V. *Prodromi.*—A few fragments only were written.

VI. *Philosophia Secunda.*—Never executed.

The Essays, or *Counsels Civil and Moral*, of which ten were
published in 1597, were afterwards greatly increased in number
and extent, being especially enriched with the brighter blossoms of
their great author's matured fancy. In this respect—that his
fancy was more vivid in age than in youth—the mind of Bacon
formed an exception to the common rule; for, in general, the fancy
of a young man grows less bright as his reason grows strong, just
as the coloured petals of a flower fade and drop to make room for
the solid substance of the fruit. Though often stiff and grave,

even where a lighter style would better suit his theme, as in treating of Gardens and Buildings, the "Essays" stand, and have always stood, among the finest works of our prose literature. What Hallam says of this classic book should not be forgotten: "It would be derogatory to a man of the slightest claim to polite letters, were he unacquainted with the 'Essays' of Bacon."

ON LEARNING.

Learning taketh away the wildness, and barbarism, and fierceness of men's minds: though a little superficial learning doth rather work a contrary effect. It taketh away all levity, temerity, and insolency, by copious suggestion of all doubts and difficulties, and acquainting the mind to balance reasons on both sides, and to turn back the first offers and conceits of the kind, and to accept of nothing but examined and tried. It taketh away vain admiration of anything, which is the root of all weakness: for all things are admired, either because they are new, or because they are great. For novelty, no man wadeth in learning or contemplation thoroughly, but with that printed in his heart, "I know nothing." Neither can any man marvel at the play of puppets, that goeth behind the curtain, and adviseth well of the motion. And as for magnitude, as Alexander the Great, after that he was used to great armies, and the great conquests of the spacious provinces in Asia, when he received letters out of Greece, of some fights and services there, which were commonly for a passage or fort or some walled town at the most, he said, "It seemed to him that he was advertised of the battle of the frogs and the mice, that the old tales went of;"—so certainly, if a man meditate upon the universal frame of nature, the earth with men upon it, the divineness of souls excepted, will not seem much other than an ant-hill, where some ants carry corn, and some carry their young, and some go empty, and all to and fro a little heap of dust. It taketh away or mitigateth fear of death, or adverse fortune; which is one of the greatest impediments of virtue, and imperfections of manners. For if a man's mind be deeply seasoned with the consideration of the mortality and corruptible nature of things, he will easily concur with Epictetus, who went forth one day, and saw a woman weeping for her pitcher of earth that was broken; and went forth the next day, and saw a woman weeping for her son that was dead; and thereupon said, "Yesterday I saw a fragile thing broken, to-day I have seen a mortal thing die." And therefore Virgil did excellently and profoundly couple the knowledge of causes and the conquest of all fears together.

● ❡

CHAPTER XII.

BENJAMIN JONSON.

Born 1574 A.D..........Died 1637 A.D.

Early days.	The great hit.	Dying gloom.
Trowel and pike.	Tavern life.	Death.
On the stage.	Eastward Hoe.	Chief works.
The fatal duel.	Brilliant days.	Illustrative extract.

A SQUARE time-worn stone, bearing the words, " O rare Ben
Jonson," marks the spot where the remains of a great English
dramatist, second only to his friend Shakspere, lie buried in
Westminster.   Not far from this simple but suggestive monument
the poet was born in 1574, a few days after the death of his
father, who was a clergyman.   A hard and rugged life lay before
the fatherless boy, and his sorrows soon began.   His mother
having married a bricklayer—not so great a descent from her former
marriage as might at first sight seem to us, for the lower clergy
were then the equals only of servants and tradesmen—young Ben
was taken from his studies at Westminster School, and forced to
carry a hod among his father's workmen.   The sturdy boy, who
had a soul above brick and mortar, rebelled at this, and in no
long time was shouldering a pike on the battle-grounds of the
Low Countries.   The rough life that he saw, during this phase of
his changeful story, had a powerful influence upon his character
and habits.   When in later times he mingled among the silken
courtiers of Elizabeth and James, he never lost a certain bearish-
ness of temper and braggart loudness of tone, which he had caught
in early days in the revels of the bivouac and the guard-room.
His short soldier-life over, he appears to have entered St. John's
at Cambridge, where he stayed some little time.

And then, driven perhaps by poverty, perhaps by natural tastes
and the desire to shine, he went on the stage, making his first
appearance on the boards of a theatre near Clerkenwell.   This

plunge into the troubled waters of an actor's life might have cured him of his passion for the stage, for it was a miserable failure. But he clung to the vocation he had embraced; and to his poor earnings as a third or fourth rate actor he began to add the still more precarious gains of a theatrical author. And all this when he was only twenty years of age.

So early did he find his life's work. Some men, whose names hold an honourable place among our chief English writers, scarcely taking pen in hand, except to write a common letter, until the snow of age began to fall upon their heads, have produced their great works in the winter of their days. Ben Jonson was not of these: almost before the down of manhood had darkened on his lip, the hand, that had already held the trowel and the pike, took up the pen.

A duel with a brother actor, whom unhappily he killed, exposed him to the charge of murder, and he lay for some time in jail. Soon after his release he sprang at once into fame by the production of his well-known and still-acted play, *Every Man in his Humour*. How strange it seems to us, who reverence the name so deeply, to read that William Shakspere was one of the company who acted this comedy at the Globe in 1598. We can hardly realize the fact that the writer of "Hamlet" and "Macbeth" was only a third-rate player. 1598 A.D.

Jonson followed up this successful hit with eager industry, and for some time every year produced its play. The greatest men of the day became the intimates of the roistering author. At the Mermaid Club, founded by Raleigh, and adorned by the membership of Shakspere and other great brothers of the dramatic craft, Jonson was a leading wit. Like his burly namesake of the eighteenth century, he was a man of solid learning and great conversational powers; and his social qualities, kindled by the old sack, which he loved too well, made him a most attractive companion. The Falcon at Southwark and the Old Devil at Temple Bar were the favourite tavern-haunts of Ben and his brilliant friends.

This rough and roaring life was chequered by several noteworthy events. The publication of a comedy called *Eastward Hoe*, which in 1605 proceeded from the pens of a literary partnership of three—Jonson, Chapman, and Marston,—excited the anger of King James by some hits at the unwelcome presence of the Scotch in England. For his share in this work Jonson went to prison with his friends, and for some time our poet's nose and ears were in considerable danger. But the storm blowing over, he regained his freedom. In 1619, after receiving the appointment of poet-laureate, he travelled on foot to Scotland, whence his family had come, and there he paid a three weeks' visit to Drummond of Hawthornden.

The composition of court masques and lighter poems filled up some easy years of Jonson's life, which was agreeably varied by visits to his distinguished friends, correspondence with learned men at home and abroad, and the collection of rare books—a pursuit in which he took especial pleasure. But debt and the ravages of paralysis upon a frame he had never spared, cast a gloom over his last years. The malice of a former friend, Inigo Jones, the archi-tect, shut the golden doors of court life against the poor sick laureate. His salary, never well paid, came dribbling in so slowly that he was compelled to write begging letters to some of his noble friends; who, to their honour be it said, did not refuse their aid. So the bright life dimmed, and flickered, and went out. On the 6th of August 1637 he died; and three days after was buried in an upright posture in the north aisle of Westminster Abbey. A workman, hired for eighteen pence by the charity of a passer-by, cut upon the grave-stone covering the poet's clay the four short words which form his only epitaph.

The works of Jonson, numbering in all about fifty, may be classed under four heads: his Tragedies, stately, cold, and classical; his Comedies, full of the coloured fire of real life, and abounding in varieties of character, which are rendered the more striking by a very decided tinge of exaggeration;* his Masques and Interludes, forming the bulk of his writings, and nearly all produced during his brilliant days at court; and his finely written Prose notes,

* He has hence been styled the "humorous poet;" not in our modern sense of that word, but as a skilful painter of those subtile shades of temper which are called "humours."

containing some good sound criticism upon Bacon and other men of literary renown. Studding his dramatic works, like gems of the purest water and the finest cutting, are numerous songs, which have not been surpassed by any of our English lyrists. His principal tragedies are *Catiline* and *Sejanus,* founded upon two of the darkest pages of Roman history. *Every Man in his Humour,* *The Alchemist,* and *Volpone* are his finest comedies; and an unfinished pastoral, *The Sad Shepherd,* touched with the gloom of his dying days, may well stand beside these works, if we can judge of the half-done picture, when the colours are dry upon the palette, and the brush has fallen for ever from the painter's hand. His prose notes bore the odd title, *Timber ; or, Discoveries made upon Men and Matter.*

CAPTAIN BOBADIL AND THE ARMY.

(FROM "EVERY MAN IN HIS HUMOUR.")

Bobadil.—I will tell you, sir, by the way of private, and under seal, I am a gentleman, and live here obscure, and to myself; but were I known to her Majesty and the lords (observe me), I would undertake, upon this poor head and life, for the public benefit of the state, not only to spare the entire lives of her subjects in general, but to save the one-half, nay, three parts of her yearly charge in holding war, and against what enemy soever. . . . . I would select nineteen more, to myself, throughout the land ; gentlemen they should be of good spirit, strong and able constitution ; I would choose them by an instinct, a character that I have : and I would teach these nineteen the special rules, as your punto, your reverso, your stoccata, your imbroccato, your passado, your montanto, till they could all play very near, or altogether as well as myself. This done, say the enemy were forty thousand strong, we twenty would come into the field the tenth of March, or thereabouts, and we would challenge twenty of the enemy ; they could not in their honour refuse us ; well, we would kill them ; challenge twenty more, kill them ; twenty more, kill them ; twenty more, kill them too ; and thus would we kill every man his twenty a day, that's twenty score ; twenty score, that's two hundred ; two hundred a day five days, a thousand ; forty thousand ; forty times five, five times forty, two hundred days kills them all up by computation. And this will I venture my poor gentleman-like carcass to perform, provided there be no treason practised on us, by fair and discreet manhood ; that is, civilly by the sword.

CHAPTER XIII.

OTHER WRITERS OF THE THIRD ERA.

POETS.

Thomas Tusser.	John Ford.	William Camden.
Robert Greene.	Thomas Carew.	Hakluyt and Purchas.
Robert Southwell.	William Browne.	King James I.
Samuel Daniel.	Robert Herrick.	Joseph Hall.
Michael Drayton.	Francis Quarles.	Robert Burton. —
Christopher Marlowe.	George Herbert.	Thomas Dekker.
Sir Henry Wotton.	James Shirley.	Lord Herbert.
John Donne.	Richard Crashaw.	James Ussher.
Beaumont and Fletcher.	Sir John Suckling. ✗ '98	John Selden.
G. and P. Fletcher.		Thomas Hobbes.
Philip Massinger.	PROSE WRITERS.	Izaak Walton.
William Drummond.	Thomas Wilson.	James Howell.

POETS.

THOMAS TUSSER, born in Essex about 1523, wrote an agricultural poem, called the *Five Hundred Points of Good Husbandry*, which in simple verse gives a good picture of English peasant life at that day. He died about 1580.

ROBERT GREENE, one of Shakspere's predecessors in the dramatic art, was born at Norwich or Ipswich about 1560. Having received his education at Cambridge, he travelled in Italy and Spain, and on his return to London plunged deep into the lowest debauchery. From about 1584 his pen was busied in the production of plays and love-pamphlets, which soon made him very popular. A surfeit of pickled herrings and Rhenish wine threw him into a mortal sickness, during which he was supported by a poor shoemaker. His miserable and premature death took place in 1592. More than forty works are ascribed to his pen. He takes rank among our early English dramatists, next below the vigorous Marlowe.

ROBERT SOUTHWELL, whose short and suffering life began in 1560, was a native of St. Faiths in Norfolk. Educated at the English college of Douay, he entered the Society of Jesuits at sixteen. In 1584 he returned to England as a missionary, and there he laboured for eight years in secret, penal laws being then extreme. Arrested at last, he lay in prison for three years, and in 1595 was hanged at Tyburn tree. His poems, of which the longest are *St. Peter's Complaint* and *Mary Magdalene's Funeral Tears*, being chiefly written in prison, have a tone of deep melancholy resignation.

SAMUEL DANIEL, born in 1562 near Taunton in Somersetshire, was a contemporary of Shakspere and Jonson. His principal poems are, *A History of the Wars between the Houses of York and Lancaster*, and a dialogue in defence of learning, styled *Musophilus*. His education was received at Oxford; he was afterwards tutor to Anne Clifford, who became Countess of Pembroke; and with other court preferments he held a post somewhat like that of our poet-laureate. His death took place in 1619 on a farm in his native shire. Shut in his garden-house in Old Street, St. Luke's, he gave up the best part of a quiet, studious life, to the composition of those graceful and pensive works, whose style obtained for him the name of "The well-languaged Daniel."

MICHAEL DRAYTON, author of the *Polyolbion*, is thought to have been born in Warwickshire about 1563, and to have begun life as a page. This threw him into the society of noble patrons, by whom his talents were soon recognised. The "Polyolbion," finished in 1622, takes a poetical ramble over England, collecting together, in thirty ponderous books, descriptions of scenery, wild country legends, antiquarian notes, and various other gleanings from the land. In spite of an unhappy subject, the genius of a true poet shines out in many passages of this work. Among Drayton's other works are historical poems entitled the *Baron's Wars* and *England's Heroical Epistles*, and an exquisitely comical fairy piece called *Nymphidia*. Dying in 1631, he found a tomb in the Poets' Corner of Westminster Abbey.

CHRISTOPHER MARLOWE merits somewhat longer notice than any other of our earliest dramatists, for it was he who prepared the way for the mighty creations of Shakspere, by establishing the use of a lofty and polished blank-verse in our English plays. Born at Canterbury in 1563-4, he passed to Cambridge, where he

graduated as M.A. in 1587.   Like some other wild-living college
men of that day, he took to the stage as a means of earning his
daily bread, and, what perhaps he valued more, of paying his daily
tavern-bill.   The riotous, licentious life of this gifted man, came to
a sad and speedy end.   He had barely reached the age of thirty
when he died, the victim of a low pot-house scuffle.   A serving-
man, whom he was struggling to stab, seizing his wrist, turned
the point of his own dagger upon himself.   It pierced through
his eye to the brain, and he died of the wound not long afterwards.

Marlowe's first great play, *Tamburlaine the Great*, is thought to
have been brought out while the author's name was still on the
Cambridge books.   Then followed the *Life and Death of Dr.
Faustus*, in which noble justice is done to the weird story that
haunts the memory of the great printer of Mayence.   *The Jew of
Malta*, and *Edward II.*, an historical drama, are the chief remaining works of Marlowe.   The first of these probably suggested
Shakspere's Shylock, while the second may have turned the pen of
our greatest dramatist into the field of English history.   Though
much disfigured with bombastic rant, the style of Marlowe, when
uplifted by a great theme, often reaches a grandeur and a power
to which few poets attain.

SIR HENRY WOTTON, a gentleman of Kent, born there at Bocton
Hall in 1568, may be named among the poets of his time.   He
was ambassador at Venice, and afterwards Provost of Eton—the
friend of Izaak Walton, and an early discoverer of Milton's tran-
scendent merit.   The *Reliquiæ Wottonianæ* were published in
1651, twelve years after the author's death.

JOHN DONNE, Dean of St. Paul's, was born in London in 1573.
He deserves remembrance as a very learned man, who began the list
of what critics call the Metaphysical poets.   Beneath the artificial
incrustations which characterize this school, Donne displays a fine
vein of poetic feeling.   He is also noted in our literary history as
the first writer of satire in rhyming couplets.   Upon his death in
1631 his body was buried in Westminster Abbey.

FRANCIS BEAUMONT and JOHN FLETCHER united their high

talents in the production of fifty-two plays. In this dramatic partnership Beaumont probably followed the bent of his mind by writing chiefly tragedy. Fletcher, a lighter and more sunny spirit, was fonder of the comic muse. Beaumont, the son of a judge, was born in Leicestershire in 1586; he studied at Oxford and the Inner Temple, but was cut off in the bloom of manhood in 1615. Fletcher, a bishop's son, was born in 1576, and died of the plague in 1625. The works of these men were very popular in their own day, even more so than those of Shakspere and Jonson. They have about them an elegance, a spirit, and a light amusing wit, reflecting the gay sprightliness of the upper classes to which their authors belonged; but they are also deeply stained with that viciousness of thought and speech which then prevailed in even the highest circles of English society.

GILES and PHINEAS FLETCHER were cousins of the dramatist. Phineas, who was Rector of Hilgay in Norfolk, lived from 1584 to 1650. Giles, who was Rector of Alderton in Suffolk, was the younger; but the dates of his birth and death are uncertain. *The Purple Island* of Phineas is a poem descriptive of the human body with its rivers of blood, and the human mind, of which Intellect is prince. From the pen of Giles came *Christ's Victory and Triumph*, a sacred poem—a work of much higher merit as a whole.

PHILIP MASSINGER, a great dramatist of his day, was born about 1584. Of his life we know absolutely nothing, but that he spent a year or two at Oxford; wrote plays for the London theatres after 1604; like many of his theatrical brethren found his money sometimes running low; and one morning in 1640 was found dead in his bed at Southwark. Eighteen of his plays have lived; but only one, *A New Way to Pay Old Debts*, is now brought upon the stage. Sir Giles Overreach, a greedy, crafty money-getter, is the great character of this powerful drama. A calm and dignified style, with little passionate fire, characterizes the pen of Massinger.

WILLIAM DRUMMOND of Hawthornden, near Edinburgh, born in 1585, was the finest Scottish poet of his day. Living by the romantic Esk, he caught a deeper inspiration from its beauty.

Though not a poet-laureate by appointment, he had all the feelings of one, and lavishly poured forth his sweet verses in praise of royalty. *The Flowers of Zion, Tears on the Death of Moeliades* (Prince Henry), *The River of Forth Feasting,* and his *Sonnets,* are his chief poetical works.   Ben Jonson paid him a visit at Haw-thornden, and the Scottish poet has been blamed for making notes, not always complimentary, of his rough guest's habits and character.   These notes, however, he did not publish himself. Drummond died in 1649.

JOHN FORD, a Devonshire man, born in 1586, was another of the brilliant dramatic brotherhood adorning this period.   Deep tragedy was Ford's excellence.   Uniting dramatic authorship with his practice as a lawyer, he contrived to avoid those abysses of debt and drink in which many brightening stars of the time quenched their young lustre.   Hallam says that Ford has "the power over tears;" but his themes are often so revolting, that compassion freezes into disgust.   Three of his tragedies are the *Brother and Sister, Love's Sacrifice,* and *The Broken Heart.*   He wrote also an historical play, *Perkin Warbeck.*   Ford died about 1639.

THOMAS CAREW, born in 1589, of an ancient Gloucestershire family, was one of the brilliant courtier poets who clustered round the throne of the first Charles.   His lyrics are, on the whole, graceful and flowing, though often deeply tainted with immorality and irreligion.   The masque, *Cœlum Britannicum,* is a work from his pen produced by order of the king.   The thoughtless gaiety and license of his life cost him many bitter tears, as he lay in 1639 upon his death-bed.

WILLIAM BROWNE, born in 1590, was a native of Tavistock in Devonshire.   He wrote pastoral poetry, taking his inspiration from Spenser.   His life was chiefly spent in two noble families, those of Caernarvon and Pembroke.   *Britannia's Pastorals* is the name of his chief work.   It is rich in landscape painting, but utterly deficient in the display of character.   Browne died in 1645 at Ottery-St-Mary in his native shire.

ROBERT HERRICK, poet and divine, was perhaps the sweetest of the lyrists who sang in the seventeenth century.   Born in Cheapside, London, in 1591, and educated at Cambridge, he became in 1629 Vicar of Dean Prior in Devonshire.   During the Civil War and the Commonwealth he lived at Westminster, but at the Restoration went back to his green Devonshire parish, an old man of almost seventy, tired and sick, no doubt, of the convivial life he had spent among the London taverns.   He died in 1674.   There is a cheerful grace, a light and happy sparkle in the poetry of Herrick; many of his lyrics are matchless.   *To Blossoms, To Daffodils, Gather the Rosebuds while ye may*—names like these suggest the sources whence his verses draw their many-coloured beauty. Flowers, birds, fruit, gems, pretty women, and little children are his favourite themes.

FRANCIS QUARLES, born in 1592 in Essex, having occupied some courtly positions, became Chronologer to the City of London. Though a keen Royalist, suffering the loss of his dear books and manuscripts in that cause, his poetical works, which form an extravagant specimen of the Metaphysical school, have something of the Puritan tone about them.   He died in 1644.

GEORGE HERBERT, Rector of Bemerton in Wiltshire, and younger brother of Lord Herbert of Cherbury, was born at Montgomery Castle, Wales, in 1593.   Before entering the Church he lived a gay life at court.   He, too, wrote in the strained style of Donne's school; but his chief work, *The Temple*, a collection of sacred poems, is filled with solemn, saintly music.   His pure and active life came to an untimely end in 1632.

JAMES SHIRLEY, born in London in 1596, was the last of the Elizabethan dramatists.   Possessing less fire and force than the rest, he excels them in purity of thought and expression.   The true poet shines out in many passages of his plays.   He gave up the curacy of St. Albans, when he embraced the Roman Catholic faith; and, after a vain attempt to get up a school in that town, he went to London to write for bread.   The great fire of 1666 burned him out of house and home; and a little after, in one of the suburbs of London, his wife and he died on the same day.

RICHARD CRASHAW was a Fellow of Peterhouse College, Cambridge, and took holy orders.   In France he became a Roman

Catholic, and, having passed to Italy, was made a Canon of Loretto. His religious poetry, and his translations from Latin and Italian, are of the first order, though somewhat marred by the affectations of the time. This scholarly poet died in Italy about 1650.

SIR JOHN SUCKLING, born in 1609, came at eighteen into a great fortune. Having served under the Swedish banner in the Thirty Years' War, he returned to England, to shine as a brilliant but passing meteor in the court of Charles the First. More desirous, perhaps, to win the fame of a skilful gamester and richly dressed gallant than of a literary man, he yet, in the quieter hours of a feverish life, produced some beautiful lyrics, brilliant outpourings of a poetic genius that could not be repressed. Detected in a plot to set Strafford free, he fled to France, where he died before 1642, having, it is thought, committed suicide by poison. His *Ballad on a Wedding*, and many of his songs are exquisite specimens of their kind.

PROSE WRITERS.

THOMAS WILSON was a Fellow of King's College, Cambridge, and afterwards Dean of Durham, who wrote about 1553 a *System of Rhetoric and Logic*, considered to be the first critical work upon the English tongue. He strongly recommends the use of a simple English style.

WILLIAM CAMDEN, the antiquary and writer of history, was born in London in 1551, and received his higher education at Oxford. Much of his earlier life was spent in connection with Westminster School, in which he was successively Second and Head-master. He afterwards became Clarencieux King-at-arms. The *Britannia* is his great work. Written in Latin, it is especially devoted to a description of the antiquities of his native land. He wrote, besides other works, Latin narratives of *Queen Elizabeth's reign* and the *Gunpowder Plot*. He died in 1623.

RICHARD HAKLUYT and SAMUEL PURCHAS were two English clergymen, who, in the reigns of Elizabeth and James I., compiled books of travel and geographical discovery. Hakluyt's chief work, of which the third volume was completed in 1600, comprised an account of all the *Principal Voyages undertaken within the previous* 1500 *years.* He was an associate and helper of Sir Walter Raleigh in the work of colonizing North America. The chief work of the other writer, bearing the quaint title of *Purchas his Pilgrims,* appeared in 1625. Another volume, entitled *Purchas his Pilgrimage,* had been already published. Hakluyt died in 1616 ; Purchas, about 1628.

KING JAMES I. of England got rid of his superfluous learning in the shape of certain literary works. Among his productions three are specially remembered, but rather for the amusement than the delight which they afford. His *Dæmonologie* defends his belief in witches in a most erudite dialogue. His *Basilicon Doron* was written in Scotland to leaven Prince Henry's mind with his own notions and opinions. His *Counterblast to Tobacco* lifts a strenu-ous but often very comical voice against the growing use of that plant. Poems, too, in both English and Latin came from this royal pen.

JOSEPH HALL, Bishop of Norwich, was born in Leicestershire in 1574. Distinguished as the author of vigorous poetical satires, he deserves yet greater praise for his sermons and other prose writings. His *Contemplations on Historical Passages of the Old and New Testament* and his *Occasional Meditations* form his chief works. He died at a good old age in 1656.

ROBERT BURTON, a native of Lindley in Leicestershire, was born in 1578. Though Rector of Segrave in his own shire, he lived chiefly at Christ-church College, Oxford, where he wrote his famous work, *The Anatomy of Melancholy, by Democritus Junior.* This strangely quaint and witty book, which is crammed with learned quotations, and with curious gleanings from works that few men ever read, became a public favourite at once. Laurence Sterne has been convicted of stealing brilliants from Burton to mingle with the tinsel and the paste of his own sentimentalities. A short poem on Melancholy, containing twelve stanzas, opens the "Anatomy." Burton's life was chequered with deep melan-choly moods, to relieve which he wrote his famous book. He died in 1640.

THOMAS DEKKER, a wild and penniless dramatist who produced

above twenty plays, wrote, among other prose works, *The Gull's Hornbook*, a satirical guide to the follies of London life, which was published in 1609. Dekker died about 1638.

LORD HERBERT of Cherbury was born in 1581 at Eyton in Shropshire, and was educated at Oxford. Though noted for his deistic works, of which the chief is entitled *De Veritate*, he deserves our kindly remembrance for his *Life and Reign of Henry VIII.*, published in 1649. *Memoirs of his own Life* were printed more than a century after his death, which took place in 1648.

JAMES USSHER, Archbishop of Armagh, was born in Dublin in 1581. While Professor of Divinity in Trinity College, Dublin, he became noted as a theologian and controversialist. A treatise, called *The Power of the Prince and Obedience of the Subject*, written in the reign of Charles I., fully displayed his Royalist opinions. In 1641 he was obliged by the war in Ireland to take refuge at Oxford, and, after many changes of abode, he died in 1656 at Ryegate in Surrey. He won his chief fame, as a chronologer, by the publication (1650–54) of the *Annals*, a view of general history from the Creation to the Fall of Jerusalem.

JOHN SELDEN, born in 1584 near Tering in Sussex, earned the distinguished praise from Milton of being "the chief of learned men reputed in this land." Educated at Oxford, he studied law in the London schools. Besides several histories and antiquarian works written in Latin, he was the author of an English book called *A Treatise on Titles of Honour*, which, published in 1614, is still highly valued by heralds and genealogists. His *History of Tithes* (1618) excited the rage of the clergy and drew a rebuke from the King. As a member of the Long Parliament, he took a leading part in the politics of the day, but was opposed to the Civil War. Appointed in 1643 Keeper of the Records in the Tower, he continued to write until his death in 1654. Some time after his death his secretary, who had been acting the Boswell to this Puritan Johnson, published the *Table-talk* that had dropped from his learned lips during twenty years.

THOMAS HOBBES was born at Malmesbury in 1588. Some years of his earlier life were spent in travelling on the Continent as tutor to Lord Cavendish, afterwards Earl of Devonshire. After a residence at Chatsworth, he was obliged to hide himself and his Royalist doctrines at Paris in 1640; and there some years later he became mathematical tutor to the Prince of Wales. He published four works, dealing with politics and moral philosophy, which gave deep offence to the friends of religion and constitutional government. The principal of these works he called *Leviathan* (1651); and the key-note of his whole system, there developed, is the doctrine that all our notions of right and wrong depend on self-interest alone. Works of a different kind from the pen of Hobbes are his *Translation of Homer in Verse*, and his *Behemoth, a History of the Civil Wars*. He died in December 1679.

IZAAK WALTON, who wielded pen and fishing-rod with equal love and skill, was born at Stafford in 1593. He kept a linen draper's shop in Cornhill, and then in Fleet Street, London; retired from business in 1643, and lived afterwards for forty years to enjoy his favourite pursuit. His memory is dear to every lover of our literature for the delightful book he has left us, redolent of wild-flowers and sweet country air—*The Complete Angler, or Contemplative Man's Recreation* (1653). *The Lives of Donne, Wotton, Hooker, George Herbert, and Bishop Sanderson*, written with beautiful simplicity, remain also as fruits of honest Izaak's old age. He died in 1683 at the age of ninety.

JAMES HOWELL, born in Caermarthenshire about 1596, spent much of his life travelling on the Continent—as agent for a glass-work—as tutor to a young gentleman—and as a political official. Returning home, he was made in 1640 clerk to the Council; was imprisoned in the Fleet by order of the Parliament; became historiographer-royal in 1660, and died six years later. His *Familiar Letters* (1645), giving, in lively, picturesque language, sketches of his foreign observations, mingled with philosophical remarks, have gained for him the reputation of being the earliest contributor to our epistolary literature. He wrote altogether about forty works.

FOURTH ERA OF ENGLISH LITERATURE.

CHAPTER I.

PURITANS AND CAVALIERS—THEIR INFLUENCE UPON
ENGLISH LITERATURE.

Puritan and Cavalier.	Gallantry in the field.	Hatred of amusement.
Dress of the Cavaliers.	Their writings.	Sincerity.
Their wild life.	Puritan habits.	Greatest literary names.

JOSTLING in London streets, and scowling as they passed each
other on leafy country roads; grappling in deadly conflict upon
many a battle-field from Edgehill to Naseby, resting upon hacked
sword or bloody ash-wood pike only till the leaping heart was
still enough to begin the strife again—Puritans and Cavaliers
stand out in violent contrast during that period of English history
which is filled with the great central struggle of the seventeenth
century. Close and deadly though their occasional collision, the cur-
rents of their domestic lives flowed far apart;—the one, a brilliant
stream flashing along its noisy way, and toying with its flowery
banks, all unheeding of the great deep to which its waters ran ;—
the other, a dark, strong, and solemn river, sweeping sternly on to
its goal between rugged shores of cold grey stone.

The violence of the opposition between Puritan and Cavalier
was strikingly expressed by the difference of their dress and of
their amusements. The Cavalier (the word was borrowed from
the Spanish) in full dress wore a brilliant silk or satin doublet
with slashed sleeves, a falling collar of rich point lace, a short
cloak hanging carelessly from one shoulder, and a broad-leafed

low-crowned hat of Flemish beaver, from which floated one or two graceful feathers. His broad sword-belt, supporting a Spanish rapier, was a marvel of costly embroidered-work. A laced buff coat and silken sash sometimes took the place of the doublet; and when the steel gorget was buckled over this, the gallant Cavalier was ready for the fray. Long waves of curled hair, rippling on the shoulders, formed a graceful framework for the finely moulded features of a high-bred English gentleman; and to this class of the nation the Cavaliers for the most part belonged. But, unhappily, these silks and ringlets filled the taverns and surrounded the gaming-tables of London by night and day. Great fortunes were lost then, as in later times, on a single throw of the dice; and many a fair-plumed hat was dashed fiercely with curses in the mud, when the half-sobered reveller, staggering with torn and wine-splashed finery out of the tavern into the cold grey light of the breaking day, found every gold piece vanished from his shrunken purse. Well might he pluck at the dishevelled love-lock—special eye-sore to the Puritans—which hung over his pallid brow, and curse his drunken folly. Such a life lived many of the Cavaliers. Tennis, billiards, drinking, masquerading, dressing, intriguing, composing and singing love songs, filled their days and their nights. Madly the whirlpool spun round with its reckless freight of gaily dressed debauchees, who, seeing one and another wasted face sink from view, only drowned the cry of dying remorse in a wilder burst of revelry. A few were flung out from the fatal circles with ruined fortune and broken health, to find nothing left them but a painful dragging out of days in some lonely country farm-house; or, if the pure air and quiet hours restored them, a life of exile, as a soldier in some foreign service, and then, perhaps, a grave in unknown soil. Yet even all this vicious round could not destroy the pluck of Englishmen. Gallantly and gaily did Rupert's horsemen, the very flower of the Cavaliers, ride in the face of hailing bullets upon the Puritan musketeers. While we condemn the vices of the Cavaliers, and pity the wretched end of so many of these brilliant English gentlemen, we cannot help respecting the bravery of the men who rallied so loyally round

the banner of their erring king, and, for the cause of monarchy,
spilt their blood on English battle-fields with the same careless gaiety as if they were pouring out bumpers of red wine in the
taverns by St. Paul's.

The literature of the Cavaliers, we may almost guess, did not,
for the most part, go very deep. The poetry was chiefly lyric,—
the sparkling, spontaneous effusions of a genius, that poured
forth its sweet and living waters in spite of overwhelming floods
of wine and dense fumes of tobacco-smoke.   Herrick, Suckling,
Waller, and the unhappy Lovelace were the chief poets of the
Cavaliers; and the works of all are stamped with characters that
proclaim their birth-place and their fostering food. The Cavalier
was graceful and gay, polite and polished; so are the verses of
Lovelace and his brother bards.   The Cavalier was dissipated, and
often vicious; there are many works of these men that bear
deepest stains of immorality and vice.   History, on the Cavalier
side, is best represented by Lord Clarendon; theology, by the witty
Thomas Fuller and the brilliant Jeremy Taylor.   The quaint
oddities of the former divine, and the gentle pictures, rich in
images of loveliness, with which the sermons of the latter are
studded, afford the most pleasing examples of English literature
written in the atmosphere of Cavalier life.

Of a totally different stamp were the Puritan and his writings.
Instead of the silk, satin, and lace which decked his gay antagonists, he affected usually a grave sobriety of dress and manners,
which should place him at the utmost possible distance from the
fashion of the vain world from which he sought to separate himself. His tastes were simple, his pleasures moderate, and his
behaviour reverent and circumspect.   Living in an atmosphere of
habitual seriousness, the Bible was much in his hands and its
sacred words often on his lips; while, disdaining lighter recreations,
he often found his chief enjoyment in the hearing of sermons
and the singing of psalms.   As in other days of high religious
fervour, his children at their baptism were called by sacred names,
either drawn from the genealogical lists of Old Testament times,
or expressive of his Christian faith and hope.   That the perfor-

mance of the stage, such as it then was, steeped in a shameless licentiousness which shocked alike good men of every party, should be the object of his utter abhorrence, was a matter of course; but with it were rejected other sports and pastimes of a less questionable kind, but which were still, in his view, inseparably mixed up with sin—as the mistletoe, the boar's head, and the country games around the May-pole, decorated with green and flowing boughs. Opposed, in short, to the riotous and dashing Cavaliers, both in political and religious views, the Puritans strove to draw the line as sharply as possible between themselves and their gaily attired antagonists, and to stand in every respect as far apart from these godless revellers as they could. They went too far, undoubtedly; but they were, in point of morality and religion at least, on the right side of the dividing line; and we can easily forgive the austere tone in which Sergeant Zerubbabel Grace, discoursing to his troopers, proclaimed the truths of the Bible, when we remember that the same brave and honest soldier gave good proofs of his sincerity, by avoiding the ale-house and the dicing-room, and living in constant fear of Him who said, "Swear not at all."

A profound religious thoughtfulness was the root, in the character of the English Puritans, out of which grew their great works of the pen.

The period of the Civil War was too full of hurry and bloodshed to be prolific in any but controversial writings. One princely work, indeed, the *Areopagitica* of Milton, lifted its lofty voice above the clash of swords and the roll of musketry, its noble eloquence undimmed by the blackening sulphur-smoke. Liberty was the grand stake, for which the English Puritans were then playing at the game of war; and there was among them one, the grandest intellect of all, who could not stand idly by and see professing champions of the sacred cause—fellow-soldiers by his own side in the great battle of freedom—lay, in their blindness, the heavy fetter of a *license* on the English press. To Milton the freedom of human thought and speech was a far grander aim than even the relief of the English people from the tyranny of Charles Stuart.

When the Civil War was over, and Charles rested in his bloody grave, the day of Roundhead triumph came. Yet not the proudest period of the Puritan literature. Pure in many things, as its name proclaimed it, the Puritan mind needed to pass through a fiery furnace before its dross was quite purged away, and the fine gold shone out with clearest lustre.

While the Cavalier poets had been stringing their garlands of artificial blossoms in the heated air of the Stuart court, Milton had been weaving his sweet chaplets of unfading wild-flowers in the meadows of Horton. It was not in the nature of things that the great Puritan poet should pass through the trying hours of conflict and of triumph without many stains of earth deepening on his spirit. To purge these away, required suffering in many shapes—blindness, bitterness of soul, threatening ruin, and certain narrowness of means. Yet bodily affliction and political disgrace could not break the giant's wing; they but served to give it greater strength. From a fall which would have laid a feebler man still in his coffin, Milton arose with his noblest poem completed in his hand. And Milton's noblest poem is the crown and glory of our English literature. What more needs to be said of Puritan influence upon English letters than that Puritan Milton wrote the *Paradise Lost?*

Puritanism acted powerfully, too, upon our English prose, finding its highest expression under this form in the works of John Bunyan and Richard Baxter. Here, also, the fervour of religious earnestness leavens the whole mass. A massive strength and solemn elevation of tone, form the grand characteristics of a school in which the naked majesty of the Divine perhaps too much overshadows the tenderness and gentleness of the human element. The stern work of those sad times was little fitted to nourish in the breasts of good men those feelings from which bright thoughts and happy sunny affections spring; but the worst enemy of these remarkable men cannot deny, that the main-spring of the Puritan mind, as displayed in written works and recorded actions, was a simple fear of God, and an over-mastering desire to fulfil every duty, in the face of any consequences, no matter how perilous or painful.

CHAPTER II. ·

THOMAS FULLER.

Born 1608 A.D................Died 1661 A.D.

Birth and education.	Collecting materials.	Death
Love of peace.	End of the war.	Worthics of England.
The Civil War.	Rector of Waltham.	Character of his works.
In the field.	Late honours.	Illustrative extract.

"WORTHY old Fuller," "quaint old Thomas Fuller," are the affectionate names by which this witty English divine is often called. He was the son of a Northamptonshire clergyman, and was born in 1608 at Aldwinckle, a place rendered illustrious in later days by the birth of the poet Dryden. Passing from under the tuition of his father, he entered Queen's College, Cambridge, in his thirteenth year. Ten years later he became a Fellow of Sidney Sussex. To follow the steps by which he rose in the Church, would be out of place here; it is sufficient to say, that when he was little more than thirty years of age he had already won a distinguished reputation in the London pulpits, and had become Lecturer at the Savoy.

The clouds of the Civil War, charged with fire and blood, were fast darkening over Britain, as Fuller laboured in this prominent sphere. Remembering that his Master had said, "Blessed are the peace-makers," he lost no opportunity of striving to reconcile the parties, that were every day drifting further apart. His sermons all pointed to this great and noble end; his conversation in society was all woven of this golden thread. At last the deluge burst upon the land; and the eloquent clergyman, upon whom the Parliament looked with jealous eyes, was forced to leave his pulpit, and betake himself to Oxford, where the King had fixed his court. Fuller's moderation had obtained for him in London, with the Parliament at least, the name of a keen Royalist; but now in the head-quarters of the royal party, all hot for carnage, the same peace-loving temper caused him to be accused of a Puritan taint. His books and manuscripts, dear companions of his quietest hours, were taken from him; and there was no resource left him but to join the royal army in the field. As chaplain to Lord Hopton, he moved with the royal troops from place to place, fulfilling his sacred duties faithfully, but employing his leisure in the collection of materials for a literary work. Wherever the tents were pitched, or the soldiers quartered, he took care to note down all the old legends afloat in the district, and to visit every place within reach, which possessed any interest for the historian or the archæologist. No better preparation could have been made for the composition of *The Worthies of England;* and when we add to his own personal observations the gleanings of a wide correspondence, we shall form some idea of the industrious care with which Fuller built up a work that has contributed so largely to make his name famous. Camp life seems to have kindled something of warlike ardour in the peaceful chaplain's breast; for we read that, when Basing Hall was assailed by the Roundheads under Waller, after the battle of Cheriton Down, Fuller, who had been left by his patron in command of the garrison, bestirred himself so bravely in its defence, that the besiegers were repulsed with heavy loss. After the downfall of the royal cause he lived for some years at Exeter, constantly engaged in preaching or writing. *Good Thoughts in Bad Times,* and *Good Thoughts in Worse Times* are the titles of the two books which he is said to have written in this capital of south-western England.

After about two years of wandering he found himself once more in London, a worn man in what was in truth a changed place. For some time he preached where he could, until he obtained a permanent pulpit in St. Bride's, Fleet Street. Then, having

1648
A.D.

passed the examination of the "Triers," he settled down in 1648 at Waltham Abbey in Essex, to the rectory of which he had been presented by the Earl of Carlisle. During the bloody year which followed, and the eleven years of interregnum, his pen and voice were busy as ever in the cause of truth.

In spite of Cromwell's interdict he continued to preach, and in 1656 his *Church History of Britain from the Birth of Christ to the Year* 1648 was given to the world.

The Restoration brought him once more prominently into view. He received again his lectureship at the Savoy, and his prebendal stall at Salisbury; he was chosen chaplain to the King, and created Doctor of Divinity by the authorities of Cambridge. But Fuller's day on earth was near its close. This gleam of sunshine, which followed the grey mist of its afternoon, was brief and passing. Scarcely had he worn these honours for a year, Aug. 16, when he sank into the grave, smitten by a violent fever, **1661** which was then known as "the new disease." Two hun- A.D. dred of his brother ministers in sad procession followed his coffin to the tomb.

Thomas Fuller is chiefly remembered for two works,— his "Church History of Britain," published in 1656, and his "Worthies of England," published the year after his death. The latter is his greatest work. Begun during his wanderings with the royal army, and continued through all the changes of his after life, this quaint, delightful collection of literary odds and ends, deals not alone with the personal history of eminent Englishmen, as the name would seem to imply, but also with botany, topography, architecture, antiquities, and a host of other things connected with the shires in which they were born. The queer but very telling wit of Fuller sparkles in every line. He possessed in an eminent degree that curious felicity of language which condenses a vast store of wisdom into a few brief and pithy words; so that maxims and aphorisms may be culled by the hundred from the pages of his books. We have lately had the "Wit and Wisdom of Sydney Smith," from a London publisher; a still better book would be the "Wit and Wisdom of Thomas Fuller." The "Church History" was condemned in the author's own day for its "fun and quibble;" but there was nothing venomous or foul in the fun of Fuller, which has well been called "the sweetest-blooded wit that was ever infused into man or book." As well might we chide the lark for its joyous song, as this gentle parson for his pleasant jokes and quaint conceits. Besides the works already mentioned, Fuller wrote *The History of the Holy War*, *The Holy and the Profane States*, *A Pisgah View of Palestine*, and very many *Essays*, *Tracts*, and *Sermons*.

THE SEA.

(FROM "THE HOLY STATE.")

Tell me, ye naturalists, who sounded the first march and retreat to the tide, "Hither shalt thou come, and no further?" Why doth not the water recover his right over the earth, being higher in nature? Whence came the salt, and who first boiled it, which made so much brine? When the winds are not only wild in a storm, but even stark mad in an hurricane, who is it that restores them again to their wits, and brings them asleep in a calm? Who made the mighty whales, which swim in a sea of water, and have a sea of oil swimming in them? Who first taught the water to imitate the creatures on land, so that the sea is the stable of horse-fishes, the stall of kine-fishes, the sty of hog-fishes, the kennel of dog-fishes, and in all things the sea the ape of the land? Whence grows the ambergris in the sea? which is not so hard to find where it is as to know what it is. Was not God the first ship-wright? and have not all vessels on the water descended from the loins (or ribs rather) of Noah's ark? or else, who durst be so bold, with a few crooked boards nailed together, a stick standing upright, and a rag tied to it, to adventure into the ocean? What loadstone first touched the loadstone? or how first fell it in love with the North, rather affecting that cold climate than the pleasant East, or fruitful South or West? How comes that stone to know more than men, and find the way to the land in a mist? In most of these, men take sanctuary at *occulta qualitas* (some hidden quality), and complain that the room is dark, when their eyes are blind. Indeed, they are God's wonders; and that seaman the greatest wonder of all for his blockishness, who, seeing them daily, neither takes notice of them, admires at them, nor is thankful for them.

CHAPTER III.

JEREMY TAYLOR.

Born 1613 A.D.........Died 1667 A.D.

Preaching.	Return to London.	Difficulties of the poet.
Rise of Taylor.	Crosses to Ireland.	Death.
The Civil War.	Trouble.	Taylor's style.
The Welsh school.	The Restoration.	Chief works.
Pen-work.	Bishop of Down.	Illustrative extract.

THERE is no reason why the picturesque and the fanciful should be excluded from the oratory of the pulpit. As Christianity is emphatically the religion of man, and imparts to every element of his nature at once its highest culture and its noblest consecration, so there is no faculty or power within him which does not admit of being devoted to its service. Within its sacred and truly catholic pale, the poet, the philosopher, the logician, the man of sentiment and the man of abstract thought have each his place. Even the greatest of the apostles would be "all things to all men, if by any means he might save some." It was on this principle that Jeremy Taylor devoted the stores of his rich and brilliant fancy to the service of the Cross—lending all the charms of beauty to set forth the sanctity of truth. He strove to teach as did that gentle Saviour whose minister he was; and therefore the lilies of the field and the birds of the air, the dashing sea, the roaring wind, the weeping sky, and a thousand other strong and lovely things scattered around him in the world, supplied him with lessons, whose dear familiar beauty charmed his hearers, and still charms his readers into rapt attention.

This "poet among preachers," the son of a poor but well-descended surgeon-barber, was born at Cambridge in 1613. Having received his elementary education at the Grammar-school of his native town, he, when not yet fourteen, entered Caius College as a sizar,—the humblest class of students. When he had studied at Cambridge for some years, he went to London ; and there, by his handsome face and still finer style of preaching, he attracted the notice of the great Archbishop Laud, who was then in the full blaze of power. Under the patronage of so noted a man the advancement of Taylor was rapid. Laud earnestly wished to establish him at Oxford; and in 1636 secured for him a fellowship in All Souls College. In the following year he became, through Juxon, Bishop of London, the rector of Uppingham in Rutlandshire; and to that quiet parsonage, two years later, he brought home his first wife, Phœbe Langdale. Three years passed by—years of mingled joy and sorrow; for they made him the father of three sons, but took from him his gentle wife.

Then came the storm of the Civil War; and in the wreck of the throne the fortunes of Jeremy Taylor suffered shipwreck too. His life at this period presents a striking resemblance to the life of Fuller. Like that witty priest, he joined the royal party at Oxford, accompanied the troops to the field in the capacity of chaplain, and took an active share in the hard work of the war. In the battle fought at Cardigan he was made prisoner by the Roundheads. His release, however, soon followed; and, having no longer a home among the rich woodlands of Rutlandshire—for his rectory had been sequestrated by the Parliament—he resolved to cast his lot in the mountain-land of Wales, and calmly wait for better times. There, at Newton-hall in Caermarthenshire, he set up a school in conjunction with two accomplished friends, who like himself had fallen upon evil days. Time slid away; King Charles was beheaded, and Oliver assumed the purple robe of Protector. Far away from the great centres of learning and distinction, girdled round by the huge Cambrian mountains, the Chrysostom of our English literature lived a peaceful but very busy life. His good friend John Evelyn, and his kind neighbour the Earl of Carbery, stretched out willing hands to help him in his need. His marriage with a lady, who possessed an estate in Caermarthen, relieved him from the wearing toil of the school-room. But if his life grew easier, he certainly did not relax in the work for which he was best fitted.

Ever labouring with his pen, he sent forth from his secluded dwelling-place book after book, enriched with the choicest fancies of a most poetic mind.   But even the privacy of his life could not keep him entirely safe; fine and imprisonment fell heavily on him at various times during the ascendency of the Puritans, against whom he spoke and wrote on some occasions very strongly.   At last, probably weary of a retirement which did not shield him from his foes, he returned to London in 1657.   An invitation from the Earl of Conway induced him, in the following year, to settle in the north of Ireland, where he officiated as lecturer at Lisburn, and also at Portmore, a village on the shores of Lough Neagh. He fixed his residence at the latter place.   Here, too, Puritan resentment found him out.   An informer gave evidence that the minister of Lisburn had used the sign of the cross in baptism. Arrested with violence, Taylor was hurried in deep mid-winter to answer before the Irish Council for his act.   Exposure and anxiety brought on a fever, which did him the good office of softening the sentence of the court.

Soon afterwards visiting London on literary business, he signed the Royalist declaration of April 24, 1660, and in the following month the joy-bells, which rang in the Restoration of the second Charles, sounded a note of preferment to Taylor.   The bishopric of Down and Connor, to which was afterwards   Aug. added the see of Dromore, rewarded the eloquent   **1660** preacher, whose Royalist zeal had never languished.   Yet,   A.D. after all, this mitre was but the badge of an honourable, but not an easy exile, in which Taylor spent his remaining years.   A hard and thankless office it must have been for an English bishop to superintend an Irish diocese at that day. His nation and his faith were both unpopular.   Congregations, driven by the terror of strict penal laws, crowded the churches every Sunday to hear a service which many of them could not understand, and which most of them regarded with the strongest dislike.   Many of his clergy, also, appointed under the old system of things, looked jealously on the authority of a bishop.   Battling with difficulties so many and so great, Taylor must often have sighed after his quiet parsonage at Uppingham, or even after his school-room at Newton-hall. But he did his duty nobly in a most difficult position, until an attack of fever cut him off at the early age of fifty-five. His death took place at Lisburn in 1667.

Hallam characterizes the style of Jeremy Taylor's sermons as being far too Asiatic in their abundance of ornament, and too much loaded with flower-garlands of quotation from other, especially classical, writers. Yet the great critic assigns to the great preacher the praise of being "the chief ornament of the English pulpit up to the middle of the seventeenth century,"—an admission which does much to blunt the point of his censure.

Taylor does, undoubtedly, sometimes run riot in sweet metaphors, and lose his way in a maze of illustrations ; but, even so, is it not pleasanter and better to wander through a lovely garden, although the flowers *are* sometimes tangling together in a brilliant chaos and tripping us as we walk, than to plod over dry and sandy wastes, where showers, if they ever fall, seem only to wash the green out of the parched and stunted grass ?

Jeremy Taylor's most popular devotional work is his *Holy Living and Holy Dying.* Other works of the same class are *The Life of Christ* and *The Golden Grove;* of which the latter is a series of meditations named after the seat of Earl Carbery, his neighbour in Wales. These were all written in his Welsh retreat. There, too, he wrote a generous, liberal, and most eloquent plea for toleration in religious matters, entitled *The Liberty of Prophesying;* * in the dedication of which he refers with pathetic beauty to the violence of the storm which had "dashed the vessel of the Church all in pieces," and had cast himself, a shipwrecked man, on the coast of Wales. His last great work, styled *Ductor Dubitantium,* treats of the guidance of the conscience, and is still considered our great standard English book on casuistry. But Taylor's style is not well suited to make clear a subject so difficult and intricate; nor does the plan, which the author lays down, aid in giving distinctness to his teaching.

---

* *Prophesying* is here used in the sense of preaching. Compare its use in certain parts of the New Testament.

ON PRAYER.

Anger is a perfect alienation of the mind from prayer, and therefore is contrary to that attention which presents our prayers in a right line to God. For so have I seen a lark rising from his bed of grass, and soaring upwards, singing as he rises, and hopes to get to heaven, and climb above the clouds; but the poor bird was beaten back with the loud sighings of an eastern wind, and his motion made irregular and inconstant, descending more at every breath of the tempest than it could recover by the libration and frequent weighing of his wings, till the little creature was forced to sit down and pant, and stay till the storm was over; and then it made a prosperous flight, and did rise and sing, as if it had learned music and motion from an angel, as he passed sometimes through the air, about his ministries here below. So is the prayer of a good man: when his affairs have required business, and his business was matter of discipline, and his discipline was to pass upon a sinning person, or had a design of charity, his duty met with the infirmities of a man, and anger was its instrument ; and the instrument became stronger than the prime agent, and raised a tempest, and overruled the man; and then his prayer was broken, and his thoughts were troubled, and his words went up towards a cloud ; and his thoughts pulled them back again, and made them without intention; and the good man sighs for his infirmity, but must be content to lose that prayer, and he must recover it when his anger is removed, and his spirit is becalmed, made even as the brow of Jesus, and smooth like the heart of God ; and then it ascends to heaven upon the wings of the holy dove, and dwells with God, till it returns, like the useful bee, loaden with a blessing and the dew of heaven.

CHAPTER IV.

EDWARD HYDE, EARL OF CLARENDON.

Born 1608 A.D..........Died 1674 A.D.

Two old pillars.	His second exile.
Early days of Hyde.	Death.
Begins public life.	Milton and Clarendon.
His first exile.	History of the Rebellion
The Restoration.	Illustrative extract.

FORMING the door-posts of a stable-yard, attached to the Three Kings' Inn in Piccadilly, there stand, or stood a short time since, two old defaced Corinthian pillars, chipped, weather-stained, drab-painted, and bearing upon their faded acanthus crowns the sign-board of the livery-stables. Ostlers lounge and smoke there; passers-by give no heed to the poor relics of a dead grandeur; and the brown London mud bespatters them pitilessly from capital to base, as rattling wheels jolt past over the uneven pavement. These pillars are all that remain of a splendid palace, which was reared upon that site by the famous Edward Hyde, Earl of Clarendon and Lord High Chancellor of England. It was built at an unhappy time, when England could but ill spare the £50,000 sunk in its gorgeous stone-work, and when England's King and Chancellor were hated by the people with a bitter hatred. So it was nicknamed Dunkirk House, and Tangier Hall, and insulting couplets were chalked upon its gates by a howling rabble, who shivered its windows with stones, when the Dutch cannon were heard in the estuary of the Thames. Clarendon, who built it, was then near the day of his fall.

Already he had seen heavy reverses. When he left the pleasant lawns of Dinton in Wiltshire, where he was born in 1608, to study at Oxford for the Church, and afterwards to pore over ponderous law-books in the old chambers of the Middle Temple, he little foresaw either his splendid rise or his sad decline. Still less

did he dream, in those golden days of youth, that out of the dark
days of his second exile would come a book, which should gild
his name with even brighter lustre than statesmanship or devotion
to his king could win for him. A chequered reputation on the
page of history, and two old pillars in Piccadilly, might have been
all that remained of the great lawyer's life-work, had not his
brilliant pen raised a monument of eloquence, imperishable while
the English language lives.

As member for Wootton Basset he began his political career in
1640, having previously, though enjoying a considerable private
fortune, devoted himself so earnestly to the practice of the law as
to win by it much renown and many friends. His rise to royal
favour was very speedy. Having aided the King most materially
by writing several important papers, he was knighted in 1643, and
made Chancellor of the Exchequer. But in spite of all that the
swords of the Cavaliers or the eloquence of Hyde could do, the cause
of Charles declined, and it was judged right that the Prince
of Wales should leave England. Hyde accompanied the   **1646**
royal boy to Jersey, where after some time he commenced   A.D.
his great *History of the Rebellion.* It would be out of
place here to trace the wanderings of his first exile. At the Hague
he heard of the Whitehall tragedy. At Paris he shared the
poverty of the royal Stuart—sometimes with neither clothes nor fire
to keep out the winter cold, and often with not a *livre* he could
call his own. All that the unfortunate, lazy, dissipated, uncrowned,
and kingdomless monarch could do to recompense the fidelity of
this devoted servant, he did. He made him his Lord Chancellor
—an empty name written on an empty purse, as things went then.

But soon came the Restoration with its pealing bells and
scattered flowers. Hyde, created Earl of Clarendon,
became a real Lord Chancellor, entitled to sit on the   **1660**
actual woolsack. Then for seven years he was the ruling   A.D.
spirit of English politics, and he shares in many of the dark
stains, which lie upon the memory of King Charles II. The feeling
of the nation grew strong against him. He lost the royal favour.
In August 1667 he had to give up the Great Seal; and, with a trial

for high treason hanging over his grey head, he fled down to the
coast, and took ship at the pretty village of Erith for the French
shore. Louis proved unfriendly to the fallen statesman. From
place to place the old man wandered, finding solace only in his
pen. Seven years passed wearily by, gout racking his feeble
frame. A plaintive petition in his last days entreated his heartless
master's leave to die at home. "Seven years," he wrote, "was a
time prescribed and limited by God himself for the expiration of
some of his greatest judgments; and it is full that time since I
have, with all possible humility, sustained the insupportable weight
of the king's displeasure. Since it will be in nobody's power
long to prevent me from dying, methinks the desiring a
place to die in should not be thought a great presumption."
No answer came; and when the year 1674 was near its
close, Clarendon breathed his last at Rouen.

1674
A.D.

The great Cavalier—prince of historical portrait painters—outlived the great Puritan—prince of epic poets—but a few days.
Born in the same year, Clarendon and Milton stood all their lives
apart, towering in rival greatness above their fellows in the grand
struggle of their century. The year of the Restoration, which
brought wealth and splendour to the Cavalier, plunged the blind
old Puritan in bitter poverty. But a few years more, and the great
Earl, too, was stricken down from his lofty place, and sent a home-
less wanderer to a stranger's land. To both, their sternest discipline
was their greatest gain; for when the colours of hope and gladness
had faded from the landscape of their lives, and nothing but a waste
of splendourless days seemed to stretch in cheerless vista before
them, they turned to the desk for solace, and found in the exercise
of their literary skill, not peace alone, but fame. Milton wrote
most of his great Poem in blindness and disgrace; Clarendon completed his great History during a painful exile.

Clarendon's "History of the Rebellion" (mark the Cavalier in
the last word of this title) is not in all things a faithful picture of
those terrible days, red with civil and with royal blood. Nor is
this wonderful, for the writer was absent from his native land during a great part of the eventful strife, which he designates by so

pointed a name. It is very unequally written, here adorned with a passage of most picturesque and glowing eloquence, and there marred by a "ravelled sleave" of sentences, tangled together in utter defiance of grammatical construction. Yet he is never, even in his most slovenly passages, obscure. It has been well remarked that his language is that of the speaker, not of the writer; and if we remember Hyde's training at the bar, we shall cease to wonder at his off-hand, careless style. When he sits down to paint the character of some celebrated man, his pencil seems dipt in the brightest hues, and, as touch after touch falls lovingly on the canvas, we feel that a master's hand is tracing the growing form. The History was not published until 1707 ; his *Life and the Continuation of the History*, not until 1759. Another remarkable work of Clarendon is his *Essay on an Active and Contemplative Life.*

CHARACTER AND DEATH OF LORD FALKLAND.

(FROM THE "HISTORY OF THE REBELLION.")

When there was any overture or hope of peace, he would be more erect and vigorous, and exceedingly solicitous to press anything which he thought might promote it; and sitting among his friends, often after a deep silence, and frequent sighs, would, with a shrill and sad accent, ingeminate the word Peace, peace; and would passionately profess, "that the very agony of the war and the view of the calamities and desolation the kingdom did and must endure, took his sleep from him, and would shortly break his heart." This made some think, or pretend to think, "that he was so much enamoured of peace, that he would have been glad the King should have bought it at any price ;" which was a most unreasonable calumny ;—as if a man that was himself the most punctual and precise in every circumstance, that might reflect upon conscience or honour, could have wished the King to have committed a trespass against either. . . . . .

In the morning before the battle, as always upon action, he was very cheerful, and put himself into the first rank of the Lord Byron's regiment, then advancing upon the enemy, who had lined the hedges on both sides with musketeers ; from whence he was shot with a musket in the lower part of the belly, and in the instant falling from his horse, his body was not found till the next morning; till when, there was some hope he might have been a prisoner, though his nearest friends, who knew his temper, received small comfort from that imagination. Thus fell that incomparable young man, in the four-and-thirtieth year of his age, having so much despatched the true business of life, that the eldest rarely attain to that immense knowledge, and the youngest enter not into the world with more innocency : whosoever leads such a life, needs be the less anxious upon how short warning it is taken from him.

(15)   13

CHAPTER V.

JOHN MILTON.

Born 1608 A.D..........Died 1674 A.D.

PERHAPS the finest sentence in that noble fragment of an English History, by which the dead Macaulay yet speaks to a grateful, reverent nation, is a sentence thus recording the glory of John Milton :—

"A mightier poet, tried at once by pain, danger, poverty, obloquy, and blindness, meditated, undisturbed by the obscene tumult which raged all around him, a song so sublime and so holy that it would not have misbecome the lips of those ethereal Virtues whom he saw, with that inner eye which no calamity could darken, flinging down on the jasper pavement their crowns of amaranth and gold."

If Milton had written not one line of verse, his richly jewelled and majestic prose would have raised him to a lofty rank among the Raleighs and the Bacons, the Taylors and the Gibbons of our English tongue ; and if he had dropped the poet's lyre for ever, when he exchanged the green shades of Horton and the crystal skies of Italy for the smoke and din of London life and the heat of a great controversial war, the songs already sung by the youthful Puritan bard had won a chaplet of unfading bays, at least as bright as those that decorate the brows of Dryden and of Pope.   But, when we add to these achievements the sublime and solemn anthem of his blind old age, the lustre of his life's work brightens to such intensity, that there is but one name in the long roll of English writers which does not grow dim in the surpassing radiance of his fame.

Shakspere and Milton dwell apart from all, in a loftier region of their own. Great Consuls in the mighty republic of English letters, to them alone belong the honours of the ivory chair, the robe with purple hem, and the rod-surrounded axe.

In the reign of Elizabeth a certain John Mylton was under-ranger of Shotover Forest, not far from Oxford. This was the poet's grandfather. A strict Roman Catholic, he disinherited his son for adopting the Protestant faith; and this son, also a John Milton, having gone to London, set up, as a scrivener or notary-public, at the sign of the Spread Eagle in Bread Street. There, in the intervals of his professional will-drawing and money-lending John Milton the scrivener wrote trifling verses and composed elaborate pieces of music. Under the wings of this Spread Eagle, which seems to have shadowed a very com- **1608** fortable, happy home, was born, on the 9th of December A.D. 1608, John Milton the poet, son of a Puritan scrivener, and grandson of a Roman Catholic ranger;—receiving from his father literary tastes and a love of music; and from his mother a kind, gentle nature, and the sad inheritance of weak eyes.

The Puritan influences, amid which the boy grew up, moulded his character to a shape it never lost. Having received his earlier education at home, from a Scotchman, Thomas Young, he went at about twelve years of age to St. Paul's school, which was then under the direction of a Mr. Gill. Even at that unripe age Milton's studious tastes showed themselves. Night after night he was up over his books till past twelve, and neither watering eyes nor increasing headaches could daunt the brave young worker. We cannot but be pained when we think of this intense application, by which Milton laid the foundation of the wonderful learning displayed in "Paradise Lost." The midnight studies of the child cost the old man his enjoyment of heaven's light and earth's colouring. Yet even here there was a blessing in disguise; for the affliction which quenched the light of the body's eye, deepened and strengthened the vision of that inner, spiritual eye, " which no calamity could darken."

While yet a school-boy, Milton could write capital Latin and Greek, either in verse or prose; and knew something, too, of

Hebrew. He had read with delight the poems of Spenser, and Sylvester's translation of the Frenchman, Du Bartas; and had tried his boyish pen on English verse by translating the 114th and 136th Psalms.

Christ's College, Cambridge, being chosen for the higher instruc-

1624
A.D.

tion of the youthful poet, he went thither in 1624 as a minor pensioner. His tutor was Chappel, afterwards Provost of Trinity College, Dublin, and Bishop of Cork. What was the ground of dispute we cannot exactly tell, but a quarrel took place between tutor and pupil, so serious that Milton had to leave his college for a while.* This incident Johnson exaggerates into rustication, insinuating on the same page that Milton was whipped at Cambridge. It is true that the rod, plied in the lower schools with systematic cruelty, had not yet been quite abandoned in the college class-room; but there is not sufficient ground for believing that Milton was flogged at college, merely because flogging at college was not quite done away with in his youthful days.

The delicate beauty of the student's face, with its shell-like pink and white, and the rolling masses of silken auburn hair, parted in the middle, that framed its oval contour, excited the jeers of some rougher class-mates, who called him "The Lady of the College." They might well have spared their mockery, for the blonde beauty was going to outshine them all, and even then was showing signs of a wondrous genius in its dawn. In the "winter wild" of 1629, Milton's twenty-first year, he composed his magnificent *Ode on the Morning of Christ's Nativity*, which ranks among the finest specimens of lyrical poetry that any age or nation has produced. Yet Johnson, in his Life of Milton, does not even mention this grand burst of song!

1632
A.D.

Having completed his course, and taken his degree of M.A., he left Cambridge in 1632, to spend five calm delightful years in his father's country house at Horton in Buckinghamshire.

It is impossible to doubt that the lovely pictures of Eden-life,

---

* It has been maintained by some keen and able reasoners that Milton never left his college at all.

which we find in the fourth and some succeeding books of "Paradise Lost"—sunny days and innocent enjoyments, shadowy rose-bowers, gentle labours amid vine and orchard, delicate fruit repasts, and sweet scenes of rosy morning and silver moonlight— were drawn from early memories of the Horton glades and gardens, idealized by the bright sunlight of poetic fancy.

Deep study, quiet country walks, and poetic composition, broken now and then by a run to London for books, or tuition in music and mathematics, filled up the softly flowing days of the poet's rural life.

At Horton and on the Continent Milton spent the vacation period of his life—a happy six years' holiday intervening between his Cambridge study and his London school; and five poems, round which the scent of the hawthorn hedge is ever fresh and sweet, were the exercises which gave a zest to the enjoyment of these bright and careless years. *L'Allegro, Il Penseroso, Arcades, Comus,* and *Lycidas* were written at Horton. The country breezes seem to have swept off the grey shadows of the Cambridge rooms, and to have called forth his love of nature in buds and blossoms of the richest luxuriance. How many verses were woven in the fragrant meadows, all embroidered with wild flowers, or by the chime of the silver stream, we do not know; but the odours and the colours of sweet rural life breathe and brighten in every line.

How curiously the life one lives is reflected in his works ! As the sea wave takes the colour of the sky above it, the multitudinous billows of thought that roll in every human soul are tinged with the hues of the outward life. Place the *Ode on the Nativity* side by side with *L'Allegro,* and mark the contrasted tints. Residence within the " studious cloisters pale" has given to the one a stern grey awfulness, a pure classic beauty, and a grave learnedness, which have but little in common with the frolicsome play and brown, healthy, country life, that laugh and gambol in the other.

His mother's death in 1637 broke the sweet charm that had bound him to Horton. There was nothing now to prevent him from starting upon his Continental tour, and accordingly, in the following year, armed with advice and letters from Sir Henry Wotton, the Provost of Eton, he crossed the

1633
A.D.

straits to France.　We shall not follow him minutely on his journeyings.　He was absent from England for fifteen months, during which he travelled through France and Italy, residing for a time in some of the principal cities.　At Paris he met Hugo Grotius, the great Dutchman; at Florence he visited the blind old Galileo, who then lay in the prison of the Inquisition for daring to speak what he believed about the stars; at Rome he heard Leonora Baroni sing, and was welcomed with remarkable attention in the first circles of society; at Naples, beyond which he did not go, he was guided through the city by the Marquis of Villa, the friend and biographer of Tasso.　The influence which Italian scenery, sculpture, and music had in kindling the imagination of the grave English Puritan and storing his memory with a wealth of classic thoughts, that gave shape and colour to the ideas he had drawn from books among the woods of Horton, formed a most important element in the education of the poet for his great work.　Amid his recollections of foreign travel,—scenic, artistic, literary, historic, classic,—there stole, too, a tinge of love, whose purple light yet lingers on his *Italian Sonnets.*　It was at Florence that the fair-cheeked Englishman met a beauty of Bologna, whose black eyes subdued his heart, and whose voice completed the conquest by binding it in silver chains—chains which it cost him a pang to break before he could tear himself away.　After visiting

1639
A.D.

Venice and Geneva, among other places, he returned by way of France to England.　Amid all the license and vice of Continental life, as it then was, he passed pure and unstained, returning with the bloom of his young religious feelings unfaded, like the flush of English manhood on his cheek. The thought of writing an epic poem appears to have ripened to a purpose in Italy; but he had not yet chosen his great theme. The story of Arthur, or some other hero of ancient British days, seems at this time to have been floating before his mind.

The toils of a teacher's life, and the composition of many prose works filled up the chief part of those ten years which elapsed between Milton's return from abroad and his appointment as Foreign Secretary (1639-1649).　His poetic muse was all but silent.　Six of these years were spent in a retired garden-house, up an entry off Aldersgate Street. There, with a few leaves and blossoms round him, shut in from the noisy street, he read with his pupils—among them his own nephews, the Phillipses—an extensive course, comprising several uncommon classics, some Hebrew, a sprinkling of Chaldee and Syriac, mathematics and astronomy—not omitting the Greek Testament and some Dutch divinity on Sundays.   His pen was at first almost wholly taken up with his intensely bitter attacks upon Episcopacy, opening in 1641 with a pamphlet on *Reformation in England*, and closing with the best of the series, his *Apology for Smectymnuus.**   To the seclusion of Aldersgate Street, Milton, a man of thirty-five, brought home his first bride—Mary, the daughter of Richard Powell, a Royalist Justice of the Peace, living at Forest Hill near Shotover.   It was a hasty mar-   **1643** riage, and far from a happy one.   The young wife, who   A.D. seems not to have fully counted the cost of such a change, had Cavalier notions of housekeeping and social life, very unlike the quiet frugality of Milton's home.   She missed the dancing and the laughter of Forest Hill.   When the friends who had brought her home left the house, its gloom seemed to deepen tenfold; her grave and studious husband never thought of leaving his books and pen for a while, to cheer her loneliness until she became used to a domestic climate so unlike that which she had left.   In a few weeks she returned to her father's house, seemingly to pay a short visit, but inwardly resolved to leave her serious bridegroom and his gloomy garden-house to keep each other company.   He wrote, and got no reply; he sent, and his messenger was ill-treated. It was a clear case that John Milton was deserted by his wife.

His four *Works on Divorce*, which were published in 1644 and 1645, are evidently the fruits of this matrimonial misery.   Sweeter fruit, however, than these sour produc-   **1644** tions marks the former year; for then was addressed   A.D. to the Parliament the celebrated *Areopagitica*, finest of all his

---

* *Smectymnuus* is a word made up of the initials of the five names of those Puritan ministers who joined the strife on Milton's side.   They were—Stephen Marshall, Edward Calamy, Thomas Young, Matthew Newcome, and William (UUilliam) Spenstow.

prose compositions.   His *Tractate on Education* appeared in the same year.

The estrangement between Milton and his wife having lasted for two years, a reconciliation took place in the house of a friend. Mary Milton, flinging herself in tears at her husband's feet, was once more taken to his home, which was now a large house in Barbican.   So completely was the breach healed, that the husband's door was opened to her ruined family, driven from Forest Hill by the fortunes of the Civil War; and in Milton's house old Richard Powell soon died.

His pupils having decreased in number about this time, the poet thought it prudent to take a backward step by removing into a smaller house.   We soon find him in Holborn, where his residence had an entrance into Lincoln's Inn Fields.   Here he wrote part of his *History of England*, and probably some of his compilations; and here, while the axe was falling on the neck of Charles Stuart, **1649** he was correcting the last proofs of a work entitled *The* A.D. *Tenure of Kings and Magistrates*, which argued the lawfulness of that terrible deed, whose red stain can never be effaced from the annals of those sad times.   Published a week or two after the tragedy of Whitehall, the "Tenure" excited such admiring attention that the office of Foreign or Latin Secretary to the Council, worth about £290 a year, was offered to the author. Thus opened a new era of Milton's life.

The period of eleven years, coming between the Regicide and the Restoration, presents perhaps the deepest contrasts of light and shadow that we find in the chequered life of Milton.   Appointed Secretary of Foreign Tongues, he removed to Charing Cross, and afterwards to the official apartments at Whitehall, which he occupied for about eighteen months.   His direct duties were not heavy, consisting merely in conducting the foreign correspondence of the Council in Latin, which was then the language of diplomacy. But his pen was also required to do higher work than the writing of state papers.   The blood of an English king, crying from an English scaffold, had roused rage and horror throughout Europe; and Milton was selected by the Parliament to front the storm, and

lay it if he could.   In reply to the sad description of the suffering
king, which was presented by the well-known *Eikon Basilikē*, he
wrote his *Eikonoklastes* (Image-breaker); in which, reviling the
memory of Charles with a rancour alike unbecoming and unchris-
tian, he smites with a rude and heavy hand the defender of dead
majesty.   To this period also belong his two great Latin works,
Defences for the People of England; in which the voice of the
Puritan is uplifted with somewhat more of dignity, and certainly
with greater power.   The first " Defence" was written in answer to
Salmasius of Leyden, a philologer of European fame; whom the
triumphant reply is said to have smitten so sorely to the heart,
that he died of the blow.   But controversies like these are pitiful
sights.   It is sad to see a magnificent genius like Milton stooping
to fling those paving-stones of abuse — " rogue, puppy, foul-
mouthed wretch "—which come ready to the hand of every sot
and shrew in England.

Why we do not know, but Milton soon left his Whitehall
lodgings for a pretty garden-house in Petty France, Westminster,
with an opening into St. James's Park.   There about 1653 two
heavy afflictions fell upon the poor man.   He lost his wife, Mary,
who, with all her faults, had, since their reconciliation, kept his
house prudently and well; and that paralysis of the optic nerve,
which had been coming on for years, left him totally blind.
Many symptoms had foretold the calamity.   He saw an iris
round the candle ; his left eye, when used alone, diminished the
size of the objects he looked at; things swam before his gaze; and
at night, when he lay down and closed his eyes, there
came for a time a flash of light and a play of brilliant   **1654**
colours.   A blind and widowed man, with three little   A.D.
girls under eight to look after, and a heavy load of public
pen-work to do, presents a sorrowful spectacle.   Such was Milton's
case in 1654.

In two or three years he married again ; but his second wife,
Catherine Woodcock, whom he dearly loved, died in fifteen months
after their union.   So his daughters grew up wild and undisci-
plined, to cost their father many a heart-ache in his declining days.

His blindness did not involve the loss of his office as Foreign Secretary.   An assistant, and afterwards a colleague, aided him in the performance of his duties.   This colleague, in 1659, was his friend Andrew Marvell, who received, as Milton himself then did, the sum of £200 a year.

In spite of the gloom which blindness and bereavement had cast over the garden-house in Petty France, and the worries caused by those poor boisterous hoidens, whose mother was dead, Milton must have enjoyed many hours of sober tranquillity there. His fame had spread far beyond the borders of his own land. To Continental strangers, Cromwell and Milton, the man of action and the man of thought, were the representative men of England —the great British lions, who were then really worthy of a visit and a view.   A few literary friends, too, often came to cheer his leisure hours.   And, better than all, before the added darkness of poverty and despair deepened upon him, he had begun to soar on wing sublime into those starry realms of thought, below which he had too long been walking with folded pinions, busied with common cares and soiled with earthly stains.   The first lines of *Paradise Lost* were lying in his desk.

The last state paper written by Milton bears date May 15th, 1659.   None but the most important work of the Foreign Office was done by his pen in the later years of the Commonwealth.

The Restoration brought gloom and terror to the household of the Puritan poet, who had written too many bitter things

1660   of the slain father to be easy in his mind at the return

A.D.   of the exiled son.   For a time he was forced to hide himself in a friend's house in Bartholomew Close.   But influential admirers exerted their interest for him ; and though the "Eikonoklastes" and the "Defences" were burned by the common hangman, the writer was included in the Act of Indemnity, and got leave to settle down into safe obscurity.   Obscurity it might have been to a common man, but to Milton it proved the brightest period of his life.   The fresh laurels of the Cambridge student,— the pastoral sweetness of the Horton poet,—the polished graces of the traveller,—the triumphs of the keen and bitter controversialist,

—the fame of the accomplished Latin Secretary,—all grow dim beside the lustrous achievements of that blind old man, who was often to be seen on sunny days, in a coat of coarse grey cloth, sitting at the door of a mean house in Artillery Walk near Bunhill Fields.   Through all changes and perils his unfailing solace must have been the composition of his great work.   A young Quaker, Thomas Ellwood, came often of an afternoon to read Latin to the helpless poet ; and this good friend it was who secured for him that cottage at Chalfont in Buckinghamshire, where the Miltons took refuge from the Great Plague that ravaged London in 1665.   The Quaker, who was tutor in a rich family of Chalfont, called upon the poet some time after he had settled down in his new abode.   During the visit Milton, calling for a manuscript, handed it to Ellwood, and bade him take it home to read.   It was the newly finished poem of **1665**
A.D.
Paradise Lost.   Returning it, after a while, to his blind friend, Ellwood said, " Thou hast said much here of Paradise Lost, but what hast thou to say of Paradise Found ?"   This casual remark led to the composition of the minor epic, *Paradise Regained.*

When the terrors of the Plague had passed, Milton returned to Bunhill Fields, prepared to dispose of his great poem.   It seemed in many ways an unfortunate time for so heavy a venture.   The Great Fire of 1666 had just laid the shops and dwellings of nearly all London in ashes.   And wares, made to find a ready sale in that day, needed to be highly spiced with choice blasphemies and gross obscenity.   At length, however, a bookseller was found who consented to buy the poem.   And a very hard bargain indeed did Mr. Samuel Simmons drive with Ex-secretary Milton.   The terms agreed upon were these : £5 in hand, £5 on the sale of 1300 copies of the first edition, and two similar sums on the sale of a like number of the second and third editions,— no edition to exceed 1500 copies.   The poem was pub- **1667** lished in 1667, in the form of a small quarto, at three **A.D.** shillings.   Milton was dead when the third edition of " Paradise Lost " appeared in 1678, and his widow surrendered all her claims on Simmons for the sum of £8. Thus, in all, to Milton and his heirs, there came only £18* for this greatest poem of modern ages !

There is extant, in the poet's own handwriting, a receipt for the second sum of £5, dated 1669, which shows that at least 1300 copies of the book had gone off in its first two years. That scrap of worn paper sufficiently refutes the statement, so often advanced in former days, that to all the other woes heaped on Milton's grey head, the neglect of the reading public was added as a last and worst infliction. Few sacred epics would command a larger sale even in these book-devouring days. Though Charles and his glittering voluptuaries preferred the whimsical adventures of Hudibras to the lofty strains of "Paradise Lost," there were thousands of true-hearted Puritans in England to read and love the noble verses of that veteran scholar, who had stood by the great Oliver in the palmy days of the Commonwealth, and had done with his pen for England's glory, at least as much as the rugged Lord Protector had ever done with that weighty sword he bore.

In 1670 appeared Milton's *History of England,* and in the following year *Paradise Regained* and *Samson Agonistes* were published in a thin octavo. His last three years were occupied in preparing for the press several minor works in Latin and in English. The clouded close of his life was calm and peaceful, on the whole, although his undutiful daughters caused him much vexation. His third wife, Elizabeth Minshull, a young woman whom he had married soon after the Restoration, tended his declining years with careful affection.

Such a picture of old Milton's daily life as that which we sub-

---

* Some say £23 in all; but it is very unlikely that Simmons would go beyond the original £20 agreed on as the price of the poem. During Milton's life he received *two* payments of £5; when the 1300 copies of the second edition were sold, his widow became entitled to the third £5; and she seems, rather than wait for the sale of the stipulated number of the third edition, to have preferred £3 in hand in addition to the sum due. This seems to us the meaning of her giving up all her claims on Simmons in 1678 for £8. If she had already received the fourth sum of £5, her claims had ceased to exist; and only by supposing that this fourth sum of £5 was included in the £8, can the total reach £23. The third edition was published in 1678, and no money was due on it until 1300 copies had been sold. Hence the fourth £5 cannot have formed a part of the final settlement of £8.

join possesses a peculiar value, in enabling us to bring nearer to our hearts the great English epic poet, who ranks with Homer, with Virgil, and with Dante.

"An ancient clergyman of Dorsetshire, Dr. Wright, found John Milton in a small chamber, hung with rusty green, sitting in an elbow-chair, and dressed neatly in black; pale, but not cadaverous; his hands and feet gouty, and with chalk-stones." *

"In his latter years he retired every night at nine o'clock, and lay till four in summer, till five in winter; and if not disposed then to rise, he had some one to sit at his bed-side and read to him. When he rose he had a chapter of the Hebrew Bible read for him; and then, with of course the intervention of breakfast, he studied till twelve. He then dined, took some exercise for an hour,—generally in a chair, in which he used to swing himself,—and afterwards played on the organ or the bass-viol, and either sang himself or made his wife sing, who, as he said, had a good voice, but no ear. He then resumed his studies till six, from which hour till eight he conversed with those who came to visit him. He finally took a light supper, smoked a pipe of tobacco, and drank a glass of water, after which he retired to rest." †

So calmly passed the days of the blind old poet, until, a month before the completion of his sixty-sixth year, he passed away from earth with scarcely a pang. It was on Sunday, **1674** the 8th of November, that the sad event occurred. Gout, A.D. his old foe, had for some time been wearing him away; and for months he knew that his life on earth was drawing to an end. His body was laid beside his father's dust in the church of St. Giles, Cripplegate.

The following list contains the names of Milton's chief works, with the dates and places of their composition or publication :—

POEMS.

Ode on the Nativity,	...	Composed in 1629, Cambridge.		
L'Allegro, ...	...	...	Doubtful,	Horton.
Il Penseroso,	...	...	—	—	—
Arcades, ...	...	...	—	1634,	—

* Richardson.　　　　† Keightley, following Aubrey.

Comus, ...	Composed in 1634, Horton.
Lycidas, ...	— 1637, —
Italian Sonnets, ...	— 1638–9, Florence.
Paradise Lost, ...	Published in 1667, London.
Paradise Regained, ...	— 1671, —
Samson Agonistes, ...	— — —
English Sonnets, ...	Various times and places.

PROSE WORKS.

Of Reformation in England, ...	Composed in 1641, London.
Prelatical Episcopacy, ...	— — —
Apology for Smectymnuus, ...	— 1642, —
Areopagitica, ...	— 1644, —
Tractate on Education, ...	— — —
The Tenure of Kings, ...	— 1649, —
Eikonoklastes, ...	— — —
Defensio pro Populo Anglicano,	— 1650, —
Defensio Secunda, ...	— 1654, —
History of England, ...	Published in 1670, —
De Doctrinâ Christianâ, ...	— 1823, * —

L'Allegro and *Il Penseroso* are two companion pictures of life at Horton, where they were written. No ecstasies of joy or sorrow are there depicted, but those moods of mirth and pensiveness which chased each other across the poet's mind, like lights and shadows across a summer landscape.

Arcades, a short pastoral masque, which was originally performed at Harefield Park before the Dowager-Countess of Derby, consists of three songs and a speech by the Genius of the wood. Some consider "Arcades" to be only a fragment.

Comus is an exquisite masque, founded on an actual occurrence. Its plot is this : A beautiful lady, lost in a wood, is brought under the spells of the magician Comus. Her fate seems sealed, until a kindly spirit appearing in guise of a shepherd to her brothers, who are vainly seeking their sister, gives them a root called haemony, by means of which they set at defiance the power of the enchanter. They dash into the palace, interrupt the progress of a delicious banquet, save their sister, and put to flight Comus and

* The Latin manuscript was found in a press in the State-paper Office in 1823, wrapped in an envelope with other papers of Milton. The publication of an English version gave origin to Macaulay's brilliant Essay on Milton in the Edinburgh Review (August 1825).

his attendant rabble. The masque was acted at Ludlow Castle by the children of the Earl of Bridgewater, then President of Wales.

Lycidas is a sweetly mournful pastoral,—a poem "In Memoriam,"—written on the death of Milton's college friend, King, who was drowned when crossing to Ireland in a crazy vessel.

Paradise Lost.—For seven years Milton laboured at the composition of his greatest work (1658–1665); but for twice seven years or more the vast design must have been shaping itself into its wonderful symmetry within the poet's brain.

The subject was not chosen rashly or with haste, and nowhere could be found a theme richer in material for genius to work upon, or more deeply fraught with a sad human interest. Many themes, no doubt, were carefully weighed, only to be rejected. Those stories of ancient Britain, which Geoffrey of Monmouth has collected, early caught the poet's attention and held it long. We can fancy his patriotic heart thrilling proudly and gladly with the thought of rearing upon the unknown graves of Arthur and his knights a great literary monument, at which the British people gazing, should learn to love the sleeping warriors evermore. But with growing years and wisdom this idea lost its charms, a change which inspired those lines at the beginning of the Ninth Book :—

> "Since first this subject for heroic song
> Pleased me, long choosing and beginning late ;
> Not sedulous by nature to indite
> Wars, hitherto the only argument
> Heroic deemed ; chief mastery to dissect
> With long and tedious havoc fabled knights,
> In battles feigned ; (the better fortitude
> Of patience and heroic martyrdom
> Unsung ;) or to describe races and games,
> Or tilting furniture, emblazoned shields,
> Impresses quaint, caparisons and steeds,
> Bases and tinsel trappings, gorgeous knights
> At joust and tournament; then marshalled feast
> Served up in hall with sewers and seneschals ;
> The skill of artifice or office mean !
> Not that which justly gives heroic name
> To person, or to poem."

The first rough sketches of the poem took the shape of a

tragedy or mystery on the "Fall of Man." Two such draughts are among the Cambridge manuscripts. But the tragic form was luckily soon abandoned for the epic.

The burning lake—the council of the fallen spirits—the ordaining of the plan of salvation—Satan's voyage to the earth—Eden and its gentle tenants—their pure and happy life—Raphael's visit and discourse upon the war of the angels and the creation of the world—Adam's tale of his own awaking to life, and his first meeting with the lovely Eve—the temptation and the fall—Satan's triumphant return to hell, and the sudden fading of exultation under the first stroke of his doom—the intercession of the Son—the mission of Michael to eject the guilty pair—the revelation of the future to Adam in a vision—and the sad departure of our first parents from their happy garden, now guarded by the sword of God,—such are the salient points in the magnificent plan developed in the twelve books of the "Paradise Lost."

Interesting glimpses of Milton's life occur in the opening passages of certain books. Most pathetic of these is the sad but beautifully patient lament of the old man upon his blindness at the beginning of the Third. The poet's love of music, which amounted to an absorbing passion, inspired some of the grandest outbursts of his song.

Hallam says, "The conception of Satan is doubtless the first effort of Milton's genius. Dante could not have ventured to spare so much lustre for a ruined archangel, in an age when nothing less than horns and a tail were the orthodox creed." The magic power of Milton's genius conjures up before us a winged, colossal, fire-eyed shape, whose size we do not know, but are left to guess dimly at by comparison with the hugest objects. His shield is like the moon seen through a telescope; compared with the spear, which helps his painful steps over the burning marl, the mast of a mighty ship dwindles to a wand. We find no definite outline of shape, no distinct measurement of size. Vague dimness and colossal immensity deepen the awfulness of the portrait, raising it infinitely far above the absurd caricature of a terrible subject, to which Hallam's sarcasm refers.

The Adam and Eve of "Paradise Lost" are beautiful creations of poetic fancy, founding on Bible truth. They are true man and woman—not poetic ideals which are never realized in human life.

And what grand conceptions, painted as only true genius can paint, are those dreadful impersonations of Sin and Death, that bar the Arch-fiend's way at Hell's nine-fold gates! Dimness is here again a wonderful power in the poet's hand. The King of Terrors is thus described in the Second Book :—

> " The other shape,—
> If shape it might be called, that shape had none
> Distinguishable in member, joint, or limb,
> Or substance might be called that shadow seemed,
> For each seemed either : black it stood as night,
> Fierce as ten Furies, terrible as Hell,
> And shook a dreadful dart ; what *seemed* his head
> The *likeness* of a kingly crown had on."

There are in this fearful image only three points on which the mind can fasten,—the colour, black—a dreadful dart—the likeness of a kingly crown : all else is shapeless cloud.

The verse in which this noblest of English poems is written, flows on with a deep and solemn current, not broken, as the blank-verse of a dramatist must be, into various alternations of rapid and of pool—quick, brilliant dialogue, and smooth, extended soliloquy or speech—but holding the even tenor of its way amid scenes of surpassing terror and delight, changing its music and its hue as it rolls upon its onward course. Awful though its tone is, when the glare of the fiery gulf falls red upon its stream, or the noise of battling angels shakes its shores, it breathes the sweetest pastoral melody as it glides on through the green and flowery borders of sinless Eden.

Paradise Regained, a shorter epic in four books, owed its origin to Ellwood's suggestion at Chalfont. It describes in most expressive verse the temptation and the triumph of our Saviour, and is said to have been preferred by the poet himself to his grander work. Yet it must be reckoned inferior both in style and interest to its great predecessor, although the authorship of so fine a poem would have made the fame of a meaner bard.

Samson Agonistes is a dramatic poem, cast in the mould of the old Greek tragedies, for which Milton had a deep admiring love. It has, like the Greek plays, a chorus taking part in the dialogue. Samson's captivity, and the revenge he took upon his idolatrous oppressors, form the argument of the drama. It was the last great sun-burst of Milton's splendid poetic genius. Such a theme pos-sessed an irresistible attraction for the mind of an intellectual and imaginative Samson, himself smitten with blindness, and fallen in his evil days amid a revelling and blasphemous crowd, that jibed with ceaseless scorn at the venerable Puritan, whose grey eyes rolled in vain to seek the light of heaven.

Sonnets.—Many of Milton's sonnets are very fine. One of the noblest is that burst of righteous indignation evoked by the mas-sacre of the Waldenses. Cromwell and Milton felt alike in this momentous affair: while the Lord Protector threatened the thunder of English cannon, the Latin Secretary launched the thunders of his English verse against the cruel Piedmontese.

The *Areopagitica* is Milton's greatest prose work. Never has the grand theme of a free press been handled with greater elo-quence or power. Here we see how true a figure is that fine image by which Macaulay characterizes Milton's prose,—"A perfect field of cloth of gold, stiff with gorgeous embroidery."

SATAN TO BEELZEBUD.

(PARADISE LOST, BOOK I.)

"Is this the region, this the soil, the clime,"
Said then the lost archangel, "this the seat
That we must change for heaven? this mournful gloom
For that celestial light? Be it so! since he,
Who now is Sovran, can dispose and bid
What shall be right: farthest from him is best,
Whom reason hath equalled, force hath made supreme
Above his equals. Farewell, happy fields,
Where joy for ever dwells! Hail, horrors! hail,
Infernal world! and thou, profoundest Hell,
Receive thy new possessor! one who brings
A mind not to be changed by place or time.
The mind is its own place, and in itself
Can make a Heaven of Hell, a Hell of Heaven.

What matter where, if I be still the same,
And what I should be,—all but less than he
Whom thunder hath made greater ?   Here at least
We shall be free ; the Almighty hath not built
Here for his envy ; will not drive us hence :
Here we may reign secure ; and in my choice
To reign is worth ambition, though in Hell :
Better to reign in Hell, than serve in Heaven.
But wherefore let we then our faithful friends,
The associates and copartners of our loss,
Lie thus astonished on the oblivious pool,
And call them not to share with us their part
In this unhappy mansion ; or once more,
With rallied arms, to try what may be yet
Regained in Heaven, or what more lost in Hell ?"

THE ANGELS.

(PARADISE LOST, BOOK III.)

No sooner had the Almighty ceased, but all
The multitude of angels, with a shout
Loud as from numbers without number, sweet
As from blest voices, uttering joy, Heaven rung
With jubilee, and loud hosannas filled
The eternal regions.   Lowly reverent
Towards either throne they bow, and to the ground,
With solemn adoration, down they cast
Their crowns inwove with amarant and gold—
Immortal amarant, a flower which once
In Paradise, fast by the tree of life,
Began to bloom ; but soon for man's offence
To Heaven removed, where first it grew, there grows,
And flowers aloft, shading the fount of life,
And where the river of bliss, through midst of Heaven,
Rolls o'er Elysian flowers her amber stream :
With these, that never fade, the spirits elect
Bind their resplendent locks inwreathed with beams ;
Now in loose garlands thick thrown off, the bright
Pavement, that like a sea of jasper shone,
Impurpled with celestial roses smiled.
Then, crowned again, their golden harps they took—
Harps ever tuned, that glittering by their side
Like quivers hung ; and, with preamble sweet
Of charming symphony, they introduce
Their sacred song, and waken raptures high :
No voice exempt—no voice but well could join
Melodious part ; such concord is in Heaven.

CHAPTER VI.

OTHER WRITERS OF THE FOURTH ERA.

POETS.	Charles Cotton.	Algernon Sidney.
Sir William Davenant.		Robert Boyle.
Edmund Waller.	PROSE WRITERS.	Sir William Temple
Henry Vaughan.	John Gauden.	John Ray.
Sir John Denham.	Sir Thomas Browne.	John Tillotson.
Richard Lovelace.	Ralph Cudworth.	Isaac Barrow.
Abraham Cowley.	John Evelyn.	Samuel Pepys.
William Chamberlayne.	Andrew Marvell.	Robert South.

SIR WILLIAM DAVENANT, born in 1605 at Oxford, where his father kept a tavern, became laureate on the death of Ben Jonson. He was a keen Royalist, and in the Civil War suffered many changes of fortune. While an exile in France he wrote part of the tedious heroic poem *Gondibert*, which is the chief work now associated with his name. During the Commonwealth, while on board a ship bound for Virginia, he was arrested by the sailors of the Parliament, and confined at Cowes and in the Tower. Milton is thought to have aided in obtaining his release; and Davenant, we are told, repaid the kindness, when the Restoration changed the fortunes of the poets. Resuming his old occupation, the management of a theatre, Davenant spent his last years in peace, and died in 1668.

EDMUND WALLER, born in 1605, is one of the brilliant, courtly, superficial poets, who flourished under the rule of our two Kings Charles. The rich and well-born youth was a member of Parliament at eighteen. At first he took the popular side, but in the Civil War, being detected in a Royalist plot, he suffered imprisonment and fine. After a sojourn in France, he came home to celebrate in verse the glory of Cromwell; and not long afterwards, in a poem of inferior merit, to welcome the returning Stuart king. He then sat for Hastings, for various other places in successive parliaments, and at eighty years of age for a Cornish borough. He died and was buried in 1687 at Beaconsfield, where, little more than a century later, the body of the great Edmund Burke was laid in the grave. Waller's verses are smooth, elegant, and polished; but they are little more. His speeches in Parliament were, in general, excellent and telling.

HENRY VAUGHAN, born in Brecknockshire in 1614, was first a lawyer and then a physician. His chief merit lies in his *Sacred Poetry*. But, with much deep feeling, it has all the faults of the Metaphysical school, many of them in an exaggerated form.

SIR JOHN DENHAM, the author of *Cooper's Hill*, was born in 1615 at Dublin, the son of the Chief Baron of Exchequer in Ireland. At Oxford he became acquainted with the most brilliant and dissolute of the young Cavaliers, and with these he afterwards gambled away the fortune left him by his father. " Cooper's Hill " is a descriptive poem, varied by the thoughts suggested by such striking objects in the landscape as the Thames, Windsor Forest, and the flats of Runnymede. It is a good specimen of local poetry. Like all the Royalist party, he rose in fortune and favour at the Restoration, becoming then a surveyor of royal buildings and a Knight of the Bath. He died in 1668. A poor tragedy, the *Sophy*, founded on incidents in Turkish life, was also written by him.

RICHARD LOVELACE, born in a knightly mansion in 1618, was the most unhappy of the Cavalier poets. For his gallant struggles in the cause of his king, he suffered imprisonment, during which he collected and published his *Odes and Songs*. The marriage of his sweetheart with another,—she thought that he had died of his wounds in France,—broke his hopes and his heart ; and through the years of the Commonwealth he continued to sink, until in 1658 he died, a ragged and consumptive beggar, in an alley near Shoe Lane. His poetry resembles Herrick's, but with less sparkle and more conceit.

ABRAHAM COWLEY, born in London in 1618, was the son of a stationer in Cheapside. He became a Fellow of Trinity College, Cambridge. Like Pope, he wrote poems in early boyhood, and published a volume when only thirteen. His Royalist principles caused him to be expelled from Cambridge ; and, after some time at Oxford, he went with Queen Henrietta to France, where he lived for twelve years. Disappointed after the Restoration in his hopes of preferment, he retired to Chertsey by the Thames, where his old timbered house is still pointed out. There he lived, in studious quiet but not content, for seven years, when in 1667 a neglected cold killed him after a fortnight's illness. He wrote *Miscellanies*, the *Mistress* or *Love Verses*, *Pindaric Odes*, and the *Davideis*, an heroic poem upon David. His light sparkling renderings of Horace and Anacreon are his happiest efforts. In many of his works there is a constant straining after effect, which has been well named *wit-writing*. His prose is simple, pure, and animated. No poet of his day was more popular than Cowley, who is now but little read.

WILLIAM CHAMBERLAYNE, of Shaftesbury in Dorset, born in 1619, wrote two long poems, which Campbell rescued from obscurity. They are *Love's Victory*, a tragi-comedy; and *Pharonnida*, an heroic poem. The latter, especially, contains some fine and varied scenes. Chamberlayne died in 1689. A country doctor practising at Shaftesbury, he associated little with the great men of his day.

CHARLES COTTON, the witty poet-friend of Walton, was a Derbyshire man, born there in 1630. His father, Sir George, left him the encumbered estate of Ashbourne. Cotton was always in money difficulties; but his light, easy nature enabled him to pass through life unsoured. The Dove, a noted trout-stream of his native shire, was the great resort of Cotton and his old friend Izaak, to whom many of his poems were addressed. The poet died in 1687.

PROSE WRITERS.

JOHN GAUDEN was born in 1605, at Mayfield in Essex, and was educated at St. John's, Cambridge. He is considered, upon satisfactory evidence, to have written the celebrated work, *Eikon Basiliké*,* or *the Portraiture of His Most Sacred Majesty* (Charles I.) *in his Solitude and Sufferings*, which came out some days after

* The Royal Image.

the king's death. Some still think that Charles wrote the book himself: it was published under the royal name. But Gauden's complaining letters to Clarendon, coupled with other evidence, seem to prove that this Royalist clergyman was the author of the "Eikon." Fifty editions were sold in one year. Milton, in his *Eikonoklastes* (Image-breaker), smote the "Eikon" with his weighty pen: but it bravely stood the blow. Gauden, who was made, under Charles II., Bishop of Exeter, and afterwards Bishop of Worcester, died in 1662.

SIR THOMAS BROWNE, born in London in 1605, was a physician in practice at Norwich. His works—*Religio Medici*, or the Religion of a Physician (1642),—*Pseudodoxia Epidemica*, or Vulgar Errors (1646),—and *Hydriotaphia*, a treatise on the Sepulchral Urns of Norfolk (1658)—display, perhaps, the most extreme specimens our literature affords of that style, loaded with heavy Latin words, which was so dear to Dr. Johnson's pen. Coleridge, with whom Browne was a favourite author, praises the enthusiasm and entireness with which the eccentric doctor handles every subject he takes up. Browne died in 1682.

RALPH CUDWORTH, born in 1617, was Regius Professor of Hebrew at Cambridge. He published in 1678 a great work, entitled *The True Intellectual System of the Universe;* in which he maintains that there is an Almighty, All-wise God,—that there is an everlasting distinction between justice and injustice,—and that the human will is free. This work was intended to combat widespread atheistic doctrines. A treatise on *Eternal and Immutable Morality*, also from Cudworth's pen, appeared after his death; and many of his manuscript works are preserved in the British Museum. He died in 1688.

JOHN EVELYN, born in 1620 to the enjoyment of a good fortune, spent his abundant leisure in popularizing science. The *Sylva*, which contains an account of forest trees and their uses, proved the means of stirring up proprietors to plant oak-trees largely over the country, for use in ship-building. *Terra*, a work on agriculture, appeared in 1675. But the most interesting of Evelyn's works is his *Diary*, which presents us with a clear view of English life, especially under Charles II., and a description of all great public events, in which the writer had any interest. The "Diary" was not published till 1818. Evelyn's snug house and beautiful gardens at Deptford were shamefully abused by his imperial tenant, the Czar Peter, who used often to amuse himself by riding on a wheelbarrow through a great holly hedge. Evelyn died in 1706.

ANDREW MARVELL, Milton's friend, wrote both poetry and prose. He was born in Lincolnshire in 1620–21. Upon finishing his education at Cambridge, he travelled, and afterwards acted as secretary to the embassy at Constantinople. In 1657 he became assistant to Milton, the Latin Secretary. As member for Hull, he is said to have refused a bribe of £1000 offered by Charles II. His treatise on *Popery and Arbitrary Government in England* was, perhaps, the greatest effort of his pen. His poems are marked with elegance and pathos. In 1678 he died, it was rumoured, by poison.

ALGERNON SIDNEY, son of the Earl of Leicester, was born about 1621. He was a colonel of cavalry in the Parliamentary army during the Civil War; but was no friend to Cromwell, whose assumption of power he condemned. After the Restoration he remained on the Continent for seventeen years; and then, having received a pardon from the King, he returned to see his aged father. Placing himself in opposition to the court, he was beheaded in 1683, on a charge of conspiracy against the government. A folio of 462 pages, entitled *Discourses on Government*, is the only important work of Sidney that we possess. It was written in opposition to the doctrine of divine right. The establishment of a republic in England was Sidney's life-long dream.

ROBERT BOYLE, son of the Earl of Cork, was born at Lismore in 1627. Distinguished for his researches in Chemistry and Natural Philosophy, he was one of the original members of the Royal Society. Air and the air-pump were his favourite subjects. His numerous works consist of philosophical treatises, and several works on religious topics. His *Occasional Reflections on Several Subjects*, published in 1665, gave origin to Swift's well-known caricature, *Meditation on a Broom-stick*. Boyle died in 1691.

SIR WILLIAM TEMPLE, noted as the negotiator of the Triple Alliance, and as that English envoy at the Hague who arranged the marriage between William of Orange and the Princess Mary of England, was born in London in 1628. His scheme of a Council of Thirty, to bring the perplexed government of Charles II. into order, proved a failure. During the intervals of public life Temple wrote many clear and musical *Essays* on various subjects, among which we may note those on the *Netherlands*, *Government*, and *Learning*. Gardening, too, his favourite recreation, employed his pen. His last days were spent at Moor Park in Surrey, where young Jonathan Swift was for a time his secretary. He died in 1699.

JOHN RAY, a blacksmith's son, born in 1628, at Black Notley in Essex, was a very celebrated naturalist. His *General History of Plants*, and his popular work on the *Wisdom of God in the Works of Creation* are his chief productions. Birds, fishes, insects, and quadrupeds, all attracted the attention of Ray ; but botany was his favourite study. He died in 1705.

JOHN TILLOTSON, who became Archbishop of Canterbury after the Revolution, was originally the son of a Puritan clothier at Sowerby near Halifax, where he was born in 1630. His associations at Cambridge, and certain books he read, gradually led to a change of views ; and he entered the Church of England after 1662. He first became celebrated as a preacher at St. Lawrence's in the Jewry. Having held the primacy for only three years, he died in 1694. His *Sermons*, sold after his death for nearly £3000, are his only literary remains. They are strong and sensible, but often without much literary grace.

ISAAC BARROW, the predecessor of Newton in his mathematical professorship at Cambridge, was born in London in 1630. His father was a linen-draper. Barrow was a man of versatile talent. Anatomy, chemistry, mathematics, astronomy, Greek, optics, and theology,—all engaged his attention at various times ; and in all he did well. His literary works are chiefly mathematical and theological. The former are in Latin ; the latter, consisting of sermons and polemical treatises, were written with much care, and are remarkable for easy fertility of thought. Barrow died of fever in 1677, having attained the honourable stations of Master of Trinity, and Vice-Chancellor of his University.

SAMUEL PEPYS, son of a London tailor, rose, by the help of his cousin Montagu, to be Secretary to the Admiralty under Charles II. and James II. He is worth remembrance as the writer of a most amusing *Diary*, originally kept in short-hand, which depicts the life of the time even to the minutest details of dinners, lace, and coat-buttons. The vanities and faults of the writer himself are displayed with comical unconcern. But the poor fellow had little notion that readers of the nineteenth century would. have many a hearty laugh over his secret memoranda. He died in 1703.

ROBERT SOUTH, reputed to have been the wittiest of the old English divines, was the son of a London merchant, and was born in 1633 at Hackney. Educated at Oxford, he was chosen Public Orator in 1660. Besides being chaplain to Lord Chancellor Clarendon and rector of Islip in Oxfordshire, he held some other valuable livings. South's wit, unhappily, was often mixed with venom. Extreme in his opinions, he held all Nonconformists in abhorrence. But his love of royalty was fully as strong as his attachment to the National Church. No clergyman of his day exceeded him in the fervour of those sermons in which he maintained the doctrines—so delightful to the Stuarts—of passive obedience and divine right. South died in 1716. In spite of his intolerance as a public preacher, he bore the private reputation of a good and charitable man.

FIFTH ERA OF ENGLISH LITERATURE.

FROM THE DEATH OF MILTON IN 1674 A.D. TO THE FIRST PUBLICATION OF THE TATLER IN 1709 A.D.

CHAPTER I.

THE COURT OF CHARLES II.

Poison.	Spread of vice.
French influence.	The theatres.
Shamelessness.	The poison too strong.
A sad picture.	What Burke said.

IT is not our purpose to present a minute picture of the court-life, rotten to the very core, which blighted English morals and English literature during the reign of the second Charles. But, to preserve the completeness of our plan, this painful and repulsive subject must be touched upon; for there are many of our English writers whose spirit cannot be fully understood unless we know at least a little of the moral air they breathed, and the fountains from which they drank their inspiration. Mephitic air and poisoned streams they truly were from which the courtly authors of the Restoration Era drew the sustenance and productive power of their minds. The little band of Puritan authors, folded in the mantle of righteousness, stood apart,—untainted and serene.

These Puritans, when in the ascendant, had with an iron hand crushed down many amusements, the desire of which is a natural appetite of man, and had thus created a hunger and a longing for the forbidden things, which became an unappeasable frenzy when the Restoration brought a change. The nation then plunged madly into the opposite extreme. And when we remember that from France, with the restored King, there came a troop of new fashions and amusements, which were but the old vices of human nature tricked out in modern attire, we shall see what kind of food the royal Court provided for the famished people.

An utter absence of shame marked the mode of life in this most wicked age. It was not that gambling as high, drinking as deep, adulteries as vile, had not been in other reigns. What stamps the reign of Charles II. with a deeper brand of infamy is the fact, that there was no attempt to throw even the thinnest veil over the evil that was rampant everywhere. The blush of innocence seemed almost forgotten in the court-circles of England. Men and women were alike immoral—nay, depraved.

On Sunday the first of February, 1685—the night before Charles was seized with his mortal illness—the great gallery of Whitehall presented a scene of "inexpressible luxury and profaneness, gaming and all dissoluteness," which may be taken as a specimen of what had been witnessed there a thousand times before during his disgraceful reign. The king sat talking with three of his mistresses. A French page, on whom the royal hand delighted to shower presents of ponies, guineas, and fine clothes, sang love-songs to the group. At a large table close by, where two thousand yellow guineas were heaped into a great bank, sat twenty of the profligate courtiers playing basset, then the fashionable game at cards. This went on, as it had been going on for five and twenty years, in the full gaze of all who chose to come and see. Little wonder that the poison should spread right and left, sinking down to the lowest classes of the people; and still less wonder that such shameless, undisguised licentiousness, should be faithfully reflected in the plays and the books, which were written in the hope of extracting smiles and gold from the beautiful profligates and high-born gamesters who surrounded the sullied throne.

Whitehall, as was natural, gave the tone to all English society; and books are but the reflection of what society thinks and does.

So the vices of Whitehall were mirrored in many of the chief writings of the time. All the Comedies, and much of the Poetry, written from the Restoration to the close of the century, and later too, are disgustingly vicious. It took many a long year to root out the poisonous weeds that, sown in this age, spread their tangling fibres through the best soils of English poetry. Even yet the English stage has hardly been cleansed from the pollutions heaped upon it by the play-wrights, who manufactured highly-flavoured vice for the delectation of the wicked men and women that hung by the skirts of the worst of our Stuart kings.

When the theatres were re-opened at the Restoration, a new splendour was thrown around their performances. The female characters began to be personated by women. Rich dresses, beautifully painted scenes, and fine decorations, added to the attractions of the drama a dazzling effect, unknown in earlier times. Crowds flocked nightly to the play: and how were they entertained? Almost all duties to God and to man were held up to public mockery. Virtue in every form, especially truth and modesty, came in for the largest share of the comedian's jeering; the strongest sympathies of the audience were stirred, and their loudest applause drawn forth, by the triumph of the profligate, and the ridicule cast upon the victims of his success.

The plays of Dryden are nearly all tainted with the poisons that floated thick in the social atmosphere of the time; but those of Wycherley are, perhaps, the most diseased specimens of our dramatic literature that have lived to the present day. The satires, songs, and novels of the period also bear the brand and scars of vice, and flaunt them openly in the eyes of all. The writers of such things penned them without compunction; and there were few who thought it shame to *read* of vicious deeds, which sun and moon saw *done* by night and day without a blush or a pang of conscience. Yet there are things more dangerous than this brazen effrontery, this shameless show of iniquity. Men grow disgusted and surfeited with the grossness of paraded

sin.   Edmund Burke was a great and wise man ; but he
said a very foolish and pernicious thing, when, at the close of his
indignant outburst in memory of the fallen Queen of France, he
told the world that " vice itself loses half its evil by losing all its
grossness."   Never was a greater falsehood spoken.   The vice
which is draped in the garb of virtue, or has the varnish of an
outward refinement laid over its leprosy, is tenfold more infectious
and destructive than the shameless wickedness which wears no
veil to hide its loathsome front.

CHAPTER II.

SAMUEL BUTLER.

Born 1612 A.D..........Died 1680 A.D.

Butler's poem.	Marriage.
Birth and education.	Turns author.
Clerk at Earl's Coomb.	Disappointed.
Better days.	His death.
Household of Luke.	Character of his work.
Taking notes.	Illustrative extract.

AFTER the Restoration of King Charles II. had thrown the Puritans into the shade, a man of almost fifty years, who had seen the bloody drama of the Revolution played out, and had been thrown by the changes of those troubled years into close contact with both Cavaliers and Roundheads, wrote a poem which cast even deeper ridicule upon the men of the steeple-hat and the sad-coloured dress than all the studied mockeries of a plumed and ringleted court could do. The man was Samuel Butler; the poem was *Hudibras*. What Shakspere is among English dramatists, Milton among English epic poets, Bunyan among English allegorists, Butler is among the writers of English burlesque—prince and paramount.

He sprang from a lowly stock. His father farmed a few acres in the parish of Strensham in Worcestershire; and there the poet came to life in 1612. His schooling he got in Worcester; but the want of money prevented him from enjoying the benefit of a college education, although he is thought to have resided for some time at Cambridge, hovering round the halls of learning without being able to find an entrance there.

His abilities, however, gained him a few friends. He spent some time at Earl's Coomb in his native shire, acting as clerk to Justice Jeffreys; and his leisure hours, while he held this humble post, were devoted, not alone to study, but also to the refining enjoyments of music and painting. Not long ago some sorry daubs, patching the broken windows of a house at Earl's Coomb, were shown as the productions of the poet's pencil. If these were his, they only afforded another proof, in addition to the myriads we already have, that there are few men who can excel in more than one branch of art or study.

It was a happy day for Butler, which transferred him to the mansion of the Countess of Kent. We do not know in what capacity he served this rich and noble lady; but there he found— what, no doubt, deeply gladdened the heart of the rustic scholar— the free use of a fine library, and the conversation of a learned man, Selden, who then managed the affairs of that household. Here he lived—how long we cannot say—revelling in books of all kinds, and often repaying by literary help the kindness of the scholarly steward.

Butler's life, as it has come down to us, is full of gaps. Knocked about from one employment to another, he acquired by his very misfortunes that rare and varied knowledge of human life which he displays so admirably in "Hudibras." The next scene in which he appears is the grave household of Sir Samuel Luke, a strict Puritan of Bedfordshire, who held a county office—that of scout-master—under Cromwell. The atmosphere which Butler here breathed must have been somewhat uncongenial; yet it was his residence among the Puritans that prepared him for his famous work, supplied material for his fine word-pictures, and sharpened his stinging pen. Little did the Roundhead knight and his quiet household think that the poor tutor, whose bubbling, irrepressible wit, no doubt often scandalized the circumspect decorum of the dining-hall, was, like a traitor in the camp, taking silent notes, soon to be printed with a vengeance.

Another gap, and Butler re-appears as secretary to the Earl of Carbery, the President of Wales, who conferred on him the stewardship of Ludlow Castle. It was then after the Restoration, and brighter days seemed to be dawning for the Royalist wit. So good were his prospects, that, although there must have been grey hairs under the huge bush of false curls which it was then the fashion to wear, he ventured to marry, as he thought, a fortune. But ill-luck still pursued him; his wife's money vanished through the failure of the securities, and Butler found himself as poor as ever. Then it was that he first came before the public as an author. The first part of "Hudibras" was **1663** published, and sprang at once into fame. The moment A.D. was most propitious, for the degraded Puritans afforded a favourite mark for the shafts of courtly ridicule. The loud insulting laugh of the Cavalier party rang everywhere, as they read verses which chimed in with every feeling they had. The Merry Monarch was so tickled with the debates between the Presbyterian justice and the Independent clerk, that he often quoted witty couplets from the book. Yet fame did not mend the fortunes of poor Butler. He got promises from his noble friends, but he got little more; and in 1680 he died obscurely in Rose Street, Covent Garden, having suffered deeply from the bitter pangs of that hope deferred, which maketh the heart sick.

" Hudibras" is justly considered the best burlesque poem in the English language. For drollery and wit it cannot be surpassed. Written in the short tetrameter line, to which Scott has given so martial a ring, its queer couplets are at once understood and easily remembered—none the less for the extraordinary rhymes, which now and then startle us into a laugh. What can we expect but broad satiric fun in a poem in which we find a canto beginning thus :—

> " There was an ancient sage philosopher,
> That had read Alexander Ross over."

The adventures of Don Quixote, no doubt, suggested the idea of this work. Sir Hudibras, a Presbyterian knight, and his clerk, Squire Ralpho, sally forth to seek adventures and redress grievances, much as did the chivalrous knight of La Mancha and his trusty Sancho Panza. Nine cantos are filled with the squabbles, loves, and woes of master and man, whose Puritan manners and opinions are represented in a most ludicrous light.

THE LEARNING OF HUDIBRAS.

> He was in logic a great critic,
> Profoundly skilled in analytic;
> He could distinguish, and divide
> A hair 'twixt south and south-west side;

On either which he would dispute,
Confute, change hands, and still confute;
He'd undertake to prove by force
Of argument a man's no horse;
He'd prove a buzzard is no fowl,
And that a lord may be an owl—
A calf, an alderman—a goose, a justice—
And rooks, committee-men and trustees.
He'd run in debt by disputation,
And pay with ratiocination:
All this by syllogism, true
In mood and figure, he would do.
For rhetoric, he could not ope
His mouth but out there flew a trope;
And when he happened to break off
I' th' middle of his speech, or cough,
H' had hard words, ready to show why,
And tell what rules he did it by:
Else, when with greatest art he spoke,
You'd think he talked like other folk;
For all a rhetorician's rules
Teach nothing but to name his tools.
But, when he pleased to shew 't, his speech
In loftiness of sound was rich;
A Babylonish dialect,
Which learned pedants much affect:
It was a party-coloured dress
Of patched and piebald languages;
'Twas English cut on Greek and Latin,
Like fustian heretofore on satin.
It had an odd promiscuous tone,
As if he had talked three parts in one;
Which made some think, when he did gabble,
Th' had heard three labourers of Babel;
Or Cerberus himself pronounce
A leash of languages at once.

CHAPTER III.

JOHN BUNYAN.

Born 1628 A.D..........Died 1688 A.D.

Youth of Bunyan.	Rebuked for cursing.	Life in Bedford Jail.
His soldier life.	Begins to preach.	Last years and death.
His marriage.	Arrested.	The Pilgrim's Progress.
First convictions.	Pleading of his wife.	Illustrative extract.

A BOOK which little children love to read, may safely be pronounced a good book. In our English literature there are two works that have been tried for many score of years by this unfailing test, and have never been found wanting. These are the *Pilgrim's Progress* of Bunyan and the *Robinson Crusoe* of Defoe. For many generations golden heads and rosy cheeks have been bent over the never-tiring pages; nor can we imagine a time when children shall cease to care about the perilous travels of Christian, or shall not grow half-afraid, yet filled with a strange delight, when they read of Friday's footstep in the sand.

That famous Puritan tinker, who wrote the " Pilgrim's Progress," was born in the village of Elstow, a mile from Bedford, in the year 1628. He was emphatically a man of the people. Few have passed through so fierce an ordeal of mental struggle and religious horror. He tells us in his *Grace Abounding to the Chief of Sinners*, a sort of religious autobiography, that even at the age of nine or ten, fearful dreams, and thoughts of the burning lake and the devils chained down to wait for the great Judgment, haunted him at intervals. Then, when the pain lulled, he plunged into sin, running riot in many vices at an early age. While yet a boy, he enlisted in the army of the Parliament, and saw some service in the war. He tells us of a narrow escape he had. At a certain siege—the siege of Leicester, it is said—he was selected as sentinel for a certain post, and was on the point of going out to mount guard, when another soldier asked leave to go instead of him.

Bunyan agreed; and the poor fellow, who took his place, was shot dead with a bullet through the brain. Yet in spite of this, and two escapes from drowning, he grew more careless still.

At the age of nineteen he married a young woman of his own rank in life. They had, he tells us, "neither dish nor spoon betwixt them;" but she brought to his humble home two religious books, and she herself had found the Pearl of great price. Faithfully and lovingly this tender wife dealt with the wayward boy, until she led him to read these good books, the legacy of her dying father, and brought him with her to church. There one Sunday he heard a sermon on the duties of that day, and the sin of breaking in on its holy calm, which flashed a new light into his soul. With a heavy heart he went home; and when, as usual, he went out in the afternoon on the village green to play cat with his roistering associates, and in the full flush of the game had struck the piece of wood one blow away from the hole—suddenly as in old times a hand wrote on the wall of the Chaldean palace —these words darted into his mind, "Wilt thou leave thy sins and go to heaven, or have thy sins and go to hell?" Although he got a momentary shock, yet Bunyan still remained unimpressed, until, about a month later, he was cursing at the shop window of a neighbour so horribly as to draw a severe rebuke from the woman of the house, who was herself of the worst character. Such a check from such lips silenced the blasphemer, who, standing with down-hung head, wished, as he touchingly says, "that he was a little child again, that his father might learn him to speak without this wicked way of swearing." He then began to read the Bible and to amend his life—repenting, among other things, of his dancing, his ale-quaffing, and his bell-ringing. The first two might, certainly, lead to sin, but we cannot class the third among great offences. Yet we must not smile at Bunyan's fears lest the bells might fall and kill him, for earnestness like his is too rare and too sublime for ridicule. However, the incident which made the deepest impression on Bunyan's soul, and which must certainly be looked on as the turning-point in his life, was his happening to overhear a conversation about the new birth

among three or four poor women sitting at a door in Bedford.
So thankfully did they speak of what God, through Jesus Christ,
had done for their souls, and so lovingly did they quote the Bible
words, that Bunyan went away feeling as he had never felt before,
and unable to think of anything but the conversation he had heard.

Thus, knot after knot, the bonds of sin were cut from his soul,
and John Bunyan became a new man.   About the year 1656 he
commenced to preach in the villages of Bedfordshire, having
already been for three years a member of a Baptist congregation.

With slight interruption he continued this good work until the
Restoration, when he was arrested as a holder of conven-
ticles, which were then declared unlawful. By Justice Win- **1660**
gate he was committed to Bedford Jail, where, in spite of a   A.D.
noble effort made by his second wife to obtain his release,
he remained for twelve years.   Within a chamber of the old Swan
Inn that faithful wife, with blushing face but undaunted heart,
pleaded before the judges and the gentlemen of the shire for her
prisoned husband. " Will your husband leave preaching?" said
Judge Twisden. " My lord," said the noble woman, " he dares not
leave preaching so long as he can speak." And so Bunyan lay in
jail, his wife and children weaving laces, upon which he fixed tags,
to get them daily bread. Happily for us, his jailer was a kind-
hearted man, disposed to deal as gently as he could with his
ward. Bunyan had two books with him—the Bible and " Fox's
Book of Martyrs," which he studied constantly and deeply. He
had also pen and ink, with liberty to use them; and thus it was
that to these years of cell-life we owe our matchless allegory, *The
Pilgrim's Progress*—the joy of childhood and the solace of old age
—a book second only to the Bible.   Towards the end of the twelve
years the rigour of Bunyan's confinement was relaxed ; he was allowed
to go out into the town ; and once he went to London. And through
all he preached at every opportunity, often meeting his little flock
under the silent stars, where the trees cast dark shadows   **1672**
upon the sleepy Ouse.   His last year in jail is memorable   A.D.
for his ordination in the room of his old minister and
friend, Mr. Gifford. Then, released by the aid of Barlow, Bishop of

Lincoln, who knew him by his books and his preaching, he held his services in a barn at Bedford, which was purchased for £50, and fitted up as a chapel. There he laboured with voice and pen for sixteen years, often visiting London, where the churches were always crowded to the doors when he preached. A

1688 journey under heavy rain from Reading to London brought
A.D. on a fever, of which he died in his sixty-first year. A

hundred years ago, a green decaying grave-stone, on which was inscribed in faint lettering, " Here lies John Bunyan," was pointed out in the cemetery at Bunhill Fields.

Macaulay's opinion of Bunyan is worth remembrance. In a fine review of Southey's edition, he says that "Bunyan is as decidedly the first of allegorists, as Demosthenes is the first of orators, or Shakspere the first of dramatists." The adventures of Christian need no description. They are told in plain, unvar. nished English, which pretends to no excellence of style, and yet has a power that more polished language often lacks. Bunyan, a common working-man, had no thought of style as he wrote. All he desired was, to place vividly before his readers certain pictures, which he himself saw almost as clearly as if he had been Christian trudging on a real highway, instead of Bunyan writing within dark prison walls. And this he has done with such marvellous skill, that we, too, feel the green grass of the Delectable Mountains beneath our feet, and shudder as the awful darkness of the Valley of the Shadow of Death closes around us. First published in 1678, this wonderful book ran through ten editions in seven years. It has since been printed in countless thousands, and has been translated into all the chief tongues of earth.

The *Holy War*, which describes the siege and capture of the city of Mansoul by Diabolus, is another allegory from the pen of Bunyan, also written within his cell at Bedford.

THE VALLEY OF THE SHADOW OF DEATH.

(FROM "THE PILGRIM'S PROGRESS.")

I saw then in my dream, so far as this valley reached, there was, on the right hand, a very deep ditch; that ditch it is into which the blind have led the blind in all ages, and have both there miserably perished. Again, behold, on the left hand, there was a very dangerous quag, into which even if a good man falls, he finds no bottom for his feet to stand on: into that quag King David once did fall, and had no doubt therein been smothered, had not He that is able plucked him out. The pathway was here also exceeding narrow, and therefore good Christian was the more put to it: for when he sought, in the dark, to shun the ditch on the one hand, he was ready to tip over into the mire on the other; also, when he sought to escape the mire, without great carefulness he would be ready to fall into the ditch. Thus he went on, and I heard him here sigh bitterly; for besides the danger mentioned above, the pathway here was so dark, that oft-times when he lifted up his foot to set forward, he knew not where, or upon what, he should set it next. About the midst of the valley I perceived the mouth of Hell to be; and it stood also hard by the way-side. And ever and anon the flame and smoke would come out in such abundance, with sparks and hideous noises, that he was forced to put up his sword, and betake himself to another weapon, called *all-prayer*. So he cried, in my hearing, *O Lord, I beseech thee, deliver my soul.* Thus he went on a great while, yet still the flames would be reaching towards him. Also he heard doleful voices, and rushings to and fro; so that sometimes he thought he should be torn to pieces or trodden down like mire in the streets.

CHAPTER IV.

RICHARD BAXTER.

Born 1615 A.D...............Died 1691 A.D.

Early life.	Secession.
Kidderminster.	Busy life.
The Civil War.	His trial.
Defends monarchy.	Chief works.
Tempted.	Illustrative extract.

No name stands higher in the history of our theological literature than that of Richard Baxter, the great Puritan divine. Born in 1615 at Rowdon, a village in Shropshire, he passed, after some desultory work at school, and a course of private theological study, into the ministry of the Church of England. During the nine months after his ordination, which took place when he was twenty-three, he held the mastership of the Free Grammar School at Dudley. Then, having acted as curate of Bridgenorth **1640** for a while, he settled down in 1640 in the parish of A.D. Kidderminster, where his untiring devotion to his flock, and the deep earnestness of his sermons, soon won for him a considerable name. Already some of those oaths, which worked such fatal mischief in the Church at that day, had crossed the path of Baxter; but he had passed them by unheeded. So long as his conscience told him that he was rightly doing his Christian work, he troubled himself little to obey every letter of the ritual laid down for his observance.

The Civil War then broke out; and although he was the friend of monarchy, his religious leanings caused him to side with the Parliament. He became a chaplain in the Roundhead army, followed his regiment through many scenes of blood, and yet always preserved the character of a peace-maker, as befitted a true soldier of the Cross. Standing midway between two extremes of conflicting opinion, he incurred, as such good men have often incurred, the suspicion of both parties. While he loved royalty, he disliked the conduct of the King; but, for all his dislike, it was with a heart full of sorrow that he beheld the discrowned head of Charles degraded to a bloody death. And when the throne lay overturned in the tempest of Revolution, the pastor of Kidderminster, standing face to face with the great Oliver himself, dared, with a noble courage, to lift his voice in defence of that ancient monarchy, which has ever been the glory of the land. Meek and moderate though he was, and much as he loved peace, he was too good and too honest a man to bate one jot of the principles which he held dearer than life or fame.

Soon after the Restoration, Clarendon tried to tempt him with an offer of the bishopric of Hereford; but he steadily refused this and other golden baits. Baxter was a Trimmer in religion as in politics; he loved the name, for he held it to be synonymous with "peacemaker." Believing that Episcopacy was in many respects a good and lawful system, he yet sided with the Presbyterians in denying the absolute need of ordination by a bishop. And he further agreed with the Presbyterians in adopting the Bible as the sole guide of man in faith and conduct. Accordingly, when the Act of Uniformity was passed in 1662, this good man had no resource but to leave the bosom of the National **1662** Church. Taking shelter at Acton in Middlesex, he A.D. spent several years in active literary work, suffering heavy penalties more than once for his strict adherence to the simple worship, which he believed to be right and true in the sight of God. We cannot follow him through the trials of those troubled years. After the Indulgence of 1672 his life was chiefly spent in London, where he preached and wrote with incessant industry. There were many days and weeks when his pulpit was silent; for the Nonconformists, among whom he was a leader, were ground from time to time to the very dust by the infatuated Stuarts. But his pen was always busy; and at length it goaded his enemies into open war.

A passage in his *Commentary on the New Testament*, complaining bitterly of the sufferings inflicted on the Dissenters, was held to be

sufficient ground for a charge of sedition against the veteran minister, now worn down by age and illness. The trial came on at Guildhall, before that bloated drunkard, who, a little later, stained the pure ermined robe of English justice deep red in the slaughter
1685 of the Bloody Assizes. All attempts on the part of
A.D. Baxter and his lawyers to obtain a hearing were roared down by the brutal Jeffreys. "Richard, Richard, dost thou think we will let thee poison the court ? Richard, thou art an old knave. Thou hast written books enough to load a cart, and every book as full of sedition as an egg is full of meat." From such a judge, and a servile jury, there was no escape. Pronounced "Guilty" after a moment's conference, the old man was sent to jail, because he could not pay the heavy fine imposed upon him; and he lay in the King's Bench prison for nearly eighteen months. Soon after his release, which was obtained by the kindness of Lord Powis, he had the joy of seeing the great second Revolution usher in a brighter day of civil and religious freedom. Then, full of years and crowned with their good works, he descended into an honoured grave, December 8th, 1691.

His published writings, which were nearly all upon divinity, reached at least to the enormous number of one hundred and sixty-eight. In the quietude of his study at Kidderminster he composed those two works of great practical power, by which he is best known, *The Saints' Everlasting Rest*, and *A Call to the Unconverted*. We have also from this gifted pen *A Narrative of his Own Life and Times*, to which Johnson and Coleridge agree in awarding the highest praise. The wonder of Baxter's laborious life becomes yet greater, when we remember that, like our Saxon Alfred and other illustrious men, he had to struggle through nearly all his years with a delicate and feeble frame. How he spent his vacation hours, when heavy sickness compelled him to snatch a little rest, may be judged from the following passage :—

BAXTER REGRETS HIS HASTE IN WRITING.

Concerning almost all my writings, I must confess that my own judgment is, that fewer, well studied and polished, had been better; but the reader, who can safely censure the books, is not fit to censure the author, unless he had been upon the place, and acquainted with all the occasions and circumstances. Indeed, for the *Saints' Rest*, I had four months' vacancy to write it, but in the midst of continual languishing and medicine; but, for the rest, I wrote them in the crowd of all my other employments, which would allow me no great leisure for polishing and exactness, or any ornament; so that I scarce ever wrote one sheet twice over, nor stayed to make any blots or interlinings, but was fain to let it go as it was first conceived: and when my own desire was rather to stay upon one thing long than run over many, some sudden occasions or other extorted almost all my writings from me; and the apprehensions of present usefulness or necessity prevailed against all other motives ; so that the divines which were at hand with me still put me on, and approved of what I did, because they were moved by present necessities as well as I; but those that were far off, and felt not those nearer motives, did rather wish that I had taken the other way, and published a few elaborate writings; and I am ready myself to be of their mind, when I forget the case that I then stood in, and have lost the sense of former motives.

CHAPTER V.

JOHN DRYDEN.

Born 1631 A.D..........Died 1700 A.D.

Brick and marble.	His great Satire.	Will's coffee-house.
Dryden's early life.	Religio Laici.	Alexander's Feast.
Astræa Redux.	Change of creed.	The Fables.
Writing for the stage.	The Hind and Panther.	His death.
His prose.	Loses the laurel.	French influences.
Literary income.	Translates Virgil.	Illustrative extract.

DR. SAMUEL JOHNSON, borrowing a classic metaphor, which de-scribes what Augustus did for Rome, says in reference to English poetry, that Dryden found it brick and left it marble. Let it not be forgotten that Johnson, in his "Lives of the Poets," (a most unsafe book,) has ignored Shakspere and vilified Milton. To the mental eye of the ponderous critic, "Paradise Lost" and "Macbeth" were built of common brick, while Dryden's Satires and Fables shone with the lustre of Parian stone. We condemn the compari-son as wholly exaggerated, and partly untrue; and yet we would not for a moment deny Dryden's exalted rank as a poet and a master of the English tongue.

Our knowledge of Dryden's early life is meagre. Born of Puri-tan parents, on the 9th of August 1631, at Aldwinckle in Northamptonshire, he received his school education at Westminster, under Dr. Busby, of birchen memory. Then, elected a Westminster scholar, he passed to Trinity College, Cambridge, where, no doubt, he wrote English verses, as he had often done at school. But he seems to have passed without marked distinction through his college course.

1631
A.D.

When the great Oliver died, the young poet created some sen-sation by a copy of verses which he wrote upon the sad event. Two years later, he celebrated the restoration of Charles Stuart, in a poem called *Astræa Redux.* So sudden a change of political principle has been harshly blamed; but we can scarcely censure young Dryden for feeling, as all England felt at the time, that a load of fear had rolled away when Charles came back from exile to fill his father's throne.

Inheriting only a small estate of £60 a year, Dryden was com-pelled to take to literature as a profession, devoting his pen at first to the service of the newly-opened theatres. *The Wild Gallant* was his first play. His marriage with Lady Elizabeth Howard took place about the opening of his theatrical career.

Then play after play came flowing from his fertile pen; all tainted, sad to say, with the gross licentiousness of that shameful age; and cramped, like the shape of a tight-laced fashionable, into rhyming couplets, which were but a poor substitute for the noble music of Shakspere's blank-verse. In all, during eight and twenty years Dryden produced eight and twenty plays; among the chief of which we may note *The Indian Emperor* (1667), and *The Conquest of Granada* (1672). This dramatic authorship was then the only field in which an author could hope to reap a fair crop of guineas, for the sale of books was as yet miserably small. It is sad to contemplate a man of genius driven to waste the elec-tric force of his mind upon a kind of writing for which his talents were but slightly fitted—sad to see the composer of one of the finest English odes, and of satires that rival the master-pieces of Juvenal, forced to drudge for a dissolute green-room, and to play the rhyming buffoon for a coarse and ribald pit. Nor was this the only evil. Mean passions were engendered by this pitiful struggle for popular applause. Poor Elkanah Settle, a rhymster of the day, one of Rochester's creatures, who was afterwards impaled on the point of Dryden's satiric pen, incurred great John's wrath by some slight successes in the dramatic line, which the silly man had prefaced with a puny war-blast of defiance. The torrent of abuse, which Dryden poured round this shallow brain, would better become a shrewish fishwife than one of England's greatest bards.

Let us turn from the mournful sight of wasted and degraded genius to Dryden's other works. Though writing so busily for the stage, he had yet found spare hours to produce his *Annus*

Mirabilis, a poem on the year of the Great Fire, and his *Essay on Dramatic Poesy;* in the latter of which he labours hard but vainly to prove that rhyme is suited to tragedy.   The Essay is a valuable piece of criticism, which derives additional charms from the elegance of its prose and its frank avowal of Shakspere's surpassing genius.   And here, dismissing Dryden's prose, we may say that few English authors have written prose so well.   His *Prefaces* and *Dedications*—things which, though now nearly banished from our books, were then most elaborate pieces of writing—are brilliant and polished essays upon various topics of literature and art.

Not unprofitably did Dryden fight the battle of life with his pen.   His dramatic work brought him over £300 a year; in 1670 he became poet-laureate (worth £100 a year and a tierce of wine), and royal historiographer (worth another £100 a year.)   The pity is, that for this £500 a year he had to dip his pen in pollution, on peril of losing the favour of a wicked Court.

At fifty, Dryden's genius was in full bloom.   In 1681 he produced that marvellous group of satiric portraits which forms the first part of *Absalom and Achitophel.*   Old Testament names, borrowed from David's day, denote the leading men of the corrupted English court.   Monmouth was Absalom; Shaftesbury, Achitophel; Buckingham, Zimri. *   And never has poet winged more terrible weapons of political warfare than the shower of bright and poisoned lines that fell on the luckless objects of Dryden's rage.   Conscious for the first time, after this great effort, of the dreadful wounds his pen could give, the poet did not henceforth spare its use.   Other satires, *The Medal*, launched against Shaftesbury alone, and *Mac Flecknoe*, hurled at the head of poet Shadwell, speedily followed ; but neither of these came up in poetry or point to his great satire of 1681.

1681

A.D.

The poem, *Religio Laici*, written about this time, displays the author's mind convulsed with religious doubts.   A severe mental struggle resulted in his abandonment of Protestantism for the Roman Catholic faith; an event which, unhappily for his repu-

---

* The satirist had a special grudge against Buckingham, who, in 1671, brought out a farce called *The Rehearsal*, in which Dryden and his heroic dramas were held up to public ridicule.

tation, occurred at a time when such a change was the high road to royal favour. It is right, however, to say, that the pension of £100, which some believe him to have received as the reward of his defection, had been already granted by Charles, and was now merely restored by James. On the whole, the change seems to have been one for which Dryden had deeper motives than the desire of gold or royal favour. He reared his children, and died in the Roman Catholic faith. In a beautiful allegory, *The Hind and Panther*, he exhibits his new-born affection for the Church of his adoption, which he paints as a "milk-white hind, immortal and unchanged." The Church of England is represented by the panther, "the fairest creature of the spotted kind"; while dissenting sects play their various parts as bears, hares, boars, and other animals. In spite of the grotesque antithesis involved in making wild beasts discuss theology, it affords a splendid specimen of Dryden's chief quality—his power of reasoning in rhyme.

When William and Mary ascended the English throne, Dryden, who thus lost his laureateship with its guineas and its wine, sank into a bookseller's hack, depending for daily bread almost entirely upon his pen. He then undertook a work for which his genius was quite unfitted—the translation into English verse of the sweet and graceful Virgil. The verses of the Latin poet have the velvet bloom, the dewy softness, the delicate odour of a flower; the version of the Englishman has the hardness and brilliance of a gem : and, when we find only flowers cut in stone, where we expect to see flowers blooming in sweet reality—no matter how skilful the lapidary, how rich the colouring, or pure the water of the jewel—admiring the triumph of art, we miss the sweetness of nature, and long to exchange the rainbow play of coloured light for the stealing fragrance and tender hues of the living blossom. For this heavy task of turning the Georgics and the Æneid into English pentameters, the work of three toilsome years, the poet received £1200. The translation **1697** was published in 1697. It was not his first task of the A.D. kind. The year before, he had translated part of Juvenal and all Persius; and, earlier, had employed his pen upon scattered poems from Horace, Ovid, and Theocritus. We think sorrowfully of the old man toiling at his desk upon this heavy task, often pursuing the "sad mechanic exercise" with little heart; for we believe he must have felt that his English rendering did not breathe the true spirit of Virgil's verse. Yet, in spite of such occasional clouds, the sunset of his life was fair. He was the great literary lion of his day; and no country stranger, of any taste for letters, thought his round of London sights complete, unless he had been to Will's Coffee-house in Russell Street, where, ensconced in a snug arm-chair, by the fire or out on the balcony, according to the season, old John sat, pipe in hand, laying down the law upon disputed points in literature or politics. Happy was the favoured rustic who could boast to his admiring friends that he had got a pinch of snuff from the great man's box!

During these sunset years he wrote his finest lyric—the *Ode for St. Cecilia's Day*, which is generally known as *Alexander's Feast*, and which, notwithstanding Hallam's unfavourable opinion, still remains a favourite; and not without deserving to be so. It cost him a fortnight's toil. Changing his metre with the variations of his theme, the poet sweeps the strings of the fierce and softer passions of the human breast; or, to use another figure, choosing with rapid and skilful finger the brightest threads from what is to many the tangled skein of our English tongue, he weaves of them a brilliant tapestry, glowing with a succession of fair and terrible pictures. No English poem better illustrates the wonderful pliancy of the tongue we speak. But it takes a master's touch to weave the threads as Dryden did; his silk and gold would change in meaner hands to grey hemp and rusted wire.

The composition of his *Fables* occupied the poet's last two years. For this work, of about twelve thousand lines, he received somewhat more than £250 from Jacob Tonson, who sold books at the Judge's Head in Chancery Lane. "The Fables" rank with Dryden's finest works. Consisting of tales from Boccaccio and Chaucer, dressed in modern diction, they are, unhappily, often stained with a deeper tinge of licentiousness than even the originals possess.

After a life of literary toil, productive of many splendid works, yet scarcely one whose splendour is not crusted over with the foul, obscuring fungus of a vicious age, Dryden let fall his pen from a dying hand. At sixty-eight, a neglected inflammation of the foot carried him off after a short illness. His body was buried in Westminster Abbey, where his name may be read among the names of many wiser and purer men.

May 1,
1700
A.D.

Most of this poet's faults sprang from the corrupting spread of French influences. Ever since the days of the Confessor and the Conqueror, France has been the arbiter of English fashions in the way of dress: our British ladies still prize the bonnets, silks, and gloves of Paris and Lyons far beyond those of their native land. Little harm in all this. But it was a black day for England, when the ship which carried Charles the Second to a throne bore also over the narrow sea a cargo of French vices and false tastes, to spread their poison through court and coffee-house, and even to mingle with the ink that dropped from the poet's pen. The trick of writing tragedies in rhyme—the trick of intermingling firm, strong English sense, with tinsel-scraps of French, like *fraicheur* and *fougue*—the trick of often substituting cold, glittering mannerisms, for the sweet fresh light of natural language—are the chief symptoms of this foreign disease in Dryden's work. In that marble palace which, according to Johnson, he reared from the rude blocks of the English tongue, there are too many gilded cornices and panellings from Versailles. Yet in this foreign adornment he was far surpassed by his imitator and admirer of the next generation, little Alexander Pope, who unquestionably ranks *facile princeps* among the painters and decorators of the literary guild.

CHARACTER OF SHAFTESBURY.

(FROM "ABSALOM AND ACHITOPHEL.")

Of these the false Achitophel was first ;
A name to all succeeding ages curst :
For close designs and crooked counsels fit ;
Sagacious, bold, and turbulent of wit ;

Restless, unfixed in principles and place ;
In power unpleased, impatient of disgrace :
A fiery soul, which, working out its way,
Fretted the pigmy body to decay,
And o'er-informed the tenement of clay.
A daring pilot in extremity ;
Pleased with the danger when the waves went high,
He sought the storms ; but, for a calm unfit,
Would steer too nigh the sands to boast his wit.
Great wits are sure to madness near allied,
And thin partitions do their bounds divide ;
Else why should he, with wealth and honour blest,
Refuse his age the needful hours of rest ?
Punish a body which he could not please ;
Bankrupt of life, yet prodigal of ease ?
And all to leave what with his toil he won,
To that unfeathered two-legged thing—a son.

CHARACTER OF BUCKINGHAM.

Some of their chiefs were princes of the land :
In the first rank of these did Zimri stand ;
A man so various that he seemed to be,
Not one, but all mankind's epitome :
Stiff in opinions, always in the wrong,
Was ev'rything by starts, and nothing long ;
But, in the course of one revolving moon,
Was chemist, fiddler, statesman, and buffoon.
Blest madman ! who could ev'ry hour employ
With something new to wish, or to enjoy.
Railing and praising were his usual themes ;
And both, to shew his judgment, in extremes :
So over-violent, or over-civil,
That every man with him was God or devil.
In squandering wealth was his peculiar art ;
Nothing went unrewarded but desert :
Beggared by fools, whom still he found too late,
He had his jest, and they had his estate.
He laughed himself from court, then sought relief
By forming parties, but could ne'er be chief ;
For, spite of him, the weight of business fell
On Absalom and wise Achitophel ;
Thus, wicked but in will, of means bereft,
He left not faction, but of that was left.

CHAPTER VI.

JOHN LOCKE.

Born 1632 A.D..........Died 1704 A.D.

Literary greatness.	Tutor to the Ashleys.	His death.
Birth and education.	Exile in Holland.	The Essay.
Studies medicine.	The Revolution.	Minor works.
Diplomacy.	Public employments.	Illustrative extract.

LOCKE's great work, *An Essay concerning Human Understanding*, has done more than any other book to popularize the study of mental philosophy. He, therefore, well deserves a place among the great names of English literature.

Born in 1632, at Wrington near Bristol, he received his education at Westminster School, and Christ Church, Oxford; and in the halls of that venerable college he learned, as the illustrious Bacon had learned at Cambridge, to dislike the philosophy of old Aristotle, at least when applied to the production of mere wordy bubbles by the schoolmen of Western Europe. Choosing the profession of medicine, he bent his great mind to the mastery of its details; but the feebleness of his constitution prevented him from facing the hard and wearing work of a physician's life. Well for England that it was so; else one of the greatest of our mental philosophers might have drudged his life away in the dimness of a poor country surgery, had he not most luckily possessed a pair of delicate lungs. So the thin student turned diplomatist, and went to Germany as secretary to Sir Walter Vane. Declining an invitation to enter the Church, he afterwards found a home in the house of Lord Ashley, where he acted as tutor to the son, and afterwards to the grandson, of his patron. The last-named pupil became that distinguished moralist whose lofty periods delighted the *literati* of Queen Anne's reign. To the fortunes of Lord Ashley, who received the earldom of Shaftesbury in 1672,

Locke attached himself with tender fidelity ; and with these fortunes his own brightened or grew dark. At the table of his noble friend he met the first Englishmen of the day; and when, in 1675, fears of consumption led him to seek health in the sunnier air of France, his residence at Montpelier and at Paris brought him into contact with many eminent French scholars and literary men. When Shaftesbury regained power in 1679, he called Locke to his side ; and when misfortune came, the Earl and his faithful friend found a refuge in hospitable Holland. There Locke lived for six years (1682–88), enjoying the society of learned friends,—especially the weekly meeting which they established for the discussion of philosophical questions,—and patiently bringing on towards its end the great book, which has made his name famous. It mattered little to the invalid scholar, in his quiet lodging at Amsterdam, that his name had, by command of the King, been blotted out from the list of Christ Church men. A real danger threatened him, when the English ambassador demanded that he, with many others, should be given up by the Dutch government, as aiders and abettors of Monmouth in that ill-fated invasion which ended on the field of Sedgemoor. But the clouds blew past, and the Revolution soon re-opened his native land to the exile. A man so distinguished would have been a strong pillar of William's throne, had his health permitted him to engage actively in the public service. As it was, he became a Commissioner of Appeals at £200 a year, and afterwards, for a short time, one of the members of the Board of Trade ; but London fog and smoke soon drove the poor asthmatic old man into the purer air of the country. Oates in Essex,

1704 the mansion of his friend, Sir Francis Masham, opened
A.D. its kindly doors to him ; and there, with his Bible in his hand, he faded gently out of life. We cannot help loving the simple and unpretending scholar, with a heart full of the milk of human kindness, who did life's work so humbly, yet so well.

Locke's *Essay*, published in 1690, was the fruit of nearly twenty years' laborious thought. One day, while he was conversing with five or six friends, doubts and difficulties rose so thick around the subject of their talk, that they could not see their way. Locke, to use his own words, proposed that "it was necessary to examine their own abilities, and see what objects their understandings were, or were not, fitted to deal with." So the four books of the "Essay" began, and his exile enabled him to bring them to a close. In clear, plain, homely English, sometimes rather tawdrily dressed with figures of speech, he lays down his doctrine of ideas, which he derives from two great sources—sensation and reflection. The third book, which treats of words, their defects and their abuse, is considered to be the most valuable part of this celebrated work.

His chief minor works are, *Letters concerning Toleration*, written partly in Holland—two *Treatises on Civil Government*, designed to maintain the title of King William to the English throne— *Thoughts concerning Education*, in which he deals not only with book-learning, but with dress, food, accomplishments, morality, recreation, health, all things that belong to the development of the mind or the body of a child—and a sequel to this, called *The Conduct of the Understanding*, which was published after his death.

THE POWER OF PRACTICE.

Some men are remarked for pleasantness in raillery; others, for apologues, and apposite, diverting stories. This is apt to be taken for the effect of pure nature, and that the rather, because it is not got by rules, and those who excel in either of them, never purposely set themselves to the study of it as an art to be learnt. But yet it is true, that at first some lucky hit, which took with somebody, and gained him commendation, encouraged him to try again, inclined his thoughts and endeavours that way, till at last he insensibly got a facility in it without perceiving how; and that is attributed wholly to nature, which was much more the effect of use and practice. I do not deny that natural disposition may often give the first rise to it; but that never carries a man far without use and exercise, and it is practice alone that brings the powers of the mind as well as those of the body to their perfection. Many a good poetic vein is buried under a trade, and never produces anything for want of improvement. We see the ways of discourse and reasoning are very different, even concerning the same matter, at court and in the university. And he that will go but from Westminster Hall to the Exchange, will find a different genius and turn in their ways of talking; and one cannot think that all whose lot fell in the city were born with different parts from those who were bred at the university or inns of court.

CHAPTER VII.

OTHER WRITERS OF THE FIFTH ERA.

POETS.	John Owen.	William Penn.
Earl of Roscommon.	Edward Stillingfleet.	Robert Barclay.
Earl of Dorset.	Thomas Burnet.	Daniel Defoe.
Sir Charles Sedley.	Thomas Sprat.	Matthew Henry.
Earl of Rochester.	Lady Rachel Russell.	Richard Bentley.
Thomas Otway.	William Wycherley.	Sir John Vanbrugh.
Matthew Prior.	William Sherlock.	John Arbuthnot.
John Philips.	Gilbert Burnet.	William Congreve.
PROSE WRITERS.	John Strype.	George Farquhar.
Henry More.		

POETS.

WENTWORTH DILLON, Earl of Roscommon, born in 1634, was the nephew of Strafford. He wrote, according to Pope, the only unspotted poetry in the days of Charles II. His chief work is called *An Essay on Translated Verse;* he also translated Horace's *Art of Poetry*, and wrote minor poems. He died in 1685.

CHARLES SACKVILLE, Earl of Dorset, born about 1637, wrote, among other songs, one beginning, *To all you ladies now at land,* which he composed at sea the night before a battle. He held high posts at court under Charles II. and William III. His verses were only occasional recreations. He is rather to be honoured for his patronage and aid of such men as Butler and Dryden than for his own compositions. He died about 1705.

SIR CHARLES SEDLEY, born in 1639, was in his prime during the reign of Charles II. His *Plays*, and especially his *Songs*, are sparkling, light and graceful, with perhaps more of the true Cavalier spirit in them than the works of contemporary lyrists display. He took a prominent part in bringing about the Revolution of 1688. Thirteen years later (1701) he died.

JOHN WILMOT, Earl of Rochester, was born in 1647. His early death at thirty-three, brought on by his own wild and drunken profligacy, left him but a short time to win a writer's fame.

Yet some of his *Songs* have lived, though most of them are stained too deeply with the vices of the man who wrote them, to permit their circulation in our purer days.

THOMAS OTWAY, the greatest dramatic name of Dryden's age, was born in 1651, at Trotting in Sussex. The son of a clergyman, he was educated at Winchester and Oxford. From the halls of Oxford he passed to the London stage ; but had only small success as an actor. Not so when he took up the dramatist's pen. Almost the only gleam of prosperity that favoured the poet shone in 1677, when, by the interest of the Earl of Plymouth, he was made a cornet of dragoons, and shipped off to Flanders. But he soon lost his commission by dissipation, and returned to his play-writing. He died in 1685, a poor and wasted debauchee, who had yet, by his tragedies, greatly surpassed the laboured dramas of Dryden, and had come not far short of the most pathetic scenes in Shakspere. Three years before his death he produced *Venice Preserved*, the play for which his name is still honoured on the English stage. The *Orphan* is a powerful but indelicate tragedy.

MATTHEW PRIOR, born in 1664, at Abbot Street in Dorsetshire, rose from humble life—his uncle kept a tavern at Charing Cross—to be secretary at the Hague, ambassador to the Court of Versailles, and a Commissioner of Trade. The kindness of the Earl of Dorset, who found the little waiter of the Rummer Inn reading Horace one day, enabled him to enter St. John's, Cambridge, of which college he became a Fellow.· He won his place in the diplomatic service by writing, in conjunction with Montagu, *The Town and Country Mouse*, a burlesque upon Dryden's "Hind and Panther." Prior's best known poems are light occasional pieces of the Artificial school. His longest and most laboured work is a serious poem, called *Solomon*. After having lain, untried, in prison for two years, accused by the Whigs of treasonable negotiation with France, he lived on the profits of his poems and the bounty of Lord Oxford, at whose seat of Wimpole he died in 1721.

JOHN PHILIPS, author of *The Splendid Shilling* and other works, was born in 1676, the son of the Archdeacon of Salop. During his short life—he died in 1708, aged thirty-two—he wrote several poems in the intervals of his medical studies. "The Splendid Shilling" imitates and tries to parody the style of Milton.

PROSE WRITERS.

HENRY MORE, born in 1614, lived a hermit-life at Cambridge, much as the poet Gray did in later days. He was a great admirer of Plato, and wrote much on metaphysical subjects, of which the mistier kind had a strong attraction for his pen. *The Mystery of Godliness—The Mystery of Iniquity—The Immortality of the Soul* are among the themes he dealt with. More died in 1687. He wrote poems also, of which the principal is called *Psychozoia, or Life of the Soul.*

JOHN OWEN, born in 1616, at Stadham in Oxfordshire, was a great favourite with Cromwell, who took him to Dublin and to Edinburgh, and caused him to be made Vice-Chancellor of Oxford. He was long the leading minister of the Independent body. Among his numerous, but far from graceful writings, we may name *An Exposition of the Hebrews; A Discourse of the Holy Spirit;* and *The Divine Original of the Scriptures.* This amiable and learned man, whom even his opponents could not dislike, died in 1683.

EDWARD STILLINGFLEET, whose life extended from 1635 to 1699, became Bishop of Worcester in 1689. He wrote *Origines Sacrae, or a Rational Account of Natural and Revealed Religion,* and also a *Defence of the Trinity;* the latter in reply to part of Locke's Essay. Stillingfleet's *Sermons,* too, are justly remembered for their good sense and force of style.

THOMAS BURNET, Master of the Charter-house, was born in 1635, and died in 1715. His chief work, originally in Latin, but rendered into English in 1691, was *The Sacred Theory of the Earth.* Written in a day when geological science was yet unborn, it is, of course, full of error and wild speculation ; but its eloquence and picturesque grandeur of style redeem it from oblivion. Burnet's other principal works were, *Archæologia Philosophica—On Christian Faith and Duties*—and *The State of the Dead and Reviving.* He held some peculiar religious views, which debarred him from pre-ferment in the Church.

THOMAS SPRAT, born in 1636, at Fallaton in Devonshire, was educated at Wadham College, Oxford, and became Bishop of Rochester in 1684. He wrote with remarkable eloquence a *History of the Royal Society; An Account of the Rye-house Plot;* and a short *Life of Cowley.* Sprat died in 1713.

LADY RACHEL RUSSELL, the daughter of the Earl of Southampton, and the devoted wife of that Lord William Russell who was beheaded in 1683 for an alleged share in the Rye-house Plot, deserves remembrance here for her beautiful *Letters.* They were published fifty years after her death, which took place in 1723.

WILLIAM WYCHERLEY, born in Shropshire in 1640, belongs to the most shameful period in the history of the English people and their literature. Educated as a lawyer, he abandoned his profession for the worst dissipations of London life. His *Comedies,* upon which his reputation as a literary man is founded, reflect the pollutions of the writer's mind. When it is said that they were all the fashion with the wits and beauties of Charles the Second's court, their character becomes clear at once. Wycherley died in 1715.

WILLIAM SHERLOCK, Dean of St. Paul's, and known as the author of a *Practical Discourse concerning Death,* was born in 1641. He wrote much against the Dissenters. His *Vindication of the Trinity* involved him in a controversy with South. He wrote also a treatise *On the Immortality of the Soul.* Sherlock died in 1707.

GILBERT BURNET, born at Edinburgh in 1643, was the son of a Scottish judge. Having graduated at Aberdeen, Gilbert entered the Church. Minister of Salton in Haddingtonshire—Professor of Divinity at Glasgow—preacher in the Rolls Chapel, London—an exile on the Continent, residing chiefly at the Hague—he became, at the Revolution, Bishop of Salisbury, as a reward for his adherence to William of Orange. His literary fame rests principally on his historical works—the *History of the Reformation,*

and the *History of My Own Times.* The latter, sketching the Civil
War and the history of Cromwell, enters with greater minuteness
into the period between the Restoration and the Treaty of Utrecht.
Burnet's work on the *Thirty-nine Articles* is his chief theological
treatise. He died in 1715.

JOHN STRYPE, born in 1643, deserves remembrance for his
biographical and antiquarian works. *Lives of Cranmer, Cheke, Grindal, Whitgift,* and many others, proceeded from his pen, besides the
Annals of the Reformation, and *Ecclesiastical Memorials.* He
was a clergyman of the Church of England, and held many posts,
the last being a lectureship at Hackney. He died in 1737, aged
ninety-four.

WILLIAM PENN, the son of the celebrated admiral, was born in
1644. Though more distinguished as a colonist than as an author,
he wrote several treatises in defence of Quakerism. *No Cross No
Crown, The Conduct of Life,* and *A Brief Account of the People
called Quakers,* are among his works. He died in 1718.

ROBERT BARCLAY, born in 1648, at Gordonstown in Moray,
followed his father, Colonel Barclay, in joining the virtuous and
God-fearing sect, then called Quakers, but now known as Friends.
His *Apology* for these persecuted Christians is a remarkable theological work. He died in 1690.

DANIEL DEFOE, born in 1661, was the son of a London butcher.
After trying various occupations,—hosier, tile-maker, and woollen-
merchant—he devoted himself to literature, and took up pen
on the Whig side. For his political attacks he suffered the pillory, imprisonment, and fine. But his greatest efforts were works
of fiction, of which *Robinson Crusoe,* published in 1719, is the
chief. No English writer has ever excelled him in his power of
painting fictitious events in the colours of truth. His simple
and natural style has much to do with this. *The Relation of
Mrs. Veal's Apparition,* prefixed to *Drelincourt on Death,* affords,
perhaps, the best specimen of Defoe's wonderful power of clothing
fiction with the garb of truth. He died in 1731, leaving behind
him many debts, and a host of works amounting to two hundred
and ten books and pamphlets.

MATTHEW HENRY, born in Flintshire in 1662, studied law, but afterwards became a Nonconformist minister. Chester and Hackney were the scenes of his labour. His name is now remembered chiefly for that *Commentary on the Bible*, which his death in 1714 prevented him from finishing.

RICHARD BENTLEY, who was born in 1662 and died in 1742, became Master of Trinity College, Cambridge, and Regius Professor of Divinity in that university. He has been called the greatest classical scholar England ever produced. Editions of *Horace, Terence,* and *Phædrus* are among his principal works. He also edited *Milton,* but with very small success.

SIR JOHN VANBRUGH, born about 1666, was a sugar-baker's son, who produced architectural designs, and wrote witty but licentious comedies. Under Queen Anne he was Clarencieux King-at-arms; and under George I., Comptroller of the royal works. *The Provoked Wife* is, perhaps, his best play. Blenheim and Castle Howard were his chief works as an architect. Vanbrugh died in 1726.

JOHN ARBUTHNOT, born in Kincardineshire in 1667, was noted in London as a physician, a writer, and a wit. He wrote, besides several other things, much of *Martin Scriblerus,* published in Pope's works—the *History of John Bull* (1712), which was a fine piece of ridicule aimed at Marlborough—treatises on the *Scolding of the Ancients,* and the *Art of Political Lying.* The very titles of his works express their humorous tone. He was physician in ordinary to Queen Anne, and died in 1735.

WILLIAM CONGREVE was an exception to the common lot of his dramatic brethren, for he lived and died in opulence and ease. Born in Yorkshire about 1670, he became at twenty-two a dramatic author. But he had the good fortune to obtain several government situations, which, when swelled by the emoluments of the secretaryship of Jamaica, received in 1715, were worth about £1200 a year. The same calamity that darkened the old age of Milton, fell on the latter days of Congreve ; but the licentious dramatist had not the same pure, angelic visions, to solace his hours of blindness as passed before the mental eye of the great Puritan.

Congreve wrote one tragedy, *The Mourning Bride.*   His comedies are steeped in vice.   How much this writer was idolized in his own day, may be judged from the strange honours paid by a Duchess of Marlborough to his memory.   Having caused images of the dead poet to be made, one of ivory and one of wax, she placed the former daily at her table, and caused the feet of the latter to be regularly blistered and rubbed by her doctors, as had been done for the gouty limbs of the dying man, when he was a member of her household.   Congreve's life came to a close in 1729.   ·

GEORGE FARQUHAR, born in Londonderry in 1678, was an actor, a military officer, and a writer of comedies.   His chief plays are *The Recruiting Officer* (1706), and *The Beaux' Stratagem* (1707). He died in his thirtieth year.   Wycherley, Vanbrugh, Congreve, and Farquhar form a group of comic dramatists, who reflect vividly in their works the glittering and wicked life which courtiers and fashionables lived during the half century between the Restoration and the accession of the Guelphs.

SIXTH ERA OF ENGLISH LITERATURE.

FROM THE FIRST PUBLICATION OF THE TATLER IN 1709 A.D. TO THE PUBLICATION OF PAMELA IN 1740 A.D.

CHAPTER I.

NEWSPAPERS AND SERIALS.

Earliest newspapers.	Parliamentary debates.	Reviews.
Papers of the Civil War.	Early reporting.	Magazines.
London Gazette.	The Times.	Encyclopædias.
The Newsletter.	High pressure.	Periodical writers.
Liberty of the Press.	Addison and Steele.	A literary contrast.

THE *Acta Diurna* of ancient Rome, the *Gazetta* of Venice, and the *Affiche* of France contained the germs from which grew the modern newspaper or journal. Small sheets or packets of news began to appear in England during the reign of James I.; and when the Thirty Years' War set all Britain on the *qui vive*, one of these, entitled *The News of the Present Week*, was established in 1622, to give the latest particulars of the great Continental struggle. This may be considered our first *regular* newspaper. The earlier news-pamphlets had no fixed time of publication.

The Civil War between Charles and his Parliament gave a political tone to this infant journalism. Each party had several organs; and a furious paper war kept pace with the sterner conflict that convulsed the land. Very curious and often comical are the titles of these news-books—for papers they can scarcely be called, being chiefly in the form of quarto pamphlets. Once, twice, thrice a week there came out a host of bitter and malicious *Scotch Doves, Parliament Kites, Secret Owls;* and when the *Weekly*

Discoverer saw the light, at once there sprang up a rival, *The Weekly Discoverer Stripped Naked.* *Mercurys* of many sorts abounded on both sides.

The reigns of Charles II. and his brother James were fruitful in newspapers of small size, and generally of short life. The fantastic folly of the age was often reflected in both title and contents. How we should laugh now at the appearance of a paper entitled, as was one of these, *News from the Land of Chivalry, being the Pleasant and Delectable History and Wonderful and Strange Adventures of Don Rugero de Strangmento, Knight of the Squeaking Fiddlestick.* Macaulay tells us that the quantity of matter contained in one of these publications during a whole year was not more than is often found in two numbers of the "Times." Of *The London Gazette,* which came out on Mondays and Thursdays, "the contents generally were a royal proclamation, two or three Tory addresses, notices of two or three promotions, an account of a skirmish between the imperial troops and the Janissaries on the Danube, a description of a highwayman, an announcement of a grand cockfight between two persons of honour, and an advertisement offering a reward for a strayed dog. The whole made up two pages of moderate size."

At this time the *Newsletter* did the work of our daily papers. News was to be learned chiefly in the coffee-houses, which were thronged all day long by the idle men, and for some hours were frequented by even the busiest men, in the capital. The evening before post-day, the correspondents of the country districts gathered all the scraps of intelligence they had collected in their daily rambles into the form of a letter, which went down duly by the post to enlighten justices of peace in their offices, country rectors in their studies, village tradesmen and neighbouring farmers in the sanded tap-rooms of rustic ale-houses. When we remember the slowness of communication a hundred and fifty years ago, it will not seem wonderful that the country was a week or a fortnight behind the town in the current history of the times. To us, who have electric wires and penny papers, this would seem intolerable.

It is not our purpose here to enter into a detailed account of the growth of the English newspaper. To do so would carry us far beyond our available space. The press, when freed in 1694 from restrictions on its liberty, advanced with rapid strides. There was something of a check, when the Tory government in 1712 laid a stamp-tax on newspapers—a halfpenny on half a sheet, a penny on a whole sheet, and a shilling on every advertisement. But through all checks its onward progress was steady and sure.

Yet it was not until the end of the eighteenth century that the parliamentary debates began to be reported at any length. Nor was it without a fierce struggle that the London printers won this important right. Of those who did stout battle for the public in this contest, William Woodfall was most prominent. A meagre summary at first, and some days later, an elaborate version of the speeches, some perhaps written, but many certainly retouched, by Dr. Johnson or other leading *littérateur* of the day, formed the parliamentary debate as it appeared in print before Woodfall's reporting began. Having set up the *Diary* in 1789, this extraordinary man would listen for many hours, from the strangers' gallery in St. Stephen's, to the progress of the debate, and then, going to the printing office, would write off from memory all that he had heard. His report sometimes extended to sixteen columns —each not, of course, containing anything like the matter of a column in the "Times" of our day, but yet large enough to make the feat a rare and remarkable instance of what the educated memory can retain. This, however, was too much for a man to do for more than a few years. There are, indeed, few men who could do it at all. The employment of several reporters to divide the labour, and the subsequent introduction of reporting in shorthand, enabled the papers to furnish earlier and more accurate accounts of what was done in the Houses of Parliament.

On the first of January 1788 appeared the first number of *The Times*, the new form of the little *Daily Register*, that had already been for three years in existence. It was a puny, meagre thing, compared with its gigantic offspring, which is delivered damp from the press at thousands of London doors every morning before early breakfast-time, and before the sun has set has been read over nearly all England. But it grew and throve; and when in 1814 the power of steam was employed to work the press, the foundation was laid of the magnificent success this giant sheet has since achieved. A newspaper paying, as the "Times" does, between £40,000 and £50,000 a year for paper-duty alone, is indeed a wonderful triumph of human energy, and a colossal proof of the reading-power of our age.

There is something feverish about the rate at which the drums of the newspaper press revolve now-a-days. At ten or eleven o'clock at night some noted member of the House—a Gladstone or a Palmerston, a Derby or a Disraeli—gets upon his legs to speak. For two hours he enchains the House with his eloquence, and, perhaps, concludes by turning back on his foes the weapon aimed at the very heart of his party. At twelve or one, in some brightly lighted room in Printing-House Square, an editor sits down to his desk, with a digest of this very speech before him, to tear it to pieces or applaud it to the skies, as it may happen to chime or clash with his own opinions on the question of debate. Not far away sit the keen-eyed reporters, busied with their task of transcribing their short-hand notes for the press. On for the bare life race all the busy pens. The wheels of the brain are all whirring away at top speed and highest pressure. At last article and reports are finished. Then arises the rattle of composing-sticks and type. The great drum of Hoe's machine, and its satellite cylinders, begin their swift rounds; and before eight o'clock in the morning the bolt of the Thunderer has fallen on the speech-maker or his foes, as the case may be.

Journalism employs thousands of able pens over all the kingdom, and has done much to lift the literary profession from the low position in which all but its most prominent members lay during a great part of the last century. Let us now turn to take a brief view of the rise of those other periodicals, whose abundance and excellence form one of the leading literary features of the present age.

Although Defoe's *Review*, begun in 1704, was, strictly speaking, the first English serial, it was not until Richard Steele and Joseph Addison began to write the pleasant and eloquent papers of *The Tatler*, that the foundation of our periodical literature was firmly laid. *The Spectator* followed—a yet nobler specimen of the early and now old-fashioned serial. Then came, at various intervals throughout the eighteenth century, and with varying fortunes, *The Gentleman's Magazine*, *The Guardian*, and *The Rambler*,— the last of which was written nearly all by Samuel Johnson ; and in Scotland, *The Mirror* and *The Lounger*, to which Henry Mackenzie was the principal contributor.

The older periodicals, which now lie upon our tables, date for the most part from the early years of the present century. We take the Reviews first for a few words of comment. Earliest, and in former times most brilliant of these large Quarterlys, was *The Edinburgh Review*, whose Whig principles are symbolized by the buff and blue of its pasteboard cover. One day in 1802, Sydney Smith, meeting Brougham and some other young Liberals at Jeffrey's house, which was then a high flat somewhere in Buccleuch Place, Edinburgh, proposed to start a Review. The happy idea took the fancy of all present; and the first number of the "Edinburgh" soon appeared. Its circulation reached in 1813 to 12,000 or 13,000 copies. This periodical was afterwards enriched by the stately and magnificent essays of the historian Macaulay.

When the Tories saw the success and felt the power of the "Edinburgh," they in 1809 started *The Quarterly Review*, which has ever since been growing in public favour. John Gibson Lockhart, the son-in-law and biographer of Sir Walter Scott, was for many years editor of the "Quarterly." *The Westminster Review* began in 1824 to represent Radical opinions. These serials and their younger brethren, appearing every quarter in thick volumes at a comparatively high price, contain articles on the leading books and political questions of the day. A great work is often singly reviewed; but the usual plan adopted is to collect a number of works bearing on a topic of prominent interest, and upon these to found an essay of tolerable length. Recently, a lighter sort of

review artillery has been brought into the literary and political
battle-field. Discarding the heavy guns, fired at long intervals,
as lumbering and comparatively ineffective, the writers of *The
Saturday Review* and its tribe discharge weekly volleys of stinging rifle-balls and smashing round-shot from their light twelve-
pounders, often with tremendous effect. *The Athenæum* stands at
the head of the weekly reviews, which are devoted solely to literature, science, and art.

The Magazine, which is generally a monthly serial, though dealing somewhat in light reviewing, aims rather at the amusement
and instruction of its readers by a dozen or so of original articles,
including tales, sketches, essays, and short poems. *Blackwood,
Fraser, The New Monthly, The Dublin University, Bentley,* and
Tait are the older favourites; but, within a year or two, there has
come upon our tables a flood of cheaper periodicals of this class,
and, riding on the highest crest of the wave, the rich maize-coloured
Cornhill, which numbers its readers by the hundred thousand, and
supplies for a solitary silver shilling a monthly crop of heavy
golden grain, reaped from the finest brain-soils in the land.

A class of serials, deserving a longer notice than we can give
them here, are the Encyclopædias. Chief of these is the *Encyclopædia Britannica*, of which the eighth edition has just been
completed, enriched with articles from the first pens in Britain.
The *Edinburgh Encyclopædia*, edited by Sir David Brewster, is
valuable for its scientific articles. *Lardner's Cyclopædia* contains a valuable series of histories,—part of England by Mackintosh, Scotland by Scott, and Ireland by Moore.

No men have done more for periodical literature than the Messrs.
Chambers of Edinburgh. They enjoy the credit of having set on
foot the cheapest form of serial by the publication in 1832 of
their *Journal*, which has lived through a long career of usefulness,
and is flourishing still in almost pristine vigour amid a host of
younger rivals.

We have in this chapter glanced along the whole course of our
serial literature up to the present day, because we shall not have
an opportunity of returning to the subject, and no historical

sketch of English literature would be complete without such a view. Laying down the last number of the "Quarterly" or the "Cornhill," we bethink us of the little leaf, on which, a hundred and fifty years ago, poor Dick Steele and stately Mr. Addison wrote the first magazine and review articles, that deserve the name in English literature; and are filled with wonder at the vast increase of the kind. There are many Addisons and very many Steeles among the literary men of our day; but so great is the supply of healthy, graceful English writing, and so much have matters altered in the way of remunerating literary men, that the Commissioners of Stamps and the Secretaries of State are not chosen by Lord Palmerston from among the contributors to *Blackwood* or *All the Year Round.* Then, there is the pleasant thought to compensate for this want of fame and of political promotion, that every man of letters, who can use his pen well, and can sit steadily at his desk for some hours a day, is sure of earning a comfortable livelihood, and holding a respectable place in society. In Queen Anne's day, it was Addison and Steele, Pope and Swift, and a few more, who got all the fame and the guineas, who drank their wine, and spent their afternoons in the saloons of the great; while the great majority of authors starved and shivered in garrets, or pawned their clothes for the food their pens could not win. In Victoria's reign there are few political prizes, but there is widespread comfort; and the man qualified to live by pen-work, is sure of finding that work to do, if to his ability he but adds the all-important qualities of industry and common sense.

CHAPTER II.

JOSEPH ADDISON.

Born 1672 A.D..........Died 1719 A.D.

Birth and school days.	Political rise.	Married life.
At Oxford.	The Tatler.	Retirement and death.
Foreign travel.	The Spectator.	Thackeray's Addison.
The Campaign.	Tragedy of Cato.	Illustrative extract.

WHEN Joseph Addison was born in 1672, his father was rector of Milston, near Amesbury in Wiltshire. He received the best part of his education at the Charter-house in London, a school which has sent forth many of our first wits and literary men. It was there that he met Dick Steele, a good-hearted, mischief-loving Irish boy; and the juvenile friendship, cemented no doubt by numerous tart transactions and much illegal Latin-verse making, was renewed at college and in later life. At the age of fifteen Addison left school for Queen's College, Oxford; two years later he obtained a scholarship in Magdalen, where his Latin poems won for him considerable renown.

His first flight in English verse was an *Address to Dryden* (1694), by which he gained the great man's friendship,—no slight matter to a newly fledged poet, whose face was hardly known in the coffee-houses. Dryden admitted his *Translation of part of the Fourth Georgic* into a book of Miscellanies. Other poems followed from the same pen. Some verses in honour of the King, though poor enough, won the favour of Lord Somers, through whom they reached the royal hand; and the fortunate writer received a pension of £300 a year, that he might cultivate his classic tastes by travel on the Continent. So, with a full purse and the reputation of being the most elegant scholar of his day in England, Addison set out upon the grand tour. From Italy he wrote a poetical *Letter to Lord Halifax*, which is looked upon as the finest of his works in English verse.

1699
A.D.

King William's death, however, stopping his pension, cut short his travelled ease; and home he came, a poor yet cheerful scholar, to wait quietly for fortune in a shabby lodging up two pair of stairs in the Haymarket.   While he lay thus under eclipse, the great battle of Blenheim was fought; and being employed by Treasurer Godolphin to write a poem in praise of the event, his performance of the task gave such satisfaction to the Ministry, that he was soon made Commissioner of Appeals.   The lucky poem, known as *The Campaign*, chanted loudly the praises of Marlborough, who is compared, in a passage that took the whole town by storm, to an angel guiding the whirlwind.   Mr. Commissioner Addison changed by-and-by into Mr. Under-Secretary of State; Mr. Under-Secretary, into the Secretary for Ireland; the Secretary for Ireland, into one of His Majesty's principal Secretaries of State (1717), the last being the greatest eminence reached by Addison in that most slippery profession of politics.

To mount so many rounds of the ladder took him a full dozen of years, during which his pen had been doing its finest work. Though he made his literary *début* as a poet, he achieved his highest fame as the writer of some of the sweetest and most artless prose that adorns our literature.

In the spring of 1709 his old school-fellow, Steele, started a triweekly sheet called *The Tatler*, which for a penny gave a short article and some scraps of news.   Addison, who was then in Ireland, wrote occasionally for this leaf.   But when the "Tatler," after living for nearly two years, gave place to the more famous daily sheet, called *The Spectator*, Addison became **1711** a constant contributor, and by his prose papers exalted the   A.D. periodical to the highest rank among the English classics.

There, on the tray beside the delicate porcelain cups, from which beauty and beau sipped their fragrant chocolate or tea by the toilette-table in the late noonday, lay the welcome little sheet of sparkling wit or elegant criticism, giving a new zest to the morning meal, and suggesting fresh topics for the afternoon chat in the toy-shops or on the Mall.   Addison's papers were marked with one of the four letters, C. L. I. O.—taken either from the Muse's name, or from the initial letters of Chelsea, London, Islington, and the Office, places where the papers were probably written. The *Essays on Milton*, the *Vision of Mirza*, and the account of *Sir Roger de Coverley's Visit to London*, may be taken as some of the finest specimens of what Addison's graceful pen could do. The "Spectator" lasted for 635 numbers, continuing to appear, with one break of eighteen months during which *The Guardian* ran its course, until the end of 1714. The first sketch of Sir Roger we owe to the pen of Steele; but it was a character such as the gentle Addison loved, and Addison is certainly the painter, in full length, of the good old bachelor baronet, full of whims and oddities, simple as a child and gentle as a woman, who lives in our hearts among the most prized of the friends we make in books, and whom we always honour as a true gentleman, though we sometimes steal a good-natured laugh at his rustic softness.

Since Addison's return from Italy, four acts of a Roman drama had been lying in his desk. Profiting by the temporary stoppage of the "Spectator," upon the completion of the seventh volume in 1712, he set to work upon the unfinished play, and soon gave *Cato* to the stage. It was performed for the first time at Drury **1713** Lane in April 1713, to a house crammed from pit to ceiling **A.D.** with all the wits and statesmen of the capital. We, who live in days when Kean writes himself F.S.A., and every buckle and shoe-tie of the wardrobe, in our better theatres at least, must pass the scrutiny of men deeply skilled in all the fashions of antiquity, smile at the incongruity of Cato in a flowered dressing-gown and a black wig that cost fifty guineas; and the brocaded Marcia in that famous hoop of Queen Anne's time, which has revived in the crinoline of Victoria's gentle reign. But Cato, thus attired, was not laughed at; for it was the theatrical fashion of the day to dress all characters in wig and hoop, exactly like those worn by the people of quality, who took snuff or flirted the fan in the resplendent box-row. A similar anachronism was com-mitted by the old Norman romancers, who turned every hero—no matter whether he was Abraham or Alexander—into a steel-clad knight of the Middle Ages. "Cato" was a great success. All

Addison's friends were in ecstasies of delight; and even the Tories allowed that the author was a man of too pure and elevated genius to be mixed up with common political quarrels. People stood knocking at the theatre doors at noon, and for more than a month the play was performed every night. Time has greatly abated the reputation of this drama. Like Addison's own nature, it is calm and cold; undeniably excellent as a piece of literary sculpture, full of fine declamation and well-chiselled dialogue, but falling far below the natural greatness of "Macbeth" or "Julius Cæsar." We remember Addison chiefly as the kindly genius who wrote the most charming papers of the "Spectator;" his own generation idolized him as the author of "Cato."

Almost a year before his appointment as Secretary of State, he married the Countess-Dowager of Warwick, and took up his abode in Holland House. The union was not a happy one between the cold and polished scholar, and the gorgeous, dashing woman of rank, who probably never found out how sweet and pure a spirit burned beneath the ice of her husband's outward manner. The quiet, lonely man, loved to escape from the gilded saloons of Holland House into the city, where he wandered through the clubs, or sat with some old friend over a bottle of wine. And here it must be said—gladly would we avoid it if we could—that the great Joseph Addison was often in his lifetime the worse for wine. The same hand that wrote "Mirza," and won for the "Spectator" its honoured place on English book-shelves, is found writing glee-fully to a friend at Hamburg about the choice old hock that had set it shaking. Let us be gentle in our blame, for it was the vice of the age. The pity is, that so fair a reputation should suffer from this sorry stain.

Addison's power lay in his pen; as a public speaker he broke down completely. This defect, coupled with the decay of his health, induced him to retire from office with a pension of £1500 a year. Asthma rapidly weakened him; symptoms of dropsy appeared; and he soon lay upon his death-bed. "See," said he to his son-in-law, "how a Christian can die!" And then this gentle spirit, that, amid many faults and weaknesses, had ever cherished a deep, reverential gratitude to God, passed at forty-eight from this troubled life, let us humbly trust, to that golden city of everlasting peace, which needs no sun to light it, for the Lamb is the light thereof.

1719
A.D.

No better close for this slight sketch could be found than the charming picture of Addison in his prime, which we owe to Thackeray's brilliant pen.*

" Addison wrote his papers as gaily as if he was going out for a holiday. When Steele's ' Tatler' first began his prattle, Addison, then in Ireland, caught at his friend's notion, poured in paper after paper, and contributed the stores of his mind, the sweet fruits of his reading, the delightful gleanings of his daily observation, with a wonderful profusion, and, as it seemed, an almost endless fecundity. He was six-and-thirty years old : full and ripe. He had not worked crop after crop from his brain, manuring hastily, subsoiling indifferently, cutting and sowing and cutting again, like other luckless cultivators of letters. He had not done much as yet; a few Latin poems—graceful prolusions; a polite book of travels; a dissertation on medals, not very deep; four acts of a tragedy, a great classical exercise; and the 'Campaign,' a large prize poem that won an enormous prize. But with his friend's discovery of the 'Tatler,' Addison's calling was found, and the most delightful talker in the world began to speak. . . . . His writings do not show insight into or reverence for the love of women, which I take to be, one the consequence of the other. He walks about the world watching their pretty humours, fashions, follies, flirtations, rivalries; and noting them with the most charming archness. He sees them in public, in the theatre, or the assembly, or the puppet-show; or at the toy-shop, higgling for gloves and lace; or at the auction, battling together over a blue porcelain dragon, or a darling monster in japan; or at church, eyeing the width of their rivals' hoops, or the breadth of their laces, as they sweep down the aisles. Or he looks out of his window at the Garter in St. James's Street, at Ardelia's coach, as she blazes to the drawing-room with her coronet and six footmen; and remem-

* See English Humorists of the Eighteenth Century, Lecture II.

bering that her father was a Turkey merchant in the city, calcu-
lates how many sponges went to purchase her ear-rings, and how
many drums of figs to build her coach box; or he demurely
watches behind a tree in Spring Garden as Saccharissa (whom he
knows under her mask) trips out of her chair to the alley where
Sir Fopling is waiting."

SKETCH OF WILL WIMBLE.

(SPECTATOR, NO. 108.)

As I was yesterday morning walking with Sir Roger before his house, a
country fellow brought him a huge fish, which, he told him, Mr. William
Wimble had caught that very morning; and that he presented it with his service
to him, and intended to come and dine with him. At the same time he delivered
a letter, which my friend read to me as soon as the messenger left him.

"SIR ROGER,

"I desire you to accept of a jack, which is the best I have caught
this season. I intend to come and stay with you a week, and see how the perch
bite in the Black river. I observed with some concern, the last time I saw you
upon the bowling-green, that your whip wanted a lash to it; I will bring half
a dozen with me that I twisted last week, which I hope will serve you all the
time you are in the country. I have not been out of the saddle for six days
last past, having been at Eton with Sir John's eldest son. He takes to his
learning hugely.

"I am, Sir, your humble servant,
"WILL WIMBLE."

This extraordinary letter, and message that accompanied it, made me very
curious to know the character and quality of the gentleman who sent them;
which I found to be as follow:—Will Wimble is younger brother to a baronet,
and descended of the ancient family of the Wimbles. He is now between forty
and fifty; but being bred to no business and born to no estate, he generally lives
with his eldest brother as superintendent of his game. He hunts a pack of dogs
better than any man in the country, and is very famous for finding out a hare.
He is extremely well versed in all the little handicrafts of an idle man. He
makes a May-fly to a miracle; and furnishes the whole country with angle-rods.
As he is a good-natured, officious fellow, and very much esteemed on account of
his family, he is a welcome guest at every house, and keeps up a good correspondence among all the gentlemen about him. He carries a tulip root in his
pocket from one to another, or exchanges a puppy between a couple of friends,
that live perhaps in the opposite sides of the country. These gentleman-like
manufactures and obliging little humours make Will the darling of the country.

CHAPTER III.

SIR ISAAC NEWTON.

Born 1642 A.D..........Died 1727 A.D.

Newton's fame.	Master of the Mint.
Early life.	Loss of his papers.
College career.	High honours.
The Principia.	English works.
M.P. for Cambridge.	Illustrative extract.

ALTHOUGH Newton's fame does not rest upon his contributions to English literature, we need make no apology for presenting here a brief view of the life and works of that Englishman who wrote the *Principia*, and won for his native land the fame of having given birth to the greatest natural philosopher the world has ever seen.

The hamlet of Woolsthorpe, eight miles south of Grantham in Lincolnshire, was the birth-place of Isaac Newton. His father farmed a small estate. During his school-life at Grantham and elsewhere, a remarkable taste for mechanics led him to spend his leisure in the construction of such things as model wind-mills and water-clocks; but his progress in his studies was very slow, until a strange accident produced a change. The boy above him gave him a heavy kick in the stomach one day; and this so roused the energies of young Isaac, that he worked industriously until he got above his injurer. He then continued his successful career until he stood at the head of his class.

At seventeen he entered Trinity College, Cambridge, became ultimately a Fellow, and in 1669 succeeded Dr. Barrow as Lucasian Professor of Mathematics. Here were performed most of those splendid optical experiments which placed the science of light on new foundations. Here and at Woolsthorpe, where he sometimes spent a while, he busied himself with those sublime investigations, resulting in his discovery of that grand law of universal gravitation which the stars obey, as they wheel in huge ellipses round a central sun, and which at the same time guides the fall of the tiniest leaflet that flutters dead to the earth in the silence of an autumn wood.

In 1672 Newton was elected a member of the Royal Society, which was then an infant association, only twelve years old. Through the studious years that followed, his great work—a Latin treatise entitled in full, *Philosophiæ Naturalis Principia Mathematica*—was slowly but steadily growing to completeness. It was published in 1687, at the expense of the **1687** members of the Royal Society, who were justly proud of A.D. the distinguished author. In the following year the University of Cambridge returned him as one of the members who represented her in Parliament—an honour which he enjoyed more than once. But through all these years of honour and success he remained a comparatively poor man, until in 1695 he received his appointment as Warden of the Mint, a post worth about £600 a year. This he held for four years, when he was promoted to be Master, with a salary of more than double what he had been receiving as Warden.

In 1692 occurred that distressing accident which some believe to have shaken his great mind for a time. The commonly received story—and a pretty one it is, often quoted to show how a gentle patience adorned the character of this great philosopher—runs thus : One winter morning, having shut his pet dog Diamond in his study, he came back from early chapel to find all his manuscripts upon the theory of colours, notes upon the experiments of twenty busy years, reduced to a heap of tinder. The dog had knocked down a lighted candle and set the papers in a blaze. " Ah ! Diamond, Diamond, little do you know the mischief you have done," was the only rebuke the dog received—though, as a Cambridge student writing in his diary at that very time tells us, "Every one thought that Newton would have run mad."

High honours crowned the later life of the philosopher ; of these the chief were his election in 1703 as President of the Royal Society, an office conferred on him every succeeding year until his death; and his knighthood in 1705, under the royal hand of good Queen Anne. His long life, more fruitful, perhaps, in great wonders of scientific discovery than that of any other man in ancient or modern times, came to a close at Kensington in 1727, when the old man had passed his eighty-fourth year.

From the long list of Newton's works, the principal of which were written in Latin, some English publications may be selected. The first edition of his *Optics* (1704) appeared in his own tongue. A work entitled, *The Chronology of Ancient Kingdoms Amended*, was printed after the author's death. And, more interesting than either, both as affording a favourable specimen of Newton's literary power, and a proof how deeply this great interpreter of nature's laws was fascinated by the shadowy mysteries of prophecy, is the theological treatise, styled *Observations upon the Prophecies of Daniel and the Apocalypse of St. John*, which his executors published in 1733.

THE LANGUAGE OF PROPHECY.

For understanding the prophecies, we are, in the first place, to acquaint ourselves with the figurative language of the prophets. This language is taken from the analogy between the world natural and an empire or kingdom considered as a world politic.

Accordingly, the whole world natural, consisting of heaven and earth, signifies the whole world politic, consisting of thrones and people; or so much of it as is considered in the prophecy. And the things in that world signify the analogous things in this. For the heavens, and the things therein, signify thrones and dignities, and those who enjoy them; and the earth, with the things thereon, the inferior people; and the lowest parts of the earth, called Hades or Hell, the lowest or most miserable part of them. Whence, ascending towards heaven, and descending to the earth, are put for rising and falling in power and honour; rising out of the earth or waters, and falling into them, for the rising up to any dignity or dominion, out of the inferior state of the people, or falling down from the same into that inferior state; descending into the lower parts of the earth, for descending to a very low and unhappy state; speaking with a faint voice out of the dust, for being in a weak and low condition; moving from one place to another, for translation from one office, dignity, or dominion to another; great earthquakes, and the shaking of heaven and earth, for the shaking of dominions, so as to distract or overthrow them; the creating a new heaven and earth, and the passing away of an old one, or the beginning and end of the world, for the rise and reign of the body politic signified thereby.

CHAPTER IV.

SIR RICHARD STEELE.

Born 1675 A.D..........Died 1729 A.D.

Addison and Steele.	Comedies.	Politics.
Dick at school.	His letters.	The Crisis.
In the Guards.	The Tatler.	Improvidence.
Captain Steele.	The Spectator.	His death.
The Christian Hero.	Steele's wit.	Illustrative extract.

WHEN Addison returned from the Continent with a head much better furnished with classic thoughts and elegant scholarship than was his purse with guineas, foremost among the few faces that presented themselves at the door of his dingy lodging in the Haymarket, was the round good-humoured countenance of an old schoolfellow and college friend, formerly Dicky Steele of the Charterhouse, but now rollicking Captain Richard Steele of Lucas's Fusiliers. The two names—Addison and Steele—are inseparably linked together, from the partnership of the two men in those periodical essays out of which have grown our *Blackwoods* and our *Cornhills*, our *Edinburghs* and our *Quarterlys*.

Steele, the son of a man who acted as Secretary to the Duke of Ormond, then Lord-Lieutenant of Ireland, was born about 1675 in Dublin. During his school-days at the Charter-house in London, he was the admiring junior of Addison, whom he afterwards joined at Oxford, being entered at Merton College in 1692. Leaving Oxford without a degree, he enlisted, much against the wishes of all his friends, as a private in the Horse Guards, dazzled by the splendour of the richly laced scarlet coats and the white waving plumes of that gallant corps. This rash step cost him a fortune; for a wealthy Irish relative, indignant at the news, cut the name of the reckless fellow out of his will. But his agreeable manners, and frank, open joviality, won him many friends. Ormond, in

whose troop he rode, obtained a cornetcy for him; he became
secretary to Colonel Lord Cutts; and ultimately was made a
captain in Lucas's Fusiliers.

During the wild life he spent about town with his brother
officers, stung sometimes by his upbraiding conscience, he wrote and
published a devotional work, called *The Christian Hero*, by which
he intended to correct his errors and force himself to pull up in
time. But his only reward was the laughter of the town; for the
idea of a fast-living soldier, who could never resist the attractions
of the Rose Tavern or the delight of beating the watch at midnight, appearing in print as a religious character, seemed to have
in it something irresistibly comic. Yet for the time Steele was
sincere in his intentions of reform. He soon, however, appeared
as an author in a different line. Three comedies from his pen—
The Funeral, The Tender Husband, and *The Lying Lover*—were
performed in 1702, and the two following years. The sober tone
of the last having drawn down a storm of hisses from the audience, Steele in disgust withdrew from dramatic authorship. A
greater task than the writing of second-rate plays was in store for
his genial pen.

Between the failure of the "Lying Lover" and the first issue of
the "Tatler," Steele married his second wife, Prue, Miss
1707 Scurlock of Caermarthenshire, who, by preserving some
A.D. four hundred letters from her husband, written chiefly in
taverns and coffee-houses, has enabled us to form truer
ideas of the man Dick Steele than we could get from any other
source. There we have displayed the inner life of the improvident
rake, whose dissipation does not sour the sweetness of his nature,
who is often detained from home by some mythical business, and
softens his announcement of delay by a little present to his wife of
tea or walnuts, or a guinea or two, when his purse is not in its
normal condition of emptiness. He held at this time the appointment of Gazetteer, which he afterwards exchanged for the post of
Commissioner of Stamps. The former office, by giving him an
early command of foreign news, enabled him to commence the publication of the "Tatler" in 1709.

The 12th of April in that year marks the opening of a great era in English literature,—the birth of the first English periodical worthy of the name. Three times a week, on the post-days, this penny sheet came out, and was scattered through town and country. After a while Addison lent his aid to his old school-fellow, and, when *The Tatler* had told his tale to a second New Year, after a short silence of two months, the greater *Spectator* arose to fill the vacant space. Here it was that Addison's genius shone in its fullest lustre; and, though Steele's good-natured wit welled out as fresh and natural as ever in the papers of the "Spectator," he suffers somewhat by contrast with his greater friend. Among other gems of this favourite classic, we owe to Steele's pen the first sketch of the members who composed the Spectator Club. Addison has made Sir Roger all his own, yet Steele certainly first placed the portrait upon canvas.

1709
A.D.

We have already called Steele's wit fresh and natural. It came with no stinted flow. He wrote as he lived, freely and carelessly, scattering the coinage of his brain, as he did his guineas, with an unsparing hand. All who read his papers, or his letters to Prue, cannot help seeing the good heart of the rattle-brain shining out in every line. We can forgive, or at least forget, his tippling in taverns and his unthinking extravagance, bad as these were, in consideration of the loving touch with which he handles the foibles of his neighbours, and the mirth without bitterness that flows from his gentle pen.

Between the seventh and eighth volumes of the "Spectator" *The Guardian* appeared, Steele and Addison being still the chief contributors. Steele's entry upon parliamentary life, as member for Stockbridge, relaxed his efforts as an essayist. Though he was afterwards concerned in other periodicals,—the *Englishman*, the *Reader*, &c.,—neither his purse nor his reputation won much by them.

It was a stirring time in politics, and Steele was not the man to be behindhand in the fray. His pamphlet, *The Crisis*, raised so great a storm against him that he was expelled from the House

of Commons for libel.   The death of Queen Anne, however, produced a change.   Under the new dynasty Dick became Sir Richard
Steele, Governor of the royal Comedians, Surveyor of the royal
stables at Hampton Court, and Member of Parliament for Borough-
bridge in Yorkshire.   In the House he spoke often and well; at
home in Bloomsbury or elsewhere he wrote spicy articles, gave
splendid dinners,—of course running up heavy bills, which he
always meant to pay, but somehow never did.   Addison, who had
lent his easy-going friend £1000, had to pay himself by selling
Steele's country-house at Hampton, furniture and all, putting his
own money in his pocket, and handing the balance to poor Dick,
who, no doubt, was very glad to get a little ready cash for the
duns that knocked daily at the door.   Steele's very successful
comedy, *The Conscious Lovers*, acted at Drury Lane in 1722,
brought him a large sum; but even that could do little to melt
the millstone of debt hanging round the unfortunate author's
neck.   His difficulties increased.   Paralysis struck the haggard,
anxious spendthrift.   Giving up all he had to his creditors, he
hid himself at Llangunnor in Wales, where he still had a shelter
from the storm that his own improvidence had raised.   There,
forgotten except by angry shopkeepers whom he could
1729 not pay, poor Steele breathed his last in 1729.   His
A.D.   dying years were dependent on the bounty of his creditors.—Let us learn the lesson of his life, grieving that the
affectionate soul, who loved to make all around him happy, should,
through his own easy negligence, have suffered so bitter pangs at
the last.

ORIGINAL SKETCH OF SIR ROGER DE COVERLEY.

(SPECTATOR, NO. 2.)

The first of our society is a gentleman of Worcestershire, of an ancient descent,
a baronet, his name Sir Roger de Coverley. His great-grandfather was inventor
of that famous country-dance which is called after him. All who know that
shire are very well acquainted with the parts and merits of Sir Roger. He is a
gentleman that is very singular in his behaviour; but his singularities proceed
from his good sense, and are contradictions to the manners of the world only as he
thinks the world is in the wrong. However, this humour creates him no enemies,

for he does nothing with sourness or obstinacy; and his being unconfined to modes and forms makes him but the readier and more capable to please and oblige all who know him. When he is in town, he lives in Soho Square. It is said he keeps himself a bachelor by reason he was crossed in love by a perverse beautiful widow of the next county to him. Before this disappointment, Sir Roger was what you call a fine gentleman,—had often supped with my Lord Rochester and Sir George Etherege, fought a duel upon his first coming to town, and kicked bully Dawson in a public coffee-house for calling him youngster. But, being ill-used by the above-mentioned widow, he was very serious for a year and a half; and though, his temper being naturally jovial, he at last got over it, he grew careless of himself, and never dressed afterward. He continues to wear a coat and doublet of the same cut that were in fashion at the time of his repulse, which, in his merry humours, he tells us has been in and out twelve times since he first wore it. He is now in his fifty-sixth year, cheerful, gay, and hearty; keeps a good house both in town and country; a great lover of mankind; but there is such a mirthful cast in his behaviour, that he is rather beloved than esteemed. His tenants grow rich, his servants look satisfied, all the young women profess love to him, and the young men are glad of his company. When he comes into a house he calls the servants by their names, and talks all the way up stairs to a visit. I must not omit, that Sir Roger is a justice of the quorum; that he fills the chair at a quarter-session with great abilities, and three months ago gained universal applause by explaining a passage in the game Act.

CHAPTER V.

ALEXANDER POPE.

Born 1688 A.D..........Died 1744 A.D.

Pope's verse.	Translation of Homer.	The Dunciad.
His early life.	Villa at Twickenham.	Essay on Man.
Sets up as poet.	His filial love.	Personal traits.
Wycherley.	Lady Mary Montagu.	His death.
Essay on Criticism.	Quarrel with Addison.	Other works.
Rape of the Lock.	Town and country.	Illustrative extract.

PRINCE of the Artificial school of English poetry stands the Roman Catholic poet, Alexander Pope, whose brilliant and versatile powers were best displayed in *The Rape of the Lock* and *The Dunciad.*

Pope's father was a well-to-do linen-draper in the Strand, who gave up business in disgust at the shadow which the Revolution had flung upon his Church, and, retiring to Binfield, on the skirts of Windsor Forest, locked up his fortune of £20,000 in a box, from which he took the needful guineas as often as his purse ran low.   Banks were then in their infancy; and the seizure which Charles II. had made of the public funds was too fresh in remembrance to make a government investment seem safe.   His **1688** delicate boy, Alexander, born in 1688, passed under some A.D.   priestly tutors, but never enjoyed a college training.

Before he was twelve the little invalid wrote an *Ode to Solitude*, marked with a thoughtfulness beyond his years; and after loitering for four summers longer among the picturesque woodlands near his home—spending summer and winter alike in a constant round of studies, rambling but deep—he boldly embraced the perilous vocation of a poet, and at sixteen began to haunt the London coffee-houses in that character.   Admiration of Dryden was the grand passion of his boyhood; and when the great monarch of letterdom, seated in his easy-chair at Will's, was one day pointed out by a good-natured friend to the pale, wistful boy, who had already drunk deep into the old man's poetry, we can well imagine the occasion marked with bright red letters in the childish memory. From admiration to imitation, somebody or other says, is but a step. Pope's versification was moulded after Dryden's " long-resounding line."

Wycherley, a battered old literary rake, was young Pope's first caresser; but in the coffee-room at Will's or Button's—head-quarters of the author-craft—the boyish writer of the *Pastorals*, which were as yet only handed about in manuscript, got many a kind shake of the hand and hearty slap on the shoulder from greater and better men than old Wycherley.

The poet soared to yet higher fame, when in 1711 his cele-brated *Essay on Criticism*, begun two years earlier, issued from the press. This performance, wonderful for a youth **1711** of twenty-one, contains many fine passages. The well- A.D. known lines, illustrating the agreement of sound with sense, afford a striking specimen of the ease with which Pope wields his native speech. Then followed a sacred poem, *The Messiah*, which appeared in No. 378 of the *Spectator;* and, not long after, came those pathetic verses, *An Elegy on an Un-fortunate Lady,*—which, we are told, mourn the suicide of a rash girl, who had cherished a violent passion for the sickly poet.

The theft of a lady's ringlet by her lover produced the happiest effort of Pope's poetic skill. Lord Petre was the delinquent, and Miss Arabella Fermor the injured fair one. The silly trick having led to a coolness between the families, Pope set to work, inspired by the wish to reconcile the estranged frowners by a good hearty laugh. Thus came into being that epic in miniature, *The Rape of the Lock*, which presents the most brilliant speci- **1713** men of the mock-heroic style to be found in English verse.* A.D. We may read the reign of Anne through in many books of history without receiving anything like so clear and vivid an impression of what was then fashionable life, as we derive from

---

* The two original cantos were written in 1711, but in 1713 the poem appeared in its present shape.

the five cantos that tell the woes of Belinda. The *machinery* of
the poem, as critics call the introduction of supernatural beings
into the action of the plot, Pope took from the Rosicrucian doctrine, that the four elements are filled with sylphs, gnomes, nymphs,
and salamanders. Most comically does this airy by-play come to
act upon the progress of the story, reaching, perhaps, the climax of
its humour in the exquisitely absurd idea of a poor sylph who was
so eager to save the imperilled lock that she gets between the
scissor blades and is snipped in two. After a fierce battle, in
which Belinda, armed with a deadly bodkin, leads the van, the
severed tress flies up to take its place among the golden stars.

In *The Epistle of Eloisa to Abelard* we find the poet wasting his
pathos upon an unhappy theme. *The Temple of Fame*, a fine
piece of descriptive writing founded on Chaucer's "House of
Fame," though written earlier, was published about this period of
his life.

At twenty-four Pope undertook his most extensive, most profitable, yet assuredly not his greatest work. "It is a pretty poem,
Mr. Pope; but you must not call it Homer," was the terse and
true remark of the great scholar Bentley upon the volumes sent
him by the poet. Many hundred verses were written on backs of
letters and chance scraps of paper, sometimes at the rate of fifty
lines a day. Begun in 1712 and finished in 1725, the *Iliad* and
the *Odyssey* together, after deducting the cost of some help which
he got in the notes and the translation of the latter, brought the
poet a handsome fortune. Not sixty years before, a blind old man
in the same great city had sold the greatest epic of modern days
for £18. Pope, whose poetic fame grows pale before the splendour of Milton's genius, as the stars die out before the sun,
pocketed more than £8000 for a clever translation. Like Dryden.
translating Virgil, Pope did little more than reproduce the sense
of Homer's verse in smooth and neatly balanced English couplets,
leaving the spirit behind in the glorious rough old Greek, that
tumbles on the ear like the roar of a winter sea.

With the money thus obtained Pope had the good sense to buy
a villa at Twickenham, standing on five acres of land. The hours

which were not given to his desk, were spent in laying out his flower-beds, and adorning his famous grotto with such things as red spar, Cornwall diamonds, Spanish silver, and lava from Vesuvius. Here, by the gentle Thames, his later years were spent; here Swift, Bolingbroke, Gay, Arbuthnot, and a host of the most brilliant men of the day, paid him frequent visits; and it is, at least, one tender trait in the character of a poet who has not had very many kind sayings lavished on him, that here his old mother found a warm welcome and a well-cushioned chair in her declining days.

Pope's love-making was as artificial as his verse, but not so successful. His professed passion for Lady Mary Montagu, of letter-writing renown, suddenly changed its hue, rosy love turning into pallid rage. So bitter, indeed, did the little man's remarks grow after his repulse, that the lady used to call her *quondam* swain "The wicked wasp of Twickenham."

Of course, Pope and Addison often met. When the poet first came to town, a boy and little known, he danced attendance for a good while upon the great Oxford scholar. He wrote an admirable prologue for the tragedy of "Cato." But gradually a coolness arose between these celebrated men. Some think that Addison was jealous of Pope's brightening fame; others think that Pope's peevish temper, often the accompaniment of a sickly frame, took offence at some slight censures passed upon his "Essay on Criticism." Whatever may have been its cause, the estrangement grew to a crisis, when Pope issued a spiteful pamphlet against old John Dennis, who had published certain "Remarks on the Tragedy of Cato." Addison, vexed at the tone of the reply, although the lance was broken in his own quarrel, hastily said, that if he answered the "Remarks" at all, he would do it as a gentleman should. This Pope never forgave; and the gulf grew wider when Tickell, Addison's close friend, began a translation of Homer, which seemed to the suspicious eyes of Pope a wilful rivalry of his great work, secretly done by Addison, but put out for appearance' sake under Tickell's name.

The *Odyssey* and the editing of *Shakspere* occupied the pen of

Pope for some years after his removal to Twickenham in 1718.
His weakly frame could not stand the wear and tear of city life,
as authors then lived. Thoroughly sick of spending night after
night till two or three o'clock over punch and Burgundy, in rooms
choking with tobacco smoke, the poet wisely separated himself
from the hard-living set, to which he had at first belonged, and
gave up his spare hours to the pure enjoyments of his garden and
his grotto.

The publication of his *Miscellanies* (1727–8), in which Swift also
took a share, brought round the heads of the offending authors an
angry swarm of scribblers, buzzing like wasps whose nest has been
rashly invaded. Then the real power of the crippled poet flashed
out in full lustre. Seizing each wretched insect with the firm
yet delicate hold of a skilful entomologist, he ruthlessly pinned
it, in the full gaze of the world's scorn, on the sheets of
the immortal *Dunciad*. There the unfortunate creatures
still hang and wriggle; and there, while English books
are read, they shall remain. This epic of "Dunces"
(hence its name) celebrates the accession of a king—at first Shaksperian Theobald, but in a later edition dramatic Cibber—to the
vacant throne of Dulness, and describes the sports of authors,
booksellers, and critics, before the newly crowned monarch. The
fourth and last book is terribly severe upon the trifling education
of the day, the "black blockade" of college dons suffering not a
little from the satiric lash. The literary profession did not recover
for many a day from the onslaught of this bitter pen. To starve
in a Grub Street garret became, in the opinion of the public, the
sure destiny of every man who took to letters for a livelihood;
and even now, when poets sometimes get their guinea a line, the
name has not altogether lost, in the minds of many an honest
merchant or yeoman, its old associations with threadbare coats, a
tendency to drink, and a general lack of half-crowns.

The "Dunciad," first published in 1728, was enlarged in the
following year; and in 1742 was completed by the addition of
the fourth book. The dethronement of Theobald, to make room
for Cibber, proved a great blunder; for the satiric lines, which

1729
A.D.

pierced poor Theobald to the bone, fell blunt and pointless off a man of totally different character.

A frequent visitor at the Twickenham villa was Lord Boling-broke, well known as a politician, a libertine, and a sceptic. Gradually the poison of his talk found its way into Pope's mind, and a metrical system of morals, *The Essay on Man*, sprang from the envenomed seeds. Condemning the opinions of the Essay, we cannot but admire its versification; but let us not forget that deadly serpents often lie coiled under the freshest leaves and sweetest blossoms of poetry.

Graceful and flowing *Imitations of Horace* were among Pope's latest works. Through all this poet's life of fifty-six years he was delicate and frail. The wonder is that soul and body kept together so long. When the poor little man got up in the morning, he had to be sewed into stiff canvas stays, without which he could not stand erect; his thin body was wrapped in fur and flannel; and his meagre legs required three pairs of stockings to give them a respectable look. After he grew bald, which happened early in life, a velvet cap became his favourite head-dress. On company days he wore a black velvet coat, a tie-wig, and a little sword. When he stayed with a friend, all the servants were kept in a bustle to answer Mr. Pope's never-ceasing calls. The house was roused up at night to make him coffee, or bring him paper, lest he might lose a happy thought. Poor fellow! his fussiness was a foible easily pardoned; and as to his temper, when we re-member that his life—to use his own sad words—was " one long disease," we can overlook the acid and the sting in remembrance of the pain. The little spider—so he describes his own meagre figure —that could spin webs of verse so brilliant and so deadly, lived with simple elegance upon £800 a year; paring his housekeeping with, perhaps, too close a hand, but cherishing to the last beneath his kindly roof the good old mother whom he loved so well.

His death took place at Twickenham on the 30th of May, 1744. Asthma and other diseases had so worn away his strength, that the moment of his decease could not be perceived.

1744
A.D.

Pope's Letters, first published, as he tried to make the world believe, against his will, are well worth the reading; but his finest piece of prose is the *Preface* to his edition of Shakspere. Two of his well-known works have not yet been named—*Windsor Forest* and the *Dying Christian to his Soul*. The former, bright with hues caught in woodland rambles, presents glowing pictures of the scenery and sports which he had witnessed in the green glades of Windsor during the days of his dreamy, studious boyhood. The latter, perhaps the feeblest effort of his great pen, is a stiff and puerile rendering of the Emperor Adrian's last trembling sigh.

FROM "THE RAPE OF THE LOCK."

For lo! the board with cups and spoons is crowned,
The berries crackle, and the mill turns round:
On shining altars of Japan they raise
The silver lamp; the fiery spirits blaze:
From silver spouts the grateful liquors glide,
While China's earth receives the smoking tide;
At once they gratify their scent and taste,
And frequent cups prolong the rich repast.
Straight hover round the fair her airy band:
Some, as she sipped, the fuming liquor fanned;
Some o'er her lap their careful plumes displayed,
Trembling and conscious of the rich brocade.
Coffee (which makes the politician wise,
And see through all things with his half-shut eyes)
Sent up in vapours to the baron's brain
New stratagems the radiant lock to gain.
Ah! cease, rash youth; desist ere 'tis too late;
Fear the just gods, and think of Scylla's fate!
Changed to a bird, and sent to flit in air,
She dearly paid for Nisus' injured hair!
  But when to mischief mortals bend their will,
How soon they find fit instruments of ill!
Just then, Clarissa drew, with tempting grace,
A two-edged weapon from her shining case;
So ladies, in romance, assist their knight,
Present the spear, and arm him for the fight.
He takes the gift with reverence, and extends
The little engine on his fingers' ends;
This just behind Belinda's neck he spread,
As o'er the fragrant steams she bent her head.

Swift to the lock a thousand sprites repair,
A thousand wings, by turns, blow back the hair!
And thrice they twitched the diamond in her ear;
Thrice she looked back, and thrice the foe drew near.
Just in that instant, anxious Ariel sought
The close recesses of the virgin's thought:
As on the nosegay in her breast reclined,
He watched the ideas rising in her mind.
Sudden he viewed, in spite of all her art,
An earthly lover lurking at her heart.
Amazed, confused, he found his power expired,
Resigned to fate, and with a sigh retired.
  The peer now spreads the glittering forfex wide
To enclose the lock; now joins it, to divide.
E'en then, before the fatal engine closed,
A wretched Sylph too fondly interposed;
Fate urged the shears, and cut the Sylph in twain
(But airy substance soon unites again),
The meeting points the sacred hair dissever
From the fair head, for ever, and for ever!

CHAPTER VI.

JONATHAN SWIFT.

Born 1667 A.D..........Died 1745 A.D.

A tragedy.	Stella and Vanessa.	Gulliver's Travels.
Education.	Takes up his pen.	Madness.
Dependence.	The Tale of a Tub.	His death.
Life at Temple's.	Dean of St. Patrick's.	His poems.
King William's offer.	Drapier's Letters.	Illustrative extract.

THE life of the famous Dean Swift is a great tragedy. Through all the acts a dark gigantic genius moves, an intellectual Saul, towering by head and shoulders above his fellows, and possessed of an evil spirit, which does not quite abandon its wretched prey even when a pall of darkness settles on his ruined mind, and that dreadful silence of three years begins to unfold itself between a lurid life and the slumber of the narrow grave.

Swift was a Dublin man by birth, being born there in Hoey's Court in 1667. But his parents and his ancestors were English. His father, a mere bird of passage in Dublin, where he had come in the hope of getting some practice as a lawyer, died seven months before Jonathan's birth. At his uncle's expense he went to Kilkenny School, and then to Trinity College, Dublin ; but in neither did he distinguish himself above the average run of students. Indeed, his degree of B.A. was of the lowest class, a narrow escape from the disgrace of being plucked, which roused him to studious resolves. And to the steady industry of the next seven years he owed almost all the learning he ever had.

Dependence had all this while been burning like an acrid poison into the proud boy's soul. But his lessons in the hard school of adversity were not yet over. His uncle's death in 1688 flung him upon the world, and forced him to seek a shelter at Moor Park in the household of Sir William Temple, with whom his mother was slightly connected. Here for many years Swift continued to eat bitter bread; waiting and looking out into the dim future for the time when he could break his chains, and smite tenfold for every stripe he had received. Standing mid-way between the elegantly selfish Sir William, who wrote and gardened and quoted the classics, and the liveried sneerers of the servants' hall, poor Swift gnawed at his own heart in disdainful silence, writhing helplessly under the lofty chidings of his Honour, and the vulgar insolence of his Honour's own man. We can well imagine the working of the swarthy features, the deadly concentrated light of the terrible blue eye, and the convulsive starts of the ungainly limbs, as those continual streams of petty scorn and malice trickled on the spirit of the morbidly sensitive youth, who felt them like molten lead, yet could not or dared not take revenge. At Temple's Swift met King William, who, walking in the garden, showed him how the Dutch cut their asparagus, and offered to make him a captain of horse. One cannot help wishing that Swift had accepted the troop. We should not, most probably, have had *Gulliver's Travels* on our shelves, but the sabreing of French dragoons might have acted as a safety-valve to the poisonous humours which so many years of bondage had generated in his breast; and the red coat would not have burned him to the bone, as the priest's cassock did, scorching him, as the poisoned shirt scorched Hercules, until the wretched man burst into shrieks of foaming rage.

In an evil hour Swift, who had already graduated as M.A. at Oxford, crossed to Dublin, took holy orders, and became prebend of Kilroot in Connor at £100 a year. But the life **1693** of a country parson was even worse misery to Swift than the A.D. wretchedness of Moor Park. Thither, accordingly, he returned, humbling himself in the dust before the great baronet. Then he became involved in his mysterious love-affair with Hester Johnson, daughter of Sir William's housekeeper, better known by Swift's pet name of Stella, whose black curls and loving eyes threw their spells around the lonely Levite.

Let us glance forward along the course of this strange and seemingly unfinished life, over which, from its very beginning, the

black shadow of final insanity cast a gloom, and see how the sad
story of Swift's attachments comes to a close.   Stella he seems to
have loved deeply, but not so well that he could bend his gigantic
ambition to a public marriage with her.   By-and-by, before he
became Dean of St. Patrick's in Dublin, a girl named Esther
Vanhomrigh fell in love with him, and was encouraged by the
flattered savage, who wrote poems in her praise.   This lady was
the unhappy Vanessa of his verse.   The two hearts, thus moved
with a strange tenderness for one who had little of the amiable in
his nature, were kept dangling round him by the cruel genius,
like silly moths round a lamp, until one after the other they were
burned to ashes.   It is said that Swift and Stella were secretly
married in the Deanery garden; but the unfeeling man would not
avow the union to the world, and she sank at last into the grave
of sorrow.

The death of Temple in 1699 sent Swift to Ireland as the chaplain of Lord Berkeley.   He soon became rector of Agher, and vicar
of Laracor and Rathbeggan in Meath.   But in his thirty-fourth
year he took his place in the ranks of political penmen
1701 by writing a pamphlet on the Whig side.   His pen was
A.D.   the lever, by which he meant to raise Jonathan Swift to
the pinnacle of clerical or political greatness.   It certainly
won for him the adoration of a country, and one of the highest
niches in the temple of our literature; but it could not raise a
mitre to his head, and he crushed it in his angry grasp till it began
to drop nothing but gall.

One of his three great works was the extraordinary *Tale of a
Tub;* which was published, according to the author's state-
1704 ment, in order to divert the followers of Hobbes, author
A.D.   of the *Leviathan,* from injuring the vessel of the State,
just as sailors were wont to fling out a tub in order to
turn aside a whale from his threatened dash upon their ship.
The *Leviathan,* he says, "tosses and plays with all schemes of
religion and government, whereof many are hollow, and dry, and
empty, and noisy, and wooden, and given to rotation."   Three
brothers—Peter, Martin, and Jack—receive from their dying father

coats, which, if carefully kept clean, will last them all their lives.
As the fashions change, they add to the simple coat shoulder-
knots, gold lace, silver fringes, embroidery of Indian figures,
twisting the meaning of their father's will so as to give a seeming
sanction to these innovations. Peter (evidently the apostle of
that name, here taken to represent the Roman Catholic Church)
locks up the will, assumes the style of a lord, and wears his
coat proudly, as it is. His brothers, stealing a copy of the docu-
ment, leave the great house, and begin to reform their coats.
Martin (Luther) goes to work cautiously in stripping off the
adornments, and leaves some of the embroidery alone lest he may
injure the cloth. But Jack (Calvin) in his hot zeal plucks off all at
once, and in so doing splits the seams, and tears away great pieces
of the coat. Thus does Swift depict the corruptions of early
Christianity, and the results of the Reformation, in a satire of
uncommon power and strange, mad drollery. His sympathies are
all with Martin, and Peter gets off better than Jack.

Disappointed in his hopes of preferment, Swift deserted from
the Whig ranks, and soon his shot began to plough through the
lines he had left. We cannot attempt to name the bitter and
caustic pamphlets that were hurled by the renegade against his
former friends. But his new allies dared not make a bishop of
the man who had written the "Tale of a Tub." The
Deanery of St. Patrick's, Dublin, received in 1713, was **1713**
the utmost they could do for him. And a short time A.D.
afterwards the Tory government fell, leaving no resource
to the disappointed Dean but to hide himself and his baffled hopes
in Dublin. To a great and troubled spirit, such as Swift's, exile
from the centre of conflict was a doom little better than burial
alive.

For about six years he lived quietly, but not contentedly, in Dublin,
employing his pen on various subjects. Then the rage against
England, which had been festering in his heart through all these
years, burst out. A pamphlet appeared advocating strongly the use
of Irish manufactures in Ireland ;—undoubtedly a laudable work,
if we could forget that it sprang more from hatred to England

than love to Ireland. It took the fancy of the Irish people,—a
fancy which was kindled into flames of enthusiastic admiration,
when the same pen produced in a Dublin newspaper a series of
Letters signed M. B. Drapier, in which the Irish were warned
against exchanging their gold and silver for the bad half-
1724 pence and farthings of Wolverhampton Wood, who had
A.D. obtained a patent empowering him to coin £180,000
worth of copper for circulation in Ireland. No one would
take the bad money ; all attempts to bring the writer to trial were
unsuccessful, though everybody knew that the Drapier and the
Dean were the same man. Swift became the idol of the nation,
possessed of unbounded influence over the rabble. " If," said
he to an archbishop who blamed him for kindling a riotous flame,
" if I had lifted up my finger, they would have torn you to
pieces."

Who has not read *Gulliver's Travels?* and what young reader
has not been startled to learn, when its fascinating pages were
devoured, that it is a great political and social satire, filled with
the mad freaks of a furious, fantastic, and cankered genius. Greatness and wisdom mark every page of the wonderful fiction ; but
such greatness and wisdom are often the attributes of a
1726 fiend. The dwarfs of Lilliput, the giants of Brobdignag,
A.D. the philosophers of Laputa, the magicians of Glubbdubdrib,
afford much amusement, although we can never get entirely
rid of the harsh and iron laugh of the narrator, whose mockery
chills us as we read. Of the last voyage we may shortly say, that
none but a bad man could have imagined its events, and none but
impure minds can enjoy such revolting pictures. Hatred of men
has never, in any age or land, so polluted the current of a literature
as when Swift committed to paper his foul and monstrous conception of the Yahoo. The strange, wild book, published anonymously in 1726, had great success, and was read by high and
low.

Long ago, sitting over his books on a garden-seat at Moor Park,
he had caught a giddiness and deafness, which afflicted him at
intervals through all his life. The attacks became more frequent

after Stella's death. His temper, always sullen, grew ferocious. Yet he continued to write until 1736. Avarice and his savage moods thinned the circle of his visitors by quick degrees; and, when deafness shut him out from the world of human talk, his mind, flung in upon itself, darkened into madness. What a terrific picture! the lonely grey-haired lunatic hurrying for ten hours a day up and down his gloomy chamber, as if it were a cage and he a chained wild beast; never sitting even to eat, but devouring, as he walked, the plateful of cut meat which his keeper left for him at meal-time. Such were Swift's last sad days. Stella was well avenged. After three years of almost total silence, he died in October 1745. A pile of black marble marks his burial-place in St. Patrick's; but a more striking monument of the wrecked and wretched genius stands in one of Dublin streets—Swift's Hospital for idiots and incurable madmen, for the building and endowment of which he bequeathed nearly all his fortune.

Swift's fame rests on his pure and powerful prose. He seems to have hated foreign words as he hated men, and has given us such nervous, bare, unadorned, genuine English, as we get from no other pen. But he wrote verses too—coarse, strong, and graphic. *Morning*, *The City Shower*, a *Rhapsody on Poetry*, and *Verses on my Own Death* are amongst his best poetic compositions.

GULLIVER'S BOATING IN BROBDIGNAG.

The queen, who often used to hear me talk of my sea-voyages, and took all occasions to divert me when I was melancholy, asked me whether I understood how to handle a sail or an oar, and whether a little exercise of rowing might not be convenient for my health. I answered, that I understood both very well; for although my proper employment had been to be surgeon or doctor to the ship, yet often upon a pinch I was forced to work like a common mariner. But I could not see how this could be done in their country, where the smallest wherry was equal to a first-rate man-of-war among us, and such a boat as I could manage would never live in any of their rivers. Her majesty said, if I would contrive a boat, her own joiner should make it, and she would provide a place for me to sail in. The fellow was an ingenious workman, and, by my instructions, in ten days finished a pleasure-boat, with all its tackling, able conveniently to hold eight Europeans. When it was finished, the queen was so delighted, that she ran with it in her lap to the king, who ordered it to be put in a cistern full of water with me in it by way of trial; where I could not manage my two sculls,

or little oars, for want of room.   But the queen had before contrived another
project.   She ordered the joiner to make a wooden trough of three hundred feet
long, fifty broad, and eight deep, which being well pitched, to prevent leaking,
was placed on the floor along the wall in an outer room of the palace.   It had a
cock near the bottom to let out the water, when it began to grow stale ; and two
servants could easily fill it in half an hour.   Here I often used to row for my
own diversion, as well as that of the queen and her ladies, who thought themselves well entertained with my skill and agility.   Sometimes I would put up
my sail, and then my business was only to steer, while the ladies gave me a gale
with their fans ; and when they were weary, some of the pages would blow my
sail forward with their breath, while I showed my art by steering starboard or
larboard, as I pleased.   When I had done, Glumdalclitch always carried back my
boat into her closet, and hung it on a nail to dry.

CHAPTER VII.

OTHER WRITERS OF THE SIXTH ERA.

POETS.	~ John Gay.	Samuel Clarke.
Nicholas Rowe.	Richard Savage.	Lord Bolingbroke.
Isaac Watts.	Robert Blair.	Bishop Berkeley.
Ambrose Philips.	John Dyer.	Lady Mary Montagu.
Thomas Parnell.		Earl of Chesterfield.
Thomas Tickell.	PROSE WRITERS.	Lord Kames.
Allan Ramsay.	Earl of Shaftesbury.	

POETS.

NICHOLAS ROWE, born about 1673 in Bedfordshire, was educated for the law, his father's profession. His plays, of which the chief are *The Fair Penitent* and *Jane Shore*, won for the young lawyer the notice of the great. His social qualities endeared him to his literary friends. Upon the accession of George I. he was made Poet-laureate, and held other more lucrative public offices. Rowe died in 1718, and was buried in Westminster Abbey. Pope, Swift, and Addison were prominent among his friends. He is also remembered as the first editor of Shakspere worthy of the name.

ISAAC WATTS, born in 1674 at Southampton, became at twenty-four assistant minister of an Independent congregation at Stoke Newington. But his weak health prevented him from retaining this position. The last thirty-six years of his long life were spent in Abney House, whose kind owner, Sir Thomas Abney, was his warmest friend. Here he wrote the beautifully simple *Hymns*, which have made his name familiar to childhood. His works on *Logic*, and *The Improvement of the Mind*, show that he could write English prose also with clearness and force. He died in 1748.

AMBROSE PHILIPS, born in 1675 in Shropshire, received his education at St. John's, Cambridge. He was the real original

(15)   19

Namby Pamby,—a nickname which was given to him on account of the complimentary versicles he was fond of addressing to his friends and their babies. His *Pastorals*, though much praised in his own day, have not held their place in public favour. Philips was bitterly satirized by Pope. He died in 1749.

THOMAS PARNELL, of English descent, but born in Dublin in 1679, became archdeacon of Clogher, and, through the influence of his friend Swift, vicar of Finglas. He lived chiefly in London. *The Hermit* is the poem for which he now lives among the great names of English literature. He died and was buried at Chester in 1718.

THOMAS TICKELL, one of Addison's most intimate friends, born near Carlisle in 1686, wrote the pathetic ballad of *Colin and Lucy*. He undertook that translation of the *Iliad* which deepened Pope's feeling towards Addison into something akin to hatred. Tickell served Addison as secretary, and in 1724 went to Ireland as Secretary to the Lords-Justices. He died at Bath in 1740. He wrote an allegorical poem called *Kensington Gardens*, besides many papers in the *Spectator* and the *Guardian*.

ALLAN RAMSAY, who was born in 1686 and died in 1758, was a native of Leadhills, a Lanarkshire village. Most of his long life was passed in Edinburgh, where he was a wig-maker, and then a bookseller. His circulating library was the first that was established in Scotland. The small quaint house, on the slope of the Castle Hill, called Ramsay Lodge, was his residence during his last twelve years. Allan's shop was a favourite lounge of the poet Gay, when he came to Edinburgh. Ramsay's pastoral drama, *The Gentle Shepherd*, first published in 1725 and written in the strong broad Doric of North Britain, is the finest existing specimen of its class. His songs, too, have endeared him to the Scottish heart. *The Yellow-haired Laddie* and *Lochaber no More* are two of his most popular lyrics.

JOHN GAY, a Devonshire man of good family, born in 1688, was at first apprenticed to a silk-mercer in the Strand. But his wishes soared higher, especially after he took up the poet's pen. As domestic secretary to the Duchess of Monmouth, he found more leisure for writing, and rapidly brought out several poems and dramatic pieces. For about two months he held the position of Secretary to the Embassy at Hanover. But he was not fitted for business of any kind, and found his proper sphere when he was permitted to nestle down in a corner of the Queensberry household as a humble friend and domestic joker. "There," says Thackeray, "he was lapped in cotton, and had his plate of chicken and his saucer of cream, and frisked, and barked, and wheezed, and grew fat, and so ended." *The Shepherd's Week*, a series of comic pastorals; *Trivia, or the Art of Walking the Streets of London;* and *The Fan*, in three books, are among his works. But his fame rests chiefly on his artless, pleasant *Fables*, his song of *Black-eyed Susan*, and his *Beggars' Opera*. Gay died of fever in 1732.

RICHARD SAVAGE, born about 1697 in London, was the illegitimate child of noble parents. His history is a miserable tale. Drink and debauchery plunged him lower and lower, until in 1743 he was found dead in his wretched bed within Bristol Jail, where he lay a prisoner for debt. *The Wanderer* is his principal work; written in 1729, during a short glimpse of sunshine which he enjoyed in Lord Tyrconnel's mansion.

ROBERT BLAIR, born in 1699 at Edinburgh, became at thirty-two minister of Athelstaneford in East Lothian. Before that event he had composed his fine blank-verse poem, *The Grave*, but it was not published till 1743. A private fortune enabled Blair to cultivate society above what usually falls to the lot of a country minister. He died in 1746.

JOHN DYER, painter, poet, and clergyman, was born in Caermarthenshire about 1698, and died in 1758. He wrote *Grongar Hill, The Ruins of Rome*, and *The Fleece;* works which, especially the first, entitle him to a high place among descriptive and picturesque poets.

PROSE WRITERS.

ANTHONY ASHLEY COOPER, Earl of Shaftesbury, was born in London in 1671. In fine, sonorous, and elaborate English he discussed the great themes of metaphysics, most difficult of all sciences. His belief in a "moral sense, by which virtue and vice —things naturally and fundamentally distinct—are discriminated, and at once approved of or condemned, without reference to the self-interest of him who judges," is the salient point in his philosophical system. His works, published in three volumes, bear the name, *Characteristics of Men, Manners, Opinions, and Times.* He died at Naples in 1713.

SAMUEL CLARKE, Newton's friend, was born at Norwich in 1675. A graduate of Cambridge, he entered the Church, in which he held important livings both in his native town and in Westminster. His works are chiefly on such theological and metaphysical subjects, as *The Being and Attributes of God, Natural and Revealed Religion, The Immortality of the Soul,* and *The Trinity.* This learned and worthy man died in 1729. His refusal to accept the lucrative post of Master of the Mint, vacant by Newton's death, because it would interfere with his clerical duties, shows the unworldliness of his devotion to the sacred office he had chosen.

HENRY ST. JOHN, Viscount Bolingbroke, born at Battersea in 1678, received his education at Eton and Oxford. He was noted as a cold-hearted profligate, as an unfortunate politician, and as a writer of much eloquence, but of unfixed and shifting principles, both in religion and philosophy. In the reign of Anne he was Secretary of State. But the accession of the Guelphs drove him to France, where he joined the Pretender. A pardon enabled him in 1723 to return to England; but he was obliged again to retire across the Straits. During those days of exile in France some of his chief works were written : *Reflections on Exile, Letters on the Study of History,* and a *Letter on the True Use of Retirement.* He afterwards wrote at Battersea *Letters on the Spirit of Patriotism,* and the *Idea of a Patriot King.* From Bolingbroke Pope got much of that ethical system unfolded in the *Essay on Man.* Bolingbroke died in 1751.

GEORGE BERKELEY, made Bishop of Cloyne in 1734, was then fifty years of age. He was born in 1684 at Thomastown, in the county Kilkenny.   He is noted among our metaphysical writers, especially for his *Theory of Vision*, and those works which embody and display his *theory of ideas.*   He strives, but in vain, to prove that all sensible qualities, hardness, figure, extension, &c., are mere *ideas* in our own minds, and have no existence at all in the things we call hard, &c.—a dangerous and unsound doctrine.   Berkeley died at Oxford in 1753.   His English is simple, scholar-like, and clear.

LADY MARY WORTLEY MONTAGU, daughter of the Duke of Kingston, was born in 1690, and at twenty-two was married to Edward Wortley Montagu.   Her residence for two years (1716–18) at Constantinople, where her husband was English ambassador, gave her an opportunity of seeing life in many varieties, and her graceful, graphic *Letters*, descriptive of travel and foreign fashions, abound with light and most agreeable reading.   Her amusement at Pope's silly declaration of love for her threw her into a hearty burst of laughter, which made the little poet ever afterwards her mortal foe.   She died in 1761, and her " Letters " were first printed two years later.   She conferred a great benefit on England by the introduction of inoculation for the small-pox, a practice she had noticed among the Turkish poor.

PHILIP STANHOPE, Earl of Chesterfield, born in 1694, wrote a series of *Letters* to his son, which had a great sale in the years succeeding the author's death.   They are just such Letters as a polished infidel man of fashion would write, and depict anything but the true notion of gentlemanhood.   A brilliant polish on the surface would atone, according to the maxims of Chesterfield, for any rottenness, however great, within.   He died in 1773.

HENRY HOME, born in 1696, assumed the title of Lord Kames, when in 1752 he ascended the Scottish bench.   The work for which his name is best known is that entitled *The Elements of Criticism*, in which he founds the art upon the principles of human nature.   He wrote other metaphysical and several legal works.   He died in 1782.

SEVENTH ERA OF ENGLISH LITERATURE.

FROM THE PUBLICATION OF PAMELA IN 1740 A.D. TO THE DEATH OF JOHNSON IN 1784 A.D.

CHAPTER I.

LITERARY LIFE IN THE EIGHTEENTH CENTURY.

Phases of author-life.	Success of a few.
Walpole no bookman.	Waiting on managers.
Life of well-to-do writers.	The great man's hall.
Grub Street hacks.	Dedications.
Passage from Macaulay.	Booksellers' shops.

As we look back upon that remarkable era of our literature which runs through Queen Anne's reign and far into that of George the First, we see two phases of author-life—the one rich and brilliant—the other dark, poor, and wretched. There are no middle tints—nothing but bright light and deepest shadow. If an author made a hit, up he went to the very top of the tree, where the golden fruit grew and the sunlight of courtly favour played ever warmly round him; if he failed to attract attention, there was nothing for even the most hard-working hack but to plod on with as much hope as he could muster, grubbing in the earth around its roots for the wretched food that scarcely kept his bones from starting through the skin.

But the artificial system of encouragement, by which men who wrote well, became, without the possession of other qualifications, Ambassadors, Commissioners, Surveyors, or Secretaries, did not last long. Walpole, a man who cared little for books and less for their writers, came into office, and almost at once the whole literary profession sank, with a few exceptions, into indigence and obscurity. The exceptions can easily be counted. Pope had made enough by his "Homer" to live snugly at Twickenham; so he was independent of Walpole or any other man. Richardson, the novelist, lived on the profits of his extensive business as a printer. Young, to be sure, got a pension; and Thomson, after tasting the worst miseries of author-life, got £100 a year from the Prince of Wales and a sinecure office worth other £300. But they were a mere handful of the writers who swarmed in London during the last century. Nearly all the rest lived from hand to mouth; a life so wretched and precarious, that Grub Street, in which they herded together, has become a name inseparably associated with rags and hunger.

The mode of life among prosperous writers has been indicated with sufficient clearness in the chapters on Addison and Steele. They wore the clothes, drank the wine, played the games, and resorted to the haunts of fine gentlemen in the time of Anne. They tapped their snuff-boxes, and offered the perfumed pinch with the true modish air, in the dainty drawing-rooms of Covent Garden and Soho Square. They paid their twopence at the bar of the fashionable coffee-houses, and lit their long clay pipes at the little wax tapers that burned on the tables among the best company in London.

There were literary men, however, of Addison's own time, but more especially of a later day, to whom the penny or twopence paid for admission to the coffee-house was often the price of a meal. These poor strugglers were glad to get any kind of work that pen could do. They compiled indexes and almanacs; they wrote puffing reviews and short notices of books; they kept a stock of prefaces and prologues always on hand, one of which they gladly sold for half-a-crown. They edited classic authors with notes, and translated works from French, Italian, Latin, or Greek, for fewer guineas than the thin fingers that held their worn-out stump of a goose-quill. It was a red-letter day with them, when one of their articles was accepted by the proprietor of the *Gentleman's Magazine.* And all this drudgery was in many cases imbittered by the con-

sciousness that they were fitted for higher work, and the feeling
that their daily battle for a crust and a garret was wearing out the
brain by sheer stress of over-work and under-pay.

Such a life, with its miseries and its fierce rushes into mad
debauchery, whenever a driblet of money came, is thus painted by
Macaulay in one of his Essays: "All that is squalid and miserable
might now be summed up in the word Poet. That word denoted
a creature dressed like a scare-crow, familiar with compters and
spunging-houses, and perfectly qualified to decide on the comparative merits of the Common Side in the King's Bench prison,
and of Mount Scoundrel in the Fleet. Even the poorest pitied
him. And they well might pity him. For if their condition was
equally abject, their aspirings were not equally high, nor their
sense of insult equally acute. To lodge in a garret up four pair
of stairs; to dine in a cellar among footmen out of place; to translate ten hours a day for the wages of a ditcher; to be hunted by
bailiffs from one haunt of beggary and pestilence to another, from
Grub Street to St. George's Fields, and from St. George's Fields
to the alleys behind St. Martin's Church; to sleep on a bulk in
June and amidst the ashes of a glass-house in December; to die
in an hospital and to be buried in a parish vault, was the fate of
more than one writer, who, if he had lived thirty years earlier,
would have been admitted to the sittings of the Kitcat or the
Scriblerus Club, would have sat in Parliament, and would have
been intrusted with embassies to the High Allies; who, if he had
lived in our time, would have found encouragement scarcely less
munificent in Albemarle Street or in Paternoster Row.

"As every climate has its peculiar diseases, so every walk of
life has its peculiar temptations. The literary character, assuredly,
has always had its share of faults,—vanity, jealousy, morbid sensibility. To these faults were now superadded the faults which are
commonly found in men whose livelihood is precarious, and whose
principles are exposed to the trial of severe distress. All the vices
of the gambler and of the beggar were blended with those of the
author. The prizes in the wretched lottery of book-making were
scarcely less ruinous than the blanks. If good fortune came, it

came in such a manner that it was almost certain to be abused. After months of starvation and despair, a full third night or a well-received dedication filled the pocket of the lean, ragged, unwashed poet with guineas. He hastened to enjoy those luxuries with the images of which his mind had been haunted, while he was sleeping amidst the cinders and eating potatoes at the Irish ordinary in Shoe Lane. A week of taverns soon qualified him for another year of night cellars. Such was the life of Savage, of Boyse, and of a crowd of others. Sometimes blazing in gold-laced hats and waistcoats; sometimes lying in bed because their coats had gone to pieces, or wearing paper cravats because their linen was in pawn; sometimes drinking Champagne and Tokay; sometimes standing at the window of an eating-house in Porridge island to snuff up the scent of what they could not afford to taste; they knew luxury; they knew beggary; but they never knew comfort. These men were irreclaimable. They looked on a regular and frugal life with the same aversion which an old gipsy or a Mohawk hunter feels for a stationary abode, and for the restraints and securities of civilized communities. They were as untamable, as much wedded to their desolate freedom, as the wild ass. They could no more be broken in to the offices of social man than the unicorn could be trained to serve and abide by the crib. It was well if they did not, like the beasts of a still fiercer race, tear the hands which ministered to their necessities. To assist them was impossible; and the most benevolent of mankind at length became weary of giving relief which was dissipated with the wildest profusion as soon as it had been received. If a sum was bestowed on the wretched adventurer, such as, properly husbanded, might have supplied him for six months, it was instantly spent in strange freaks of sensuality, and, before forty-eight hours had elapsed, the poet was again pestering all his acquaintances for twopence to get a plate of shin of beef at a subterraneous cook-shop. If his friends gave him an asylum in their houses, those houses were forthwith turned into taverns. All order was destroyed; all business was suspended. The most good-natured host began to repent of his eagerness to serve a man of genius in distress, when he heard his guest roaring for fresh punch at five o'clock in the morning."

Through such a life some, like Samuel Johnson, struggled up to competence and fame; but by far the greater number perished prematurely, worn out with the toils and fiery fevers of the rugged and perilous way; and there was not a man of those who passed safely through the furnace, but bore the deep scars of the burning with him to the grave.

Men who lived thus on the verge of starvation, would not, as we may well suppose, be very nice in their taste, or very choice in the expressions which they hurled at a political or literary foe. They needed to be kept in order; and many brethren of the literary craft were, therefore, no strangers in the eighteenth century to the pillory and the scourge.

When an author had finished a play, his first care was to carry the precious manuscript to the most likely manager he knew; and to this great man he confided it with many low bows and cringing civilities. Weeks—perhaps months—passed by; and the theatrical season drew near its close. Still no missive from the theatre. With fear and trembling the threadbare, haggard author presents himself at the stage door, and is ushered, after some delay, into the presence of the autocrat. He humbly ventures to remind His Dramatic Highness of the play left there many months ago; and is rewarded for the sickening suspense he has endured, and the abject humility he has had to assume in making his approaches to the presence, by the cool assurance that such a thing has been utterly forgotten until that moment. And sure enough, after tumbling over heaps of similar papers, the dusty manuscript is found lying as it was left, tied up with the very red string which the wretched dramatist had begged from his landlady to encircle the all-important roll. He is a lucky man if this second reminder induces the manager to read and accept the play; the chances are that it is returned unread, with the consolatory remark that dozens of authors have been so treated during the season. If he has heart and pluck enough to persist, the only hope of really getting his work put on the stage, is to curry favour with some nobleman's

valet, who may induce his Lordship to read the play and recommend it to a manager.   One poor fellow, who had danced attendance
thus upon a leading London.manager for many months, at last
grew sick of the constant drain upon his temper and his patience,
and demanded his play again.   It could not be found.   Fruitless
search was made,—it was gone.   And when the broken-spirited
literary hack ventured to complain of such treatment, the irritated
manager, thrusting his hands into a drawer, drew out a bundle of
manuscript plays with, " Choose any three of these for your miserable scribble, and let me hear no more of it or you."

Equally trying to the spirit, and yet more galling in the abject
humility it demanded, was the hanging on at a great man's door,
or the waiting in a great man's hall to pluck my Lord by the sleeve
as he passed to his carriage, and beg a subscription for a forthcoming volume of poetry or prose.   Success in such an undertaking
depended much upon the number of half-crowns the poor author
could afford to invest in buying the good-will of .the porter or confi-
dential footman of His Grace or Sir John.   Not even the highest
literary man was free from this humiliation of cringing before the
great.   No book appeared without a fulsome dedication or flattering apostrophe addressed to some person of quality, as the phrase
then went, whose footman came smirking to the author's dingy
room a few days after publication with a present of five, or ten,
or twenty guineas—the sum varying according to the amount of
flattery laid on the belauded name, or perhaps oftener according
to the run of luck which the gratified fashionable had happened
to meet at the card-table of the night before.

In such miserable ways alone could the author of the eighteenth
century eke out the poor pittance which the booksellers of the
time—Tonson, Lintot, or Curll—could or did afford to pay for
original works.   But we must not suppose, as we might be led to
suppose if we judged alone from the works of disappointed authors,
that every London bookseller of the day was a kind of trading
ogre, who fattened on the blood and brains of the writers he employed.   The sale of books in general was small and slow.   The
circle of book-readers was narrow; but still narrower was the

circle of book-buyers.   Indeed many men never bought books at all ; but when any work came out of which they wished to get a sight, they went to the bookseller's shop day after day, and for a small subscription obtained leave to read at the counter. Marking their page where they left off in the afternoon, they came back again and again, until the volume was finished.   This prac- tice, which crowded the shops and stalls of the booksellers a hundred years ago with a floating population of readers, laid the foundation of those useful circulating libraries and reading-clubs which so abound in modern days.

CHAPTER II.

JAMES THOMSON.

Born 1700 A.D.........Died 1748 A.D.

The Seasons.	Sophonisba.	Cottage at Richmond.
Early life.	On the Continent.	His death.
Arrives in London.	Secretary of Briefs.	The Castle of Indolence.
Winter.	Pensioned.	Illustrative extract.

EVERY one has read Thomson's *Seasons;* comparatively few have read his *Castle of Indolence.* Yet the latter is the finer piece of literary workmanship. The subject of the former comes home to every heart,—we like to find our own thoughts and feelings pictured in the books we read ; and so the poem of the Seasons, displaying in glittering blank-verse the changeful beauty of the year, has come to be read by old and young, and loved by all.

The poet's father was minister of Ednam in Roxburghshire; and there in 1700 James was born. Having received his elementary education at the Grammar School of Jedburgh, he became a student in the University of Edinburgh. Nothing of importance marked his progress there, until one day in the Divinity classroom he paraphrased a psalm in language so brilliantly figurative as to excite the wonder of the class and draw forth a rebuke from the professor, who cautioned him against the use of such highflown diction in the pulpit. This was the turning-point in the youth's career; forthwith he abandoned his studies for the Church, wrote poetry more diligently than before, and, upon the slightest encouragement from a friend, went to seek his fortune among the literary men of London.

A raw Scotchman, newly landed in London streets, was then the butt of every Cockney witling, and the sure prey of every city thief. Thomson did not escape; for as he gaped along the street, his letters of introduction, which he had carefully knotted into his handkerchief, were stolen from his pocket. But he did not de-

spair.   When his poem of *Winter*, of which his friend Mallet
thought very highly, was finished, he offered the manu-
1726 script to several booksellers without success; until at last
A.D.   a Mr. Millar bought it for three guineas.   It appeared in
1726.   Poets in those days, if they desired success, were
forced, as we have just seen, to dance attendance on the great.
Having selected some rich or powerful man, they wrote a dedication, crammed with compliments, which often drew from the flattered magnate a purse of guineas, far outweighing the niggard pay
they got from their booksellers.   Thomson in this way received
twenty guineas from Sir Spencer Compton.   Quickly "Winter"
grew into public favour.   One literary amateur and another read
it, and buzzed the praises of the new poet everywhere.   The
panorama of the completed *Seasons* soon followed this success.
Thomson tried his pen, too, upon tragedy; but *Sophonisba* perished
from the stage in a few nights, killed by the echo of one weak line.

"O Sophonisba! Sophonisba, O!"

wrote the poor poet;

"O Jemmy Thomson! Jemmy Thomson, O!"

cried some critical mocking-bird; and the mischief was done, for
all London rang with a ready laugh.

In 1731 Thomson set out for the Continent, as tutor to the son
of Sir Charles Talbot, afterwards Lord Chancellor.   Having travelled through France, Switzerland, and Italy with his pupil, he
returned to England and published a poem on *Liberty*, which he
wrongly considered to be his greatest work.   About the same time
he received from his patron Talbot the easy place of Secretary of
Briefs in Chancery.   When the Chancellor died, the Secretary lost
office; although it is said that he might have retained it by soliciting
the favour of the incoming minister.   The loss of this appointment
drove the poet again to pen-work.   He wrote for the stage two
tragedies, which proved failures.   But the Prince of Wales granted
him a yearly pension of £100; and he was, besides, made Sur-
veyor-General of the Leeward Islands,—from which office, after
paying a man to do the work, he drew about £300 a year.

So the fat and lazy poet found at last a snug haven in which to spend his few remaining days. A pretty cottage at Richmond, filled with good furniture and well supplied with wine and ale, was the last home of Thomson. There, lounging in his garden or his easy-chair, he brought to a close his greatest poem, *The Castle of Indolence*, lavishing on its polished lines the wealth of his ripened genius. This latest effort was published in May 1748. One day in the following August, after a sharp walk out of town, which heated him, he took a boat at Hammersmith for Kew. On the water he got chilled—neglected the slight cold, as many do—became feverish—and in a few days was dead.

The plan and style of Thomson's *Seasons* are too well known to need much comment. Many fine episodes of human life relieve the stillness and deepen the interest of the ever-changing pictures of natural scenery which fill this beautiful poem. A certain roughness and crudity, disfiguring many passages of the original work, were removed by the poet, as years developed more fully his artistic skill. So many, indeed, were the changes and corrections, that the third edition of the "Seasons" may be looked upon almost as a new work. Thomson's style becomes occasionally inflated and wordy; but, as to the ring of his blank-verse, it has been well said, that, with all its faults, it is his own—not the echo of another poet's song.

"The Castle of Indolence," an allegory written in the stanza and the style of Spenser, affords a noble specimen of poetic art. No better illustration could be given of that wonderful linking of sound with sense, which critics call *onomatopœia*. Stanza after stanza rolling its dreamy music on the ear, soothes us with a soft and sleepy charm. Like Tennyson's Lotus Eaters, the dwellers in this enchanted keep lie steeped in drowsy luxury. The good knight Industry breaks the magician's spell; but (alas for the moral teaching of the allegory!) we have grown so delighted with the still and cushioned life, whose hours glide slumberously by, that we feel almost angry with the restless being who dissolves the delicious charm. No man or boy need hope to be lured into early rising by the study of this poem. That Thomson's *forte* lay in description, is clearly shown in both his leading works. On such a theme as Indolence he wrote *con amore;* for no man could better enjoy the *dolce far niente* of the lazy Italian than he could himself. And when, after some hard battling with the stern realities of life, he had settled himself down in his quiet nest at Richmond—itself a Cottage of Indolence—all circumstances were most favourable to the composition of his great work. It took its colours from his daily life. With £400 a year and nothing to do for it—lying down and rising when he liked—sauntering in the green lanes around his house, or sucking peaches in sunny nooks of his little garden—he mused and wrote and smoothed his verses, undisturbed by anything which could mar the music of his song.

STANZAS FROM "THE CASTLE OF INDOLENCE."

In lowly dale, fast by a river's side,
With woody hill o'er hill encompassed round,
A most enchanting wizard did abide,
Than whom a fiend more fell is nowhere found.
It was, I ween, a lovely spot of ground:
And there a season atween June and May,
Half pranked with spring, with summer half imbrowned,
A listless climate made, where, sooth to say,
No living wight could work, ne cared even for play.

Was nought around but images of rest:
Sleep-soothing groves and quiet lawns between;
And flowery beds that slumberous influence kest,
From poppies breathed; and beds of pleasant green,
Where never yet was creeping creature seen.
Meantime unnumbered glittering streamlets played,
And hurled everywhere their waters sheen;
That, as they bickered through the sunny glade,
Though restless still themselves, a lulling murmur made.

Joined to the prattle of the purling rills,
Was heard the lowing herds along the vale,
And flocks loud bleating from the distant hills,
And vacant shepherds piping in the dale:
And now and then sweet Philomel would wail,
Or stock-doves 'plain amid the forest deep,
That drowsy rustled to the sighing gale;
And still a coil the grasshopper did keep;
Yet all these sounds yblent inclined all to sleep.

Full in the passage of the vale above,
A sable, silent, solemn forest stood,
Where nought but shadowy forms was seen to move,
As Idlesse fancied in her dreaming mood ;
And up the hills, on either side, a wood
Of blackening pines, aye waving to and fro,
Sent forth a sleepy horror through the blood ;
And where this valley winded out below,
The murmuring main was heard, and scarcely heard, to flow.

A pleasing land of drowsy-head it was,
Of dreams that wave before the half-shut eye ;
And of gay castles in the clouds that pass,
For ever flushing round a summer sky:
There eke the soft delights, that witchingly
Instil a wanton sweetness through the breast,
And the calm pleasures, always hovered nigh ;
But whate'er smacked of noyance or unrest,
Was far, far off expelled from this delicious nest.

CHAPTER III.

SAMUEL RICHARDSON.

Born 1689 A.D..........Died 1761 A.D.

Birth and education.	King's Printer.	Sir Charles Grandison.
Boyish life.	Begins to write.	Value of such works.
Bound apprentice.	Pamela.	His death.
Thrives in business.	Clarissa Harlowe.	Illustrative extract.

SAMUEL RICHARDSON, the first parent of that countless tribe, the modern novel, was a joiner's son. Born in Derbyshire in 1689, the little fellow went to a village school, where he became a great favourite with his class-fellows by the exercise of his remarkable gift of story-telling. Ragged and bare-footed the little circle may have been that hemmed in the boy-novelist with its line of berry-brown cheeks and sun-bleached hair; but it was a pleasant picture for the old printer to look back upon through the lens of many years, as the beginning of his fame. We have a companion picture in the group that gathered so often in the Yards of the Edinburgh High School round little Walter Scott, clamorous for another story out of the teeming brain and glowing fancy, which were destined to delight the world with the richly-coloured fictions of a riper time. Nor was it only among the school-boys of the village that young Sam Richardson was a favourite. His quiet, womanly nature, made him love the society of the gentler sex; and while his rougher audiences were scattered through the woods enjoying the savage glories of bird-nesting, or were filling the village green with their noisy games at fives or hockey, he sat, through spring afternoons and long summer evenings, the centre of a little group of needle-women, who sewed and listened while he read some pleasant book, or told one of his enchaining tales. Three of these kind girl-friends put his abilities to another use, when they secretly begged him to write their love-letters for them, or at least to put what they had already written into a polished shape. In these occupations of his boyhood we can easily trace the germs, which grew in later years into *Pamela* and *Clarissa Harlowe*.

In his fifteenth year young Richardson was bound apprentice to Mr. John Wilde, a London printer. And thenceforward his career of prosperity in trade and of advancement in civic dignity resembles strongly the upward progress of the honest apprentice, as delineated by Hogarth's graphic pencil. During his seven years of servitude he is honoured and trusted by his master, who calls him " the pillar of the house." His seven years over, he remains for some time as foreman among the old familiar types and presses. Then, setting up in business for himself in Salisbury Court, Fleet Street, he marries his master's daughter, and rises high in the estimation of the booksellers; for he possesses all the qualities most prized in a man of business, and, in addition, a certain literary faculty, which lifts him high above the mere mechanical craftsman. He continues in a small way to use the pen he had found so telling in the service of the Derbyshire lasses. Booksellers whom he knew used often to ask him for a preface or a dedication for the books he was printing. And so this honest London printer flourished and throve, winning, by his gentle, feminine kindness, the good-will of all around him, and amassing, by steady industry and attention to his trade, a very considerable fortune. His position as a business man may be judged from the fact, that the printing of the Journals of the House of Commons was given to him while he was yet comparatively young. He was elected Master of the Stationers' Company in 1754; and, six years later, he bought one-half share in the patent of King's Printer.

But it is not as King's Printer that we remember Samuel Richardson with such reverent affection. When more than fifty years of this printer's life had passed, a talent, which had been slumbering almost unknown in the keen business brain, awoke to active life. A couple of bookselling friends requested him to draw up a series of familiar letters, containing hints for guiding the affairs of common life. Richardson undertook the task, but, inspired with the happy idea of giving a deeper human interest to the letters, he made them tell a connected story, which he justly thought would barb the moral with a keener and surer point. In a similar way the "Pickwick Papers," perhaps the most humorous book in English fiction, grew into being. A young writer, who had already furnished picturesque sketches of London life to an evening paper, was invited by a publishing firm to write some comic adventures in illustration of a set of sporting plates. He began to write, and, losing sight very soon of the original idea of the work, he produced the narrative over which so many hearty, honest laughs have been enjoyed.

The subject of Richardson's first novel, *Pamela, or Virtue Rewarded*, is the domestic history of a pretty peasant girl who goes out to service; and, after enduring many mishaps and escaping many dangers, becomes the wife of her rich young master. A simple, common theme, and quite unlike the subject-matter of those heavy, affected, licentious romances, which had hitherto supplied readers of fiction with poisonous amusement in their leisure hours. It is surprising with how much truth Richardson has painted the life of this persecuted girl. That spice of the woman in his own nature, to which reference has been already made, and his early love for the playful and innocent chat which beguiles the gentle toil of a circle of happy girls, busy with their needle-work or knitting, give a peculiarly feminine colouring to the pictures of Pamela's life. Little more than three months were occupied with the composition of the first part of this book. It appeared in 1740, and became the rage at once. Five editions were sold within the year. The ladies went wild with rapture over its pages, and began almost to idolize the successful author. The appearance of "Pamela" has been chosen, in our plan, as the opening of a new era in English literature. It marks the turning of the tide. The affectation and deep depravity of the earlier school of fiction had been slowly wearing away. People were sick, without knowing it, of the paint and patches, the brocades and strutting airs, which disguised the foul spirit lurking under the garb of romance; and when a simple tale

1740
A.D.

appeared, whose faults we are disposed to magnify by a contrast
with our purer books, the reäction commenced, and a flood
began to rise, whose even, steady flow, has cleansed the deepening
channels of our literature from many pollutions.

"Pamela" was followed in 1748 by a yet greater work, *The
History of Clarissa Harlowe.* So powerful was the hold with
which this first of our great novelists had grasped the public
mind, that during the progress of " Clarissa," he was deluged with
letters, entreating him to save his heroine from the web of
misery he was slowly weaving round her. Happily for his own
fame, he turned a deaf ear to such requests, and has added to our
literary treasures a grand tragedy in prose, of which the catastrophe has been worthily compared to "the noblest efforts of
pathetic conception in Scott, in our elder dramatists, or in the
Greek tragedians."

In less than five years, Richardson was ready with the first
volumes of his third great work, *Sir Charles Grandison;* in which,
adopting a similar epistolary style, he paints with the same minuteness of touch the character of a gentleman and a Christian.
Here, it must be confessed, he somewhat fails ; for we get very tired
of the long-winded and ceremonious Sir Charles, and his prim
sweetheart. The truth seems to be, that Richardson hardly drew
Sir Charles from the life ; for although well to do as a citizen of rich
London, he had not the *entrée* of those drawing-rooms, where one
or two genuine Grandisons mingled with scores of gaily dressed
and foully cankered Lovelaces.

Few read Richardson's novels in this fast age ; for their extreme
length and minuteness of description,—in which there appears
something of a womanish love of gossip—repel any but earnest
students of English fiction. Our appetite for such tedious works
has been spoiled by the banquets which Scott and Thackeray
and Dickens have spread before us. But when we compare
" Pamela " and " Clarissa " with the works that had preceded them,
leaving out of sight those modern fictions which have since enriched
our libraries, we shall be better able to appreciate the value of such
productions, and we shall be less disposed to cavil at their faults,

which stand clearly out in the light of modern refinement. Their naturalness and comparative purity of tone made them a precious boon to reading England in the day when they were written.

Richardson's last years were spent in his villa at Parson's Green, where the ladies, whose friendship he had won by his gentle life and charming books, vied with one another in soothing the last hours of the good old man. He died in 1761, at the ripe age of seventy-two.

PAMELA AT CHURCH.

Yesterday we set out, attended by John, Abraham, Benjamin, and Isaac, in fine new liveries, in the best chariot, which had been cleaned, lined, and new harnessed; so that it looked like a quite new one; but I had no arms to quarter with my dear lord and master's, though he jocularly, upon my noticing my obscurity, said that he had a good mind to have the olive branch quartered for mine. I was dressed in the suit of white, flowered with silver, a rich head-dress, and the diamond necklace, ear-rings, &c., I mentioned before : and my dear sir, in a fine laced silk waistcoat of blue Paduasoy, and his coat a pearl-coloured fine cloth, with gold buttons and button-holes, and lined with white silk; and he looked charmingly indeed. I said, I was too fine, and would have laid aside some of the jewels; but he said, it would be thought a slight to me from him, as his wife; and though I apprehended that people might talk as it was, yet he had rather they should say anything, than that I was not put upon an equal foot, as his wife, with any lady he might have married.

It seems the neighbouring gentry had expected us, and there was a great congregation; for (against my wish) we were a little late, so that, as we walked up the church to his seat, we had many gazers and whisperers: but my dear master behaved with so intrepid an air, and was so cheerful and complaisant to me, that he did credit to his kind choice, instead of shewing as if he was ashamed of it: and I was resolved to busy my mind entirely with the duties of the day ; my intentness on that occasion, and my thankfulness to God for His unspeakable mercies to me, so took up my thoughts, I was much less concerned than I should otherwise have been, at the gazings and whisperings of the congregation, whose eyes were all turned to our seat. When the sermon was ended, we stayed the longer, for the church to be pretty empty ; but we found great numbers at the doors, and in the porch; and I had the pleasure of hearing many commendations, as well of my person as my dress and behaviour, and not one reflection, or mark of disrespect.

CHAPTER IV.

HENRY FIELDING.

Born 1707 A.D.............Died 1754 A.D.

Pamela.	Joseph Andrews.	His chief works.
Early life.	A police magistrate.	The life they describe.
Studies law.	Breaking up.	Nature of his plots.
Writes on politics.	His death	Illustrative extract.

MINGLED with the delighted murmur of praise and congratulation which welcomed Richardson's "Pamela," there rang a mocking laugh from the crowd of scamps and fast men, who ran riot in London streets, beating the feeble old watchmen, and frightening timid wayfarers out of their wits. To such men virtue was a jest; and among the loudest laughers was a careless, good-humoured, very clever lawyer of thirty-five, called Harry Fielding. Richardson scarcely heeded—for he must have expected—the jeers of the aristocratic coffee-houses; but he was bitterly mortified at Fielding's laughter, for that mad wag laughed on paper, and in 1742 gave the world the novel of *Joseph Andrews*, a wicked mockery of those virtuous lessons which the respectable printer of Salisbury Court had endeavoured to inculcate by his first book.

The life of Fielding has in it much of the same colouring and scenery as the life of Dick Steele—a thoroughly congenial spirit, gay, careless, improvident, witty, and excessively good-natured. Lady Mary Montagu well knew of whom she was writing, when she described Fielding as one who forgot every evil, when he was before a venison pasty and a flask of champagne.

He was born in 1707, at Sharpham Park in Somersetshire. His father was a general in the army, and his mother was the daughter of a judge. General Fielding, who was a grandson of the Earl of Denbigh, set an example of extravagance, which his celebrated son was but too ready to imitate. A broken residence at Eton and Leyden gave Harry a kind of rambling education; but, no supplies coming from home, he was obliged at the age of twenty to cut his studies short, and try to make his bread by writing for the London stage. He entered literary life as a composer of light comedies and farces; but in this department he gained no great renown.

About 1735 he married Miss Cradock, who brought him £1500, upon the strength of which, and a small estate left him by his mother, he retired to the country for a time. But only for a time. Two years sufficed to scatter to the winds almost every guinea he had; and he came up to town again, to enter the Middle Temple, and there complete his long suspended

1740   study of the law. Called to the bar in 1740, he struggled
A.D.   for a while with the opening difficulties of a lawyer's career; but few briefs came his way, and his pen was the chief bread-winner of the household. It was principally as a pamphleteer, or political writer, in defence of the Hanoverian succession, that he employed his literary powers during this period of his life. In our day, he would have written telling leaders for the *Times*, or rather for the *Saturday Review*.

Then came that tide in the current of his life, which, taken at the flood, bore him on, if not to fortune, at least to lasting fame. Richardson published "Pamela;" and Fielding ridiculed the sentimentalism of the work in his *Joseph Andrews*. This start

1742   in the novel-writing line took place in 1742. The char-
A.D.   acter of Parson Adams is justly considered to be Fielding's master-piece of literary portraiture.

Now fairly embarked as a successful novelist, and fully awake to the powers of that pen, long degraded to petty uses, he continued to produce the works inseparably associated with his name. His political connections, however, were still kept up. For a while he edited a journal directed against the Jacobites, who, in 1745, showed a front so threatening. And in 1749 he was appointed, through the interest of Lord Lyttelton, one of the Justices of Peace for Middlesex and Westminster. This position, similar in nearly all respects to that of a London police-magistrate, brought him in fees amounting to not quite £300 a year.

But though the emoluments of the office were small, and obtained by unpleasant drudgery, his position yet enabled him to observe phases of low and criminal life, which supplied fine material for his darker sketches of English society.

Unhappily, this active man never could shake off the habits of dissipation he had contracted in his early life; and such bore, in middle age, their necessary fruits. Dropsy, jaundice, and asthma seized him in their dreadful grip, and, after a vain struggle for health in England, he sailed in 1754 for Lisbon, to try **1754** the effect of a warmer climate. All was useless. His A.D. life's strength was gone. In the autumn of that year he died in the city of his exile, and was buried there in the cemetery of the British Factory.

In spite of the coarseness and indelicacy which mar its pages, Fielding's novel of *Tom Jones* is recognised as a work of remarkable genius. Written in his first year of magistrate life, it contains scenes and characters which could be drawn only from the daily experiences of the police-bench. *Jonathan Wild* and *Amelia* are the principal remaining fictions of this great artist. The former depicts the career of a thief, who turns thief-catcher and ends his days upon the gallows. The latter commemorates the domestic virtue either of the novelist's first wife, or of that amiable maid-servant, who sorrowed so deeply for the loss of her mistress, that, in gratitude and tender concern for his motherless children, he made her their second mother. And he never regretted the step, for she did her duty with loving faithfulness both to him and them.

The life described in Fielding's books was—let us be thankful for the change—totally unlike the life we now live. Much of the fun was of the roughest physical kind—practical jokes that would now-a-days fill our courts of law with actions for assault and battery, and violent altercations in road-side inns, which generally ended in a row, involving everybody present, to the serious detriment of eyes and limbs. The *mêlée* of fishwives, cabbage-mongers, and policemen, which enlivens every second or third scene of the comic business in our Christmas pantomimes, affords us a specimen of the same boisterous humour. Everything is pelted about, and everybody beats everybody else, until the noisy crowd is hustled off the stage, and the scene or chapter ends. The tedious mode of travelling, especially the crawling of the stage waggon or slow coach of those days, necessarily gives a striking prominence to inn-life; for those who travelled much, a hundred years ago, spent one-third of their nights in the Maypoles and Blue Dragons that lined every road. The highwayman, too, is sure to figure wherever the progress of travellers is depicted. And here the novelist has ample scope for displaying the courage of his hero, or the cowardice of some braggart soldier, who has been swearing and twirling his moustache fiercely ever since the coach set out, but who turns pale, and with shaking hand fumbles silently for his purse, when the ominous pistol-barrel shows its dark muzzle at the coach window.

Fielding's early practice as a writer for the stage formed his first literary training for the great works that have made his name famous. We may safely hazard the conjecture, that his novels would have wanted much of their brilliant, changeful play, and skilful development of story, if his pen had not been well practised already in the farces and vaudevilles of his dramatic days. A play may be viewed, not improperly, as the skeleton of a novel. The frame-work of dialogue is there, which, being filled up and clothed with passages of description, grows into the full work of fiction. A play acted on the stage before us, and a novel in the hand, from which we read, address the mind through different channels, but with like result. In a play, we see the bustling movement of the plot, the varied dresses of the actors, and the painted scenery amid which they play their parts; and, combining these with the spoken words, we trace the outline of each individual character, and become wrapped in the interest of the story. In the novel, action, costume, and scenery are depicted by those descriptive passages, of which Sir Walter Scott was so fine a painter.

PARTRIDGE AT THE PLAY.

As soon as the play, which was *Hamlet, Prince of Denmark*, began, Partridge was all attention, nor did he break silence till the entrance of the ghost; upon which he asked Jones: "What man that was in the strange dress; something," said he, "like what I have seen in a picture. Sure it's not armour, is it?" Jones answered: "That is the ghost." To which Partridge replied, with a smile: "Persuade me to that, sir, if you can. Though I can't say I ever actually saw a ghost in my life, yet I am certain I should know one if I saw him better than that comes to. No, no, sir; ghosts don't appear in such dresses as that neither." In this mistake, which caused much laughter in the neighbourhood of Partridge, he was suffered to continue till the scene between the ghost and Hamlet, when Partridge gave that credit to Mr. Garrick which he had denied to Jones, and fell into so violent a trembling that his knees knocked against each other. Jones asked him what was the matter, and whether he was afraid of the warrior upon the stage. "O la! sir," said he, "I perceive now it is what you told me. I am not afraid of anything, for I know it is but a play; and if it was really a ghost, it could do one no harm at such a distance, and in so much company; and yet if I was frightened, I am not the only person." "Why, who," cries Jones; "dost thou take me to be such a coward here besides thyself?" "Nay, you may call me coward if you will; but if that little man there upon the stage is not frightened, I never saw any man frightened in my life. Ay, ay; go along with you! Ay, to be sure! Who's fool, then? Will you? Who ever saw such foolhardiness? Whatever happens, it is good enough for you. Oh! here he is again! No further! No, you've gone far enough already; further than I'd have gone for all the king's dominions!" Jones offered to speak, but Partridge cried: "Hush, hush, dear sir; don't you hear him?" And during the whole speech of the ghost, he sat with his eyes fixed partly on the ghost, and partly on Hamlet, and with his mouth open; the same passions, which succeeded each other in Hamlet, succeeding likewise in him.

CHAPTER V.

TOBIAS SMOLLETT.-

Born 1721 A.D.........Died 1771 A.D.

Early life.	Peregrine Pickle.	On his travels.
Surgeon's mate.	Visits Scotland.	Humphrey Clinker
Coarse satires.	Edits a Review.	Smollett's sailors.
Roderick Random.	Writes history.	Illustrative extract.

THIRD among the grand old masters of English fiction, both in
date of appearance as an author and in rank as a novelist, comes
Tobias Smollett. Born in 1721, at Dalquhurn-house near Renton,
in Dumbartonshire, and educated at the Grammar School of Dumbarton and the University of Glasgow, this boy of gentle blood
entered upon life as an apprentice to Mr. Gordon, an apothecary
in Glasgow. His grandfather, Sir James Smollett of Bonhill, who
had borne the expenses of his education, having died without
leaving him any further provision, the youth of nineteen made
his way up to London, carrying among his few shirts a tragedy,
called *The Regicide*, which he fondly hoped would raise him at
once to the pinnacle of fame and fortune. How many poor
fellows have toiled nightly for months over a crazy desk, and
have then trudged weary miles up to the Great Babylon with the
same high hope burning in their young hearts ! And how many,
a dozen years after that sanguine, light-hearted journey to town,
have found nothing left of those bright hopes but a few smoulder-
ing embers amid the grey ashes of a disappointed life !

The Regicide being refused by the London managers, Smollett
had to fall back upon the profession he had learned from Gordon.
Finding the stage doors shut against him, he sought the humble
position of surgeon's mate in the navy, and was, after some time,
appointed to an eighty-gun ship. It was thus that he acquired
his wonderful knowledge of sailors and sailor-life. His ship forming one of the fleet which was despatched against Carthagena with

so disastrous a result, he had an opportunity of witnessing and feeling the horrors of naval warfare. The story of the expedition may be found in his novel of *Roderick Random*, and also in his *Compendium of Voyages and Travels.* During a short residence in Jamaica he met Miss Lascelles, the lady who afterwards became his wife.

Upon his return to London in 1744 he endeavoured to establish himself as a medical man; but the attempt was unsuccessful. Betaking himself more eagerly to the pen, when the lancet failed him, he wreaked his revenge upon those whom he considered his foes, by the publication in 1746 of *Advice*, a satire, which has been well characterized as possessing all the dirt and vehemence of Juvenal, with none of that writer's power. All through life Smollett's unhappy temper preyed upon his own spirit, and made enemies of some who might otherwise gladly have befriended the struggling genius. He was one of those poor men who aim too high at the outset of their career, and who for ever after their first failure are possessed with the haunting monomania, that all the world has entered into an envious plot to slight their works and deprive them of their justly-earned fame.

Another coarse and bitter satire, *The Reproof*, in which actors, authors, and critics were abused without stint or measure, produced a yet deeper feeling of disgust against the irritable surgeon, —a feeling which the publication of *Roderick Random* in 1748 could scarcely abate. This first novel at once **1748** stamped Smollett as one worthy to rank with the great A.D. masters who were then plying the novelist's pen. But his works are evidently the creations of a somewhat inferior mind. There are, indeed, in Smollett's books an innate coarseness and an unscrupulous love of the indelicate, which we do not find in the works of Richardson or Fielding. Theirs is rather the coarseness of the age in which they lived; Smollett's is the coarseness of a man the fibre of whose moral nature was as rough as the roughest sacking.

His second novel, *Peregrine Pickle*, followed in three years. It is disfigured by the same faults as its predecessor. Another attempt to get into medical practice—this time at Bath—having ended as before, he took a house at Chelsea, and became an author by profession. If he could have flung away the hedgehog prickles of his temper along with his rusty lancet, he might have gathered round him a circle of loving and admiring friends. But the soured surgeon grew sourer still. His pen worked busily on. *Ferdinand Count Fathom*, the career of a sharper, and a translation of *Don Quixote*, occupied some four years, which bring us to one of the few sunny spots we meet in this gloomy, battling life. He visited Scotland ; felt the arms of his old mother again round his neck ; saw the crystal Leven and the oak-woods of Cameron once more ; talked of *auld lang syne* with former school-fellows and boyish playmates ; and then hurried back to his *alter ego*, sitting with knitted brow and bitter pen at a desk in southern England.

Smollett's sixteen remaining years were years of incessant literary occupation. He undertook to edit the *Critical Review ;* an office for which he was ill qualified, since of all men, an editor ought not to be quarrelsome. Endless were the scrapes into which the abuse of his editorial functions brought him. Admiral Knowles had him fined £100, and imprisoned for three months, as the author of a scurrilous libel. While he was in jail he wrote a tiresome English imitation of Don Quixote's adventures, entitled *Sir Launcelot Greaves*. Turning his pen from fiction to history, he produced, in the brief period of fourteen months, a *Complete History of England*, from the landing of Cæsar to the treaty of Aix-la-Chapelle; to which he afterwards added chapters carrying the work down to 1765. The latter part of this flowing History was taken to supplement the greater work of the historian Hume. In a few old-fashioned libraries Hume and Smollett even still stand shoulder to shoulder as the great twin authorities on English history, although the light of modern research has detected errors and flaws by the hundred in their finely-written story.

Wilkes and Smollett had a tilt about Lord Bute's ministry, in which the latter, defending the *quondam* tutor of royalty, suffered severely. The last years of the novelist, imbittered by the death of his only child, a girl of fifteen, were chiefly spent in restless travel. Visiting France and Italy, he vented his increasing spleen upon even the crumbling ruins of old Rome, and the exquisite statue of the Venus de Medici. The poor peevish author was hastening to his end; but before he sank beneath this life's horizon, his genius shot forth its brightest beam. Disappointed in his last earthly hope—that of obtaining a consulship on some shore of the Mediterranean, where his last hours might be prolonged in a milder air—he travelled to the neighbourhood of Leghorn, and, settling in a cottage there, finished *Humphrey Clinker*, which is undoubtedly his finest work. Lismahago is the best character in this picture of English life; Bath is the principal scene, upon which the actors play their various parts. Scarcely was this brilliant work completed, when Smollett **1771** died, an invalided exile, worn out long before the allotted A.D. seventy years.

His pictures of the navy-men who trod English decks a century ago, are unsurpassed and imperishable. Trunnion, the one-eyed commodore; Hatchway and Bowling, the lieutenants; Ap-Morgan, the kind but fiery Welsh surgeon; Tom Pipes, the silent boatswain, remain as types of a race of men long extinct, who manned our ships when they were, in literal earnest, wooden walls, and when the language and the discipline, to which officers of the royal navy were accustomed, were somewhat of the roughest and the hardest.

Smollett wrote poetry also, but it hardly rises above mediocrity. His *Ode to Independence*, his *Lines to Leven Water*, and his *Tears of Scotland*, present the most favourable specimens of his poetic powers.

AN UNEXPECTED REUNION.

As we stood at the window of an inn that fronted the public prison, a person arrived on horseback, genteelly though plainly dressed in a blue frock, with his own hair cut short, and a gold-laced hat upon his head. Alighting, and giving his horse to the landlord, he advanced to an old man who was at work in paving the street, and accosted him in these words: " This is hard work for such an old man as you." So saying, he took the instrument out of his hand, and began to thump the pavement. After a few strokes, "Have you never a son," said he, "to ease you of this labour?" "Yes, an' please your honour," replied the senior, "I have three hopeful lads, but at present they are out of the way." "Honour not me," cried the stranger; "it more becomes me to honour your grey hairs. Where are those sons you talk of?" The ancient pavier said, his eldest son was a captain in the East Indies, and the youngest had lately enlisted as a soldier, in hopes of prospering like his brother. The gentleman desiring to know what was become of the second, he wiped his eyes, and owned he had taken upon him his old father's debts, for which he was now in the prison hard by.

The traveller made three quick steps towards the jail; then turning short, "Tell me," said he, "has that unnatural captain sent you nothing to relieve your distresses?" "Call him not unnatural," replied the other; "God's blessing be upon him! he sent me a great deal of money, but I made a bad use of it; I lost it by being security for a gentleman that was my landlord, and was stripped of all I had in the world besides." At that instant a young man, thrusting out his head and neck between two iron bars in the prison window, exclaimed: "Father! father! if my brother William is in life, that's he." "I am! I am!" cried the stranger, clasping the old man in his arms, and shedding a flood of tears—"I am your son Willy, sure enough!" Before the father, who was quite confounded, could make any return to this tenderness, a decent old woman, bolting out from the door of a poor habitation, cried: "Where is my bairn? where is my dear Willy?" The captain no sooner beheld her than he quitted his father, and ran into her embrace.

CHAPTER VI.

THOMAS GRAY.

Born 1716 A.D..........Died 1771 A.D.

Birth and education.	Professor of history.
At Cambridge.	The Elegy.
Foreign travel.	His famous Odes.
Settles at Cambridge.	Other works.
His tastes and studies.	Illustrative extract.

THE poet Gray was born in noisy Cornhill on a December day in 1716. His father, a money-scrivener, was a bad man, so violent in temper that Mrs. Gray, separating from him, joined her sister in opening a shop in Cornhill for the sale of Indian goods. To the love of this good mother Thomas Gray owed his superior education. Her brother being a master at Eton, the lad went there to school, and found among his class-fellows young Horace Walpole, with whom he soon struck up a close friendship. Many a time, no doubt, Walpole, Gray, and West, another *chum* of the scrivener's son, did their Latin verses together, and many a golden summer evening they passed merrily with bat and ball in the meadows by the smoothly flowing Thames.

In 1735 he entered as a pensioner at Peter-house, Cambridge, his uncle's college. And for three years he lingered out his life there, chained to a place whose laws and lectures he felt to be most irksome. Mathematics were his especial disgust; but the classics he loved with no common love, and studied with no common zeal. His school-fellow Walpole was at Cambridge too; and when in 1738 Gray left without a degree, the two friends agreed to set out on a Continental tour. Together they saw France and Italy; the poet wandering with delight amid the ruins of the great past; the *con-noisseur* ransacking the old curiosity shops of Rome and Florence in search of rare pictures and choice medallions, such as in later days he piled up in dainty confusion under the roof of Strawberry

Hill. Their tastes being thus dissimilar, it is no wonder that Walpole and Gray quarrelled and separated after some time.

Gray returned to England, and, upon his father's death, he settled down at Cambridge, where most of his after life was spent. It has been already said that he hated the ways of the place, which, in his opinion, never looked so well as when it was empty; but there were *books* in abundance on the shelves of its noble libraries, and their silent yet speaking charms—he knew no other love—bound the poet for life to the banks of the Cam. Here, like a monk in his cell, he read and wrote untiringly. A glance round his study would, no doubt, have shown his tastes. Between the leaves of a well-used Plato or Aristophanes there might often have been found, drying for his *hortus siccus*, some rare wild flowers, which he had gathered in the meadows by the Cam. Books on heraldry and architecture shouldered the trim classics on his loaded book-shelves, while such things as sketches of ivied ruins, a lumbering suit of rusty armour, or a collection of curious daggers and pistols hanging on the crowded walls, most probably displayed the antiquarian tastes of the inmate.

A quiet life, like that the poet led, has almost no history. Besides such salient points as the appearance of his various works, there are only three events worthy of notice in his later years. These events were—his removal in 1756 to Pembroke Hall from Peter-house, caused by the annoyance of some madcap students; his refusal in 1757 of the laurel, vacant by Cibber's death; and his appointment in 1768 to the professorship of Modern History at Cambridge. His chief trips were to London, where he lodged near the British Museum, and explored its literary treasures with a student's patient love; to Scotland, where he met the poet Beattie; to the English lakes in 1769; and to Wales in the autumn before his death. This sad event took place in 1771. He had been breaking up for many months, when gout, settling in his stomach, cut him off with a sudden attack.

Gray is best known by his famous *Elegy Written in a Country Church-yard*, whose solemn stanzas roll out their muffled music, like the subdued tolling of a great minster bell. Corrected and re-corrected line by line, as were all this poet's works, it yet shows no sign of elaboration—its melancholy grace is the perfection of art. There are writers with whom a slovenly style stands for nature, and rude unpruned stanzas for the fairest growths of poetry. Gray was not of these. His classically formed taste was too pure and too fastidious to be content with anything but carefully polished verses: and we therefore have to thank him for giving us, in the " Elegy," as noble a specimen of grave and scholarly English as our literature affords. This poem was published in 1750.

But the triumph of his genius may be viewed in his two magnificent Odes, *The Progress of Poesy*, and *The Bard*. The subject of the latter is the terrific malison of a Welsh bard, escaped from the massacre at Conway, who, standing on an inaccessible crag, prophesies the doom of the Norman line of kings, and the glories of the Tudors. This done, he springs from the rock to perish in the foaming flood below. The chief facts of early English history have never been so finely woven into poetry as in " The Bard."

Among his other poems we may notice his *Ode to Spring; Hymn to Adversity ;* his much admired *Ode on a Distant Prospect of Eton;* and some light, humorous verses, on *Mr. Walpole's Cat.* His chief prose writings are *Letters*, written in a clear, elegant, and often most picturesque style.

OPENING STANZAS OF THE "ELEGY."

The curfew tolls the knell of parting day,
The lowing herd winds slowly o'er the lea,
The ploughman homeward plods his weary way,
And leaves the world to darkness and to me.

Now fades the glimmering landscape on the sight,
And all the air a solemn stillness holds,
Save where the beetle wheels his droning flight,
And drowsy tinklings lull the distant folds ;

Save that from yonder ivy-mantled tower
The moping owl does to the moon complain
Of such as, wandering near her secret bower,
Molest her ancient solitary reign.

Beneath those rugged elms, that yew-tree's shade,
Where heaves the turf in many a mouldering heap,
Each in his narrow cell for ever laid,
The rude forefathers of the hamlet sleep.

The breezy call of incense-breathing morn,
The swallow twittering from the straw-built shed,
The cock's shrill clarion, or the echoing horn,
No more shall rouse them from their lowly bed.

For them no more the blazing hearth shall burn,
Or busy housewife ply her evening care :
No children run to lisp their sire's return,
Or climb his knees the envied kiss to share.

Oft did the harvest to their sickle yield,
Their furrow oft the stubborn glebe has broke ;
How jocund did they drive their team a-field !
How bowed the woods beneath their sturdy stroke !

Let not Ambition mock their useful toil,
Their homely joys and destiny obscure ;
Nor Grandeur hear with a disdainful smile
The short and simple annals of the poor.

The boast of heraldry, the pomp of power,
And all that beauty, all that wealth e'er gave,
Await alike the inevitable hour :—
The paths of glory lead but to the grave.

CHAPTER VII.

DAVID HUME.

Born 1711 A.D..........Died 1776 A.D.

Boyhood of Hume.	History of England.
Law and commerce.	Character of the work.
First books.	Hume's prosperity.
Paid occupation.	Scepticism and errors.
Advocates' Library.	Illustrative extract.

DAVID HOME, the first of his family to write himself Hume, was a cadet of a distinguished Scottish house, and was born at Edinburgh in April 1711. After passing through the classes in the College of his native city, he nominally began the study of the law ; but, as he tells us himself, he was devouring Cicero and Virgil, while his friends fancied he was poring over Voet and Vinnius. Literature ousted law, and commerce had no better fortune. A few months among the sugar-houses of Bristol, far from weaning young Hume from his literary tastes, only deepened his love of study, and his desire to be a man of letters.

From Bristol he crossed to France, where he wrote his first work, *A Treatise of Human Nature*, published in London in 1738. It was an utter failure, not having achieved even the distinction of being abused. His second work, *Moral and Philosophical Essays*, composed partly in Scotland, met with tolerable success.

All this time he had been living on the slender means he got from home. But in 1745 an occupation, well paid to make up for its unpleasantness, fell in his way. He became the companion of the young Marquis of Annandale, whose mind was somewhat affected. Having held this charge for about a year, Hume accepted the position of secretary to General St. Clair, in whose suite he visited Vienna and Turin, seeing foreign life under most favourable auspices, and mixing in the first Continental circles.

After his return to Britain he lived for two years in his brother's house, engaged chiefly in the composition of his *Political Discourses* and his *Inquiry Concerning the Principles of Morals.*   In 1752 he undertook the charge of the Advocates' Library in Edinburgh; not so much for the sake of the nominal salary then attached to the office, as for the great command of books which such a position gave him.

There he seems first to have formed the idea of writing that *History of England* which made him famous.   The work grew to completeness in a most irregular fashion.   Afraid at first to face so long a story as the entire range of English history, he began with the accession of the Stuart race.   The first **1754** volume, closing with the Regicide, appeared in 1754. A.D.   Only forty-five copies were sold in a twelvemonth !   His sympathy for the slain king and Thorough-grinding Strafford excited a cry of disapproval and rebuke from almost every sect and every party.   So deeply did he feel this mortifying reception of his book, that, but for a French war breaking out, he would have hidden himself, with changed name, in some country town of France, and there have tried to forget his native land, and the defeat of his literary ambition.   But the ill wind of that French war, which gave us Canada, also blew to our libraries the remaining volumes of Hume's *England.*   The second, treating of the years between the Regicide and the Revolution, came out in 1757.   The tide had turned.   Everybody began to read and praise the book.   The year 1759 saw the publication of the third volume, containing the history of the Tudors ; and two other volumes, in 1762, added the narrative of earlier events, and brought the work to a triumphant close.   For ease, beauty, and picturesque power of style, there was then nothing like it in the range of English historical literature : and for these qualities it yet holds an honoured place on our book-shelves.   Yet the day of Hume as an authority on English history has long gone by.   The light of modern research has detected countless flaws and distortions in the great book, which was carefully, even painfully, revised as to its style, but which was formed in great part of a mass of statements often gathered from very doubtful sources, and heaped together, almost unsifted and untried. The diligence of that eminent modern historian, who often read a quarto volume to obtain material for a single sentence, and travelled a hundred miles to verify a solitary fact, was utterly unknown to David Hume. He wrote exquisitely; but he sometimes spent the beauty of his style upon mere chaff and saw-dust. Much the same thing it was, as if a jeweller should frame a costly casket and grace it with every adornment of art, that its rich beauty might at last enshrine a few worthless pebbles or beads of coloured glass.

The completion of his History made Hume a famous man. The Earl of Hertford invited him to join the embassy at Paris, there to act as interim secretary. His fame had gone before him, and he became a sort of lion in the French capital. When he re-crossed the Straits of Dover, it was to find promotion awaiting him at home. For about two years he acted as Under-Secretary of State, and in 1769 he returned to spend the evening of his life in the beautiful city of his birth, "passing rich" with £1000 a year,—the result of a prudent life, and the profits of his pen. For seven years longer he enjoyed the best society Edinburgh could afford, and then, in August 1776, he died. A journey to Bath, in the spring of that fatal year, was of no avail to stop the progress of his disease.

In philosophy and in religion Hume was a sceptic. He doubted almost everything, and attacked the Christian faith, especially by striving to cut away the foundations on which our belief in miracles rests. This being so, we cannot look in his great historical work for that recognition of religion as the main-spring of civilization, which our Bible and our common sense alike lead us to require from a true historian. Unable to resist a paradox, or a strange theory, he lost his way too often in the chase of flitting, unsubstantial meteors. In his system of morality he traces the goodness and badness of human actions or motives altogether to considerations of utility. These things take much from his lustre as an ornament of English literature.

DEATH OF QUEEN ELIZABETH.

She rejected all consolation ; she even refused food and sustenance ; and, throwing herself on the floor, she remained sullen and immovable, feeding her thoughts on her afflictions, and declaring life and existence an insufferable burden to her. Few words she uttered ; and they were all expressive of some inward grief, which she cared not to reveal : but sighs and groans were the chief vent which she gave to her despondency, and which, though they discovered her sorrows, were never able to ease or assuage them. Ten days and nights she lay upon the carpet, leaning on cushions which her maids brought her : and her physicians could not persuade her to allow herself to be put to bed, much less to make trial of any remedies which they prescribed to her. Her anxious mind at last had so long preyed on her frail body, that her end was visibly approaching ; and the Council being assembled, sent the keeper, admiral, and secretary, to know her will with regard to her successor. She answered with a faint voice, that as she had held a regal sceptre, she desired no other than a royal successor. Cecil requesting her to explain herself more particularly, she subjoined that she would have a king to succeed her ; and who should that be but her nearest kins-man, the king of Scots ? Being then advised by the archbishop of Canterbury to fix her thoughts upon God, she replied that she did so, nor did her mind in the least wander from him. Her voice soon after left her ; her senses failed ; she fell into a lethargic slumber, which continued some hours, and she expired gently, without further struggle or convulsion (March 24, 1603), in the seventieth year of her age and forty-fifth of her reign.

CHAPTER VIII.

WILLIAM ROBERTSON.

Born 1721 A.D..............Died 1793 A.D.

Birth and education.	Mary Stuart.
The country minister.	History of Charles V.
Professional success.	Historic style.
Removal to Edinburgh.	History of America.
History of Scotland.	Illustrative extract.

SECOND, in date of birth, of the illustrious historic triad that graced the eighteenth century, was William Robertson, the son of a Scottish clergyman. Born at Borthwick, in Mid-Lothian, in the year 1721, he studied for the profession of his father; and at the age of twenty-two was presented to the living of Gladsmuir, in Haddingtonshire.

The quietude of his country manse was broken by few incidents, annual visits to the General Assembly at Edinburgh being, perhaps, the greatest events of the young minister's life. But the completion of every week's sermon left his pen trained to greater skill in the weaving of eloquent and dignified English sentences; and every new book, which the weekly carrier brought to the moorland manse from some dim old shop in the High Street of the metropolis, widened his views of society and civilization. In his country retirement history became his favourite study. Most ministers in his sphere are content with their pulpit-work, and their round of farm-house visits, travelling beyond the literary work required for their professional duty only to pen an occasional letter to the newspapers, or to prepare for a telling appearance, when summer calls the great Church Court into session. But Robertson was not content with this. He preached, and visited, and spoke admirably upon the great questions which in his day came to be debated in the General Assembly; but while he did these well, his leisure hours were devoted to building up a kind of reputation which these could never build. The Rev. William

Robertson, a distinguished minister of the Scottish Church, would probably long ago have been forgotten, or, at least, only confounded with all the other Robertsons that have donned the pulpit-gown; but the name of William Robertson, the historian of Scotland, of Germany, and of America, cannot perish from the annals of our literature, while history is read by Englishmen.

In 1758 the country pastor, whose "Recreations" took a shape so noble and enduring, was promoted to Lady Yester's Church in Edinburgh. And in the following year, the reading

1759
A.D.

public—especially the literary men of London—were electrified by the appearance of *A History of Scotland* from this unknown minister's pen. Dealing with the reigns of Mary Stuart and her son, down to the accession of the latter to the English throne, he described, in pure, pathetic, and dignified language, the sorrows of that wretched Scotchwoman with a French soul, who saw so little of Holyrood and so much of English jails. He stands midway between those who believe her to have been a beautiful martyr, and those who brand her as a beautiful criminal. Agreeing with all writers as to the great loveliness of this beheaded Scottish queen, he considers that the intensity and long continuance of the sorrows, darkening over her whole life until the bloody catastrophe of Fotheringay, have blinded us to her faults, and that we therefore "approve of our tears, as if they were shed for a person who had attained much nearer to pure virtue."

The minister of Lady Yester's became, in three years after the publication of this book, Principal of the University of Edinburgh; and soon received a striking mark of royal approval in his appointment as historiographer for Scotland. Not content to rest on the fame he had won, he pushed on to higher ground. His greatest

1769
A.D.

work, the *History of Charles the Fifth of Germany*, was published in 1769, ten years after the appearance of his first production. A rapid view of European politics and society previous to the accession of the great Emperor, precedes the story of the reign, which is narrated in clear, majestic English. The materials from which Robertson drew his account of this great central epoch of European history, have, since the day he wrote, been tested, and sifted, and rearranged, with all the valuable additions that time has brought. And while his great History still remains a standard work, valuable supplements stand beside it in our libraries, from which a new light shines on many portions of the character and reign of Charles the Fifth. The researches of Prescott the American historian, and Stirling of Keir, the latter of whom wrote "The Cloister Life of Charles V.," give us another notion of the man Charles than we get from the purple and gold of Robertson's portraiture.

The fault of this great historian was one common to the chief writers of his time. Filled with an exaggerated idea of the dignity of history, he trembles at the thought of descending to so mean a thing as daily life. The Emperor moves before us in all his grandeur, the rich velvet of his train sweeping in stately waves upon the marble that he treads. We know many of the laws he made, the wars he waged, the great public assemblies and pageants of which he was the brilliant central figure; but we know little of the man who dwelt within the gorgeous wrappings, for we see him as if on a lofty terrace, where he plays his magnificent part, while we stand far away at the foot of the stairs, humble spectators of the imperial drama. Of the many-hued life the people lived, we hear next to nothing. Such a treatment of history may be termed the *statuesque*, as contrasted with the *picturesque* pages of a writer like Macaulay. Stateliness and elegance are the characteristic features of Robertson's style; but, inseparable from these, we find a cold sameness and want of colour. He walks a minuet with the historic Muse; who, according to his notion of her, is a lady used only to the very best society, dressed in the perfection of the mode, her complexion heightened with the faintest brush of *rouge*, and withal too stately and precise in her manners and her gait to be charged with such crimes as naturalness or ease.

Eight years passed before his third great work—*The History of America*—appeared. The story of Columbus fascinated his pen; and nowhere, perhaps, have we a finer specimen of stately narrative than we possess in his description of the great first voyage of the Italian sailor, and his landing on the new-found western soil.

A year or two before his death, which occurred in 1793, at the Grange House, near Edinburgh, he published an *Essay on the Earlier History of India;* which, however, was founded on sources not always reliable or safe. This, indeed, is a fault more or less pervading all his works. Like Hume, he often adopted second-hand statements, without looking carefully into the evidence on which they rested; and even the grand march of a stately style can sometimes scarcely reconcile us to accept as history a narrative, of whose facts we are not sure, and whose descriptive passages may probably be, for aught we know, coloured with brighter than the natural tints, for the mere sake of rhetorical effect.

THE DISCOVERY OF AMERICA.

About two hours before midnight, Columbus, standing on the forecastle, observed a light at a distance, and privately pointed it out to Pedro Guttierez, a page of the queen's wardrobe. Guttierez perceived it, and calling to Salcedo, comptroller of the fleet, all three saw it in motion, as if it were carried from place to place. A little after midnight, the joyful sound of "Land! land!" was heard from the *Pinta*, which kept always ahead of the other ships. But having been so often deceived by fallacious appearances, every man was now become slow of belief, and waited in all the anguish of uncertainty and impatience for the return of day. As soon as morning dawned, all doubts and fears were dispelled. From every ship an island was seen about two leagues to the north, whose flat and verdant fields, well stored with wood, and watered with many rivulets, presented the aspect of a delightful country. The crew of the *Pinta* instantly began the *Te Deum*, as a hymn of thanksgiving to God, and were joined by those of the other ships with tears of joy and transports of congratulation. This office of gratitude to Heaven was followed by an act of justice to their commander. They threw themselves at the feet of Columbus, with feelings of self-condemnation, mingled with reverence. They implored him to pardon their ignorance, incredulity, and insolence, which had created him so much unnecessary disquiet, and had so often obstructed the prosecution of his well-concerted plan; and passing, in the warmth of their admiration, from one extreme to another, they now pronounced the man whom they had so lately reviled and threatened, to be a person inspired by Heaven with sagacity and fortitude more than human, in order to accomplish a design so far beyond the ideas and conception of former ages.

As soon as the sun arose, all their boats were manned and armed. They rowed towards the island with their colours displayed, with warlike music, and other martial pomp.   As they approached the coast, they saw it covered with a multitude of people, whom the novelty of the spectacle had drawn together, whose attitudes and gestures expressed wonder and astonishment at the strange objects which presented themselves to their view.   Columbus was the first European who set foot on the New World which he had discovered.   He landed in a rich dress, and with a naked sword in his hand.   His men followed, and, kneeling down, they all kissed the ground which they had so long desired to see.   They next erected a crucifix, and prostrating themselves before it, returned thanks to God for conducting their voyage to such a happy issue.   They then took solemn possession of the country for the crown of Castile and Leon, with all the formalities which the Portuguese were accustomed to observe in acts of this kind in their new discoveries.

CHAPTER IX.

OLIVER GOLDSMITH.

Born 1728 A.D..........Died 1774 A.D.

BUFFON's well-known saying, "*Le style est l'homme,*" is by no man better illustrated than by Oliver Goldsmith. A guileless good-nature, a kind and tender love for all his human brotherhood, a gay, unthinking hopefulness, shine clearly out from every page he wrote. The latter half of his short life of forty-five years was spent in a continuous struggle for daily bread; his earlier years were full of change and hardship. Yet sneers and buffets, drudgery and debt, had no power to curdle the milk of human kindness in this gentle heart.

Charles Goldsmith, a Protestant clergyman, was trying to live on £40 a year at the little village of Pallas or Pallasmore, in the county of Longford, when in 1728 his famous son Oliver was born. Before the child was two years old, the living of Kilkenny West, worth nearly £200 a year, rewarded this good parson for his virtues and his toils; and the family in consequence removed to a commodious house at Lissoy, in the county of Westmeath. Here little Oliver grew up, went to the village school, and had a severe attack of small-pox, which left deep pits in his poor face. When he went to higher schools, at Elphin, Athlone, and Edgeworthstown, the thick, awkward, pale, and pock-marked boy was knocked about and made fun of by his cruel seniors, until the butt began to retort sharp arrowy wit upon those who sneered at his ugly face or uncouth movements.

In 1745 he passed the sizarship examination at Trinity College, Dublin, being placed last on the list of the eight successful candidates. The sizar of those days, marked by a coarse black sleeveless gown and a red cap, had to do much servile work—sweeping the courts, carrying the dishes up from the college kitchen, and waiting upon the Fellows as they dined. The kindness of his uncle Contarine, who had paid most of his school bills, followed him to college too; but even with this aid, when the Reverend Charles Goldsmith died in 1747, his son Oliver was left not far from starvation in the top room of No. 35. Here we detect his first literary performances. Writing street-ballads for five shillings apiece, he used to steal out at night to hear them sung and watch their ready sale in the dimly lighted streets. Here, too, we see the early symptoms of that benevolence, which was almost a mental disease, for it was seldom that the five shillings came home with the hungry student,—some of the hard-earned money had gone to the beggars he had met upon the way. Hated and discouraged by his tutor, he grew idler than ever,—took his full share in the ducking of a bailiff,—tried for a scholarship, and failed,—was knocked down by his tutor,—ran away,—was brought back to college by his brother,—took a very low **1749** B.A. in 1749,—and then went home to his mother's little A.D. cottage at Ballymahon for two years.

We cannot trace minutely his attempts to be a tutor, a clergyman, a lawyer, a physician. During his stay in Edinburgh, whither he went in 1752 to study medicine, his name was better known among his fellow-students as a good story-teller, and one who sang a capital Irish song, than for any distinctions he won in the class-rooms of the professors. His two winters in the Scottish capital were followed by a winter at Leyden, where he lived chiefly by teaching English. One day, after spending nearly all the money he had just borrowed from a friend, in buying a parcel of rare tulip-roots for his uncle Contarine, he left Leyden "with a guinea in his pocket, but one shirt to his back, and a flute in his hand," to make the grand tour of Europe, and seek for his medical degree.

Between February 1755 and February 1756 he travelled

through Flanders, France, Germany, Switzerland, and Italy—very
often trudging all day on foot, and at night playing merry tunes
on his flute before a peasant's cottage, in the hope of a supper and a
bed—for a time acting as companion or governor to the rich young
nephew of a pawnbroker—and in Italy winning a shelter, a little
money, and a plate of macaroni by disputing in the Universities.
His degree of M.B., on which his claim to be called Doctor Goldsmith rests, was probably received during these wanderings either
at Louvain or at Padua.   No one can regret this twelvemonth's
walk, who has read *The Traveller*, or those chapters in the Vicar
of Wakefield which depict the career of a *Philosophic Vaga-
bond.*

And then began that struggle in the troubled waters of London life, which closed only when the struggler lay coffined in
Brick Court.   Before he settled down to the precarious work of
making a livelihood by his pen, he made a desperate attempt to
gain a footing in his own profession.   In a shop on Fish Street
Hill he worked for a while with mortar and pestle as an apothecary's drudge.   He then commenced practice among the poor of
Southwark ; a scene of his life during which we catch two glimpses
of his little figure,—once, in faded green and gold, talking to an
old school-fellow in the street; and again, in rusty black velvet,
with second-hand cane and wig, concealing a great patch in his
coat by pressing his old hat fashionably against his side, while
he resists the efforts of his poor patient to relieve him of the
encumbrance.   In the printing-office of Richardson the novelist
he was for a time reader and corrector to the press ; and he was afterwards usher in Dr. Milner's school at Peckham,—a position in which
he was far from being happy.   One day Griffiths the book-
1757   seller, dining at Milner's, proposed to give him board
A.D.   and a small salary if he would write for the *Monthly
Review.*   Accepting the offer, he contributed many papers
to that periodical; but he complained that the bookseller, or the
bookseller's old wife, tampered with every one of them.   Returning
in a few months to the old usher-life at Dr. Milner's, he felt a
passing gleam of prosperity, when he received his appointment

as surgeon to a factory on the Coromandel coast; but, for some unexplained reason, this hope of permanent employment came to nothing. As a last chance, he presented himself at Surgeons' Hall in a suit of clothes obtained on Griffiths' security, in order to pass as a surgeon's mate in the navy; but fortunately for the readers of the "Vicar" and "Sweet Auburn," he was plucked. This last hope broken in his eager grasp,
he was driven to the pen once more. His rejection at **1758** Surgeons' Hall may thus be viewed as marking his real A.D. entrance upon the literary profession.

A garret in a miserable, tottering square, called Green Arbour Court, which was approached by a flight of stone stairs, styled suggestively "Break-Neck-Steps," had lately become his home. This dirty room, furnished with a mean bed and a single wooden chair, witnessed the misery of the would-be surgeon's mate on the night of his rejection, and saw him, thoughtless of all but burning pity, go out, four days later, to pawn the clothes he had got on the bookseller's security, in order to help his poor landlady, whose husband had just been seized by bailiffs. There he wrote reviews and memoirs for Smollett's periodical. There he was visited by Percy of the "Reliques," who found him writing his first important
work, *An Inquiry into the Present State of Polite Learning* **1759** *in Europe.* He was soon engaged to write a three-penny A.D. periodical, which was to appear every Saturday under the title of *The Bee.* It was a *blue* book, utterly unlike the ponderous tomes so called now, for it was full of wit and graceful writing. But it did not take. Still the busy pen worked on. "The British Magazine," edited by Smollett, was enriched with several *Essays* by Goldsmith. Among these we find some of his most charming shorter pieces; of which the Reverie in the Boar's Head at Eastcheap, and the story of the Shabby Actor, picked up in St. James's Park, are oftenest read and best liked. Soon in the "Public Ledger," a newly sprung paper, there appeared a series of Letters, describing a Chinaman's impressions of English life, which attracted considerable notice. These productions of Goldsmith's pen were afterwards published in a collected form as *The Citizen of the*

(15)   22

World. And if the hack of Green Arbour Court had written no more than these Letters, contributed twice a week to the "Ledger" for a guinea apiece, he might, as the creator of Beau Tibbs and the Man in Black, claim a high place among our English classics.

The night of the 31st of May 1761 was memorable in Wine Office Court, where Goldsmith then lived; for on that night the great Johnson ate his first supper at Goldsmith's table. Percy brought about the meeting; and Johnson, in honour of the occasion, as well as to disabuse his entertainer's mind of the idea that he was a sloven, went through the unusual ceremonies of powdering his wig and putting on clean linen.

Another visit from Johnson to Goldsmith, in the country lodging at Islington, where the latter had taken refuge from the din and dinginess of Fleet Street, stands out in violent contrast to this social evening. It was three years later. The little Irishman and the big Englishman had grown to be firm friends. Many a Monday night at seven had they shaken hands at the Turk's Head in Soho, where the famous weekly suppers of the Literary Club had already begun. One morning in 1764 an urgent message arrived from Goldsmith, begging Johnson to come to him as soon as possible. Johnson sent him a guinea, and went out to Islington immediately afterwards. He found that poor Goldsmith had been arrested by his landlady for the rent. A newly opened bottle of Madeira stood on the table, which Johnson wisely corked before he began to talk of what was to be done. Goldsmith producing a manuscript novel from his desk, down sat his friend to look over *The Vicar of Wakefield.* Struck at once with the merit of the work, Johnson went out and sold it to a bookseller for *sixty* pounds, with which the now triumphant Goldsmith discharged the debt he owed.

1764
A.D.

Fifteen months passed before an advertisement in the " St. James's Chronicle" announced *The Vicar of Wakefield* in two duodecimo volumes. The interval between sale and publication had made its author famous; for his beautiful poem of *The Traveller* had appeared not long after the distressful day at Islington. Johnson declared that it would not be easy to find anything equal to it since the death of Pope. The sister of Reynolds said, after hearing the poem read aloud, that she would never more think Dr. Goldsmith ugly. A simple saying, but very true, and very natural. The world has indorsed the utterance of that fussy, middle-aged lady. The bull-dog face, with its rugged skin, and coarse, blunt features, shines with a beauty from within, above all loveliness of flesh and blood, as we close the pages of "The Traveller," "The Deserted Village," or "The Vicar of Wakefield," and think of the little man who wrote these works. We forget that he delighted to array his small person in sky-blue and bloom-coloured coats, and to exhibit himself, as if pinned through with a long sword, in the glittering crowds that filled the gardens at Vauxhall; or, if we remember these things, it is only to smile good-naturedly at the weakness of a great man. *The Vicar of Wakefield* needs no description. An exquisite naturalness is its prevailing charm. No bad man could write a book so full of the soft sunshine and tender beauty of domestic life,—so sweetly wrought out of the gentle recollections of the old home at Lissoy. It was coloured with the hues of childhood's memory; and the central figure in the group of shadows from the past, that came to cheer the poor London author in his lonely garret, was the image of his dead father. "For," says John Forster in his Life of Goldsmith, not more truly than beautifully, "they who have loved, laughed, and wept with the Man in Black of the *Citizen of the World*, the Preacher of the *Deserted Village*, and Doctor Primrose in the *Vicar of Wakefield*, have given laughter, love, and tears to the Reverend Charles Goldsmith."

Still the busy pen worked on, for the wolf was always at the door. Among the minor tasks of the *quondam* usher we find an *English Grammar*, written for five guineas; and in later days some *School Histories*, abridgments of his larger volumes. But more famous works claim our notice.

His comedy of *The Good-Natured Man*, acted in 1768, brought him nearly £500; which, with the true Grub Street improvidence, he scattered to the winds at once. He bought those chambers in Brick Court, Middle Temple, where **1768** A.D.

the last act of his life-drama was played out. He furnished them
in mahogany and blue moreen. He gave frequent dinners and
suppers, startling all the quiet barristers round him with noisy
games at blind-man's buff and the choruses of jovial songs. He
was constantly in society with Johnson, Burke, and Reynolds,
and lived far beyond his means.

In May 1770 appeared his finest poem, *The Deserted Village*.
Before August closed, a fifth edition was nearly ex-
1770 hausted. The village, "sweet Auburn," whose present
A.D. desolation strikes the heart more painfully from the lovely
pictures of vanished joy the poet sets before us, was that
hamlet of Lissoy where his boyhood had been spent. The soft
features of the landscape,—the evening sports of the village train,
—the various noises of life rising from the cottage homes,—the
meek and earnest country preacher,—the buzzing school,—the
white-washed ale-house,—attract by turns our admiration as we
read this exquisite poem. And not least touching is this yearning
utterance, spoken from the literary toiler's deep and solitary heart :—

> In all my wanderings round this world of care,
> In all my griefs—and God has given my share—
> I still had hopes my latest hours to crown,
> Amidst these humble bowers to lay me down ;
> To husband out life's taper at the close,
> And keep the flame from wasting by repose :
> I still had hopes, for pride attends us still,
> Amidst the swains to show my book-learned skill,—
> Around my fire an evening group to draw,
> And tell of all I felt, and all I saw ;
> And as a hare whom hounds and horns pursue,
> Pants to the place from whence at first he flew,
> I still had hopes, my long vexations past,
> Here to return—and die at home at last.

The emphatic words of poor dying Gray, who heard " The Deserted Village" read at Malvern, where he spent his last summer in
a vain search for health, must be echoed by every feeling heart,—
" 'That man *is* a poet."

Debt now had Goldsmith fast in its terrible talons. He worked
on, but was forced to trade upon his future,—to draw heavy ad-

vances from his booksellers in order to meet the pressing wants of the hour. He undertook a *History of England*, in four volumes; a *History of the Earth and Animated Nature*, largely a translation from Buffon; *Histories of Greece and Rome*; and wrote a second successful comedy, *She Stoops to Conquer*, which was first acted in 1773.

The last flash of his genius was the short poem, *Retaliation*, written in reply to some jibing epitaphs, which were composed on him by the company met one day at dinner in the St. James's Coffee-house. Garrick's couplet ran thus:—

> " Here lies poet Goldsmith, for shortness called Noll,
> Who wrote like an angel, but talked like poor Poll."

And certainly in the reply poor Garrick suffers for his unkindness; for never with so light but so perfect a touch was the skin peeled from any character.

With hands yet full of unfinished work, Goldsmith lay down to die. An old illness seized him. Low fever set in. He took powders against the advice of his doctors, and died, after nine days' sickness, on the 4th of April 1774. "Is your mind at ease?" asked the doctor by his bed-side. "No, **1774** it is not," was the sad reply. At last the spendthrift author A.D. had lost "his knack of hoping," as he used to call the unthinking joyousness of his nature. His debts and the memory of his reckless life cast heavy shadows on his dying bed. In the spirit of that sublime prayer, which we learn to say at our mother's knee in the season of life when, in truth, "we take no thought for the morrow," let us hope that the gentle, thoughtless, erring nature, which gave and forgave so much on earth, found in Heaven that mercy which every human spirit needs.

THE FAMILY PICTURE.

(FROM " THE VICAR OF WAKEFIELD.")

My wife and daughters, happening to return a visit at neighbour Flamborough's, found that family had lately got their pictures drawn by a limner, who travelled the country, and took likenesses for fifteen shillings a head. As this family and ours had long a sort of rivalry in point of taste, our spirit took the alarm at this stolen march upon us, and, notwithstanding all I could say, and I said much, it was resolved that we should have our pictures done too. Having, therefore,

engaged the limner, (for what could I do?) our next deliberation was to show
the superiority of our taste in the attitudes. As for our neighbour's family,
there were seven of them, and they were drawn with seven oranges,—a thing
quite out of taste, no variety in life, no composition in the world. We desired
to have something in a brighter style, and, after many debates, at length came a
unanimous resolution of being drawn together, in one large historical family-
piece. This would be cheaper, since one frame would serve for all ; and it would
be infinitely more genteel, for all families of any taste were now drawn in the
same manner. As we did not immediately recollect an historical subject to hit
us, we were contented each with being drawn as independent historical figures.
My wife desired to be represented as Venus ; and the painter was requested not
to be too frugal of his diamonds in her stomacher and hair. Her two little ones
were to be as Cupids by her side ; while I, in my gown and bands, was to present her with my books on the Whistonian Controversy. Olivia would be drawn
as an Amazon, sitting upon a bank of flowers, dressed in a green joseph, richly
laced with gold, and a whip in her hand. Sophia was to be a shepherdess,
with as many sheep as the painter could put in for nothing ; and Moses was to
be dressed out with a hat and white feather.

Our taste so much pleased the squire, that he insisted on being put in as one
of the family, in the character of Alexander the Great at Olivia's feet. This
was considered by us all as an indication of his desire to be introduced into the
family, nor could we refuse his request. The painter was therefore set to work,
and, as he wrought with assiduity and expedition, in less than four days the
whole was completed. The piece was large, and it must be owned he did not
spare his colours ; for which my wife gave him great encomiums. We were all
perfectly satisfied with his performance ; but an unfortunate circumstance, which
had not occurred till the picture was finished, now struck us with dismay. It
was so very large that we had no place in the house to fix it ! How we all came
to disregard so material a point is inconceivable ; but certain it is we had all
been greatly remiss. This picture, therefore, instead of gratifying our vanity,
as we hoped, leaned in a most mortifying manner against the kitchen wall,
where the canvas was stretched and painted, much too large to be got through
any of the doors, and the jest of all our neighbours. One compared it to Robinson Crusoe's long-boat, too large to be removed ; another thought it more
resembled a reel in a bottle ; some wondered how it could be got out, but still
more were amazed how it ever got in.

CHAPTER X.

SAMUEL JOHNSON.

Born 1709 A.D..........Died 1784 A.D.

Picture of Johnson.	Rambler and Idler.	Life of Johnson.
Birth and education.	The Dictionary.	Lives of the Poets.
Struggles of his youth.	Rasselas.	His last years.
Starts for London.	The pension.	His style.
A bookseller's hack.	James Boswell.	Letter to Chesterfield.

A HUGE and slovenly figure, clad in a greasy brown coat and coarse black worsted stockings, wearing a grey wig with scorched foretop, rolls in his arm-chair long past midnight, holding in a dirty hand his nineteenth cup of tea. As he pauses to utter one of his terrible growls of argument, or rather of dogmatic assertion, commencing invariably with a thunderous " Sir," we have leisure to note the bitten nails, the scars of king's evil that mark his swollen face, and the convulsive workings of the muscles round mouth and eyes, which accompany the puffs and snorts foreboding a coming storm of ponderous English talk. Such was the famous Doctor Samuel Johnson in his old age, when he had climbed from the most squalid cellars of Grub Street to the dictatorial throne of English criticism—such the man who wrote *Rasselas* and *London*, who compiled the great *English Dictionary*, and composed the majestically moral pages of the *Rambler*.

This celebrated son of a poor man, who used to spread his little book-stall on market-day in Lichfield to tempt the louts of Staffordshire, was born in that town on the 18th of September 1709. From infancy the child struggled with constitutional disease, which weakened his eyes and left indelible seams across his little face. The father gave his poor afflicted boy all he could—a liberal education ; and upon this foundation—the best for fame that can ever be laid—the work of a great and noble lifetime began to rise.

Slowly, obscurely, and with many heavy falls, did the ill-dressed, ugly, clumsy youth begin to take his first steps towards the kingship of English letterdom. Having received his elementary education chiefly at Stourbridge, he entered Pembroke College, Oxford. But his dying father could spare no more money to the lad, so a degree could not be taken then. He must wait until he has earned a higher title with his pen. One terrible foe, with which poor Johnson had to battle through all his life, must not be forgotten, when we strive to estimate the greatness of his triumph over circumstances. Fits of morbid melancholy often seized him, which, as he says, " kept him mad half his life." Penniless, diseased, ill-favoured, but half educated, and touched with terrible insanity, the youth of twenty-two stood on the threshold

1731
A.D.
of the mean house, within which his father lay dead, looking out upon a world, that seemed all cold and bare and friendless to his gaze. No wonder that his earlier portrait shows a thin cheek and saddened brow, with lines of suffering already round the wasted lips.

Trudging on foot to Market Bosworth in Leicestershire, he became usher in a school. It would not do; by natural temperament he was totally unfitted for the work. We then find him translating for a bookseller in Birmingham; and after a while marrying a Mrs. Porter, the widow of a mercer there, who had £800.[*] With this money he attempted to start a school of his own near Lichfield; but he could not gather pupils enough to pay the rent and keep his wife in comfort. So, packing up his little

1736
A.D.
stock of clothes and books, he set out in March 1736 for London, accompanied by a former pupil, fresh-coloured, good-humoured, little Davy Garrick, who was going up to study law in Lincoln's Inn, but in whose brain the foot-lights were already shining far more brightly than briefs or pleadings at the bar. It was just as well for the theatre-going folks of England that the little Huguenot's head did not become a wig-block, on which to air a covering of grey horse-hair.

So up to London went the dapper pupil and his great hulking

---

[*] Mrs. Johnson died on the 17th of March 1752, to the deep and lasting grief of her husband, and was buried at Bromley.

master; and there they parted, to meet occasionally, but each to go his several way. And Johnson's was a hard and perilous path. We have already given a picture of literary life in those days. The worst miseries of such a life were endured by Johnson. For six-and-twenty years the pen scarcely ever left his hand. How often he and Savage wandered foot-sore all night through the streets of London, unable to hire the meanest shelter; how often they spent their last penny on a little loaf, which they tore with wolfish teeth, we cannot tell. But we know that miseries like these were commonly endured by men of letters in Johnson's day, and that he had his full share of such bitterness and want. It was for Cave the bookseller that he chiefly drudged, enriching the "Gentleman's Magazine" with articles of various kinds. His poem *London*, a satire in imitation of Juvenal, laid the foundation of his literary fame, by establishing him in the good graces of the booksellers. For this work Dodsley gave him ten guineas. A *Life of Savage* (1744) was followed by a second satire in Juvenal's manner, *The Vanity of Human Wishes* (1749); but these are only the most notable works in a vast crowd of minor writings, which occupied the days and nights of these busy years. His tragedy of *Irene*, begun in his teaching days, was brought upon the stage in 1749; but it failed to hold its ground.

Johnson's name is inseparably associated with the *Rambler*, a periodical of the "Spectator" class, which appeared twice a week between March 1750 and March 1752. Only four of the papers proceeded from other pens. There was some strange sympathy between the bulky frame of the essayist and the ponderous words that came from his ink-bottle; and in the pages of the "Rambler" there is certainly much of wordy weight. He reäppeared as an essayist, after the lapse of six years, in a lighter periodical called the *Idler*, which ran to 103 numbers, closing with its last sheet the chequered list of single-article serials, which had opened with the "Tatler's" pleasant talk.

While writing for the "Rambler," and for some years before the starting of that heavy serial, Johnson had been steadily at work upon his *Dictionary of the English Language*. There was no such work in English literature; and when Johnson undertook to finish the herculean labour in three years, he had but a slight notion of the toil that lay before him.   He was to receive for the completed work £1575; a comparatively small sum when we recollect that it took him seven years to bring his labour to a close, and that he had to pay several copyists, who sat in his house in Gough Square, in a room fitted up like a lawyer's office, working away at the slips of paper on which the various words, definitions, and quotations were jotted down roughly by the great lexicographer himself. The name we have just used sounded sweet to the ear of classical John-son, who was never so happy as when piling these huge blocks of antiquity into English sentences.   The "Dictionary" was a great work, but necessarily imperfect.   In etymology it is very defective; for of those Teutonic languages from which come three-fifths of our English, he knew next to nothing.

When Johnson's mother died, he devoted the nights of a single week to the composition of a book, which paid the **1759** expenses of her funeral.   This was *Rasselas*, a tale of **A.D.** Abyssinia, in which much solid morality is incul-cated in language of "a long resounding march."   But there is no attempt on the part of the author to identify himself with Oriental modes of thought.   The *heik* and *burnoos* of the Eastern prince and philosopher cannot conceal the old brown coat and worsted stockings of the pompous English moralist.   The grey wig peeps from below the turban.   In a word, Johnson talks at us throughout the entire book; he talks sensibly and well, but we cannot believe in the thin disguise of tawny cheek and mus-lin robes.   If we could imagine Johnson "doing" the Nile, as modern English travellers are apt to call their boating up that noble river; and for a freak, donning the native dress, and staining his cheeks with the printers' ink of which he knew so much; we might be able, perhaps, to conceive how such grand declamations, as certain paragraphs we know of in Rasselas, came to be spoken among the lotuses and river-horses of the African highlands.

The great turning-point of Johnson's life, at which he comes out from darkness, or at least from dim twilight, into bright and steady light, is that May day in 1762 on which he received the happy news that the king had conferred on him a pension of £300 a year. Thenceforward he wrote less, but talked con- **1762** tinually. We know all about the Johnson of this later A.D. period. The Johnson who starved with Savage, is a dim shadow; but the burly Doctor who lived in Bolt Court, and thought no English or Scottish landscape at all comparable to the mud-splashed pavement and soot-stained houses of Fleet Street, is almost a living reality, with whom any evening we please we may sit for hours to hear him talk. We know even how he ate his dinner—with flushed face and the veins swollen on his broad forehead. We know that he puffed, and grunted, and contradicted everybody, reviling as fools, and blockheads, and barren rascals all who dared to differ from his Literary Highness. We know that he had secret stores of orange-peel, hoarded we know not why— and that he never was happy unless he had touched every post he passed in the streets, when walking to and from his house. We know that he bore marks of scrofula, and was troubled with St. Vitus's dance. And we know that he sheltered with unchanging kindness in his house a peevish old doctor, a blind old woman, and a negro, with some of whom it was often hard to bear. We know no other author as this old man is known. For in 1763 he became acquainted with James Boswell, Esquire, a Scottish advocate of shallow brain but imperturbable conceit, the thickness of whose mental skin enabled him to enjoy the great Englishman's society, in spite of sneers and insults hurled by day and night at his empty head. Not a perfect vacuum, however, was that head; for one fixed idea possessed it—admiration of Samuel Johnson, and the resolve to lose no words that fell from his idolized lips. Nearly every night when Boswell went home he wrote out what he remembered of the evening's talk; and these notes grew ulti- mately into his great *Life of Johnson*. To this fussy, foolish man, the butt and buffoon of the distinguished society into which he had pushed himself, we owe a book which is justly held to be the best biography in the English language. Of other men, whose lives have been written, we possess pictures; of Johnson we have a photograph,—accurate in every line and descending to the minutest details of his person and his habits. Having spoken thus far of the man, we shall shortly sum up the chief events of his closing life, and leave the full story to be gathered from the pages of Boswell's marvellous book.

His degree of LL.D., conferred' in 1765 by the University of Dublin, was confirmed some years later by his own Alma Mater. In 1765 he published his edition of Shakspere, the preface to which is one of the best specimens of his prose we have. In the autumn of 1773 he made a tour through eastern Scotland and the Hebrides; and from his Letters to Mrs. Thrale he afterwards constructed his *Journey to the Hebrides*. In 1775 he visited Paris.

The Lives of the Poets, finished in 1781, formed the last of his important works. Beginning with Cowley, he writes of the leading poets down to his own day. His unfair view of Milton has been already noticed. In truth, Johnson seems never to have felt the full meaning of the word " poet." He was himself a master of pentameter rhymes, smooth, lofty, full-sounding; and we strongly suspect that the skilful manufacture of such appeared to him the highest flight of poetic genius. If he had any poetic fancy at all, it must have been of the clumsiest and palest kind, grey with London smoke and smothered in Latin polysyllables. Let no young reader take his knowledge of the English poets from Johnson's Lives, if he would know the true proportions of our bards. Some of his dwarfs are giants; many of his giants have dwindled into dwarfs.

Burke, Garrick, Gibbon, Reynolds, Goldsmith, and many others of the first men in London, were the constant associates of great King Samuel. Of these, Garrick was the only man who had known him almost from the first. The Thrales—a rich brewer and his wife—opened their hospitable house to the Doctor in his declining years. Streatham became more his home than the lonely chambers in Bolt Court. Here he drank countless cups of tea, had his friends from London out to see him, and was, in fact, a second master of the house. But the end was creeping on. One friend after another dropped into the grave. And after two years of complicated disorders—paralysis, dropsy, asthma, and the old melancholy

—he joined the company of illustrious dead that sleep in silence under the stones of Westminster Abbey. On Monday the 13th of December 1784 his last breath was drawn, at his own house in London.

Dr. Johnson's English style demands a few words. So peculiar is it, and such a swarm of imitators grew up during the half century of his greatest fame, that a special name—Johnsonese—has been often used to denote the march of its ponderous classic words. Yet it was not original, and not a many-toned style. There were in our literature, earlier than Dr. Johnson's day, writers who far outdid their Fleet Street disciple in recruiting our native ranks with heavy-armed warriors from the Greek phalanx and the Latin legion. Of these writers Sir Thomas Browne was perhaps the chief. Goldy, as the great Samuel loved to call the author of the " Deserted Village," got many a sore blow from the Doctor's conversational sledge-hammer; but he certainly contrived to get within the Doctor's guard and hit him home, when he said, " *If you were to write a fable about little fishes, Doctor, you would make the little fishes talk like whales.*" Macaulay tells us that when Johnson wrote for publication, he did his sentences out of English into Johnsonese. His Letters from the Hebrides to Mrs. Thrale are the original of that work, of which the "Journey to the Hebrides" is a translation; and it is amusing to compare the two versions. " When we were taken up stairs," says he in one of his letters, " a dirty fellow bounced out of the bed on which one of us was to lie." This incident is recorded in the Journey as follows : " Out of one of the beds, on which we were to repose, started up, at our entrance, a man black as a Cyclops from the forge." Sometimes Johnson translated aloud. " The Rehearsal," he said, very unjustly, " has not wit enough to keep it sweet." Then, after a pause, " It has not vitality enough to preserve it from putrefaction."

One of the most natural pieces of English that ever came from Johnson's pen, was his letter to Lord Chesterfield, written in a proud and angry mood to reject the offered patronage of that nobleman. We subjoin it, in preference to heavier specimens of Johnson's style.

February 7th, 1755.

My Lord,

   I have been lately informed, by the proprietor of *The World*, that two papers, in which my *Dictionary* is recommended to the public, were written by your Lordship. To be so distinguished is an honour which, being very little accustomed to favours from the great, I know not well how to receive or in what terms to acknowledge.

  When, with some slight encouragement, I first visited your Lordship, I was overpowered, like the rest of mankind, by the enchantment of your address, and could not forbear to wish that I might boast myself *Le vainqueur du vainqueur de la terre,*—that I might obtain that regard for which I saw the world contending; but I found my attendance so little encouraged that neither pride nor modesty would suffer me to continue it. When I had once addressed your Lordship in public, I had exhausted all the art of pleasing which a retired and uncourtly scholar can possess. I had done all that I could; and no man is well pleased to have his all neglected, be it ever so little.

  Seven years, my Lord, have now passed since I waited in your outward rooms, or was repulsed from your door; during which time I have been pushing on my work through difficulties, of which it is useless to complain, and have brought it at last to the verge of publication, without one act of assistance, one word of encouragement, or one smile of favour. Such treatment I did not expect, for I never had a patron before. The shepherd in Virgil grew at last acquainted with Love, and found him a native of the rocks. Is not a patron, my Lord, one who looks with unconcern on a man struggling for life in the water, and when he has reached ground, encumbers him with help?

  The notice you have been pleased to take of my labours, had it been early, had been kind; but it has been delayed till I am indifferent, and cannot enjoy it; till I am solitary, and cannot impart it; till I am known, and do not want it. I hope it is no very cynical asperity, not to confess obligations when no benefit has been received; or to be unwilling that the public should consider me as owing that to a patron, which Providence has enabled me to do for myself.

  Having carried on my work thus far with so little obligation to any favourer of learning, I shall not be disappointed though I should conclude it, if less be possible, with less; for I have been long wakened from that dream of hope in which I once boasted myself with so much exultation,

My Lord,

Your Lordship's most humble, most obedient Servant,

SAM. JOHNSON.

CHAPTER XI.

OTHER WRITERS OF THE SEVENTH ERA.

POETS.		
William Shenstone.	James Macpherson.	Horace Walpole.
William Collins.	Charles Churchill.	Hugh Blair.
Mark Akenside.	Thomas Chatterton.	Gilbert White.
The Wartons.		Samuel Foote.
John Home.	PROSE WRITERS.	Sir William Blackstone.
William Mason.	Philip Doddridge.	Adam Smith.
Thomas Percy.	John Wesley.	Junius.
Erasmus Darwin.	Thomas Reid.	Adam Ferguson.
William Falconer.	Laurence Sterne.	James Boswell.
James Beattie.	David Garrick.	William Paley.

POETS.

WILLIAM SHENSTONE, born in 1714, at Leasowes in Shropshire, after receiving his higher education at Pembroke College, Oxford, retired to spend his days upon those acres, of which his father's death had left him master. His chief works are the *Schoolmistress*, "a descriptive sketch, after the manner of Spenser;" and the *Pastoral Ballad*, which is considered the finest English specimen of its class. Shenstone died at Leasowes in 1763.

WILLIAM COLLINS, one of our finest writers of the Ode, was the son of a hatter at Chichester, and was born there in 1721. He enjoyed the advantage of a classical education at Winchester, and at Magdalen College, Oxford. *The Passions*, and his *Odes to Liberty* and *Evening*, are his finest lyrical pieces. His *Oriental Eclogues*, written at college, afford a specimen of his powers in another style—that of descriptive writing. After a short life, clouded with many disappointments, Collins sank into a nervous weakness, which continued until his death in 1759.

MARK AKENSIDE wrote the *Pleasures of Imagination*. He was the son of a butcher at Newcastle-upon-Tyne, where he was born in 1721. In 1744 he took his degree of M.D. at Leyden. His great poem had already appeared. He enjoyed some practice as a physician; but his chief support was derived from the liberality of a friend. Akenside died somewhat suddenly in 1770 of putrid sore throat.

The WARTONS, a father and two sons, were poets and poetical critics during part of the last century. The father was Professor of Poetry at Oxford,—an office which was also held by his second son, Thomas, (1728–1790.) Thomas Warton's chief poem was *The Pleasures of Melancholy*, published when he was only nineteen; but his greatest work was his *History of English Poetry*. He became poet-laureate in 1785. An elder brother, Joseph, who was head-master of Winchester School and afterwards a prebend of St. Paul's, also wrote poems, but of inferior merit. His *Ode to Fancy* may be considered a favourable specimen of his style.

JOHN HOME, a well-known dramatist, was born at Leith in 1722. He became minister of Athelstaneford, but when he wrote the tragedy of *Douglas*, he had to resign his living. Lord Bute having conferred on him a sinecure office and a pension, together worth about £600 a year, on this comfortable income he enjoyed the best literary society of the Scottish capital. Of all his works, *Douglas* alone has lived. Home died in 1808.

WILLIAM MASON, born in Yorkshire in 1725, was a close friend of the poet Gray, whose acquaintance he made at Cambridge. Mason wrote many odes and dramas; but *The English Garden*, a blank-verse poem in four books, was his chief composition. After the death of Gray he edited the Poems, and published the *Life and Letters* of his friend. Mason died in 1797.

THOMAS PERCY, Bishop of Dromore, deserves our gratitude for his collection of ballads, published in 1765 under the title of *Reliques of English Poetry*. These old songs, revived and often supplemented by the collector, gave a strong impulse to the genius of Scott and other poets. Percy, a Shropshire man, lived from 1728 until 1811. Before obtaining the bishopric of Dromore he was Dean of Carlisle.

ERASMUS DARWIN, the poet-laureate of botany, was born in 1731, at Elston near Newark. Having received his education at Cambridge, and taken a medical degree at Edinburgh, he began to practise as a physician at Lichfield. His principal poem, *The Botanic Garden*, appeared in three parts between 1781 and 1792. His reputation as a poet has greatly declined. He died in 1802.

WILLIAM FALCONER, born at Edinburgh in 1732, was the son of a barber. His early life at sea prepared him for the composition of his fine poem, *The Shipwreck*. The "Britannia," of which he was second mate, was wrecked off Cape Colonna. He was afterwards a midshipman and purser in the Royal Navy. In 1769 or early in 1770, the "Aurora," on board of which he was then serving, foundered, with the loss of all hands, it is supposed, in the Mozambique Channel. Thus the poet of *The Shipwreck* died amid the waves, whose power he so finely painted.

JAMES BEATTIE, born in 1735, at Laurencekirk in Kincardineshire, was educated at Marischal College, Aberdeen. His fame as a poet rests upon *The Minstrel*, published in 1771. Written in the Spenserian stanza, it depicts beautifully the opening character of Edwin, a young village poet. Beattie, who became at an early age Professor of Moral Philosophy and Logic at Marischal College, died of paralysis in 1803.

JAMES MACPHERSON, a Scottish Chatterton of maturer growth who did *not* commit suicide, was born in 1738, at Kingussie in Inverness-shire, and was educated at Aberdeen. In 1762 and 1763 he gave to the world two epic poems, *Fingal* and *Temora*, which he professed to have translated from materials discovered in the Highlands of Scotland. The opinion generally received now is, that he *discovered* them in his own desk, written on his own paper with his own pen. They present, in florid and highly coloured prose, stirring pictures of old Celtic life. Many years of Macpherson's life were spent in London as a political writer. At Belleville, a property which he bought in his native parish, he died in 1796.

CHARLES CHURCHILL, born in Westminster in 1731, was a dissipated and disgraced clergyman, who wrote biting and fluid poetry of an inferior order. The *Rosciad*, *Night*, and the *Prophecy of Famine* are among his most noted works. He died of fever at Boulogne in 1764.

THOMAS CHATTERTON, "the marvellous boy that perished in
his pride," was the son of a schoolmaster at Bristol. There the
young poet was born in 1752.   Educated in the most humble way,
he entered an attorney's office at fourteen.   The covers of old school-
books left by his dead father were formed of valueless parchment
deeds, taken from an old chest in the muniment room of
a Bristol church.   Among these remains of " Mr. Canynge's
Coffre," Chatterton pretended to have found fragments of ancient
poems, sermons, and articles descriptive of the city churches, &c.
They were all written by himself, in the old lettering and spelling,
upon stained parchments.   The boy of seventeen went up to
London to write for bread and fame.   He toiled hard, but sank
into infidelity and intemperance.   One effort to save himself from
this whirlpool—an application for the position of surgeon's mate
in Africa—failed.   He sent most of his money home to his mother
and sisters, with glowing accounts of his prospects.   But his
prospects proved a deceptive *mirage.*   Soon, stung to the core of his
proud heart by neglect and increasing want, he formed the desperate
resolve of suicide.   One August day in 1770 the lad, not yet
eighteen, took a dose of arsenic, and died amid the fragments of
his torn papers.   Picturesque description is the leading charm of
his poems.

PROSE WRITERS.

PHILIP DODDRIDGE, remarkable as a theological writer, was
born in London in 1702.   Much of his life was spent at Northampton, where for many years he had a flourishing school.   His
Rise and Progress of Religion in the Soul, his *Passages in the Life*
of Colonel Gardiner, and his *Family Expositor,* are all popular
and standard works.   Dr. Doddridge died at Lisbon in 1751.

JOHN WESLEY, born in 1703, at Epworth in Lincolnshire, was
famous as the most eminent of the founders of Methodism.   He
was educated at the Charter-house and at Christ Church, Oxford,
and afterwards became Fellow of Lincoln College.   There, with
his younger brother Charles, he joined a few seriously disposed students in private meetings for prayer and in visiting

the sick and poor.   In conjunction with George Whitefield, a celebrated pulpit orator, whose electric eloquence startled thousands into serious thought, he travelled about and preached with an earnestness little understood in that day.   His best-known works are his *Journal* and his *Hymns;* in the latter of which his brother gave him important aid.   John Wesley died in 1791.

THOMAS REID, born in 1710, at Strachan in Kincardineshire, held in succession the professorships of Moral Philosophy at Aberdeen and Glasgow.   His *Inquiry into the Human Mind* (1764) was an effective reply to Hume's sceptical doctrines. `Essays on the Intellectual and Active Powers of Man* came afterwards from his pen. Reid died in 1796.

LAURENCE STERNE, author of *Tristram Shandy* and *The Sentimental Journey*, was born in 1713, at Clonmel.   Educated at Cambridge, he entered the Church, becoming rector of Sutton and a prebend of York.   The living of Stillington also added to his income after his marriage.   The publication of "Tristram Shandy," beginning in 1759, closed in 1762.   His *Sentimental Journey* was the fruit of his second Continental tour, undertaken in 1765.   Uncle Toby, Corporal Trim, Dr. Slop, Yorick the parson, the widow Wadman, and Susannah are the leading creations of his imagination.   Fine humour and delicate pathos appear in Sterne's works; but the grace of these is often marred by the affected glitter of his style and the indecent hints, which betray the wolf in sheep's clothing, the profligate hidden in the parson's gown.   He has been charged with wholesale pillaging from Burton and other old authors.   Sterne died in 1768 in a London lodging-house, with no one by his bed but a hired nurse.

DAVID GARRICK, the famous actor and theatrical manager, employed his pen sometimes in the writing of plays, of which the best are *The Lying Valet* and *Miss in her Teens*.   Born at Lichfield in 1716, Garrick came up to London with Johnson, studied law, embarked afterwards in business as a wine-merchant, but found his fitting sphere in 1741, when he became an actor by profession. He died in 1779.

HORACE WALPOLE, the third son of the well-known statesman,

was born in 1717. He sat in Parliament for twenty-six years, but never made any figure as a politician. Much of his time and his snug income of £4000 a year went in the decoration of his villa at Twickenham, well known as Strawberry Hill. His tastes were eminently Gothic. Not content with realizing a Gothic mansion in the turrets and stained-glass windows of Strawberry Hill, he wrote a singular Gothic romance, called *The Castle of Otranto*. But his racy sparkling *Letters* and *Memoirs* of his own time, unrivalled in their way, give him his chief title to a place among the best English writers. Walpole, who became Earl of Orford in 1791, died six years later.

HUGH BLAIR, born at Edinburgh in 1718, is best remembered for his polished *Sermons* and his *Rhetorical Lectures*. Having filled in succession the pulpits of three Edinburgh churches, and held an honoured place in the best circles of that city, he died there in 1800.

GILBERT WHITE, a country clergyman, born in 1720, has made his Hampshire parish well known through all the land, especially to young readers, by his charming book, *The Natural History of Selborne*. This simple-minded earnest man has painted, in sweet and natural language, the busy life around his daily walks. White died in 1793.

SAMUEL FOOTE, born in 1721 and educated at Oxford, shone as an actor and dramatic writer. In 1747 he commenced his theatrical career. *The Minor* and *The Mayor of Garratt* may be named among the twenty plays he gave to the English stage. Foote, who was unrivalled for a mimicry that did not spare the chief characters of his own day, died in 1777.

SIR WILLIAM BLACKSTONE, a celebrated lawyer, born in London in 1723, published in 1765 a popular law-book, entitled *Commentaries on the Laws of England*, which is still reckoned the great standard work on that subject. He died in 1780, being then a judge in the Court of Common Pleas.

ADAM SMITH was born in 1723, at Kirkcaldy in Fifeshire. He was Professor of Moral Philosophy at Glasgow, and afterwards a Commissioner of Customs. His great work, *The Wealth of Nations*, showing that *labour* is the only source of the opulence of nations, laid the foundation of the important science of Political Economy. This book appeared in 1776. Adam Smith had previously published a metaphysical work, *The Theory of Moral Sentiments.* He died in 1790.

JUNIUS, the *nom de plume* of an unknown writer, who wrote in *The Public Advertiser* a series of political *Letters*, commencing January 21st, 1769. For fierce invective, piercing, brilliant sarcasm, and appropriate imagery, these "Letters" remain unrivalled. Who Junius was is still a mystery, although Sir Philip Francis, born at Dublin in 1740, who was chief clerk in the War Office between 1763 and 1772, is the man in whose favour the evidence is strongest.

ADAM FERGUSON, who was born in 1724, held in succession two professorships in the University of Edinburgh. He wrote, among other works, *The History of Civil Society*, and *The History of the Roman Republic.* He died in 1816.

JAMES BOSWELL, born in 1740, was the son of a Scottish judge. Attaching himself to Dr. Johnson, this conceited and foolish man took notes of the great man's conversation, which he afterwards embodied in his famous *Life of Johnson.* No better biography has ever been written. Boswell died in 1795.

WILLIAM PALEY, born at Peterborough in 1743, having received his higher education at Christ's College, Cambridge, entered the Church of England, in which he rose to be Archdeacon of Carlisle. His chief works were *Elements of Moral and Political Philosophy*, (1785); *Horæ Paulinæ*, (1790); *View of the Evidences of Christianity*, (1794); and *Natural Theology*, (1802). His style is simple and homely, but very clear. Paley died in 1805.

EIGHTH ERA OF ENGLISH LITERATURE.

FROM THE DEATH OF JOHNSON IN 1784 A.D. TO THE DEATH OF SCOTT IN 1832 A.D

CHAPTER I.

SOME NOTES ON POETRY AND CRITICISM.

Poetry and prose.	Use of figures.	The Unities.
English metre.	Essence of poetry.	Lyric poems.
Inverted order.	Epic poems.	Poetic "Schools."
A higher language.	Dramatic poems.	Objective and subjective.

WHEN we turn from Milton's "Paradise Lost" to Macaulay's "History of England," we perceive at once a difference in the language of the two. The one we call poetry; the other, prose. And when we recollect that we do not talk, at least most of us do not talk, to our friends in the same style as that in which Milton describes the Council of Infernal Peers, or Macaulay the Relief of Londonderry, we perceive that language assumes a third, its lowest form, in the conversation that prevails around our dinner tables, or upon our pleasant country walks. Of the three shapes that language takes — poetry, literary prose, colloquial prose—poetry is, undoubtedly, the chief.

Taking English poetry in the common sense of the word, as a peculiar form of language, we find that it differs from prose mainly in having a *regular succession of accented syllables*. In short, it possesses *metre* as its chief characteristic feature. Every line is divided into so many *feet*, composed of short and long syllables arranged according to certain laws of prosody. With a regular foot-fall the voice steps or marches along the line, keeping time like the soldier on drill, or the musician among his bars. In many languages syllables have a *quantity*, which makes them intrinsically long or short; but in English poetry that syllable alone is long on which an *accent* falls. Poets, therefore, in the use of that license which they have, or take, sometimes shift an accent, to suit their measure. *The inversion of the order of words*, within certain limits, is a necessary consequence of throwing language into a metrical form. Poetry, then, differs from prose, in the first place, in having metre; and, as a consequence of this, in adopting an unusual arrangement of words and phrases. The object of inverting the order, however, is often not so much to suit the metre as to give additional emphasis or rhetorical effect.

But we find more than this in poetry, else poetry and verse are one and the same thing. That they are *not*, we know to our cost, when we are compelled to wade through some of those productions which throng our booksellers' windows at times,—without, all *mauve* and gleaming gold—within, all barrenness and froth.

We must have, in addition to the metrical form, the use of uncommon words and turns of expression, to lift the language above the level of written prose. Shakspere, instead of saying, as he would, no doubt, have done in telling a ghost-story to his wife, "The clock then striking one," puts into the mouth of the sentinel, Bernardo, "*The bell then beating one.*" When Thomson describes the spring-ploughing, the ox becomes a *steer*, the plough is the *shining share*, and the upturned earth appears in his verse as the *glebe.* The use of periphrase (the round-about mode of expression) here comes largely to the poet's aid. Birds are *children of the sky, songsters of the grove, tuneful choirs,* &c.; ice is a *crystal floor,* or a *sheet of polished steel.* These are almost all figurative forms, and it is partly by the abundant use of *figures* that the higher level of speech is gained.

Yet there is something beyond all this. Smoothly the metre may flow on, without a hitch or hinderance—brilliantly the tropes may cluster in each shining line—lofty as a page of the "Rambler" may be the tone of the faultless speech—yet, for all, the composition may fall short of true poetry. There is a something, an essence, which most of us can feel when present, or at once detect the lack of, which is yet entirely indefinable. We are as little able to define the essence of poetry as to describe the fragrance of a rose, or the nature of that mysterious fluid which shows itself in a flash of lightning and draws the needle towards the north. Let us be content to enjoy the sweet effect of that most subtile cause, which has baffled the acutest thinkers in their attempts to give it " a local habitation and a name." Lying, as it does, in the thought, we can no more express it in words than we can assign a shape or colour to the human soul. It is the electric fluid of the soul, streaming always through the world of thought and speech and writing, flashing out occasionally into grand thunder-bursts of song and the lightning play of true genius. Some minds are highly charged with the brilliant essence —*positive* minds, an electrician would call them: others are *negative* to the last degree. Some minds, as good conductors, can easily receive and give out the flow of thought; very many have no conducting power at all, being incapable alike of enjoying the pleasures of poetry, or of communicating those pleasures to other minds.

All poetry, so far as its form goes, may be classed, for purposes of convenience, under three heads—Epic, Dramatic, and Lyric. Blair defines the Epic poem to be " a recital of some illustrious enterprise in a poetic form." To this it may be added that the epic poem is generally composed in the highest form of verse that the prosody of the language possesses—in a word, in the *heroic* measure of the tongue. Milton's " Paradise Lost" is undoubtedly the great epic of the English tongue, founded upon one of the loftiest themes that could employ any pen, and written in that stately blank-verse, that noble iambic pentameter, which holds the place in our tongue that is held in Greek and Latin by the hexameter of the " Iliad" and the " Æneid."

Dramatic poetry assumes the form that we commonly call a play, breaking into the two branches,—Tragedy and Comedy. We can easily single out a great example here among our English authors; for one name—that of Shakspere—stands far above the crowd of his brother dramatists. Without being at all strictly true, there is a good deal of sense in a familiar mode of distinguishing tragedy from comedy—namely, that a tragedy completes its plot with the *death* of the principal characters, while a comedy is sure to end in their *marriage*. The tragedy, like the epic poem, generally adopts the leading measure of the tongue; the language of prose better suits the lower level of comedy, which depicts the scenes of every-day life rather than the great sufferings or great crimes that form the proper material for a tragic poem. A tragedy, in its usual form, contains five acts, each act consisting of a variable number of scenes. The third, or central act, is the natural place for the *crisis* of the plot; and the fifth for the *catastrophe*, or wind-up smash of the whole. Thus, in "Hamlet," the play-scene and the fencing-scene are so arranged, that we have a central point as well as a final point of interest; and in "Julius Cæsar," the murder at the Capitol and the battle of Philippi are placed upon the same artistic principle. By writers of the Artificial school much attention is paid to preserving the three unities of action, place, and time. The need of making all the incidents tend to one great centre of the plot, and thus preserving the unity of action, is very manifest; for nothing is more confusing than the attempt to carry on several plots within the same play. But the need of sticking always to one place, and of confining the time supposed to pass in the dramatic story to the few hours actually spent in the representation of the play, does not so manifestly appear, when we find our greatest dramatist continually violating both of these unities without in the least marring the effect of his magnificent creations.

Of Lyric poetry, which is composed chiefly of songs and short poems, such as might be set to music, the works of Robert Burns afford our finest example. Thomas Moore, too, in his "Irish Melodies" has given us some splendid lyrics; but there is in these considerably more of the artificial than we find in the sweet fresh verses of the Ayrshire peasant.

We have used the word "school" in speaking of poetry. It is applied, as well in literature as in art, to a set of men whose works are founded on a certain known principle, which appears in all as a distinctive feature.   Thus we have that Metaphysical or Unnatural school, of which the poet Donne was head-boy ; we have the Artificial or French school, represented by Dryden and Pope ; the Transition school, of which Thomson, Gray, and Collins are good specimens ; the Lake school, deriving its name from the fact that its founders, Wordsworth, Southey, and Coleridge, lived for the most part among the lakes of northern England ; and the German school, of which Tennyson and Longfellow are the modern exemplars.   These are the "schools" to which most frequent reference is made by critics.

We close this rambling chapter with another note.   Two metaphysical words, *objective* and *subjective*, have been much used of late in reference to the poetic treatment of a theme.   The former expresses chiefly the picturing of outward life, as perceived by the senses of the observer, or realized by his fancy: of this style, Scott is one of the greatest masters.   The latter denotes that kind of poetry which gives, instead of the outward scene, the various thoughts and feelings excited by it in the poet's mind.   For example, let a *deserted house* be the subject.   The objective poet paints the moss-grown steps—the damp-stained walls—the garden tangling with a wilderness of weeds—the rusty hinges of the door —the broken or dirt-incrusted panes of the closed windows ; while the subjective poet broods over the probable history of its scattered tenants, or, attracted by a solemn resemblance, conjures up the image of a human body—this house of clay we all inhabit —deserted by its immortal inmate—its eyes, "those windows of the soul," closed and sealed up in the long sleep of death.

CHAPTER II.

EDWARD GIBBON.

Born 1737 A.D.............Died 1794 A.D.

Evening in the Capitol.	His first work.	The great subject.
The Acacia Walk.	The History begun.	Style and treatment.
Early life and education.	Life at Lausanne.	Radical evils.
Changes of creed.	Death of Gibbon.	Illustrative extract.

On an October evening in the year 1764, a young English gentleman of twenty-seven resolved to write a book of history. His own words tell us of the romantic circumstances in which the great resolve was made :—

"As I sat musing amidst the ruins of the Capitol, while the barefooted friars were singing vespers in the Temple of Jupiter, the idea of writing the Decline and Fall of the city first started to my mind."

The same man, Edward Gibbon, has thus described the completion of his great work at Lausanne, when he had passed his fiftieth year :—

"It was on the day, or rather night, of the 27th of June 1787, between the hours of eleven and twelve, that I wrote the last lines of the last page in a summer-house in my garden. After laying down my pen, I took several turns in a *berceau*, or covered walk of acacias, which commands a prospect of the country, the lake, and the mountains. The air was temperate, the sky was serene, the silver orb of the moon was reflected from the waters, and all nature was silent. I will not dissemble the first emotions of joy on the recovery of my freedom, and perhaps the establishment of my fame. But my pride was soon humbled, and a sober melancholy was spread over my mind, by the idea that I had taken an everlasting leave of an old and agreeable companion; and that, whatsoever might be the future date of my History, the life of the historian must be short and precarious."

Gibbon was born in the year 1737, at Putney in Surrey The delicate boy received much of his early education from his aunt; and when he went to Westminster School at the age of twelve, ill health prevented him from giving very close attention to his studies. In 1752 he became a gentleman commoner of Magdalen College, Oxford,—arriving at that seat of learning, as he tells us himself, "with a stock of erudition that might have puzzled a doctor, and a degree of ignorance of which a school-boy would have been ashamed." The key to this statement we find in the fact, that, while too ill for study during his school-days, he had been devouring works of all sorts, especially enjoying with the keenest relish books of history and geography. As was the case with Walter Scott, the mind of the youthful invalid never lost the colouring with which these sick-bed readings had saturated its fibres. At Oxford, Gibbon led a wild and idle life for fourteen months, when, as the result of his private reading, he turned to the Roman Catholic Church. This change closed his university career.

After spending a year in the house of a Protestant clergyman at Lausanne in Switzerland, where his father had placed **1754** him, he returned to the Protestant Church, expressing his A.D. belief in the commonly accepted truths of Christianity. But there is reason for more than fear that any change he made was made as a mere matter of form. The truth seems to be, that Gibbon had read himself into infidelity; and in his History he makes very light indeed of Christianity as a motive power in the civilization of man.

His five years at Lausanne made him a perfect master of French, and considerably advanced his neglected Latin studies. Some time after his return to England he published his first work, a little French treatise, entitled *Essai sur l'Etude de la Littérature;* which, in England at least, was soon forgotten. Acting for a while as captain in the Hampshire Militia, he gained considerable insight into modern military tactics; and we can easily fancy the great historian of the Roman Empire pausing, pen in hand, as he sat in after years in his summer-house by the blue waters of Lake Leman, writing the story of some mediæval battle, to think of the days when he used to drill his grenadiers in the barrack-yards of England.

When his father died in 1770, leaving him an estate much hampered with debt, he settled in London, and began to write. From the outset of the work he felt the magnitude and difficulty of the theme. All was dark and doubtful. Three times he composed the first chapter, and twice he composed the second and third, before he felt satisfied with them; but, as he advanced, what seemed to be a chaos of tangled facts, mixed in hopeless confusion, grew under his shaping hand into an orderly and beautiful narrative; and before he had gone very deep into his subject, his gorgeous and stately style had grown so familiar to his pen, that he made no second copy of what he wrote, but sent the first manuscript direct to the printer. In 1776, when he had been already two years in Parliament as member for Liskeard, the first volume of *The Decline and Fall of the Roman Empire* **1776** was published; and the author sprang at once into   A.D. literary fame. In five years (1781) the second and third volumes made their appearance; soon after which the historian, disappointed in his hopes of a permanent government post, retired to the house of a literary friend at Lausanne, where he wrote the rest of the work.

His life at Lausanne was simple and studious. Rising before eight, he was called from his study to an English breakfast at nine. He then shut himself up among his books and papers till half-past one, when he dressed for the two o'clock Swiss dinner, at which a friend or two often joined the table. Light reading, chess, or visiting filled up the interval between dinner and the assemblies. A quiet game of whist and a supper of bread and cheese passed the evening hours, and eleven o'clock saw all in bed. This life, with slight interruption, Gibbon lived for the four years which he spent in the completion of his great work. After the publication of the last volumes, which he saw through the press in 1788, he returned to Lausanne, and did not leave it until the death of Lady Sheffield in 1793 brought him hastily to London, in order to console the bereaved husband, who was his most intimate friend. In little more than six months after he had left his Swiss retirement, he died in London, of a disease which had long been preying on his strength (January 16, 1794).

Viewed simply as a literary performance, "The Decline and Fall of the Roman Empire" must be regarded, in spite of its defects and errors, as the noblest historical work in the English language. When we remember the immensity of the subject,—the history, during nearly thirteen centuries, not only of the two great branches of the Roman Empire, but of all the various nations that played a part in the grand drama of which Rome and Constantinople were the central scenes—we are struck with astonishment at the courage of the mind that could grapple with a theme so gigantic. We think of Gibbon, sitting down to compose that memorable first chapter for the first time, as of some strapping woodsman, who, on the outskirts of a spreading forest, strikes his bright axe deep into the bark of the first tree. A wilderness of tangling boughs and thorny underwood, pathless and unexplored, lies stretching out before his gaze. But day by day the clearing grows wider. The fallen timber is shaped for use and beauty. The corn-patch waves its golden plumes every season in a larger circle. Gardens and cultured farms smile, where before the sunlight could scarcely shine through a rank, unfruitful thicket.

From the reign of the Antonines to the fall of Constantinople the narrative extends, filling much of that great gap which long severed the history of ancient Rome from the history of modern Europe. The style is lofty, musical, sometimes pompous in its gorgeous stateliness. No man has better understood the power of the picturesque in historical composition ; and throughout the entire work the law of historical *perspective,* by which events and characters receive their due proportion of space, is wonderfully maintained. From the range of his deep and varied reading he drew materials for the splendid panorama he has unfolded to our view. The manners and customs of peoples, the geography of countries, the science of war, the systems of law, the progress of the arts, are all woven with masterly skill into the brilliant tissue of events.

But in this great book there are deep-rooted and terrible evils. Without denying the evidences of Christianity, the historian loses no opportunity of slighting its power and sneering at its purity. Utterly ignoring the work of a Divine hand in the wonderful spread of the gospel of Christ, he traces the development of the Christian system only to secondary causes, and dwells at length, and with a seeming pleasure, on the corruptions of the early Church, as if these had grown out of the system itself, instead of being the foul fun- guses of human sin. His chapters on the spread of Christianity have nothing in them of the fire with which he describes the blood-stained marches of Mahomet and Tamerlane. Then he has not only the sneer of the Voltaire school, but that deep depravity of imagination which made them revel in licentious and disgust- ing details. Such faults as these, coupled with the fact that his acquaintance with the Byzantine historians is considered to have been but superficial, are abiding blots on this great literary achieve- ment.

THE ATTACK ON CONSTANTINOPLE.

At daybreak, without the customary signal of the morning gun, the Turks assaulted the city by sea and land ; and the similitude of a twined or twisted thread has been applied to the closeness and continuity of their line of attack. The foremost rank consisted of the refuse of the host,—a voluntary crowd, who fought without order or command ; of the feebleness of age or childhood, of peasants and vagrants, and of all who had joined the camp in the blind hope of plunder and martyrdom. The common impulse drove them onwards to the wall : the most audacious to climb were instantly precipitated ; and not a dart, not a bullet, of the Christians was idly wasted on the accumulated throng. But their strength and ammunition were wasted in this laborious defence. The ditch was filled with the bodies of the slain,—they supported the footsteps of their com- panions ; and of this devoted vanguard the death was more serviceable than the life. Under their respective bashaws and sanjaks the troops of Anatolia and Romania were successively led to the charge : their progress was various and doubtful ; but, after a conflict of two hours, the Greeks still maintained and improved their advantage ; and the voice of the Emperor was heard encouraging his soldiers to achieve, by a last effort, the deliverance of their country. In that fatal moment the janizaries arose, fresh, vigorous, and invincible. The Sultan himself on horseback, with an iron mace in his hand, was the spectator and judge of their valour. He was surrounded by ten thousand of his domestic troops, whom he reserved for the decisive occasion ; and the tide of battle was directed and impelled by his voice and eye. His numerous ministers of justice were posted behind the line, to urge, to restrain, to punish; and if danger was in the front, shame and inevitable death were in the rear, of the fugitives. The cries of fear and of pain were drowned in the martial music of drums, trumpets, and attaballs; and experience has proved, that the mechanical operation of sounds, by quickening the circulation of the blood and spirits, will act on the human machine more forcibly than the eloquence of reason and honour. From the lines, the galleys, and the bridge, the Ottoman artillery thundered on all sides; and the camp and city, the Greeks and the Turks, were involved in a cloud of smoke, which could only be dispelled by the final deliverance or destruction of the Roman Empire.

CHAPTER III.

ROBERT BURNS.

Born 1759 A.D..........Died 1796 A.D.

The lyrist's power.	Poems published.
Birth of Burns.	In Edinburgh.
His scanty schooling.	At Ellisland.
Following the plough.	At Dumfries.
Bound for Jamaica.	Illustrative extract.

ROBERT BURNS was an Ayrshire ploughman. But beneath the
" hodden grey" of the peasant's dress there shone poetic fire as
pure and bright as the world has ever seen. . The faults of the
man are forgotten, or at least forgiven, for the sake of a surpassing music, which, sounding first from the smoky interior of a
clay-built cabin, has spread its sweetness into every home, not in
Britain only, but wherever the English tongue is heard. Yet
other and sterner scenes than the domestic circle are even more
deeply blessed by this enchanting influence. Soldiers on the
dusty march or round the red logs of the bivouac fire—sailors in
the long dark nights at sea amid washing waves and creaking
cordage—trappers and woodmen in the ancient forests of the New
World—miners crushing quartz in the golden bed of the Sacra-
mento or the Fraser—shepherds galloping from huge flock to flock
over the boundless pastures of Australia—have all had their loneliness cheered, their rugged natures softened, and the crust, which
gathers on the human heart through years of sin and hardship,
melted into tender tears, by the gentle or spirit-stirring magic of
Robert Burns's songs. No lyrist goes home to the heart so straight
as he.

Thirty-seven years of sorrow and struggle, chequered with one
or two brief flickering gleams of apparent prosperity, made up the
poet's span of life. He was born on the 25th of January 1759,
in a mud cabin not far from the Bridge of Doon, in the Ayrshire

(15) 24

parish of Alloway.   His father, a gardener, who had struggled
into a humble business as a nurseryman on his own account,
built with his own hands the clay walls within which Robert first
saw the light.   Going to school at six years of age, the boy battled
his way stoutly through the mysteries of English reading, pot-hooks
and hangers, the multiplication table, and other sorrows of the young,
until at eleven years of age he had acquired a very fair degree of
elementary education.   It was all his good father could give him;
and when it became necessary to employ the young hands in the
labour of a farm, Mount Oliphant, to which the family removed in
1767, some occasional evening studies rubbed away the rust that
will come, and added a little to the scanty stock of knowledge
already gained.   "A fortnight's French," which the simple rustic
was fond of parading in his letters, and a summer quarter at land-
surveying, completed all the instruction the poet ever got, beyond
what he was able to pick up from a few books that lay on his humble
shelf.   The Spectator, Alexander Pope, and Allan Ramsay were
there; and by-and-by Thomson, Shenstone, Sterne, and Mackenzie
joined the little company of silent friends.

But out on the fields of Mossgiel, amid the birds and wild-
flowers of a Lowland farm, he learned his finest lessons, and conned
them with all his earnest heart, as he held the handles of the
plough.   A little heap of leaves and stubble, torn to pieces by the
ruthless ploughshare, one cold November day, exposes to the frosty
wind a poor wee field-mouse, that starts frightened from the ruin.
The tender heart of the poet-ploughman swells and bubbles into
song.   And again, when April is weeping on the field, the crushing
of a crimson-tipped daisy beneath the up-turned furrow, draws
from the same gentle heart a sweet, compassionate lament, and
exquisite comparisons.   Poems like those to the Mouse and the
Daisy, are true wild-flowers, touched with a fairy grace, and breathing a delicate fragrance, such as the blossoms of no cultured garden
can ever boast.

But the ploughing that led to the production of these poems was
profitless in other respects.   In vain Robert and his brother Gilbert
toiled " like galley-slaves."   In vain their mother looked after the

dairy and the eggs. Things became so bad on the farm that the poet resolved to sail for Jamaica, in the hope of obtaining a steward-ship on some sugar-plantation. Desirous both to raise the need-ful funds and to leave behind some lasting memorial of himself, which might prevent his name from being utterly forgotten in the land of his birth, he had six hundred copies of his poems printed at Kilmarnock, and scattered among the **1786** shops of a few booksellers. The little volume went off A.D. rapidly; and nearly twenty guineas chinked in the poet's purse, after paying all expenses of the edition. His passage was taken in the first ship that was to sail from the Clyde; his chest was on the way to Greenock; a farewell to the bonnie banks of Ayr was breathed in his touching song, *The gloomy night is gather-ing fast;* when a *letter* changed the current of his life, and kept the poet in his native land. It was to a friend of Burns from Dr. Blacklock of Edinburgh, himself a poet, giving such praise as the modest rustic had not dared to hope for.

True to his impulsive soul, he turned his back at once on the Clyde, and in November 1786 arrived in Edinburgh with very few shillings, and not a letter of recommendation to win a friend. But his book, which was there before him, unlocked the doors of the first Edinburgh mansions to the peasant who had so sweet a note. Burns became the rage. Earls, grave historians, popular novelists, moral philosophers, listened with applause to his fresh and bril-liant talk; asked select friends to meet him at dinner; subscribed for the second edition of his poems, by which he cleared nearly £500; and then, when the gloss had worn off their plaything, and some fresh novelty had sprung up among them, this man, of whom his country is now so proud, in whose honour, not two years ago, every Scottish bell pealed joyously all day long, and every Scottish heart grew kinder all the world over, was looked coldly on, neglected, and forgotten :—but not until the poison of a capricious flattery had sown deadly seeds in the poet's soul.

The rest of his life-story, except for the immortal works his later years produced, is a tale of deep sadness, and had best be briefly told. Having taken the farm of Ellisland, about a hun-

dred acres on the Nith not far from Dumfries, he married Jean
Armour, to whom he had long been attached, and settled down to
a country life once more.   This phase of his career opened in June
1788.   Some time afterwards, by the interest of a friend, he
obtained the office of exciseman for the district in which he lived.
The sum he derived from this employment—never above £70 a
year—but ill repaid him for the time its duties cost, and the dangers of that unsettled, convivial life, to which his excitable nature
was thus exposed.   After struggling for more than three years
with the stubborn soil of Ellisland, and vainly trying to raise good
crops while he looked after the whisky stills, he gave up the farm,
and in 1791 went to live at Dumfries, upon his slender income as
a gauger.

A third edition of his poems, enriched with the inimitable *Tam
o' Shanter*, which he had written at Ellisland, came out two years
later.   But there were then not many sands of his life-glass to
run.   Sickness, debt, " the proud man's contumely," and the fell
gripe or bitter dregs of those dissipated habits to which his ardent,
passionate nature was but too prone, cast heavy clouds upon the
closing scene of his short, pathetic life.   He died at Dumfries on
the 21st of July 1796.

It is chiefly for his *Songs* that the memory of Robert Burns
is so dear to his countrymen.   But the lines already noticed
To a Daisy and *a Mouse;* the beautiful domestic picture of
The Cottar's Saturday Night; the noble *Elegy on Captain Matthew
Henderson;* the mad, low-life revelry of *The Jolly Beggars;* and,
above all, the serio-comic tale of *Tam o' Shanter*, with its market-
day carouse, its ride through the stormy midnight, its horrible
witch-dance within the old Kirk of Alloway, and its thrilling
escape of the rash farmer and his old grey mare;—these are works
which fully display the versatile genius of Robert Burns, and raise
him to the highest rank among our British bards.   Most of his
poems were written in Lowland Scotch; but in a mood more than
commonly pathetic, he rises to an English style, so refined and
beautiful, that we almost wonder where a Scottish peasant could
have learned the pure and lofty strain.

TO A MOUNTAIN DAISY.

Wee, modest, crimson-tipped flower,
Thou's met me in an evil hour;
For I maun crush amang the stoure
   Thy slender stem:
To spare thee now is past my power,
   Thou bonnie gem.

Alas! it's no thy neibor sweet,
The bonnie Lark, companion meet,
Bending thee 'mang the dewy weet,
   Wi' spreckled breast,
When upward-springing, blithe, to greet
   The purpling east!

Cauld blew the bitter-biting north
Upon thy early, humble birth;
Yet cheerfully thou glinted forth
   Amid the storm,
Scarce reared above the parent earth
   Thy tender form.

The flaunting flowers our gardens yield,
High sheltering woods and wa's maun shield;
But thou beneath the random bield
   O' clod or stane
Adorns the histie stibble-field,
   Unseen, alane.

There, in thy scanty mantle clad,
Thy snawie bosom sun-ward spread,
Thou lifts thy unassuming head
   In humble guise;
But now the share uptears thy bed,
   And low thou lies!

Such is the fate of artless maid,
Sweet flow'ret of the rural shade!
By love's simplicity betrayed,
   And guileless trust,
Till she, like thee, all soiled, is laid
   Low i' the dust.

Such is the fate of simple bard
On life's rough ocean luckless starred!
Unskilful he to note the card
   Of prudent lore,
Till billows rage, and gales blow hard,
   And whelm him o'er.

Such fate to suffering worth is given,
Who long with wants and woes has striven,
By human pride or cunning driven
            To misery's brink,
Till wrenched of every stay but Heaven,
                    He, ruined, sink!

Even thou who mourn'st the daisy's fate,
That fate is thine—no distant date ;
Stern Ruin's ploughshare drives, elate,
            Full on thy bloom,
Till crushed beneath the furrow's weight
                    Shall be thy doom !

CHAPTER IV.

EDMUND BURKE.

Born 1730 A.D..........Died 1797 A.D.

Early days.	Trial of Hastings.
Called to the bar.	The French Revolution.
Literary life.	Death of his son.
Dublin Castle.	Last days at Gregories.'
In Parliament.	Illustrative extract.

EDMUND BURKE, first of our political writers and among the greatest of our orators, was born in 1730, in a house on Arran Quay, Dublin. His father was an attorney, who enjoyed a large and thriving practice. Many of Edmund's early days were spent in the county of Cork, not far from the ruined walls of Kilcolman, where his namesake Spenser had lived and written, and whence the poet had fled a broken-hearted man. In his twelfth year young Burke was sent to school at Ballitore in Kildare ; and there, under a skilful master, Abraham Shackelton the Quaker, he studied for about two years.

Trinity College, Dublin, where his picture holds an honourable place on the wall of the Examination Hall, received him as a student in 1743. To shine at the English bar was his young ambition; and so he was entered at the Middle Temple in 1747. But he never became a lawyer; his great genius soon found its fitting sphere in a statesman's life. In the meantime, however, he began to write his way to fame. An imitation of Lord Bolingbroke's style, *The Vindication of Natural Society*, was followed by his well-known *Essay on the Sublime and Beautiful.* Having married Miss Nugent of Bath, on the strength of an allowance of £200 a year from his father and what his pen could make, he formed additional literary engagements with the bookseller Dodsley. For a sketch of *American History* in two volumes he received fifty guineas ; and was paid at the rate of £100 a volume for the *Annual*

Register, which first appeared in 1759. So, writing for daily bread, and struggling manfully with many difficulties, cheered by the love of his wife and his little son, Burke toiled onward and upward, never letting go the hope of fame.

His entrance on political life may be dated from his appointment in 1761 as private secretary to "Single Speech" Hamilton, who then became Chief Secretary for Ireland. The atmosphere of Dublin Castle did not long agree with the clever young Whig, who threw up a lately conferred pension of £300 a year, broke with Hamilton, and returned to London, where a brilliant career awaited him.

Having been appointed private secretary to the Marquis of Rockingham, who became Prime Minister in 1765, Burke in the following year entered Parliament as member for Wend-

1766
A.D.
over in Buckinghamshire. At the age of thirty-six he stood for the first time on the floor of St. Stephen's Chapel, whose walls were to ring so often during the next eight-and-twenty years with the rolling periods of his grand eloquence, and the peals of acclamation bursting alike from friend and foe. Among the great men who then sat upon the benches of the ancient hall, Burke at once took a foremost place. The triumphs of his eloquent tongue we cannot follow here, for it is ours to mark only the achievements of his brilliant pen. In the stirring years of the American War he poured out the opulence of a richly-stored mind in many noble orations; but the crown of his glory as an orator was won in the great Hall of Westminster, where, in the presence of the noblest and the fairest, the wisest and most gifted of the land, he uttered the thunders of his eloquence in the impeachment of Warren Hastings, Governor-Gene-

1788
A.D.
ral of India. Opening the case in February 1788 in a speech of four days, he continued his statement during certain days of April, and wound up his charges with an address, which began on the 28th of May and lasted for the nine succeeding days. As he spoke, the scenery of the East—rice-field and jungle, gilded temple and broad-bosomed river, with a sky of heated copper glowing over all—unfolded itself in a brilliant

picture before the kindled fancy of his audience; and when the sufferings of the tortured Hindoos and the desolation of their wasted fields were painted, as only Burke could paint in words, the effect of the sudden contrast upon those who heard him was like the shock of a Leyden jar. Ladies sobbed and screamed, handkerchiefs and smelling-bottles were in constant use, and "some were even carried out in fits."

Another great subject filled his thoughts during his last years. He foresaw the hurricane that was blackening over France, and, when it broke in fury, he wrote his greatest work, 1790 entitled *Reflections on the Revolution in France;* in which A.D. he lifts a powerful voice to warn England against cherishing at home the fatal seeds that were bearing so terrible a harvest across the waves of the Channel.

From the ceaseless toil of a statesman's life Burke sometimes stole away to his gardens at Gregories, near Beaconsfield, where, so far back as 1768, he had purchased an estate for £20,000. A heavy blow at last fell on his grey head, and bowed it with sorrow to the grave. His dear son Richard, who had been for thirty-six years the light of his eyes, sank under a rapid consumption. With some of Milton's glorious words upon his lips, this gifted man died in the arms of his great father. The world was then all darkness to Edmund Burke. But a little ago it was June, and he had sat for the last time in the Commons, glory- 1794 ing in the thought that he had a gallant son to fill the A.D. place he was leaving empty. It was now an August day —a marble mask of that son lay before him in an unclosed coffin, but the spirit had left the clay.

In his retreat at Beaconsfield he still continued to write, producing during his last two years some of his best works. A pension having been conferred on the veteran statesman, two of the Peers thought fit to find fault with the richly-deserved honour. It would have been wise for the Duke of Bedford and the Earl of Lauderdale to let the old lion die in peace. They thought that he was toothless, until he rose with gnashing fangs and tore the wretches limb from limb. The *Letter to a Noble Lord,* called forth by this ungenerous attack, stands next to the "French Revolution" as a specimen of Burke's powerful style.   Other works of his last years were *Letters on a Regicide Peace* and *Observations on the Conduct of the Minority*.   At last he began to sink daily, for his heart was still bleeding for his son.   In vain for four months **1797** the waters of Bath were tried.   He returned home to die, **A.D.** and was laid in a vault under Beaconsfield Church, beside the dust of his darling Richard.

MARIE ANTOINETTE.

(FROM THE "FRENCH REVOLUTION.")

It is now sixteen or seventeen years since I saw the Queen of France, then the Dauphiness, at Versailles; and surely never lighted on this orb, which she hardly seemed to touch, a more delightful vision.   I saw her just above the horizon, decorating and cheering the elevated sphere she just began to move in—glittering like the morning star, full of life, and splendour, and joy.   Oh, what a revolution! and what a heart must I have to contemplate without emotion that elevation and that fall!   Little did I dream, when she added titles of veneration to those of distant, enthusiastic, respectful love, that she should ever be obliged to carry the sharp antidote against disgrace concealed in that bosom; little did I dream that I should have lived to see such disasters fallen upon her in a nation of gallant men, in a nation of men of honour and of cavaliers.   I thought ten thousand swords must have leaped from their scabbards to avenge even a look that threatened her with insult.   But the age of chivalry is gone.   That of sophisters, economists, and calculators has succeeded ; and the glory of Europe is extinguished for ever.   Never, never more shall we behold that generous loyalty to rank and sex, that proud submission, that dignified obedience, that subordination of the heart, which kept alive, even in servitude itself, the spirit of an exalted freedom.   The unbought grace of life, the cheap defence of nations, the nurse of manly sentiment and heroic enterprise is gone !   It is gone,—that sensibility of principle, that chastity of honour, which felt a stain like a wound, which inspired courage whilst it mitigated ferocity, which ennobled whatever it touched, and under which vice itself lost half its evil by losing all its grossness.

CHAPTER V.

WILLIAM COWPER.

Born 1731 A.D..........Died 1800 A.D.

The sensitive-plant.	Madness.	Tirocinium.
A kind mother.	The Unwins.	Last days.
Misery at school.	Life at Olney.	Letters.
Studies the law.	Earliest poems.	Illustrative extract.
The clerkship in the Lords.	The Task.	

IF we compare our English literature to a beautiful garden, where Milton lifts his head to heaven in the spotless chalice of the tall white lily, and Shakspere scatters his dramas round him in beds of fragrant roses, blushing with a thousand various shades—some stained to the core as if with blood, others unfolding their fair pink petals with a lovely smile to the summer sun,—what shall we find in shrub or flower so like the timid, shrinking spirit of William Cowper, as that delicate sensitive-plant, whose leaves, folding up at the slightest touch, cannot bear even the brighter rays of the cherishing sun ?

The Reverend Doctor John Cowper, a royal chaplain, the son of a judge, and the nephew of a lord-chancellor, was rector of Great Berkhamstead in Hertfordshire, when his son William was born there in 1731. A tender mother—a lady of the highest descent—watched the infancy and childhood of the boy. Her hand it was that wrapped his little scarlet cloak around him, and filled his little bag with biscuits, every morning before he went to his first school. By her knee was his happiest place, where he often amused himself by marking out the flowered pattern of her dress on paper with a pin, taking a child's delight in his simple skill. He was only six years old when this fond mother died; thus early upon the childish head a pitiless storm began to beat. More than fifty years after the day on which a sad little face, looking from the nursery window, had seen a dark hearse moving slowly from the door, an old man, smitten with incurable madness but then enjoying a brief lucid interval, bent over a picture, and saw the never-forgotten image of that kindest earthly friend, from whom he had so long been severed, but whom he was so soon to join in the sorrowless land.   There are no more touching and beautiful lines in English poetry or prose than Cowper's *Verses to his Mother's Picture.*

The circumstance to which his morbid nervousness and melancholy may most of all be traced, is full of warning for the young. The poor motherless boy of six was sent to a boarding-school at Market Street in Hertfordshire, where a senior pupil, whose brutality and cowardice cannot be too strongly condemned, led the child a terrible life for two years, crushing down his young spirit with cruel blows and bitter persecution.   It was a happy release, when he was removed from this scene of misery to the house of an eminent oculist, for the treatment of his eyes, which the poor little fellow had probably cried into a state of violent inflammation.   His seven years at Westminster School were less unpleasant to the timid boy, though there too he had to take his full share of buffeting and sneers.

The law being his appointed profession, he entered an attorney's office at eighteen, and there spent three years.   This period and a few succeeding years formed almost the only spot of sunshine in the poet's life.   Many a hearty laugh echoed through the gloomy office, where Cowper and his fellow-apprentice—afterwards Lord-Chancellor Thurlow—made believe that they were studying the English law.   Called to the bar in 1754, he lived for some time an idle, agreeable life, in his Temple chambers, writing a little for the serials of the day, and taking a share in the wit-combats of the "Nonsense Club," which consisted nearly altogether of Westminster men.   It was during this part of his life that he fell in love with his cousin Theodora,—a passion the unfortunate issue of which gave a darker colouring to the naturally sombre spirit of the young lawyer.

A relative presented him in the year 1763 to a valuable clerkship in the Lords, which required the holder of the office to appear frequently before the House. The idea of such a thing was, in Cowper's own words, "mortal poison" to his shrinking nature. A more private post—that of Clerk of the Journals of the House of Lords—was then substituted for the **1763** former gift; but, most unexpectedly, the presentee was A.D. summoned to the bar to be examined as to his fitness for the post. Obliged to face the future horror of this examination, while for months he worked hard to prepare himself for passing it creditably, his mind gave way,—he tried to kill himself; and a private asylum at St. Albans became for eighteen months the refuge of the afflicted man.

A deep religious melancholy was the form of his mental disease ; an awful terror that his soul was lost for ever, beyond the power of redemption, hung in a thick night-cloud upon his life. Three times after the first attack the madness returned,—for nearly four years previous to 1776—for about six months in 1787—and during his last six years, from 1794 to 1800.

The friendship of the Unwins was the great blessing of his life. At Huntingdon he became intimate with this kind family, then consisting of the Reverend Morley Unwin, his wife, son, and daughter ; and the friendship grew so strong, that Cowper went in 1766 to live in their calm and cheerful home. **1766** The good clergyman was killed in the following year by A.D. a fall from his horse, and the widow and her daughter went to live at Olney in Buckinghamshire. Thither Cowper accompanied them, for he was now unalterably one of the quiet household.

Here the timid spirit nestled in a pleasant home. A walk with his dog by the reedy banks of the placid Ouse, to admire the white and gold of the water-lilies that floated on the deep stream —a round of visits to the cottages of the neighbouring poor—the composition of some hymns for his friend John Newton, the curate of the parish,—filled up his peaceful days for a time. But the terrible shadows were thickening again round his brain. A second fit of madness came in 1773, and all was dark for more than three years.

When light once more broke through the clouds, the need of some graver and more constant work made the man of fifty, who had already produced light occasional verses, take pen in hand, and sit down seriously to write a book of poems.   For recreation he had his flowers, his pet hares, his landscape drawing, and his manufacture of bird-cages; but poetry now became the serious business of his life.

His first volume was issued in 1782.   It contained three grave and powerful satires, *Truth, Table-talk,* and *Expostulation,* **1782**   with poems on *Error, Hope, Charity,* and kindred subjects, A.D.   written chiefly in pentameter rhymes.   No great success rewarded this first instalment of Cowper's poetic toil; but at least two men, whose good opinion was worth more than gold, saw real merit in the modest book.   Johnson and Franklin recognised in the recluse of fifty a true and eminent poet.

But higher efforts lay before the literary hermit.   The widow of Sir Robert Austen, coming to live at Olney, soon became intimate with the melancholy Cowper.   To cheer him, she told the story of *John Gilpin,* whose comical equestrianism became the subject of a famous ballad.   In this rattling tale and other minor pieces, as well as in numberless satiric and ironical touches scattered through the mass of his poems, we catch gleams of a sunny humour lurking below the shy and sensitive moods which wrapt the poet from public gaze.   To Lady Austen, Cowper owed the origin of his greatest work, *The Task.*   She asked him to write some blank-verse, and playfully gave him the *Sofa* as a subject.   Beginning a poem on this homely theme, he produced the six books **1785**   of *The Task,* which took its name from the circumstances A.D.   of its origin.   From a humorous historical sketch of the gradual improvement of seats, the three-legged stool growing into the softly cushioned sofa, he glides into the pleasures of a country walk, and following out the natural train of thought, draws a strong contrast between rural and city life, lavishing loving praise upon the former.   The second book, entitled *The Time-piece,* opens with a just and powerful denunciation of slavery, and proceeds to declare the blessings and the need of peace among the nations

A noble apostrophe to England, and a brilliantly sarcastic picture of a fashionable preacher are among the more striking passages of this book. Then come *The Garden, The Winter Evening, The Winter Morning Walk,* and *The Winter Walk at Noon,* full of exquisite description and deep kindliness. Mirrored in these beautiful poems, we see the peaceful recreations and the gentle nature of this amiable afflicted man. We learn to reverence him for his wisdom, to love him for his human tenderness, and to sympathize pitifully and deeply with the overshadowing sorrow of his fitful life.

Accompanying "The Task," which appeared in 1785 to take the hearts of all Englishmen by storm, was a review of schools, entitled *Tirocinium,* strongly recommending private tuition in preference to education at a public school. The sad experience of his own early school-days was, without doubt, the root from which this poem sprang.

Dissatisfied with Pope's version of the great Greek epics, Cowper now undertook to *translate Homer into English verse;* and by working regularly at the rate of forty lines a day, he accomplished the task in a few years. A passing attack of his old malady laid him by for a while during the progress of this work. The "Homer" appeared in 1791 ; and a revised edition, altered and corrected to a great extent, followed in 1799. Kind friends of his youth drew round the poor old man in his last years. His cousin, Lady Hesketh, induced him to remove to a villa at Weston, about a mile from his well-loved Olney. But the last and thickest cloud was darkening down. About 1794 the gloom of madness fell again upon his mind, and only for very brief intervals was there any light, until the ineffable brilliance of a higher life broke upon his raptured gaze. A sad sight it must have been to see the grey-haired sufferer standing by the coffin, where his faithful friend of many years—the kind, devoted Mary Unwin—lay in the last marble sleep. She died 'in 1796; and in less than four years the gentle poet, whom her roof-tree had sheltered, and her gentle ministerings had cheered and solaced for April 25, fully thirty years, closed his eyes for ever on the earth, **1800** which had been to him indeed a place of many sorrows. A.D.

A pension of £300 a year from the king had comforted his declining days.   He was able before death to revise his "Homer," and to leave in the little poem of *The Castaway*—descriptive of a sailor's death, who had been washed overboard in the mid Atlantic —the last sad wail of his noble lyre.   Already the darkness of the Valley of the Shadow of Death was on his soul, when he sang the concluding words :—

> "We perished, each alone ;
> But I beneath a rougher sea,
> And whelmed in deeper gulfs than he."

To forget *Cowper's Letters*, in a sketch of his literary life, would be unpardonable.   Southey, his best biographer, calls him "the best of English letter-writers;" and there is no exaggeration in the praise.   Loathing from his soul, as he tells us, all affectation, he writes to his friends in fine simple English words, which have caught their lustre, as style must always do, from the beauty of the thoughts expressed.   A sweet, delicate humour, plays throughout these charming compositions, like golden sunlight on a clear and pebbled stream.

APOSTROPHE TO WINTER.

(FROM "THE TASK," BOOK IV.)

O Winter ! ruler of the inverted year,
Thy scattered hair with sleet like ashes filled,
Thy breath congealed upon thy lips, thy cheeks
Fringed with a beard made white with other snows
Than those of age, thy forehead wrapped in clouds,
A leafless branch thy sceptre, and thy throne
A sliding car, indebted to no wheels,
But urged by storms along its slippery way,
I love thee, all unlovely as thou seem'st,
And dreaded as thou art !   Thou hold'st the sun
A prisoner in the yet undawning east,
Shortening his journey between morn and noon,
And hurrying him, impatient of his stay,
Down to the rosy west. . . . . .
No rattling wheels stop short before these gates;
No powdered pert, proficient in the art
Of sounding an alarm, assaults these doors

Till the street rings; no stationary steeds
Cough their own knell, while, heedless of the sound,
The silent circle fan themselves, and quake :
But here the needle plies its busy task,
The pattern grows ; the well-depicted flower,
Wrought patiently into the snowy lawn,
Unfolds its bosom; buds, and leaves, and sprigs,
And curling tendrils, gracefully disposed,
Follow the nimble fingers of the fair;
A wreath, that cannot fade, of flowers that blow
With most success when all besides decay.
The poet's or historian's page by one
Made vocal for the amusement of the rest;
The sprightly lyre, whose treasure of sweet sounds
The touch from many a trembling chord shakes out;
And the clear voice symphonious, yet distinct,
And in the charming strife triumphant still,
Beguile the night, and set a keener edge
On female industry;—the threaded steel
Flies swiftly, and unfelt the task proceeds.
The volume closed, the customary rites
Of the last meal commence.   A Roman meal !
Such as the mistress of the world once found
Delicious, when her patriots of high note,
Perhaps by moonlight, at their humble doors,
And under an old oak's domestic shade,
Enjoyed, spare feast ! a radish and an egg.
Discourse ensues, not trivial, yet not dull,
Nor such as with a frown forbids the play
Of fancy, or proscribes the sound of mirth:
Nor do we madly, like an impious world,
Who deem religion frenzy, and the God
That made them an intruder on their joys,
Start at his awful name, or deem his praise
A jarring note.

CHAPTER VI.

GEORGE GORDON, LORD BYRON.

Born 1788 A.D..........Died 1824 A.D.

Parentage.	Attack and reply.	Leaves England for ever.
At Aberdeen.	Childe Harold.	Italian life.
The little lord.	A London lion.	Later works.
Harrow and Cambridge.	Turkish tales.	In Greece to die.
Hours of Idleness.	Unhappy marriage.	Illustrative extract.

In the year 1790 a profligate and dissipated captain in the Guards abandoned his wife and a little child of two years in the stony wilderness of London. The officer's name was John Byron; his wife was Catherine Gordon of Gight in Aberdeenshire. *He* went abroad to die: *she* went north to Aberdeen with her little lame boy to live as well as she could on £130 a year.

There, in Scottish schools, the boy received his early education, until an announcement reached the small household in the city of granite, that, by the death of his grand-uncle, "Geordie" was a lord, and owner of Newstead Abbey in Nottinghamshire. At **1798** once his weak, capricious mother, was seized with a desperate A.D. horror of her son's lameness, which had existed from his birth. In vain she tried quacks and doctors. The foot remained unchangeably distorted, and to the last a look at the deformity stabbed Byron like a dagger. Less than two years at a Dulwich boarding-school, and some time at Harrow, prepared the young lord for entering Trinity College, Cambridge, in 1805. Already the youth of seventeen, thoroughly spoiled by his foolish mother, who flung things at him one moment, and strained him to her breast the next, had been neglecting his regular studies, but eagerly devouring other books of every class and kind. Oriental history seems early to have fascinated his taste; and this early love gave its own colouring to his chief poetical works. Already, too, another love than that for books had been tinging his spirit with its hues. The lame but handsome boy was only fifteen, when he met that Mary Chaworth, whose coldness towards him was the first rill of lasting bitterness that mingled with the current of his life. The beautiful *Dream*, which we find among his minor poems, tells the sad story of this boyish love and its results.

The young lord's life at Cambridge lasted about two years, during which he made some firm friends among the students, but annoyed and estranged the college Dons by his irregularities. Among other freaks, he kept bull-dogs and a bear in his rooms, the latter of which he introduced to visitors as in training for a fellow-ship. His lameness did not prevent him from taking a full share in athletic sports. At school he had loved hockey and cricket better than the Latin poets. At college, and during his residence at Newstead, before he came of age, he was passionately fond of boating. A large Newfoundland dog was his invariable companion during the lonely cruisings he enjoyed.*

During his leisure hours at school and college he had been penning occasional verses, which appeared at Newark in 1807, in a little volume entitled *Hours of Idleness.* Very boyish and very weak these verses were, but they hardly merited **1807** the weighty scorn with which an Edinburgh reviewer A.D. noticed them within the year. Stung to the quick by this article, with the authorship of which Lord Brougham is charged, the "noble minor" retorted in a poem, *English Bards and Scotch Reviewers*, which showed the world that the abused versicles were but the languid recreations of a man in whose hand, when roused to earnest work, the pen became a tremendous and destructive weapon.

Two years of foreign travel (1809–1811), led the poet through scenes whose beauty and historic interest inspired the first two cantos of *Childe Harold's Pilgrimage.* Though Byron was only one-and-twenty when he set out upon this tour of Spain and Turkey, the shadow of disappointed love had long been brooding upon his heart. In spite of his own repeated denials, we cannot

---

* The Epitaph on this dog, especially the last line, affords a strange glimpse of the poet's misanthropic pride.

help identifying the writer with this gloomy Childe Harold, who had exhausted in revelry and vice the power of enjoying life. Not that Byron at this early stage felt within his breast only the cold and lifeless embers of wild passions, which had burned themselves to death ; but the poor young fellow, smarting sorely under his early sorrow, and feeling that his talents were of no common kind, grew into that diseased state of mind which leads a man to believe that it is a fine thing to hate all the world and care for nothing— to be utterly *blasé* and done-up, and alone and uncared-for.   So he pictures Childe Harold to have been ; and the same unpleasant character is reproduced in nearly all his portraitures of men. When the first two cantos of this noble poem were published in

1812   1812, the author, who only five years earlier had been
A.D.   sneered at as a weakling, rose by unanimous consent to the head of the London literary world.   In his own words, he awoke one morning to find himself famous. As the Ayrshire peasant had been caressed by the fashionables of Edinburgh, the aristocratic and handsome Byron was idolized in the saloons of London.

His life, as a man of fashion and a literary lion, lasted for about three years.   During this time he took his seat in the House of Lords, and made three speeches without producing any marked effect.

The material gathered during his travels being yet far from exhausted, he wrote those fine Turkish tales, which kindled in the public mind of England an enthusiastic feeling towards modern Greece.   *The Giaour* and *The Bride of Abydos* appeared in 1813 ; *The Corsair* and *Lara*, in the following year.   The two former are written in that eight-syllabled line which suits so well the narration of stirring and romantic adventures.   In the latter he adopted the rhyming pentameters of Dryden and Pope, but gave them a music and a colour all his own.   In all four the inevitable and unwholesome Byronic hero,—sallow, wasted, dark-haired, mysterious, ill-humoured,—casts his chill upon us.   Childe Harold has wound a crimson shawl round his high, pale brow, has donned the snowy capote, has stuck ataghan and silver-mounted pistols in his belt, and in full Greek dress glooms at us with his melancholy eyes.

Byron's marriage with Miss Milbanke took place in 1815. Almost from the beginning there were disagreements, and in a twelvemonth the union was dissolved. One daughter, Ada, to whom are addressed the touching lines which open the third canto of "Childe Harold," reminded the unhappy parents of what their home might have been.

Having produced *The Siege of Corinth* and *Parisina* amid the miseries of his last months in London, where he was abused in the papers and hissed in the streets for his conduct to his wife, he left England in disgust in the spring of 1816, and never saw his native land again. Restless and miserable years they were that filled up the allotted span of poor Byron's life. He passed—a lonely wanderer, with many a poisoned arrow rankling in his memory and heart—over the blood-stained ground of Waterloo, amid the snowy summits of the Jura echoing with frequent thunder, into the beautiful Italian land, to find in the faded palaces of Venice and the mouldering columns of Rome fit emblems of his own ruined life,—but, alas! not to read these lessons of the dead past with a softening and repentant soul. At Venice, at Ravenna, at Pisa, and at Rome, he lived a wicked and most irregular life, writing many poems, for which he received many thousand pounds, but descending, as he sank morally, into a fitful and frequently morbid style, too often poisoned with reckless blasphemy and unconcealed licentiousness.

His greatest work, *Childe Harold's Pilgrimage*,* was finished in 1818. The third canto was written at Geneva; the fourth and last, chiefly at Venice. The Spenserian **1818** stanza takes a noble music in the skilful hand of Byron. A.D. The view of modern Rome, the starlight vision of the bleeding Gladiator, and the address to the Ocean, which no familiarity can ever rob of its sublime effect, are the finest passages of the closing poem.

Of course Byron tried his pen at dramatic writing. Almost every poet does. But the author of "Childe Harold" and the

* *Childe* is an old English word, signifying a *knight.* Byron at first intended to give an antique cast to the diction of the poem.

"Corsair" had not the power of *going out of himself*, which a successful dramatist must possess. That dark and morbidly romantic
figure, of whom we have spoken before, haunts us through all the
Mysteries and *Tragedies* which this unhappy genius produced in
the later years of his shadowed life. *Cain* and *Manfred* are the
most powerful of these works; but they afford, especially the
former, a terrible view into the workings of a mind steeped in
rebellious pride and misanthropy. *Marino Faliero, The Two
Foscari, Sardanapalus, Werner, Heaven and Earth*, and *The
Deformed Transformed*, are the principal remaining dramas from
Byron's pen.

His last great literary effort was the composition of his most
dangerous work, *Don Juan*. Dangerous, we say, because it
is draped and garlanded with passages of exceeding beauty and
sweetness. It stands, a fragment of unfinished toil, a sad memento of lofty genius debased to the foulest use. Never were
shining gold and black mire so industriously heaped together.
It seems as if the unhappy bard, tired of hating his fellow-mortals,
had turned with fierce mockery upon himself, to degrade and
trample on that very genius upon which was based his only claim
to admiration, and which alone can save from ridicule his scornful
isolation of himself.

Byron's last enterprise flings a somewhat pathetic light upon
his closing days. The Greece whose ancient glories and whose
lovely shores had formed a chief theme of his earlier song, had
risen at length from her ignoble bondage. The War of Independence had begun. Sailing from Leghorn in 1823, Byron
landed in Cephalonia, and soon passed to Missolonghi. With
money, with advice, with encouragement, and with bodily service,
he began to work eagerly in the cause of his adopted land.
Difficulties were thick around him; for wild lawlessness was everywhere, and fierce quarrels occurred in the Greek army every
day. In a few months he did much to overcome these troubles,
and was looking forward with eagerness to leading an attack on
Lepanto, when fever, rising from the marshes of Missolonghi,
seized in its deadly gripe his enervated and toil-worn frame.

He died on the 19th of April 1824 ; and three days later, his
turbulent Suliotes gathered, pale and tearful, round his
coffin, to hear the funeral service read. The body of   **1824**
the poet was carried to England, and interred in the   A.D.
family vault at Hucknall, near Newstead.

The Prisoner of Chillon, a sweetly mournful sketch written at
Geneva; *The Lament of Tasso; The Prophecy of Dante; Beppo,*
a light tale of Venetian life; *Mazeppa;* and the terrible *Vision
of Judgment,* written in mockery of a like-titled poem by Southey,
with whom he had a deadly feud, complete the list of Byron's
more important works.

ADDRESS TO THE OCEAN.

(FROM "CHILDE HAROLD.")

Roll on, thou deep and dark-blue ocean—roll !
Ten thousand fleets sweep over thee in vain;
Man marks the earth with ruin—his control
Stops with the shore; upon the watery plain
The wrecks are all thy deed, nor doth remain
A shadow of man's ravage, save his own,
When, for a moment, like a drop of rain,
He sinks into thy depths with bubbling groan—
Without a grave, unknelled, uncoffined, and unknown.

His steps are not upon thy paths—thy fields
Are not a spoil for him—thou dost arise
And shake him from thee; the vile strength he wields
For earth's destruction thou dost all despise,
Spurning him from thy bosom to the skies,
And send'st him, shivering in thy playful spray
And howling to his gods, where haply lies
His petty hope in some near port or bay,
And dashest him again to earth :—there let him lay

The armaments, which thunder-strike the walls
Of rock-built cities, bidding nations quake
And monarchs tremble in their capitals ;
The oak leviathans, whose huge ribs make
Their clay creator the vain title take
Of lord of thee, and arbiter of war :
These are thy toys, and as the snowy flake,
They melt into thy yeast of waves, which mar
Alike the Armada's pride, and spoils of Trafalgar.

Thy shores are empires, changed in all save thee.
Assyria, Greece, Rome, Carthage—what are they?
Thy waters wasted them while they were free,
And many a tyrant since; their shores obey
The stranger, slave, or savage; their decay
 Has dried up realms to deserts;—not so thou,
Unchangeable save to thy wild waves' play—
 Time writes no wrinkle on thine azure brow—
Such as Creation's dawn beheld, thou rollest now.

Thou glorious mirror, where the Almighty's form
Glasses itself in tempests; in all time,
Calm or convulsed—in breeze, or gale, or storm—
Icing the pole, or in the torrid clime
 Dark-heaving, boundless, endless, and sublime—
The image of Eternity—the throne
Of the Invisible; even from out thy slime
The monsters of the deep are made; each zone
Obeys thee; thou goest forth, dread, fathomless, alone.

And I have loved thee, Ocean! and my joy
Of youthful sports was on thy breast to be
Borne, like thy bubbles, onward; from a boy
I wantoned with thy breakers—they to me
Were a delight; and if the freshening sea
Made them a terror—'twas a pleasing fear;
For I was as it were a child of thee,
 And trusted to thy billows far and near,
And laid my hand upon thy mane—as I do here.

CHAPTER VII.

GEORGE CRABBE.

Born 1754 A.D...........Died 1832 A.D.

A line of Byron.	Five pounds wanted.	The Village.
Aldborough.	In London.	A country parson's life.
Treasured verses.	Kindness of Burke.	Theme of Crabbe.
Pills and plasters.	The Library.	Illustrative extract.

" NATURE's sternest painter, yet the best," wrote Lord Byron of the poet Crabbe.   It was a just and generous compliment, deriving additional value from the brilliance of the pen that traced the words.

Well might George Crabbe be a painter of stern and gloomy scenes, for with these he had been familiar from earliest childhood. His first recollections were of a flat and ugly coast, bordered with slimy rock-pools, washed by discoloured waves, and tenanted only by a race of wild, amphibious, weather-beaten men, who, for the most part, added to their lawful calling as fishermen the yet more hazardous occupation of the smuggler.   Such was the scenery, and such were the people round Aldborough in Suffolk, where in 1754 he was born.   His father, the salt-master or collector of salt duties in that little town, treated his   **1754** son George, as he seems to have treated everybody else,   A.D. with considerable harshness.   But the boy had early found a consolation for the passing griefs of childhood.   He used to cut out for his private reading the occasional verses of a periodical, for which his father subscribed.   Over and over again the treasured scraps were conned, until the happy owner began to imitate their simple music.

The life of Crabbe, before settling down into the quietude of a rural parish, presents pleasant and painful scenes.   The boy of fourteen, who had already got some grounding in classics and mathematics, was apprenticed to a surgeon at Wickham Brook, near Bury St. Edmund's. Here he met with such ill-treatment, that it was thought right to remove him to another master, at Woodbridge in his native shire. Secretly, amid all discouragements and sorrows, the young poet, even when he was rolling pills or grinding nauseous drugs in a mortar, had been cultivating his new-found talent for making verses. In the house of his hard taskmaster he had "filled a drawer with poetry." And, while at Woodbridge, he won a prize for a poem on *Hope*, which was proposed by the proprietor of a certain magazine. The success of this maiden effort sealed the future fate of Crabbe. Thenceforward for life he was a poet; and in a short time, after a brave attempt to establish himself in his profession at Aldborough, he was drawn by an irresistible magnetism into the then perilous struggles of literary life in London.

This is the strangest period of his story. An apothecary's shopman and a country clergyman have nothing wonderful about their daily lives. But there is often a romance about the career of a literary adventurer, especially during his earlier struggles, which possesses a remarkable fascination. Even the first step Crabbe took towards getting to London was original and odd. He had no money. He sat down and wrote a letter, asking the loan of five pounds from Mr. Dudley North, whose brother had once contested the town of Aldborough at an election. The money came. A sloop bound for London was in the harbour, and soon the ex-surgeon stood in the solitude of those busy streets.

There he went through the old routine of hard work and bitter rejection, in the midst of which so many earnest, hopeful hearts have failed and broken. His poems were refused; a publisher, to whom he had intrusted the issuing of a work on his own account, failed; his money was nearly gone; and want stared him in the face. Just at this crisis he thought of his letter to North and the cordial reply. At once acting on the recollection, he wrote, enclosing poems, to the Prime Minister, the Lord Chancellor, and others. No answer came. He would try the great Edmund Burke. With a beating heart he knocked at the statesman's door one night, handed in a letter, and then went in pitiable agitation to walk to

and fro on Westminster Bridge, till the lamps went out along the
river, and the red dawn began to glimmer in the east. Burke's
kindness was prompt and real. Appointing a time for Crabbe to
call, he looked over the manuscripts; picked out two, *The Library*
and *The Village;* good-naturedly pointed out some passages in need
of change ; and, better than all, took the works to Dodsley's shop
and recommended them to that eminent bookseller. Going further
still, he brought the poet out to Beaconsfield, where he introduced
him to some of the first men of the day. The tide had turned,
and thenceforward there was no struggle in the peaceful life of
Crabbe.

In 1781 *The Library* was published. Lord Chancellor Thurlow
became his friend, though tardily. At Burke's suggestion the poet
qualified himself for entering the Church, and was ordained in the
August of 1782. The *quondam* surgeon went back to Aldborough
as curate of the parish, with every prospect of competence and
fame. His good friend Burke did not forget the struggler he had
saved from want, or worse than want. The statesman's influence
having obtained for him the domestic chaplaincy in the household
of the Duke of Rutland, he exchanged Aldborough parsonage for
Belvoir Castle. Then appeared in 1783 *The Village*, the
revisal of which was among the last works of Dr. John- **1783**
son's toilsome life; and so decided was the success of   A.D.
the poem, that its publication may be regarded as the
seal of George Crabbe's fame. Presented by Thurlow with
two small livings in Dorsetshire, the successful poet married
without delay that gentle Suffolk girl who had waited for him so
long.

The quiet current of his days then flowed on without any striking
change or remarkable sorrow, except the gentle regrets of moving
occasionally from one parish to another, and that one darkest cloud
of his life, the loss of his affectionate wife. In 1785 he published
The Newspaper; and then his name was not seen in the publishers'
lists for two-and-twenty years. The flowers, insects, and rocks of his
parish, wherever he might be, engaged much of his studious love.
With his sons, whom he taught at home, he read French and

Italian books, and took long walks through the fields. Such pursuits, combined with the unflagging labour of the pen, filled those hours of the country clergyman that were not given to the duties of his sacred office.

His most successful work, *The Parish Register*, appeared in 1807 ; and three years later came *The Borough*, in which, perhaps, we find his most powerful painting. About a year after the loss of his wife, which befell him in 1813, he was presented by the Duke of Rutland to the living of Trowbridge in Wilt-

1814   shire, worth ·£800 a year. There he wrought at his last
A.D.   great literary task, *The Tales of the Hall*, which were published in 1819, and for which, with the remaining copyright of his poems, he received the large sum of £3000. There, too, he died at a ripe old age, on the 3rd of February 1832.

The English poor—their woes, weaknesses, and sins—form the almost unvarying theme of Crabbe's poetry. Himself a poor man's son, he could not help, whenever he visited the hovels or the parish workhouse at Muston or at Trowbridge, recollecting the days when he had played with ragged boys down by the shipping in the little harbour of Aldborough ; or when he had stood by the sick-beds of labourers and boatmen, a poor country surgeon living a more wretched and precarious life than many of his patients. He had been himself within the veil of the poor man's life—he had himself felt many of the sorrows that smite the poor; and thus it was that he could produce, with such marvellous truth and minuteness of detail, those grey photographs of humble village life which extorted Byron's expressive line. The distinguishing feature of his poetry is the wonderful minuteness of his descriptive passages. One of the most objective of our poets, he described faithfully all that he saw, and little seems to have escaped his searching ken. Upon the sea he dwells with especial love. It was almost the only beautiful object that met his young eyes at Aldborough ; and whether he writes of it as the gentle, sunny thing, that taps lazily at the side of a stranded ship, or the fierce and powerful element that sweeps in white fury over sharp and splintered rocks. some

of his finest lines flow and brighten in its praise. He has been
called a " Pope in worsted stockings ;" which simply means, when
we get rid of the faint flavour of the wit, that he wrote in the
pentameter couplet of which Pope was so fond, and that he wrote
about the poor. Otherwise, there is as slight similarity between
the testy little invalid of Twickenham, and the mild, venerable
rector of Trowbridge, as between the powdered and brocaded
Belinda of the one, whose tress is severed by the daring scissors,
and the sweet, rustic, rosy-cheeked Phœbe Dawson of the other,
who trips smiling across the village green.

ISAAC ASHFORD.

(FROM "THE PARISH REGISTER.")

Next to these ladies, but in nought allied,
A noble peasant, Isaac Ashford, died.
Noble he was, contemning all things mean,
His truth unquestioned and his soul serene.
Of no man's presence Isaac felt afraid ;
At no man's question Isaac looked dismayed :
Shame knew him not, he dreaded no disgrace ;
Truth, simple truth, was written in his face.
Yet while the serious thought his soul approved,
Cheerful he seemed, and gentleness he loved ;
To bliss domestic he his heart resigned,
And with the firmest, had the fondest mind.
Were others joyful, he looked smiling on,
And gave allowance where he needed none;
Good he refused with future ill to buy,
Nor knew a joy that caused reflection's sigh.
A friend to virtue, his unclouded breast
No envy stung, no jealousy distressed—
Bane of the poor ! it wounds their weaker mind
To miss one favour which their neighbours find.
Yet far was he from stoic pride removed ;
He felt humanely, and he warmly loved:
I marked his action when his infant died,
And his old neighbour for offence was tried ;
The still tears, stealing down that furrowed cheek,
Spoke pity plainer than the tongue can speak.
If pride was his, 'twas not their vulgar pride,
Who, in their base contempt, the great deride;

Nor pride in learning, though my clerk agreed,
If fate should call him, Ashford might succeed;
Nor pride in rustic skill, although we knew
None his superior, and his equals few:
But if that spirit in his soul had place,
It was the jealous pride that shuns disgrace;
A pride in honest fame, by virtue gained,
In sturdy boys to virtuous labours trained;
Pride in the power that guards his country's coast,
And all that Englishmen enjoy and boast;
Pride in a life that slander's tongue defied,—
In fact, a noble passion, misnamed pride.

CHAPTER VIII.

SIR WALTER SCOTT.

Born 1771 A.D..........Died 1832 A.D.

Four periods.	Waverley.	Visit to Italy.
First associations.	Succeeding novels.	The dropping of the pen.
At school and college	Abbotsford.	Death and burial.
Translates Lenore.	The crash.	List of chief works.
Border Minstrelsy.	Killing work.	His poetry.
Life at Ashestiel.	Life of Napoleon.	Word-painting.
The Last Minstrel.	Woodstock.	Historical novels.
Clarty-Hole.	Paralysis.	Illustrative extract.

WHETHER we estimate him by the enormous amount of literary work he accomplished, or by the splendour of the fame that he achieved, Scott must be reckoned beyond question the greatest writer that the nineteenth century has yet produced. Before he began to pour his wonderful series of novels from a well of fancy that seemed without measure and without depth, he had already won a brilliant and lasting renown as a poet of chivalry and romance.

As the object of this chapter is to present a clear and vivid sketch of Scott's life, we shall best avoid confusion by dividing that life into four great periods, to be touched on in succession, reserving for the close a short account of the principal works with which this magnificent genius endowed his country and the world.

I. From his birth in 1771 to his entrance on literary life in 1796 by the publication of Bürger's *Lenore*, translated from the German. This period, extending over twenty-five years, includes his early life, his education, his apprenticeship, and his first appearance as an advocate.

II. From 1796 to the publication of *Waverley* in 1814. This period of eighteen years, from his twenty-fifth to his forty-third year, includes the publication of his chief poems, and his editions of Dryden and of Swift. It was a time of growing fame.

III. From 1814 to the great catastrophe of 1826, when he sat
    down, a man of fifty-five, to write off a debt considerably
    above £100,000. During these twelve years, the brightest
    of his life, he produced his finest novels, and built on the
    banks of Tweed his mansion of Abbotsford.

IV. From 1826 to his death, a period of six years, devoted to
    constant literary toil, rendered doubly painful towards the
    end by the consciousness of decaying powers, and the shocks
    of mortal disease.   Literally, Scott wrote himself to death.
    The noble genius, straining every nerve under an over-
    whelming burden, burst his heart and fell, just when the
    goal of his honourable hopes began to rise clearly into view.

In a house at the head of the College Wynd in Edinburgh
        Walter Scott was born, on the 15th of August 1771.
1771   His father was a respectable Writer to the Signet; his
A.D.   mother, Anne Rutherford, was the daughter of an eminent
        Edinburgh physician.   When a toddling bairn of only
eighteen months, a severe teething fever deprived him of the power
of his right leg.   The earliest recollections of the child were of a
fairer kind than the College Wynd, or even George's Square, to
which the family soon removed, could afford.   The delighted eyes
of the poor lame little fellow, as he lay among his intimate friends
the sheep, on the grass-cushioned crags of Sandy-Knowe, saw, below,
the windings of the silver Tweed, and the grey ruins of Dryburgh
nestling among dark yew trees; and in front the purple summits of
" Eildon's triple height." And this scene, the first he was conscious
of gazing upon, was to the last most fondly loved of all.   With
Tweed, above all other names, the memory of Scott is imperishably associated.   And upon that warm September day when
his spirit fled, " the gentle ripple of Tweed over its pebbles" was
almost the last earthly sound that fell upon his dying ear.

At the High School of Edinburgh he spent some years, having
entered Luke Fraser's second class in 1779, and passed to the
tuition of the rector, Dr. Adam, in 1782.   He did nothing remarkable in the class-rooms; but in the yards of the High School

he was very popular, on account of his powers as a story-teller. We should not forget, however, that he won Dr. Adam's attention by some clever poetical versions from Horace and Virgil. Indiscriminate reading was the grand passion of his boyhood. He tells us how he found some odd volumes of Shakspere in his mother's dressing-room, where he sometimes slept, and with what absorbing delight he sat in his shirt reading them by the light of the fire, until he heard the noise of the family rising from the supper-table. Spenser, too, was an especial favourite with him, read many a time, during holiday hours, in some sheltered nook of Salisbury Craigs or the Blackford Hills.

After a short attendance at the Latin, Greek, and Logic classes of the Edinburgh University, he was apprenticed to his father in 1786. Of Greek he knew next to nothing. He was well read in Shakspere and Milton ; but took especial delight in such writers as Spenser, Boccaccio, and Froissart. Nothing, he says, but his strong taste for historical study, a study that never grew weak, saved his mind at this time from utter dissipation. A dangerous illness, arising from the bursting of a blood-vessel, which occurred about the second year of his apprenticeship, gave him several months of almost uninterrupted reading, and deepened the colouring caught from old chivalrous romance, which remained to the last the characteristic of his mind.

When his apprenticeship was duly served, he studied for the bar, and in July 1792 donned the wig and gown of a Scottish advocate. But this honourable garb was to him little more than a matter of form; for the practice of law, which never yielded him £200 a year, was soon given up for more congenial and illustrious toils.

The literary career of Scott opens with the publication of his *Translations from Bürger*. The study of German having become fashionable in Edinburgh some years earlier, Scott, with other young lawyers, loungers of the "Mountain," as their idling bench in the Parliament House was called, formed a class for the study of that language. Having heard of "Lenore," the young student procured a copy, and one night after supper sat down to translate the thrilling tale. It was published, with "The Wild Huntsman," a **1796** rendering from the same author, in the autumn of 1796.   **A.D.**

402 LIFE AT ASHESTIEL.

A cottage at Lasswade soon received Scott and his young
French bride, whose maiden name was Charlotte Carpenter, or
Charpentier; and there the lawyer-poet lived happily by the lovely
Esk, occasionally varying his literary labours by the stirring details
of military drill on Portobello sands; for he now wore scarlet, as
quarter-master of the Edinburgh Light Horse. We all know
how the galloping and wheeling of these cavalry drills, with
braying trumpets, flashing steel, and the wild excitement of the
headlong charge, must have kindled martial fire in the breast of
the author of " Marmion."

In 1799 Scott was appointed, by the influence of the Duke of
Buccleuch, Sheriff-deputy of Selkirkshire, poetically called Ettrick
Forest. With the income of this office—£300 a year
1804 —and some little fortune held by his wife, he soon
A.D. established himself at the farm of Ashestiel on the Tweed,
not far from the Yarrow, a literary man now by profession. This house, where he resided for the greater part of nearly
eight years, stood in an old-fashioned garden fenced with holly
hedges, and on a high bank, which was divided from the river he
loved so well only by a narrow strip of green meadow. Already
he had raised his name in literary circles by the publication of
several noble ballads and three volumes of the *Border Minstrelsy*,
filled partly with original poems, but chiefly with pieces gathered
during those tours in southern Scotland, which he called his "raids
into Liddesdale."

His life at Ashestiel may serve as a specimen of his routine to
the last, when he was in the country. Rising at five, he lit his
own fire (if it was cold weather), dressed with care, and went out
to see his favourite horse. At six he was seated at his desk in
his shooting-jacket, or other out-of-doors garb, with a dog or two
couched at his feet. There he wrote till breakfast-time, at nine
or ten; and by that hour he had, in his own words, "*broken the
neck of the day's work.*" A couple of hours after breakfast were
also given to the pen, and at twelve he was "his own man"—free
for the day. By one he was on horseback, with his greyhounds
led by his side, ready for some hours' coursing; or he was gliding

in a boat over some deep pool on Tweed, salmon-spear in hand,
watching in the sunlight for a silver-scaled twenty-pounder.* Such
sports, varied with breezy rides by green glen and purple moorland, closed the day, whose early hours had been given to the
battle of Flodden, or the romantic wanderings of Fitzjames.

It was at Ashestiel that his first great poem—*The Lay of the
Last Minstrel*—was completed. Published in January .
1805, this noble picture of the wild Border life of by-   **1805**
gone days raised the Sheriff of Ettrick Forest to an exalted   A.D.
rank among British poets. The grey-haired Harper, who
timidly turned his weary feet towards the iron gate of Newark,
and tuned his harp to such glorious strains, is one of the finest
creations of our poetical literature. This tale was but the first
of a series of picturesque romances, couched in flowing verse of
eight syllables, and coloured with the brightest hues of Highland
and knightly life, that proceeded during the next ten years from
Scott's magic pen. Of these enchanting poems we shall here
name only *Marmion* and *The Lady of the Lake.* Another important work of this period was his *Life and Works of Dryden,*
which, published in eighteen volumes in 1808, cost him much
toil during the three years he spent upon it.

The dream of being a Tweedside laird began, with his
brightening fame and growing wealth, to take a definite shape.
In 1806 he had been appointed one of the Clerks of Session,
in room of old Mr. Home; promotion which did not at once
increase his income, but gave him the prospect of £800 a
year, in addition to his salary as sheriff, upon the death of his
predecessor. Accordingly, he purchased the farm of
Clarty-Hole, consisting of about a hundred acres, stretch-   **1811**
ing for half a mile along the Tweed, not far from the   A.D.
foot of the Gala. This ill-named and not very well-
favoured spot formed the nucleus of Abbotsford. One piece of
neighbouring land after another was added,—a mansion was
built, which has been called " a Gothic romance embodied in
stone and mortar,"—the bare banks of Tweed were clothed with

---

* In that day even sheriffs plied the *leister.*

plantations of young wood, and the fair dream of the poet's life was fast shaping itself into a grand and apparently solid reality. But this is all in anticipation of our story.

The year after his removal to Abbotsford, which took place in 1812, a letter from the Lord Chamberlain offered him the laureate-ship, in the name of the Prince Regent. This honour Scott declined with respectful thanks. He was meanwhile toiling hard at his *Life and Works of Dean Swift*.

But a power, greater than even himself was conscious of, had lain all this time sleeping in his brain. Fragments of an historical tale in prose, which was designed to give a picture of old Scottish life and manners, had been lying for years in his cabinet, when one day, as he was searching for some fishing-tackle, he came upon the almost forgotten sheets. It was then the autumn of 1813. Though engaged in finishing his edition of Swift, he set to work upon the tale. The greater part of the first volume was done during the ensuing Christmas vacation, and " the evenings of three summer weeks " completed the remaining two. A gay party of young men were sitting over their wine in a house in George Street upon one of those summer evenings, when the host drew attention to a window, where a solitary hand appeared, working without stay or weariness at a desk, and tossing down page after page of manuscript upon a rising heap. " It is the same every night," said young Menzies; " I can't stand the sight of it when I am not at my books. Still it goes on unwearied,—and so it will be till candles are brought in, and nobody knows how long after that." It was Walter Scott's hand, writing the last volumes of " Waverley," seen as he sat in a back room of that house in North Castle Street—No. 39—which was long his Edinburgh residence.

When the work was finished, the manuscript was copied by John Ballantyne, in whose printing concern Scott had, many years earlier, become a partner ; and then *Waverley, or 'Tis Sixty Years Since*, was given to the world, but without the author's name. A cruise on board the Light-house yacht to Shetland and Orkney and round among the Hebrides, which filled two summer months of the same year,

July 7, 1814 A.D.

supplied him with materials for his fine poem, *The Lord of the Isles*, published in the following January.

The success of " Waverley " was immediate and remarkable, although it appeared in what publishers call the *dead season*. " Who wrote the nameless book ? " became the great literary question of the day ; and when, from the same hidden hand, there came a series of new novels, brilliant and enchaining as no novels had ever been before, the marvel grew greater still. Most carefully was the secret kept. One of the Ballantynes always copied the manuscript before it was sent to press. For a time Scott was not suspected, owing to the mass of other literary work he got through ; but, in Edinburgh at least, long before his own confession at the Theatrical Fund Dinner in 1827 rent a then transparent veil, the authorship of the Waverley novels was no mystery.

Elated by this success, and feeling like a man who had come suddenly upon a rich and unwrought mine of gold, Scott began to build and to plant at Abbotsford, and to buy land with all the earnestness of a most hopeful nature. His industry never relaxed ; nor did his public duties ever suffer from the severe desk-toil that he went through every day. While *Guy Mannering, The Antiquary, Rob Roy, The Heart of Mid-Lothian, Ivanhoe, Kenilworth,* and many other works, were in progress, he sat daily during the winter and spring in the Court of Session, attended to his duties as Sheriff, gave dinners in Castle Street, or went to " refresh the machine" and entertain his friends at Abbotsford. Never had a hard-working *littérateur* so many hours to give to his friends. When the morning's task was over in the little back parlour in Castle Street—a neat and orderly room, with its blue morocco books in dustless regularity, and its well-used silver ink-stand shining as if new— he took his drive, or frolicked with his dogs, until it was time to show his bright and happy face in the drawing-room of some friend. And at Abbotsford there was no difference in the desk-work ; but when that was done, he went with the ardour of a boy into the sports and pleasures of rural life, or walked out among his young trees with his unfailing retinue of dogs frisking about his feet. And none was happier than that hard-featured and

faithful old forester, Tom Purdie, whom Scott's kindness had
changed from a poacher into a devoted servant, when he saw the
green shooting-coat, white hat, and drab trousers of the jovial
Sheriff appearing in the distance on the path that led to the
plantations. The decoration of the interior of his mansion by the
Tweed, and the collection of old armour, foreign weapons, Indian
creases and idols, Highland targets, and a thousand such things,
dear to his chivalrous and antiquarian tastes, occupied many of
his busiest and happiest hours. Upon his armory and his woodlands, his house and grounds, his furniture and painting, he spent
thousands of pounds; and to meet the expenses of such costly
doings, and of the free hospitality to which his generous nature
prompted him — doing the honours for all Scotland, as he
said—he coined his rich and fertile brain into vast sums—the
prices of his magical works. Unhappily, much of this money
was spent before it was earned; and the ruinous system of receiving bills from his publishers as payment for undone work,
when once entered upon, grew into a wild and destructive habit.
Author and publishers, alike intoxicated by success, became too
giddy to look far into the future. Yet that retributive
future was coming with swift and awful pace. As they neared
the cataract, the smooth, deceitful current, bore them yet more
swiftly on. At last the money panic of 1825 came with its
perils and its crashes. Hurst and Robinson went down. Then
followed Constable and Ballantyne. Scott's splendid fortune,
all built of paper now utterly worthless, crumpled up like a torn
balloon; and the author of the Waverley Novels stood,
1826 at fifty-five years of age, not penniless alone, but
A.D.   burdened, as a partner in the Ballantyne concern, with
        a debt of £117,000. Nobly refusing to permit his credi-
tors—or rather the creditors of the firm to which he belonged—
to suffer any loss that he could help, he devoted his life and his
pen to the herculean task of removing this mountain-debt. Thus
opens the last, the shortest, and the saddest of the four periods
into which we have marked out this great life.

Already his strong frame had been heavily shaken by severe

illness. Especially in 1819—the year after he accepted the offer of a baronetcy—jaundice had turned the slightly grey hair, that fringed his conical forehead, to snowy white. The first symptoms of apoplexy had appeared in 1823. Yet the valiant soul was never shaken by the failing of the once sturdy frame. Amid the gloom of his commercial distresses—under the deeper sorrow of his wife's death, which befell him in the same sad year—he worked steadily and bravely on. Every day saw its heavy task performed; and he seldom laid aside his pen until he had filled *six* large pages with close writing, which he calculated as equal to *thirty* pages of print.

Some months before the crash, he had entered upon a new and much more laborious kind of work. He had undertaken to write a *Life of Napoleon Buonaparte*. Formerly, with head erect and left hand at liberty for patting his stag-hound Maida, or other canine occupant of his "den," he had been used to write sheet after sheet of a novel with the same facile industry as on that summer evening when the young advocates in George Street saw the vision of a hand. But now he had to gather books, pamphlets, newspapers, letters, and all other kinds of historical materials round his writing-table, and painfully and slowly, note-book in hand, to wade through heavy masses of detail in search of dates and facts. Before, he had read for pleasure; the old man had now to read, often with aching head and dim eyes, for the materials of his task. Heavy work for any one; heavier for him, who had been used to pour forth the riches of his own mind without trouble and without research. Both morning and evening must now for the most part be given to literary toil.

Woodstock was the first novel he wrote after his great misfortune; and its sale for £8228—it was the work of only three months—gave strength to the hopes of the brave old man, that a few years would clear him from his gigantic debt. But the toil was killing him. The nine volumes of his "Life of Napoleon" were published in 1827. Essays, reviews, histories, letters, and tales, among the last that series called *The Chronicles of the Canongate*, poured from the unresting pen as fast as they had ever done in its strongest days. His delightful *Tales of a Grandfather*, in which for the first time a picturesque colouring was given to history intended for the perusal of the young, were among the works of his declining years. *Count Robert of Paris* and *Castle Dangerous* were the last of his published novels. What he called *The Opus Magnum*, a reprint of his novels with explanatory introductions and notes historical and antiquarian, may also be named as one of the chief tasks in the closing life of the novelist.

At last, in the midst of his toil, there came a day—February 15th, 1830—when he fell speechless in his drawing-room under a stroke of paralysis. From that time he never was the same man, and " a cloudiness " in his words and arrangement shows that the shock had told upon the mind. Fits of apoplexy and paralysis occurred at intervals during that and the following year; and, as a last hope, the worn-out workman sailed **1831** in the autumn of 1831 for Malta and Italy. He lived A.D. at Naples and at Rome for about six months; and in the former city he spent many of his morning hours in the composition of two novels, *The Siege of Malta*, and *Bizarro*, which were never finished, and which last feeble efforts of a mind shattered by disease his friends wisely did not judge it right to publish. On his way home down the Rhine the relentless malady struck him a mortal blow. His earnest wish was to die at Abbotsford, the loved place that had cost him so dear; and there he soon found himself with his grandchildren and his dogs playing round the chair he could not leave.

Perhaps the saddest scene of all this sad time—sadder even than the kneeling family round the dying bed—was the last effort of the author to return to his old occupation. On the 17th of July, awaking from sleep, he desired his writing materials to be prepared. When the chair, in which he lay propped up with pillows, was moved into his study and placed before the desk, his daughter put a pen into his hand; but, alas! there was no power in the fingers to close on the familiar thing. It dropped upon the paper, and the helpless old man sank back to weep in silence.

Little more than two months later, on the 21st of September

1832, this great man died, as he had wished to die, at Abbotsford, with all his children round his bed; and on the fifth day after death his body was laid beside the dust of his wife in Dryburgh Abbey, whose grey walls he had seen among the yews from his grassy seat on the crags of Sandy-Knowe.

Some of Scott's chief works have been named in sketching his life. We subjoin here, for more accurate reference, a chronological list of the most important. Any one who has glanced over the catalogue of his writings appended to his Life by Lockhart, will know how useless it would be to give a complete list in a book like this :—

The Lay of the Last Minstrel,*	1805
Marmion,*	1808
Life and Works of Dryden, ...	—
The Lady of the Lake,*	1810
Vision of Don Roderick,*	1811
Rokeby,*	1812
Life and Works of Swift, ...	1814
Waverley, ...	—
The Lord of the Isles,*	1815
Guy Mannering, ...	—
The Antiquary, ...	1816
The Black Dwarf and Old Mortality, ...	—
Rob Roy, ...	1817
The Heart of Mid-Lothian, ...	1818
Bride of Lammermoor, ...	1819
Legend of Montrose, ...	—
Ivanhoe, ...	—
The Monastery, ...	1820
The Abbot, ...	—
Lives of the Novelists, ...	—
Kenilworth, ...	1821
Fortunes of Nigel, ...	1822
Peveril of the Peak, ...	1823
Quentin Durward, ...	—
Redgauntlet, ...	1824
The Talisman, ...	1825
Letters of Malachi Malagrowther, ...	1826
Woodstock, ...	—
Life of Napoleon, ...	1827
Tales of a Grandfather—First Series, ...	—

* These are poems.

Though *facile princeps* in his own peculiar realm of poetry, Scott's brilliant renown rests chiefly on his novels. The same love of chivalrous adventure and mediæval romance colours his best works in both branches of literature. The author of "Marmion" and "The Lady of the Lake" was just the man to produce, in maturer age and with finer literary skill, the changeful, pathetic brilliance of "Waverley," and the courtly splendour of "Kenilworth." Of his poems, "The Lady of the Lake" is perhaps the best. Nothing could surpass, for vivid force, the meeting and the duel between the disguised king and the rebel chieftain, Roderick Dhu; or that rapid flight of the Fiery Cross over mountain and moor, by which the clansmen are summoned to the tryst. The opening of Michael Scott's grave, in the "Lay of the Last Minstrel," and the battle of Flodden, at the close of "Marmion," are pictures that none but true genius could paint. The fine songs, scattered through the works of Scott, afford further evidence of his great poetic powers. Who does not know and delight in *Young Lochinvar* and *Bonnie Dundee?*

Scott was eminently a painter in words. The picturesque was his forte. Witness the magnificent descriptions of natural scenery —sunsets, stormy sea, deep woodland glades—with which many of his chapters open. But his portraitures surpass his landscapes. For variety and true painting of character he was undoubtedly the Shakspere of our English prose. What a crowd of names, "familiar as household words," come rushing on the mind, as we think of the gallery of portraits his magical pencil has left for our endless delight and study! There is scarcely a class of old Scottish life without its type in this collection. Dominie Sampson—Nicol Jarvie—Jeanie Deans—Edie Ochiltree—Jonathan Oldbuck—Meg Dods—Dandie Dinmont—Dugald Dalgetty —their descendants (typical, of course) may still be found by the banks of Forth and Clyde and Tweed.

Of the twenty-nine tales which form the Waverley Novels, the

greater part have an historical ground-work. Scottish history and
Scottish soil were invested by the genius of Scott with a new
lustre. Tourists came from all parts of the world to see the places
where Fitz-James, Rob Roy, and Jeanie Deans had played their
fancied parts. Nor was the Wizard himself forgotten amid the
romance of the magical scenes his genius had conjured up.
.Abbotsford is still one of the sights of Scotland. But Scott was
not the man to work a vein until it began to yield a base, inferior
ore. When he felt that he had fallen below the level of his earlier
poetical works, he turned to prose ; and when " Waverley," " The
Antiquary," " Old Mortality," " Rob Roy," " The Heart of Mid-
Lothian," and so forth, had gone deep into the pictured life of Scottish
history and society, he felt that it was time to break new ground.
So, turning to English annals, he reproduced in "Ivanhoe" the brilliant, chivalrous days of the Lion-hearted King. And then followed several novels founded upon the most striking eras of
English history. Of these, " Kenilworth," a picture of Elizabeth
and her court—" The Fortunes of Nigel," dealing with London life
in the reign of James the First—" Peveril of the Peak," a story of
the Restoration era—and " Woodstock," a tale of Cromwell's time
—may be named as the chief specimens. " The Talisman" carries
us to the East during the third Crusade, and " Quentin Durward"
introduces us to the French court during the reign of that strange
mixture of cruelty, cunning, and superstition, King Louis XI. So
the theme was varied, and thus the interest was maintained. Well
might Byron say of this wonderful master of fiction, " He is a
library in himself."

The chief work of actual history by Scott is his " Life of
Napoleon." It is not a satisfactory performance. Written too near
the time of which it treats to be quite impartial, it also bears in
many places the marks of haste and imperfect execution. The training through which Scott had been going for the previous ten years,
was not of a kind to fit him for working with perfect patience
upon a theme so vast and difficult. The laborious research and
the careful balancing of conflicting evidence, which such a work
required, were not the things to which Scott had been accustomed

in his literary toils. The complete change of literary habits involved in this work has been noticed during the progress of our
sketch.

KNIGHTHOOD IN THE LISTS.

(FROM "IVANHOE.")

At length, as the Saracenic music of the challengers concluded one of those
long and high flourishes with which they had broken the silence of the lists, it
was answered by a solitary trumpet, which breathed a note of defiance from the
northern extremity. All eyes were turned to see the new champion whom these
sounds announced; and no sooner were the barriers opened than he paced into
the lists. As far as could be judged of a man sheathed in armour, the new
adventurer did not greatly exceed the middle size, and seemed to be rather
slender than strongly made. His suit of armour was formed of steel, richly
inlaid with gold; and the device on his shield was a young oak-tree pulled up by
the roots, with the Spanish word *Desdichado*, signifying Disinherited. He was
mounted on a gallant black horse; and as he passed through the lists he gracefully saluted the Prince and the ladies by lowering his lance. The dexterity
with which he managed his steed, and something of youthful grace which he displayed in his manner, won him the favour of the multitude, which some of the
lower classes expressed by calling out, "Touch Ralph de Vipont's shield!—
touch the Hospitaller's shield; he has the least sure seat; he is your cheapest
bargain!"

The champion, moving onward amid these well-meant hints, ascended the
platform by the sloping alley which led to it from the lists, and, to the astonishment of all present, riding straight up to the central pavilion, struck with the
sharp end of his spear the shield of Brian de Bois-Guilbert until it rang again.
All stood astonished at his presumption, but none more than the redoubted
knight, whom he had thus defied to mortal combat, and who, little expecting so
rude a challenge, was standing carelessly at the door of the pavilion.

When the two champions stood opposed to each other at the two extremities
of the lists, the public expectation was strained to the highest pitch. Few
augured the possibility that the encounter could terminate well for the Disinherited Knight; yet his courage and gallantry secured the general good wishes
of the spectators.

The trumpets had no sooner given the signal than the champions vanished
from their posts with the speed of lightning, and closed in the centre of the lists
with the shock of a thunderbolt. The lances burst into shivers up to the very
grasp; and it seemed at the moment that both knights had fallen, for the shock
had made each horse recoil backwards upon its haunches. The address of the
riders recovered their steeds by use of the bridle and spur; and having glared on
each other for an instant with eyes which seemed to flash fire through the bars
of their visors, each made a demivolt, and, retiring to the extremity of the lists,
received a fresh lance from the attendants.

A loud shout from the spectators, waving of scarfs and handkerchiefs, and general acclamations, attested the interest taken by the spectators in this encounter ; the most equal, as well as the best performed, which had graced the day. But no sooner had the knights resumed their station than the clamour or applause was hushed into a silence so deep and so dead, that it seemed the multitude were afraid even to breathe.

A few minutes' pause having been allowed, that the combatants and their horses might recover breath, Prince John with his truncheon signed to the trumpets to sound the onset. The champions a second time sprang from their stations, and closed in the centre of the lists, with the same speed, the same dexterity, the same violence, but not the same equal fortune as before.

In this second encounter, the Templar aimed at the centre of his antagonist's shield, and struck it so fair and forcibly, that his spear went to shivers, and the Disinherited Knight reeled in his saddle. On the other hand, that champion had, in the beginning of his career, directed the point of his lance towards Bois-Guilbert's shield, but, changing his aim almost in the moment of encounter, he addressed it to the helmet, a mark more difficult to hit, but which, if attained, rendered the shock more irresistible. Fair and true he hit the Norman on the visor, where his lance's point kept hold of the bars. Yet, even at this disadvantage, the Templar sustained his high reputation ; and had not the girths of his saddle burst, he might not have been unhorsed. As it chanced, however, saddle, horse, and man rolled on the ground under a cloud of dust.

CHAPTER IX.

OTHER WRITERS OF THE EIGHTH ERA.

POETS.
Samuel Rogers.
James Hogg.
James Montgomery.
Thomas Moore.
Robert Tannahill.
Thomas Campbell.
Felicia Hemans.
Reginald Heber.
Leigh Hunt.
Kirke White.
Percy Shelley.
John Keats.
  Supplementary List.

DRAMATISTS.
Hannah More.
Brinsley Sheridan.
Joanna Baillie.
  Supplementary List.

HISTORIANS.
William Roscoe.

Sir James Mackintosh.
John Lingard.
Thomas M'Crie.
James Mill.
Henry Hallam.
William Napier.
  Supplementary List.

NOVELISTS.
Henry Mackenzie.
Frances Burney.
Maria Edgeworth.
John Galt.
Frances Trollope.
  Supplementary List.

ESSAYISTS AND CRITICS.
William Cobbett.
John Foster.
William Hazlitt.
Sydney Smith.
Lord Jeffrey.
Charles Lamb.

Savage Landor.
  Supplementary List.

SCIENTIFIC WRITERS.
Jeremy Bentham.
Dugald Stewart.
David Ricardo.
Thomas Brown.
Sir Humphry Davy.
Sir John Herschel.

THEOLOGIANS AND SCHOLARS
Adam Clarke.
Robert Hall.
Edward Irving.
Richard Porson.

TRAVELLERS.
James Bruce.
Mungo Park.
Edward Clarke.

TRANSLATORS.

OWING to the multitude of names that crowd upon us as we approach our own day, we must, in this and the similar chapter of the Ninth Era, depart from the simple division into Poets and Prose Writers, hitherto adopted in the last chapter of each period, and class authors under nine heads, viz., Poets, Dramatists, Historians, Novelists, Essayists and Critics, Scientific Writers, Theologians and Scholars, Travellers, and Translators. Those names which limited space prevents us from noticing at any length, will form a list at the end of each section.

POETS.

SAMUEL ROGERS, a London banker, whose reputation as a poet stands very high, was born in 1763, at Stoke Newington, a metropolitan suburb. His chief poems are *The Pleasures of Memory*

(1792); *Columbus* (1812); *Human Life* (1819); and *Italy*, of which the first part appeared in 1822. A graceful and gentle spirit fills the poetry of Rogers. His love for the beautiful in nature and in art led him to delight in "a setting sun, or lake among the mountains," and at the same time to fill his house in St. James's Place with the finest pictures wealth could buy. The breakfasts he gave in this pleasant home used to draw some of the first men in London round his table. Never weary of benevolence, especially to the literary struggler, this kindly, clever man, lived far into the present century, dying in 1855.

JAMES HOGG, the Ettrick Shepherd, was born in Selkirkshire in 1770. He began by writing songs, and gathered some pieces for Scott's "Border Minstrelsy." *The Queen's Wake*, a legendary poem published in 1813, stamped him as a true poet. Among the ballads supposed to be sung to Queen Mary is the exquisite fairy tale, *Kilmeny*. From the nature of his themes, this poet may be classed with Spenser, as a bard of romantic and legendary strain. *Madoc of the Moor*, in Spenser's stanza, and *The Pilgrims of the Sun*, in blank-verse, are among the most important of his later works. Many of his songs are very fine; and several novels, too, came from his untaught pen. As a farmer he was unsuccessful, like Burns. His chief residence was a cottage at Altrive, where he died of dropsy in 1835.

JAMES MONTGOMERY, well known as the author of two richly descriptive poems, *Greenland* and *The Pelican Island*, was born in 1771, at Irvine in Ayrshire. Much of his life was spent in the wearing toil of a journalist, as editor of the *Sheffield Iris*. He was twice imprisoned for imputed libels. In addition to the works already named, he wrote *The Wanderer in Switzerland, The West Indies, Prison Amusements, The World before the Flood*, and many other poems. He died in 1854, having long enjoyed a pension of £200 a year.

THOMAS MOORE was born in Dublin on the 28th of May 1779. At fourteen he contributed verse to a magazine. Having studied at Trinity College, he entered the Middle Temple in London as a student of law. His first important literary undertaking

was a *Translation from Anacreon*, published in 1800. The works
for which he is chiefly remembered are his *Irish Melodies*, exquisite
specimens of polished and most musical verse; and his *Lalla
Rookh* (Tulip-check), a glittering picture of Eastern life and thought.
Shutting himself up in a Derbyshire cottage with a pile of books
on Oriental history and travel, he so steeped his mind in the
colours of his theme, that he is said to have been asked by one
who knew Asia well, at what time he had travelled there. *The
Fudge Family in Paris*, a sparkling satire, and *The Epicurean*, a
romance of Oriental life in poetic prose, deserve special mention
among the works of Moore. Burns and Moore stand side by side
as the lyrists of two kindred nations. But the works of the latter,
polished and surpassingly sweet as they are, have something of
a drawing-room sheen about them, which does not find its way
to the heart so readily as the simple grace of the unconventional
Ayrshire peasant. The Muse of the Irish lawyer is crowned with
a circlet of shining gems; the Muse of the Scottish peasant wears
a garland of sweet field-flowers. Moore lived a brilliant, fashionable life in London, and died in 1852.

ROBERT TANNAHILL, born at Paisley in 1774, was in early life
a weaver. His Scottish songs, among which may be named
Gloomy Winter's now awa, and *Jessie the Flower o' Dunblane*, are
remarkable for sweetness and power. The return of his poems
by a publisher, to whom he had sent them, so preyed upon his
sensitive mind, that it gave way and he drowned himself in a
neighbouring brook (1810).

THOMAS CAMPBELL was a native of Glasgow. Born there in
1777, he distinguished himself at the University by his poetical
translations from the Greek. Tuition and booksellers' work supported him, until he made a hit in 1799 by his *Pleasures of Hope*,
which was written in a dusky Edinburgh lodging. His other
great poem, *Gertrude of Wyoming*, a tale of Pennsylvania, appeared
in 1809. Fine as these are, however, they are surpassed by his
smaller poems, many of which, such as *Hohenlinden* and *Lord
Ullin's Daughter*, are extraordinary specimens of scenic power, or
picturing in words. Such noble naval lays as *The Battle of the*

Baltic, and *Ye Mariners of England,* obtained for him a government pension. In prose he won considerable praise for the critical notices attached to his *Specimens of the British Poets.* He edited the "New Monthly Magazine" for ten years. He died in 1844.

FELICIA HEMANS (maiden name, Browne) was born at Liverpool in 1793, the daughter of a merchant. Amid the lovely scenery of Wales her youth was spent. Her marriage with Captain Hemans was far from happy. Appearing before the public as a poetess in her fifteenth year, she continued at intervals to produce works of exquisite grace and tenderness, until some three weeks before her death, which took place in Dublin on the 16th of May 1835. *The Forest Sanctuary* is her finest poem; but to name those lyrics and shorter poems from her pen, which live in the memory like favourite tunes, would be an endless task. Such are *The Voice of Spring, The Graves of a Household, The Battle of Morgarten, The Palm Tree,* and *The Sunbeam.* Her tragedy, *The Vespers of Palermo,* though abounding in beauty, has not enough of dramatic effect to suit the stage.

REGINALD HEBER was born in 1783, at Malpas in Cheshire. Educated at Oxford, and there distinguished for both Latin and English verse—especially for his fine prize poem, *Palestine*—he became a Fellow of All Souls' College, and entered the Church. In 1809 he published *Europe, or Lines on the Present War.* Appointed Bishop of Calcutta in 1823, he was in the full career of active usefulness, when he died suddenly in his bath one morning at Trichinopoly, having worn the mitre only three years. This gentle poet is, perhaps, best known by such sweet missionary hymns as that beginning, "From Greenland's icy mountains."

LEIGH HUNT, born in 1784, at Southgate in Middlesex, went to school at Christ's Hospital with Charles Lamb. Poetry and journalism began early to employ his lively pen. In 1808 Hunt and his brother started *The Examiner,* a weekly paper, in which he made some statements about the Prince Regent that led to his imprisonment for libel. Turning his cell and prison-yard into a little bower of sweet flowers, he lived there for two years, receiving visits from Byron, Moore, and other sympathetic friends. His

Italian poem, *A Story of Rimini*, was published after his libera-
tion. His visit to Italy, and alliance with Byron in the publication
of *The Liberal* were unfortunate undertakings. A narrative poem
called *The Palfrey*, and a drama, *A Legend of Florence*, are among
his other works. His prose *Essays, Sketches*, and *Memoirs* have all
the characteristics of his verse—a light picturesque gracefulness
being the prevailing quality of both. He died in 1859.

HENRY KIRKE WHITE, the son of a butcher, was born at Nottingham on the 21st of August 1785. At fourteen he was apprenticed to a stocking-weaver; but, disliking the trade, he afterwards
entered an attorney's office. A silver medal, awarded him for a
translation of Horace, which was proposed in the *Monthly Preceptor*,
confirmed the boy's desire to cultivate poetry. In 1803 he published a volume of poems, the chief piece in which was called *Clifton
Grove*. The notice of Southey cheered the young poet's heart, and
the kindness of new friends enabled him to enter St. John's College,
Cambridge, as a sizar. There he wrought so hard to win the
honours of scholarship and science, that he died in 1806, a victim
to intense study acting on a somewhat delicate frame. Southey
edited his *Remains*, consisting of poems on various subjects and
letters to his friends.

PERCY BYSSHE SHELLEY, a baronet's son, born in 1792 at Field
Place in Sussex, lived a short, unhappy life. The young student
of romance wrote two novels while yet a school-boy. Expelled
from Oxford for his atheism, he wrote at eighteen a poem called
Queen Mab, full of power and beauty, but debased in its very grain
and ground-work by rank infidelity and blasphemy. *Alastor, or
the Spirit of Solitude*, a poetical picture of his own lawless and unresting soul; *The Revolt of Islam*, written in his country-house
at Great Marlow in Bucks; *Prometheus Unbound*, a classic
drama, mystical and impious, written under the blue Roman sky
amid bowers of fragrant blossom; and *The Cenci*, a powerful but
repulsive tragedy, form the leading works of this brilliant, wayward, ill-fated youth. Some of his minor poems, among which
we may specify *The Cloud, The Skylark*, and the delicious *Sensitive
Plant*, actually overflow with lyrical beauty both of thought and

language. Delicacy of constitution forced him to the sweet air of
Italy, where he saw a good deal of Byron. Boating was his
favourite recreation; and one July day in 1822, returning from
Leghorn, a squall overset his little craft in the Gulf of Spezzia,
and he perished in the waves.

JOHN KEATS, born in London in October 1795, was early
bound apprentice to a surgeon. Cultivating poetry with great
earnestness, he published *Endymion, a Poetic Romance*, in 1818.
A severe and scornful review of this first effort, which appeared
in the " Quarterly," struck like a dagger to the heart of the sensitive
poet, and probably hastened his death. Before consumption, which
was a family disease, slew this brilliant young " singer of the senses,"
he had written *Hyperion, The Eve of St. Agnes, Lamia, Isabella*,
and other poems, which showed that his untrained, over-luxuriant
imagination, springing from the root of true genius, could be
pruned into the production of works well worthy to live. Keats
died at Rome on the 27th of December 1820, and was buried in the
Protestant Cemetery there, under a sweet carpeting of violets and
daisies. When the body of drowned Shelley drifted ashore, a
volume of Keats was found in the pocket of his brine-soaked coat.
He had already shown his love for the young surgeon-poet by an
elegy called *Adonais*.

Supplementary List.

MICHAEL BRUCE.—(1746-1767)—Portmoak, Kinross—a schoolmaster—*Lochleven;
An Elegy written in Spring.*

SIR WILLIAM JONES.—(1746-1794)—London—a Judge in the Supreme Court in
Bengal—*Song of Hafiz; Hindoo Wife.*

JOHN LOGAN.—(1748-1788)—Soutra, Mid-Lothian—a Scottish minister—*The
Cuckoo; The Country in Autumn; Runnimede.*

ROBERT FERGUSSON. —(1751-1774)—Edinburgh—a lawyer's clerk—poet of Scottish
town life—*Guid Braid Claith; To the Tron Kirk Bell.*

WILLIAM GIFFORD.—(1756-1826)—Ashburton, Devonshire—*The Baviad; The
Mæviad*—Editor of " Quarterly."

WILLIAM SOTHEBY.—(1757-1833)—London—a dragoon officer—*Orestes, Saul,
Italy;* translations from *Wieland, Virgil, and Homer.*

WM. L. BOWLES.—(1762-1850)—King's-Sutton, Northamptonshire—canon of
Salisbury—*Sonnets; Sorrows of Switzerland; Missionary of the Andes.*

JAMES GRAHAME.—(1765-1811)—Glasgow—curate of Sedgefield, Durham—*The
Sabbath; Mary Queen of Scots.*

ROBERT BLOOMFIELD.—(1766–1823)—Honington, near Bury St. Edmunds, Suf-
    folk—*The Farmer's Boy; Rural Tales; Mayday with the Muses.*
J. HOOKHAM FRERE.—(1769–1846)—diplomatist—*Most Interesting Particulars
    relating to King Arthur, by the Brothers Whistlecraft.*
HON. WM. R. SPENCER.—(1770–1834)—author of *Beth Gelert* and minor poems;
    translator of *Lenore.*
MARY TIGHE.—(1773–1810)—Miss Blackford—county of Wicklow, Ireland—
    Psyche, in six cantos.
JOHN LEYDEN.—(1775–1811)—Denholm, Roxburghshire—*Scenes of Infancy; The
    Mermaid; Ode to a Gold Coin.*
JAMES SMITH.—(1775–1839)—London—solicitor—in conjunction with his brother
    Horace wrote *Rejected Addresses,* in imitation of popular authors.
GEORGE CROLY.—(1780–1860)—Dublin—Rector of St. Stephen's, Walbrook—*Paris
    in 1815; Angel of the World; Catiline,* a tragedy; *Salathiel,* a romance.
ALLAN CUNNINGHAM.—(1784–1842)—Blackwood, Dumfries-shire—Chantrey's as-
    sistant—*Scottish Songs; Sir Marmaduke Maxwell; The Maid of Elvan;
    Life of Wilkie.*
WILLIAM TENNANT.—(1785–1848)—Anstruther, Fife—professor at St. Andrews
    —*Anster Fair; Thane of Fife; Dinging Down of the Cathedral.*
EBENEZER ELLIOTT.—(1781–1849)—Masborough, Yorkshire—iron-founder—*Corn
    Law Rhymes.*
RICHARD BARHAM.—(1788–1845)—Canterbury—an Episcopal clergyman—*In-
    goldsby Legends,* in prose and verse; *My Cousin Nicholas,* (a novel).
JOHN KEBLE.—(1790–1866)—Episcopal clergyman—Professor of Poetry at
    Oxford—*The Christian Year.*
CHARLES WOLFE.—(1791–1823)—Dublin—Episcopal minister—*Burial of Sir John
    Moore; Jugurtha in Prison.*
ROBERT POLLOK.—(1799–1827)—Muirhouse, Renfrewshire—theological student
    —*The Course of Time,* a sacred epic.

DRAMATISTS.

HANNAH MORE, the daughter of a Gloucestershire schoolmaster, was born in 1745. Her three tragedies, produced under Garrick's encouragement, were *The Inflexible Captive, Percy,* and *The Fatal Falsehood.* Of these, "Percy" is the best. She is also remembered for her very numerous *Tales* and other prose works, many of which treat of female education. Of the former, *Coelebs in search of a wife,* was remarkably popular. She died in 1833.

RICHARD BRINSLEY SHERIDAN, distinguished as a manager, dramatist, and statesman, was born in Dublin in 1751. At twenty-four he produced *The Rivals,* in which Captain Absolute and Mrs. Malaprop are well-known characters. But his greatest work was *The School for Scandal*, which, produced in 1777, is justly regarded as the finest comedy of our later literature. *The Duenna*, an opera; *The Critic*, a witty farce, containing the capital character of Sir Fretful Plagiary ; and *Pizarro*, an adaptation from Kotzebue's American drama, may be named among his other works. Sheridan's chief political appearance was his great speech on the impeachment of Hastings. He died in 1816.

JOANNA BAILLIE was born in 1762, at the manse of Bothwell in Lanarkshire. Her dramatic works, written during thirty-eight years, fill many volumes; but they are nearly all fitter to be read than acted. She commenced in 1798 a *Series of Plays on the Passions*, intending to make each passion the central theme of a tragedy and a comedy. Sir Walter Scott considered her to be most successful in the delineations of Fear. *De Montfort* is the only one of Miss Baillie's plays that has been put upon the stage. *Count Basil* is a drama of similar stamp. She wrote also fine Scottish songs and many minor poems. She died at Hampstead in 1851.

Supplementary List.

RICHARD CUMBERLAND.—(1732–1811)—Cambridge—secretary to Board of Trade —comedies, *The West Indian ; The Wheel of Fortune.*

GEORGE COLMAN.—(1733–1794)—Florence—manager of Covent Garden and the Haymarket theatres—comedies, *The Jealous Wife; The Clandestine Marriage.*

THOMAS HOLCROFT.—(1745–1809)—London—pedler, jockey, shoemaker, actor, author—comedies. *The Road to Ruin ; The Deserted Daughter.*

GEORGE COLMAN the Younger.—(1762–1836)—London—manager of the Haymarket and Examiner of plays—comedies, *John Bull; Heir at Law ; Poor Gentleman*— comic poems, *Newcastle Apothecary, Lodgings for Single Gentlemen*, &c.

CHARLES R. MATURIN.—(Died in 1824)—curate of St. Peter's, Dublin—*Bertram*, a tragedy ; and *Women*, a romantic novel.

HISTORIANS.

WILLIAM ROSCOE, originally an attorney, but afterwards a banker, was a native of Liverpool, born there in 1753. Devoting himself early to literature, he produced a poem on slavery, called *The Wrongs of Africa*. But he soon turned to the work for which he was better suited. In 1796 he published in two volumes *The Life of Lorenzo de Medici;* and nine years later, in 1805, *The Life and Pontificate of Leo X.,* a great work, but received with less enthusiasm than "Lorenzo." He represented Liverpool in Parliament for some time. The failure in 1816 of the bank in which he was a partner, plunged him in difficulties. He died in 1831.

SIR JAMES MACKINTOSH was born in 1765, at Aldourie House, on the banks of Loch Ness. Called to the English bar in 1795, he won considerable renown by his defence of Peltier, went out to India as Recorder of Bombay, and in seven years retired on a pension of £1200. Amid the whirl of public life he did something with his pen, as if to show what he might have done in greater quiet and with greater industry. Some articles in the "Edinburgh Review," a *Dissertation on Ethical Philosophy* for the "Encyclopædia Britannica," part of a *History of England* for Lardner's "Cyclopædia," and a short *Life of Sir Thomas More,* are almost the only works of Mackintosh. His brilliant conversation caused him to be much sought after in society, and thus little time was left for the labour of the pen. He died rather suddenly in 1832.

JOHN LINGARD, born at Winchester in 1771, was the author of a *History of England* from the invasion by the Romans to the abdication of James II., of which the first volumes appeared in 1819. Such a work, written by a Roman Catholic priest, as Lingard was, must naturally discuss the Reformation and kindred subjects from a hostile point of view; but, making this allowance, Lingard's "History" is a calm and learned narrative, especially valuable in those chapters which deal with the Anglo-Saxons and their life. A smaller work, on *The Antiquities of the Anglo-Saxon Church,* displays a deep insight into this distant period of our national history. Lingard died in 1851, at Hornby, near Lancaster.

THOMAS M'CRIE, celebrated as the author of the *Life of John Knox,* was born in 1772, at Dunse in Berwickshire. The "Life of Knox," first published in 1813, deals not only with the man, but with the stirring times of which he was a central figure. A *Life of Andrew Melville* proceeded also from the pen of this eminent

Scottish clergyman. M'Crie's condemnation of Sir Walter Scott's picture of the Covenanters, as displayed in "Old Mortality," drew from the illustrious novelist a reply in the shape of a review of his own work in the "Quarterly." The biographer of Knox lived, respected and beloved, until 1835.

JAMES MILL, born in 1773, at Logie Pert, near Montrose, is noted as a metaphysician, political economist, and historian. His great work, in the last capacity, was a *History of British India,* which was published in five volumes in 1817–18. Mill advocated many of the progressive views of Jeremy Bentham. He died in 1836.

HENRY HALLAM, the son of the Dean of Wells, was born in 1778, and received his education at Eton and Christ Church, Oxford. He has worthily won the praise of being "the most judicial of our great modern historians." A great brother-labourer in the same toilsome field, Macaulay, pays him the high compliment of accepting any fact vouched for by him, as almost certain to be correct. Having studied in the Inner Temple, he was called to the bar, and soon became a Commissioner of Audit. Besides his early contributions to the "Edinburgh Review," he wrote three great historical works, which have raised him to the very highest literary rank. These are,—*View of Europe during the Middle Ages,* (1818), extending from the middle of the fifth to the end of the fifteenth century; *The Constitutional History of England,* from the accession of Henry VII. to the death of George II., published in 1827; and *An Introduction to the Literature of Europe* in the fifteenth, sixteenth, and seventeenth centuries, which appeared in 1837–38. Outliving his sons by many years, this great historian died in 1859.

WILLIAM NAPIER, born in 1785, at Castletown in Ireland, went through the bloody scenes of *The Peninsular War,* of which he produced a most accurate and graphic History, between 1828 and 1840. Southey's History of the same war is comparatively clumsy. Colonel Sir W. Napier wrote also *The Conquest of Scinde,* and *The Life of Sir Charles Napier.* He died February 12th, 1860.

Supplementary List.

DAVID DALRYMPLE.—(1726-1792)—Lord Hailes—Edinburgh—a Scottish judge—*Annals of Scotland*, from Malcolm III. to the accession of the Stuarts.

GEORGE CHALMERS.—(1742-1825)—Fochabers, Elgin—barrister in America—*Caledonia* (Antiquities and Early History of Scotland); *Life of Queen Mary; Life of Sir David Lyndsay.*

WILLIAM MITFORD.—(1744-1827)—London—colonel of South Hampshire Militia and member of Parliament—*History of Greece*, from an anti-democratic point of view.

WILLIAM COXE.—(1747-1828) — London—Archdeacon of Wilts—*History of Austria; Memoirs of Walpole and Marlborough.*

JOHN PINKERTON.—(1758-1825)—Edinburgh—a lawyer—*History of Scotland*, before the reign of Malcolm III. and under the Stuarts; *The Scythians or Goths.*

MALCOLM LAING.—(1762-1818)—Orkney—a Scottish lawyer—*History of Scotland*, from 1603 to 1707; *Dissertations on the Gowrie Plot and the Murder of Darnley.*

SHARON TURNER.—(1768-1847)—a London solicitor—*History of the Anglo-Saxons; History of England during the Middle Ages.*

PATRICK FRASER TYTLER.—(1791-1849)—Edinburgh—son of Lord Woodhouselee, author of *Universal History—History of Scotland*, from Alexander III. to the Union of the Crowns in 1603; *Lives of Scottish Worthies; Life of Raleigh.*

NOVELISTS.

HENRY MACKENZIE, born in Edinburgh in 1745, and educated there, published in 1771 a novel called *The Man of Feeling*, in which the prominent character is Harley. *The Man of the World* is an inferior work. Sterne was Mackenzie's model; but the disciple has more true feeling in his books than the master. Having held for some time the office of Comptroller of Taxes for Scotland, Mackenzie, who was a lawyer by profession, died in 1831.

FRANCES BURNEY (MADAME D'ARBLAY), was the daughter of Dr. Burney, author of the *History of Music*, and was born in 1752, at Lynn Regis in Norfolk. In early life she wrote a novel called *Evelina, or a Young Lady's Entrance into the World*, which, being published in 1778, raised its author to great popularity. This was her best work. *Cecilia* (1782) is more highly finished, but less interesting. After her marriage with Count D'Arblay, a French refugee, had freed her from the "splendid

slavery" of keeping Queen Charlotte's robes, she wrote a tragedy and
two novels, but of greatly inferior merit.   She died in 1840, and,
two years later, appeared her *Diary and Letters*, edited by her niece.

MARIA EDGEWORTH, born in 1767, at Hare Hatch, near Reading in Berkshire, spent nearly all her life at Edgeworthstown, in
the county of Longford.   Taught chiefly by her father, Richard
Lovell Edgeworth, author of several educational and engineering
works, she began her career as a novelist in 1801 with *Castle
Rackrent*, a tale of Irish extravagance.   At intervals appeared
*Belinda, Popular Tales, Leonora, Tales of Fashionable Life,
Patronage*, and a host of other fictions, the series closing in 1834
with *Helen*.   The hollowness of frivolous, fashionable life, as it
then was, and the racy varieties of real Irish character, are
depicted in these novels with marvellous skill.   In 1823 Miss
Edgeworth paid a visit to her admirer and brother-artist, Sir
Walter Scott, at his mansion of Abbotsford.   She died in 1849,
aged eighty-three.

JOHN GALT, born in 1779, at Irvine in Ayrshire, spent his
youth in an unsettled way.   A custom-house clerk at Greenock, a
law-student at Lincoln's Inn, a traveller for health about the shores
of the Mediterranean, a writer for the stage, a merchant at Gib-
raltar, he at last found his proper sphere in the production of
Scottish novels.   *The Ayrshire Legatees* (1820), and *The Annals
of the Parish* (1821), were followed by *Sir Andrew Wylie, The
Entail, The Last of the Lairds*, and, after a visit to Canada on
commercial business, by *Lawrie Todd*.   Having spent a life of constant literary toil, he died in 1839, at Greenock, shattered by
repeated shocks of paralysis.

FRANCES TROLLOPE, the daughter of an English clergyman, was
born in 1790.   She was past fifty when, in 1832, she entered
the literary field by her work entitled *The Domestic Manners of
the Americans*, in which she satirizes most severely the people
of the States.   Her first novel was *The Abbess* (1833).   Then
followed from her fertile pen a whole army of fictions and books
of travel, sometimes pouring into the libraries at the rate of nine
volumes a year.   Perhaps the best of these are *The Vicar of*

Wrexhill (1837), *The Widow Barnaby* (1839), and *The Ward of Thorpe Combe* (1842). She ceased to write about 1856, and died in 1863 at Florence; but her sons, Anthony and Tom, by their literary industry and talent, still uphold the honour of the well-known name.

Supplementary List.

JOHN MOORE.—(1729–1802)—Stirling—physician in Glasgow and London—father of the hero of Corunna—*Zeluco*; *Edward*.

CHARLOTTE SMITH.—(1749–1806)—Surrey—*The Old English Manor-house*; *Emmeline*.

SOPHIA LEE—(1750–1824)—and her sister HARRIET—(1766–1851)—*The Canterbury Tales* and dramas.

ELIZABETH INCHBALD.—(1753–1821)—near Bury St. Edmunds—an actress—*A Simple Story*; *Nature and Art*; plays.

WILLIAM GODWIN.—(1756–1836)—Wisbeach, Cambridgeshire—at first a Dissenting minister—*Caleb Williams*; *St. Leon*.

ELIZABETH HAMILTON.—(1758–1816)—Belfast—a merchant's daughter—*Cottagers of Glenburnie*.

WILLIAM BECKFORD.—(1759–1844)—son of a London millionaire—*Vathek, an Arabian Tale*.

ANN RADCLIFFE.—(1764–1823)—London—novelist of the Terrific school—*Romance of the Forest*; *Mysteries of Udolpho*; *The Italian*.

R. PLUMER WARD.—(1762–1846)—held office in the Admiralty—*Tremaine, or the Man of Refinement*; *De Vere*; *De Clifford*.

AMELIA OPIE.—(1769–1853)—Miss Alderson of Norwich—wife of the painter Opie—*Father and Daughter*; *Tales of the Heart*; *Temper*.

MATTHEW GREGORY LEWIS.—(1773–1818)—London—*The Monk; Bravo of Venice; Tales of Wonder* (poems) ; *The Castle Spectre* (a play).

JANE AUSTEN.—(1775–1817)—Steventon, Hampshire—a clergyman's daughter—*Pride and Prejudice*; *Mansfield Park*; *Persuasion*.

MARY BRUNTON.—(1778–1818)—Miss Balfour of Burrey in Orkney—an Edinburgh minister's wife—*Self-Control*; *Discipline*.

JAMES MORIER.—(1780–1849)—Secretary of Embassy in Persia—*Hajji Baba; Zohrab; The Mirza*.

THOMAS HOPE.—(died 1831)—a rich English merchant of Amsterdam—*Anastasius, or Memoirs of a Modern Greek*.

MARY FERRIER.—(1782–1854)—Edinburgh—daughter of a Clerk of Session—*Marriage*; *The Inheritance*; *Destiny*.

LADY MORGAN.—(1786–1859)—Sydney Owenson—Dublin—an actor's daughter and a physician's wife—*The Wild Irish Girl*; *O'Donnell*.

THEODORE HOOK.—(1788–1842)—London—dramatist, novelist, journalist—*Gilbert Gurney*; *Sayings and Doings*; *Jack Brag*.

MARY MITFORD.—(1789–1855)—Alresford, Hampshire—*Our Village*; *Belford Regis*.

COUNTESS OF BLESSINGTON.—(1790–1849)—Miss Power—Knockbrit, near Clon-mel—*The Repealers; Belle of a Season; Victims of Society; Idler in Italy; Idler in France.*

ANNA PORTER.—(1780–1832)—*Don Sebastian;* and JANE PORTER—(1776–1850) —*Thaddeus of Warsaw; Scottish Chiefs.*

THOMAS C. GRATTAN.—(born 1796)—Dublin—*Highways and Byways; Heiress of Bruges; History of the Netherlands.*

MARY SHELLEY.—(1797–1851)—Miss Godwin—the poet's second wife—*Franken-stein.*

ESSAYISTS AND CRITICS.

WILLIAM COBBETT, born in 1762, at Farnham in Surrey, attracted considerable notice by his sturdy, fresh English writings. First a field-labourer, he became afterwards a soldier, rising to the rank of serjeant-major. After the passing of the Reform Bill he was elected member for Oldham, but failed as a public speaker. *Rural Rides, Cottage Economy*, works on *America*, and articles in the *Political Register* form his chief literary remains. These have an especial value, as illustrating a fine type of the English peasant mind. Cobbett died in 1835.

JOHN FOSTER, a farmer's son, was born in 1770, near Halifax in Yorkshire. He began public life as a Baptist preacher. His literary reputation rests partly on his articles in the *Eclectic Review*, but more especially on his four *Essays*, which were first published in 1805 in the form of letters. The Essays are—On a Man's Writing Memoirs of Himself; On Decision of Character; On the Epithet Romantic; On Evangelical Religion rendered less accept-able to Persons of Taste. He died in 1843.

WILLIAM HAZLITT, a brilliant and refined critic, was born in 1778, at Maidstone. Originally a painter, he became in 1803 author by profession, and through all his life contributed largely to the periodicals of the day. *His Life of Napoleon* was his most elaborate work. But he is chiefly celebrated for his *Characters of Shakspere's Plays*, his *Table-Talk*, and his *Lectures upon the English Poets*. Hazlitt died of cholera in 1830.

SYDNEY SMITH, born in 1771, at Woodford in Essex, earned, by his sayings and his works, the reputation of a brilliant wit. Entering the Church, he was at various times curate in a village on Salisbury Plain, a tutor in Edinburgh, a London preacher, rector of Foston-le-Clay in Yorkshire, of Combe Florey in Somersetshire, and then a canon of St. Paul's. In 1802 he took a share in originating the *Edinburgh Review*, of which he was the first editor. His *Letters on the Subject of the Catholics, by Peter Plymley*, are, perhaps, the finest example we have of wit used as a political weapon. In Yorkshire, where he wrote these Letters, he lamented the solitude of his position, as being "ten miles from a lemon." His *Letters to Archdeacon Singleton* and *Letters on the Pennsylvanian Bonds* display the same wonderful power of sly and telling drollery. He died in February 1845.

FRANCIS LORD JEFFREY, a distinguished critic, was born in Edinburgh on the 23d of October, 1773. He became an advocate in 1794. Soon after the establishment of the *Edinburgh Review* he assumed the editorship, and in that position he continued, writing the chief poetical articles, until 1829, when he retired, on being elected Dean of the Faculty of Advocates. Raised to the bench in 1834, he died in 1850.

CHARLES LAMB, born in London in 1775, remained in heart a Londoner to the last. Becoming at seventeen a clerk in the India House, this gentle, stuttering recluse, devoted his life to the care of his sister Mary, who at dinner one day, in a fit of hereditary madness, stabbed her mother to death with a knife. He was a school-fellow and an attached friend of Coleridge, whose poetry prompted his own attempts in verse. He wrote *John Woodvil*, a tragedy; *Tales Founded on the Plays of Shakspere*, and occasional poems. But his literary fame rests chiefly upon *Essays by Elia*, which appeared originally in the " London Magazine." The delicate grace and flavour of these papers cannot be described. Retiring on a pension from his clerkship in 1825, "Coming home for ever on Tuesday week," as he tells Wordsworth in a letter, he spent the ten remaining years of his life chiefly at Enfield. He died in 1835 of erysipelas, caused by a fall which slightly cut his face.

WALTER SAVAGE LANDOR, born in 1775, at Ipsley Court in Warwickshire, died at Florence in 1864, having outlived the generation to which he belonged. Besides *Gebir*, an epic, *Count Julian*, a tragedy, and various minor poems, he produced a prose work, *Imaginary Conversations*, for which his name is most renowned. His later works, *The Last Fruit off an Old Tree*, and *Dry Sticks Fagoted*, especially the second, bear evident marks of a decayed and corrupted genius.

Supplementary List.

HORNE TOOKE.—(1736–1812)—son of a London poulterer—a lawyer—tried for high treason in 1794—*Epea Pteroenta, or The Diversions of Purley.*

WILLIAM COMBE.—(1741–1823)—*Letters of the late Lord Lyttelton; Tour of Dr. Syntax* (verse).

ARCHIBALD ALISON.—(1757–1838)—Episcopal minister in Edinburgh—*Essay on Taste.*

ISAAC D'ISRAELI.—(1766–1848)—son of an Italian Jew—*Curiosities of Literature; Quarrels of Authors; Calamities of Authors.*

HENRY LORD BROUGHAM.—(1778–1868)—Edinburgh—*Articles in Edinburgh Review; Observations on Light; Statesmen of George III.; England under the House of Lancaster.*

SIR EGERTON BRYDGES.—(1762–1837)—editor of *Retrospective Review; Censura Literaria*, an account of Old English Books; *Letters on the Genius of Byron.*

JOHN WILSON CROKER.—(1780–1857)—Galway—secretary to the Admiralty—*Articles in the Quarterly;* edited *Boswell's Life of Johnson; Lord Hervey's Memoirs of the Court of George II.*

SCIENTIFIC WRITERS.

JEREMY BENTHAM, born in 1748, was the son of a London solicitor. Beginning his literary career in 1776 with a *Fragment on Government*, founded on a passage in Blackstone, he continued through a long life to write upon law and politics. His grand principle of action, which he wished to push to a dangerous extreme, was "the greatest happiness to the greatest number." He died in 1832.

DUGALD STEWART, born in Edinburgh in 1753, became in 1780 Professor of Moral Philosophy in that University. His chief works, founded on the views of Reid, were *The Philosophy of the Human Mind; a Dissertation on the Progress of Metaphysical and Ethical Philosophy* (written for the "Encyclopædia Britannica"); and a *View of the Active and Moral Powers of Man.* His *Outlines of Moral Philosophy* form a favourite elementary text-book on that subject. He died in his native city in 1828.

DAVID RICARDO, born in London in 1772, was the son of a Dutch Jew. In the midst of his business as a thriving stock-broker, he found time to write several works on political economy. His pamphlet on *The High Price of Bullion* was his first publication. But his fame rests on a treatise called *The Principles of Political Economy and Taxation* (1817), which ranks next in importance to Adam Smith's "Wealth of Nations." Ricardo died in 1823, after some sessions of parliamentary life.

THOMAS BROWN, successor of Dugald Stewart, was a native of Galloway, born in 1778. After some practice as a physician, he found in 1810 a more congenial sphere in the work of the Moral Philosophy chair. His *Lectures on the Philosophy of the Human Mind* are his chief production. He also published some graceful poetry. He died in 1820.

SIR HUMPHRY DAVY, born in 1778, at Penzance in Cornwall, became distinguished as a chemist, and read many valuable papers before the Royal Society, upon the results of his researches. Most of these were published in the *Transactions* of the Society. His great invention of the safety-lamp won for him in 1818 a baronetcy. In general literature he was the author of *Salmonia, or Days of Fly-Fishing,* and *Consolations in Travel, or The Last Days of a Philosopher.* He died in 1829.

SIR JOHN HERSCHEL, born in 1790, at Slough, near Windsor, received his education at St. John's, Cambridge. He is one of our most eminent scientific men. Among his many works we may name *Treatises on Sound* and *Light;* and, yet more popular, his *Discourse on Natural Philosophy* in Lardner's "Cyclopædia," and his *Outlines of Astronomy,* of which the original was published in the same work. He was Master of the Mint for some time, and lived for four years at the Cape, engaged in an astronomical survey of the southern hemisphere.

Supplementary List.

GEORGE COMBE.—(1788-1858)—an Edinburgh Writer to the Signet—*Essays on Phrenology ; The Constitution of Man.*

JOHN ABERCROMBIE.—(1781-1844)—Aberdeen—an eminent Edinburgh physician —*The Intellectual Powers and the Investigation of Truth ; Philosophy of the Moral Feelings.*

ALEXANDER WILSON.—(1766-1813)—originally a Paisley weaver—*American Ornithology.*

J. RAMSAY M'CULLOCH.—(1790-1864)—Galloway—in the Stationery Office— *Elements of Political Economy ; Dictionary of Commerce ; Statistical Account of the British Empire.*

THEOLOGIANS AND SCHOLARS.

ADAM CLARKE, the son of a schoolmaster at Moybeg in Derry, where he was born in 1760, won great renown as an Oriental scholar and Biblical critic. He was a Wesleyan Methodist. *A Commentary on the Bible* and a *Bibliographical Dictionary* are his chief works. He died of cholera in 1832.

ROBERT HALL, born in 1764, at Arnsby in Leicestershire, was a distinguished Baptist preacher. Two of his leading publications were, *An Apology for the Freedom of the Press,* and *A Sermon on Modern Infidelity.* Perhaps his finest sermon was that upon the *Death of the Princess Charlotte.* Hall died at Bristol in 1831.

EDWARD IRVING, a tanner's son, was born in 1792, at Annan in Dumfries-shire. Having assisted Dr. Chalmers in Glasgow, he removed to Cross Street Church, London, where his preaching created an extraordinary sensation. Many of his *Sermons* and *Lectures* were published. Charged in 1830 with heresy, he was soon deposed, and in 1834 died in Glasgow of consumption.

RICHARD PORSON, son of a parish-clerk in Norfolk, and born there in 1759, won great renown at Cambridge, where he was Professor of Greek. His critical pen was especially engaged upon *Euripides, Homer, Æschylus,* and *Herodotus. Adversaria, or Notes and Emendations of the Greek Poets,* was published after his death. In college-life he was notorious for deep drinking, and noted for his pungent sarcasms. He died in 1808.

Books of travel and geographical discovery have come, within the last hundred years, to form a very large and important section of our literature. JAMES BRUCE of Kinnaird (1730–1794), the brave seeker for the sources of the Nile, and MUNGO PARK (1771–1805), that young surgeon of Selkirkshire who explored the basin of the Niger and died in its waters, have left us narratives of their adventures. The works of the latter possess much simple literary grace. Lieutenant CLAPPERTON, RICHARD LANDER of Niger fame, BURCKHARDT a Switzer, and BELZONI an Italian, added greatly to our knowledge of Africa. Dr. EDWARD CLARKE of Cambridge (1769–1822), a polished and obser-vant scholar, wrote a valuable account of his travels through the East, including Russia, Tartary, Turkey, Greece, Palestine, and Egypt. FORSYTH, EUSTACE, MATHEWS, Lady MORGAN, and many others, contributed works on Italy. The Polar Regions have found describers in nearly all those brave officers who have tried to penetrate the icy seas. Among such, PARRY, Ross, the lamented FRANKLIN, and SCORESBY the whale-fisher, stand out prominently. SILK BUCKINGHAM, in Asia Minor and Arabia; MALCOLM, MORIER, OUSELY, and KER PORTER, in Persia; FRASER, among the Hima-layas; STAUNTON, BARROW, and ELLIS, in China; Captain BASIL HALL, all over the Pacific and round its shores; INGLIS, in Nor-way, France, Switzerland, and among the Pyrenees and Spanish Sierras—are a few of the leading travellers, who, during this era of our literature, added valuable works to the geographical shelf of our libraries.

The number of translating pens employed upon the Greek and Roman authors is beyond counting. PHILIP FRANCIS (died 1773) translated *Horace* and *Demosthenes;* THOMAS MITCHELL (1783–

1845), devoted his classic skill to *Aristophanes;* while in our own time Professor BLACKIE, besides Goethe's *Faust,* has given us *Æschylus* in an English dress; and THEODORE MARTIN, of Bon Gaultier fame, has lately translated the Odes of *Horace* and the lyrics of *Catullus.* The gentleman last named is also well known for his translations from the Danish and the German. In the latter he has been associated with Professor Aytoun.

A noble version of *Dante* by the Rev. HENRY FRANCIS CARY (1772–1844); *Ariosto* by WILLIAM ROSE (1775–1843); *Calderon* the Spanish dramatist by DENIS F. M'CARTHY; the *Lusiad* of Camoens the Portuguese poet by WILLIAM MICKLE (1734–1788); and *Poems* from the same author by Viscount STRANGFORD (1780–1855); Goethe's *Faust* and Schiller's *Song of the Bell* by Lord ELLESMERE (1800–1857); Bürger's *Lenore,* Lessing's *Nathan,* Goethe's *Iphigenia,* and Schiller's *Bride of Messina,* by WILLIAM TAYLOR (1765–1836); *Russian, Polish, Magyar, Bohemian Poetry* by Sir JOHN BOWRING (born 1792);. *Norse* and *Icelandic Tales* by DASENT,—are far from exhausting the list of our best translations. *Bohn's Library* contains a most valuable set of these works, almost all of the highest stamp.

NINTH ERA OF ENGLISH LITERATURE.

FROM THE DEATH OF SCOTT IN 1832 A.D. TO THE PRESENT TIME.

CHAPTER L

PRINTING BY STEAM.

The old press.	Statement in the *Times*.
Earl Stanhope.	König's machine.
König.	Cowper and Applegath.
Nicholson.	Statistics.
An anxious night.	Scene in Printing-House Square.

THE clumsy press, with which William Caxton and Wynkyn de Worde printed off their black-letter volumes in the Almonry or Red-pale at Westminster, continued with slight alterations to supply Britain with the works of Shakspere, Milton, Dryden, Pope, Goldsmith, Cowper, in a word, of all the writers who adorned our literature until the present century was some years old.

Its great improver was Charles, third Earl Stanhope, who, born in 1753, devoted much of his aristocratic leisure to the study of machinery. The chief change he made was "in forming the entire press of iron, the plate being large enough to print a whole sheet at once, instead of requiring a double action." The blank paper, being placed upon a frame-work, is folded down upon the newly inked types, which lie in a "form" upon a horizontal slab. Paper and type being wheeled, by the turning of a handle, under a heavy square plate of metal, this, called the *platten*, is, by means of a lever, brought down upon the paper, pressing it suddenly and strongly against the type. The printed sheet is wheeled out; another takes its place; and so the work of the Stanhope press proceeds.

A Saxon clockmaker, called König, who could find no Continental printers to take up the subject of an improved press, came to London with his plans about the year 1804. He found the presses there throwing off 250 single impressions in an hour; and setting steadily to work in the face of many difficulties, he persevered until he had constructed a printing *machine* capable of being worked by steam. Already, about the year 1790, a Mr. Nicholson had taken out a patent for printing by revolving cylinders, one of which was surrounded with type, and the other with soft leather, so that a sheet, passing between them, received the impression. It remained for König to apply this principle to the steam machine; and so considerable was his success, that in 1814 Mr. John Walter of the *Times*, alive to everything in the shape of literary progress, gave him a commission to set up his cylinders on the premises of the great Daily.

This was a dangerous move, needing the utmost caution; for the infuriated pressmen, maddened by the prospect of hand-labour in printing being superseded by machinery, would have torn to pieces both inventor and invention, had they got any inkling of the work that was going on, not many yards away. When all was ready, the pressmen were told one night to wait for news expected from the Continent, and at six o'clock on a   Nov. 29, dark November morning, Mr. Walter came in among   **1814** them with the damp sheets in his hand, to tell them   A.D. that the *Times* was already printed off by *steam;* that if they meant violence, he was ready for them; but that if they kept quiet, their wages should be continued until they got work elsewhere. Taken completely aback, they looked in amazement at the paper which he distributed among them, and without a struggle they yielded to the power of this friendly foe. And ever since that anxious night the clank of the engine and the rushing of white hot steam have been heard amid the multitudinous noises of Printing-House Square.

The following announcement appeared in the *Times* of that

same November morning:—"The reader now holds in his hands
one of the many thousand impressions of the *Times* newspaper,
which were taken last night by a mechanical apparatus. That
the magnitude of the invention may be justly appreciated by its
effects, we shall inform the public that after the letters are placed
by the compositors, and enclosed in what is called a 'form,' little
more remains for man to do than to attend and watch this unconscious agent in its operations. The machine is then merely supplied with paper; itself places the form, inks it, adjusts the paper
to the form newly inked, stamps the sheet, and gives it forth to
the hands of the attendant, at the same time withdrawing the
form for a fresh coat of ink, which itself again distributes, to meet
the ensuing sheet, now advancing for impression: and the whole
of these complicated acts are performed with such a velocity and
simultaneousness of movement, that no less than 1100 sheets are
impressed in one hour."

König's first machine, although an undoubted stride far beyond
the Stanhope press, was comparatively clumsy and complicated.
Its worst point was the inking apparatus, in which no fewer than
forty wheels were always at work. The type was laid on a flat
surface, and the impression was taken by passing it under a large
cylinder. He afterwards improved the machine, so as to accomplish the printing of the sheet on both sides.

A simpler machine by Cowper and Applegath was introduced
in 1818, which, in order to secure *register*—a technical name
for the perfect coincidence of the printed matter on opposite sides
of the same sheet—had, between the printing cylinders, two
drums, under and over which the paper was passed. Still the
march of improvement continued. A four-cylinder machine, also
by Cowper and Applegath, began in 1827 to print at the rate of
about 5000 copies in an hour. Napier also made many improvements. The process of inking became simpler, and so
1848 the work went on, until in 1848 Applegath set up a
A.D. machine, which consisted of a great central upright drum,
surrounded by eight smaller cylinders also vertical, bound
in cloth, and connected by toothed wheels with the central mass.

so that the rate of revolution should be uniform in all the nine. The type was arranged in vertical columns upon the great drum. Every cylinder had its own inking apparatus. Eight workmen, standing on elevated stages before eight piles of blank paper, supplied sheet after sheet to the tape fingers of the monster, which, drawing the paper down to a cylinder, passed it round, and carried it off impressed. About 12,000 copies in an hour were thus produced. Hoe of New York is now the engineer, who supplies *Times*, *Scotsman*, and all our leading newspapers with their huge wonder-working machines.

On the 7th of May 1850, the *Times* and its *Supplement* contained 72 columns, or 17,500 lines, made up of more than one million types. Two-fifths of this matter were written after seven in the evening. Here are some notes of the night's work :—

Supplement sent to press	...	...	7.50 P.M.
First form of the paper do.	...	...	4.15 A.M.
Second form do. ...	...	...	4.45 "
7000 papers printed off before	...	...	6.15 "
21,000 do. do.	...	...	7.30 "
34,000 do. do.	...	...	8.45 "

The entire impression of this gigantic newspaper, for one day, was therefore completed in about *four* hours.

But even 1850, near as it looks, is behind the age in newspaper life. Let us see how the *Times* is worked in 1861. And here we need make no apology for borrowing the words of a graphic describer, who is himself, if we mistake not, thoroughly familiar with the scene he depicts.*

"The printing-house of the *Times*, near Blackfriars Bridge, forms a companion picture to Gutenberg's printing-room in the old abbey at Strasbourg, and illustrates not only the development of the art, but the progress of the world during the intervening centuries. Visit Printing-House Square in the day-time, and you find it a quiet, sleepy place, with hardly any signs of life or movement about it, except in the advertisement office in the corner, where people are continually going out and in, and the clerks have a

* From " The Triumphs of Invention and Discovery," by J. Hamilton Fyfe.

busy time of it, shovelling money into the till all day long. But come back in the evening, and the place will wear a very different aspect. All signs of drowsiness have disappeared, and the office is all lighted up, and instinct with bustle and activity. Messengers are rushing out and in, telegraph boys, railway porters, and 'devils' of all sorts and sizes. Cabs are driving up every few minutes and depositing reporters, hot from the gallery of the House of Commons or the House of Lords, each with his budget of short-hand notes to decipher and transcribe. Up stairs, in his sanctum, the editor and his deputies are busy preparing or selecting the articles and reports, which are to appear in the next day's paper. In another part of the building the compositors are hard at work, picking up types, and arranging them in 'stickfulls,' which being emptied out into 'galleys,' are firmly fixed therein by little wedges of wood, in order that 'proofs' may be taken of them. The proofs pass into the hands of the various sets of readers, who compare them with the 'copy' from which they are set up, and mark any errors on the margin of the slips, which then find their way back to the compositors, who correct the types according to the marks. The 'galleys' are next seized by the persons charged with the 'making-up' of the paper, who divide them into columns of equal length. An ordinary *Times* newspaper, with a single inside sheet of advertisements, contains seventy-two columns, or 17,500 lines, made up of upwards of a million pieces of type; of which matter about two-fifths are often written, composed, and corrected after seven o'clock in the evening. If the advertisement sheet be double, as it frequently is, the paper will contain ninety-six columns. The types set up by the compositors are not sent to the machine. A mould is taken of them in a composition of brown paper, by means of which a 'stereotype' is cast in metal, and from this the paper is printed. The advertisement sheet, single or double, as the case may be, is generally ready for the press between seven and eight o'clock at night. The rest of the paper is divided into two 'forms,'—that is, columns arranged in pages and bound together by an iron frame, one for each side of the sheet. Into the first of these the person who 'makes up' endeavours to put all the early news, and it is sent to press usually about four o'clock. The other 'form' is reserved for the leading articles, telegrams, and all the latest intelligence, and does not reach the press till near five o'clock.

"The first sight of Hoe's machine, by a couple of which the *Times* is now printed, fills the beholder with bewilderment and awe. You see before you a huge pile of iron cylinders, wheels, cranks, and levers, whirling away at a rate that makes you giddy to look at, and with a grinding and gnashing of teeth that almost drives you deaf to listen to. With insatiable appetite the furious monster devours ream after ream of snowy sheets of paper, placed in its many gaping jaws by the slaves who wait on it, but seems to find none to suit its digestion, for back come all the sheets again, each with the mark of this strange beast printed on one side. Its hunger never is appeased,—it is always swallowing and always disgorging; and it is as much as the little 'devils' who wait on it can do, to put the paper between its lips and take it out again. But a bell rings suddenly, the monster gives a gasp, and is straightway still and dead to all appearance. Upon a closer inspection, now that it is at rest, and with some explanation from the foreman, you begin to have some idea of the process that has been going on before your astonished eyes.

"The core of the machine consists of a large drum, turning on a horizontal axis, round which revolve ten smaller cylinders, also on horizontal axes, in close proximity to the drum. The stereotyped matter is bound, like a malefactor on the wheel, to the central drum, and round each cylinder a sheet of paper is constantly being passed. It is obvious, therefore, that if the type be inked, and each of the cylinders be kept properly supplied with a sheet of paper, a single revolution of the drum will cause the ten cylinders to revolve likewise, and produce an impression on one side of each of the sheets of paper. For this purpose it is necessary to have the type inked ten times during every revolution of the drum; and this is managed by a very ingenious contrivance, which, however, is too complicated for description here. The feeding of the cylinders is provided for in this way: Over each cylinder is a

sloping desk, upon which rests a heap of sheets of white paper.
A lad—the ‘layer-on’—stands by the side of the desk and pushes
forward the paper, a sheet at a time, towards the tape fingers of
the machine, which, clutching hold of it, drag it into the interior,
where it is passed round the cylinders, and printed on the outer
side by pressure against the types on the drum.   The sheet is
then laid hold of by another set of tapes, carried to the other end
of the machine from that at which it entered, and there laid down
on a desk by a projecting flapper of lath-work.   Another lad—the
‘ taker-off ’—is in attendance to remove the printed sheets at certain intervals.   The drum revolves in less than two seconds ; and
in that time, therefore, ten sheets—for the same operation is performed simultaneously by the ten cylinders—are sucked in at one
end and disgorged at the other, printed on one side, thus giving
about 20,000 impressions in an hour."

We have taken the *Times* as the best example of these wonderful improvements in the art of printing, both because the working
of that paper is upon a colossal scale, and it therefore well
deserves to be noticed first, and because almost every improvement came into earliest play in the machine-room at Printing-
House Square.   The influence of the great change—the substitu-
tion of the steam *printing-machine* for the hand-worked *printing-
press*—has been felt in every corner of the land, where a cheap
book or a penny newspaper has found its way ; and it must be
indeed a sequestered nook into which these have not pushed
themselves in Britain.   So that famous and tremendous word,
"The Press," at whose sound blusterers have suddenly grown
meek as lambs, and Cruelty has pocketed his whip, trying to look
innocent and kind, is now a sort of misnomer ; for the *Press* is
actually rusting in lumber-rooms, or, at best, printing off the cloudy
hand-bills of a country town, while the place of power is held by the
Machine, which roars and struggles and puffs by day and night in
the accomplishment of its enormous task.   Such a change has half
a century produced in Caxton's art and mystery !   How the old
mercer would stare and rub his eyes, if these eyes could open now
upon a modern printing-room in any of our great publishing concerns !

CHAPTER II.

SAMUEL TAYLOR COLERIDGE.

Born 1772 A.D...........Died 1834 A.D.

A great dreamer.	Nether Stowey.	Shelter at Highgate.
Early life.	The Ancient Mariner.	Christabel.
A light dragoon.	Visits Germany.	Other works.
Bound for America.	Unsettled life.	Illustrative extract.

COLERIDGE, a magnificent dreamer, has left us only a few fragments to show what his life-work might have been, had industry
been wedded to his lofty genius. We think of him as of some
rarely gifted architect, before whose mind's eye visions of sublime
temples were continually floating, but whose realized work consists
of a few pillars and friezes, exquisitely beautiful, indeed, but lying
on the chosen site unfinished and unset.

Born at Ottery St. Mary in Devonshire, on the 21st of October
1772, this youngest child of a poor country vicar entered the
hard school of an orphan's life at Christ's Hospital. There, within grey old walls, began his cherished friendship with the gentle
Charles Lamb. Already, under the long blue coat of "the inspired
charity-boy," the nature of the man was burning. He dreamed
away his days; he read books of every kind with insatiable relish,
until history, novels, even poetry, began to pall upon his taste,
and nothing but metaphysics could afford any delight to the boy
of fifteen. The sonnets of Bowles, however, struck a chord,
whose vibration filled his young soul with untold pleasure.
During the two years of his residence at Cambridge, whither he
went in 1791 as an exhibitioner of Jesus College, his habits
deepened. Ideals, ever floating before his mind, sadly im-
peded the *real* work of the student. His first success—a gold
medal for Greek verse—was followed by some defeats, which,
coupled with a little debt and his admiration for revolutionary

France, caused him to abandon a college life without taking his degree.

Starving in London, he enlisted in the 15th Light Dragoons under the name of Comberbach, and spent four wretched months in trying to fathom the mysteries of drill and stable-work. The discovery of his classical attainments by the captain of his troop, who observed some Latin words written under his saddle as it hung upon the wall, led to his release from this position.

We then find him at Bristol, with his new friend Southey and four other young enthusiasts, building a splendid castle in the air. They were to sail over the Atlantic to the banks of the Susquehanna, and there to found a *Pantisocracy,* or domestic republic, where all goods should be property in common, and the leisure of the work-men should be devoted to literature. Only one thing was wanted to carry out the scheme—money. Failing this, the pretty bubble burst. Probable starvation by the Avon, instead of republican case and plenty by the Susquehanna, was the stern reality which now pushed its dark face into the dreamer's life. His **1795** pen, employed by a Bristol bookseller, kept off this ugly A.D. shape; and soon the struggler added to his difficulties by an early marriage with a girl, whose sister became Southey's wife. Poor Lovell, who died very soon, had already wedded the third of these Bristol Graces.

A cottage at Nether Stowey in Somersetshire, nestling at the foot of the Quantock hills, received the youthful pair, who resided there for about three years. Out of this, the brightest period in a desultory life, blossomed some of the finest poetry that Coleridge has written. An *Ode to the Departing Year,* and that piece entitled *France,* which Shelley loved so well, are among the productions of this peaceful time. But finer than these are two works of the same period, which deserve more than passing mention. *The Rime of the Auncient Marinere* was written at Stowey, and there *Christabel* was begun.

"The Ancient Mariner" is a poem in the simple, picturesque style of the old ballad. The tale—told to a spell-bound wedding-guest by an old sailor, who, in a few vivid touches, is made to stand before us with grey beard, glittering eyes, and long, brown, skinny hands—enchains us with strange and mystic power. The shooting of the albatross, that came through the snowy fog to cheer the crew—the red blistering calm that fell upon the sea— the skeleton ship with its phantom dicers driving across the sun in view of the thirst-scorched seamen—the lonely life of the guilty mariner on the rolling sea amid the corpses of his ship- mates—the springing of good thoughts at the sight of the beau- tiful water-snakes sporting "beyond the shadow of the ship"—the coming of sleet, and rain, and a spectral wind—and the final deliverance from the doomed vessel, are among the pictures that flit before us as we read—shadows all, but touched with weird light and colour, as from another world.

A visit to Germany (1798), the expense of which was defrayed by the Wedgewoods of Staffordshire, deepened the hues of mys- ticism already tinging the spirit of Coleridge. His translation of Schiller's *Wallenstein* was the principal result of his residence in that land of learning and romance. Upon his return to England in 1800, he took up his abode in Southey's house at Keswick, and with some temporary interruptions he continued to make the Lakes his head-quarters for ten years. He wrote largely for *The Morning Post;* during a visit to Malta in 1804 he acted as sec- retary to the governor of that island; he came home to deliver his eloquent and profound criticisms on *Shakspere* to a London audi- ence, and to issue the weekly essays of the short-lived *Friend,* which ceased after a few numbers, as had happened to the *Watch- man,* a similar venture of the old Bristol days. During these many changes, his opinions, both political and religious, had veered completely round. Once a Red Republican, he was now a keen upholder of the throne; once a Unitarian preacher at Taunton and Shrewsbury, he now acknowledged his firm belief in the Trinity.

In 1810 he bade good-bye to the Lakes, and went to live in Lon- don with various friends, who could forgive and pity the thriftless, erring man for the sake of his splendid genius. His natural sloth and dreaminess were increased by the destructive habit of opium-eating, or rather laudanum-drinking, **1810 A.D.**

which he had formed while using the drug as a medicine.   Deeper
and deeper he plunged into those abysses of German metaphysics
towards which he had been gradually drifting. Various convulsive
efforts at hard work were made by him at times, but all his great
plans dissolved into vapour and vanished.   The roof of Gilman, a
friendly surgeon at Highgate, sheltered the dreamer during his last
nineteen years; and there the old man used for hours to pour out
his wonderful talk in a stream, which was often turbid and slow,
but which sometimes broke into a brilliant run, or discovered,
through its clear crystal, the rich sands of gold and shining gems
below.   At Highgate he died in July 1834.

Carlyle's portrait of Coleridge "sitting on the brow of Highgate
Hill," to be found in his " Life of Sterling," is remarkably vivid :—
" Brow and head were round, and of massive weight; but the face
was flabby and irresolute. The deep eyes, of a light hazel, were as full
of sorrow as of inspiration; confused pain looked mildly from them,
as in a kind of mild astonishment. The whole figure and air, good
and amiable otherwise, might be called flabby and irresolute; expressive of weakness under possibility of strength. He hung loosely
on his limbs, with knees bent, and stooping attitude; in walking,
he rather shuffled than decisively stepped; and a lady once remarked, he never could fix which side of the garden-walk would
suit him best, but continually shifted, in cork-screw fashion, and
kept trying both. A heavy-laden, high-aspiring, and surely much-
suffering man. His voice, naturally soft and good, had contracted
itself into a plaintive snuffle and sing-song; he spoke as if preaching—you would have said preaching earnestly, and also hopelessly, the weightiest things. I still recollect his 'object' and
'subject,'—terms of continual recurrence in the Kantean province; and how he sung and snuffled them into 'om-m-mject'
and 'sum-m-mject,' with a kind of solemn shake or quaver, as
he rolled along."

His noble fragment, *Christabel*, has been already named. Begun
at Stowey, and continued upon his return from Germany, by the
advice of Byron it was given to the world in 1816 in its unfinished
loveliness. Both Byron and Scott have echoed the irregular music

of its verse, though with peculiar variations. It is a tale of strange witchcraft. A sweet and innocent girl, praying for her lover's safety beneath a huge oak-tree outside the castle gate, under the dim moon-light of an April sky, is startled by the appearance of a witch, dis-guised as a richly-clad beauty in distress. The gentle Christabel asks the wanderer into the castle; the disguise is there laid aside; some horrible shape smites the poor hospitable maid into a trance; and the blinking glance of the witch's small, dull, snake-like eyes, shot suddenly at the shuddering victim, clouds the innocent blue of her eye with a passive imitation of the same hateful look. In dealing with mystic themes like this, Coleridge was master of a spell over thought and language, such as no other writer has ever possessed. But his inspiration came in gusts, and fragments grew around him at such a rate that soon the difficulty of choosing what to finish caused all to remain undone. His life was a succession of beginnings which never saw an end. He went to college, but took no degree. He prepared for emigration, but did not start. He got married, but left others to support his wife and children. At twenty-five he planned an epic on the Destruc-tion of Jerusalem; but to-morrow—and to-morrow—and to-morrow—passed without one written line. A great genius with a great in-firmity—the twinhood of mental strength and feebleness — he claims at once our reverence and our deep compassion.

Besides the works already named there are two which cannot be forgotten, as examples of the varied powers of this great poet. For simple tenderness and depth of natural feeling his little love-song of *Genevieve* cannot be surpassed. And the *Hymn before Sunrise in the Vale of Chamouni*, of which we quote some lines, has in it an exultant sublimity akin to Milton's song. While the melody of *Genevieve* most resembles the sighing of "a lonely flute," stealing through the odours of the summer dusk, this *Hymn to Mont Blanc* swells through the darkness of the Alpine morning up to the rosy summit of the snow, with all the tumultuous music of a vast organ, pealing in unison with the chorus of ten thousand rejoicing throats.

Coleridge's *Lectures on Shakspere* have been already named.

The review of Wordsworth's poetry, which may be found in his *Biographia Literaria*, has been pronounced to be "perhaps the most philosophical piece of criticism extant in the language." Though able to penetrate deep into the mysteries of Shakspere's power over tears and laughter, he had himself no genuine dramatic faculty. His tragedies, *Remorse* and *Zapoyla*, contain some noble passages, but we read them with cold, unkindling souls.

FROM THE HYMN AT CHAMOUNI.

Thou first and chief, sole sovran of the vale !
O struggling with the darkness all the night,
And visited all night by troops of stars,
Or when they climb the sky, or when they sink !
Companion of the morning star at dawn,
Thyself earth's rosy star, and of the dawn
Co-herald ! wake, O wake, and utter praise !
Who sank thy sunless pillars deep in earth ?
Who filled thy countenance with rosy light ?
Who made thee parent of perpetual streams ?
   And you, ye five wild torrents fiercely glad !
Who called you forth from night and utter death,
From dark and icy caverns called you forth,
Down those precipitous, black, jagged rocks,
For ever shattered, and the same for ever ?
Who gave you your invulnerable life,
Your strength, your speed, your fury, and your joy,
Unceasing thunder and eternal foam ?
And who commanded—and the silence came—
Here let the billows stiffen, and have rest ?
   Ye ice-falls ! ye that from the mountain's brow
Adown enormous ravines slope amain—
Torrents, methinks, that heard a mighty voice,
And stopped at once amid their maddest plunge !
Motionless torrents ! silent cataracts !
Who made you glorious as the gates of heaven
Beneath the keen full moon ? Who bade the sun
Clothe you with rainbows ? Who, with living flowers
Of loveliest blue, spread garlands at your feet ?
God ! let the torrents, like a shout of nations,
Answer ! and let the ice-plains echo, God !
God ! sing ye meadow-streams with gladsome voice !
Ye pine groves, with your soft and soul-like sounds !
And they, too, have a voice, yon piles of snow,
And in their perilous fall shall thunder, God !

CHAPTER III.

ROBERT SOUTHEY.

Born 1774 A.D.........Died 1843 A.D.

Early life.	Banks of the Greta.	Leading poems.
Pantisocrata.	Hard work.	Kehama.
Lisbon and law.	The Laurel.	Prose works.
Thalaba.	Last years.	Illustrative extract.

ROBERT SOUTHEY, a linen draper's son, was born in Wine Street, Bristol, on the 12th of August 1774. After passing through various local seminaries, he went in 1788, at the expense of his uncle, the Reverend Herbert Hill, to the celebrated school of Westminster. From that school he was expelled four years afterwards, owing to the share he had taken in an article against flogging, which appeared in a magazine conducted by the senior boys. Entering Balliol College, Oxford, in 1792, he spent a couple of years in general reading and industrious verse-making, carrying from the University, according to his own account, a knowledge of but two things as the fruit of his imperfect undergraduate course—how to row and how to swim.

At Oxford he met Coleridge, and these "birds of a feather," both smitten by the widening swell of the French Revolution, rank Republicans in political creed, and Unitarians in religious profession, formed, in conjunction with others, the wild American scheme spoken of in the sketch of Coleridge. Southey, Coleridge, and their friend Lovell, another of the *Pantisocrats*, became the husbands of three sisters of Bristol; all of whom were gathered in a while under Southey's roof, for Lovell soon died, and Coleridge in his vast dreamings often forgot the real duty of supporting his wife and children.

Already Southey's pen had been busily at work. At college he had composed an epic poem, *Joan of Arc*, for which that kindly bookseller of Bristol, Cottle, now gave the young husband fifty guineas. A volume of poems, written in conjunction with Lovell under the names of Bion and Moschus, had previously appeared; and a wild, revolutionary piece, *Wat Tyler*, had been written in a fit of republicanism. The last-named work was surreptitiously published many years afterwards by a bookseller, who wanted to annoy the Laureate, then a celebrated man.

Between his two visits (1795 and 1800) to Lisbon, where his uncle was chaplain of the British Factory, he studied law at Gray's Inn, advancing, to use his own expression, "with sufficient rapidity in Blackstone and Madoc." The latter was an epic poem. This divided love could not last, and so Blackstone was at last given up, while Madoc advanced to completion. Before settling down to these temporary and uncongenial studies, he had published *Letters from Spain and Portugal*, the offspring of his first visit to the Peninsula.

In 1801 appeared the first of a series of great poems, intended to illustrate those various systems of mythology, which are so rich in poetic ore. Although its sale was slow, this work did much to raise the author's literary fame. Called *Thalaba, the Destroyer*, it depicts, in blank-verse of very irregular length but of great music, the perils and ultimate triumph of an Arabian hero, who fights with and conquers the powers of Evil. A splendid moonlight shining on the Eastern sands, with two figures—a sad mother and a weeping boy—wandering in the pale radiance, is the opening picture of a poem which abounds in brilliant painting. For the copyright of this work, which was finished in Portugal, Southey received a hundred guineas.

After one more effort towards a permanent settlement in some recognised position—the acceptance of a private secretaryship to the Irish Chancellor of Exchequer, worth £350 a year, which

1804
A.D.

he kept for only six months—he became a literary man by profession, and in 1804 fixed his residence on the banks of the Greta near Keswick, in the heart of the Lake country. Coleridge was already there, settled for so long a time as a being ever on the wing could settle; and

Wordsworth lived about fourteen miles off, at Mount Rydal, near Ambleside.

Already his incessant industry had begun, but it now deepened into a life-long habit, until the busy brain wore itself out, and the workman could but wander without purpose and without power among the books, which he had gathered with patient love around the walls of his writing-room. Few events of any note, beyond the publication of his various works, marked the life of this busy author. In a letter to a friend he thus describes a day, and most of his days were similarly spent :—

" Three pages of history (of Portugal) after breakfast (equivalent to five in small quarto printing) ; then to transcribe and copy for the press, or to make any selections and biographies (for " Specimens of the British Poets "), or what else suits my humour till dinner-time. From dinner-time till tea I read, write letters, see the newspaper, and very often indulge in a siesta. After tea I go to poetry (he was now writing the " Curse of Kehama "), and correct and re-write and copy till I am tired ; and then turn to anything else till supper. And this is my life."

No wonder that a friend should say in deep astonishment, on hearing of such incessant toil, " But, Southey, tell me, when *do* you *think ?* "

We postpone for a little a notice of his various works. When Pye died in 1813, Southey received the Laurel which Scott had just declined. In 1821 Oxford conferred on him the degree of LL.D. A pension of £300 a year was granted to him in 1835 by Sir Robert Peel, who had already offered him a baronetcy. His first wife having died in 1837, he contracted a second marriage two years later with the poetess, Caroline Bowles, who was then an elderly lady of fifty-two, and whose four years of married life were given to the tendance of the poor Laureate, already, like the elm-tree pointed to by Swift—himself the saddest example of so terrible an end—*beginning to die at the top.* During the last three years of Southey's life his over-wrought mind was a total blank. He died at Greta on the 21st of March 1843.

The poetry of Southey, though not of the very highest order,

displays undoubted genius.   His ambition as a poet was great;
and few could have made more of the unmanageable themes
he selected.   *Madoc*, a Welshman's supposed discovery and conquest of Mexico (1805);   *The Curse of Kehama*, a tale of the
Hindoo mythology (1810); and *Roderick, Last of the Goths*, a
blank-verse epic on early Spanish history (1814), are his principal
poems, besides those already named.   Among many others we
may mention *The Vision of Judgment*, which provoked Byron's
terribly sarcastic echo; and his latest efforts in verse, *All for Love*,
and *The Pilgrim of Compostella*.   His Lakist tendencies can best
be observed in his minor poems and ballads, of which *Lord William*,
Mary the Maid of the Inn, and *The Old Woman of Berkeley* are
well-known specimens.

  " The Curse of Kehama " is his finest poem.   In verse of most
irregular music, but completely suited to his fantastic theme, he
leads us to the terrestrial paradise,—to the realms below the sea,
—to the heaven of heavens, and, in a sublime passage, through
adamantine rock, lit .with a furnace glow, into Padalon, the Indian
Hades. We follow the strange career of Kehama, a Hindoo rajah,
who by penance and self-inflicted torture raises himself to a level
with Brahma and Vishnu; we suffer with the poor mortal, who
is burdened with the spell of a terrible curse laid on him by the
enchanter, and we rejoice in his final deliverance and restoration
to his family.   Various Hindoo gods, a ghost, a benevolent spirit,
and a woman, who receives immortality at the end, are among the
dramatis personæ.   Scenery and costume, situations and sentiments, are alike in keeping with the Oriental nature of the work.
But, for all its splendour and all its correctness as a work of art,
it is so far removed from the world in which our sympathies lie,
that few can fully appreciate this noble poem, and perhaps none
can return to it with never-wearied love, as to a play of Shakspere
or a novel by Scott.

  Southey was a remarkable writer of English prose.   His *Life
of Nelson* (1813) is a model of its kind.   Clear, polished, and
thoroughly unstrained, a language flowed from his practised pen
which few English writers have surpassed.   *A History of Brazil*

(1st vol. 1810); *Lives of John Wesley, Chatterton, Kirke White*, and *Cowper*; a *History of the Peninsular War* (1st vol. 1823); *Colloquies on Society* (1829), a strange and not over-wise book, giving an account of conversations between Montesinos (Southey himself) and the ghost of Sir Thomas More, who visits him at Keswick; *Lives of the British Admirals* for Lardner's "Cyclopædia" (1833); and *The Doctor* (1834), stand out prominently amid a host of articles for the *Quarterly*, and occasional papers on almost every subject, which filled up the *idle* hours of this most indefatigable author. Like Johnson he was living from "hand to mouth," until a pension placed him above the fear of want; but he could not then give up the habits of incessant study and literary toil, which had grown to be his second nature. He was never so happy as when he sat amid his books, pen in hand, adding newly-written sheets to the pile of manuscript already lying in his copy-drawer.

A VOYAGE THROUGH THE SKY.

(FROM "KEHAMA.")

Then in the ship of heaven Ereenia laid
　The waking, wondering maid;
The ship of heaven, instinct with thought, displayed
　Its living sail, and glides along the sky.
　　On either side, in wavy tide,
The clouds of morn along its path divide;
The winds that swept in wild career on high
Before its presence check their charmed force;
The winds that loitering lagged along their course
　Around the living bark enamoured play,
Swell underneath the sail, and sing before its way.

That bark, in shape, was like the furrowed shell
Wherein the sea-nymphs to their parent-king,
On festal day, their duteous offerings bring.
　Its hue?—Go watch the last green light
Ere evening yields the western star to night;
Or fix upon the sun thy strenuous sight
Till thou hast reached its orb of chrysolite.
　The sail, from end to end displayed,
　Bent, like a rainbow, o'er the maid.

An angel's head, with visual eye,
Through trackless space directs its chosen way;
  Nor aid of wing, nor foot, nor fin,
Requires to voyage o'er the obedient sky.
Smooth as the swan when not a breeze at even
  Disturbs the surface of the silver stream,
Through air and sunshine sails the ship of heaven.

Recumbent there the maiden glides along
    On her aërial way,
How swift she feels not, though the swiftest wind
    Had flagged in flight behind.
  Motionless as a sleeping babe she lay,
    And all serene in mind,
Feeling no fear; for that ethereal air
With such new life and joyance filled her heart,
    Fear could not enter there:
For sure she deemed her mortal part was o'er,
And she was sailing to the heavenly shore;
And that angelic form, who moved beside,
Was some good spirit sent to be her guide.
    *   *   *   *   *
Through air and sunshine sails the ship of heaven;
  Far, far beneath them lies
The gross and heavy atmosphere of earth;
    And with the Swerga gales
    The maid of mortal birth
At every breath a new delight inhales.
And now toward its port the ship of heaven
Swift as a falling meteor shapes its flight,
Yet gently as the dews of night that gem
And do not bend the hare-bell's slenderest stem.
Daughter of earth, Ereenia cried, alight:
This is thy place of rest, the Swerga this,—
  Lo, here my bower of bliss!
He furled his azure wings, which round him fold
  Graceful as robes of Grecian chief of old.
The happy Kailyal knew not where to gaze;
  Her eyes around in joyful wonder roam,
  Now turned upon the lovely Glendoveer,
    Now on his heavenly home.

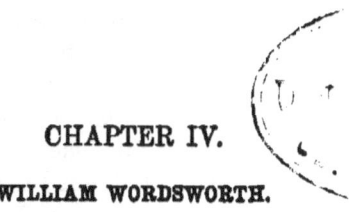

CHAPTER IV.

WILLIAM WORDSWORTH.

Born 1770 A.D..........Died 1850 A.D.

The Lake School.	Coleridge.	Works of later years.
Wordsworth's style.	By the Lakes.	Some minor poems.
Early life.	Rydal Mount.	His last years.
His maiden work.	The Excursion.	Illustrative extract.

WORDSWORTH was the great master of the Lake School,* in which
Coleridge and Southey were also prominent members.   Choosing
the simplest speech of educated Englishmen as a vehicle for the
expression of their thoughts, and passing by with quiet scorn the
used-up subjects of the Romancists—the military hero waving his
red sword amid battle smoke ; the assassin watching from the
dark shadow of a vaulted doorway his unconscious victim, who
strolls, singing in the white moonlight, down the empty street ;
the lover, " sighing like furnace with a woeful ballad made to his
mistress's eyebrow," and kindred themes—the poets of the Lake
School took their subjects often from among the commonest things,
and wrote their poems in the simplest style.   Bending a reverent ear to the mysterious harmonies of nature, to the ceaseless
song of praise that rises from every blade of grass and every dew-
drop, warbles in the fluting of every lark, and sweeps to heaven
in every wave of air, they found in their own deep hearts a
musical echo of that song, and shaping into words the swelling of
their inward faith, they spoke to the world in a way to which the
world was little used, about things in which the world saw no
poetic beauty.   The history of a hard-hearted hawker of earthen-
ware and his ass, the adventures of Betty Foy's idiot son, and

* The Lake School derived its name from the fact that its three most conspicuous members, Wordsworth, Southey, and Coleridge, lived chiefly by the English lakes. Originally a
contemptuous name, it has gradually come to be the recognised title of Wordsworth and
his disciples.

the wanderings of an old pedler, are among the themes chosen by
Wordsworth for the utterance of his poetic soul. As of old the
Puritans had done in political and domestic life, the Lakists went too
far in their disdain for the conventional ornaments and subjects of
poetry. But their theory, a healthful one, based on sound principles,
made an impression on the British mind deeper and more lasting
than many think. Like that *ozone* or electrified oxygen in the
natural air, upon which, say chemists, our health and spirits depend,
its subtle influence is ever stealing through the atmosphere of
our national thought, quickening the scattered germs of a truer
and purer poetic philosophy than has yet prevailed. As all advocates of a new theory are apt to do, Wordsworth ran at first into
an almost ridiculous extreme of simplicity, both in the selection of
his subjects and his treatment of them. His ballads, on their first
publication, raised a perfect storm of disdainful laughter among the
critics of the day,—laughter which he heard serenely, conscious
that he was right in the main, and that time alone was needed to
insure the triumph of his views. But here it must be remembered,
that the language in which his highest thoughts found their fitting expression is not by any means a common-place language.
When telling the tale of Johnny Foy, the idiot who stayed out all
night, he may properly enough descend to humble strains like
these :—

> " And now she's at the doctor's door,
>   She lifts the knocker, rap, rap, rap
>   The doctor at the casement shows
>   His glimmering eyes that peep and doze !
>   And one hand rubs his old night-cap."

But when higher themes attract his pen, as, for example, in that
noble simile, among the finest our poetry contains,—

> " I have seen
> A curious child, who dwelt upon a tract
> Of inland ground, applying to his ear
> The convolutions of a smooth-lipped shell,
> To which, in silence hushed, his very soul
> Listened intensely : and his countenance soon

Brightened with joy ; for, murmuring from within,
Were heard sonorous cadences, whereby,
To his belief, the monitor expressed
Mysterious union with its native sea :
Even such a shell the universe itself
Is to the ear of Faith,"—

his style is elevated far above the level of our common speech, as a poetic style must always be, that takes its tone and colour from the lofty thoughts which it embodies.

Wordsworth, an attorney's son, was born on the 7th of April 1770, at Cockermouth in Cumberland. Both father and mother died while he was yet a boy ; and when his school education was considered, by the uncle under whose guardianship he passed, to be sufficiently advanced, he was sent in 1787 to St. John's College, Cambridge. There, during the four years of his undergraduate course, he read a good deal, studied Italian, wrote poetry, and, when the welcomed vacations released him from what he considered to be an irksome and narrow course of study, went upon various tours—that in the autumn of 1790 being directed to France and Switzerland, although the tempest of Revolution was then raging with great fury. In the following year, having graduated, he went again to France, with a soul on fire in her cause. There he stayed for fifteen months, and there he might have perished by the guillotine in the growing ardour of his sympathy for the Girondists, had not his return to England in 1792 changed the current of his life.

His friends wished him to enter the Church; but he was born to be a poet and nothing else. The love of poetry was the grand passion of his heart, gaining strength as the flame of republicanism wasted and died with the coming of maturer years.

In 1793 appeared a modest book of descriptive verse, containing two poems in the heroic couplet, entitled *An Evening Walk* and *Descriptive Sketches* of walks among the Alps. This maiden appearance of the poet Wordsworth revealed to thinking minds the rise of a new star, destined to shed a brilliant lustre on the land. Coleridge, a kindred spirit, was especially struck with the merit of the work.

1793
A.D.

The need of earning a livelihood had turned the young poet's thoughts to the law and the career of a journalist, when, happily for the literature of the nineteenth century, the kindness of Calvert, a dying friend, who left him £900 and a pressing request that he would devote himself to poetry, marked out another future for the man of twenty-five.

Settling down in Somersetshire with his sister, he wrote *Salisbury Plain* and a tragedy called *The Borderers,* and soon afterwards made the acquaintance of Coleridge. When the latter took up house at Nether Stowey, his new friend, in order to be near him, removed to Alfoxden, three miles off; and they lived thus in constant association with each other. A volume called *Lyrical Ballads* appeared in 1798, containing twenty-three pieces, the first being the "Ancient Mariner," and the rest poems by Wordsworth. It fell all but dead from the press.

After a tour in Germany, Wordsworth settled with his sister in a cottage at Grasmere, among those hills whose blue peaks had bounded the world of his childhood. There he resided for nine years, during which his marriage and the commencement of his great philosophical poem, of which we have but two instalments, were the chief occurrences. The payment of £8500 by the Earl of Lonsdale, in settlement of a debt due to his father, enabled him at the time of his marriage to look forward with composure to a life undisturbed by the cares of money-getting,—a circumstance of no small importance to the successful cultivation of that calm and thoughtful poetry towards which his native genius was inclined. In 1808 he removed to Allan Bank, and in 1813 to

1813   Rydal Mount, both places lying in sight of those sweet

A.D.   lakes, and under the shadow of those old hills, which have become inseparably associated with his name and memory.

At Rydal Mount, " a cottage-like building, almost hidden by a profusion of roses and ivy," from whose grassy lawn a silver gleam of Windermere could be caught to the south, the poet spent the greater half of his life. About the time of his removal to this charming residence, the office of Distributor of Stamps for the county of Westmoreland, the salary of which was £500 a year, with no very heavy duties attached to it, made a considerable addition to his private means. He owed his appointment to the influence of Lord Lonsdale.

In the following year he published his noblest poem, *The Excursion*, which brought him little or no money, and drew down upon him the wrath of the critics, Jeffrey of the "Edinburgh" leading the hostile van. "This will never do," wrote the great Athenian lawyer; but alas for his prophecy! *this* (*i.e.*, "The Excursion") has been *doing* ever since, making its way steadily **1814** upwards, like a star that climbs into the clear sky A.D. above masses of cloud hung upon the horizon, and sheds its mild yet penetrating light with growing power as it climbs. When we examine the structure of this great work—only a fragment, let it be remembered, of a vast moral epic, to be called *The Recluse*, in which the poet intended to discuss the human soul in all its deepest workings and its loftiest relations—we find no dramatic life, and little human interest; and to this feature of the poem, as well as to the novelty of finding subtle metaphysical reasoning embodied in blank-verse, its original unpopularity must be ascribed. Even still, though yearly widening, the circle of those who read the "Excursion" is small; for it is a poem written only for the thinking few. Those who read poetry as some do, only for the *story*, will be hipped and desperately bored by the grave musical philosophy of the old Scotch pedler and his friends. Yet it is not all a web of subtle reasoning, for there are rich studies from nature and life scattered plentifully over its more thoughtful ground-work. Coleridge, who was his friend's truest and finest critic, describes the higher efforts of Wordsworth's pen as being characterized by "an austere purity of language, both grammatically and logically." No English poet, who has dealt with lofty themes, is more thoroughly English in both his single words and his turns of expression.

The chief remaining works of this great writer are *The White Doe of Rylstone* (1815), a tragic tale founded on the ruin of a northern family in the Civil War; *Peter Bell* (1819), a remarkable specimen of the Lakist writings, which he dedicated to

Southey;* *Sonnets on the River Duddon; The Waggoner*, dedicated to Charles Lamb; *Memorials of a Tour on the Continent; Ecclesiastical Sonnets; Yarrow Revisited, and other Poems;* and *The Prelude*, a fragment of autobiography, describing the growth of a poet's mind, which was not published until the author was dead. In the composition of *Sonnets*, a poetic form of which he was remarkably fond, he has not been excelled by the finest of the old masters. As he says of Milton, we may say of himself with regard to the sonnet,—

> " In his hand
> The thing became a trumpet, whence he blew
> Soul-animating strains."—

"Wordsworth's sonnet never goes off, as it were, with a clap or repercussion at the close ; but is thrown up like a rocket, breaks into light, and falls in a soft shower of brightness."

Some of his minor poems, displaying his genius in its simple beauty and unaffected grace, are *Ruth*, a touching tale of Love and Madness; *We are Seven*, a glimpse of that higher wisdom which the lips of childhood often speak; the classic *Laodamia*, clear-lined and graceful as an antique cameo; and those *Lines on Revisiting the Wye*, of which we quote a part, rich in the calmly eloquent philosophy that formed the golden woof of all he wrote.

In 1842 the old man, then past seventy, resigning his public office to his son, received a pension of £300 a year; and in 1843, on the death of Southey, he became poet-laureate. Seven years

April 23,
1850
A.D.

later, he sank into the grave, dying a few days after the completion of his eightieth year. His remains were laid in the churchyard of Grasmere, by the side of his darling daughter, who had been taken from him three years before.

---

* One of the finest examples of Wordsworth's direct simplicity of expression occurs in the description of Peter's utter want of sympathy with the beauty of Nature,—

> " A primrose by a river's brim,
> A yellow primrose was to him,
> And it was nothing more."

THOUGHTS ON REVISITING THE WYE.

Oh ! how oft,
In darkness, and amid the many shapes
Of joyless daylight, when the fretful stir
Unprofitable, and the fever of the world,
Have hung upon the beatings of my heart,
How oft in spirit have I turned to thee,
O silvan Wye ! thou wanderer through the woods—
How often has my spirit turned to thee !
And now, with gleams of half-extinguished thought,
With many recognitions dim and faint,
And somewhat of a sad perplexity,
The picture of the mind revives again,
While here I stand, not only with the sense
Of present pleasure, but with pleasing thoughts
That in this moment there is life and food
For future years.   And so I dare to hope,
Though changed, no doubt, from what I was when first
I came among these hills; when, like a roe,
I bounded o'er the mountains, by the sides
Of the deep rivers, and the lonely streams,
Wherever nature led ; more like a man
Flying from something that he dreads, than one
Who sought the thing he loved.   For nature then—
The coarser pleasures of my boyish days
And their glad animal movements all gone by—
To me was all in all—I cannot paint
What then I was.   The sounding cataract
Haunted me like a passion; the tall rock,
The mountain, and the deep and gloomy wood,
Their colours and their forms were then to me
An appetite; a feeling and a love
That had no need of a remoter charm,
By thought supplied, or any interest
Unborrowed from the eye.   That time is past,
And all its aching joys are now no more,
And all its dizzy raptures.   Not for this
Faint I, nor mourn, nor murmur; other gifts
Have followed,—for such loss, I would believe,
Abundant recompense.   For I have learned
To look on nature, not as in the hour
Of thoughtless youth, but hearing oftentimes
The still sad music of humanity,
Nor harsh nor grating, though of ample power
To chasten and subdue.   And I have felt

A presence that disturbs me with the joy
Of elevated thoughts; a sénse sublime
Of something far more deeply interfused,
Whose dwelling is the light of setting suns,
And the round ocean, and the living air,
And the blue sky, and in the mind of man;
A motion and a spirit that impels
All thinking things, all objects of all thought,
And rolls through all things.   Therefore am I still
A lover of the meadows and the woods
And mountains, and of all that we behold
From this green earth,—of all the mighty world
Of eye and ear, both what they half create
And what perceive; well pleased to recognise
In nature, and the language of the sense,
The anchor of my purest thoughts, the nurse,
The guide, the guardian of my heart, and soul
Of all my moral being.

CHAPTER V.

THOMAS BABINGTON, LORD MACAULAY.

Born 1800 A.D..........Died 1859 A.D.

Macaulay's fame.	Called to the bar.	History of England.
His lineage.	Political life.	The Peerage.
His college life.	Out in India.	Lays of Ancient Rome.
Article on Milton.	Beaten at Edinburgh.	Illustrative extract.

DISTINGUISHED as a descriptive poet by his fine *Lays of Ancient Rome*, and yet more distinguished as a master of English prose by his *Essays* and his noble *History of England*, Macaulay stands prominent among the highest literary names of the nineteenth century. When, amid the Christmas festivities of 1859, a mournful whisper crept into almost every home in the land, telling of his death, there were few hearts so thoroughly engrossed by the pleasures of the passing hour as not to send a thought of affectionate sorrow into that quiet room at Kensington, where the great Historian and Essayist—the only man whom England ever made-a lord for the power of his pen—lay mute and still among his cherished books and the half-written sheets of his unfinished volume.

Macaulay was of Scottish lineage, being a descendant of the Macaulays of Lewis in Ross-shire. His grandfather, John, was a Presbyterian minister. His father, Zachary, who spent part of his life in Jamaica, became well known for his exertions in opposition to the hateful slave-trade. At Rothley Temple in Leicestershire, the seat of Zachary's brother-in-law, a rich English merchant and member of Parliament, the future historian was born in 1800, and was named Thomas Babington, after the uncle in whose house he first saw the light.

Young Macaulay's career as a student of Trinity College, Cambridge, was crowned with high honours. Entering in 1818, he obtained in the following year the Chancellor's medal for a poem called *Pompeii;* in 1821 he received a similar distinction for a poem on *Evening*, and was, besides, elected to the Craven scholarship; and he had been for a year Fellow of Trinity when, in 1825, he took his degree of Master of Arts.   And in the arena of the Union Debating Society, where the keenest and brightest minds of Cambridge met to display their skill in fence, few could measure weapons with Babington Macaulay.   Such honours formed no unfitting prelude for the career of literary and political renown upon which he entered without delay.   While yet an undergraduate, he had contributed to *The Etonian*, a short-lived serial conducted by Praed, his most formidable rival at the Union ; and had also, in company with that author of "Quince" and the "Red Fisherman," written for *Knight's Quarterly Magazine.*   Here his first public laurels were won.   But the young student of law—he was now working away at Lincoln's Inn in preparation for his call to the bar—before donning the legal robe, had achieved a success of which many older men might well be proud.   Milton's newly-found treatise on "Christian Doctrine" having been rendered into English, Macaulay contributed to

1825
A.D.

an August number of the " Edinburgh Review " that article on *Milton*, which must be regarded as the starting-point of his literary fame.   It was brilliant even to excess.   The writer himself, when the added skill and taste of nearly twenty years had chastened his style, condemned this article, as being "overloaded with gaudy and ungraceful ornament."   But its appearance was felt, by all the reading public, to mark the rising of a new star of uncommon lustre above the horizon ; and it is easier to forgive an excess of real brilliance, which, we know, coming years must purify and subdue, than to endure a poverty of light, or, still worse, that display of pinchbeck jewels, glittering with affected lustre, of which our young literature is too full.

About six months after the appearance of *Milton*, the writer was called to the English bar.   We pass lightly over his professional and political career.   His Whig friends soon made him a

Commissioner of Bankruptcy. He took his seat in 1830 as member for Calne. He spoke often and with great power in the battle of the Reform Bill, and won considerable reputation as an orator, although his delivery was monotonous and he lacked some of the *physical* qualities of a telling speaker. His orations were rather brilliant political essays than great outbursts of natural eloquence, like the speeches of Chatham or Burke. From 1832 to 1834 he was member for Leeds. And then he went out to India as legal adviser to the Supreme Council of Calcutta, his principal business there being the preparation of a new penal code of Indian law. The formation of this code led him to the investigation of Indian history, a study which bore fine fruit in his Essays on *Lord Clive* and *Warren Hastings*, the principal literary results of the two years and a half which he spent in the East. Many of his best articles in the "Edinburgh" came home by the Indian mail, recreations of his leisure at Calcutta. In 1839 Macaulay, then newly returned from India, became member for Edinburgh, upon taking office under Lord Melbourne as Secretary at War, and this connection with the Scottish capital lasted for eight years. Under Lord John (now Earl) Russell, he was in 1846 appointed Paymaster-General of the Forces; but, in the following year, his vote in favour of the Maynooth grant having given offence to some of the Edinburgh electors, he was beaten at the poll by Mr. Cowan.

The defeat was a victory. Macaulay the member for Edinburgh, sinking out of public view for two years, emerges as Macaulay the historian of England. Living chiefly at the Albany, and spending many of his mornings among the literary treasures of the British Museum, quartering himself for weeks at a country ale-house in the village of Weston Zoyland, that he might write his stirring and vivid description of the battle of Sedgemoor on the very spot, he devoted all his strength to more enduring work than Essays in the "Edinburgh Review." The first two volumes of *The History of England from the Accession of James the Second*, published in 1849, were received with an **1849** enthusiasm fully equal to the reception of Gibbon's A.D.

Decline and Fall. The plan was a great one. " I purpose to write the history of England from the accession of King James the Second down to a time which is within the memory of men still living," are the opening words of the opening chapter. He has brought the work down only to the death of William the Third, and that with gaps in the concluding and imperfect volume. We cannot say that a History from the time of James the Second down to the battle of Waterloo or the death of blind old King George, written by so great a pen within the compass of half-a-dozen volumes, would have been a book of little interest to the general reader, for we know what brilliant summaries of historical periods, all glowing with colour and filled with life, the Essayist has given us ; but a summarized History would greatly lack the charm with which the volumes of Macaulay enchain us, as we pass in review the panorama of court and camp and council-room and country-house, unfolded to our delighted gaze. To condense the Rebellion of Monmouth, the Trial of the Bishops, the Siege of Derry, the Battle of the Boyne, or the Massacre of Glencoe into fewer pages, would be to squeeze out most of the splendid colouring that reminds us of Titian or Tintoretto, and scatter to the winds those little traits of personal appearance and individual action—those glimpses of weather, scenery, costume, and domestic life—which make authentic history read, in his pictured pages, like a tale of romance. One of Macaulay's favourite maxims—how greatly in description the particular excels the general—is finely exemplified by all his writings. The third and fourth volumes of the History were published in 1855. Cartloads of copies left the publisher's ware-room, and the presses could hardly work quick enough to keep pace with the demand. The last volume, published in the present year (1861), is formed of such manuscripts as were found among his papers after death, partly revised, partly in original roughness (which, however, surpasses the elaborate smoothness of most other men). The Death-bed of Dutch William is the last scene described; but the narrative of the fifth volume is not continuous, it being wisely thought better to leave the fragments as the dead artist's hand had left them, than to link these fragments together with pieces of inferior workman-ship.

The first chapter of this noble work contains a rapid but masterly view of earlier English history, becoming more detailed and pic-turesque as that period of which Cromwell is the central figure widens on the historian's view. The second chapter depicts the shameful reign of the second Charles. The third—among all, most characteristic of Macaulay's historical treatment—shows us the cabbages and gooseberry bushes growing close to the country squire's hall door in 1685 ; leads us through the shrub-wood, with here and there a woodcock, which covered the site of now brilliant, busy Regent Street; introduces us to the literary gossips at Will's Coffee-house, and the grave surgeons who clustered round Garra-way's tables; carries us in a Flying Coach at the wonderful rate of forty miles a day along roads thick with quagmires and infested with highwaymen ; brings us even into the crowded jails, festering with dirt, disease, and crime;—gives us, in short, such a picture of old England in the days of the Stuarts as no writer had ever given us before. From novels, plays, pictures, maps, poems, diaries, letters, and a hundred other such sources, with patient industry he collected his materials for this remarkable view of English life. Then, after an overture so magnificent, the brilliant drama, on which the black curtain fell sadly soon, opens with the death of King Charles the Second.

The slight put upon Macaulay by the electors of Edinburgh was somewhat atoned for in 1852, when they returned him as their member, although he issued no address and stooped to solicit no vote. For four years he continued to represent that city in Parliament; but his day of public life was nearly over,—he was fast breaking prematurely down. Resigning his seat in 1856, he entered the Upper House in the following year as Baron Macaulay of Rothley Temple, having received his peerage chiefly as a fitting tribute to his eminent literary merit. **1859** He wore the coronet little more than two years, dying on A.D. the 28th of December 1859.

We have spoken of Macaulay's prose. The little poetry he has left us affords almost equal delight, and is equally worthy of close and careful study. Having tried his youthful pen in the composition of stirring ballads from English and French history, such as *The Armada* and the *Battle of Ivry*, on his return from India he resumed this style in his noble *Lays of Ancient Rome*, which were published in 1842. The four Lays,—*Horatius Cocles, The Battle of Lake Regillus, Virginius,* and *The Prophecy of Capys*—are imaginative reproductions, in the English ballad style and measure, of those old songs which Niebuhr justly believes to have formed the early history of Rome. For marvellous power over the picturesque —a single line, sometimes even a single *word*, suggesting a landscape or a group—these Lays have never been surpassed by any poems of their kind. The free swing of the melody, streaming on in a rush of Saxon words, such as alone can trace vivid pictures on an English page, has a mingling of warlike fire, thoroughly in keeping with the character of the plain, hardy, bronze-cheeked, iron-limbed plebeians of the early Republic, who are supposed to listen to and be kindled by the song.

THE BURIAL-PLACE OF MONMOUTH.

In the meantime many handkerchiefs were dipped in the Duke's blood; for by a large part of the multitude he was regarded as a martyr, who had died for the Protestant religion. The head and body were placed in a coffin covered with black velvet, and were laid privately under the communion-table of Saint Peter's Chapel in the Tower. Within four years the pavement of the chancel was again disturbed; and hard by the remains of Monmouth were laid the remains of Jeffreys. In truth, there is no sadder spot on the earth than that little cemetery. Death is there associated not, as in Westminster Abbey and Saint Paul's, with genius and virtue, with public veneration and imperishable renown; not, as in our humblest churches and church-yards, with everything that is most endearing in social and domestic charities; but with whatever is darkest in human nature and in human destiny,—with the savage triumph of implacable enemies,—with the inconstancy, the ingratitude, the cowardice of friends,—with all the miseries of fallen greatness and of blighted fame. Thither have been carried, through successive ages, by the rude hands of gaolers, without one mourner following, the bleeding relics of men who had been the captains of armies, the leaders of parties, the oracles of senates, and the ornaments of courts. Thither was borne, before the window where Jane Grey was praying, the mangled corpse of Guilford Dudley. Edward Seymour, Duke of Somerset and Protector of the realm, reposes there by the brother whom he murdered. There has mouldered away the headless trunk of John Fisher, Bishop of Rochester and Cardinal of Saint Vitalis, a man worthy to have lived in a better age, and to have died in a better cause. There are laid John Dudley, Duke of Northumberland, Lord High Admiral; and Thomas Cromwell, Earl of Essex, Lord High Treasurer. There, too, is another Essex, on whom nature and fortune had lavished all their bounties in vain, and whom valour, grace, genius, royal favour, popular applause, conducted to an early and ignominious doom. Not far off sleep two chiefs of the great house of Howard, Thomas, fourth Duke of Norfolk, and Philip, eleventh Earl of Arundel. Here and there, among the thick graves of unquiet and aspiring statesmen, lie more delicate sufferers; Margaret of Salisbury, the last of the proud name of Plantagenet, and those two fair Queens who perished by the jealous rage of Henry. Such was the dust with which the dust of Monmouth mingled.

CHAPTER VI.

SHERIDAN KNOWLES.

Born 1784 A.D.........Died 1862 A.D.

The modern drama.	Chief plays.
Early life.	Pensioned.
Hazlitt's help.	Preaching.
Goes on the stage.	Poetic style.
At Waterford.	Illustrative extract.

ALTHOUGH the English drama has fallen from its high estate, a few men still remind us in this nineteenth century that we are the countrymen of Shakspere, of Jonson, and of Massinger. Among such may be named Sheridan Knowles, the author of *Virginius;* Henry Taylor, the author of *Philip van Artevelde;* and Thomas Noon Talfourd, the author of *Ion.* That dramatic writing may not be entirely without a representative name in this last era of our literary history, we take the first and most prolific of these dramatists as the subject of a brief sketch.

James Sheridan Knowles was born in the year 1784, in Anne Street, Cork. His father was an English master and teacher of elocution there. During the boyhood of the dramatist the family removed to London, where the spirit of poetry began to stir in his heart, when he was about twelve years old. Writing a play for his boy friends, he conducted the performance himself. Then came from the new-fledged pen an opera, a ballad called *The Welsh Harper,* and a Spanish tragedy. But what more than all gave the genius of young Knowles its decided literary bent, was the notice with which the distinguished critic Hazlitt honoured him. Many a clever boy has written plays and poems at twelve or fourteen without turning out a Sheridan Knowles. Hazlitt, however, brought the boy to his house, made him known to Coleridge and to Lamb, and did him the invaluable kindness of criticising his juvenile productions, and cultivating his dramatic tastes.

It was in the Crow Street Theatre of Dublin that Knowles made his *début* upon the stage. He did not take with the audience; in fact, his first appearance was an utter failure. Yet we find him persevering in his efforts to be an actor; and it was well for his fame that he did persevere, for his stage-experience must have greatly aided him in the preparation of his popular dramas. Conjoining, as did his far greater prototype Shakspere, the occupations of actor and dramatic author, he knew, from daily habit and observation, what was required to make a play *tell* upon the house. None but a practical teacher can produce a thoroughly good and useful school-book; and, granting him to possess the requisite brains, we may reasonably expect the actor to produce a more effective play than the working lawyer, or the author who never leaves his desk.

In a theatrical company at Waterford, to which Knowles was for some time attached, he met Edmund Kean, who filled the principal part in his first-acted play, called *Leo the Gipsy*. There, too, the publication of a small volume of poems, entitled *Fugitive Pieces*, brought the literary struggler a little money and some reputation.

But Belfast was the opening scene of his decided success in the walk he had chosen. While engaged there as a teacher of elocution and grammar, he produced a drama called *Brian Boroihme*, which was received in the local theatre with enthusiastic applause.

And then came the first of his great plays, *Caius Gracchus*. **1815** Spurred on by success, for which he had long been bat- A.D. tling and hoping, he continued his dramatic authorship.

Virginius was the next production of his facile pen. Though offered to Kean—indeed it is said to have been written at his request—it was not first acted at Drury Lane, but came out under less favourable auspices in Glasgow. There it had a most successful run. Macready soon got hold of it, studied it, played it, and made his own fortune and the fame of Knowles. According to the opinion of Hazlitt, the author's old friend and mental father—

no mean authority on a point of dramatic criticism—"Virginius" was Macready's greatest character. *William Tell; The Beggar of Bethnal Green; The Hunchback; The Wife, a Tale of Mantua; Love;* and several other popular and successful plays, added, during the next twenty-three years, to the fame that Knowles had already won. In many of these he played the leading character himself. Crossing the Atlantic in 1836, he found in America the warmest welcome and the kindest appreciation of his professional talent.

When his health began to fail, application having been made to the Government by a number of dramatic authors, and also by some Glasgow merchants, a pension of £200 a year was granted to him in 1849.

Since the close of his professional life he has. written a couple of novels, of which we shall say no more than that they are unworthy of his earlier fame; and has also displayed his controversial power in two works, *The Rock of Rome,* and *The Idol Demolished by its own Priest.* So long as his health permitted, he acted in his later years as a lay preacher of the Baptist persuasion; and after some time of decaying strength he died at Torquay in 1862.

The dramatic style of Sheridan Knowles was modelled after the Elizabethan plays, especially those of Philip Massinger. And here, with all our admiration for the effectiveness and artistic construction of *Virginius* and *Tell,* we must confess that the model seems at times to peep out too plainly, and that we would rather have Knowles writing in his own proper and natural manner than be obliged to look upon him sometimes as a second-hand Massinger, revived on the stage of the nineteenth century, but speaking after the fashion of those days when the *Globe* and the *Rose* were in all their primitive glory. The poetry of Knowles is not of the intense school, but "sparkles through his plays, mildly and agreeably; seldom impeding with useless glitter the progress and development of incident and character, but mingling itself with them, and raising them pleasantly above the prosaic level of common life."

FROM "WILLIAM TELL."

Scaling yonder peak,
I saw an eagle wheeling near its brow,
O'er the abyss.   His broad expanded wings
Lay calm and motionless upon the air,
As if he floated there, without their aid,
By the sole act of his unlorded will,
That buoyed him proudly up.   Instinctively
I bent my bow : yet kept he rounding still
His airy circle, as in the delight
Of measuring the ample range beneath
And round about ; absorbed, he heeded not
The death that threatened him.   I could not shoot—
'Twas Liberty ! I turned my bow aside,
And let him soar away.
            Heavens ! with what pride I used
To walk these hills, and look up to my God,
And think the land was free.   Yes, it was free—
From end to end, from cliff to lake, 'twas free—
Free as our torrents are that leap our rocks
And plough our valleys without asking leave ;
Or as our peaks that wear their caps of snow
In very presence of the regal sun.
How happy was I then ! I loved
Its very storms.   Yes, I have often sat
In my boat at night, when midway o'er the lake—
The stars went out, and down the mountain-gorge
The wind came roaring.   I have sat and eyed
The thunder breaking from his cloud, and smiled
To see him shake his lightnings o'er my head,
And think I had no master save his own.
—On the wild jutting cliff, o'ertaken oft
By the mountain-blast, I've laid me flat along ;
And while gust followed gust more furiously,
As if to sweep me o'er the horrid brink,
Then I have thought of other lands, whose storms
Are summer flaws to those of mine, and just
Have wished me there ;—the thought that mine was free
Has checked that wish ; and I have raised my head,
And cried in thraldom to that furious wind,
Blow on !—this is the land of Liberty !

CHAPTER VII.

ALFRED TENNYSON.

Born 1810 A.D.................Still living, 1869 A.D.

Tennyson's fame.	Poems of '42.	Made Laureate.
Timbuctoo.	The Princess.	Maud.
First publications.	In Memoriam.	Idylls of the King.
Poems of '33.	A change of scene.	Illustrative extract.

NOT always has the Laurel been given to him most worthy of
that royal honour; but when the reverend brow of Wordsworth
drooped in death, there was none fitter to succeed " the old man
eloquent" than the English gentleman who now wears the wreath.
By consent of all, Alfred Tennyson stands at the head of English
poets in the passing generation.   In his own department of literature he is the representative man of the age—caressed by critics,
admired by all, imitated by not a few.   Rare are the poems published now-a-days untouched with the light of this master-mind,
whose pure and steady radiance has been diffusing itself in ever-
widening circles for more than thirty years.

A Lincolnshire clergyman, rector of Somersby, had three
sons—Frederick, Charles, and Alfred.   All have written poetry,
the third and greatest of the three being the present Laureate.
Tennyson's poetic career may be said to have begun in 1829,
when, as an undergraduate of Trinity College, Cambridge, he won
the Chancellor's medal for a poem in English blank-verse upon
the somewhat unpromising theme of *Timbuctoo.*   About the same
time he joined his brother Charles in the publication of *Poems
by two Brothers.*

But in 1830 a bolder step was taken.   A Cornhill publisher
announced a modest volume, bearing on its title-page the
1830   words *Poems, chiefly Lyrical, by Alfred Tennyson,* in which
A.D.   such pieces as *Mariana in the Moated Grange, Claribel,*
and *The Ballad of Oriana,* showed that a minstrel of brilliant

promise was trying his 'prentice hand upon the lyre of English song.

Undaunted by the frigid reception of his first venture, Tennyson published a second volume in 1833, containing, besides corrected reprints of some former poems, many new compositions, which marked a striking advance both in thought and style. Those who then read for the first time *The Lady of Shalott*, *The Miller's Daughter*, *Ænone*, *The Lotus Eaters*, and, above all, *The Queen of the May*, an exquisitely touching picture of a pretty wilful village girl fading away amid the brightening blossoms of an English spring, felt that a new well of poetic thought had burst out to gladden and make green the arid roads of modern life. One part of a poet's lofty mission is to battle with that tendency to the common-place and the matter-of-fact, which belongs to a money-getting age, by affording such nutriment to the imagination as may keep its fair shoots from withering away in the hot and dusty struggle of our daily lives. And no English poet of modern days has more nobly fulfilled this exalted function than he who has given us the sweet fruits of genius that have just been named.

The critics of 1833 were unkind and unjust to the youthful singer; and for nine years the sweet voice was silent. But it was not the silence of an idle life. *Locksley Hall* was unfolding its pathetic and passionate beauty. *The Gardener's Daughter* and *Dora* were budding into life. *Lady Clara Vere de Vere*, one of the sternest rebukes ever levelled at the cold arrogance and deadly cruelty of high-born beauty, was in preparation. And such fragmentary poems as *Morte d'Arthur* and *Godiva*, dealing with the chivalrous and feudal times of old England, were giving earnest of what the minstrel might do in some future day, should he choose his theme from that dim past, through whose mists we see in broken outline, with here and there a glimpse of brilliant colour shining through a rift, confused groups of giant men, whose life was summed up in the battle, the tilt-yard, the chase, and the carouse. When in 1842 appeared two volumes, containing the poems to which we have referred with many others of remark-   **1842** able beauty, the victory was won. Another King Alfred   **A.D.**

was crowned in England, whose realm has wider bounds and whose sceptre has another power than the sceptre and the realm of the illustrious Saxon.

Tennyson's next work was published in 1847,—a fanciful poem of the epic class, written in blank-verse, entitled *The Princess, a Medley*. At a little pic-nic on the grassy turf within a ruin, seven college men tell the tale in turn, and

> " The women sang
> Between the rougher voices of the men,
> Like linnets in the pauses of the wind. "

A prince and princess are betrothed, but have never met. He loves the unseen beauty; she, influenced by two strong-minded widows, hates the thoughts of marriage, and founds a University for girls. Disguised in female dress, the prince and two friends don the academic robe of lilac silk, and mingle with the gentle under-graduates. All goes well—lectures are duly attended—until upon a geological excursion the princess falls into a whirling river, and is snatched from the brink of a cataract by her lover. The secret being thus discovered, the pretenders are expelled, in spite of a life saved. Then comes war between the kingdoms; the prince is struck senseless in the strife; and as Ida, the Head of the College, moves round the sick-bed, where he lies hovering between life and death, a new light dawns upon her. She begins to feel that the gentle ministrations of home are a fitter study for her sex than the quadrature of the circle or the properties of amygdaloid. By degrees

> " A closer interest flourished up,
> Tenderness touch by touch, and last, to these,
> Love, like an Alpine harebell hung with tears
> By some cold morning glacier; frail at first
> And feeble, all unconscious of itself,
> But such as gathered colour day by day. "

We never think of characterizing the poem by adjectives like "sublime" or "magnificent," for it pretends to no such qualities as these express. " Exquisite," " beautiful," " graceful," " tender," are rather the words we choose. A delicate playfulness runs through every page, like a golden thread through rich brocade. But with the sweet satiric touch there often mingles a tone of deep social wisdom, which exalts the poem far above mere prettiness. Some of the intervening lyrics are the perfection of lingual music, especially those lines descriptive of the dying echo of a bugle-note sounded amid the rocky shores of a lake.

Early in life a great sorrow had fallen upon Tennyson. Arthur Henry Hallam, the historian's son, who had been the poet's bosom friend at college and had been affianced to his sister, died in 1833 at Vienna. Stunned by the heavy blow, the surviving friend long refuses to be comforted; and the black shadow of the pall and the coffin broods upon his soul. But merciful time works its cure. The shadows turn grey, are touched with light, and at last roll off in golden clouds. "The sad mechanic exercise" of weaving verses in memory of his dead companion restores the mourner to himself, and brings him back to take renewed pleasure in the days that pass. But the gaiety of youth is gone; the graver brow and somewhat saddened voice tell of one who has **1850** drunk of that bitter cup, which Infinite Wisdom often pre- A.D. pares to purify the soul and fit it for higher deeds. Such were the circumstances in which this work—the history of a human sorrow—was composed. Not until 1850 did the group of poems, which, to the number of one hundred and twenty-nine, make up the tributary *In Memoriam*, appear in a printed volume. The stanza, in which all are written, is the well-known eight-syllabled quatrain; to which a very simple modification of rhyme, an exchange between the third and fourth lines, imparts an uncommon tone,—

> " I hold it true whate'er befall ;
> I feel it when I sorrow most ;
> 'Tis better to have loved and lost
> Than never to have loved at all."

The lost friend, dying at Vienna, was borne to England and buried in the chancel of Clevedon Church in Somersetshire. How beautifully these circumstances are woven together in the following lines, which condense in their simple language the spirit of all the scenery round that lonely tomb :—

> " The Danube to the Severn gave
>   The darkened heart that beats no more ;
>   They laid him by the pleasant shore,
> And in the hearing of the wave.
>
> There twice a day the Severn fills ;
>   The salt sea-water passes by,
>   And hushes half the babbling Wye,
> And makes a silence in the hills."

Tennyson's early life amid the fens of Lincolnshire and Cambridge led him to paint, in his earlier poems, the features of such landscapes as are common there. The barren moor—the tangled water-courses, embroidered with brilliant flowering weeds—the great mere, shimmering in the frosty moonlight—the pool, fringed with tall sword-grass and bristling with bulrushes, meet us continually in his first volumes. But his manhood has been spent in a different scene. At Farringford in the Isle of Wight, on the road from Alum Bay to Carisbrook, he has resided for many years, amid green undulating woodland, thick with apple-trees, and fringed with silver sand and snowy rocks, on which the light-green summer sea and the black waves of winter flow with the changeful music of their seasons. The landscape of southern England, where green and daisied downs take the place of the grey wolds to which his young eyes were accustomed, is often painted in his later works. Within his quiet home by the sea the stalwart, dark-bearded poet lives among his children and his books, strolling often, no doubt, beyond the privet-hedge that bounds his lawn and garden, but seeing little society except that of a few chosen friends.

When Wordsworth died in 1850, the vacant laurel was worthily conferred on the author of " Locksley Hall " and " The Princess." His *Ode on the Death of Wellington*, which is **1850** the chief work he has produced in his official capacity, A.D. though somewhat monotonous, sounds in many passages like the roll of the muffled drums that startle Nelson in his sleep beneath the pavement of St. Paul's, as the car of bronze bears a dead soldier to his side.

Maud and other Poems were published by Tennyson in 1855. "Maud" is scarcely so fine a work as many that preceded it from the same pen. A squire's daughter, wooed by a new-made lord, prefers another gentleman, who is somewhat of the Byronic stamp. The serenade or invocation, sung by the lover as he waits at dawn for Maud among the roses and lilies in the Hall garden, after the guests of the evening have gone, is full of passionate fire and delicacy of thought. In the duel, which results from the discovery of their meeting, Maud's brother is killed, and her sweetheart has to flee the land. The Crimean war is then hauled most incongruously into the dream,—for it is now the dream of a dead man,—and "the blood-red blossom of war with a heart of fire," flaming from the cannon's mouth, lights up the concluding scene of a wild, ill-jointed tale, rich, however, in such splendours of English expression as few but Tennyson can produce.

We now notice, very briefly, the Laureate's latest work, of his longer poems undoubtedly the best.* Turning his gaze back into that dim past from which he had already drawn one or two striking scenes, he reproduced the shadowy court at Caerleon, where King Arthur and his knights won their dusky-bright renown. He has succeeded admirably in setting before us the brilliant and the darker sides of that old and well-nigh for- **1859** gotten life, in the four tales which form *The Idylls of the* A.D. *King.* The delicate *Enid*, riding in her faded silk before her cruel lord,—the sweet and faithful *Elaine* gazing tenderly on the shield of her absent knight,—the crafty beauty, *Vivien*, weaving her spells round old wizard Merlin to shear him of his strength, and shrieking, as the forked lightning splinters an oak hard by,—and, finest picture of all, the guilty Queen Guinevere lying in an agony of remorse at the feet of Arthur, her tear-wet face crushed close to the convent floor, and her dark, dishevelled hair floating in the dust, while the noble forgiveness of the injured King and his sad farewell pierce her to the very soul,—these are the subjects of the song. The "Idylls" are in blank-

---

* We must look upon "In Memoriam" rather as a group of elegies—a funeral wreath of mingled asphodel and yew—than as a single poem.

verse, whose fine polish and sweetly-varied music prove the Laureate to be a consummate master of that noble instrument in skilful hands,—the English tongue.

Enoch Arden, a touching domestic story of humble life, has been the chief offspring of Tennyson's muse in recent years. The same volume contains *Aylmer's Field*, some minor poems of which the principal are *Tithonus* and the *Northern Farmer*, and a few *Experiments* in various metres unsuited to the genius of the English language.

MEETING OF ENID AND GERAINT.

(FROM "THE IDYLLS OF THE KING.")

Then rode Geraint into the castle court,
His charger trampling many a prickly star
Of sprouted thistle on the broken stones.
He looked, and saw that all was ruinous.
Here stood a shattered archway, plumed with fern ;
And here had fall'n a great part of a tower,
Whole, like a crag that tumbles from the cliff,
And, like a crag, was gay with wilding flowers :
And high above, a piece of turret stair,
Worn by the feet that now were silent, wound
Bare to the sun ; and monstrous ivy-stems
Claspt the grey walls with hairy-fibred arms,
And sucked the joining of the stones, and looked
A knot, beneath, of snakes,—aloft, a grove.

　　And while he waited in the castle court,
The voice of Enid, Yniol's daughter, rang
Clear through the open casement of the Hall,
Singing : and as the sweet voice of a bird,
Heard by the lander in a lonely isle,
Moves him to think what kind of bird it is
That sings so delicately clear, and make
Conjecture of the plumage and the form ;
So the sweet voice of Enid moved Geraint,
And made him like a man abroad at morn,
When first the liquid note beloved of men
Comes flying over many a windy wave
To Britain, and in April suddenly
Breaks from a coppice gemmed with green and red,
And he suspends his converse with a friend,
Or it may be the labour of his hands,

To think or say " There is the nightingale ;"
So fared it with Geraint, who thought and said,
"Here, by God's grace, is the one voice for me."
  It chanced the song that Enid sang was one
Of Fortune and her wheel, and Enid sang :

"Turn, Fortune, turn thy wheel and lower the proud ;
Turn thy wild wheel, through sunshine, storm, and cloud ;
Thy wheel and thee we neither love nor hate.

"Turn, Fortune, turn thy wheel with smile or frown ;
With that wild wheel we go not up or down ;
Our hoard is little, but our hearts are great.

"Smile, and we smile, the lords of many lands ;
Frown, and we smile, the lords of our own hands ;
For man is man, and master of his fate.

"Turn, turn thy wheel above the staring crowd ;
Thy wheel and thou are shadows in the cloud ;
Thy wheel and thee we neither love nor hate."

  " Hark ! by the bird's song you may learn the nest,"
Said Yniol ; "enter quickly." Entering then,
Right o'er a mount of newly-fallen stones,
The dusky-rafter'd, many-cobweb'd Hall,
He found an ancient dame in dim brocade ;
And near her, like a blossom vermeil-white,
That lightly breaks a faded flower-sheath,
Moved the fair Enid, all in faded silk,
Her daughter.

CHAPTER VIII.

CHARLES DICKENS.

Born 1812 A.D..........Still living, 1869 A.D.

Two great novelists.	The Pickwick Papers.	Later works.
Dickens' father.	Nicholas Nickleby.	Christmas stories.
The attorney's office.	Little Nell.	Ugly heroes.
Reporting.	In America.	His later style.
Sketches by Boz.	David Copperfield.	Illustrative extract.

THERE are two distinguished living authors, who divide the honour of being called, "First novelist of the day." Charles Dickens and William Makepeace Thackeray stand side by side on that proud eminence, each with his multitude of admirers; each striving with the other in a fair and generous rivalry; each more than willing to acknowledge how justly the applause of the nation, and those less evanescent fruits of literary toil, which chink and shine and fill the banker's book with figures, have fallen to the lot of his brother-artist. "I think of these past writers," said the present editor of the *Cornhill*, when lecturing to a London audience upon the Reverend Laurence Sterne, "and of one who lives amongst us now, and am grateful for the innocent laughter, and the sweet, unsullied page, which the author of "David Copperfield" gives to my children."

Though born at Landport, Portsmouth, where his father, John Dickens, who was connected with the Navy **1812** Pay Department, happened to be residing at the time, **A.D.** the celebrated novelist is essentially a London man; for thither the family removed upon the conclusion of the war. The pay-clerk having become a parliamentary reporter, young Charles grew up in an atmosphere likeliest of all to develop any literary tastes he possessed; for there are, perhaps, no men who acquire a truer and more intimate knowledge of public characters and new books than those who report for the London press.

When the fitting time came, Charles Dickens was placed by his father in an attorney's office ; but the occupation was very distasteful to the young man, who soon abandoned it for the more stirring life his father led. We cannot regret this little attempt upon a father's part to make his son take root in what he believed a safer soil, when we remember those fine pictures of middle-class lawyer-life, ranging from deepest tragedy to broad uproarious fun, which are scattered among the pages of "Pickwick."

After a short engagement on *The True Sun*, Dickens joined the staff of *The Morning Chronicle*, where he soon took a first rank among the reporters. He began to sketch upon paper the varied life he saw. The letter-box of a magazine—*The Old Monthly*, we believe—received one day a little manuscript, dropped in by a modest passer-by. With quickly beating heart the author of that slender scroll got hold of the fresh uncut serial, some time afterwards, and with a joy the author feels only once in life, saw himself in print. It was the first of those delightful *Sketches by Boz*,* which were soon transferred to the columns · of the *Chronicle*, and when the author's fame grew bright, were published in a separate form.

But the beginning of his fame dates from the publication of the unrivalled *Pickwick Papers*. The adventures and misadventures of a party of Cockney sportsmen formed the original idea of the book, as proposed by the publisher, and begun by Dickens. Boz was to write the chapters, and Seymour **1837** to furnish the illustrations. Glimpses of this original A.D. plan appear in Mr. Winkle's disastrous rook-shooting,— the ride and drive towards Dingley Dell,—the hot September day among the partridges, when Mr. Pickwick found the cold punch so very pleasant,—the skating scene at Manor Farm ; but as the work went on, the scope of the Papers expanded, both the sporting and the club being forgotten, or rarely referred to, in the varied

---

* Boz was a little sister's corruption of the name Moses, by which Dickens, whose young head was full of the "Vicar of Wakefield" and kindred works, used playfully to call his younger brother. It is pleasant to think that this novelist, who has depicted the quiet graces of an English home so tenderly and truthfully, should have taken the *nom de plume*, with which he signed his earliest papers, from the lispings of a little child.

pictures of life, through which we follow the fortunes of the kind old
bachelor, his three friends, and his attached servant,—the inimitable Sam Weller, an indescribable but perfectly natural compound
of Cockney slang and the coolest impudence, with rich ever-
bubbling humour and the tenderest fidelity.

Then followed *Nicholas Nickleby*, a tale crowded with finely
drawn portraits and scenes of modern English life; among which,
perhaps, the sojourn of Nicholas at the wretched Yorkshire school,
and his stay among the Portsmouth actors, are richest in character and colouring. This is generally looked upon as the finest
work from Dickens' pen.

While for a short time editor of "Bentley's Miscellany," he
contributed to its pages the striking story of *Oliver Twist*, in which
some of the lowest and vilest forms of London life are painted
with a startling truthfulness that rivals the pencil of Defoe. The
publication of "Nickleby" in monthly numbers—"putting forth
two green leaves a month," as the author expresses it in a pretty
botanical conceit—having proved very successful, a new work was
projected, to appear in the same form, and also in low-
1840   priced weekly numbers. This was *Master Humphrey's*
A.D.   *Clock*, a connected series of tales, among which there appeared *The Old Curiosity Shop*, and *Barnaby Rudge.*
The former of these—whose central figure, Little Nell, is one
of the most exquisite creations of modern fiction—contains
the finest writing that has ever come from this brilliant pen.
"Barnaby Rudge" is a tale of the last century, which mingles its
fictitious plot with the story of the Gordon Riots in London. A
wonderfully gifted raven plays no unimportant part in the stirring
drama.

A visit to America supplied material for two new works,—
American Notes for General Circulation, and *Martin*
1843   *Chuzzlewit*, a novel—in both of which he deals very
A.D.   severely with some peculiarities of Transatlantic life
and character; too severely, we may safely say, for the
tendency of Dickens in all his painting is towards caricature.
This fault is an outgrowth of his very power. Seizing in an

instant, with an intense abstraction, the odd feature or whimsical bent in any man or woman, he creates a character from that single quality, making his creation stand out in bright and startling relief as the type of a whole class. Among the English characters of Chuzzlewit, the scoundrel Pecksniff and the immortal Sairey Gamp are undoubtedly the most artistic and original.

After a twelvemonth in Italy, Dickens came home to establish and edit a morning paper, *The Daily News,* to which he contributed sketches entitled *Pictures from Italy.* But from this heavy, and to some extent thankless task, he soon returned to the more congenial field of fiction. *Dombey and Son,* the tale of a starched and purse-proud merchant, whose every thought is centred in the House (not of Commons, but of business); *David Copperfield,* the story of a young literary man struggling up to fame, as the author himself had done, through the thorny toils of short-hand notes ; and *Bleak House,* founded on the miseries of a suit in Chancery, came out in brilliant succession, to delight a million readers. "Copperfield" especially is prized as the finest of his later novels.

Upon the conclusion of "David Copperfield," Dickens undertook to conduct a weekly serial, called *Household Words,* which is now his own property, under the title of *All the* **1850** *Year Round.* To this he contributed *A Child's History* A.D. *of England,* giving a picturesque view of the national growth and fortunes. And soon after the conclusion of "Bleak House," he wrote for the same serial his tale of a Strike, called *Hard Times.*

Little Dorrit, depicting the touching devotion of a young girl to her selfish father, who is a prisoner for debt ; *A Tale of Two Cities* (London and Paris), filled with the horrors of the French Revolution ; *Great Expectations*—hinging upon the return of a convict; and *Our Mutual Friend,* are his recent works.

We should not forget, in reviewing the fruits of Dickens' busy pen, the charming series of Christmas tales which commenced in 1843 with *A Christmas Carol. The Chimes* and *The Cricket on the Hearth* are deservedly the most popular of these minor works, all of which, to be thoroughly enjoyed, should be read by the

cheery light of a Christmas fire, while the polished green and
vivid scarlet of the fresh holly boughs wink upon the parlour
wall, and the crisp snow sparkles out of doors in the frosty starlight. No finished portrait is Trotty Veck, but a slightly-filled
sketch,—what artists call a study,—yet who can forget or fail to
love the good old fellow?

On such a portrait Dickens loves to lavish his highest skill.
Choosing some character of the most unpromising outward
appearance—Smike, the starved, half-witted drudge of a Yorkshire
school; Pinch, the awkward, shambling assistant of a rascally
country architect; Ham, a rough, tar-splashed, weather-beaten
fisherman of Yarmouth; Joe, the huge, stout blacksmith, whose
dull brain can scarcely shape a thought clearly into words—he
makes us love them all, for the truth, the honesty, the sweet, guileless, forgiving spirit that lives within the ungainly frame. If
Dickens had done no more than create the Tom Pinch of "Chuzzlewit," and the blacksmith Joe of "Great Expectations," he deserves
lasting gratitude and fame. As the commonest weed, the meanest
reptile has its own beauty and its own use in the grand scheme of
Creation—as some delicate blossom or tender leaf nestles in the
nooks of every ruin, no matter how wildly or how long the storm
may have beaten on its walls, or how entirely defaced by war or
time the tracery of its stonework may have become—so man or
woman never falls so low, never grows so ugly or repulsive, never
is so thoroughly ridiculous or stupid, as utterly to lose the outlines
of that Divine image in which the ancient parents of the race were
created. And although we, with clay-dimmed eyes, cannot clearly
see why a man is ugly or a tree distorted, we must not forget
that the plainest face and the homeliest manner may cover a
noble intellect and a heart beating with tenderest pity and love
for humankind. Such we take to be the great moral of Dickens'
"sweet, unsullied page."

In some of his later works a slightly morbid desire for violent
effects has disfigured his plots and his style. He has become less
natural in colours and in grouping,—too violent in the former,
too theatrical in the latter. The rage for sensation-dramas,

for something more peppery and stimulating than a simple picture of human life, which has infected the modern stage, seems somewhat to have touched his pen. But that pen, in its own best vein, has lost none of its early power, as his latest tale has shown.

TIM LINKINWATER'S WINDOW.

(FROM "NICHOLAS NICKLEBY.")

"There is a double wall-flower at No. 6 in the court, is there?" said Nicholas.

"Yes, there is," replied Tim, "and planted in a cracked jug without a spout. There were hyacinths there this last spring, blossoming in—but you'll laugh at that, of course."

"At what?"

"At their blossoming in old blacking-bottles," said Tim.

"Not I, indeed," returned Nicholas.

Tim looked wistfully at him for a moment, as if he were encouraged by the tone of this reply to be more communicative on the subject; and sticking behind his ear a pen that he had been making, and shutting up his knife with a sharp click, said, "They belong to a sickly, bed-ridden, hump-backed boy, and seem to be the only pleasures, Mr. Nickleby, of his sad existence. How many years is it," said Tim, pondering, "since I first noticed him, quite a little child, dragging himself about on a pair of tiny crutches? Well! well! not many; but though they would appear nothing if I thought of other things, they seem a long, long time, when I think of him. It is a sad thing," said Tim, breaking off, "to see a little deformed child sitting apart from other children, who are active and merry, watching the games he is denied the power to share in. He made my heart ache very often."

"It is a good heart," said Nicholas, "that disentangles itself from the close avocations of every day, to heed such things. You were saying—"

"That the flowers belonged to this poor boy," said Tim, "that's all. When it is fine weather, and he can crawl out of bed, he draws a chair close to the window, and sits there looking at them, and arranging them all day long. We used to nod at first, and then we came to speak. Formerly, when I called to him of a morning, and asked him how he was, he would smile and say, 'Better:' but now he shakes his head, and only bends more closely over his old plants. It must be dull to watch the dark house-tops and the flying clouds for so many months; but he is very patient."

"Is there nobody in the house to cheer or help him?" asked Nicholas.

"His father lives there, I believe," replied Tim, "and other people too; but no one seems to care much for the poor sickly cripple. I have asked him very often if I can do nothing for him; his answer is always the same—'Nothing.' His voice has grown weak of late, but I can see that he makes the old reply. He can't leave his bed now, so they have moved it close beside the window; and there he lies all day, now looking at the sky, and now at his flowers, which he still makes shift to trim and water with his own thin hands. At night, when he sees my candle, he draws back his curtain, and leaves it so till I am in bed. It seems such company to him to know that I am there, that I often sit at my window for an hour or more, that he may see I am still awake ; and sometimes I get up in the night to look at the dull, melancholy light in his little room, and wonder whether he is awake or sleeping.

"The night will not be long coming," said Tim, "when he will sleep and never wake again on earth. We have never so much as shaken hands in all our lives, and yet I shall miss him like an old friend. Are there any country flowers that could interest me like these, do you think ? Or do you suppose that the withering of a hundred kinds of the choicest flowers that blow, called by the hardest Latin names that were ever invented, would give me one fraction of the pain that I shall feel when these old jugs and bottles are swept away as lumber. Country !" cried Tim, with a contemptuous emphasis ; "don't you know that I couldn't have such a court under my bed-room window anywhere but in London ?"

With which inquiry Tim turned his back, and pretending to be absorbed in his accounts, took an opportunity of hastily wiping his eyes, when he supposed Nicholas was looking another way.

CHAPTER IX.

WILLIAM MAKEPEACE THACKERAY.

Born 1811 A.D..........Died 1863 A.D.

Early life.	Pendennis.	The Virginians.
School and college.	English Humourists.	Editor of the Cornhill.
Writes for Fraser.	Henry Esmond.	Often abused.
Writes for Punch.	The Newcomes.	Character of his works.
Vanity Fair.	The Four Georges.	Illustrative extract.

THE author of *Vanity Fair* and *The Snobs of England* was born in 1811, at Calcutta. His father, descended from a good old Yorkshire family, held office in the Civil Service of the East India Company. The novelist was yet a very little child when that separation from his parents, which is the bitterest penalty attached to Indian life, took place. His own words give us a glimpse of the voyage to England. "Our ship touched at an island on the way home, where my black servant took me a walk over rocks and hills till we passed a garden where we saw a man walking. 'That is Bonaparte,' said the black: 'he eats three sheep every day and all the children he can lay his hands on.'" We can well imagine little fingers tightening round the dark hand that held them, as the pair hurried back to the ship and looks of terror glancing from the little white face back to the trees where this ogre lived.

The old Charter-house school, lovingly painted in more than one of his works, was the place of his education; and his name is the latest of those household words which that quiet cloister has given to the literature of England. After some time at Cambridge, where he did not stay to take a degree, he entered life, the heir to a fortune of many thousand pounds, resolved to devote himself to the easel and the brush. His studies in the art-galleries of Rome and some of the German cities, particularly Weimar, prepared him, unconsciously to himself, for that other painting—in pen and ink—to which his life was afterwards devoted.

The loss of a large part of his fortune made it necessary that he should be more than an amateur student of art. He entered at the Middle Temple, and began his literary career in the pages of "Fraser's Magazine." Month by month there appeared tales and sketches by Michael Angelo Titmarsh and George Fitz-boodle, Esquire; which, although slow in attracting general attention, caught the eye of such men as John Sterling, who saw in them the evidence of great talent in the bud. *The Hoggarty Diamond*, *The Paris Sketch-Book*, *The Chronicle of the Drum*, and *The Irish Sketch-Book* were among the first works of this artist-author's pencil. *Barry Lyndon*, the story of an Irish fortune-hunter, also appeared in "Fraser."

The columns of *Punch* were next enlivened by Thackeray's sketches; and no papers, in the formidable array of wit and fun, which for twenty years has been growing into volumes under the striped jacket of that distinguished criminal, have ever surpassed *Jeames's Diary*, or *The Snob Papers*. The former, inimitably rich in its spelling—which, whether the writer meant it or not, most delightfully exposes the absurdities of the *Phonetic* system— contains the history of a London flunkey, elevated to sudden wealth by speculation in railway shares. The latter, with a touch of light and seemingly careless banter, twitches the cloak from Humbug and Hypocrisy, especially as these wretched things are found in London clubs and drawing-rooms, and discloses them in all their ridiculous meanness to the scorn of honest men.

Then appeared Thackeray's first, and, in the eyes of many, his greatest novel, *Vanity Fair*. Running its course in serial numbers, it rapidly became a favourite. It was utterly unlike the fiction already on English tables. A very clever and thoroughly unprincipled governess, Becky Sharp, pushing and scheming her way into fashionable life, is certainly the heroine of the book. She personifies intellect without virtue.

1846
A.D.

Opposed to her is the sweet, amiable, pretty, but somewhat silly Amelia Sedley, who represents virtue without intellect. Pictures of Continental life mingle with London scenes; and especially we have a sketch of Brussels in those terrible days when

Waterloo thunder was in the air. Prominent among the portraitures of men in "Vanity Fair" are the fat Indian official, Jos. Sedley,
whose delicate health does not interfere with the play of his knife
and fork—the big, hulking dragoon, Rawdon Crawley, whose heart,
for all his nonsense, is in the right place — the empty dandy,
George, upon whom little Amelia wastes her sweetness—and the
unselfish and devoted William Dobbin, a kind of Tom Pinch in
regimentals.

The History of Arthur Pendennis, the second great work from
Thackeray's pen, followed in a short time. In the character of
Pendennis the novelist depicts a man full of faults and weaknesses,
who is acted on by the common influences of modern life.
Mrs. Pendennis, the hero's mother, and Laura, who, although   **1849**
too good for the scamp, finally becomes his wife, are the   A.D.
chief feminine portraits. The Major, a worldly old beau,
and that fine fellow, George Warrington, a literary man, who acts
as the good genius of Pen, are capitally drawn.

Six brilliant and appreciative *Lectures on the English Humourists of the Eighteenth Century*, dealing, among others, with Swift,
Pope, Addison, Steele, Hogarth, and Goldsmith, delighted a
fashionable London crowd at Willis's Rooms in 1851, and were
afterwards delivered by the author, both in Scotland and America.
They have since been printed, and have sold remarkably well.

Many of the literary men, whose books and manners Thackeray
discussed in the delightful gossip of these Lectures, mingle in the
mimic life of his next work, *The History of Henry Esmond, Esq.*
The days of Blenheim and Ramillies are revived. Swift, Congreve,
Addison, and Steele walk once more among men. Jacobites are
plotting for the return of those exiled princes who live across the
water. Queen Anne is on the English throne. As a work
of literary art, *Esmond* stands, perhaps, higher than either   **1852**
Vanity Fair or *The Newcomes*. The hero, who has long   A.D.
sought Beatrix Castlewood, a self-willed beauty, consoles
himself for rejection by a union with her mother, and settles down
in Virginia to write the story of his life. The novelist had a difficult task to accomplish in reconciling his readers to a plot so un-

common; but any slight revulsion of feeling which we experience at the change is amply atoned for by the eloquence of the book and its truthfulness as a piece of historical painting.

The Newcomes, Memoirs of a Most Respectable Family, edited by Arthur Pendennis, Esquire, appeared in monthly numbers, which completed their tale in 1855. The story is one of modern life. And, in all the range of fiction, nothing goes deeper to the heart than the affecting spectacle of that true gentleman, and **1855** gentlest man, old Colonel Newcome, lying, after a life of A.D. virtue and devotion, on a poor death-bed within the gloom of the old Charter-house. Amid a crowd of new and striking characters, we find here a 'lovely picture of womanhood in the sweet Ethel Newcome.

The success of the " English Humourists" induced the lecturer to try his pen a second time in this attractive field. Continuing those light and graceful sketches of later English history which form the ground-work of " Esmond," he produced a series of lectures on *The Four Georges*, which he delivered first in the States, then in London, and afterwards in several leading cities of Great Britain. These lectures have since appeared in the " Cornhill Magazine." The darker side of the Germanized English Court is here depicted. He tells with great pathos the domestic tragedy of poor old " Farmer George," third of the name, closing the sorrowful story with a passage in his own peculiar vein, full of mournful beauty and deep feeling. But the son of that blind, insane, deaf old king is treated with such contemptuous sarcasm—such fine-pointed, piercing irony, as a Thackeray alone can sprinkle or fling upon his victim. All the poor paints and feathers, in which this royal character is tricked out in contemporary books and records of his reign, shrivel and drop under the fluid flame ; and the man, poor and miserable and naked, stands disclosed to view.

The Virginians, a continuation of " Esmond," founded like **1857** that work on an historical basis, began to appear towards A.D. the close of 1857. The story embraces pictures of life in England during the reign of George the Second, and places before us the literary men and wits who thronged the coffee-houses of that time. The American War forms a part of the historical ground-work of the plot.

Nine years ago the "Cornhill Magazine" was started, with Thackeray as its editor. If his position in English letterdom had been a doubtful one, the splendid success of that serial would at once have dissolved all doubts. The circulation of the second number exceeded one hundred thousand; nor was this sudden leap over the heads of all other serials of the day a mere spasmodic effort— the sudden soaring of a blazing rocket which comes down a blackened stick. The position quickly won has been steadily maintained. In addition to his editorial duties, Mr. Thackeray contributed largely to the pages of his magazine. A short story, called *Lovel the Widower*, rather confused in its plot, and somewhat unpleasant in its heroine, yet bearing witness to the undiminished brilliance of his pen; a novel, entitled *Philip*, which ranks among his finest picturing of life and character; and those queer, delightful, rambling, thoroughly Thackerayesque *Roundabout Papers*, which many abuse but all delight in—frolics of genius "wandering at its own sweet will" through all wildernesses of topics, past and present,—were his chief works after he undertook the literary management of the "Cornhill." This eminent novelist died suddenly in his bedroom in London on the Christmas Eve of 1863.

Thackeray had his full share of abuse; but he lived, or rather wrote it down. "He sees no good in man," cried one. "Cold, sneering cynic," says another. "*Vanitas Vanitatum*, and never another theme." Cries like these, which have all but died away, were evoked by the author's earlier works, in which he devoted his pen rather to the humiliation of empty pride and the destruction of those *shams* which flourish thickly in the atmosphere of London fashion, than to the direct inculcation of virtue by the creation of virtuous models. His genius resembles some tart and sparkling wine, which has ripened with age into a mellow cordial —golden, sweet, and strong. His later works, though somewhat less pungent, possess a deeper human wisdom and a sunnier glow of benevolence.

His language is fresh and idiomatic English, abounding in the better coinage from the mint of *slang*, though never descending to its baser metals. Words that would have shocked Dr. Johnson, and which still startle gentlemen of the old school by their direct expressiveness, rise to his pen continually. And he talks to his readers out of the pleasant page he gives them with a playful, genial artlessness, which not unfrequently changes to a sudden shower of sharp, satiric hits. That which especially distinguishes his works, among the crowd of English novels that load our shelves and tables, lies in his portrayal of human character *as it is*. Painting men and women as he meets them at dinner or watches them in the park, he gives us no paragons of perfection—forms of exquisite beauty enshrining minds of unsullied purity, or that opposite ideal so familiar to the readers of romance —but men and women, with all their faults and foibles, with their modest virtues shrinking from exhibition, or their meanness well deserving the censor's lash. Illustrations by himself adorn all his larger works, displaying the same tendency to teach by apparent fun-making, and the same dislike of the conventional, which pervade the letter-press. No stranger pencil could so well convey the spirit of that delicate irony and sparkling banter which flow freely from Thackeray's pen.

DEATH OF GEORGE THE THIRD.

(FROM "THE FOUR GEORGES.")

All the world knows the story of his malady: all history presents no sadder figure than that of the old man, blind and deprived of reason, wandering through the rooms of his palace, addressing imaginary parliaments, reviewing fancied troops, holding ghostly courts. I have seen his picture as it was taken at this time, hanging in the apartment of his daughter, the Landgravine of Hesse Hombourg—amidst books and Windsor furniture, and a hundred fond reminiscences of her English home. The poor old father is represented in a purple gown, his snowy beard falling over his breast—the star of his famous Order still idly shining on it. He was not only sightless—he became utterly deaf. All light, all reason, all sound of human voices, all the pleasures of this world of God, were taken from him. Some slight lucid moments he had; in one of which the queen, desiring to see him, entered the room, and found him singing a hymn, and accompanying himself at the harpsichord. When he had finished, he knelt down and prayed aloud for her, and then for his family, and then for the nation, concluding with a prayer for himself, that it might please God to avert his heavy calamity from him, but if not, to give him resignation to submit. He then burst into tears, and his reason again fled.

What preacher need moralize on this story; what words save the simplest are requisite to tell it? It is too terrible for tears. The thought of such a misery smites me down in submission before the Ruler of kings and men, the Monarch Supreme over empires and republics, the inscrutable Dispenser of life, death, happiness, victory. " O brothers," I said to those who heard me first in America—" O brothers! speaking the same dear mother tongue—O comrades! enemies no more, let us take a mournful hand together as we stand by this royal corpse, and call a truce to battle! Low he lies to whom the proudest used to kneel once, and who was cast lower than the poorest: dead, whom millions prayed for in vain. Driven off his throne; buffeted by rude hands; with his children in revolt; the darling of his old age killed before him untimely; our Lear hangs over her breathless lips and cries, ' Cordelia, Cordelia, stay a little!'

> Vex not his ghost—oh! let him pass—he hates him
> That would upon the rack of this tough world
> Stretch him out longer!'

Hush, Strife and Quarrel, over the solemn grave! Sound, Trumpets, a mournful march. Fall, Dark Curtain, upon his pageant, his pride, his grief, his awful tragedy!"

CHAPTER X.

THOMAS CARLYLE.

Born 1795 A.D..........Still living, 1869 A.D.

Thinking in German.	Sartor Resartus.	Latter-Day Pamphlets.
Early life.	French Revolution.	Life of Sterling.
Literary start.	Lecturing.	Frederick the Great.
Craigenputtoch.	Carlyle's Cromwell.	Illustrative extract.

IT has been said that Thomas Carlyle thinks in German; which, without looking too closely into its metaphysical accuracy, may be accepted as a brief character of his remarkable mind. From the leading German writers his thoughts have caught their deepest colouring, and his style some of its most startling qualities. No English classic possesses a more strongly marked individuality on paper than does this latest of the great names of our varied and wealthy literature.

Born on the 4th of December 1795, in the parish of Middlebie in Dumfries-shire, he enjoyed the incalculable blessing of wise and pious parents in that honest farmer and farmer's wife whom he called father and mother. After attending school at Annan he passed to the University of Edinburgh, where his earnest mind was devoted chiefly to mathematical studies under Leslie. The thoughtful student became for a while a teacher, as mathematical master in a Fifeshire school, and afterwards as tutor to Charles Buller. His parents had destined him for the Church. But neither the school-room nor the pulpit was his fitting sphere. Literature soon attracting him with resistless power, he began that career of authorship which has placed his name among the first in English literature.

Some short biographies for Brewster's "Edinburgh Encyclopædia," among which were *Montesquieu, Montaigne,*
1823 *Nelson, The Pitts*—a translation of *Legendre's Geometry*
A.D.   —and, more important than any of these, as an early

indication of the future direction of his thoughts, a translation of *Goëthe's Wilhelm Meister*,—were the literary labours of 1823, his first year of pen-work.

A *Life of Schiller*, published by scattered chapters in the "London Magazine," and afterwards enlarged, was the second fruit of this Scottish sapling grafted upon German thought. It appeared in 1825 as a separate volume. During the same year the author became a married man with other resources than those of brain and pen.

For several years Craigenputtoch, a small estate about fifteen miles north-west of Dumfries,—a patch of corn-land nestling among trees in the middle of the black Galloway moors,—was the congenial home of this great man, whose mind, prone by nature and by habit to dwell apart, "wrapped in the solitude of its own originality," flamed out occasionally from its hermit-cell upon the *shams* and *flunkeyism* of that seething world, whose roar lay beyond the swelling granite hills. In this lonely nook he wrote several things for the Reviews, among which *Characteristics* and *Burns* in the "Edinburgh," and *Goëthe* in the "Foreign Quarterly," are notable. His estimate of Burns is remarkable for its sympathetic justice, and its straightforward recognition in the poet of a true manhood, swathed in wretched environments. And not less is it remarkable as our finest specimen of Carlyle's earlier manner, before he had laid aside the conventional forms of English speech for that language of splintered fire, rapid and sudden as the forked lightning, and often as jagged too, which we find in his later works.

But *Sartor Resartus* (The Patcher Repatched) was the principal result of the quiet thoughtfulness—by study-fire or on pony's back—to which the Craigenputtoch life was chiefly given up. Professing to be a review of a German work on dress, it is in reality a philosophical essay, illustrating in a very original and powerful style the transcendentalism of Fichte. Professor Diogenes Teufelsdröckh is the imaginary mouthpiece, through which Carlyle inveighs against the old clothes of falsehood and conventionalism that smother and conceal a Divine idea lying wrapped in the centre of our human life. So odd the subject and apparently grotesque the style, that London publishers looked very shy at the offered manuscript, which could find its way to the public only in fragments through the pages of "Fraser's Magazine" (1833–34).

The year 1837 is the central point in Carlyle's literary life, for then appeared *The French Revolution, a History*, written as no history had ever been written before. All the scenes in that wonderful tale of blood and tears flash out upon our gaze, as we read, with a startling vividness and distinctness of outline, entirely unlike the way in which the stately pictures of Gibbon and Macaulay grow upon the unfolding canvas, and thoroughly in keeping with the wild hurry and seeming disjointedness of the tumultuous time. Carlyle's pen has not yet outdone this brilliant historic piece. But it must not be forgotten, that those who wish to know *all* the *minutiæ* of the French Revolu-

1837 tion, must supplement their reading of Carlyle's "History"

A.D. with the study of calmer works, which aim, not so much at fixing on the mind with bright sun-darts a succession of indelible photographs, as at heaping together with quiet and careful industry all the details of the tremendous drama. Defiant of critical canons, and regarding that stately pomp of diction which some think "the dignity of history" requires, as an intolerable sham, this hater of old clothes works out his own ideas in his own way—paints with a brush of daring lawlessness—is minute at one time, even to the wart on a hero's eyebrow, at another so broad in his treatment that a single dash of colour depicts a man—violates every propriety of conventional art, historical perspective excepted—fills his pages with abrupt and startling apostrophes—often flings together a bundle of words, which, upon cool analysis, we find to be a mass of disjointed notes—drives at full swing through all school-notions of logical order and grammatical arrangement, scattering right and left into ignominious exile nominatives and verbs, articles and pronouns,—and yet strikes so surely to the brain and heart, that his pictures, printed with an instantaneous flash, live on the mental retina for ever.

The delivery of certain courses of Lectures on *German Litera-*

ture,—*The Revolutions of Modern Europe,*—and *Heroes, Hero-Worship, and the Heroic in History* (1840), combined with the production of a tract on *Chartism* (1839) and an historical contrast, entitled *Past and Present* (1843), filled up eight years between the publication of the " French Revolution " and the appearance of a second great work.

That work is entitled *The Letters and Speeches of Oliver Cromwell, with Elucidations.* A vast heap of materials, collected with painful patience from all sources, " fished up," as the collector tells us, " from foul Lethean quagmires, and washed clean from foreign stupidities—such a job of buck-washing as I do not long to repeat,"—was given to the world in fair order and modernized form, the great Puritan being made to speak from the dead past with his own voice and pen. This book, however, is no mere edition of Cromwell's works. What he modestly calls " Elucidations," the setting of these rough recovered gems, are brilliant specimens of Carlyle's historic style. His portraiture of the great Oliver, and his battle-piece of Dunbar, are well worthy **1845** of the pencil which drew Mirabeau and Marie Antoin- **A.D.** ette, the storming of the Bastille, and the shrill drum-led march of the Paris women to Versailles. That *substratum* of the Puritan or old Covenanter in his character, to which Leigh Hunt and Hannay make allusion, kindled into volcanic flame when Cromwell formed his theme. He is, indeed, himself a literary Cromwell, waging sternest war with all the force of an earnest soul against modern humbug, untruth, and noisy pretension. No wonder that this soldier of the pen, among the stanchest of our century, looking back across two hundred years of history, should recognise natural royalty in the craggy brow, solid frame, and iron soul of a Huntingdon farmer who could lead armies to certain triumph and dissolve a senate with the stamping of his foot. An electric sympathy linked the two : true manhood sharpened Cromwell's sword and true manhood guides Carlyle's pen.

The toppling thrones and surging peoples of the disastrous year 1848 stirred the impulsive oracle to a vehement utterance. The *Latter-Day Pamphlets* (1850) assailed with most galling invec-

tive and contemptuous ridicule the leading politicians and institutions of the country. The hollowness of great men and
the servility of small are lashed with a furious, stinging whip, whose
thongs, steeped in the salt of grim fantastic wit, cut and smart
to the very bone. Yet many blows are too fierce, too sweeping,
and many fall harmless upon sound and honest things.

His *Life of John Sterling* (1851), a brilliant Essayist who had
conducted the "Athenæum" for a while, and who died prematurely
in 1844, grew out of his dissatisfaction with the picture which Archdeacon Hare had given of the free-thinking curate. It is a fine
specimen of literary skill; but the sympathy which the writer
shows for the loose religious views of his friend has been heavily
blamed.

During recent years Mr. Carlyle, residing chiefly at Chelsea,
has been employed upon *The History of Friedrich II., called
Frederick the Great*. This stern soldier has been chosen as the
hero of a new work, not because the historian believes him to
have been a truly great man, but because he managed *not* to be
a liar and a charlatan, as his century was." Frederick and Voltaire
are the types of action and of thought in the eighteenth
1858 century. In 1858 the first and second volumes of
A.D.   "Frederick" appeared; but they were only preliminary
to the greater story of his reign, bringing his life
through a tangled thicket of Brandenburg and Hohenzollern
genealogy, up to the death, in 1740, of his bearish old father,
Friedrich Wilhelm. Mr. Carlyle visited the leading battle-fields
of the Seven Years' War, while collecting material for the concluding volumes of his History. Though inferior to his *French
Revolution*, this work presents here and there pictures coloured
with that lawless but potent brilliance, that wild, abrupt, impulsive
touch, which distinguish this master's style from that of all other
writers of English. Clarendon nor Gibbon nor Macaulay, all
great masters of the historic pencil and well skilled in the portraiture of men, can scarcely match, can certainly not overmatch,
that image of the great Frederick—the very Fritz himself—that
starts to life in the opening pages of Carlyle's latest work.

PORTRAIT OF FREDERICK THE GREAT.

He is a king every inch of him, though without the trappings of a king. Presents himself in a Spartan simplicity of vesture: no crown, but an old military cocked hat—generally old, or trampled and kneaded into absolute *softness* if new; no sceptre but one like Agamemnon's, a walking-stick cut from the woods, which serves also as a riding-stick (with which he hits the horse "between the ears," say authors) ; and for royal robes, a mere soldier's blue coat with red facings,— coat likely to be old, and sure to have a good deal of Spanish snuff on the breast of it ; rest of the apparel dim, unobtrusive in colour or cut, ending in high over-knee military boots, which may be brushed (and, I hope, kept soft with an underhand suspicion of oil), but are not permitted to be blackened or varnished, --Day and Martin with their soot-pots forbidden to approach. The man is not of god-like physiognomy, any more than of imposing stature or costume : close-shut mouth with thin lips, prominent jaws and nose, receding brow, by no means of Olympian height ; head, however, is of long form, and has superlative gray eyes in it. Not what is called a beautiful man ; nor yet, by all appearance, what is called a happy. On the contrary, the face bears evidence of many sorrows, as they are termed, of much hard labour done in this world ; and seems to anticipate nothing but more still coming. Quiet stoicism, capable enough of what joys there were, but not expecting any worth mention ; great unconscious and some conscious pride, well tempered with a cheery mockery of humour, are written on that old face, which carries its chin well forward, in spite of the slight stoop about the neck ; snuffy nose, rather flung into the air, under its old cocked hat, like an old snuffy lion on the watch ; and such a pair of eyes as no man, or lion, or lynx of that century bore elsewhere, according to all the testimony we have. "Those eyes," says Mirabeau, "which, at the bidding of his great soul, fascinated you with seduction or with terror." Most excellent, potent, brilliant eyes, swift-darting as the stars, steadfast as the sun ; gray, we said, of the azure-gray colour ; large enough, not of glaring size ; the habitual expression of them vigilance and penetrating sense, rapidity resting on depth. Which is an excellent combination, and gives us the notion of a lambent outer radiance, springing from some great inner sea of light and fire in the man. The voice, if he speak to you, is of similar physiognomy : clear, melodious, and sonorous ; all tones are in it, from that of ingenuous inquiry, graceful sociality, light-flowing banter (rather prickly for most part), up to definite word of command, up to desolating word of rebuke and reprobation.

CHAPTER XI.

OTHER WRITERS OF THE NINTH ERA.

POETS.

Thomas Hood.
David Macbeth Moir.
Miss Landon.
Thomas Aird.
Hon. Mrs. Norton.
Mrs. Browning.
Robert Browning.
William E. Aytoun.
Philip Bailey.
Sydney Dobell.
Alexander Smith.
  Supplementary List.

DRAMATISTS.

Sir Thomas Talfourd.
Henry Taylor.
  Supplementary List.

HISTORIANS & BIOGRAPHERS.

Sir Archibald Alison.
George Grote.
Thomas Arnold.
Bishop Thirlwall.
Sir Francis Palgrave.
John Gibson Lockhart.
John Forster.
George Henry Lewes.
David Masson.
Henry Thomas Buckle.

James Anthony Froude.
  Supplementary List.

ESSAYISTS, CRITICS, ETC.

John Wilson.
Thomas De Quincey.
Anna Jameson.
Harriet Martineau.
Sarah Ellis.
Arthur Helps.
John Ruskin.
  Supplementary List.

NOVELISTS.

Frederick Marryat.
William Carleton.
George P. R. James.
Douglas Jerrold.
Sir E. Bulwer Lytton.
Harrison Ainsworth.
Benjamin Disraeli.
Charles Lever.
Samuel Warren.
Charles Kingsley.
Charlotte Brontë.
Wilkie Collins.
Dinah Muloch.
James Hannay.
Elizabeth Gaskell.
George Eliot.

Anthony Trollope.
  Supplementary List

SCIENTIFIC WRITERS.

Sir David Brewster.
Archbishop Whately.
Sir William Hamilton.
Sir Roderick Murchison.
William Whewell.
Mary Somerville.
Hugh Miller.
John Stuart Mill.
  Supplementary List.

THEOLOGIANS AND SCHOLARS

Thomas Chalmers.
Isaac Taylor.
Henry Rogers.
John W. Donaldson.
  Supplementary List.

TRAVELLERS, ETC.

Samuel Laing.
David Livingstone.
Austen Layard.
Richard Ford.
George Borrow.
Alexander Kinglake.
Sir Emerson Tennent.
  Supplementary List.

POETS.

THOMAS HOOD, born in 1798, was the son of a London bookseller.
His literary career began in Dundee, where he contributed to a
local magazine. His works abound in sparkling wit and humour,
being crammed with the choicest puns and most whimsical
turns of thought. But his true power as a poet, unfortunately
seldom put forth, appears in such tragic pieces as *Eugene Aram's
Dream, The Song of the Shirt,* and *The Bridge of Sighs,* or

in the *Flea of the Midsummer Fairies.* A kindred spirit, Jerrold, says that "his various pen touched alike the springs of laughter and the sources of tears." Hood died in 1845.

DAVID MACBETH MOIR, born in 1798 was the Delta of *Black-wood's Magazine.* The surgeon of Musselburgh found time to culti-vate a poetic genius of the first order. A gentle melancholy is the ruling spirit of his works; but from his novel of *Mansie Wauch,* a mellow Scottish humour shines softly out. He died in 1851.

LETITIA ELIZABETH LANDON was born in 1802 at Old Brompton. Her signature of L. E. L. soon became known by her beautiful poems in the *Literary Gazette.* *The Improvisatrice* and *The Golden Violet* are among her principal works. She wrote also three novels, one of which is called *Romance and Reality.* Having married Mr. Maclean, Governor of Cape Coast Castle in Africa, she went out to that lonely home to die. One October morning in 1839, about two months after her arrival, she was found dead on her bedroom floor, having accidentally, it is thought, taken an overdose of prussic acid. Rich luxuriance of fancy is the characteristic of her poetry.

THOMAS AIRD, born in 1802, at Bowden in Roxburghshire, contri-buted many poems to *Blackwood.* He was long editor of the *Dum-fries Herald.*. *The Devil's Dream* is his noblest poem. Some racy prose sketches of Scottish character have also come from his pen.

CAROLINE NORTON (Miss Sheridan), grand-daughter of the celebrated dramatist, was born in 1808. *The Sorrows of Rosalie* —*The Undying One,* a legend of the Wandering Jew—*The Dream*—and *The Child of the Islands,* may be named among her poems. *Stuart of Dunleath* is her principal novel.

ELIZABETH BROWNING (Miss Barrett) attracted notice first by a translation of the *Prometheus Bound* of Æschylus. A long illness in early life, occasioned by the bursting of a vessel in the lungs, enabled her, by a wide and varied course of reading, and much deep, solitary thought, to prepare for the high vocation of a poet. She certainly has given us the sweetest and noblest strains of poetry that have come in the present generation from her sex. In 1846 she went to reside at Florence; and what she saw of Tuscan affairs inspired her fine political poem of *Casa Guidi Windows.*

A long poem in blank-verse, *Aurora Leigh*, depicts the maiden life
of a poetess, "the autobiography of a heart and intellect." The
principal favourites among Mrs. Browning's poems are, *The Duchess
May—Bertha in the Lane—Cowper's Grave—The Cry of the Children—Lady Geraldine's Courtship—Sonnets from the Portuguese.*
This gifted lady died in the earlier part of the year 1861.

ROBERT BROWNING, the husband of the lady just named, was
born at Camberwell in 1812. He published *Paracelsus* in 1836.
Then followed *Pippa Passes; Strafford* (1837), and *The Blot on
the Scutcheon* (1843), tragedies which proved failures on the stage;
Bells and Pomegranates; and in 1855, *Men and Women.* Obscurity is his chief fault (take *Sordello*, as an example): but the
lightning of great poetic genius shines through the clouds.
Recently (1869) he has published a new poem entitled *The Ring
and the Book.*

WILLIAM EDMONDSTOUNE AYTOUN was born in 1813 at Edinburgh. While at college his poem of *Judith* attracted the notice
of Professor Wilson. But his fame rests chiefly upon his spirit-
stirring *Lays of the Scottish Cavaliers.* He also wrote the historic
romance of *Bothwell*, and a most effective satire on modern poets,
entitled *Firmilian, a Spasmodic Tragedy, by Percy T. Jones.* He
filled the chair of Rhetoric and Belles Lettres in the University of
Edinburgh, and was also Sheriff and Vice-Admiral of Orkney. In
conjunction with THEODORE MARTIN, a parliamentary solicitor in
London, he wrote *Ballads by Bon Gaultier*, and joined the same
friend in translating the lyrics of *Goëthe.* Professor Aytoun died
in 1865.

PHILIP JAMES BAILEY, born in 1816 at Nottingham, has written
some noble but unequal poems. *Festus* is his chief work (1839).
The Angel World and *The Mystic* followed in succession, both
being in the same rapturous and exalted style. In *The Age, a
Colloquial Satire*, he tried another key, pitched as low as his
former strains were high.

SYDNEY DOBELL, whose *nom de plume* is Sydney Yendys, was
born in 1824 at Peckham Rye. In the uncongenial atmosphere
of a wine-merchant's counting-house—his father followed that

business near Cheltenham—he cultivated poetry with much success. *The Roman* (1850), was his first, and is still his best poem. *Balder—Sonnets on the War*, written in conjunction with ALEXANDER SMITH—and *England in Time of War*, complete the list of Mr. Dobell's works already published.

ALEXANDER SMITH, born in 1830 at Kilmarnock, made his fame by *A Life Drama*, written amid the toils of drawing patterns for a muslin house in Glasgow. A second volume, entitled *City Poems*, rich with the same excessive wealth of imagery, appeared in 1857. We have here the black streets of smoky Glasgow glorified with poetic light, which sometimes brightens to sublimity. The year 1861 produced mellowed fruit of his genius in a fine poem of the epic class, *Edwin of Deira*, which gives a stirring and truthful picture of Saxon life in old Northumbria. Mr. Smith, who had been for several years Secretary to the University of Edinburgh, died in 1867 at Wardie near Edinburgh, cut off at the age which proved fatal to Burns and to Byron. In a domestic novel, styled *Alfred Hagart's Household*, and a book of Essays called *Dreamthorp*, he gave proof that a poet can often write most graphic and graceful prose.

Supplementary List.

CAROLINE SOUTHEY.—(1787–1854)—Miss Bowles—Buckland, Hants—*Ellen Fitz-Arthur; The Widow's Tale; Chapters on Churchyards* (prose).

WILLIAM THOM.—(1789–1848)—Aberdeen—a weaver of Inverury—*Rhymes and Recollections*.

BRYAN PROCTER.—(1790–1868)—known as Barry Cornwall—barrister and Commissioner of Lunacy—*Marcian Colonna; Flood of Thessaly; Dramatic Scenes; Mirandola* (a tragedy).

HENRY HART MILMAN.—(1791–1868)—London—Dean of St. Paul's—*Fazio* (a tragedy); *Samor; The Fall of Jerusalem; The Martyr of Antioch; History of Latin Christianity* (prose).

JOHN CLARE.—(1793—still living)—Helpstone, Northamptonshire—a ploughman—*Poems of Rural Life; The Village Minstrel.*

HARTLEY COLERIDGE.—(1796–1849)—Clevedon, near Bristol—*Poems; Lives of Northern Worthies* (prose). DERWENT COLERIDGE.—(1800—still living)—Keswick—*Memoir of Hartley Coleridge.* SARA COLERIDGE.—(1803–1852)—Keswick—*Phantasmion.*

HAYNES BAYLY.—(1797–1839)—near Bath—lyrist—*The Soldier's Tear; I'd be a Butterfly.*

WILLIAM MOTHERWELL. — (1797–1835) — Glasgow—journalist—*Scottish Minstrelsy; Jeanie Morrison.*

ALARIC ALEXANDER WATTS. — (1799-1864) — London — journalist — *Poetical Sketches; Lyrics of the Heart.*

JOHN EDMUND READE.—dramatist and poet—*Italy; Revelations of Life; Cain* and *Catiline* (dramas).

WINTHROP MACKWORTH PRAED.—(1802-1839)—London—barrister and politician—*The Red Fisherman ; Quince.*

RICHARD HENRY HORNE.—(1803—still living)—London—*Orion*, an epic (sold at a farthing); *Cosmo de Medici* and *Death of Marlowe* (dramas).

CHARLES SWAIN.—(1803—still living)—Manchester—an engraver—*The Mind; English Melodies; Letters of Laura D'Auverne.*

THOMAS KIBBLE HERVEY (1804-1859)—Manchester—editor of the *Athenæum* —*Australia; Modern Sculpture; England's Helicon.*   •

THOMAS RAGG.—(1808—still living)—Nottingham—lace-weaver and bookseller —*The Deity; Martyr of Verulam; Heber.*

RICHARD MONCKTON MILNES—(1809-still living)—now LORD HOUGHTON—Yorkshire—politician—*Poems of Many Years; Palm Leaves; Life of Keats.*

MARTIN FARQUHAR TUPPER.—(1810—still living)—London—barrister—*Proverbial Philosophy; An Author's Mind; The Crock of Gold.*

CHARLES MACKAY.—(1812—still living)—Perth—journalist—*Voices from the Crowd; Town Lyrics ; Egeria ; The Salamandrine.*

ROBERT NICOLL.—(1814-1837)—Tullybeltane, Perthshire—editor of the *Leeds Times—Thoughts of Heaven ; Death.*

FRANCES BROWN.—(1816—still living)—Stranorlar, Donegal—*The Star of Atteghei ; Vision of Schwartz ; Lyrics.*

ELIZA COOK.—(1817—still living)—Southwark—*Melaia,* and *Lyrical Pieces.*

MATTHEW ARNOLD.—(1822—still living)—Laleham—son of Dr. Arnold—inspector of schools—*The Strayed Reveller ; Empedocles on Etna.*

COVENTRY PATMORE.—(1823—still living)—Woodford, Essex—assistant librarian, British Museum—*Tamerton Church Tower ; The Angel in the House.*

GERALD MASSEY—(1828—still living)—Tring, Hertfordshire—originally a factory boy—*Babe Christabel; Craigcrook Castle.*

· Among the many poets to whom our space prevents us from doing justice, WILLIAM BENNETT, and two Irish minstrels, DENIS FLORENCE M'CARTHY of Dublin and WILLIAM ALLINGHAM of Ballyshannon, are prominent. Of the ladies who adorn this department of our current literature it would be unpardonable to pass over ISA CRAIG, who wrote the prize poem on *Burns* in 1859 ; BESSIE PARKES, author of *Gabriel ;* MARY HUME, author of *Normiton ;* and ADELAIDE PROCTER, author of *Legends and Lyrics ;* all of whom have added new lustre to their literary fame by untiring efforts to open a wider field of employment to their sex.

DRAMATISTS.

SIR THOMAS NOON TALFOURD, born in 1795 in a suburb of Stafford, was the son of a brewer at Reading in Berkshire. Educated for the law, he rose rapidly, until in 1849 a seat on the bench rewarded his talents and his toils. Five years later, he died suddenly of apoplexy, while charging the grand jury at Stafford. The study of the Greek drama, upon which he wrote an *Essay*, guided his pen to the production of some noble works. His principal play is *Ion.* But *The Athenian Captive; Glencoe, or the Fate of the Macdonalds;* and *The Castilian,* are all dramas of powerful cast and elevated style. We also owe a *Life of Charles Lamb* to this accomplished man.

HENRY TAYLOR, born in the beginning of the present century, has contributed to the modern English drama one of its finest works, *Philip van Artevelde*, founded on the history of the famous brewer of Ghent. This noble and stately play was published in 1834. To its accomplished author we also owe a drama, founded on early English history, called *Edwin the Fair.* Mr. Taylor, who holds a senior clerkship in the Colonial Office, is author of *The Eve of the Conquest* and other poems, and of Essays entitled *Notes from Life* and *Notes from Books.*

Supplementary List.

THOMAS LOVELL BEDDOES.—(1803–1849)—son of a learned physician—*The Bride's Tragedy.*

RICHARD LALOR SHEIL.—(died 1851)—Dublin—an orator and politician—*Evadne; The Apostate.*

GILBERT ABBOTT A'BECKETT.—(1810–1856)—London—a police magistrate—many *Plays;* also *Comic Blackstone; Comic Histories of England and Rome.*

TOM TAYLOR.—(1817—still living)—Sunderland—Secretary to Board of Health—many *Comedies* and *Farces;* contributions to *Punch; Memorials of Haydon.*

WESTLAND MARSTON.—(1825—still living)—Boston, Leicestershire—*Heart of the World; Patrician's Daughter.*

ROBERT B. BROUGH.—(born 1828)—London—brewer's son—*What to Eat, Drink, and Avoid; Medea* (a burlesque), &c.

Other names worthy of honourable mention under this head are SHIRLEY BROOKS, the novelist (*Our Governess; The Creole*)—WILKIE COLLINS (*The Frozen Deep*)—MARK LEMON, editor of *Punch* (more than fifty Farces, &c.)—HENRY MAYHEW, founder of *Punch* and author of *London Labour and the London Poor* (*The Wandering Minstrel,* a farce).

HISTORIANS AND BIOGRAPHERS.

Sir Archibald Alison, born in 1792 at Kenley in Shropshire, received his education at the University of Edinburgh. Called to the Scottish bar, he was appointed in 1834 Sheriff of Lanarkshire, a position which he held up to his death in 1867. His great work is *The History of Europe from the Commencement of the French Revolution to the Restoration of the Bourbons*, published in ten volumes between 1839 and 1842. Eight volumes, carrying the work on to the *Accession of Louis Napoleon*, were afterwards added. Many errors have been detected in this great work; but in spite of imperfection it remains a remarkable monument of the historian's energy, perseverance, and literary skill. Sir Archibald, made a baronet in 1852, was also the author of *A Life of Marlborough*.

George Grote, born in 1794 at Clay Hill, near Beckenham in Kent, was educated at the Charter-house. Amid the toils of a London banking-house, he found time to prosecute historical studies with so much success, that his great work, *The History of Greece, from the earliest period to the Death of Alexander the Great*, completed in 1856, ranks with the best of our modern histories. The sympathies of the writer throughout the entire narrative are enlisted on the side of Athenian democracy.

Thomas Arnold, the celebrated head-master of Rugby, was born in 1795, at East Cowes in the Isle of Wight. Educated at Oxford, he became a Fellow of Oriel. His appointment to Rugby School took place in 1828. As an author, he was chiefly distinguished for a fragment of *Roman History*, closing with the Second Punic War. This work is modelled after Niebuhr. An edition of *Thucydides;* eight *Historical Lectures*, delivered at Oxford, where he became Professor of Modern History in 1841 ; his *Sermons* to the Rugby boys; and his collected *Essays*, complete the short list of his published works. He died suddenly at Rugby in the summer of 1842.

Connop Thirlwall, born in 1797, at Stepney in Middlesex, having studied at Trinity College, Cambridge, was called to the bar in 1825 at Lincoln's Inn. But after three years he abandoned the law for the Church, and ultimately became Bishop of St. David's. A calm and scholarly *History of Greece*, written originally for Lardner's "Cyclopædia," gives him an honourable place among British authors.

SIR FRANCIS PALGRAVE, born in London, Deputy-keeper of Public Records, produced several remarkable historical works. *The History of the Anglo-Saxons ; The Rise and Progress of the English Commonwealth ;* and especially *The History of Normandy and of England,* of which the Norman Conquest is the central subject, are his leading works. He died in 1861.

JOHN GIBSON LOCKHART, born in 1794, at Cambusnethan in Lanarkshire, is best known as the biographer of Sir Walter Scott, whose son-in-law he was. Except Boswell's " Johnson " we have no finer " Life " in the language. The diary and letters of Scott are interwoven with the story of his life, in that finished, graceful style, of which Lockhart was a thorough master. *Valerius,* a tale of Trajan's time; *Reginald Dalton,* an English story; and two other similar works, entitle Lockhart to a high place among novelists. His *Spanish Ballads* possess remarkable poetic fire; and his articles in the *Quarterly Review,* which he edited from 1826 until shortly before his death in 1854, place him in the foremost rank of English essayists and critics.

JOHN FORSTER, born in 1812 at Newcastle, was long the acting editor of the "Examiner." His literary fame rests on the *Lives of the Statesmen of the Commonwealth,* and still more surely on an admirable *Life of Goldsmith,* in which the man and his times are all produced with vivid effect. Mr. Forster is a Commissioner of Lunacy.

GEORGE HENRY LEWES, born in 1817 in London, early forsook the study of medicine for the more congenial toils of the pen. His literary talent has been directed to a great variety of subjects; and in all, his power of clothing a dry theme with living interest manifests itself clearly. His chief works are *A Biographical History of Philosophy,* and a *Life of Goëthe.* But he has also written a *Life of Robespierre; The Physiology of Common Life; The Spanish*

Drama; besides two novels, a tragedy, and serial articles without number.

DAVID MASSON, born in 1823 at Aberdeen, wrought his way steadily with his pen, through journalism and magazine-work, up to his present position as Professor of English Literature in the University of Edinburgh, and editor of " Macmillan's Magazine."   He has written *British Novelists and their Styles,* and other works; and is at present engaged upon the *Life and Times of John Milton,* of which the volume already published affords a fine sample.

HENRY THOMAS BUCKLE was the author of a remarkable *History of Civilization,* of which the second volume appeared some time ago.   To tracing the development of national intellect he has devoted patient attention, and has marshalled an array of evidence in support of his views that tells of deep and long research.   But he follows Comte, the French author of *Positive Philosophy,* in ignoring that all-wise Providence whom we gratefully recognise as the Supreme Agent in the advancement of mankind.   This is the radical fault of a learned and finely written work.   Buckle died at Damascus in 1862.

JAMES ANTHONY FROUDE, an ex-Fellow of Exeter College, Oxford, is distinguished as the author of a graphic and eloquent *History of England from the Fall of Wolsey to the Death of Elizabeth.*   In this work, Henry VIII.—the English Bluebeard, as he has been not unfitly styled—is set in a much more favourable light than in all previous histories of his reign.   Mr. Froude has for years held the editorship of " Fraser's Magazine."

Supplementary List.

LORD CAMPBELL.—(1779-1861)—Springfield, Fife—originally a reporter for the " Morning Chronicle"—Lord Chancellor of England—*Lives of the Lord Chancellors; Lives of the Chief-Justices.*

CHARLES KNIGHT.—(1790—still living)—Windsor—publisher and author—*Old Printer and Modern Press; Popular History of England; Edition of Shakspere.*

ROBERT VAUGHAN.—(about 1798-1868)—an Independent minister—*John de Wycliffe; England under the Stuarts; Revolutions of English History* (Vols. I. and II.).

AGNES STRICKLAND.—Reydon-hall, Suffolk—*Lives of the Queens of England and of Scotland.* Her sister ELIZABETH aided her in this work.

WALTER FARQUHAR HOOK.—Dean of Chichester—*Ecclesiastical Biography; Church Dictionary; Lives of the Archbishops of Canterbury* (Vol. I.)

ROBERT CHAMBERS.—(1802—still living)—Peebles—an Edinburgh publisher— *Traditions of Edinburgh; History of the Rebellion of 1745-46; Domestic Annals of Scotland.*

COSMO INNES.—Professor of History, Edinburgh—*Scotland in the Middle Ages; Sketches of Early Scottish History.*

EARL STANHOPE.—(1805—still living)—Walmer—formerly Lord Mahon—*Life of Belisarius; War of Succession in Spain; History of England from the Peace of Utrecht to the Peace of Versailles.*

SIR GEORGE CORNEWALL LEWIS. — (1806–1863) — *The Credibility of Early Roman History; Influence of Authority on Opinion.*

JOHN HILL BURTON.—(1809—still living)—Aberdeen—a Scottish advocate—*Life of Hume; Lives of Lord Lovat and Duncan Forbes of Culloden; History of Scotland.*

THOMAS ADOLPHUS TROLLOPE.—son of the celebrated lady-novelist—*Girlhood of Catherine de Medici; A Decade of Italian Women.*

WILLIAM HOWARD RUSSELL.—(1816—still living)—Dublin—Special Correspondent of the " Times"—*Letters on the Crimean War; Diary in India.*

GEORGE WILSON.—(1818–1859)—Edinburgh—chemist and lecturer—*Lives of John Reid and Henry Cavendish; Five Gateways of Knowledge* (popular science); *Life of Edward Forbes* (completed by Geikie).

SIR WILLIAM STIRLING-MAXWELL.—(1818—still living)—Kenmure, near Glasgow —Laird of Keir—*Annals of Spanish Artists; Cloister-Life of Charles V.; Life of Velasquez.*

WILLIAM HEPWORTH DIXON.—(1821—still living)—Yorkshire—barrister—editor of the " Athenæum"—*Lives of John Howard, William Penn, Admiral Blake,* and *Lord Bacon;* and *New America* (a book of travel).

HANNA'S *Life of Chalmers;* MUIRHEAD'S *Life of James Watt;* SMILES' *Life of George Stephenson;* CARRUTHERS' *Life of Pope;* MISS PARDOE'S *Lives of Francis I. and Marie de Medici;* MISS FREER'S *Reign of Henry IV. of France;* MERIVALE'S *History of the Romans under the Empire;* EYRE CROWE'S *History of France;* JAMES WHITE'S *Eighteen Christian Centuries,* and *Histories of France and England;* and GEORGE FINLAY'S *Histories of Mediæval and Modern Greece,* are among the works to which we cannot here do justice.

ESSAYISTS, CRITICS, ETC.

JOHN WILSON, born in 1785 at Paisley, was the son of a wealthy manufacturer. During his course at Magdalen College, Oxford, he won the Newdigate prize for English poetry. Settling down at Elleray, on the banks of Windermere, he enjoyed for some time the lovely scenery of the Lakes, and the friendship of Wordsworth, in whose poetic school he was a promising disciple. But changing circumstances led him to fix his residence at Edinburgh, where he was appointed in 1820 to the chair of Moral Philosophy. Like Walter Scott, he won his earliest laurels in poetry; but a greener wreath awaited him in the realms of English prose. *The Isle of Palms* (1812), and *The City of the Plague* (1816), are his chief poetical works. Under the name of Christopher North, he contributed to "Blackwood's Magazine" paper after paper, enriched with a glorious eloquence, which struck a flash of enthusiasm even from the calm, judicial Hallam. The various Essays on *Spenser* and *Homer*, the *Essay on Burns*, and those inimitably witty and brilliant conversations, known as *Noctes Ambrosianae*, afford, perhaps, the finest specimens of Wilson's prose. A collection of sweet, pathetic tales, entitled *Lights and Shadows of Scottish Life*, and a novel in the same style, *The Trials of Margaret Lyndsay*, display the gentle, almost feminine spirit, that burned within the huge, muscular frame of the literary athlete. Three years before his death, this man, of whose memory and fame Scotland may well be proud, received a pension of £300 a year. He died at Edinburgh on the 3d of April 1854.

THOMAS DE QUINCEY, born in 1786 at Manchester, was a merchant's son. Educated at Eton and Oxford, he soon embarked in literary pursuits. His most remarkable works are, *The Confessions of an English Opium-Eater*, first published in the "London Magazine;" and *Suspiria de Profundis*, contributed to "Blackwood." In reading the former papers it should be remembered that De Quincey was long a slave to the use of that deadly drug, and with difficulty tore himself—not without suffering and shattered health—from the clutch of the horrible habit. His *Lives of Shakspere* and *Pope* in the "Encyclopædia Britannica," and his *Logic of Political Economy*, are characterized, like all his works, by wonderful eloquence and thorough grasp of his subject. He died at Edinburgh in December 1859.

ANNA JAMESON, born in 1796 at Dublin, was the daughter of Murphy the painter. Her works on art rank with those of

Ruskin. Two *Hand-books*, descriptive of the Public and Private Galleries of London, were written by this accomplished woman. But her most noted works are, *Characteristics of Women*, containing an estimate of Shakspere's heroines, as just as it is beautiful; and *Sacred and Legendary Art*, including *Legends of the Monastic Orders* and *Legends of the Madonna*. Mrs. Jameson died in March 1860.

HARRIET MARTINEAU, born in 1802 at Norwich, is the author of many works on subjects of Political and Social Economy. She has written also *Society in America; Deerbrook* and *The Hour and the Man*, two novels; and *The History of the Thirty Years' Peace*. Her collection of correspondence between Mr. Atkinson and herself, under the title, *On the Laws of Man's Nature and Development*, contains a direct avowal of atheism. She has for many years resided at Ambleside, in the Lake district.

SARAH ELLIS, the daughter of a Quaker named Stickney, married in 1837 William Ellis, long a missionary in the South Sea Islands. Her chief work, *The Women of England*, appeared in the following year. Ringing the changes on this title, she produced, in succession, among other works devoted to moral instruction, *The Daughters—the Wives—and the Mothers of England*. Books of travel and several short tales have proceeded from her busy pen. Her husband is known as the author of *Polynesian Researches, History of Madagascar*, and many other works.

ARTHUR HELPS, educated at Cambridge, has grown into the favour of thoughtful readers by the pure, calm wisdom of such works as *Friends in Council* and *Companions of My Solitude*. He has given us also a *History of the Spanish Conquest of America*, a strange fiction, called *Realmah*, and two historical dramas.

JOHN RUSKIN, born in 1819 in London, is the son of a rich wine-merchant. He received his education at Christ's Church, Oxford. His first publication, *Modern Painters, by an Oxford Graduate* (1843), won instant attention by its intrepid criticisms, and yet more by its brilliant and lofty style. Turner is his especial favourite. Attracted from painting to architecture during his Continental tours, he has uttered his love for old Gothic art in two works, entitled *The Seven Lamps of Architecture* and *The Stones of Venice.* Pre-Raphaelite Art has also been defended by this bright, sharp pen. Travelling, of late, into the less flowery fields of Political Economy, he has lost his way, and has written things —papers in the "Cornhill" chiefly—which are not likely to add to his fame as a writer, or his character as a man of common sense.

Supplementary List.

JOHN PAYNE COLLIER.—(1789—still living)—London—originally a law-student and journalist—*Poetical Decameron; History of Dramatic Poetry; Life and Works of Shakspere.*

WILLIAM MAGINN.—(1794–1842)—Cork—author and journalist—*Articles in Blackwood* and *Fraser;* especially *Shakspere Papers,* and *Homeric Ballads.*

WILLIAM HOWITT.—(1795–still living)—Heanor, Derbyshire—*Book of the Seasons; Rural Life in England; Life in Germany; Two Years in Victoria.* MARY HOWITT, his wife, aided him in many works.

ALEXANDER DYCE.—(1798—still living)—Edinburgh—Episcopal clergyman—*Notes on Shakspere; Lives and Works of Elizabethan Dramatists.*

JOHN STERLING.—(1806–1844)—Kaimes Castle, Bute—conductor of the "Athenæum"—curate of Hurstmonceaux—*Essays in Athenæum* and *Blackwood; Poems; Strafford* (a tragedy).

MARY COWDEN CLARKE.—(1809—still living)—Miss Novello—*Complete Concordance to Shakspere; Girlhood of Shakspere's Heroines.*

GEORGE GILFILLAN.—(1813—still living)—Comrie, Perthshire—United Presbyterian minister in Dundee—*A Gallery of Literary Portraits; Bards of the Bible.*

SAMUEL PHILLIPS.—(1815–1854)—London—*Literary Essays in the Times; Caleb Stukely* (a novel).

GEORGE BRIMLEY.—(1819–1857)—Cambridge—Librarian of Trinity College, Cambridge—*Essays in the Spectator* and *Fraser.*

NOVELISTS.

FREDERICK MARRYAT, a captain in the Royal Navy, was born in 1792, in London. No better painter of English sailor-life has sought the favour of the reading world since Smollett gave us Trunnion and Pipes. *Frank Mildmay* (1829) was Marryat's first venture. Then came in quick succession from his fertile pen *Newton Forster—Peter Simple—Jacob Faithful—Midshipman Easy,* and a host of similar works, full of wild hilarious life and stirring adventures. Captain Marryat, whose professional daring and skill would have raised him high, apart from all literary fame, died in 1848, at Langham in Norfolk.

WILLIAM CARLETON, who has done for the gray frieze of the Irish peasant what Marryat did for the English blue-jacket, was born in 1798, at Prillick in the county of Tyrone. His father was a peasant, simple and unlearned, but overflowing with the legends and romantic tales in which the wilder parts of Ireland are so rich. Intended for a Roman Catholic priest, Carleton turned in youth to literature. His first work, *Traits and Stories of the Irish Peasantry*, appeared in 1830 without his name, and was at once successful. *Fardorougha, the Miser; Valentine M'Clutchy,* and *Willy Reilly,* are his chief remaining works : but his most pathetic and humorous passages occur in his shorter pieces. Mr. Carleton enjoyed a pension of £200 a year.

GEORGE PAYNE RAINSFORD JAMES, born in 1801 in London, was one of the most voluminous of modern English novelists. The shelves of the circulating libraries still groan under his endless volumes ; and there are readers of peculiar taste who enjoy his monotonous fictions. His great field is modern history ; and perhaps his first historical novel, *Richelieu* (1829), is his best. But to read one of James's novels is to read all. His famous opening scene of two travellers winding on horseback down a mountain road, in the red light of sunset—the one dark and elderly, the other young and fair, &c., has been often turned into fun. James acted for a time as British Consul at Richmond in Virginia; but he exchanged that post for a similar office at Venice, where he died in June 1860.

DOUGLAS JERROLD, born in London in 1803, was an actor's son. Having spent two years at sea, and worked for some time as a printer, he entered literary life as a writer for the Coburg theatre. *Black-eyed Susan* is still a stage favourite, and all his dramatic works are radiant with true wit. *Time Works Wonders*, is, perhaps, the best of them. However, Jerrold's fame rests rather upon his contributions to *Punch* and other serials. Who can forget *The Caudle Curtain-Lectures?* Such works as *St. Giles and St. James,*

(15) 33

and the *Story of a Feather*, display his power as a novelist. For some years before his death, which occurred in 1857, he edited "Lloyd's Weekly Newspaper." His son Blanchard now holds a similar position.

SIR EDWARD BULWER LYTTON, born in 1805, is the third son of General Bulwer, of Heydon Hall in Norfolk. The name of Lytton he assumed, when he succeeded, in 1843, to his mother's estate of Knebworth. Educated at Cambridge, he broke ground as a novelist in 1827, when *Falkland* (a tale tinged deeply with the red and black of Byron's style) appeared. Then came *Pelham*, *a la* Theodore Hook. We cannot attempt to follow out the list. Such unhealthy novels as *Paul Clifford* and *Eugene Aram*, in which a robber and a murderer are clothed with heroic light, afforded but small promise of successors like *The Last Days of Pompeii*, *Rienzi*, and *The Last of the Barons*, and still smaller promise of those matured works, *The Caxtons*, *My Novel*, and *What will he Do with It?*—in which the novelist, turning from baser ore, has struck upon a vein of pure and lustrous gold. Bulwer Lytton's earliest literary efforts were directed to verse-making, and more than once he has returned to this form of literature. He has tried his hand at satire in *The Siamese Twins* and *The New Timon*, and has written a long metrical romance called *King Arthur ;* but a poem on *Milton* is considered to be his best work in English verse. Among several plays from this versatile pen, *Richelieu* and *The Lady of Lyons* deserve special mention. As a politician and an orator, Sir Edward, now Lord Lytton, has won great distinction.

WILLIAM HARRISON AINSWORTH, born in 1805 at Manchester, is a powerful, but often repulsive writer of fiction. His *Rookwood* and *Jack Sheppard* are shoots of the same poisonous tree as bore Bulwer Lytton's "Eugene Aram." In such works as *The Tower of London*, *Old St. Paul's*, and *Windsor Castle*, English history has supplied the ground-work of Ainsworth's plots. He owns and edits "Bentley's Miscellany."

BENJAMIN DISRAELI, born in 1805 in London, is the son of old Isaac D'Israeli, who wrote the "Curiosities of Literature." *Vivian Grey* (1826) was his first novel ; and among the many that followed we may single out *Contarini Fleming; Henrietta Temple;* and *Coningsby*,—in the last of which he mingles politics with the usual staples of a modern novel. A fantastic kind of Eastern exaggeration—the unpruned luxuriance of a Judean vine whose branches run over the wall—characterizes both the plots and the style of Mr. Disraeli's works. As a politician, he holds a foremost rank on the Conservative side, was twice Chancellor of the Exchequer under Lord Derby, and has recently held the seals as Premier.

CHARLES LEVER, born in 1806 at Dublin, was physician to the embassy at Brussels when he wrote his first work, *The Confessions of Harry Lorrequer*. *Charles O'Malley* and *Jack Hinton*, works of the same dashing military style, followed, to the delight of thousands. The fun and frolic of Irish life, especially such life as officers see, were there depicted in most spirit-stirring style. *Roland Cashel, The Knight of Gwynne,* and *The Dodd Family Abroad*, are the best of his later fictions. Lever edited the "Dublin University Magazine" for a while, but has since resided, for the most part, in Italy. He is now Consul at Trieste.

SAMUEL WARREN, born in 1807 in Denbighshire, was Recorder of Hull, and then Master in Lunacy. He is chiefly known as a novelist by his tragical sketches in "Blackwood," entitled *Passages from the Diary of a late Physician,* and his fine novel, *Ten Thousand a Year.*

CHARLES KINGSLEY, born in 1819, at Holne Vicarage in Devonshire, studied at Magdalen College, Cambridge, and entered the Church of England. He soon became rector of Eversley, a moorland parish in Hampshire. His first important literary work was a dramatic poem, called *The Saint's Tragedy*, founded on the story of Elizabeth of Hungary (1848). A novel, entitled *Alton Locke, Tailor and Poet,* dealing with some of the problems of modern trade, and written in thorough sympathy with the working-classes, came next from his pen. *Yeast, a Problem; Phaethon, or Loose Thoughts for Loose Thinkers; Hypatia, or New Friends with an Old Face; Alexandria and her Schools,* a series of lectures delivered in Edinburgh; *Glaucus, or the Wonders of the Shore,* are among his remaining works. But his finest production is the novel, *Westward Ho!* founded on the Elizabethan sailor-life, and depicting, in connection with the fictitious history of Sir Amyas Leigh, the fortunes of Raleigh, Drake, and Hawkins, and the brilliant affair with the Armada. In addition to his brilliant prose he has produced some very fine poetry. *Andromeda* is, perhaps, the most elaborate of his later poems; but it is chiefly in lyrics that his poetic genius shines. Mr. Kingsley has been lately appointed Professor of Modern History at Cambridge.

CHARLOTTE BRONTÉ, better known by her pseudonym of Currer Bell, was one of the most original novelists of the day. The daughter of an Irish curate settled in Yorkshire, she grew up in the wilds of Haworth. After a short time as pupil and teacher in a school at Brussels, she returned to the bleak parsonage, where she commenced to write a novel. Her two sisters engaged in similar works at the same time. Charlotte's work, *The Professor*, was rejected by the London publishers; but the rejection was sweetened by encouragement to try a more saleable book. The fruit of this advice was soon beheld in *Jane Eyre* (1847), a work of startling interest and power, which at once made the author famous. *Shirley* and *Villette* are the remaining works of this woman of true genius. She married her father's curate, Mr. Nichol, in June 1854; but died in the following March, in her thirty-ninth year.

WILKIE COLLINS, born in London in 1825, is the son of the painter William Collins. He wrote his father's *Life*; a novel called *Antonina*; *The Frozen Deep*, a drama; and *The Dead Secret*. But his novel, *The Woman in White*, contributed to "All the Year Round," is undoubtedly his best work. Plunged in a mystery before the first chapter has closed, we remain dark and breathless almost to the last page of the tale. *No Name*, *Armadale*, and *The Moonstone*, are more recent fictions from his pen.

DINAH MARIA MULOCH was born in 1826, at Stoke-upon-Trent in Staffordshire. Her first novel was *The Ogilvies* (1849). Perhaps her best is *John Halifax, Gentleman* (1856).

JAMES HANNAY, born in 1827 at Dumfries, entered the navy at thirteen, and for five years (1840–45) served on board of various ships. Since the latter date he has been engaged constantly in literary work, and has won considerable distinction as a novelist and reviewer. *Singleton Fontenoy* is the most popular of his works; *Eustace Conyers* is perhaps the best. His *Lectures on Satire and Satirists*, delivered in London in 1853, have been published; and not long since appeared a selection from his brilliant *Essays contributed to the Quarterly Review*. Mr. Hannay is at present British Consul at Barcelona.

ELIZABETH GASKELL, the wife of a Unitarian minister in Manchester, contributed to our literature a remarkable picture of English factory life in her novel of *Mary Barton*, and a most interesting biography in her *Life of Charlotte Brontë*. She died suddenly in 1865.

GEORGE ELIOT (said to be Miss Evans) has produced some of the most remarkable novels of the day. Beginning her literary career with *Scenes of Clerical Life*, she afterwards took the reading public by storm, when *Adam Bede* appeared. This lady has since written *The Mill on the Floss*, and *Silas Marner, the Weaver of Ravelhoe;* but neither of these works comes up to the mimic scene, on which Adam Bede, Hetty Sorrel, Dinah Morris, and the delightful Mrs. Poyser play their varied parts of mingled fun and deep sad earnest. Her later works are *Romola, Felix Holt*, and a dramatic poem of high merit, entitled *The Spanish Gipsy*.

ANTHONY TROLLOPE, who held an important position in the General Post-Office, has followed in the steps of his famous mother. Beginning with Irish stories, he afterwards struck upon a vein but little wrought by former novelists—life among English clergymen. *The Warden; Barchester Towers; Doctor Thorne; The Bertrams; Framley Parsonage; The Claverings;* and *The Last Chronicle of Barset*, are among his chief completed works. Trollope is a most prolific novelist: his fictions possess great merit as unexaggerated pictures of modern English life among the upper-middle classes.

GEORGE MACDONALD, born at Huntly in 1826, first attracted notice by a work called *Phantastes*. He has since attained to considerable reputation as a poet and novelist. Among his recent works, which are imbued with an earnest religious spirit, we may name *Alec Forbes, David Elginbrod, Annals of a Quiet Neighbourhood*, and a volume of poems called *The Disciple*.

Supplementary List.

GEORGE GLEIG.—(1796–still living)—son of the Bishop of Brechin—Chaplain-General to the Forces—*The Subaltern; The Chelsea Pensioners.*

SAMUEL LOVER.—(1797–1868)—Dublin—a miniature painter—*Rory 'More; Handy Andy* (novels)—noted also for *Irish songs.*

JOHN BANIM.—(1800–1842)—Kilkenny—originally a miniature painter—*The O'Hara Tales.*

ANNE MARSH.—(about 1798)—Miss Caldwell of Newcastle-under-Lyne—a London banker's wife—*Two Old Men's Tales; Emilia Wyndham.*

CATHERINE GORE.—(about 1799–1861)—novelist of fashionable life—*Mothers and Daughters; Cecil, or the Adventures of a Coxcomb.*

GERALD GRIFFIN.—(1803–1840)—Limerick—journalist—*The Munster Tales; The Collegians.*

WILLIAM H. MAXWELL.—(died 1850)—captain in the army—*Stories of Waterloo; Hector O'Halloran.*

ANNA MARIA HALL.—Miss Fielding of Wexford—wife of S. C. Hall, of the Art Journal—*The Buccaneer; Lights and Shadows of Irish Life; Marian.*

ALBERT SMITH.—(1816–1860)—Chertsey—originally a medical man—lecturer on *Mont Blanc* and *China—Christopher Tadpole; Mr. Ledbury* (novels).

SHIRLEY BROOKS.—(1816—still living)—lawyer and journalist—*The Gordian Knot; Aspen Court; The Silver Cord; Sooner or Later.*

ANGUS BETHUNE REACH.—(1821–1856)—Inverness—reporter and critic—*Clement Lorimer; Leonard Lindsay; Natural History of Bores and Humbugs; Claret and Olives* (book of travel).

JAMES GRANT.—(1822—still living)—Edinburgh—served some time in the 62nd Regt.—*Romance of War; Jane Seton; Memorials of Edinburgh Castle.*

GEORGE AUGUSTUS SALA.—*Gaslight and Daylight in London; Hogarth; Seven Sons of Mammon.*

CHARLES READE.—English barrister—*Peg Woffington; Christie Johnston; N'ever too Late to Mend.*

THOMAS HUGHES.—Chancery barrister—*Scouring of the White Horse—Tom Brown's School Days; Tom Brown at Oxford* (contributed to "Macmillan ").

Modern novels are numberless, and we are forced to omit many deserving names. FRANK SMEDLEY, author of *Frank Fairleph* and *Lewis Arundel*—Captain MAYNE REID, author of the *Scalp-Hunters* and many thrilling tales of war and hunting in American wilds—Miss GERALDINE JEWSBURY, author of *Zoe* and *The Half-Sisters*—and Mrs. CATHERINE CROWE (Miss Stevens), author of *Susan Hopley* and *The Night Side of Nature,*—may serve to close the list of English novelists.

SCIENTIFIC WRITERS.

SIR DAVID BREWSTER, born in 1781 at Jedburgh, died in 1868 as Principal of the University of Edinburgh. The pen of a scientific man is not often gifted with the grace and brilliance that adorn his works. He spent twenty years (1808--1828) in editing the " Edinburgh Encyclopædia." A treatise on the *Kaleidoscope* (which he invented in 1816); a treatise on *Optics; More Worlds than One;* and especially his *Life of Sir Isaac Newton,* may be singled out from his valuable writings. Sir David was long Principal of the United College at St. Andrews.

RICHARD WHATELY, son of the Rev. Dr. Whately of Nonsuch Park in Surrey, was Archbishop of Dublin from 1831 until his death in 1863. Born in 1787, he received his education at Oriel College, Oxford, of which he became Fellow in 1811. His principal works are *Elements of Logic; Elements of Rhetoric; Lectures on Political Economy; Essays on Difficulties in the Epistles of St. Paul;* and annotated editions of *Bacon's Essays* and *Paley's Moral Philosophy,* in which the notes afford a pleasing specimen of his style.

SIR WILLIAM HAMILTON, born in 1788 at Glasgow, won his world-wide fame as a metaphysician during his twenty years' tenure of the Chair of Logic and Metaphysics in the University of Edinburgh. The son of a Glasgow professor, he passed from the college of his native town to Oxford, as the holder of the Snell Exhibition. He was called to the Scottish bar in 1813, and in 1821 was appointed to the Chair of Universal History at Edinburgh. This he exchanged in fifteen years (1836) for that position round which his learning has cast such lustre. His *Essays from the Edinburgh Review,* and his *Edition of Dr. Reid's Works,* were published during his lifetime. And after his death appeared his *Lectures,* edited by Dr. Mansel of Oxford, and Professor Veitch, now of Glasgow. Hamilton died in 1856.

SIR RODERICK MURCHISON, born in 1792, at Tarradale in Ross-shire, began life as a military officer, and served for nine years (1807–1816) in the Peninsula and elsewhere. The rest of his life has been given to geology. His great work is called *Siluria, the History of the Oldest Known Rocks Containing Organic Remains.* A work on the *Geology of Russia* resulted from his examination of the strata eastward to the Ural Mountains. Sir Roderick is now Director-General of the Geological Survey of the British Isles.

WILLIAM WHEWELL, born in 1795 at Lancaster, died in 1866 as Master of Trinity College, Cambridge. To this position he nobly fought his way from the humble station of a carpenter's son. One of the Bridgewater treatises, entitled *Astronomy and General Physics in reference to Natural Theology*, was written by him; but his greatest work is *The History and Philosophy of the Inductive Sciences*.

MARY SOMERVILLE, a Scottish lady of deep scientific learning and considerable literary skill, published in 1832 a redaction of Laplace's work, which she called *The Mechanism of the Heavens*. Her fame rests chiefly on her second work, *The Connection of the Physical Sciences*. She has also published a *Physical Geography*. Her first husband was a naval officer; her second is a Scottish minister.

HUGH MILLER, no less remarkable as a master of picturesque English prose than as a practical geologist, was born in 1802 at Cromarty. After such education as his native town could give, he went to work as a stone-mason in the neighbouring quarries. There his hammer became an instrument of magic, breaking the young workman's way into a subterranean Wonderland. A volume of *Poems* (1829), and some *Letters on the Herring Fishery*, opened his brilliant literary career. After fifteen years spent with hammer and chisel—the highest flight of his art being the cutting of epitaphs on tombstones—he became, after his marriage, accountant in a Cromarty bank. In this position about six years were spent, during which his chief literary performance was *Scenes and Legends in the North of Scotland, or the Traditional History of Cromarty*. His zeal on behalf of the Non-Intrusion principle, then agitating the Church of Scotland, led him to write two powerful pamphlets, which attracted so much notice that he was selected in 1840 to edit the *Edinburgh Witness*. This station he filled until the sad day of his death. Amid the unceasing toils and distractions of journalism, he continued to cultivate his darling study. *The Old Red Sandstone* (1841); *First Impressions of England and its People* (1847); *Footprints of the Creator* (1850); an autobiography entitled *My Schools and Schoolmasters* (1854); and *The*

Testimony of the Rocks (1857), a work which he had just completed when madness impelled him to point the fatal pistol to his heart, mark the unceasing labour through which he held his way from year to year. He shot himself on the 24th of December, 1856. *The Cruise of the Betsy*, a geological voyage to the Hebrides; and *The Sketch-book of Popular Geology*, edited by his widow, have appeared since his death. The varied splendour of his style, and the giant grasp of his mental faculties, are displayed in his grand *Mosaic Vision of Creation*, woven of such coloured shadows as may have rolled in a gorgeous panorama before the eye of the prophet, sitting upon a hill top in the lonely Midian desert.

JOHN STUART MILL, the son of the historian of India, and the author of a *System of Logic, Ratiocinative and Inductive* (1843); *Essays on Unsettled Questions of Political Economy* (1844); *Principles of Political Economy* (1848); and *Liberty* (1859), takes rank among the first thinkers of the time. His philosophy is opposed in most respects to the system of Bacon. He held, as did his father, the office of Examiner of Indian Correspondence, retiring when the Company was dissolved in 1859. Mr. Mill was born in 1806.

Supplementary List.

WILLIAM SMITH.—(1769–1839)—Churchill, Oxfordshire—founder of English geology—*Geological Map of England; Organic Remains.*

WILLIAM BUCKLAND.—(1784–1856)—Dean of Westminster—one of the Bridgewater treatises on *Geology and Mineralogy in Reference to Natural Theology.*

GIDEON MANTELL.—(1788–1852)—an English physician—*The Fossils of the South Downs; The Medals of Creation; Wonders of Geology.*

DIONYSIUS LARDNER.—(1793–1859)—*Hand-Book of Natural Philosophy and Astronomy; Museum of Science and Art;* edition of *Euclid.*

MICHAEL FARADAY. — (1794–1867) — a blacksmith's son — greatest English chemist—*Researches on Electricity;* Popular Lectures on *Chemistry of a Candle,* &c.

SIR CHARLES LYELL.—(1797—still living)—Kinnordy, Forfarshire—*Principles of Geology; Elements of Geology; Travels in North America.*

RICHARD OWEN.—(about 1803—still living)—Lancaster—a distinguished surgeon and physiologist—*History of British Fossil Mammals and Birds; British Fossil Reptiles.*

JAMES FERRIER.—(1808–1864)—Professor of Moral Philosophy at St. Andrews
—*Institutes of Metaphysic;* edition of *Wilson's Works.*

Dr. MANSEL of Oxford, author of *Limits of Religious Thought,* and joint-
editor of *Sir William Hamilton's Lectures*—Dr. MORELL, Inspector of Schools
in England, author of *A History and Critical View of the Speculative Philosophy of Europe during the Nineteenth Century*—Professor M'COSH, now President of Princeton College in the United States, author of the *Method of the
Divine Government*—Professor ALEXANDER BAIN of Aberdeen, author of *The
Senses and the Intellect; The Emotions and the Will*—and HERBERT SPENCER,
author of *First Principles of Psychology,* have made valuable contributions to
the scientific literature of the present century.

The *Dissertations,* written for the *Encyclopædia Britannica* from time to time
during the last hundred years, trace the progress of Physical and Mental Science
with remarkable clearness and effect. DUGALD STEWART and Sir JAMES MACK-
INTOSH took up Ethical Philosophy; Archbishop WHATELY dealt with the History of Christianity; while Mathematics and Physics have been treated successively by JOHN PLAYFAIR (1748–1819), Sir JOHN LESLIE (1766–1832), and JAMES
DAVID FORBES (born 1808—now Principal of the United College, St. Andrews).
Leslie wrote also a remarkable work on *Heat;* and Forbes is well known for his
books upon *Glaciers.*

THEOLOGIANS AND SCHOLARS.

THOMAS CHALMERS, born in 1780, at Anstruther in Fifeshire,
was a merchant's son. Educated at St. Andrews, he was ordained
in 1803 as minister of Kilmany in his native county. Twelve
years later (1815) he removed to Glasgow, where his splendid
fame as a pulpit orator was chiefly won. Jeffrey's striking char-
acterization best conveys the marvellous power which this wonderful man had over every audience he addressed,—"He buries his
adversaries under the fragments of burning mountains." In 1823
he went to St. Andrews as Professor of Moral Philosophy in the
United College; and in 1828 he exchanged this post for the Chair
of Divinity in the University of Edinburgh. When the Disrup-
tion of 1843 took place, Chalmers was prominent among the
founders of the Free Church of Scotland. On the 31st of May
1847 he was found dead in his bed, with no sign of suffering on
his placid face. A most interesting and graphic Life of this
eminent orator and scholar has been written by his son-in-law,
Dr. Hanna of Edinburgh. Thirty-four volumes are filled with

the gathered works of Chalmers. His *Natural Theology*, his *Evidences of Christianity*, his *Lectures on the Romans*, and his magnificent *Astronomical Discourses*, may be singled out as noble specimens of literary work. But the qualities which distinguish these pervade all his writings. From heaven and earth and sea, from the world of mind and the world of matter, he drew countless illustrations to clothe his subject in a fitting garb. He touched a pebble, and it became a gem. He looked on a scene, and it brightened into beauty or faded into gloom, as wrath or mercy lit his eye. His audience heard with *his* ears, saw with *his* vision, and followed in rapt wonder the man whose resistless spirit had flung its lightning chains around them.

ISAAC TAYLOR, born in 1787 at Lavenham, the son of an Independent minister, settled down at Stanford Rivers, not far from his home at Ongar in Essex, to write *The Natural History of Enthusiasm*. It appeared anonymously in 1829. *The Physical Theory of Another Life*, and *Ancient Christianity*, may be named among his many works. Taylor died in 1865.

WILLIAM MURE of Caldwell, born in 1799, a colonel in the Renfrewshire Militia, is distinguished for his learned and carefully written *Critical History of the Language and Literature of Ancient Greece*. In the Homeric controversy Colonel Mure sides with those who consider the Iliad and Odyssey to have been the work of a single poet. He died in 1860.

THOMAS GUTHRIE, born in 1800, at Brechin in Forfarshire, is a minister of the Free Church of Scotland. The " Times," in a review of one of his works, calls him " The greatest of our pulpit orators." Some of his principal works are, *A Plea for Ragged Schools; The Gospel in Ezekiel; The City, its Sins and Sorrows; Christ and the Inheritance of the Saints*.

JOHN WILLIAM DONALDSON, born about 1810, was the son of a London merchant. He became a Fellow of Trinity College, Cambridge, and was for many years head-master of the Grammar School of Bury St. Edmunds. His principal works, *The Theatre of the Greeks, The New Cratylus*, and *Varronianus*, have won for him a first-rate reputation among the classical scholars and philologers of the century. Dr. Donaldson, who resided latterly at Cambridge, died in the year 1861.

HENRY ROGERS, a professor in the Independent College at Birmingham, is celebrated as the author of *The Eclipse of Faith, or a Visit to a Religious Sceptic.* This work, published in 1852, deals with all the controversies and new questions in theology that have arisen in England or Germany during the last twenty years. It is a reply to Newman's *Phases of Faith.* A *Reply* and *Defence* have been exchanged between the rival champions since the publication of the "Eclipse." Mr. Rogers has contributed largely to the *Edinburgh Review;* and many of his essays have been republished.

Supplementary List.

RALPH WARDLAW.—(1779–1853)—Dalkeith—Independent minister at Glasgow— *Discourses on the Socinian Controversy.*

JOHN BIRD SUMNER.—(1780–1862)—Kenilworth—Archbishop of Canterbury— *St. Paul's Epistles; Records of Creation* (second Burnett prize); *Evidences of Christianity.*

THOMAS HARTWELL HORNE.—(1780–1862)—London—Episcopal minister and librarian in the British Museum—*Introduction to the Study of the Scriptures.*

JOHN BROWN.—(1785–1859)—minister of the United Presbyterian Church in Edinburgh—*Commentaries upon Romans, Galatians, First Peter,* &c.

HUGH M'NEILE.—(1795—still living)—Ballycastle, Antrim—rector of St. Jude's, Liverpool—a celebrated pulpit orator.

JULIUS HARE.—(1795–1855)—archdeacon of Lewes—a leader of Broad Church party—sermons on *Victory of Faith* and *Mission of the Comforter; Life of John Sterling; Niebuhr's Rome,* (trans.)

ROBERT CANDLISH.—(still living)—minister of Free St. George's, Edinburgh— *Lectures on Genesis; Scripture Characters; The Atonement; Reason and Revelation,* &c.

JOHN KITTO.—(1804–1854)—Plymouth—deaf—*Pictorial Bible; Cyclopædia of Biblical Literature; Daily Bible Readings.*

RICHARD CHEVENIX TRENCH.—(1807—still living)—Archbishop of Dublin— *Justin Martyr,* and other poems; *Notes on the Parables and Miracles; Synonyms of the New Testament; Study of Words; English—Past and Present.*

WILLIAM EWART GLADSTONE.—(1809—still living)—Liverpool—present Prime Minister—*Homer and the Homeric Age.*

SIR HENRY RAWLINSON.—(1810—still living)—Chadlington, Oxfordshire—decipherer of Assyrian inscriptions—*Outline of the History of Assyria.*

HENRY ALFORD,—(1810—still living)—London—Dean of Canterbury--edition of the *Greek Testament; Sermons and Poems.*

WILLIAM ARCHER BUTLER.—(1814-1848)—Annerville, near Clonmel—Professor of Moral Philosophy, Trinity College, Dublin—*Sermons; Lectures on Ancient Philosophy.*

ARTHUR PENRHYN STANLEY.—(1815—still living)—Alderley—Dean of Westminster—*Discourses on Corinthians; Life of Dr. Arnold; Memorials of Canterbury.*

ROBERT ANCHOR THOMPSON.—(1821—still living)—Durham—once curate of Louth in Lincolnshire—first Burnett *Prize Essay.*

JOHN TULLOCH.—(1822—still living)—Tibbermuir in Perthshire—Principal of St. Mary's College at St. Andrews—*Theism,* (second Burnett Prize); *Leaders of the Reformation; English Puritanism.*

JOHN CAIRD.—(1823—still living)—Greenock—Professor of Divinity at Glasgow —*Sermons, (Religion in Common Life).*

NORMAN MACLEOD.—minister of Barony Church, Glasgow—eloquent preacher— editor of *Good Words.*

The leaders of the Tractarian party in the Church of England (so called from the publication of *Tracts for the Times,* between 1832 and 1837) were EDWARD PUSEY and JOHN HENRY NEWMAN, the latter of whom wrote also an *Essay on the Development of Christian Doctrine.* Mr. NEWMAN has since become a member of the Roman Catholic Church. His brother, FRANCIS NEWMAN, Latin Professor in University College, London, is author of a sceptical work, *The Phases of Faith,* to which Henry Rogers replied in "The Eclipse of Faith." The well-known volume, *Essays and Reviews,* written by seven Oxford men, among whom BENJAMIN JOWETT is the leading name, represents a free-thinking section of the Church of England. J. FREDERICK DENISON MAURICE, a Cambridge man, lately Professor of Divinity in King's College, London, and well known for his association with Kingsley and others in efforts to raise the educational standard of the working classes, is the author of *Theological Essays, The Religions of the World,* and several other able works, which contain opinions 'at variance with the tenets of the Church of England, their "liberalism" sometimes going the length of heterodoxy. These opinions led to the removal of Mr. Maurice from his chair. JAMES MARTINEAU, a Unitarian minister in Liverpool, has produced some most eloquent works, among which may be named *Studies in Christianity,* and the *Rationale of Religious Inquiry.*

Cardinal WISEMAN, born at Seville in 1802, represented theology from the Roman Catholic point of view. He published an interesting contribution to general literature, entitled *Recollections of the Last Four Popes.*

TRAVELLERS AND GEOGRAPHERS.

SAMUEL LAING, of Papdale in Orkney, is the author of *A Residence in Norway* (1834-36); *A Tour in Sweden* (1838); *Notes of a Traveller* (1854). This agreeable writer is a younger brother of the Scottish historian already named.

DAVID LIVINGSTONE, born about 1817, at Blantyre in Lanarkshire, has travelled much in Africa as a missionary. His work, *Missionary Travels in South Africa*, a valuable repertory of facts concerning that region, was published in 1857. The basin of the Zambezi has been the chief scene of his explorings, and his chief discoveries have been the Victoria Falls and Lake Nyassa. In 1864 he published an account of his second expedition. He is now returning from a third expedition, to the great joy of his countrymen, who some time ago received a report of his death.

AUSTEN HENRY LAYARD, born in 1817 in Paris, is distinguished as the author of two works, *Nineveh and its Remains* (1848) ; and *Discoveries in the Ruins of Nineveh and Babylon* (1853), describing his successful excavations, especially at the former place. Sculptured bulls and lions, with wings and human heads, stand, amid many other similar works of ancient art, in the hall of the British Museum, as trophies of Mr. Layard's toil. For a time he took a prominent part in politics as member for Aylesbury, and under-Secretary for Foreign Affairs. He has lately returned to political life.

RICHARD FORD (1796–1858) wrote Murray's *Hand-Book for Spain*, and also a work entitled *Gatherings from Spain* (1846), which together form the best authority we have on the modern condition of that romantic land.

GEORGE BORROW, born near Norwich about 1800, when travelling in Spain as the agent of the Bible Society, gathered materials for a work descriptive of his personal adventures which he called *The Bible in Spain* (1844). Few books possess more vivid interest. Gipsy life has an especial attraction for his pen. His other works are *Zincali, or the Gipsies in Spain*, published before his chief book ; *Lavengro, or the Scholar, the Gipsy, and the Priest ;* and a sequel to this, called *The Romany Rye.*

ALEXANDER WILLIAM KINGLAKE, born in 1802 at Taunton, having passed through Trinity College, Cambridge, studied law at Lincoln's Inn. His book, *Eöthen*, descriptive of his travels in the East, which was published in 1850, is remarkable for its thought and eloquence. Mr. Kinglake is the author of a *History of the Crimean War*, courageous and brilliant, but in the later volumes too minute in detail.

SIR JAMES EMERSON TENNENT, born in 1804 at Belfast, is a merchant's son. Elected member for his native town in 1832, he devoted himself to political life, making literature his recreation. His books on *Modern Greece, Belgium,* and *Wine* are well known; but his great work is *Ceylon,* for which he collected materials during his five years' residence in the island as Secretary to the Colonial Government. He has been since 1852 one of the joint Secretaries to the Board of Trade.

JOHN HANNING SPEKE, a captain in the Indian army, explored (1857–62) the basin of the Upper Nile, having started from Zanzibar. He fixed the true position of the Mountains of the Moon, and in 1858 discovered the vast lake *Victoria Nyanza.* A brother officer named Grant accompanied him on his travels, and aided him in the preparation of his *Journal.* Speke was killed near Box in Wiltshire, in 1864, by the accidental discharge of his own gun. He was then only thirty-seven years of age.

SIR SAMUEL WHITE BAKER, born in 1821 in Worcestershire, undertook the exploration of the Nile by ascending its current. His brave wife accompanied him. In 1864 he discovered a very large lake, to which he gave the name *Albert Nyanza.* Baker tells the story of his explorations with much more graphic power and elegance than either Speke or Livingstone has displayed.

Supplementary List.

To the list of travellers in Spain, headed by Ford and Borrow, the name of. HENRY DAVID INGLIS (1795–1835), son of a Scottish advocate, who wrote under the name of Derwent Conway, deserves to be added. Mr. Inglis also published travels in Northern Europe, France, and Ireland.

Sir JOHN BOWRING (born in 1792 at Exeter), otherwise famous as a translator, has written an account of *Siam.* ELIOT WARBURTON (1810–1852), an English barrister who was burned in the Amazon, has left, besides some novels and memoirs, an eloquent book of Eastern travel, *The Crescent and the Cross* (1846). *China* has been "done" and described by JOHN FRANCIS DAVIS, Chief Superintendent there, and WINGROVE COOKE, Special Correspondent of the *Times;* and *Japan* by LAURENCE OLIPHANT, Secretary to Lord Elgin. The Rev. JOSIAS PORTER, now a Professor of Biblical Criticism in Belfast, is author of *Five Years in Damascus,* and Murray's *Hand-book for Palestine and Syria.* Captain SHERARD OSBORNE, author of *Stray Leaves from an Arctic Journal,* has since written *A Cruise in Japanese Waters.*

Arctic travel and discovery, during this period of English literature, are represented by many eminent names, among which those of Dr. RAE, Sir ROBERT M'CLURE, discoverer of the North-West Passage, and Sir LEOPOLD M'CLINTOCK, commander of the Fox, are prominent. Sir FRANCIS HEAD (born 1793), for some time Governor of Upper Canada, wrote a popular work upon the *Pampas and the Andes* (1826); and a Yorkshire Squire, CHARLES WATERTON (born 1782), has depicted his wonderful adventures and toils in *Wanderings in South America, the North-West of the United States, and the Antilles.*

Murray's *Hand-books,* some of which have been already named, form in themselves a most valuable geographical library. They are not the work of mere compilers, but, in nearly every case, of men who can describe clearly and gracefully what they have seen and heard in the land of which they write.

APPENDIX ON AMERICAN LITERATURE.

POETS.	NOVELISTS.	SCIENTIFIC WRITERS.
William Bryant.	Washington Irving.	Benjamin Franklin.
Lydia Sigourney.	James F. Cooper.	Supplementary List.
Henry Longfellow.	Thomas Haliburton.	
Nathaniel Willis.	Nathaniel Hawthorne.	THEOLOGIANS.
Edgar Allan Poe.	Harriet B. Stowe.	
Supplementary List.	Supplementary List.	Jonathan Edwards.
		Supplementary List.
HISTORIANS.	ESSAYISTS AND CRITICS.	
William Prescott.	William Channing.	TRAVELLERS.
George Bancroft.	Ralph Emerson.	
George Ticknor.	Edward Everett.	John L. Stephens.
John L. Motley.	Supplementary List.	Edward Robinson.
Supplementary List.		Supplementary List.

UPON the opposite shores of the Atlantic a branch of our literature is flourishing in green and vigorous youth. We subjoin a brief view of American writers and their works, following the plan which has been adopted in the foregoing chapter.

POETS.

WILLIAM CULLEN BRYANT, who divides the crown of American poetry with Longfellow, was born in 1794, at Cummington in Massachusetts. At first a lawyer, he afterwards devoted himself to journalism. His poem called *Thanatopsis* (a view of death) is full of Wordsworth's clear and pensive beauty of expression. *The Ages—Lines to a Waterfowl—Green River—The Yellow Violet* —and *The Inscription for the Entrance to a Wood*, are among his finest poems.

LYDIA HUNTLY SIGOURNEY, born in 1791, at Norwich in Connecticut, is the Mrs. Hemans of American poetry. As Miss Huntly she appeared before the public in 1815. Four years later she married a merchant of Hartford. The delicate pathos

(15)
34

of *The Dying Infant, The Emigrant Mother,* and *To-morrow,* is worthy of all praise. *Pocahontas* is her most elaborate poem. Mrs. Sigourney died in 1865.

HENRY WADSWORTH LONGFELLOW, born in 1807, at Portland in Maine, has been since 1835 Professor of Modern Languages and Belles-Lettres in Harvard College, Cambridge. He first appeared as a poet in 1840, when he published *Voices of the Night.* The study of European literature, especially that of Germany, has had a powerful influence upon his mind. Tennyson is the English writer whom he most resembles. His chief works, verse and prose, are as follows :—

<table>
<tr><td colspan="2" align="center">VERSE.</td><td align="center">VERSE—*Cont*.</td></tr>
<tr><td colspan="2">Voices of the Night.</td><td>Dante translated.</td></tr>
<tr><td colspan="2">Poems on Slavery.</td><td>New England Tragedies.</td></tr>
<tr><td colspan="2">The Spanish Student, a play.</td><td></td></tr>
<tr><td colspan="2">The Belfry of Bruges.</td><td align="center">PROSE.</td></tr>
<tr><td colspan="2">Evangeline (in English hexameters).</td><td>Outre-Mer, or Sketches from Beyond</td></tr>
<tr><td colspan="2">The Sea-side and the Fire-side.</td><td>Sea.</td></tr>
<tr><td colspan="2">The Golden Legend (mediæval).</td><td>Hyperion, a Romance.</td></tr>
<tr><td colspan="2">Hiawatha, an Indian tale.</td><td>Poets and Poetry of Europe.</td></tr>
<tr><td colspan="2">The Courtship of Miles Standish.</td><td>Kavanagh, a Tale.</td></tr>
</table>

Many translations, from Spanish, German, Swedish, Danish, and Anglo-Saxon, attest the linguistic power and poetic skill of this favourite author. On this side of the Atlantic Longfellow and Washington Irving are as well known as Tennyson and Goldsmith.

NATHANIEL PARKER WILLIS, born in 1817 at Portland, has written poetry and prose with grace and lightness. There is something of Leigh Hunt about his pen. He was the editor of the *New York Mirror.* Some of his Scriptural pieces, such as *The Leper, The Daughter of Jairus,* and *The Shunamite Mother,* are very beautiful. *Melanie* and *Lord Ivon and his Daughter* afford good specimens of his romantic style. But such sweet, natural lyrics as *Better Moments,* and *Lines to a City Pigeon,* surpass his more laboured works. In prose he produced various clever, readable, gossipy books,—*Pencillings by the Way—Inklings of Adventure—Loiterings of Travel,* &c. Willis died in 1867.

EDGAR ALLAN POE, author of that exquisite piece of mystery and music, *The Raven*, was born in 1811 at Baltimore. *Annabel Lee*, a tender lament for his dead wife, is one of the sweetest lyrics in the language. His prose tales are full of wild and absorbing interest. Reckless intemperance brought his short life to a close in 1849.

Supplementary List.

JOHN PIERPONT.—(1785)—Litchfield, Connecticut—*Airs of Palestine; Lyrics.*

RICHARD DANA.—(1787)—Cambridge, Massachusetts—*The Buccaneer; Thoughts on the Soul;* also noted as an Essayist.

CHARLES SPRAGUE.—(1791)—Boston—a bank cashier—*Curiosity; The Brothers; The Family Meeting.*

JAMES GATES PERCIVAL.—(1785)—Kensington, Connecticut—*Lyric Poems.*

FITZ-GREENE HALLECK.— (1795) — Guilford, Connecticut — *Fanny; Alnwick Castle; Marco Bozzaris.*

JAMES RUSSELL LOWELL.—(1819)—Boston—author of many serious poems (*Rhœcus, Prometheus,* &c.), but better known for the *Papers of Hosea Biglow*, abounding in Yankee fun and shrewd sarcasm.

Southey gave great praise to *Zophiel, or the Bride of Seven*, by MARIA BROOKS. CHARLES HOFFMAN, author of *The Vigil of Faith;* and JOHN GREENLEAF WHITTIER, a Quaker poet, may be added to this list.

HISTORIANS.

WILLIAM HICKLING PRESCOTT, born in 1796, at Salem in Massachusetts, is the chief of American historians. An accident at college—the throwing of a crust—deprived him almost wholly of one eye. Thus situated, he began a career of literary toil which resulted in the production of four great historical works,—*The Reign of Ferdinand and Isabella, The Conquest of Mexico, The Conquest of Peru,* and *The History of Philip II.*,—all of which have been remarkably successful. The sight of his single eye failing, he was for several years unable to read. He died of a paralytic stroke in 1859.

GEORGE BANCROFT, born in 1800, at Worcester in Massachusetts, is the author of the principal existing *History of the United States*. He was for three years (1846-49), Minister for the States at the British Court.

GEORGE TICKNOR, born in 1791 at Boston, preceded the poet Longfellow in the chair of Modern Literature at Harvard. A *History of Spanish Literature* from his pen ranks, for learning, sound criticism, and literary merit, with the very highest works of its class.

JOHN LOTHROP MOTLEY has won a high place among historians by his *Dutch Republic* and *United Netherlands*, on the latter of which he is at present engaged. He excels in vivid and pictorial description.

Supplementary List.

JOHN WINTHROP.—(1587-1649)—one of the Pilgrim Fathers—Governor of Massachusetts—*Diary of Events* in that colony down to 1644.

COTTON MATHER. — (1663-1728) — a Puritan minister at Boston — *Magnalia Christi Americana*, an Ecclesiastical History of New England.

JARED SPARKS.—(1794)—editor of the *Library of American Biography*—author of a *Life of Washington*, and an edition of *Franklin's Works*.

RICHARD HILDRETH.—(1807)—Deerfield, Massachusetts—*History of the United States; Japan as it Was and Is.*

Among various local histories, containing much valuable material, we may name *Maine*, by WILLIAMSON; *Virginia*, by CAMPBELL; *Georgia*, by STEVENS; *Kentucky*, by MANN BUTLER; and the *Indian Tribes*, by M'KENNEY and HALL.

WRITERS OF FICTION.

WASHINGTON IRVING, born in 1783 at New York, was the scion of an old Orkney family. His father was a merchant. The literary career of this Goldsmith of the States began in 1807, the year after his admission to the bar, by contributions to *Salmagundi*, a humorous serial of short life. Then came that queer, delightful burlesque of old Dutch and Swedish colonist life, called *The History of New York, by Diedrich Knickerbocker*. The management of a branch of Irving Brothers, in Liverpool, being confided to him, he crossed the Atlantic for the second time in 1815. But the house failed, and the young merchant turned author by profession. It was up-hill work at first; but Scott having pronounced a most favourable opinion upon *The Sketch-book*, which was submitted to him, the road to fame and fortune was opened at once to Geoffrey Crayon, Gentⁿ., as the author styled himself.

A list of Washington Irving's works is subjoined:—

Salmagundi	1807–8
History of New York	1809
Sketch-book of Geoffrey Crayon	1819–20
Bracebridge Hall	1822
Tales of a Traveller	1824
Life of Columbus	1828
Conquest of Granada	1829
Companions of Columbus	1831
Tales of the Alhambra	1832
Tour on the Prairies	1835
Abbotsford and Newstead Abbey	—
Astoria, Beyond the Rocky Mountains	1836
Captain Bonneville	1837
Life of Goldsmith	1849
Mahomet and his Successors	1850
Wolfert's Roost	1855
Life of Washington	1855–7

Whatever his subject—an English manor-house, with bright fires and Christmas snow—a drowsy Dutch farm-steading in Sleepy Hollow—a moonlit court in the Alhambra—the great Italian sailor —the sweet-souled Irish author—the simply noble American general —we are charmed by the poetic graces of his fancy and the liquid music of his style. For several years he resided at Madrid, collecting materials for his Spanish works. In 1830, while in England, he received one of two gold medals conferred by George the Fourth for historical eminence, Hallam receiving the other. His later life was spent at a pleasant seat—Sunnyside, by the Hudson. There he died in November 1859.

JAMES FENIMORE COOPER, born in 1789, at Burlington in New Jersey, entered, after six years of naval life, upon his brilliant career as a writer of fiction. Residing on the borders of Otsego Lake, a district thick with game and then uncleared, he wrote his first novel, *Precaution.* In two walks he has been eminently successful—Indian novels and Naval novels. Among the former, *The Last of the Mohicans, The Prairie, The Path-finder,* and *The Deer-*

slayer, are the best ; among the latter, *The Pilot*, with its noble character of *Long Tom Coffin*, stands first. Of his tales founded on the history of the American War, *The Spy* is most popular. Cooper died in 1851.

THOMAS CHANDLER HALIBURTON, a Nova Scotian judge, born about 1800, is well known as the author of the papers signed Sam Slick, illustrative of Yankee life and humour. *The Clockmaker*, *The Attaché*, *The Old Judge*, *Letter-Bag of the Great Western*, and *The Season-Ticket*, are his chief works. Judge Haliburton latterly resided in England, where he died in 1865. He also wrote an *Historical and Statistical Account of Nova Scotia.*

NATHANIEL HAWTHORNE, born about 1807, at Salem in Massachusetts, was one of the finest American novelists. His first acknowledged work was *Twice-Told Tales* (1837). Then came *Mosses from an old Manse* (1846) ; *The Scarlet Letter* (1850) ; *The House of the Seven Gables* (1851), his best novel ; and *The Blithedale Romance* (1852). His taste for psychology deeply tinged his works, the chief of which belong somewhat to the Weird school of fiction. The beauty of his language and the rich quaintness of his humour possess irresistible attractions. For a year Mr. Hawthorne was Surveyor of Customs at Salem ; and for some time he held the American Consulship at Liverpool. He died in 1864.

HARRIET BEECHER STOWE, the world-renowned authoress of *Uncle Tom's Cabin*, was born at Litchfield in Connecticut, the daughter of Lyman Beecher, an eminent Congregationalist minister. *The Mayflower* was one of her earlier works. "Uncle Tom" appeared in 1850, in the columns of a weekly paper, *The Washington National Era.* Its astonishing success was owing partly to its subject, but not a little to its graphic power. A *Key* followed the work, supplying ample evidence of its truthfulness. Mrs. Stowe then visited Europe,—recollections of her tour appearing in *Sunny Memories of Foreign Lands.* None of her later works—*Dred, The Minister's Wooing, The Pearl of Orr's Island*—have come up to "Uncle Tom" in power or popularity. *Agnes of Sorrento* (in the "Cornhill") is said to be from her pen.

Supplementary List.

CHARLES BROCKDEN BROWN.—(1771-1810)—Philadelphia—*Wieland; Ormond; Arthur Mervyn: Edgar Huntly.*

JAMES KIRKE PAULDING.—(born 1779)—associated with Irving in *Salmagundi* —*John Bull and Brother Jonathan; The Dutchman's Fireside; Westward Ho!*

JAMES HALL.—(born 1793)—Philadelphia—a judge in Illinois—*Letters from the West; Wilderness and War-Path.*

JOHN P. KENNEDY.—(born 1795)—Virginia (?)—follower of Irving—*Swallow Barn; Horse-Shoe Robinson.*

WILLIAM WARE.—(born 1797)—Massachusetts—Unitarian clergyman—*Fall of Palmyra; Probus, or Rome in the Third Century.*

ROBERT M. BIRD.—(1803-1854)—Newcastle, Delaware—a doctor of medicine— *Calavar* and *The Infidel* (Mexican romances); *Nick of the Woods; Hawks of Hawk Hollow.*

WILLIAM SIMMS.—(born 1807)—planter of South Carolina—*Guy Rivers; Beauchamp; Wigwam and Cabin.*

T. B. THORPE.—(born 1815)—Westfield, Massachusetts—*Mysteries of the Backwoods; Big Bear of Arkansas.*

Our list must close with the names of Miss SEDGWICK (*Hope Leslie*); Miss LOTHROP (*Dollars and Cents*); Miss WARNER (*The Wide Wide World* and *Queechy*); Mrs. KIRKLAND (*New Home* and *Forest Life*); and SAMUEL GOODRICH (Peter Parley), author of an immense number of tales and educational works.

ESSAYISTS, CRITICS, AND ORATORS.

WILLIAM ELLERY CHANNING, born in 1780, at Newport in Rhode Island, though ranking high amongst theologians, finds a fitter place among the most eloquent American Essayists. After a distinguished career at Harvard College, he lived for a while as a tutor in Virginia, and in 1803 was ordained minister of a Unitarian church in Boston. *National Literature, Milton, Napoleon, Fenelon, Self-Culture, The Elevation of the Labouring Classes,* are among the subjects he has written and lectured upon. Brilliant and original thoughts, clothed in language of rare fire and beauty, characterize all the works of this eminent man. *Discourses on the Evidences of Revealed Religion* form his chief theological work. One of his strongest feelings was hatred of the Slave-Trade;

and his last public utterance was upon the emancipation of British slaves in the West Indies. He died of typhus fever in 1842.

EDWARD EVERETT, born in 1794, at Dorchester near Boston, originally a Unitarian minister, became Governor of Massachusetts, American minister in London (1841–46), and Secretary of State for the United States. His literary fame rested on his *Orations and Speeches.* He wrote largely for the *North American Review*, which he edited for four years (1820–24). Everett died in 1865.

RALPH WALDO EMERSON, born in 1803 at Boston, became, after studying at Harvard, minister of a Unitarian church. This connection soon ceasing, he buried himself at Concord, to study and to write. He has spoken to the public principally through lectures, afterwards collected and published. His chief work is *Representative Men*, embracing strikingly eloquent estimates of Montaigne, Goëthe, Plato, Swedenborg, Shakspere, and Napoleon.

Supplementary List.

ALEXANDER HAMILTON.—(1757–1804)—island of Nevis—a lawyer and statesman of the Revolution—*The Fedcralist*, to which Madison and Jay also contributed.

ALEXANDER EVERETT.—(1790–1847)—Boston—elder brother of the orator—diplomatist—*Europe; New Ideas on Population; America; Essays.*

OLIVER WENDELL HOLMES.—(born 1809)—Cambridge, Massachusetts—Professor of Anatomy at Cambridge—lives now at Boston—*Poems; Autocrat at the Breakfast-Table* (essays).

MARGARET FULLER.—(1810–1850)—Cambridge, Massachusetts—Marchesa D'Ossoli—*Woman in the Nineteenth Century; Summer on the Lakes.*

HENRY THEODORE TUCKERMAN.—(born 1813)—*Thoughts on the Poets; Characteristics of Literature; Diary of a Dreamer; New England Philosophy.*

RUFUS GRISWOLD.—(1815–1857)—Benson, Vermont—Baptist minister—*Curiosities of American Literature; Poets and Prose-Writers of America.*

The Lectures of HENRY REED (drowned in the wreck of the Arctic) upon *English Literature*, and of EDWIN WHIPPLE, upon *Subjects connected with Literature and Life*, are fine specimens of eloquent and accurate criticism. THEODORE PARKER, a Unitarian minister, has written Essays upon *German Literature*, *Labour*, and the *Labouring Classes*. DANIEL WEBSTER (1782–1852), HENRY CLAY (1777–1852), and JOHN CALHOUN (1782–1850), are the leading names in American oratory. NOAH WEBSTER'S *English Dictionary*, and ANTHON'S *Editions of the Classics* belong to this section.

SCIENTIFIC WRITERS.

BENJAMIN FRANKLIN, born in 1706 at Boston, began life as a printer's boy. Steadily he rose by native genius, conjoined with industry and prudence, to a foremost place among his countrymen. *Poor Richard's Almanac*, a repertory of Proverbial Philosophy for the poor, begun in 1732, lasted for twenty-five years. This collection is otherwise known as *The Way to Wealth*. He won great fame by his scientific researches, especially into the laws of *Electricity*, the results of which are embodied in various letters and papers. He wrote also numerous *Essays, Historical, Political, and Commercial*, and an *Autobiography* of great value. His *Letters*, too, have been published. In all the great political movements of the Revolution he took a leading share; but the crown of his statesmanship was won when, as Minister Plenipotentiary at the court of France, whither he went in 1776, he secured the aid of French bayonets and cannon for the struggling Americans. He died in 1790.

Supplementary List.

JOHN JAMES AUDUBON.—(1780-1851)—son of a French admiral settled in Louisiana—travelled much—*Birds of America*.

HENRY CAREY.—(born 1793)—Philadelphia—a publisher—*The Credit System; Past, Present, and Future; Harmony of Interests; The Slave Trade*.

ORVILLE DEWEY.—(born 1794)—Sheffield, Massachusetts—Unitarian minister—*Moral Views of Commerce, Society, and Politics; The Old World and the New*.

MATTHEW F. MAURY.—(born 1806)—Virginia—captain in United States Navy—*Physical Geography of the Sea*.

THEOLOGIANS AND SCHOLARS.

JONATHAN EDWARDS, born in 1703, at East Windsor in Connecticut, ranks highest among American divines. He was licensed as a Congregationalist minister in 1722. The honourable office of President in the College of New Jersey, Princeton, was conferred on him in 1757, but in the following year he died of small pox. His principal work, *The Freedom of the Will*, is a master-piece of metaphysical reasoning. Treatises from his pen upon *The History of Redemption, True Virtue, God's Chief End in the Creation, Original Sin,* and the *Religious Affections,* also display great power of thought, "warm piety, and profound acquaintance with the Scriptures."

Supplementary List.

JOHN WITHERSPOON.—(1722-1794)—Scotland—President of Princeton College—*Ecclesiastical Characteristics.*

TIMOTHY DWIGHT.—(1752-1817)—Northampton, Massachusetts—Congregational minister, army chaplain, President of Yale College (1795-1817)—*History, Eloquence, and Poetry of the Bible; Theology Explained and Defended* (chief work); *Poems.*

CHARLES HODGE.—(born 1797)—Philadelphia—Professor of Biblical Literature at Princeton—Commentaries on *Romans, Ephesians, First Corinthians; History of the Presbyterian Church in the States.*

ALBERT BARNES.—(born 1798)—Philadelphia—Presbyterian minister—*Notes on the Gospels* and other *Commentaries.*

JOSEPH ADDISON ALEXANDER.—(1809-1860)—Philadelphia—Professor in Princeton College—chief works upon *Isaiah* and the *Psalms*—associated with Dr. Hodge in a *Commentary on the New Testament.*

HENRY WARD BEECHER.—(born 1813)—Litchfield, Connecticut—Congregationalist minister—brother of Mrs. Stowe—*Lectures; Star Papers; Life-Thoughts.*

———

TRAVELLERS.

JOHN LLOYD STEPHENS, born in New Jersey in 1805, published in 1836-37 *Incidents of Travel in Egypt, Arabia, Palestine, Yucatan, and Central America.* Italy, Greece, Turkey, Russia, Germany, and France came also within the limit of his wanderings. Overtasking his strength in surveying the Isthmus of Panama with a view to the connection of the oceans by a railway, he died in 1852, at the age of forty-seven.

EDWARD ROBINSON, born in 1794, at Southington in Connecticut, before entering on his duties as Professor of Biblical Literature in the Union Theological Seminary at New York, spent two years in the Holy Land and the surrounding countries, which on his return he described in *Biblical Researches in Palestine, Mount Sinai, and Arabia Petræa* (1841). This learned and valuable work obtained for him the gold medal of the Geographical Society.

Among American travellers of the last century, we may name JOHN BARTRAM (1701–1777), who described *East Florida;* JOHN WOOLMAN (1720–1772), a Quaker, in whose *Journal of a Tour in England* Charles Lamb delighted; JONATHAN CARVER (1732–1780), who explored the interior of North America, trying to reach the Pacific; and JOHN LEDYARD (1751–1789), who travelled both in frozen Siberia and burning Africa, dying at Cairo.

TIMOTHY FLINT, the novelist (1780–1840) contributed to this branch of American literature *The Geography and History of the Mississippi Valley*—HENRY SCHOOLCRAFT (born 1793), *Tours in Missouri, Arkansas, and the Copper Region of Lake Superior*, besides various important works upon the *Red Race in America*—and CHARLES WILKES, of the United States Navy, *A Narrative of the United States Exploring Expedition*, giving an account of travels in Chili, Peru, and the South Seas.

CALEB CUSHING's *Reminiscences of Spain;* GEORGE CHEEVER's *Pilgrim in the Shadow of Mont Blanc* and *Pilgrim in the Shadow of the Jungfrau;* BAYARD TAYLOR's *Sketches in the East;* J. T. HEADLEY's *Letters from Italy, the Alps, and the Rhine,* are among the most readable books of late American travel.

INDEXES.

GENERAL INDEX.

INDEX OF AUTHORS.

THE ROYAL SCHOOL SERIES.

A NEW SERIES OF
EDUCATIONAL WORKS.

I.

THE GEOGRAPHY AND ATLAS COMBINED. Containing a Complete Geography, Seventeen Full-coloured Maps, and Numerous Diagrams. Small Quarto. Price 1s. 6d.

"Many thanks for your new book on Geography. It is truly admirable in plan, in matter, and in execution. It will completely revolutionize the teaching of Geography, and render the study more interesting and attractive to the young than it can possibly be with our common Text-books. The information is so judiciously chosen, both in *kind* and *amount*, is so *practical*, and so clearly set forth, as to leave nothing to be desired. The Maps, too, are models of distinctness and simplicity ; and the price of the volume is amazing for cheapness. I congratulate you very sincerely on the publication of this admirable school-book."— *Extract of Letter from A. H. Bryce, LL.D., Principal of the Edinburgh Collegiate Institution, and Author of Latin and Greek Readers, &c.*

"It is the *beau-ideal* of a class-book for the young. For my pupils' sake, no less than for my own, I shall lose no time in causing the introduction of so valuable a school-book. Its merits are so manifest, that I am sure every teacher into whose hands it comes must think of it as I do."—*Extract of Letter from Dr. Collier, Author of "History of the British Empire."*

II.

THE SENIOR CLASS-BOOK OF BRITISH HISTORY. By W. F. COLLIER, LL.D. With Copious Questions. 12mo. Price 2s. 6d.

"Dr. Collier's book is unrivalled as a School History of the British Empire. The arrangement is admirable."—*English Journal of Education.*

*** *Other Volumes of the Series will shortly be announced.*

THOMAS NELSON AND SONS, LONDON, EDINBURGH, AND NEW YORK.

Awarded the Prize Medal at the International Exhibition.

NELSON'S WALL MAPS.

With Divisions and Measurements in English Miles.
Each 4 feet by 4 feet.

Beautifully Coloured and Mounted on Rollers.
Price 13s. 6d. each.

1. **EASTERN HEMISPHERE.** With Circles at intervals of 1000 English Miles, showing the distance from London.
2. **WESTERN HEMISPHERE.** With Circles at intervals of 1000 English Miles, showing the distance from London.
3. **ENGLAND.** With the Railways. Divided into Squares of 100 Miles.
4. **SCOTLAND.** With the Railways. Divided into Squares of 100 Miles.
5. **IRELAND.** With the Railways. Divided into Squares of 100 Miles.
6. **THE BRITISH ISLANDS in relation to the Continent.** Divided into Squares of 100 Miles.
7. **EUROPE.** Divided into Squares of 1000 English Miles.
8. **PALESTINE.** Divided into Squares of 10 Miles.
0. **GENERAL MAP OF BIBLE LANDS—The Journeys of the Israelites, &c.** Divided into Squares of 100 English Miles. With Plan of Jerusalem, &c.
10. **NORTH AMERICA.** Divided into Squares of 1000 English Miles.
11. **BRITISH AMERICA.** Size 3 feet 10 inches, by 2 feet 2 inches. Price 8s.

The attention of Teachers and others interested in Education is specially invited to these Maps. They will be found to possess advantages for educational purposes over any hitherto published.

Each of the Hemispheres forms a circle four feet in diameter. They are so large that, with the exception of Europe, of which a separate Map is just ready, the Geography of all the countries of the great Divisions of the Globe can be taught from them. Separate Maps of Africa, Asia, Australia, North America, and South America, will not be required in the great majority of schools.

THE FOLLOWING ARE REDUCED COPIES OF THE WALL MAPS :—

NELSON'S SCHOOL MAPS.

Price 1d. each, Plain, with Cover; 2d. each, Coloured; 3d. each, Coloured, and Mounted on Cloth.

1. EASTERN HEMISPHERE.
2. WESTERN HEMISPHERE.
3. ENGLAND.
4. SCOTLAND.
5. IRELAND.
6. THE BRITISH ISLANDS in relation to the Continent of Europe.
7. EUROPE.
8. PALESTINE.
9. BIBLE LANDS.

ENGLISH READING-BOOKS,

ADAPTED TO THE

STANDARDS OF THE REVISED CODE.

"A more interesting set of Reading-books we have never seen. We are not surprised by their great popularity and extensive sale. . . . . We have had the advantage of examining with care the entire Series, and we cannot too strongly express the sense we entertain of the taste and judgment the books display, or of their great educational value."— *The Rev. Dr. Hall (in the Evangelical Witness), Commissioner of National Education, Ireland.*

THE SERIES IS NOW COMPLETE AS FOLLOWS :—

STANDARD I.

1. **STEP BY STEP;** or, The Child's First Lesson-Book: 18mo. Parts I. and II. Price 2d. each.
2. **SEQUEL TO " STEP BY STEP."** 18mo. Price 4d.

STANDARD II.

3. **THE YOUNG READER—New No. 3.** Beautifully Illustrated. Price 6d.

STANDARDS III. & IV.

4. **NEW FOURTH BOOK.** Beautifully Illustrated. Price 10d. ; or with Book Slate, 1s.

    "Out of sight the best Elementary Reading-book we have seen."— *Museum and English Journal of Education.*

STANDARD IV.

5. **JUNIOR READER.** No. I. Post 8vo, cloth. Price 1s. 3d.

STANDARD V.

6. **JUNIOR READER.** No. II. Post 8vo, cloth. Price 1s. 6d.

STANDARD VI.

7. **THE SENIOR READER.** Post 8vo, cloth. Price 2s. 6d.

8. **THE ADVANCED READER.** Post 8vo. 400 pages. Price 2s. 6d.

    "We have no hesitation in pronouncing this the best 'Advanced Reader' that we know....The book is one of deep interest from beginning to end, and will be read by the teacher as well as the pupil with growing pleasure."— *The Museum and English Journal of Education.*

EXTRA VOLUMES.

9. **READINGS FROM THE BEST AUTHORS.** Edited by A. H. BRYCE, LL.D. 12mo, cloth. Price 1s. 6d.

10. **READINGS FROM THE BEST AUTHORS.** Second Book. Edited by A. H. BRYCE, LL.D. Post 8vo, cloth. Price 2s.

ENGLISH READING-BOOKS.

EXTRA VOLUMES.

THE LITERARY READER: Prose Authors. With Biographical Notices, Critical and Explanatory Notes, &c. By the Rev. HUGH G. ROBINSON, M.A. Cantab., Incumbent of Bolton Abbey, Canon of York, &c. 12mo, cloth, 430 pages. Price 3s.

"We scarcely ever saw so useful an aid to the study of English Literature. Instead of giving mere scraps from a great many writers, most of them of little importance, the editor has confined himself to those of the first rank, from whose most celebrated works choice passages of considerable length are quoted. The reader is thus enabled to form a good idea both of each author and the period he represents. The editor has supplied an Introductory Essay on English Literature, a Biography of each Author, and an Account of his Works, with Notes on the passages extracted, every part of his task being very ably and carefully executed."—*The Athenæum.*

HISTORY OF ENGLISH LITERATURE. In a Series of Biographical Sketches. By W. F. COLLIER, LL.D. 12mo, cloth. Price 3s. 6d.

CLASS-BOOK OF ENGLISH LITERATURE; with Biographical Sketches, Critical Notices, and Illustrative Extracts. For the use of Schools and Students. By ROBERT ARMSTRONG, English Master, Madras College, St. Andrews; and THOMAS ARMSTRONG, Edinburgh; Authors of "English Composition" and "English Etymology." Post 8vo. Price 3s.

MILTON'S PARADISE LOST AND PARADISE REGAINED. With Notes. For the Use of Schools. By the Rev. J. EDMONDSTON. 12mo, cloth. Price 2s. 6d.

THE SCIENTIFIC AND TECHNICAL READER. From the Works of Recent and Eminent Authors. 12mo. Price 2s. 6d.

THE CHEMISTRY OF COMMON THINGS. By STEVENSON MACADAM, F.R.S.E., F.G.S. With upwards of Sixty Diagrams. 12mo. Price 1s. 6d.

"It contains a very considerable amount of information, conveyed in clear and untechnical language."—*Educational Times.*

NEW CLASS-BOOK OF ENGLISH POETRY. Part I.—JUNIOR DIVISION. Small Type, Price 6d. Large Type, 1s.

PART II.—SENIOR DIVISION. Small Type, Price 6d. Large Type, 1s.

THE TWO PARTS BOUND IN ONE. Small Type, Price 1s. Large Type, 2s.

THE ENGLISH WORD-BOOK: A Manual Exhibiting the Sources, Structure, and Affinities of English Words. By JOHN GRAHAM. Price 1s.

WORD EXPOSITOR AND SPELLING GUIDE: A School Manual Exhibiting the Spelling, Pronunciation, Meaning, and Derivation of all the Important and Peculiar Words in the English Language. With Copious Exercises for Examination and Dictation. By GEORGE COUTIE, A.M. 12mo, cloth. Price 1s. 3d.

GEOGRAPHIES, ATLASES, &c.

GEOGRAPHIES.

NEW CLASS-BOOK OF GEOGRAPHY, Physical and Political. By ROBERT ANDERSON, Head Master, Normal Institution, Edinburgh. 12mo, cloth. Price 1s. 9d.

"We can speak favourably of this improved edition of a well-known work. There is a valuable introduction on physical geography, and throughout the book prominence is given to the natural features, climate, and productions of each country. One new feature, which we think good, is the employment of our own country as a standard for comparing the size, latitude, and distances of others."—*Athenæum.*

MODERN GEOGRAPHY. For the Use of Schools. By ROBERT ANDERSON. Foolscap 8vo, cloth. Price 1s. 6d.

EXERCISES IN GEOGRAPHY. Adapted to Anderson's Geography. 18mo, cloth. Price 6d.

GEOGRAPHY FOR JUNIOR CLASSES. By ROBERT ANDERSON. 18mo, cloth. Price 11d.

ELEMENTARY GEOGRAPHY. By THOMAS G. DICK. Post 8vo, cloth. Price 1s.

ANCIENT GEOGRAPHY. For the Use of Schools. With Complete Index. By ARCHIBALD H. BRYCE, LL.D. Post 8vo, cloth. Price 1s. 6d.

BIBLE GEOGRAPHY. By the Rev. W. G. BLAIKIE, D.D. With Coloured Maps. 12mo, cloth. Price 1s ; or with the Maps mounted on Cloth, 1s. 3d.

ATLASES.

With Divisions and Measurements in English Miles.

NELSON'S ATLAS OF THE WORLD. Containing 23 Large Quarto Maps, full coloured. Reduced copies of Nelson's Wall Maps. In boards. Price 2s. 6d.

NELSON'S JUNIOR ATLAS. Containing 9 Quarto Maps. Full coloured. Stiff cover. Price 1s. 6d.

NELSON'S SHILLING ATLAS. Containing 16 Maps, plain. Stiff wrapper, 4to.

ARITHMETICS.

THE STANDARD ARITHMETICS. Adapted to the New Requirements of the Committee of Council on Education. STANDARDS II., III., Price 1d. each; STANDARD IV., Price 2d.

THE FIRST BOOK OF ARITHMETIC FOR YOUNG CHILDREN By W. STANYER. 18mo. Price 3d.

THE SECOND BOOK OF ARITHMETIC. PART I. By W. STANYER. 12mo, cloth. Price 1s. 6d. With "Answers to the Exercises," Price 1s. 9d.

EXERCISES IN MENTAL AND SLATE ARITHMETIC FOR BEGINNERS. By J. COPLAND. 18mo, cloth. Price 4d.

MENTAL ARITHMETIC FOR ADVANCED CLASSES. By WILLIAM KENNEDY, Training College, Moray House, Edinburgh. 12mo. Price 6d.

SCHOOL HISTORIES.

BY W. F. COLLIER, LL.D.

OUTLINES OF GENERAL HISTORY. Post 8vo, cloth. Price 3s.

"A very useful compendium, well adapted for reference, and more readable than such works generally are."—*The Athenæum.*

HISTORY OF ROME FOR JUNIOR CLASSES. 12mo, cloth. Price 1s. 6d.

HISTORY OF GREECE FOR JUNIOR CLASSES. 12mo, cloth. Price 1s. 6d.

ENGLISH HISTORY FOR JUNIOR CLASSES. 12mo, cloth. Price 1s. 6d.

HISTORY OF THE BRITISH EMPIRE. With Tables of the Leading Events of each Period—List of Contemporary Sovereigns—Dates of Battles—Chapters on the Social Changes of each Period, &c. 12mo, cloth. Price 2s.

THE SENIOR CLASS-BOOK OF BRITISH HISTORY. With Copious Questions. 12mo, cloth. Price 2s. 6d.

HISTORY OF THE NINETEENTH CENTURY. 12mo, cloth. Price 1s. 6d.

"Extremely well adapted for giving young persons intelligent general notions respecting those events that have most largely influenced the character of the present age."—*Educational Times.*

THE GREAT EVENTS OF HISTORY, from the Beginning of the Christian Era till the Present Time. 12mo, cloth. Price 2s. 6d.

BY THE REV. J. MACKENZIE.

HISTORY OF SCOTLAND. 12mo, cloth. Price 1s. 6d.

BY THE REV. R. HUNTER.

HISTORY OF INDIA, from the Earliest Ages to the Fall of the East India Company, and the Proclamation of Queen Victoria in 1858. 232 pages, with Woodcuts. Foolscap 8vo, cloth. Price 1s. 6d. ;

BY THE REV. DR. BLAIKIE.

BIBLE HISTORY, in Connection with the General History of the World. With Descriptions of Scripture Localities. 470 pages 12mo, with Maps. Price 3s.

This volume has been prepared mainly with a view to the instruction of schools and families.

QUESTIONS ON BLAIKIE'S BIBLE HISTORY. Price 6d.

CLASSICAL SERIES.

FIRST LATIN BOOK. By Archibald H. Bryce, LL.D., of Trinity College, Dublin. Fifth Edition. 249 pages, 12mo. Price 2s.

This is intended as a First Latin Book, supplying everything which a pupil will require during his first year. It contains—

I. The leading facts and principles of Latin Grammar, with the inflexions of Substantives, Adjectives, Pronouns, and Verbs, set forth at full length ; and also a Synopsis of the Syntax of Simple Sentences.

II. A numerous set of Simple Exercises, with Lists of the Words used in them.

III. A series of easy and interesting Lessons in continuous reading, consisting of a few simple Fables of Phaedrus, &c.

IV. A Vocabulary, in which the quantities of Syllables are marked, and the derivation of words given.

The two great features in the plan of the book are—*First,* That pupils are enabled daily, and from the very first, to *make practical use* of grammatical facts and principles so soon as they are learned ; and *Secondly,* That acquisitions, when once made, are impressed by constant repetition.

Key to the above. Price 6d.

The Key will be sold to Teachers only, and all applications must be addressed direct to the publishers.

SECOND LATIN BOOK. By Archibald H. Bryce, LL.D., of Trinity College, Dublin. Fourth Edition. 384 pages. Price 3s. 6d.

This Volume is intended as a Sequel to No. I. It contains—

I. Extracts from Nepos.

II. Extracts from Cæsar.

III. Extracts from Ovid.

IV. Notes on the above, with Tables for the Declension of Greek Nouns.

V. A System of Syntax, in which the illustrative examples are taken from the Reading Lessons, and to which constant reference is made in the Notes.

VI. A full Vocabulary (proper nouns being inserted), in which are noted Peculiarities of Inflexion, Conjugation, and Comparison. Quantities are carefully marked, and Derivations given, with frequent illustrations from modern languages.

VII. Imitative Exercises on Nepos and Cæsar. Adapted to the Extracts, and illustrating the Peculiarities of Construction in each chapter.

*** It will be seen that the First and Second Latin Books supply *everything that is necessary for pupils during at least the first two years of their course, and that the expense of books is thus reduced to a minimum.*

Key to Imitative Exercises in Second Latin Book. Price 6d.

The Key will be sold to Teachers only, and all applications must be addressed direct to the publishers.

CLASSICAL SERIES.

GRAMMAR OF THE LATIN LANGUAGE. By Archibald H. Bryce, LL.D. 12mo, 268 pages. Price 2s. 6d.

In preparing this Grammar the author has endeavoured to unite simplicity of arrangement with fulness of detail—to form a book which will be entirely suited for an initiatory class, and which will at the same time supply to more advanced students all the information required, previous to a study of such larger works as those of Zumpt, Madvig, Donaldson, &c. Those questions which are of essential importance in a first course will be indicated by a variety of type.

ELEMENTARY LATIN GRAMMAR. By Archibald H. Bryce, LL.D. 12mo, 176 pages. Price 1s. 3d.

This Work is an abridgment of the larger Latin Grammar, forming part of the same Series. It is designed for the use of beginners, and of those who intend to prosecute classical studies only to a limited extent.

FIRST GREEK BOOK. By Archibald H. Bryce, LL.D. Third Edition. 222 pages. Price 2s. 6d.

The plan of the Greek Book is the same as that of the Latin, and seeks to carry out the same principles. The Extracts for Reading are such as to interest and amuse the young, consisting of selections from the Witticisms of Hierocles, from Anecdotes of Famous Men, and from the Fables of Æsop, with a few easy Dialogues of Lucian.

Key to the above. Price 6d.

The Key will be sold to Teachers only, and all applications must be addressed to the publishers.

SECOND GREEK BOOK. By Archibald H. Bryce, LL.D. 12mo, 432 pages. Price 3s. 6d.

This Second Greek Book is formed on the same plan as Dr. Bryce's Second Latin Book, and contains—

I. EXTRACTS FROM LUCIAN ; some of the easier Dialogues—18 pp.

II. ANABASIS of XENOPHON : (1.) Those sentences of Books I., II., III., which are *absolutely necessary* to carry on the narrative of the Expedition; (2) Book IV. complete, giving the most interesting portion of the Retreat of the Ten Thousand—70 pp.

III. EXTRACTS FROM GREEK TESTAMENT : the Sermon on the Mount —10 pp.

IV. Homer. Book I., line 1–235, explaining the general subject of the Iliad. Book III. Helen on the Tower, pointing out to Priam the Grecian Chiefs—100 lines. Book VI. The Parting of Hector and Andromache—134 lines. Book XXII. The Death of Hector—228 lines. Book XXIV. Priam begging Hector's dead body from Achilles—200 lines—32 pp.

V. A SYNOPSIS OF SYNTAX—40 pp.

VI. NOTES ON THE EXTRACTS—56 pp.

VII. VOCABULARY—154 pp.

VIII. IMITATIVE EXERCISES, formed on the model of each chapter, and illustrating the Syntax—30 pp.

www.ingramcontent.com/pod-product-compliance
Lightning Source LLC
Chambersburg PA
CBHW021938110726
47901CB00003B/887